INFERNIUM

KERI LAKE

INFERNIUM
Published by KERI LAKE
www.KeriLake.com

Copyright © 2022 Keri Lake

Cover art by Hang Le
Editing: Julie Belfield

Warning: This book contains explicit sexual content, and violent scenes that some readers may find disturbing.

PLAYLIST

THE SONGS THAT INSPIRED SCENES

Come Find Me - Emile Haynie, Lykki Li, Romy
This Place Is Death - Deftones
Black Out Days - Phantogram
Hymn - Rhye
Crimson & Clover - Tommy James & The Shondells
Starry Eyes - Cigarettes After Sex
Only in My Dreams - The Marias
The Sky Is Empty - Orchid Mantis
Demons - PLAZA
Her & The Sea - CLANN
I Bleed For You - Peter Gundry
Fjörgyn - Osi And The Jupiter
Tear You Apart - She Wants Revenge
In Flames - Digital Daggers
Hysteria - Muse
Immortal Lover - Andrew Bayer, Alison May
Shelter - The XX
Use Me (Slowed + Reverb) - PLAZA
NFWMB - Hozier
Melt - TENDER

Moon Ascending - PHILDEL
The Last of Her Kind - Peter Gundry
Angels - The XX
Dark Side - Ramsey
it's ok, you're ok - Bonjr
After Night - MXMS
Change (In The House of Flies) - Deftones
Holy - Roniit
Help Me - AWAY, Koda
Are You With Me - nilu
Take It Out On Me - Bohnes
The Perfect Drug - Nine Inch Nails
War of Hearts - Ruelle
We Meet In Dreams - Gothic Storm
We Gotta Get Out Of This Place - Denmark + Winter
Make Me Feel - Elvis Drew

Dear Reader,

When I started Nightshade, I had originally intended it to be a standalone. However, by the time I reached the end, I realized there was still so much story left to tell for this couple. There are a number of unanswered questions, which I weaved into this book, and as it is predominantly Jericho's POV, it will have *a lot* more world building than Nightshade (you might want to bookmark the glossary). Because of that, Infernium is thick—my longest book to date.

My hope is that when you sit down to read this monster, you'll settle in and prepare to be transported for a while, as this is not a light or easy read. There are moments of darkness, some very personal to me.

For a full list of trigger warnings, with spoilers, please visit my website: https://www.kerilake.com/inferniumtriggerlist

Thank you for taking this journey with me. This world is one of my favorites, encompassing so many gothic elements that I love. I hope you enjoy the conclusion to Jericho and Farryn's story and feel a sense of closure by the end 🖤

Love,
Keri

GLOSSARY

Aenge – An uncommon flower that grows along rivers, and carries a nectar that looks like blood

Alatum – Fallen angels whose wings have been severed by a blade with cursed steel

Amreloc aehter'nu – Eternal love

A'ryakai – A sect of angels who believe in a pure race; they hunt half breeds and demons

Av'adeih et paej – 'Go in peace' in Pri'scucian

Ba'nixium – A curse which binds one soul to another and prevents the cursed from committing murder

Bullio – a disease characterized by bone deformities and horrible lesions

Ca'ligo an a tua – Nephilim spell to cast away demons

Caelicolan – Language of the Nephilim

Cambion – Half human, half demon; can traverse planes; are immortal but can be mortally wounded; can be born cambion or turned

Casmal'zhation – A painful form of torture experienced when agreement fails to be honored

Celestial steel – Steel forged by angels which can send any being to Ex Nihilo

Con'jeszis - The binding of souls, similar to marriage, but the bond cannot be broken.

Cret'calatięsz – Summoning chalk

Chthoniac – A potent demon liquor, lethal to humans

Contiszha – A demon contingency clause

Dalgoth – the only species of demon that resist and harvest vitaeilem

Dzilagion – a sea serpent that looks like a cross between a dragon and a snake

Diablisz steel – Steel forged by the Infernal which cannot be broken by any otherworldly being

Dojzra – Humans turned into immortal slaves in the Infernal Lands; they wear a slave band and answer to a demon overlord; can traverse planes and claim mortal souls

Dominus vigilans – The lord is watching

Dra'Akon – Humans granted special powers to protect mankind; their bloodline goes back to the ancients

Enchainsz – Binding another to sexual slavery without a collar; mindless and constant sex

Empyreal coin – Currency found in both Heaven and Hell

Empyreal Debenture – An official I.O.U.

Eradyę – The barren realm of starving souls; a place where angels cannot tread as they lose their powers

Es'ra – Echoes of a past life that may manifest imperfectly

Etheriusz – The protective layer, comprised of vitaeilem, which surrounds **Etheriana** (Heaven)

Ex Nihilo – The Nothingness from which everything was made – a plane devoid of life

Fallen – Angels who were banished from the heavens

Gratisz li'brunok – Unlimited freedom granted by Empyreal Debenture

Imolz era'da amreloc - The equivalent of I love you, but translates into *for my desired, I sacrifice*

Infernal Lands – Essentially Hell, where those who cannot be redeemed are sent. It is ruled by high ranking demons; can be easily traversed by demons and cambions; memories are retained as a means of torment.

Infernium – An asylum in Nightshade, formerly the location of an ancient temple

Inflodiusz – A command to fill

Intortui – Deformed beings, infected with bullion, who are able to predict future events

Ję'untis – A body whose soul is still attached

La'ruajh - A potent elixir that masks an angel's vitaeilem

Ma'baalirhya diszhra – My most treasured possession

Mę amreloc – A feeling beyond love

Me'retrixis - A vulgar name for a female

Met'Lazan – A human chosen by the ancients with the power to translate the Omni and access vitaeilem in Etheriusz.

Mortesz ul'Lilith – Death to Lilith

Mortunath – Soulless creatures who feed on souls and whose bite can turn others into Mortunath

Nephilim – Half human, half angel; can traverse planes; are immortal but can be mortally wounded; can be born Nephilim or turned (this is very rare)

Netherium – A kingdom found in the Infernal Lands

Noc'tu umbraj – Night + shadow = Nightshade

Noxerians – A very powerful demon council who oversee overlords in the various realms and answer to the Infernal Lord.

Omni – A dangerous sigil which can restore power and regenerate severed wings; it may also grant new powers to an individual

Omniasz – The all that makes up the existence of life in all realms

Overlords – High ranking fallen angels who rule Nightshade, collect taxes and carry out punishment

Pentacrux – The militant sect of the Pentasanctori

Pentasanctori – The Holy Five, consisting of the Holy Father, The Virgin Mother, The Messiah and the Two Warriors

Pentash – Female clergy

Pentash Mother – Similar to Reverend Mother; a high-ranking female clergy member

Pentrosh – Male clergy

Pentrosh Father – Similar to monsignor, a high-ranking clergymen in the Pentacrux

Praecepsia – An ancient city believed to have existed centuries ago that mysteriously disappeared

Pri'scucian - A language that predates Enochian – the true ancient language of angels

Rur'axze – A demon's intense and sometimes painful need to be sated

Saericasz – Refers to a divine fruit that has an addicting quality and can be eaten to the point of death; a demon euphemism for vagina

Sang âysh'la cin'tchinez – Blood of five blades

Sentinel – Half demon, half angel; powerful beings who often work undercover to infiltrate the demons realm

Septier – A gift of seven

Seraphica – a potent drug made from angels' blood that mimics vitaeilem

Sigiliuz de'tei – A Pri'scucian grimoire containing the most forbidden magic

Strę vera'tu – As real as the stars

Sybil – Prophetesses or oracles who have the power of foresight

Tę nebrisz – A soul's dark energy

Tu'Nazhja – A bird whose song is so beautiful, it lures its prey to death

Vale – The barrier between the mortal realm and Nightshade

Venator - Assigned huntsmen in a village

Vinculum – A mental bond between animal and angels/demons

Vitaeilem – the life blood of angels

Vocatori – A summoner

PROLOGUE

THE BARON

Centuries ago ...

*E*very muscle in the boy's body shook, as he stared down the side of the mountain toward the ground, where the tops of trees appeared as tiny as the wooden horses he had played with as a child. The air was thinner closer to the peak, and no matter how hard and fast he breathed, he could not fill his lungs. How foolish of him to have ventured up the most dangerous mountain in all of Praecepsia.

As he stood almost swaying, the cruel words of his father chimed inside his head—the same words which had goaded him up the treacherous rock in the first place, knowing all the while that few had ever made it to the top of Mount Helios. Certainly not a boy who had only just reached his twelfth year.

"You're weak. Pathetic. No son of mine!"

The baron might have proven that he was not weak, had he not gotten stuck on the ledge of a rock with no means to climb further. The next possible foothold sat too far out of reach for him, but climbing down proved to be impossible, also, considering a faint mist of rain had turned the stony surface slippery. He knew he would be stuck on that ledge, forced to wait out the misty rain until it dried—except, the temperatures would soon drop, and with no shelter or means to stay warm, he would surely freeze to death. Of course, his mother would undoubtedly search for him and, if necessary, set the hounds to track him, but after how long? It wasn't unusual for the boy to venture into the woods for hours at a time, coming home at dusk on occasion.

Perhaps he *was* weak and pathetic, after all. What kind of imbecile would trap himself on Mount Helios with no means to climb back down?

The anger from before twisted in his stomach as he imagined his father laughing at his ignorance. He could hear the bastard's voice rattling inside his skull, and the boy slammed his palms to his ears.

"Quiet! Quiet!" he screamed in a poor attempt to silence the laughter. Teeth grinding, he closed his eyes, creating jagged flashes of light behind his tight lids. "I despise you," he whispered, his voice wobbly with the threat of tears. "You have never been a father to me. And you never will."

With renewed fervor, the boy turned toward the next foothold, twice his height above him. Perhaps he could jump.

No. If anything, he should venture downward. Closer to the ground, not farther away. He'd tried to step down before, though, and nearly lost his footing. Fortunately, he'd been able to catch himself before tumbling down to what would've surely been a painful death.

Yet, faced with the prospect of standing there all night, it was worth another try.

On a deep breath, he stepped cautiously, turning himself to face the mountain, as he'd been positioned while climbing up. With one knee bent, he lowered himself slowly, using the toe of his boot to search for the next narrow ledge. Clutching a small pocket in the rock's surface, he scarcely breathed, not wanting to throw himself off balance.

The sole of his boot hit the surface, and he released a shaky exhale, his fingers cramping from the toil of gripping tightly. He leaned carefully into the descent, reluctant to put all his weight onto the ledge below him.

His boot slipped.

He lost his hold of the pocket.

Fire burned over his belly as it slid across the jagged rock, and his elbows slammed onto the wider ledge upon which he'd stood moments before. With every ounce of strength inside of him, he pulled himself up, his muscles simmering, trembling, threatening to fail him at any moment. Still, he refused to give up. He refused to fall to his death. What mockery his father would make of it–the stupid, illegitimate boy who had made a perilous climb to prove himself.

Despite his father's allegiance to the Pentacrux, the boy had never had much faith in religion, but in that moment, he prayed. To any god willing to listen.

"Help me. Please. Show me the way back down." His words were a quiet whisper, caught on a brisk wind that had him clutching the ledge tighter than before. He toed the wall of the mountain for purchase, and with his strength waning, he managed the slightest foothold. Just enough to pull himself up so that his ribs rested against the ledge. From there, he hiked a knee up and rolled himself back onto safety.

With his forehead pressed to the rock, he swallowed a gulp and breathed deeply, his muscles stiff and aching from the pressure.

He was stuck. No way to get down. No way to climb higher.

No shelter, nor food. Only a small waterskin, the contents of which wouldn't last beyond one more day.

Unless by some miracle he was found and could be rescued, he would have to wait out the rain and pray the accompanying wind was enough to dry the rock.

Or find another way.

Defeated, the baron pushed to his feet, and once again, he could hear the laughter of his father.

No son of mine would be so foolish. You would be better off jumping to your death.

Tears stung his eyes as he stared downward, wondering if it would be painful to jump, or if he would die a merciful death before striking the ground. In the distance, he caught a flash that sent a heavy weight of dread sinking to his stomach.

No.

The lightning flashed again. Closer that time.

He pressed himself as close to the rock as he could, but his height from the ground ensured there was no safe means to escape. Should a bolt decide to strike, he would make the perfect target.

The laughter in his head grew louder.

His muscles tightened.

A black, toxic rage stirred inside of him.

Another flash, even closer than before, forced him flat against the mountain. As if it were coming right for him. What a ridiculous thought. So ridiculous, he could not help but laugh. Loud, hysterical laughter, like his father's still pounding at his skull.

Yet another bolt struck the rock beside him, and he watched as the tiny flickering jags danced across the wet surface.

He laughed harder than before. "Come for me, if you want me so badly! I am here! Here!"

The world flicked to darkness. A white-hot bolt struck his chest. Arms stretched to either side, he stood paralyzed, his body surrendering to the searing heat that shot through him. His muscles twitched on their own. His lungs locked up.

The fire released its hold, and he teetered on the ledge, helpless to catch himself.

On a stifled breath, he fell forward.

Horror seized him as he watched the rocky ground below rise toward him at a sickening speed. He opened his mouth to scream but nothing came out.

There was no stopping the inevitable fall. No saving himself.

He closed his eyes and prepared his mind for the impact.

If only he could have sprouted wings and flown right then.

No sooner had the thought struck him when a sharp slicing sound cut through the hum of wind rushing past his ears, and a fiery pain tore across his shoulder blades. Something black shuddered in his periphery, and he turned just enough to see an enormous wing stretched outward. He snapped his attention to the opposite side and observed the same. His descent slowed, but not enough to keep him from striking the rock on a hard *thunk* that buckled his knees. He tumbled and rolled down the sharp slope, which tore at his skin. The ground punched at his ribs, his spine, his legs, his arms in an erratic attack, as he barreled gracelessly over the unforgiving earth.

Until he finally rolled to a stop.

Lungs seized up, he clawed at the gritty dirt beneath him, struggling for one sip of breath. With his mouth agape, he fought to suck in the air that had gotten knocked out of his chest. The canopy of trees overhead blurred and sharpened. Black birds circled, their form merging into a single, black halo. In the center, he saw an image of his mother. Her lips moved, but he could not make out what she was saying.

He lifted his head, desperate to hear her, while panic pounded at his ribs for air.

"Breathe!" she screamed. "Breathe!"

He gasped, swallowed a gulp of cold air, and the image of her fizzled to nothing.

Rolling to his side, he coughed and choked, heaving with every inhale. Minutes passed before his muscles relented their grip and he took the first easy breath.

Beneath him lay an enormous wing with feathers lined in glinting ribbons of silver. Tiny bolts of lightning danced over their surface, and when he reached out to touch one, he hesitated, recalling that moment on the mountain's ledge when he'd been struck.

There had been stories of others less fortunate, those who'd perished at the first touch of lightning, and yet, the baron had lived. He had not only lived, he felt *invigorated*. Stronger, if such a thing were possible, but the baron knew that it was not. How could one become stronger from a strike of lightning, after all?

And yet, how could one sprout wings with a mere thought?

He stroked his finger across one of the feathers, marveling at the way the jagged bolts sparkled over his hand. Smiling at the tickling vibration that hummed beneath his skin, he twisted his hand in front of him, and with a nervous tremble, he reached back to palpate a thick bone-like structure sticking out from his shoulder blade.

He quickly retracted his hand on a shocked breath. The grotesque deformity of his flesh sent a shudder of nausea through him. Hands trembling with the cold, his chest giving a retching tug, he reached again and ran his fingers over the rigid protrusion. He let out a whimper of panic when the soft, downy fibers that ran along the bone drifted beneath the pads of his fingers.

What would his mother say when she saw him? Or worse, his father? Surely, they'd lock him in a cage. They would brand him a deviant–aberration–and hand him over to the bishop to be properly judged.

With a firm grip of the bone, he tugged as much as he was able in an effort to dislodge the odd appendage from his back, but it was no use. Aside from a small flare of pain, it would not budge.

He pushed to his feet, taking notice that his legs could hold his weight. That, somehow, his bones had not been crushed in the fall and were strong enough to accommodate the heavy wings that extended outward on either side of him. By some miracle, his legs and shoulders felt stronger than before.

Reaching around, he gripped one of the wings and pulled, grunting with the effort. The lightning played beneath his fingertips, and he released it.

He tried again with the other side. "Get off of me!"

At a crackling sound in the distant woods, he snapped to attention, and as he scanned over the forest, he heard the slicing sound from before. He turned just in time to see the wings collapse into him on a violent spasm that had him squeezing his shoulder blades together, as the wings disappeared, as quickly as they'd unfurled. To be sure, he reached back, his fingertips brushing only over the tattered threads of his torn tunic and smooth skin where the odd protrusion of bone had just been. Frowning, he ran his palm over the span of it, palpating flesh that was smooth and lacked any strange deformity.

How?

The crackling sound from before stole his attention again, and he lifted his gaze to find a small doe just beyond the trunk of a thick oak. He hoped that had been the source of the noise from earlier.

Because if anyone had happened to see what had taken place, he would surely be hunted. Aberrations were considered evil in his world.

And, without doubt, there was something very wrong with him.

1

FARRYN

One month ago ...

She's judging me. I know it.

The excessively pregnant woman stared back at me from her bright and perfectly posed world on the face of the magazine that sat out in the doctor's dreary waiting room. Wearing a lime-green strappy dress and a jubilant smile against a glowing complexion, she was certainly a far cry from my ripped jeans and T-shirt, hair pulled back in an unbrushed ponytail, face-lucky-to-have-been-washed-that-morning look. I hadn't slept the night before. Or the night before that. Or the week before that. Not since that horrible night nearly two months ago.

I closed my eyes to the flashes of memory slipping behind my eyelids–Jericho on his knees, staring up at me. The look in his eye. The sound of the sword slicing through his wings with ease. The flames. God, the intensity of the heat given off by the hellfire that claimed him. I could feel it then–the scent clogging my throat. He was gone. It seemed impossible that a simple flame could've extinguished something so powerful as him, but I'd watched it happen. I'd watched it happen every night in my dreams since then, and I was determined to find a way to bring him back.

Opening my eyes to a shield of tears, I blinked them away for fear someone might ask me what was wrong. After all, how did one explain a story like ours? In my world, Jericho was a myth–an impossibility. I not only carried his child on my own, but the weight of his loss, too.

Sleep was just one of the many normal human functions that I'd been lacking as of late. The dark circles and relentless fatigue had become as much a part of my lifestyle as the chalky nutrition drink I forced myself to guzzle three times a day for the sake of the baby growing inside of me.

Jericho's baby.

The very thought of him had the rims of my eyes tingling again, and my focus instantly returned to the woman on the magazine. Behind her stood an equally cheerful man, his arms wrapped around her, palms resting against her belly.

Jaw shifting, I sneered and looked away from them and their happy smiles. My world had grown darker. Colder. And unlike the couple on the magazine, or any of the patients in the doctor's office, I wasn't incubating a regular human child. It'd be half Sentinel, and what the hell did I know about that?

Frowning, I clutched my stomach, imagining all of the things that I'd have to learn on my own, because not even the doctor to whom I'd come to confirm the pregnancy could offer any insight. He specialized in human babies, after all. My mind was so wound around finding a way to bring Jericho back from Ex Nihilo that I really hadn't considered much about the pregnancy, at all.

Jericho. Even in the silence of my thoughts his name sent a stab of pain to my heart.

I couldn't think of him right then.

Desperate for distraction, I looked around the office,

catching sight of a painting of what appeared to be a naked woman standing in flames, chains hanging from her hands that were outstretched above her.

What the ever-loving hell?

"*Anima sola*," a silver-haired woman said beside me, her thick Spanish accent smothered by the crackled sound of *Crimson & Clover* playing on the speaker overhead. She appeared to be staring in the same direction as me, confirmed when she nodded toward the painting and said, "The woman in purgatory."

"What's her story?"

"She gave up eternal salvation for temporal love." With a wistful sigh, she tipped her head. "Not the most romantic of endings, yes?"

Sliding my gaze back toward the image, I frowned. "What the hell does that have to do with the gynecologist?"

"Miss Ravenshaw?" another voice interrupted, and I turned toward a slim blonde whose flawlessly made-up face had me agonizing over my dark circles again, as she stood in the doorway leading to the exam rooms. "Please follow me."

Mind still wracked with uncertainty of the appointment, I pushed up from the leather chair, debating whether, or not, to bolt out the door, or follow after her. A thick stack of paperwork clipped to the board in my lap nearly fell to the floor, but the older woman next to me caught it, and with a smile, handed it to me.

"Thanks." I offered, avoiding her long, yellow nails as I took the papers from her. Once I reached the nurse, I handed her the clipboard, and she took only a moment to flip through all the documents that had taken me a good thirty minutes to fill out. "Hope I didn't sign my soul away with all that paper."

With a mirthless chuckle, she tucked the clipboard under her arm and jerked her head. "This way."

Another glance back at the exit and I bit my lip, the urge to leave calling to me like an uncorked bottle of wine in the desert. Technically, the pregnancy hadn't yet been confirmed. I'd taken an at-home pregnancy test about a week before, but it had come back negative—because, I suspected, I wasn't technically pregnant with a *human* child.

Of course, I'd lied when I made the OB/GYN appointment. How could I have explained that I'd *known* I was pregnant simply because an ancient curse had been lifted?

No. No matter what, I needed to know for sure. I'd had doubts over the last few weeks. Doubts about if Nightshade had even been real. Whether Jericho had been real, or merely part of a really elaborate and fucked-up mental state.

I wanted confirmation that the baby inside of me existed.

Hands wringing my shirt, I followed after the woman who sashayed her hips in a pair of slim-fitting scrubs. The youth on her face put her in her early twenties, maybe not much younger than me, and I wondered if she'd ever had kids.

As we made our way down the corridor, passing pictures of hands holding tiny feet, palms resting on rounded stomachs, an abstract of pregnant women in a circle holding hands, I couldn't help feeling completely unrelatable, an outsider to the human race. As though I'd peeled back a curtain for a world not meant to be seen. Despite all the images we passed being designed to calm and empower, those were the last things I felt as we approached the exam room.

The blonde led me to room seven and gestured me inside. I'd taken one step in that direction, when a high-pitched ringing rattled inside my skull, and I halted in place, slamming my hands over my ears. Eyes screwed shut, I opened my jaw as the agonizing noise shot from my brain to my freaking teeth. Not a random sound, but a scream. A high-pitched scream trapped inside my head. Dizziness swept over me, and when I opened my eyes, the hallway wobbled. I lowered my hands, staring at the wall, where the paint peeled in long, curling strips from the ceiling to the floor.

What the hell?

The screaming withered.

"Miss Ravenshaw?" The voice arrived in sharp focus, and I turned to see the blonde staring back at me. Brows raised with impatience, lips curved to an unconvincing smile, she gestured into the room.

I glanced back at the walls, their surface perfectly intact, and frowned. Had I hallucinated the peeling paint?

Shaking it off, I stepped inside the room and made my way toward the type of chair that was both familiar and terrifying.

Doctor Shein wasn't my usual doc. I hadn't been able to bring myself to make the appointment with my long-time doc. There'd have been too many questions of the personal variety that I wasn't ready to explore with someone who'd first examined my inner machinery at sixteen years old. No history with Doctor Shein made the visit slightly less harrowing.

Only slightly.

Stomach gurgling from the overpowering scent of disinfectant, I hesitantly slid up onto the chair, ignoring the godforsaken stirrups. Wordless, Blondie pressed a gentle palm to my chest, urging me back onto the pillow behind me.

The sound from before reached my ears again, and when I turned toward the wall, I could see the paint curling back, just as before. Dark shadows poured out of the exposed strips, and a creeping horror tickled the back of my neck as I watched them slide over the floor.

What the—?

I double blinked at the shadows crawling toward me like eerie and supernatural animals closing in, and I squeezed my eyes shut, counting to ten. When I opened them again, only stagnant shadows cast by the light filtering through the shades stretched across the too-white floor tiles.

The touch of cold hands against my stomach snapped my attention back to the nurse, who'd lifted my shirt up to my chest. Eyes alight with what I surmised to be fascination, she ran her hands over my belly in a way that didn't feel medical.

"What are you …" Muscles in my arms turned to lead weights at my sides when I tried to push myself up on the exam bed, and wouldn't move. Panic swelled at the back of my throat. "Hey. Hey!"

Her palms roamed higher, and she slid her ice-cold hand over my neck. A sickness stirred in my gut when I felt her fingers squeeze. Hard. Harder.

"Stop! Please! Stop!" Hands plastered to my sides, I mentally begged my muscles to push her away, but they wouldn't move at my command.

Eyes riveted on my lips, she lowered her head, as if to kiss me. Through her parted lips, a black curling smoke seeped out, like a serpent snaking its way toward me. The smoke prodded my clamped lips, and I shook my head, but in spite of my efforts to fight, it breached the barrier, and the taste of burnt ash filled my mouth. Thick as honey, it oozed down the back of my throat, pulsing as it made its way into my belly. I tried to scream, but choked and gagged instead. My body convulsed.

Still standing over me, the nurse chuckled. "How does it taste, Miss Ravenshaw?" she hissed in a strange voice.

The edges of the room closed in on me. Narrower and narrower.

Until, at last, everything turned black.

"Miss Ravenshaw?" A soft voice pierced the darkness.

I opened my eyes to find myself standing in the hallway, just outside the exam room, and staring at the wall, as before.

Blondie still stood at the door, her brows winged up with concern. "Are you all right?"

Was I?

I flicked my gaze from the wall, where the paint remained intact, to the clock on the wall that read one thirty-seven in the afternoon. Shifting my attention to the exam room showed the white paper they had stretched over the chair appeared unwrinkled. Un-sat in.

What had happened?

Nothing?

Though the phantom touch of cold hands still chilled my skin, I cleared my throat and gave a nod.

No. I wasn't okay. I hadn't been okay in weeks.

Hallucinations had become commonplace throughout my day, but mostly at night, which was why I needed to confirm the pregnancy. Because what if that was a hallucination, too?

Once inside the room, Blondie directed me to a scale, where she noted my weight–about fifteen pounds lighter in recent weeks. Following other vitals, she handed me a urine cup to fill, and took some blood. The horrid paper gown sat folded on the exam chair when I returned from the bathroom, and I inwardly groaned at the thought of having to wrestle with the damn thing.

A nervous quiet settled over me when she finally exited the room, and I changed out of my clothes and into the dreaded gown to wait for the doc. Not even the paintings of the ocean, or the pastel blue of the room could temper my anxiety. Medical visits had always made me nervous, but more so then. The world didn't feel right or normal to me anymore. It felt upside down and spinning too fast. All I wanted to do was crawl into my bed and sleep, or stare out the window, as I'd done on so many days since having returned from Nightshade. As I waited, I mindlessly toyed with the locket at my neck—the one from my father that Jericho had returned to me.

A knock at the door had my spine snapping straight, and I cleared my throat, "Come in."

Doctor Shein was a white middle-aged man, with a white shirt under his white lab coat, and tufts of graying hair slicked back to make him look like an aging Ken doll. By his appearance alone, I had a sense the man was the type to question anything outside of his pristine education. Which meant I wouldn't be bringing up the strange hallucination with his nurse and whatever that was she'd breathed into my mouth.

"Miss Ravenshaw," he began. "I've a pretty tight schedule today, so I'm gonna have you lie back so we can get the ultrasound done."

"Ultrasound? Already?"

"Your urine came back negative. I'd like to have a look inside the uterus."

It took every muscle in my face to keep from frowning at what sounded completely invasive. Did all docs talk like that?

The snap of his gloves had my stomach lurching, as I settled back into the chair. Another knock and Blondie appeared again with her iPad at the ready. Feet propped in the stirrups, I watched Doc Shein prep the transducer that looked like something out of a sex toy shop, adding a condom-like sheath over it, and with hardly a hello, he pushed my knees aside and slipped the object up into me. Fingers curled around the edge of the chair bed, I cleared my throat, thighs trembling. Blondie pushed a monitor closer to him, while I tried to ignore the slimy glide of the instrument and the way he moved it around inside of me.

While he watched the screen, I watched his brows lower, his head tip. He leaned closer to the monitor, then sat back. After a twitch of the object inside of me, he leaned in closer, frowning again.

The screen itself made no sense to me. Nothing but a quarter arc of dark streaks and static noise like something out of *Poltergeist*. He curved the wand to the left in a slightly uncomfortable angle and held it there a moment, studying the screen again. He moved the wand again, but returned to that same angle studying it. Scowling. Staring. A series of unnerving expressions that repeated at least three more times. "Jenny, can you grab the other transducer for me, please?"

At his request, the blonde shuffled out of the room, returning about a minute, or two, later and handing off a second transducer.

Doctor Shein pulled the first out of me on a cold glide, prepped the second, and quickly inserted it, picking up where he'd left off with his scowling and staring and prodding that damn thing like he was jousting with my womb.

"This is … very strange."

At that, the blonde tipped her head, brows lowered just like his. She sauntered over to him, and after a moment of staring at the monitor, her brows lifted, as in surprise.

Shit. They know. They know.

I didn't even want to ask because I knew they knew. The pregnancy wasn't normal. It wasn't human.

"It isn't there," he said, interrupting my agonizing thoughts.

"What?"

The screen flickered and made an electrical zapping sound, and I felt the wand unceremoniously slip out of me again. A cracking boom echoed in the room.

Startled, I accidentally kicked Doctor Shein. Before I

could apologize, the lights flickered out and the sound of his wheels rolling over the tiles was the only warning before he knocked into the stirrups. The buzzing of electricity died out, and the lights flickered back on to show confusion plastered on the doc's and his assistant's face.

"What the hell was that?"

Hell is right. His question mirrored my thoughts, as I turned to see a dark shadow slide across the ultrasound screen. A fluttering tickle in my stomach had me clutching myself there on a gasped breath, and I silently prayed that what I'd seen was nothing more than the glitchy static noise being glitchier.

Without a word, Doctor Shein shook his head and pushed up from his chair, removing his gloves as he made his way to the sink.

Wordless.

I scooted up in my chair, pulling my knees together. "Um … is … is everything okay?"

After washing his hands, he returned to his little stool, and I lowered my legs to the edge of the bench. "The uterus appears empty, though there seems to be … something there."

I cleared my throat yet again, daring myself to ask the question, wondering if he caught movement on the screen, as well. "Some*thing?*"

"I'd be inclined to think that this was an ectopic pregnancy, but I'd have expected your urine test to be positive in that case, as far along as you claim to be. Are you certain that it was a positive test that brought you here, Miss Ravenshaw?"

"Yeah," I lied. "Two lines, right?" An unconvincing chuckle flew past my lips.

"I'll wait for the blood to confirm, but in the case of ectopic pregnancy, I'm recommending methotrexate."

"What's that?"

"It's an injection given, to stop the fetal cells from dividing. To terminate the pregnancy. Essentially."

Terminate. *Terminate?*

I shook my head. "I'm not terminating this pregnancy."

"If it's confirmed that you are, in fact, pregnant, it is imperative that you do this. Ectopic pregnancy is life-threatening."

"What do you mean *confirm*? You're telling me it *could* be ectopic. As in, you're not certain after the *ultrasound?*"

A quick glance over his shoulder toward the blonde, and he turned to me, tucking his hands into his coat pocket. "I'm afraid I don't quite know what I saw, Miss Ravenshaw. There seems to be a significant mass outside the uterus."

"Mass? Like …" I swallowed a gulp, not wanting to say it aloud and put the possibility in his head. "A tumor?"

"A tumor is something I could identify, based on having seen one before. This was … unusual. I thought maybe the transducer wasn't working properly, but it persisted onscreen with the second."

"So, what is it?"

"I'm not sure. I'd like to wait for the blood results to proceed. Another ultrasound would be in order. We'll try a different monitor and perhaps more extensive tests. In the meantime, I'll ask that you make a follow up appointment at the front desk and prepare yourself for the likelihood of termination."

No. I couldn't do that. I wouldn't. I didn't know enough about Sentinel pregnancies to make a decision like that. Maybe it was normal to have a negative test and empty uterus. Maybe every Sentinel mother experienced the weird flickering screen and shadowy movement on ultrasound. I'd watched enough death in the past couple of months–Jericho,

Garic, Remy—and I surely wouldn't be adding Jericho's baby to that list.

I hated that the two of them seemed to be studying me as if waiting for my reaction. "Is there no possible way that the baby could—"

"I'm afraid not. And prolonging it only puts you at risk. Please consider my advice on this, Miss Ravenshaw."

I'd considered, and unfortunately for him, I'd already made my decision. What I'd come to know in my time spent in purgatory was, not everything followed the rules of what should be. Some beings surpassed, or defied, our limits of science. Jericho had taught me that.

The familiar sting in my eyes and nose had me looking away, because a monstrous deluge of pain and grief was on the brink of tripping the gates and I surely didn't want to break in front of Ken and his Barbie.

I wasn't going to terminate the pregnancy. I wasn't going to take some metho crap to kill Jericho's baby. His legacy. The only thing I had left of a centuries-old love.

No matter what.

2

EVIE

Present day ...

*E*vie sat up from the rented bed of the village tavern, where she'd made her home in recent months. With an appreciative smile, she watched the blond stranger pull his leathers over an inhumanly perfect ass. A lean, muscular build gave him the body of a warrior, and his skin bore no flaws. Not even so much as a birthmark, freckle, or scar. "So, how does it work?"

Still busying himself with getting dressed, he didn't bother to glance her way, or acknowledge that she'd even asked a question. Until after an exceptionally long pause, when he looped his belt through his trousers and frowned. "How does what work?"

"Crossing the Vale? Does it hurt?"

"No."

"Is it dangerous?"

"Yes."

She nibbled her lip, quietly contemplating his frustratingly uninformative responses. "I don't care. I need to get out of here. Away from Nightshade. If what you said is true, then … perhaps my family, assuming I have a family … well, perhaps they'll take me back. So I'll do it. I'll tell you where to find Van Croix."

Lifting the sheet up over her breasts, she swallowed back the unease churning in her gut. How long she'd loved Van Croix, only to betray him like that. He'd made his choice, though.

And he'd chosen *her*. Farryn.

After months of Evie offering him affection and pleasure, she'd been cast aside like a dirty pair of underwear, for a complete stranger who'd come out of nowhere.

"And what of the woman? Farryn?" She couldn't help the animosity in her tone. The hatred she felt toward the other woman had simmered in her blood since the night Van Croix had forced Evie to leave Blackwater Cathedral. Her only home. The only shelter from the darker parts that made up Nightshade.

"You assume she still lives?"

"He would not have it any other way. The bounds of his obsession with her are nonexistent."

"She will share his fate." The finality in his words struck her like a slap. Evie had been under the impression that the angel wanted to collect on a bounty. To turn Jericho over to the heavens without harming him.

The stranger had told her a number of things in their short time together. Peculiar things that she'd always suspected to be true. That Jericho was half angel, half demon. Given the times she'd seen him in the bell tower, the long and unusual feathers she'd collected, with their silvery tips and strange vibrations, she couldn't doubt that there was something different about her former lover. And unlike Jericho's withdrawn and enigmatic behaviors, the angel she'd spent the night with had gone so far as to prove his claims, by showing Evie his own wings and the unearthly features of his body. The way he moved and flexed like a perfectly honed machine.

"What exactly is his fate, if I may ask?" she dared to ask.

"None of your concern."

"You won't harm him, though?"

"You have my word."

The knots in her stomach unfurled with relief. As much as Jericho had disappointed her, he certainly wasn't the source of her ire. "My concerns do not extend to the woman. Just so we're clear."

"Crystal."

"Very well. I mean, I don't believe in all that religious karma crap, anyway. A girl has to look out for herself, and what she did to me was unforgivable." She lifted a nail file from the nightstand beside her and, in a nervous gesture, began primping her nails. "You can find Van Croix at Blackwater Cathedral. Of course, I'm sure anyone would've been able to tell you that. Which leads me to wonder … why me?"

"Why not you?" From the small wooden table across the room, he collected his many weapons laid out there, sheathing them in holsters strapped to his hip, legs, and chest.

"Forgive my sounding crude and irresponsible, but I didn't even get your name."

He turned around, and his lips stretched to the first smile she'd seen since the night before, when he'd charmed his way to her bed. "What is yours?"

"Evie. You are truly an angel who can restore my soul and send me back?"

Finger pressed to the tip of a dagger, its hilt the most ornate she'd ever seen, he crossed the room back toward the bed. Without so much as a flicker of the blade's metal to warn her, the stranger struck her throat, severing the scream that failed to break past her lips.

Evie stared up at him, wide-eyed, catching her shocked expression in the reflection of his bright eyes.

"I'm afraid I don't salvage souls such as yours, Evie. I break them."

3

THE BARON

Centuries ago ...

*T*he boy followed the worn path that disappeared into the spectral shadows of the forest. The same path his father, Lord Praecepsia as he was known to the common folk, had taken minutes before, his fading footsteps still cast in freshly fallen snow. The trees shivered in the wind, their white limbs, thick with hoarfrost, sending a flurry down upon the baron as they loomed like old, wary guards, watching him. *Daring* him to go further.

He didn't care about the cold, nor the thick, numb sensation that tingled his cheeks and palms. The rage that burned inside of him could've ignited the surrounding forest, if not for what little control still simmered beneath the surface.

Lights from the small hovel at the end of the path flickered across the surrounding trees. The sickly aura of betrayal on the air stirred his gut as he neared, his muscles flexing, spoiling for violence. The very thought of blood on his hands, that copper tang burning his tongue, had him fighting the inexplicable urge to piss himself.

His mother had warned him to control those dark, unnatural impulses, but the boy couldn't help the venom that coursed through him. The blackness that consumed him every time he so much as thought of what his father might be doing right then.

A wolf bayed in the distance. An owl, perched on an overhead branch, watched him as he passed. And if the stories told by the village venators, or hunters, held any merit, surely, something dangerous lurked in the woods beyond. Yet, nothing could pull his attention from the small, frosted window, where he could just make out the blurred forms of two people inside.

He needed to see for himself. To lay his suspicion to rest with the truth.

As he neared with his dagger in hand, he took light steps up the wooden porch, to avoid creaking the tired wood. The images through the opaque glass moved fervently and the sounds of moans echoed from inside.

The boy breathed on the glass, the heat melting the surrounding frost, and he peered through the tiny viewing portal he'd made. His stomach gurgled, the fury in his chest expanding and pressing against his ribs.

Beyond the window, his father stood naked and hunched over his own sister, fucking her against the wooden table. She held an apple lodged in her mouth, her hands bound behind her back.

Having just turned sixteen years of age, the baron had been exposed to sexual acts himself, and he was well aware that to take a woman from behind, like an animal, was forbidden by the church. The very church that held his father in such high regard.

Shadows played on the walls, sexual scenes not matching the movements of the two, like some kind of lewd gathering, yet no one else seemed to be present in the room. Only the dark formations moving in the telling signs of sex. Whatever the shadows mimicked could not be seen. And in his distraction of them, the boy failed to immediately notice a shift in the room. The way the light dimmed.

The frost thickened on the pane. The eyes of his aunt turned white, as her irises rolled back into her head.

His father's movements turned abrupt and aggressive, the way he twitched and curled his fingers into her milk-white flesh, springing drops of blood from beneath his fingernails. He bared his teeth, and what happened next seared itself into the boy's brain.

What looked like long, black tentacles protruded from his father's body, some of which wound tightly around the woman's thighs and the legs of the table, holding her open. Another disappeared between the cheeks of her buttocks, moving in and out of her in the same rhythm as his father prodded her from behind. Yet another wrapped around her throat and, by the telling redness of her face, tightened.

A subtle movement of the older male's arm drew the boy's eyes toward black scales moving across his skin and catching a glint of light.

A monster.

Breath sawed in and out of the baron as shock hooked its claws into his lungs. What in God's name! A disembodied voice told him to *look away*, but he could not. To divert his attention might suggest that what lay before his eyes was real, but surely that could not be so. For he had seen some terrible things in his lifetime, albeit nothing so vile and absurd. The very abomination and sin, for which Bishop Venable had whipped and tormented countless others in the village. Perhaps he would have whipped the baron, as well, because there were things, queer things, that had happened to him on a few occasions. Inexplicable occurrences that defied human ability, or reason. Occurrences he would not dare speak of, lest he wanted to be dissected like the boys who, before him, had drawn Bishop Venable's conjectures.

His ability to capture lightning in his palm without burning his flesh, for one, would've surely spurred rumors throughout all of Praecepsia. And to lift boulders four times his size and hoist them well above his head. To stop time and observe objects floating in air, as if suspended by invisible strings. He knew all these aberrations about himself, and that the world did not always follow human expectations of it, and still, as he stood frozen on that porch, staring into the scene beyond the window, the cold gnawing of shock left him pondering all the many things he did not yet understand.

His father had always been a beast, a cruel and wicked man, but the young baron could never have imagined the depths of his depravity. That he could physically transform into a thing of nightmares. It wasn't possible.

He had to have been dreaming.

In spite of the cold, the baron felt a chill across the back of his neck, and he moved a step away from the glass, but not far enough to shield his view. A tickle of disgust flittered inside his chest as he watched something slither across the inside of his aunt's belly. It took only a moment to realize the tail-like structure had slithered its way down her throat.

What a godless aberration! The limb that blocked her mouth moving inside her belly!

The knife fell from his hand on a clang.

His father's head snapped in his direction.

Black, beady eyes stared back at him through the glass, and the baron backed away further, tripping over the stairs of the porch. Cold, wet snow sloshed beneath his palms, as he tumbled onto his back, never taking his eyes off the window. The shadowy form of his father appeared there, the tentacles slinking back from wherever they'd come and tucking into his body. Even across the small distance from the porch, the boy could see his father's eyes had returned to their usual color, and branches of ice-cold fear snaked beneath his skin.

He slid backward, farther away from the small house, and ran as fast as his legs would carry him into the dark woods. Chilled air burned his lungs and fire claimed the muscles in his legs. The knotty branches and bracken of the forest bed reached out for his legs, digging their ligneous claws into his skin.

The moon sat high overhead, its faint, silvery beams offering little more than slivers of light across an untrodden path. Still, the baron kept on, the chaos in his mind evolving from fear to rage.

There was no one he could tell, not a soul in Praecepsia who would believe such a thing. His father was almost as respected as Bishop Venable. To accuse would result in punishment. In being taken down into one of the undercroft dungeons, like the other boys who were never seen again.

No. He would never speak of it, that much he vowed. But he would need to protect his mother at all costs.

He would kill the evil bastard for the pain he'd caused her. The misery he'd inflicted on the kind and benevolent soul, who grew weaker with each passing day. The insult she suffered, every time she'd been forced to lay eyes on the boy's cousin, Drystan, and could undoubtedly make out the resemblance of her husband and his sister.

The boy vowed to kill his father in the most vile and painful ways--as mercilessly as the hatred Lord Praecepsia had shown toward his son.

And whatever beast lived inside of him.

It was not long before brighter light trickled through the treetops, glistening across the untouched snow. The baron had walked through the night to morning, his limbs stiff and cold, his feet aching. He paused to lean against a tree, closing his eyes to settle his mind. Except, the only thought that lingered there was his father fucking his aunt.

New rage bubbled up inside of the boy, and gritting his teeth, he slammed his fist into the trunk of the tree on which he leaned. The sound of crackling had him opening his eyes, and he lifted his gaze toward the leafy canopy above, which tottered precariously back and forth.

"Oh shit." The baron backed up a step, unsure of which way the tree would inevitably choose to fall. At the sound of splitting wood, he jumped backward, just as the pale beech toppled over, away from him, and crashed to the ground on an explosion of bracken and snow.

Wide-eyed, he stared at the splintered threads of wood, where the trunk lay completely sundered from its roots. It was not the first time the boy had done something which defied human ability and strength, and a niggling sensation of unease crept over his skin. He lifted his hands, imagining black scales and tentacle-like appendages protruding out of him.

No. He was not the same as his father. Not the same!

Movement from the corner of his eye seized his attention, and he turned to find a small mouse trapped beneath one of the fallen branches. It squirmed and squealed to no avail. The sight of it disgusted him, reminding him of his own weakness, trapped beneath his father's cruel and unyielding lordship over him. Its squeaking sounds wrapped around his senses like blades scraping over bone, and he clamped his eyes shut.

"You're weak and pathetic! Just like your mother!"

The words of his father chimed inside his head, stirring

his rage, until jagged flashes of red flickered behind his eyelids. He lifted his boot to stomp on the mouse, his keen sight picking up the reflection of his foot in the mouse's round black eyes. The animal stopped moving, staring up at him, as if accepting its fate. A thought that twisted the baron's revulsion all the more.

It was in that moment that a sound reached his ears. Soft, feminine laughter echoing through the trees. Lowering his boot and briefly sparing the mouse, he looked around for the source of the laughter, which soon turned to quiet chatter. With his hearing sharper than most, the sound could've been a few steps away, or halfway across the forest, and he followed it over fallen trees and tangles of woody debris toward a clearing, not far from where he'd stood.

At the opposite side of a meadow, a young girl in a black hooded cloak, perhaps just a few years his minor, sat atop a branchless log. Long, black plaits of hair spilled from the corners of her raised hood, a contrast to her flawless, pale skin, and his hands curled at his sides as he imagined the silky surface gliding beneath his fingertips. Beams of sunlight seemed to reach for her, as if they longed to touch her, too. At her feet, a half dozen mice scrambled about, and she tossed crumbs onto the snow, inciting a frenzy. She laughed again, and the baron's spine snapped to attention.

He wanted to capture the sound, bottle it away, so he could study its pitch and euphony. Instead, it died out to wistful humming, which turned to singing in a voice that clenched his chest. So beautiful, it pained him to listen, but he did. He watched her for far longer than he'd intended, as she sat feeding the mice.

She stopped suddenly and pointed a finger down at the creatures, as if to count them. "I could've sworn there were seven of you before. What happened to your brother? Hmmm? Has he wandered off?"

The baron glanced back at the fallen branch, where the mouse had been trapped by the fallen tree. Against all his good sense, he tromped back through the woods to where the small mouse still lay trapped by its tail. As he closed his palm around the creature, it nipped his flesh, and the baron snarled, drawing his hand back into a fist.

The sound of the girl's voice reached him again. Like a warm, soothing tea, it sent an inexplicable calm through him, and he ignored the mouse's protests as he held it in the palm of one hand and lifted the fallen branch with the other.

As though sensing his intent, the mouse squirmed less, and the baron was able to get a good look at the smashed and bloodied end of its tail. Something curled inside of him at the sight of it. Pity. He'd never felt remorseful toward an animal that way before, but the thought of the girl seeing the mouse in such a condition made him uneasy. As he ran his finger over the wound, he imagined the tail as it was before. Light flickered between his fingers, followed by a dull heat, and when he released the tail, he could see tiny bolts of lightning dance over the wound.

Frowning in confusion, he watched as the wound's edges moved on their own, toward each other, sealing the bloody flesh between. Not even a minute later, the wound appeared completely healed.

How?

He lifted his hand, staring down at his fingertips where he still felt a small vibration beneath his skin. The flickering bolts disappeared into his flesh and the sensation withered.

He uncurled his fingers from around the mouse, which stood up onto its back feet on his hand and ran its front paws over its face, cleaning itself.

It didn't try to run from him.

As if it no longer feared him.

Hand held out in front of him, he carried the mouse back

across the woods toward the clearing, where the girl still sat. The baron lowered to one knee and rested his palm against the snow, allowing the mouse to run off. At first, it didn't. Paws curled at its chest, it stared back at him with those wide, black eyes.

The baron flicked his fingers. "Go on now," he whispered. Only then did the small creature scamper off, and the boy watched it hop across the clearing toward the girl.

"There you are!" she said, tossing crumbs toward the mouse. "For a moment, I swore an owl had gotten you."

The baron quietly chuckled to himself, but as if she'd heard it, she lifted her gaze in his direction. Fortunately, he stood cloaked by the trees, yet he still slipped behind the trunk of the nearest. On spinning around, he met the tip of a blade propped beneath his chin, his father's henchman, Alaric, staring him dead in the eye. Behind him, the baron's father dismounted his horse and strode up to the boy, a wicked, bastardly smile stretched across the elder lord's face.

"It seems you like to spy." He leaned forward and, lips to the boy's ear, whispered, "Come now, Son. Let us hear just how much your keen eyes have seen."

4

FARRYN

Present

a *starless night looms over the copula, as I stare up at the dilapidated tower. Only a couple stories above, three stony-faced gargoyles peer down at me from their perches—ledges made to look like a pile of skulls beneath their clawed feet. Though they seem to be no more than masonry, there's unsettling detail in their features. Carvings so lifelike, I swear I saw one of them move as I approached the building.*

Above them, a thick fog drifts toward me, carrying on it bits of ash that sprinkle from the sky like a shaken snow globe. Pangs of heavy dread settle into my stomach, the pungent odor of something burning, thick and greasy, like meat, searing my nose.

I've been here before. But when?

A dense thickness clings to the air, slowing my muscles as an invisible force guides me up the stone stairs to the ornate iron door that awaits me. On its surface is a door knocker with the disturbing face of a devil, the eyes of which appear red. Glowing.

The sight of it sends a heavy weight of dread to my stomach, and it's when I place my hand against my belly that I notice the

34

rounded shape of it. So strange. It must've been only yesterday I was dreaming how I might look in a couple months when I started to show.

"Go inside." The feminine voice I hear is foreign, but somehow, strangely familiar.

Yet, I don't want to obey. Something tells me, if I go inside, I'm not coming out. But as if my body has cleaved itself from my mind, I enter through the door, and I'm greeted by a pale, ghostly-looking woman seated at a desk. Gray hair is neatly pinned back, and the white cap with a black stripe that she wears on her head tells me she's a nurse, though the uniform is outdated by a few decades.

I've seen her before, though I can't place where.

She glances up and smiles, teeth a sparkling white. Her expression flickers to soulless black orbs, teeth to yellowing fangs.

Stumbling back a step, I double-blink, and it's the woman's smiling face again. Did I imagine that just now?

She turns just enough to wave me on to the hallway behind her, every movement fluid, as if we were underwater.

A long, dark corridor, its end shadowed in darkness, beckons me beyond the desk's threshold.

That curling sensation in my stomach rises up again, and I swallow back a lump in my throat. Turn back! my head urges. Leave now!

Except, I can't because something is compelling me forward, in spite of that warning in my gut.

A force beyond my control.

A door on the left catches my attention as I make my way down the hall. Bars stretch across a small window, through which I peek inside to find a woman with weathered, wrinkled skin and gray hair, sitting completely naked on the floor. She rocks back and forth, staring up at the corner of the room.

I follow the path of her gaze to two amber, glowing eyes staring back from the shadows. On a gasp, I jump back, a shiver of terror coiling up my spine.

Movement flashes in my periphery, and I turn to see a young boy standing off in the middle of the corridor a few doors down from me. With black hair and blue eyes, he reminds me of Jericho. Ragged clothes, too small for his body, cling desperately to his skeletal frame. His presence is strange and unfitting here. The eerie hum in my bones tells me bad things happen in this place. Horrible things that a child should never suffer.

When I step in his direction, he spins on his heel and darts off toward the shadows.

"Hey!" I call out, but he doesn't bother to turn. I chase after him, through winding corridors whose ends are always cloaked in darkness. The boy disappears into the shadows, and I come to a halt, turning to see a door. An ominous entrance, on which 777 has been etched into the steel.

Frowning, I stare at the crude carving, certain there's meaning behind it, but I can't remember why. Whimpers from the other side stir up a deep-seated dread—something buried so deep within, I can't even say what it is that troubles me.

Save him.

In spite of the foreboding twist in my gut, I reach for the handle on the door.

"Farryn," the foreign voice from before whispers, and when I turn, there's a woman standing only a few steps away. Long, golden-spun, almost-white hair rests on her bony shoulders. Her eyes are a rich chestnut brown, drawing attention to the soft pale glow of her face. In spite of her small and fragile frame, which looks to be wracked by hunger, she carries an ethereal beauty.

"How do I know you?"

She glances down to my stomach and back, her lips stretching to a smile, and for a split second, her eyes turn black, teeth to fangs just as the nurse's had at the desk.

Tendrils of fear slither over my neck, and I back up a step, but an intense pain claws my insides, like hooks dragging across my abdomen. Paralyzing pain that has me bent over, clutching my swollen belly.

Blood splashes to the floor below me. So much blood, and when it pools over the concrete, it has a glassy, black appearance. Deep, black pools that fan out from my feet.

At a strange humming sound, I look back and find the woman twitching in place. Nausea claims the strength of my legs, and I stumble to the side, my shoulder hitting the wall. The woman rushes toward me with bared teeth and the kind of thrill in her eyes that sends a shudder to the center of my bones. She drops to her knees.

I watch in horror as she drags her hand over the blood and licks it from her palm.

Finally, screams rip from my chest.

Something bands around my midsection, pressing into the ache of my belly. I claw at whatever it is, frantic to get away, but it's strong. Too strong.

Beyond the woman, the little boy I followed stands watching, then covers his face in his little palms.

Save him.

The woman's jaw widens until unhinged to a terrifying gape, as she twists around toward the boy.

"Leave him alone! Leave my baby alone!" The band tightens at the same time that my hands shoot out to reach for him.

In my scratching and wriggling to break free of what's holding me, I look down to see that what I thought were arms dragging me away is a long, black tentacle-like appendage curling itself around my waist.

Every muscle in my body tenses.

Following the length of the tentacle, I turn to see red fiery eyes staring back at me. Eyes I've seen before. Ones that send a shudder of fear through every cell of my body.

Horns protrude from his head and curl backward, their surface covered in the same silvery tattoos that match those on his skin.

He opens his mouth to show two long fangs, their tips dripping blackness. Without warning, he snaps toward me.

❧

I awoke on a gasp to darkness, caged in arms too strong to escape. *My baby. My baby!* Kicking and squirming, I fought to break loose, but my captor only tightened his grip.

"Farryn, settle down." Though his voice was familiar and calming, I refused to settle. I needed to see the blood. *The blood!*

"Shhhh," he whispered, "It's only a dream."

"Let me go! I need to see! I need to see the blood!"

Without protest, he released me, and I shot upright. Throwing the sheets away from me, I stared down at my naked legs where not a speck of blood could be seen. I shifted on the bed, lifting up from the mattress. No blood. Nothing but crisp white sheets.

Confused, I scanned the room, but it stood only dark and quiet. A curtain fluttered at a cracked window, allowing the late winter air to breeze through. *Aunt Nelle's. I'm at Aunt Nelle's. The old bedroom I took as my own.*

A glance at the clock on the nightstand showed it was one thirty-seven in the morning. As lucidity crept over me, I recalled three nights before.

Jericho. He'd come back.

Back from Ex Nihilo.

The heady scent of sex clung to the air, the bedsheets crumpled and in disarray. I turned to find Jericho staring back at me, a look of concern on his face. Only, instead of the red glowing eyes from my dream, his was the bright blue I recognized. *He's here. I'm safe.*

Nausea gurgled in my stomach and tickled my chest, a sensation I'd grown all too familiar with. Scrambling out of bed, I slapped a hand over my mouth and darted down the hallway toward the bathroom, not caring that I didn't wear a stitch of clothing. Once inside, I slammed the door behind me and fell to my knees before the toilet just as acid shot up my throat, and I leaned forward, spewing black, viscous vomit into the bowl. Another heave sent more liquid pouring out of my mouth, splashing up into my face as it hit the water. I spat out the stringy material, and staring down at the dark-tinged fluids that gathered in a strange, swirled pattern in the water, the unease I'd felt before climbed the back of my neck. I'd read a number of pregnancy books that spoke of morning sickness, but had yet to come across any references to *black* vomit.

An all-too-familiar smoky flavor, like a burnt steak, filled my mouth and curled my stomach. The first time I'd vomited, I'd sworn I was about to die of some kind of internal bleeding. I hadn't bothered to go to the ER, because, well, what could I have said? I was impregnated with a half demon, half angel child, and vomiting black might've been perfectly normal.

A hard knock at the door startled me, and on reflex, I flushed the toilet.

"Is everything okay?" Jericho asked through the door.

"Yeah. Just a little morning sickness is all! I'll be right out!" Still weak with queasiness, I pushed up from the toilet and, with trembling hands, turned on the faucet to wash the grotesque mist of toilet water vomit from my face.

In the mirror's reflection, I caught sight of something on my side. Twisting toward the mirror showed a dark bruise there. An ache I hadn't paid attention to up until that moment, and it prompted me to turn to view the other side, where dark successive lines marked the rough grip of fingers. My thoughts drifted to the night before, when Jericho had gotten a little rough during sex. I vaguely recalled feral sounds and grunting, along with his bruising grip across my hips. More twisting showed bruises across my ass and the back of my thighs.

Jesus. It looked like we'd had an all-out brawl.

Shaking it off, I gave my teeth a thorough brushing, and gargled twice with mouthwash until the burned-ash taste no longer lingered on my tongue. Ignoring my still-gurgly stomach, I returned to the room, careful to hold my arms so he wouldn't see the bruising, as he'd surely feel remorseful over it. I didn't want him regretting his roughness. I liked the aggression in him, his fervor for sex, as much as I enjoyed his gentle nature.

The moment I stepped through the door, my eyes shot to Jericho. His muscled body lay sprawled over the mattress, white sheets covering what I already knew was an impressive lower half, and even in my shaken and nauseated state, I couldn't help but admire him while I crossed the room toward the bed. Three days he'd been with me, and I still marveled the man.

He turned to his side, as I crawled in next to him. Thick arms, *normal arms*, wrapped around me, and I allowed him to pull me into his warm body. Despite the heady scent in the room, he carried his own citrusy, masculine aroma that calmed my nerves—a scent, so delicious, I wanted to lick it from the air.

Yes, I remembered it all. We'd hardly left my bed in the three nights since his return, the two of us entangled in each other. I'd slept soundly ever since–a first for me–up until that damned dream.

Forcing myself to breathe slowly, I closed my eyes. *Just a nightmare.*

Breathe.

Rubbing a trembling hand across my brow, I urged my

head to banish those last seconds of the dream that had somehow looped through my memories.

"You have a sickness?" Jericho asked as he stroked a hand down my hair, the sound of his voice grounding me even more.

A weak chuckle escaped me. "A number of pregnant women do. It's normal." Though, I suspected vomiting black wasn't.

"It was a nightmare that woke you. Tell me about it."

"It was horrible."

We'd made the decision to leave at first light for Nightshade, so that I might rest after our marathon lovemaking, but I could've left right then, as unsettled as I felt.

"Tell me."

"I can't. I feel like if I say it, it'll be out in the universe."

"The universe doesn't require prompting to do what it wants." The air of amusement in his voice made me smile, in spite of the fear still rattling my nerves. I'd forgotten how easily I could be distracted by him.

For so many months, I'd woken from horrible dreams, to the feeling of someone watching me and unable to shake the visuals--until morning, when I'd reawaken a sleep-deprived zombie. If not for the inheritance Aunt Nelle had left me, who knew how I'd have survived, sleeping all day, trying to sleep at night.

"Tell me your dream," he said again.

I hesitated, at first, my mind fixated on all the blood. So much blood. With a shake of my head, I dismissed the thought. "Just a nightmare. It was nothing."

"You called for Syrisa." The humor in his voice from moments ago had withered to a troubling tone.

I scoffed at that. "*Syrisa?* I've never met a Syrisa in my life." Although, she could have been someone from Lustina's life that I just couldn't recall. "Did you know a Syrisa?"

"I did, yes. She was a seer from centuries ago."

"Perhaps it was *you* who called for *her*, then? Like one of the maids who pined after you, hmmm?" I teased with a smile. "Speaking of maids, Evie …"

"Is gone. The moment I realized what had happened, I ordered her out of Blackwater. And had Remy not died at the hands of Drystan, I'd have killed him myself." His eyes held a sincere and deadly resolve, as if he could've imagined such a thing right then, and I had to remind myself, for all the good in Jericho, there was a duality within him. A darkness that was as much a part of him as the raven color of his hair and the unwavering sparkle of his eye.

"He was actually trying to help me, in a weird, Remy sort of way."

"I could have lost you forever. Regardless of his intentions, I would not have spared him mercy."

"This must be your demon half speaking."

"This is my no-bullshit half speaking. Nothing will take you away from me again. Now, tell me this nightmare of yours."

His request sprang forth the image of the strange woman, who hadn't seemed familiar to me, at all—not in Lustina's memories, nor my own.

"Tell me more about this seer," I volleyed back.

Brows pulled to a frown, he stared off, but I felt the curl of his fingers around my shoulders in a possessive grip. "No one to trouble yourself over. Perhaps just a name you've stumbled upon in one of your many books."

"I've not, though. That's not a common name. And as I recall, the last book wasn't entirely fiction." I was referring to the one given to me at the bookstore in Nightshade by the mysterious Catriona, who I'd since found out was Lustina's mother. Nowhere in that text, though, did I stumble upon a Syrisa. "I just want to know who she was."

On a clearly-irritated groan, he dragged a hand down his face. "Gods be damned, you are a stubborn little bird."

The comment snagged another smile from me—the most I'd smiled in months.

"Fine. She was an accused *black witch* who suffered the most severe punishment in the history of Praecepsia. Satisfied?"

Snorting a laugh, I turned my head to the side. "Of course I'm not satisfied. You left me on a cliffhanger with that. Why are you being so strange about it?"

"I'm not being strange. Only cautious. The details surrounding her death can be unsettling."

"And yet, I dreamed of a woman who shared the same uncommon name as her. I want to hear the story."

"For seven days and seven nights, she suffered torment at the hands of the Pentacrux. They shaved her head and stripped her of clothing. Beat her. Starved her. Burned her with hot irons and flayed the skin from her back." The thought of that made me flinch, and he kissed my shoulder. "They tied her arms and legs between two posts, and a crowd watched on as feral dogs consumed her alive."

Tendrils of dread curled inside my stomach at the visual of such a thing. "Jesus. *Why?* What did they want?"

"She foretold the future, and as such, the Pentacrux viewed her as evil. Few could speak her name without a shudder for the look in her eyes when those dogs set their sights on her."

Although Lustina's memories had somewhat merged with my own, I felt little connection to that barbaric world, where punishment included dogs feeding on women. "They watched it and did nothing?"

"In fairness, she *was* dangerous. Unlike Lustina's mother, who was also accused of being a witch, there was venom in

Syrisa's blood, and magic so dark, even my bastard father feared her."

"Your father?" I couldn't recall if I'd ever heard Jericho speak of him.

"Yes. It was at his command that she was captured by the Pentacrux. He tried to make her his slave, but she would not yield to him."

"Why did they capture her?"

"Why so many questions?"

"Well, that's your fault. You got me intrigued."

With a huff, he pulled me in tight to him and ran his hand along the edge of my hip. "She began an affair with a young boy from the village. Probably no more than fourteen years old. He was betrothed to another. A girl from a very prominent family in Praecepsia who insisted that Syrisa had been possessed by demons to favor a lover so young."

Betrothed at fourteen? I'd never have survived the era in which Jericho had grown up. "How old was Syrisa?"

"At the time, she would have been thirty-two. It wasn't unusual for men to have such relationships with young girls, as a means of stature, or financial security. But Syrisa had neither. She was a lonely widow in the woods."

I grimaced at the thought that he was so young and she, so much older. Even if Jericho had a couple centuries on me, I was at least beyond puberty.

"When the guard seized her home, they found the bodies of two boys in a room beneath the floorboards in her cabin."

The visual of that sent a shudder through me. "Oh, my God. But you said they arrested her for something else. Because she foretold the future."

"Yes. Years before, she had foretold my father's demise. Why they didn't arrest her then, is a mystery to me. And so the question remains. Why did you dream of a Syrisa? What was this nightmare of yours?"

Lips clamped together, I hesitated once more to voice it, for fear of manifesting the outcome. "I dreamed I lost the baby." A tightness throbbed in my chest, and I couldn't bring myself to go into detail.

His grip tightened around me, and he kissed the top of my head. "I'm no expert on pregnancy, by any means, but I would venture to say it's normal to dream that. Perhaps it represents some latent fear inside of you."

"Maybe. But …"

"But what?"

"Well, there was another in my dream. A terrifying demon with red eyes and horns. And tentacle-like arms. I feel like I've dreamed him before."

With an abrupt twitch of his shoulder, he shifted beneath me. "Tentacle arms?"

"I didn't really see much of them. He was standing behind me. We were in a place I recognized. A recurring dream I've had. A place with endless rooms and passages that disappeared into shadows. Hidden rooms, like an enormous labyrinth."

"You have these dreams often?" he asked, running his finger up and down my arm.

"More so in the last couple of months. Well, since that night. But the rooms aren't new. And I can see the door knocker at the entrance. Devils with ghastly faces and strange gargoyles that feel like they're moving. I'm always scared to enter this place. There's such a horrible feeling that I can't leave once I go inside."

Again, I felt him twitch beneath me. "These gargoyles … are they perched upon a stone ledge of skulls?"

"Yes. You've seen them?"

"I have."

I shot my gaze to his. "Where?"

"The entrance to Infernium. It's an asylum in

45

Nightshade."

"Asylum?" I frowned at that. Yet another strange oddity. Half of my brain wanted to believe it was all a string of odd coincidences. The other half knew better. "So, this isn't a place I would've seen in Nightshade? One of those weird echoes you told me about?"

"I very much doubt you'd be here now if you had. Very few ever leave Infernium. And of those who do, no one can forget having been there."

"Why would I know of it? How could I remember such details if I've never been there?"

"I do not know the answer to that. I am equally baffled." Wearing a contemplative expression, he stroked a finger across my shoulder as he stared off toward the end of the bed.

"Did Lustina ever cross over? Is it possible it's a memory of hers?"

"I was not well-versed on crossing over back then. The only asylum in Praecepsia was run by the Pentacrux. I will admit that, although it was equally unsettling, there's a difference between those who are essentially still alive, and those who do not realize they've passed on."

Could there have been anything more terrifying than an asylum in the afterlife? A place where a soul might never have the opportunity to leave? "There is no escape from the mind, then? Whether you're alive, or dead."

"No. And too often, those who are lost, whose faith has deteriorated over time, find themselves in Infernium. Unfortunately, there are no angels looking after them there, and the most vulnerable become easy prey."

"Prey to what?"

He lifted a lock of my hair, letting it slide through his fingers. "The demons who haunt them."

"So, how does one end up in an asylum in the afterlife?"

He rolled onto his back, tucking a muscled bicep beneath his head. "The same way they do here, I suppose. Some hear voices, telling them to do unspeakable things. Some see things. Of course, they're just more in tune to what others refuse to see. Vulnerable, really."

"I've had hallucinations."

"What kind of hallucinations?"

"Things that aren't there. Eyes watching me. Paint peeling." *A nurse blowing black smoke in my face.* "It's like a dream, but when I snap out of it, they're gone."

"It's possible they're not hallucinations, Farryn. Bear in mind, you're privy to things that most are not. The infernal are probably chomping at the bit for a soul as pure as yours."

The idea of that prickled my skin. "It's only the baby that keeps them from claiming it now?"

"Yes."

Thoughts spun wild inside my head, ones I'd considered before, but didn't bother to speak aloud. "What will childbirth be like there? In Nightshade?"

"Different from here. There's a physician, skilled, but exceptionally old fashioned, who comes to the Cathedral on call."

"Human?" Given the fact so many in Nightshade had forgotten their lives and memories, it didn't seem likely their education would survive the transition to Purgatory.

"Cambion."

"Can she be trusted?"

"*He*," he clarified.

"Ah. Well, you said *skilled*, I just assumed."

"And he would only harm the baby if he happens to yearn for eternal agony himself. No cambion in his right mind would dare bring harm to a sentinel. Particularly said sentinel's only child."

"Already protective." I chuckled, the humor dying on a

sigh when I rested my hand against my still-small belly. "And if there are any complications?"

"That is a thought which has kept me up most of the evening. And so I'll ask again. Are you certain you want to leave behind what you know? What's familiar and comfortable?"

My thoughts rewound to the day in the OB's office, the one and only appointment I'd bothered to make in the last few months. "Women do home births all the time. I'll deal with the pain."

"Of that, I am certain, Tu Nazhja. However, I'm not sure *I* can deal with watching you go through that pain."

"Is pregnancy the only way to break the curse?"

"Two souls can't be claimed by the curse, so yes. Why do you ask?"

I hesitated to tell him at first, fearing the possibility that he'd tell me something I didn't want to hear. "My pregnancy test came back negative, actually. Is that normal?"

"Perhaps, yes. Your tests aren't exactly equipped to detect the complexities of what makes up a Sentinel. They test for human hormones, which may not even be detectable."

"Even if the baby is half human?"

"Who's to say how much when they first develop?"

There were so many unknowns and nothing to guide me through what was normal and abnormal. "I keep trying to imagine a version of you and I smooshed together in an adorable little cherub with dark hair and beautiful eyes."

The smile on his face faded to something serious, and I didn't have to ask to know what had soured his mood.

"Will it hurt? My transition to cambion?" I didn't look at him, knowing the question probably infuriated him even now.

"I've never watched it happen before."

"Then, how do we even know it'll happen? Maybe it's a

myth to keep nosy humans like me from–"

"It's not a myth, Farryn, and I suggest you not take it lightly. What you've signed yourself over for could be a myriad of things."

Wringing the sheet in my hands failed to calm the burgeoning anxiety that crawled over the back of my neck. The very thing I didn't want to think about. "Am I condemned to Hell?"

"Hell for humans is not a physical place, per se. There are the Infernal Lands where demons dwell, but most of hell happens inside the mind, when your demons are given free reign. When they're no longer bound by the rules of the heavens."

"What do you mean?"

"You've forgone the protection that most are given by birth. A treaty, of sorts, between Heaven and Hell. When our child is born, you will no longer fall under their protection."

"I don't understand."

"Demons are not permitted to toy with humans, any more than angels are permitted to cavort with them. When humans go out of their way to commit a crime against the heavens, as you did by having that symbol translated, they essentially forfeit the protection of the angels and open the gates to the darkest parts of the mind. Your demons consume you to the point of absolute paralysis."

Everything I'd been taught about Hell seemed like a ridiculous fairytale to me, with some caricature version of the devil. The place he was talking about sounded terrifying. Real. "Are you talking delirium?"

"Yes. When you succumb to those demons, you become vulnerable. There are five realms, one of which seeks out these vulnerable souls. It's called Eradyę. Imagine your world, but through a much darker lens. A land of death and destruction."

Holy shit, this was a lot to unpack. "But ... Xhiphias ..."

"Xhiphias answers to an overlord. Are you prepared to do the same? To take innocent life and deliver souls to those who will spend eternity tormenting them? Or to become a dojzra slave to some sadistic overlord who would have you do unspeakable things at his command?" He asked the last question through clenched teeth, as if the very thought enraged him.

Admittedly, I'd been a little naive, not really considering the consequences of bringing Jericho back from Ex Nihilo. That wasn't to say I wouldn't do it all over again. Exactly the same. In a heartbeat. "Is there no other way?"

"Of course. There are hundreds of other ways. All of them with the same outcome. Pain. Suffering. Eternal misery for a human."

"I not only brought the wrath of the heavens, but opened the gates of hell."

His muscles stiffened beneath me, and without warning, he sat upright. Abruptly. The sight of him had the hairs on my neck standing upright, the way his brows pulled tight as he stared off at seemingly nothing. It reminded me of the nights I'd woken to find Camael hissing at something only she could see at the end of my bed.

"What is it?"

Instead of answering, he continued to stare off, the deepening of his frown becoming worrisome. "They're here." His words had the hairs on my neck standing on end.

"Who?"

"The Sentinels. They must've sensed my return."

"Like, *here*-here? In my house?"

"No. I can sense when they've breached the plane." His gaze finally landed on mine, and the intensity in it sent a chill down my spine. "We have to leave tonight. Right now."

5

THE BARON

"The holy penitential tells us that confession of sin is a means of cleansing our soul. The Holy Father demands such sacrament in order that we might be purified enough to sit beside Him in the heavens. Now tell me, boy, what sins have you to confess?" Bishop Venable's voice echoed through the cold and dimly-lit room.

Cold chains dug into the baron's arms as he stood on the balls of his feet, in the center of a dank room of the church's undercroft. A place he had seen countless others—mostly boys—taken for questioning under the guise of righteous intent. His tunic and jacket had been removed, exposing his bare chest. Food had been withheld since two days prior, when his father had escorted him back to the manor and demanded a meeting with Bishop Venable. The two had prodded him to speak of what he'd seen in the woods, but the baron had known better. Had seen too many young boys go missing for confessing equally strange things. As punishment for his silence, his father had him taken to the undercroft of the church, where the two elders continued their inquisitions in private. Only one other pentrosh stood in attendance, and his cousin Drystan, whom the baron had long suspected was born from the infidelity of his father and aunt. The thought brought to mind the visual of his father's monstrous form fucking her like an animal, and the baron clenched his jaw to keep from showing his repulsion.

"Have you nothing to confess?" the bishop asked, his voice laced with stark irritation.

The baron said nothing. Did not so much as twitch, or move, or show the slightest inclination to entertain their questioning. Hunger and exhaustion gnawed at his bones, but he would not relent. Giving up his silence would result in punishment far worse than an empty stomach and weak muscles.

Except, the bishop was far shrewder a man than the baron was in his delirious state.

More conniving.

"It is to be assumed, with your lack of response, that you do not wish to cleanse your soul, and therefore, you must be infected with evil. An evil that claims your tongue!"

The baron ground his teeth at the accusation, his thoughts reverting to the night in the woods when he'd seen true evil in the flesh while watching his father fuck his sister like an animal. The black scales and tentacles. Horns and fangs. Had he told them what he had witnessed, he would have been labeled a sorcerer of evil. A prophetic seer of demons, which the Pentacrux deemed an offense to the bishop.

Yet, he could not bring himself to tell the bishop that he had seen nothing, either. Such blasphemous words burned his tongue and squeezed his muscles.

"We will rid you of this evil, boy. However long it takes, you will be cleansed."

From the corner of his eye, the baron caught a glimpse of the leather plaits of a whip hanging from the bishop's grip, knotted and menacing and hungry for flesh. A rush of adrenaline surged through his body, his arms shaking, clattering the chains.

The bishop's quiet chuckle grated his nerves. "You are stubborn, young lord. But not unbreakable to the will of The Holy Father. Evil cannot be left to fester within us, for it will grow like a violent weed and strangle the life of our good community." He ran his fingers through the leather braids in mocking. "As an act of mercy, I offer you one last opportunity to confess."

In that moment, the baron thought of his mother, could hear her voice like a soft wind caressing his ear. *Tell them you saw nothing.*

"I can't," the baron whispered to himself, but the bishop must have picked up on his words because he volleyed back, "You can and you will, lest you suffer the punishment of a heretic!"

Tell them, his mother's voice urged.

The baron lifted his gaze from the floor, catching sight of Drystan, who stared back with a piteous look in his eyes. A look that would one day turn to resentment and spite, but right then showed nothing but sympathy.

Swallowing back the rage that had climbed to the back of his throat, the baron shook harder, wanting nothing more than to set the entire room to flame. "I saw … nothing," he gritted out past clenched teeth.

"Lies!" Lord Praecepsia hissed from the corner of the room where he watched. "The boy lies! He saw something that day in the woods. And as a result, he speaks through the mouth of evil."

The baron wanted to laugh at his father. Wanted to tell him to return to the hell from which he had indisputably come, but that was exactly what they both wanted of him. Confessing would have been his death sentence.

"Perhaps you have been there, *Father*, to speak so assuredly on my behalf." Though small, the boy's insult had him smiling as he watched his father's face blanch.

"Your father fears for your soul, and as one who has borne witness to the evil corruption of young boys such as yourself, I cannot deny the telling signs of it in you." The bishop circled him to his back, and when he leaned in, the baron felt the moist steam of hot breath against his neck. "I will tear away the nefarious beast which has taken residence in your heart like the fragile wings of an insect." He stepped away, and the baron directed his gaze toward the stony floor, where bloodstains marked the punishment of others before him. "Come forth, demon of Lucifer. Come forth and reveal your wicked intent!"

The whooshing sound of leather sliced through the air and struck hard against the baron's flesh. Pain rippled over his skin, searing and hot like scorched metal. He swallowed back a whimper, not daring to give them the satisfaction of hearing his cries. Another streak of fire licked his flesh. Another whoosh and crack. His knees buckled, knuckles burning as he gripped the chain for support. More lashes followed, and the baron opened his eyes in time to see his own fresh blood mingled with stains on the floor.

"Confess! Confess now!"

He could hear the exasperation in the bishop's voice, a sound that only goaded him to remain silent.

"You will confess for the sake of your soul! Every drop of blood spilled is a testament of the devil's hold on you! It is milk for the beast."

Each strike arrived in an unbearable cadence of agony, until all at once, the baron felt a different sensation bubble up inside of him. One of anticipation.

Freedom.

He tipped his head back and spat a listless chuckle, which

was met with a gasp from the young pentrosh across the room, who stood covering his mouth with his hands.

"Your defiance does not sway me, boy. I have learned to be resolute in the face of evil. Now tell me, what will you confess? What sins burn in your belly like fire?"

Again, the young baron chuckled darkly, breathing shallow so as not to disrupt his wounds. "It is only ... the urge to piss ... on your fine shoes ... which burns inside of me."

On a growl, the bishop struck again, and when the leather bit his muscles, the baron let out a groan. "Mark my words. I will exorcize this dark creature from your soul. If it takes an entire lifetime, I will see you purified. We will reconvene after your wounds have had the opportunity to properly heal. And then, young lord, the true inquisition will begin."

With one arm wrapped around him, Drystan helped the baron lower to the soft bed mattress. The wounds on his back flared in protest, and the baron turned onto his stomach, burying his face into the mattress. The bishop had allowed him to return to the manor, but only for his father's sake.

How would the great Lord Praecepsia be perceived, had his own son been accused of heresy?

"You haven't so much as moaned. I dare say you seem content. How is that possible after such cruel punishment?" Drystan asked, daubing a wet cloth against the opened flesh.

The truth was, during punishment, his mind had raced with so many vicious thoughts, his rage as strong and unrelenting as the leather which tore at his back, that he'd barely felt the pain through the numbness. But as he lay in the aftermath, the agony poked at him with a vengeance. He searched his mind for distraction. Anything that could deter his focus from what must have been a grotesque sight to behold.

In the nothingness, a figure emerged. One with long, raven hair and skin as fair and flawless as the fresh snow. The soothing nature of her voice somehow mingled with the searing burn on his back, entwining itself like silken ribbons across a blade's edge. An inexplicable arousal throbbed in his groin, and he shifted on the bed, groaning into the pillow.

"That is the first sound of agony I've heard out of you. Dear Lord in Heaven, if you saw what I see ... well, you would surely vomit."

While the baron wanted to hate Drystan and all he represented, it so happened he was the only semblance of a friend the boy had, seeing as the baron had been cast as evil from the time he had been born. The villagers paid him respect out of stature only, because of his name and his father's position, while otherwise speaking ill of him behind his back.

"Leave, if it troubles you so much." Something had happened inside that small room in the undercroft, which stank of dried blood and suffering. As he hung from those chains, helpless and hopeless, he'd felt a mystifying exhilaration consume him. A delicious fearlessness that had curled in his stomach with every strike to his back. The visions in his head had darkened, a black, toxic fume of elation that held him captivated.

Craving.

"What troubles me is that you insist on prodding your father. Do you not know that just three nights ago, young Lord Fletcher was taken down into that very room and has not been heard from since?" Drystan dipped the blood-soaked rag into the basin of water on the table beside the bed, squeezing the pink-tinged fluids from the cloth. When he set it on a new wound, the baron's muscles flinched with the burn.

"For what *crime?*" The baron could not help the sarcasm in his voice. The boys taken to the undercroft had rarely ever committed a crime worthy of the punishment rumored to have been doled there. Punishment, for which, he could now attest.

"He claimed to have seen a tiny serpent-like creature housed within an apple."

"He was murdered for observation of a worm?"

"It was no worm. I saw it myself. And I will not dare describe the nature of it, except to say, it *was no worm.*"

"It did not matter what I said to the bishop. Whether I confessed, or remained silent. He has longed to punish me for quite some time."

A long pause followed before Drystan finally cleared his throat. "The bishop … is a … good man. Do not speak ill of him. He wants only to cleanse your soul."

"Your affections for the man are concerning to me."

"I do not have affections. It is admiration and nothing more."

Admiration. The very word became blasphemous when paired with Bishop Venable. "Let us speak of your admiration once he has meted out punishment against your flesh."

After rinsing the cloth, Drystan shook his head, his gaze directed toward the fluid in the basin that seemed more blood than water. "Forgive me for speaking candidly, My Lord, but you would avoid such punishment if you stopped inviting it. The idea that you ventured into the woods so late at night–"

"Do not endeavor to lecture me as if you have no sense for why I ventured out."

"They were together."

If there was anyone who loathed his father as much as the baron, it was Drystan. And only for the way Lord Praecepsia had always treated his mother, his own sister, like a common whore. "I am tired. Leave me."

"As you wish, My Lord." An air of disappointment clung to his tone, as he lifted the basin from the bedside table. "I will return in the morning to check your wounds." Basin in hand, he made his way to the door, and the click signaled his exit.

The baron had suffered small punishments throughout his childhood, but Drystan, as the whipping boy assigned to him, had taken most of his spankings. He'd never truly suffered such unbearable lashings that felt like his skin had been torn clean off his back. The pain had intensified since he had left the cathedral, and it was only the brisk, nighttime air which had numbed the agony on the carriage ride back to the manor. Right then, however, it pulsed with new torment, spasms that clawed at his skin with fresh pain, and he curled his fingers into the soft pillow and attempted to breathe through the cotton.

The stifling of his breaths sent a shiver through his body and a rush of blood to his cock. Intrigued by the sensation, he undid his breeches just enough to spring himself free and buried his face in the pillows once more. As he ground his hips into the mattress, the pain across his back flared and, coupled to the lack of breath, had him dizzy with euphoria.

He moaned into the cotton and imagined a soft, feminine form beneath him. One with full breasts and curves, and while the girl at the meadow could not have been more than fourteen, two years younger than him, it was her face he saw in the blackness of his mind. Her moans in that song-like voice which had coiled around his senses. He drove his groin faster into the mattress, daring himself not to take his cock in hand, but as another zap of pain streaked across his skin, he could not help it. Snaking his hand beneath him, he lifted his hips just enough to stroke his shaft, face still buried.

What in Hades had taken hold of him?

He had certainly worked himself that way before. Had eased the ache of his cock many times in the night, but never to the tune of pain and fantasy. Somehow, the two had crossed paths in his mind, creating an exquisite sensation that had his stomach flexing and his ballocks heavy and aching for release. As the pressure heightened, the air waning, he moaned harder, pumping his fist with furious determination. Thoughts reverted from the girl to the wounds on his back, and what he imagined to be a grotesque display of violence. The rage from before twisted inside of him again, and before he could process what was happening to him, a wave of dizzying ecstasy swept over him, crashing into the back of his skull on a flash of bright light. He grunted out a muffled completion into the soft cotton as jets of hot release shot forth, wetting his stomach and chest, just before he lowered his hips to the mattress, and ground out the last of it.

He'd never felt anything so intense and pleasurable in his life, but in the calm that followed, a cold sensation moved across the back of his neck. The realization that it was not pleasure alone that had brought him to such a pinnacle, but the pain. The agony and violence inflicted against him.

The thought left his stomach churning with disgust, and pulling his hand from his pants, he shuddered, repulsed and ashamed.

What had he done? Why?

Surely, there was something wrong with him. What kind of ill-minded person could think such vile fantasies?

Thoughts of his father back in the cabin sprang to mind, and the pained expression on his aunt's face while his father took her savagely. Violently. He could not imagine inflicting such torment. The baron's first time with a woman had been at the cusp of fourteen. She was a scullery maid, four years his senior, who had pulled him into a closet after a few curious glances. They'd held private trysts every night, her having taught him things about a woman's body, and how to give pleasure, as well as receive. He'd always enjoyed the satisfied smile on her face afterward. It had given him a sense of pride to know he'd learned so quickly, and she would praise his skills, referring to him as a young *adeptus*. His mother had eventually found out and promptly kicked her out of the manor, but the seed of euphoria had been planted in the baron's head. On two occasions, he'd sought out slightly older girls from the village, who were happy to oblige him, due to his title and appearance, but most wanted marriage and promises he could not keep at such a young age. Therefore, most nights had been spent stroking himself to climax, which he found most satisfying during baths when the water would wet his skin. However, at no point did he harbor a single thought of pain, or violence, during those sessions. Something had shifted inside of him. A terrifying discovery.

Was that how it would be with a woman from then on? Gleaning pleasure from her misery?

As if in punishment, a searing hot jolt like a trickle of boiling water ran down his spine and left him stiff and trembling. The worst of his wounds stretched from one shoulder blade to the other. He screwed his eyes shut and squeezed the pillow so hard, his knuckles burned. But as the heat in his hand intensified, he released the pillow to find the skinny, jagged lightning bolts dancing across his fingers.

A thought struck him then. The mouse in the woods with the crushed tail.

He had healed it with his own hands.

A narrow trench across his arm was the evidence of an errant lash from one of the leather braids, and he set his finger over it, imagining his flesh as it was before his punishment. He focused hard on the image in his mind, and felt warmth beneath his palm. A strange, wet sound had him opening his eyes, and when he lifted his hand, he watched with morbid fascination, as the wound's edges stretched toward each other, sealing the gash from one end to the other, until nothing remained. Not a single indication that a whip had ever touched him there. No cut, nor bruise, nor scar.

Confounded, he stared down at his hand again, then rested it at his shoulder, unsure if the healing required direct contact with the wound itself. In spite of that, he imagined his back, the entirety of it, healed and flawless as it was before that night. The same wet sound he had heard moments ago reached his ears. A tightness stretched across his back, but he felt no pain. On the contrary, a cool, soothing sensation blanketed his abused flesh, and he lay against the pillow once more, reveling in it. It wasn't long before the feeling faded, and he hesitated a moment, then pushed up from the bed, tucking his manhood back into his breeches.

There was no pain.

No agonizing burn.

He ran across the room to the embellished golden mirror, which his mother had purchased from Venice. There, he twisted enough that he could see nearly half his back was free of any bleeding wounds, before he checked the other half, noting the same.

Healed, just as he'd healed the mouse's tail in the woods.

The baron lifted his hands, staring down at them, his mind swirling with so many questions. The most prominent of which being, what else could they do?

6

FARRYN

*T*he old-fashioned, claw-foot tub made for an ominous piece of furniture in the small bathroom, where I stood wringing the oversized T-shirt I'd worn as a nightgown. We'd already handed off Camael to the neighbor lady. Much as I'd have wanted her to come along, I didn't think she'd be willing to damn near drown without clawing my eyeballs out.

Shirtless, Jericho sat on the edge of the tub, turning the dials to adjust the temperature, and as the water filled the basin, a knot formed in my stomach.

For years, I'd lived in the house and couldn't bring myself to bathe in that tub. It wasn't just bathtubs, either. Sometimes, if I held my face toward the shower spray for too long, the panic would rise up inside my chest, reminding me of that godawful day when my father had held me underwater. Even then, a visual flashed through my mind, the sounds of my screams muted beneath the surface.

"Papa! I can't breathe! I can't breathe! Stop!"

Eyes clamped, I shook the memory free and breathed in

through my nose, out through my mouth, just like my therapist had taught me.

"So, um …" I gulped back the fear climbing up the back of my throat. "How do we do this?"

Brows creased with concern, he ran his hand over the water's surface, and I watched as ripples chased after. "Come here."

"You could just tell me first."

"Come, Farryn. Sit." He patted one of his muscled thighs, and I wondered if he'd use them to wrangle me into the water.

A burn streaked across my lip where I bit down too hard, and I stepped toward him, my pulse hammering as I neared the half-filled tub. Before I could jolt back, his hand gripped me, and he yanked me onto his lap, facing away from the water. He ran a hand through my hair and pulled me to his lips. "This isn't going to be easy, okay? You have to trust me. And do everything I tell you. Understand?"

The cold inside my chest expanded. I did trust him. I just didn't trust the water wouldn't get all vindictive for not having killed me the last time someone tried to do the job. "How do we even know this is for the best, anyway? I mean, maybe I'm not safe anywhere."

He moved a lock of hair from my face, tucking it behind my ear. "Whether here, or there, makes no difference in terms of your safety. It is only that there, I have a small advantage, without the Sentinels breathing down my neck."

"And if they decide to seek me out there?"

"Let them. I will watch every one of them burn. In fact, let them send their *legions* of angels and demons." Finger hooked beneath my chin, he guided my eyes to his. "Any god or devil foolish enough to lay claim to you will suffer my unforgiving wrath. You are mine, Farryn. *Mine.* There is no compromise, no bargain that could possibly change what has already been decided. Understand?"

I blew out a shaky breath and nodded.

"Good. You must trust me. Trust that I won't let anything, or anyone, hurt you."

"I do, but … why drowning?"

"The Vale exists between life and death. When you fell from the roof, there was a point at which you traversed that line. It is both fragile and precise. Too far over the edge, and you could traverse in death."

"Can we, like … knock me out, or something?"

"I don't want to risk that you'll inhale and drown. But I have an idea. You'll trust me, yes?"

Again, I nodded, because I did trust him, even if I was terrified out of my mind.

"Good." Fingers lodged in my hair, he pulled me to his lips for the kind of slow and lazy kiss that felt out of place for the dread simmering in my gut. "Put your arms over your head."

Limbs trembling, I raised my arms up and felt his warm palms skim over my stomach, as he raised my T-shirt up and peeled it away, tossing it onto the floor.

Hand cradling the back of my head, he pressed himself forward, forcing me backward as he lowered me into the tub, but instinct throttled my muscles, and I gripped his arm, clawing at his flesh.

"Wait! Wait, wait, wait."

He didn't wait, though, and before I knew it, I was submerged to my breasts, every cell quivering with terror while I clung to him for dear life.

"I can't. I can't do this, Jericho! Please."

"Shhhh," he whispered. "I'm right here, Farryn. I will not hurt you."

Panting hard, I curled myself around his bicep and

wrapped my arms around his neck tight enough to pull up from the water.

"Darling, relax. Just breathe and relax."

Still barnacled to his body, I rested my forehead on his shoulder and attempted to breathe, as he said.

"Close your eyes. We're going to play a little game."

"What game?" I asked in a shaky voice.

"You're going to lie back, head beneath the water's surface."

Wordless, I shook my head, and if my fingers could've possibly dug any deeper, I was certain I'd have been clutching his bones.

"You're not relaxed, Tu Nazhja. If you're not relaxed, this isn't going to work, and it has to. The line between life and death is far too fragile for panic. You're stronger than this."

Tears welled in my eyes, frustration and terror battling inside my head.

"Focus on my voice. Can you do that?"

I gave a small nod, ignoring the way my chest expanded and filled with cold panic.

"I want you to lie back a little. You can hang onto me, but lie back."

Muscles burning with hesitation, I reluctantly leaned back, and he leaned with me until the cold porcelain pressed into my spine, the edge of the tub resting against my nape.

"Good girl," he whispered, stroking my hair back, before he planted a kiss on my forehead. "Now close your eyes."

I licked my bone-dry lips and did as he asked, shutting out the sight of the water at my breasts.

"Breathe."

Drawing in a long breath, I felt his hand stroke my hair again.

"I'm going to make you relax, and I want you to focus on

me. My words. My touch. It's all I want you to think about. Nothing else. Understand?"

"I'll try."

"Not good enough. There is only me and nothing else. Say it."

"There is only you and nothing else."

"Good. Just breathe."

As my mind took in his words, swallowed them like a lifeline, he shifted, jostling the water, and on a gasp, I clutched him tighter. I squeezed my eyes shut, not wanting to see the frustration on his face.

"Relax, Farryn. Picture yourself floating above this water. Into the air. Safe."

"I'll feel *real* s-s-s-safe if you l-l-l-lift me out of here."

His dark chuckle offered only a minor distraction from the distressed gurgling of my stomach. "The way you're clutching to me, I'd be inclined to, but that isn't going to save you. Now focus. Picture yourself through my eyes. Naked. Perfect. Wet."

A sudden warmth pulsed beneath my skin, and not just because of his words. The feeling hooked itself inside my muscles, stirring an ache between my thighs. I'd felt it before, that day in his office when I could hardly sit still as he'd interrogated me.

"Y-y-you're glamouring me right now?"

"I take offense to that word."

"I … I c-c-c-can't."

"You can and you will." Palm gliding down my stomach, he only exacerbated the sensation, and I moaned in protest. "Don't try to fight me, Farryn. I will devour every one of your senses until all you know is my voice and my touch."

While my head fought to focus on the water bobbing at my chest, a current rooted deep beneath my flesh pulled and contracted in a throbbing sensation. Brows pinched, I tried to ignore the tingles dancing across my bones. My fingernails bit into his muscles, and I released an agonized sound, desperate to grind myself against something. "Jericho," I whispered. "What're you doin'?" My voice held a drunken slur, and as a tickle in my belly tugged at my thighs, I let out a quiet moan.

Lips trailed along the edge of my jaw, and he paused, grazing his teeth across my earlobe. He skated his palm lower, snaking his finger between my thighs, and caressed my swollen and too-sensitive flesh. "Spread your legs. Show me where it aches."

The sensation overwhelmed me, the fear of the water coupled to the intensity building low in my stomach. An urge pulled at my knees, and I fell into mindless submission, retreating into the dark space behind my eyes. Cool porcelain pressed into the back of my knees with the vague awareness that he'd draped my legs over the opposite edges of the tub.

"Did I ever tell you the Pri'Scucian word for this?" He circled his fingers over my sensitive flesh, featherlight, just enough to distract my head from the water.

My back bowed on a sharp exhale, the buzz of his touch sending little shocks of pleasure to my muscles. "No."

"*Saericasz*. Death's fang. In our language, it's a sweet fruit that smells and tastes absolutely mouthwatering. Like delicious warm silk against the tongue."

In spite of the tremble of fear still running through me, I let out a shaky breath, as he tunneled his finger deeper into my seam and spread the flesh.

"When it's ripe, the nectar inside of it spills into your mouth, and its flavor is so addicting, you could eat to the point of death." Flicking his finger over my clit sent a wire of tension through my muscles, and my stomach curled with the uncontrollable twitching of my thighs. "Fucking hell, if you could see what I see right now. I'm starving for your *saericasz.*" His voice echoed inside the darkness, sending another pulse of electricity beneath my skin. In an act of mercy, he rubbed his fingers up and down my seam, the unexpected rush of pleasure spiraling up my spine, and I arched upward. "Yes, that's it," he praised.

"Please, Jericho."

"Tell me what you need." A hum of what felt like electricity danced over his fingers as he slid them toward that singular place begging to be filled.

Instead of answering, I rolled my head against the edge of the tub, using his body to push my hips upward. A whine slipped past my lips, quieted by his hungry mouth. His tongue brushed over mine, the soft and gentle caress of a master kisser.

"Take a breath," he said against my lips.

The moment my lungs filled with air, he sealed it off, kissing me harder, and the world muted beneath the water's surface.

Panic gurgled at the back of my throat, my objection swallowed by his unrelenting mouth. He shoved two fingers up inside of me, and the pulses of electricity swallowed the ache as he pumped in and out of me. My muscles relented the fight, and I fell into bliss of his fucking me with his hand. My thighs trembled where they remained draped over the edge of the tub, toes curling with every drive of his fingers. In my mind's eye, I was staring down at the scene, and I drifted into a blinding pleasure.

A tug of my chest begged for air.

I pushed upward.

He held me down with his lips, his body immovable, his fingers unforgiving. In the silence of my mind's eye, I could see the silvery tattoos on his body twitching over hardened muscles as he drove into me. The sweat beaded at his hairline. The scent of raw sex perfumed the air alongside the primal sounds he'd made while fucking me earlier. I could feel his desperation seeping into me, the need for release which had mirrored my own.

I convulsed, agitating the water around me, the air cool across my breasts when I arched into him. The water lubricated every glide of his finger, and I envisioned the pained expression he always wore just before he'd come. A cross between agony and bliss—a look that set my soul on fire.

Darkness seeped in.

The need for air punched at my chest with fierce determination.

I clawed at him.

Screamed against his mouth still pressed to mine.

In that moment, I dared to open my eyes, and through the watery layers above me, I saw red. A red, angry, glowing eye, and two horns curled outward from Jericho's forehead. Not Jericho. A demon.

Precious gulps of water bubbled past my lips as I let out a scream. Fingers dug into my throat, and he squeezed just enough to let me know how easily he could snap my neck. I clawed harder, but something wicked moved through me. A burning in my thighs. A hunger in my belly. In spite of my fear, in spite of the way he looked, a greater force pulled me into submission. Death? Was I dying?

The sensation, so intense, had me closing my eyes, when I should've been fighting for my life.

Snap out of it, Farryn!

What the hell was wrong with me, that I would abandon my fight for whatever need raked through me with an unrelenting intensity.

A cold rush of adrenaline pumped through my veins, and something wound tight in my stomach. So fucking tight, I could do little more than shake, muscles stiff and cramping.

My body was in full-on chaos, muscles locked, lungs burning for one sip of air, while a cramping knot in my belly grew bigger with his relentless fingering. Euphoria heightened. Tension curled through me like a poisonous vapor, withering my resistance. Waning senses told me I was on the verge of blacking out. A flash of blinding light exploded behind my eyes, the heat racing straight to my toes.

Blackness filtered in only a split second before my body was thrust upward at a dizzying speed. The stinging water racing over my skin, while I bulleted like a torpedo through an aqueous wall.

I gasped on a jolt and breathed in the ice-cold air that inflamed my lungs. A coughing spasm clinched my chest in a crushing blow against my ribs. I frantically inhaled, desperate for oxygen, and opened my eyes to the pale white moon and stars overhead.

Muscles weak and flaccid, weighed by a numbing cold that felt like boulders dangling from my fingertips, I settled into a calm and let the heavy liquid blanket pull me down.

Deeper.

A strong arm banded around me, an unflinching grip keeping my head above water. I turned just enough to see the glint of silvery tattoos wrapped across my naked chest.

Panic jolted through me, and I flapped my arms to get away, letting out a weakened gasp of fear. Twisting, I caught a glimpse of his eye. The unusual pale blue, without a hint of red. And at his forehead, no horns.

Only Jericho. My Jericho.

Had I hallucinated the demon I'd seen?

Wearing a confused expression, he pulled me into him, and it was only when I was tucked safely against his warm body that I noticed we were bobbing in a pitch-black sea. While he wore the sweats I'd given him, I had nothing. No bra, no panties, and no idea why I hadn't thought of that small detail before, but I was grateful not to have the added weight of clothes.

"We m-m-made it?" The words rasped from my rigid jaw, chased by the steam of my exasperated breath. My muscles felt on the cusp of a constant shiver.

"You were perfect," he said before kissing me. "So fucking perfect."

Smiling at that I wrapped my arms tightly around him, frantic for the heat that radiated off his wet skin. "How are y-y-y-you so w-w-w-warm?" Needing every part of me in contact with him, I hooked my legs around his body and climbed him like a damn tree in search of warmth.

"Demon blood." He guided my head back and stared down at me. "How was it?"

"I'm not s-s-s-stupid enough to think an orgasm cured my f-f-f-fear, but it sure as hell made for an intense distraction."

"I have my methods." A wickedly handsome smile curved his lips, while his free hand roamed over my skin, leaving a wake of heat that settled down into my bones, and I shivered in his grasp.

Looking around showed the cliff behind us, and Black-water Cathedral looming overhead like a dark and ominous watcher. As the heat from his body slowly leached into mine, I melted against him, taking a moment to breathe deep. "So, now we just have to swim to the cliff."

"Cake."

"Easy for you to say. You at least have pants on. And didn't almost die of some kinky erotic asphyxiation."

Hoisting me around his body so I straddled his back, he took the first stroke toward the cliff, when something sharp brushed the back of my calf. On a gasp, I twitched against him, turning in time to catch the moon's light glistening over iridescent scales along a sharp black curve that disappeared beneath the surface.

"Jericho! There's something–"

A tight grip of my ankle yanked me off Jericho's back. I sucked in a breath, just before I slipped into an ice-cold casket of water. Thrusting my hands up above me, I reached out for the surface as it shot out of my grasp.

The alarm inside of me took over, and I clawed for it. For my life and the life inside of me, because goddamn it, I wasn't going down like that. Not after having survived the bathtub.

Except, my fight was futile against whatever held me, clinging to my leg in a burning grip. I only knew whatever it might be, it was enormous—that much I could make out from the terrifying curve of its fin which reminded me of a dragon's spine.

No.

No!

The moment I resigned myself to breathe in the water, rather than face whatever it might've had in mind for me, a sharp release sent me floating upward again. An arm hooked beneath me, which I prayed belonged to Jericho, but his body yanked free of mine, and I climbed the numbing water to the surface.

Once breached, I twisted around, searching for him across a placid blackness. "Jericho!" I cried out, biting back tears. "Jericho!"

Peering down into the water was no use, as I couldn't even see my own legs below me. "Jericho!"

My wheezing was the only sound in the deafening silence. A creeping chill crawled up my spine, my body growing heavy in the cold. I'd never make it to the shoreline. Not with my limbs frozen.

An impossibly bright flash of light from below was the only warning, before the water around me shifted and jostled my form. A blast of heat shot through my body, melting away the cold like a block of ice held over an open flame. With a guarded breath, I waited.

Until, at last, a figure emerged, and with the last shred of energy left in me, I plowed through the water toward him as fast as I could. Even in the dark, I could make out three deep gashes across his neck and shoulder. The agony twisting his face told me it was painful, but he pulled me toward him anyway.

"What was that thing?" I asked, noticing the temperature of the water had changed to tepid.

"*Dzilagion*," he said in a hoarse voice. "It's a sea serpent whose ass I'd have easily kicked a few months ago." He touched a finger to his wound and groaned. "It should not have even gotten a hit in."

Not a minute later, a bubbly sound drew my attention toward a monstrous vortex behind him, where an enormous black beast bobbed up to the surface. A scream escaped me, and I dug my nails into Jericho, until I realized it wasn't moving but curled into itself, as if it'd died that way. As Jericho described, its long serpent-like body, with spiked fins along the spine, gave it the appearance of a creepy dragon snake, about the size of a whale shark.

With one arm wrapped around me, Jericho dragged me through the water as he swam toward the cliff, and though it was significantly faster than I'd have managed to swim, I felt compelled to help him and shoulder some of the burden with my heavy, useless arms as a weak paddle.

"I thought it was … going to drag me … into the depths … of Hell." The toil of swimming, even in warmer water, left me struggling to hold conversation.

"Close enough. It would've consumed you slowly. Kept you alive inside a pocket in its mouth, where its saliva would've basically broken you down over time."

That horrific image slowed my stride, and a shiver raced down my spine. "Seriously?"

"Seriously."

I glanced over my shoulder. "You *did* kill it ... right?"

"I did. At the expense of my energy." An air of frustration clung to his tone, and I could tell he wasn't interested in talking about it anymore. It didn't take a psychiatrist to see his lack of power troubled him. Forget that he saved me from what I was certain was the most horrific way to die. Ever.

It wasn't long before we reached the shore of Blackwater Cliff, and I stumbled to my feet, the wintry wind stealing my breath as, hands crossed over as much of my nakedness as I could cover, I followed him toward a cave. Once inside, he pulled me after him, into the dark depths, where I felt twice as vulnerable as when we were in the water. He stopped to lift a lamp from a bracket on the stone wall and lit it with an attached flint striker. Once illuminated, the cave proved to be an entryway of some sort, and it was in the light that I could see the depth of Jericho's injury, glistening with deep crimson blood.

"Your w-w-wound," I managed through chattering teeth.

"I'll worry about it later. We need to get you warm."

It was only the scratchy sensation of fabric against my fingers that prompted me to look down at myself to find a signature gray Blackwater dress covering me. Yet, the cold still nipped at my skin as if I were naked. Frowning, I glanced up at him and back to the dress. "How?"

"It's only an illusion."

"You mean, I'm not really wearing this?"

"No. But don't worry." Lips curved to a grin, he gave a squeeze of my ass, and I let out a squeal. "Only I know." A quick kiss, and he led me toward a heavy steel door, where he pressed his palm to its surface and muttered something in a language I didn't understand.

The door clicked and opened, and a chamber on the other side held what appeared to be an elevator, though like the gate on the very first night that I'd arrived, there weren't any buttons to press. Jericho threw back an iron door and stepped inside the small box. I followed in after, and the moment I turned, the door closed on its own and the clank of metal signaled the cart's upward ascent with a jerk that caught me off balance.

"Does anything make sense here?" I asked, scanning over the walls for any sign of how the thing moved.

"Rarely." Backing me into the wall behind me, he gripped my face and hiked my leg up onto his hip. With his body pressed against me, I noticed a slight tremble in his muscles, before fervent lips devoured my next breath in a kiss. The elevator stopped, as if he'd willed it. "I could've lost you back there, Farryn. Fuck!"

Stroking a hand down his hair, I shook my head. "No. I knew you'd come for me. I had no doubt of that."

"I'm weak. Practically mortal."

"Now you're just being mean. Besides, that wasn't a small insect you crushed back there. That thing was huge."

"That thing is a *puppy* compared to our real threats."

That was the scariest freaking puppy I'd ever seen.

"You're going to restore your powers. You'll have your wings again. I'm not all that religious, but I have faith in that."

He ran his thumb across my cheek, his eye locked on my lips. "What I wouldn't give to see the world as you do. Such illuminating hope must be blinding at times."

An echo of memory struck me with the sarcasm in his tone. The biting snip of the boy from long ago. Memories of my former life had begun to arrive more frequently as of late. More so during the weeks when he was imprisoned in Ex Nihilo and my days had been consumed with thoughts of him. "It wasn't long ago that my world was as dark as yours."

His jaw twitched, his grip tighter on my jaw. "While I know those few months you suffered placed an unbearable weight on you, that time was a mere blink in the *centuries* I waited for you to be reborn. You may have damned your soul, but I have committed unthinkable crimes and sunk to unfathomable depths. I do not wish that pain on you. Ever."

"You told me of Praecepsia. And while I'll never understand what drove you to kill innocents, I can't bring myself to condemn you for it entirely."

Gaze cast from mine, he breathed hard through his nose. "Praecepsia was only the beginning."

I took his words to mean he'd killed more. Thousands more, if the silvery tattoos all over his body were anything to go by. He'd once told me they were markings left for every soul he'd taken. "I'm cold."

He stared down at me, as if trying to read my thoughts. "Of course." The elevator lurched into motion again, my stomach still twisting with his confession. The bold side of me wanted to ask what came after Praecepsia, but the shadows behind his eye assured I didn't want to know.

After a relatively short ascent, the elevator slowed to a stop once again. I practically held my breath as the doors opened to the empty foyer, where the dim light of the chandelier flickered overhead.

"Is anyone here?" Jericho asked the question burning in my mind.

A sound of movement echoed from the upper floor, followed by breaking glass, a loud curse, and more movement. Anya appeared at the top of the stairwell, the sight of her making me smile, until a shiver coiled through me, and the inclination to cover myself sent a needling panic over my skin. Not even Jericho's reassurance that I appeared fully clothed could stop me from feeling buck naked.

"Master? You've returned! And Miss Ravenshaw! Oh, my

heavens, both of you!" Lifting the skirt of her dress, she hobbled down the stairs. "Girls! The Master and Miss Ravenshaw have returned!"

My muscles eased a little when Anya didn't appear to be shocked or even to take notice of my breasts in all their glory.

Familiar faces peeked out over the banister and from rooms down corridors. When Anya finally reached us, she offered a respectful nod toward Jericho, then, throwing out her arms, wrapped me in the most awkward hug of my life, given my lack of *clothes*.

"I can't tell you how happy I am to see the both of you again! Oh!" Her hands smoothed over my back, and as she pulled away, she ran her palm over my arm, frowning. "How strange. This fabric feels ice cold. And soft as skin."

I didn't have to look at him to know Jericho was holding back what I imagined to be a wolfish grin. "My skin was damp when I put it on."

Wearing a look of disbelief, she continued to stroke my arm, just missing my exposed breast, and I prayed the roof would cave in right then. "Your hair is sopping wet, too. Did you go for a swim?"

"Yeah. One of those polar plunge deals." Crossing my arms over myself, I shivered, rubbing my shoulders for warmth.

With a confused expression, Anya turned to Jericho. "Sir, that's quite a scratch on your neck! We'll have to get that looked at by the doc!"

"No, no. Some antiseptic and a bandage will be fine." It was then I noticed the blood had become darker than before, reminding me of the day I'd cleaned Remy's wound.

Concerned, I peered closer, wondering if perhaps Anya was right, after all. "Those do look pretty deep."

After a quick glance toward me and back to Anya, Jericho asked, "The dogs. How are they?"

"All three seem to have mourned your loss, Master. They rarely chase so much as a rabbit these days. Once that wound is cleaned, perhaps the two of you can pay them a visit. I'm certain it'll lift their spirits."

"Yes, I'd like to see them."

The chill still rattled my bones as they spoke, and I caught Anya glancing back at me a couple times, as if my teeth had chattered too loudly.

"Very well, I'll have the kitchen staff make you a nice big welcome home feast. It is so wonderful to have you back."

"Thank you. If you'll excuse me, I don't know about Miss Ravenshaw, but I could use a hot shower and some fresh clothes."

God, the sound of hot water on my skin right then was heavenly. "I could definitely use a hot shower and some fresh clothes." At the winging up of Anya's brows, I cleared my throat. "Separately, of course."

"Of course." The wily curve of her smile had me paranoid, looking away for fear she'd suspect something about the pregnancy. "We've kept the linens laundered along with the clothing, in hopes you'd return soon. The night you disappeared was … chaos. Complete chaos. The dogs were going crazy. We kept hearing awful noises, and there was monstrous thunder in the sky."

Had they missed the whole battle between Drystan and Jericho, and the godawful nightmare of him bursting into flames before my eyes?

"You didn't see anything else? Anything strange like bolts of lightning touching down?"

Or maybe hundreds of those mutated creatures, the Alatum, stampeding across the property? The fire Jericho had started had held them back for a short time, of course, but surely they'd gotten around it.

"Lightning? Not that I saw myself, no. Only heard the thunder. We *did* have an impressive wildfire. Took nearly a week to burn itself out, and as a result, Misty Hollow is now being called Dreary Hollow by all the locals."

It was odd that they hadn't even witnessed a moment so utterly heartbreaking as Jericho losing his wings and bursting into flames, as if it'd never happened.

At a tug of my arm, I looked down to see Jericho's hand gripping my wrist–urging me to cut the conversation short. "We'll catch up a bit later, Anya. I have *so* much to tell you."

"Yes, we must. Go. Get washed up and change into something cozy, and I'll see to it you're well-fed."

"Thank you." Jericho led me up the staircase to the second floor, but instead of dumping me in my old bedroom along the way, he dragged me farther, around the corner, toward his room.

"So, you think Anya was entirely obtuse to this absurd dress illusion just now?" I asked, hustling to keep up with his brisk pace when my legs still felt like frozen boulders.

"Humans in this realm aren't entirely privy to our kind. They see things as natural phenomena. Ones they can explain."

"She's seen the Alatum before. The glowing eyes."

"In her mind, it's nothing but an animal."

"Then, why do I see them?"

"We've already established that you are the exception, as one of the living. But you see by choice." We arrived at his bedroom door, which he clicked open before releasing my arm. As he strode toward the adjacent bathroom, I closed the door behind me.

"By choice? What do you mean? I can see what they can't because I want to?"

"Yes. That's exactly right," he said over his shoulder, just before he slipped inside the bathroom and tossed me his robe.

Slipping it over myself, I trailed after him, stopping in the doorway and watching him rummage through a cupboard. "All they have to do is want to see, and they can?"

"Yes. But doing so would force them to accept that the world isn't what they thought it was, and that they're no longer living, of course. While that fact may come easy for some, for others, it's not possible." He set bandages and a white linen cloth onto the bathroom counter and tilted his head in the mirror, examining the gashes on his throat.

Arms crossed, I leaned against the doorframe. "When I first arrived in Nightshade, I watched Anya handle a man in a way that made me question whether, or not, she was human, at all."

"They might unknowingly manipulate our laws of physics, but it doesn't mean that they have the desire to understand why, or how."

I pushed off the doorframe and swiped the cloth from the counter, urging him to sit on the edge of the tub. "That seems awfully *unaware*."

Balancing himself on the edge of the black stone tub, he quirked a brow. "As are most humans in the earthly realm. Some are aware of our presence. Others chalk it up to coincidences, or the supernatural."

It was true. Even with a father as crazy as mine, I'd chosen not to believe him for a number of years.

"The asylum you spoke about. You said they end up there because they do see what others refuse."

"Yes. Their minds are a bit more open to things most find inexplicable. This also makes them slightly easier prey for the demons who wish to consume them."

I'd already been plagued a number of times by things

others refused to see. Things my father had been labeled crazy for seeing.

"What is it?" Jericho asked, as if he'd sensed my worry.

"Xhiphias told me that was the first step in my change." Setting the cloth to his wound, I gently daubed at blood, noting the way he didn't so much as flinch. "That I would see things. Hear things. He said it would only last days, but ... what if it doesn't? What if it persists?" My father had succumbed to visions and voices, which Aunt Nelle had chalked up to declining mental health. It made sense, but remained a fear of mine. As his daughter, would I one day suffer as he did?

"What are you afraid of, Farryn? Truly afraid of? Turning cambion, or becoming like your father?" With a gentle grip, he took the soaked cloth from my hand and set it aside.

I rested my hand against my stomach, imagining myself as my father. Dragging me out into the cold to chase symbols on bubblegum. Obsessing over his work. Even knowing now that every bit of his studies was valid and real, it didn't take away the lifetime of humiliation, loneliness and isolation. "I'm afraid of not knowing the difference between what's real and what isn't. What if none of this is real right now, and I'm sat in the corner of a room somewhere dreaming it up."

He raised his hand in the air and, taking hold of my wrist, pressed our palms together. "Do you feel that? The warmth? The hum of life inside of me?" The tiniest vibration tickled my palm, and with a slight smile, I nodded. *Strę vera'tu,* he said in an accent that sent a flutter to my stomach. Something about those words felt oddly familiar to me.

"What does it mean?"

"It's a Pri'Scuscian incantation which roughly translates to *as real as the stars.*"

"It's beautiful."

"There is a belief that reality is what we choose to see,

even if it doesn't seem real to the rest of the world. Even if all of this is a lie, it doesn't matter. If ever your eyes should deceive you, though, and you're scared of not knowing what is real and what isn't, speak the words and I will bring you back."

Not wanting to voice my insecurities, I turned toward the sink and, noting only bandages there, and frowned. "Do you have antiseptic? I'm pretty sure that wound will need stit–" I turned back to face him, eyes wide on seeing a flickering light beneath his palm where he held it to the wound.

The flickering died out, and he removed his hand to reveal smooth, flawless skin. As if the creature in the water hadn't so much as scratched him.

"Wow. I didn't know you could do that at will." I leaned forward, studying the perfect, intact texture of his skin, and ran my finger over its surface.

"I didn't know I had enough juice left in me to accomplish it, either."

"I swore I was going to have to sew this up. Can all demons and angels heal themselves?"

"No. Not all. The Fallen, in particular, lose their ability when their power is stripped from them. Mine is weak, but apparently still present."

"So cool." Twisting back toward the counter, I lifted the bandage set out there. "What's the point of this?"

"Maintaining appearances." He swiped the bandage out of my hand, and his eye seemed to catch on something, the abrupt way his movements came to a halt. The moment his brows pinched together, I knew what it was. The ache at either side of my throat bore the ghostly echo of where his fingers had dug themselves into my flesh back in the bathtub. "How did this happen? The Dzaglion?"

No. I recalled the ache there before the scuffle with the serpent, and it had only grabbed my ankle before releasing me. "When you grabbed my throat in the tub. It felt *slightly* aggressive."

A shocked and remorseful expression claimed his face. "I grabbed your throat?"

"You don't remember that?"

"I must've been lost in the moment. I hurt you?"

Touching a hand there pulled me back into those moments, when all I'd been able to feel was intense pleasure. "I didn't register any pain at the time. Of course, I was drowning and freaking out, so maybe I was numb to it all."

With quick hands, he tipped my chin back, further examining what must've been small bruises left behind. I was glad for the robe so that he couldn't see the ones left on my back and ass. After a whisper-soft stroke of his finger across my skin, he flinched and released me, the confusion on his face pinching to a look of absolute misery. In lowering his arms, he must've caught sight of something, as he examined his flesh.

Along his forearm were four long black markings that looked like scratches. How it was possible for his frown to deepen even more than before was a mystery.

"Did the serpent do that?" I studied the clean edges of the markings that almost looked like he'd tattooed them there.

"No. The markings on my neck were clearly different."

It was true. The marks on his neck had bled and oozed, their edges much more lacerated as with claws. "What would leave behind black markings like that?"

"I'm not entirely sure."

"There was one other thing." I hesitated to say anything more, as agonized over it as he looked. Particularly since I hadn't quite worked out whether or not I had hallucinated it in my panic of drowning. "I thought maybe it was just light reflecting off the water, but you had horns. And black skin. And your eye turned red."

Staring off, he ran a finger along the perimeter of his eye. "Red?" His hand curled into a fist, and he looked away, as if he were trying to hide it right then. "Fuck."

"What is it?"

"While I was trapped in Ex Nihilo, I was plagued by visions."

"What kind of visions?"

"Of turning." Staring off, he seemed to lose himself in thoughts, his one eye unfocused. "Without my wings, the strength of my vitaeilem declines. I become more susceptible to the demon half of me. My *father's* half." Jericho rarely, if ever, spoke about his father.

"Did I know him in the past?" Given the many coincidences and memories that'd unlocked in recent months, I no longer hesitated to claim Lustina's existence as my own. Unfortunately, mention of his father didn't jog any recollection of him.

"You met him on a few occasions. He was there the night of your murder and played just as much a part as Bishop Venable."

"And was he also burned by the fire you set to Praecepsia?"

"No." Jericho rubbed a hand down his face and shook his head. "He and his sister mistress escaped."

"To where?"

"Nightshade, for a while. For centuries, I tracked him. I ventured to the bowels of Hell. A place drenched in the blood of angels. I saw things." With a twitch of his eye, he lowered his gaze and shook his head. The way his shoulders bunched with tension told me whatever he'd seen still set him on edge. "Horrific things that seared themselves inside of my head for the centuries that followed. Things I will never speak of."

"Did you find your father?"

"No. I spiraled deeper into the pitch-black world of desolation. It was your rebirth which saved me." He drew in a deep inhale and exhaled an easy breath. "A moment that felt like the first breath after having been buried alive. I will not become like him. I would sooner tear the still-beating heart out of my chest."

"You're not like him."

"But I could choke you while you were in distress? And that I don't recall a moment of it?" He turned away, as if he couldn't even look at me.

While I had faith that he wouldn't have hurt me, the fact that he didn't remember *was* a little troubling. "With the return of your wings, does that mean you'd be able to better control the demon half?"

"My whole life has been a balancing act between the two. It was the teaching of my mother and an old mentor who helped me learn to suppress those thoughts and feelings. And while the violence was always there beneath my skin, taunting me, it never sank its hooks in me. I could always grasp something good. Losing you shifted that balance for me, and I suspect that more malevolent half of me got a taste of freedom. So, to answer your question, I can only hope."

Taking his hand in mine, I gave a gentle tug. "Come on. Take a bath with me?"

"I don't think that's wise."

Frowning, I studied his vexed expression, desperately wishing I could read his thoughts right then. "Jericho, what happened ... it could've been a combination of things. The sexual tension. The urgency. The adrenaline."

"It is the sexual trigger that concerns me most. It's a very powerful catalyst for my species."

"We were together the first night you came back, though."

"I wasn't holding you under water, Farryn."

"Okay, you could've easily killed me, and you didn't. What kept you from doing so?"

"I don't even remember grabbing your neck, that's what is so concerning. I don't know what made me stop." Brows pinched tight, he lowered his gaze to the floor. "Until I understand whether this is a lingering effect of Ex Nihilo, or something much worse, a little distance between us is best."

Though my body had warmed from its earlier chill, a cold sensation stirred in my chest. One I knew all too well. I'd first felt it when I was thirteen and had worked up the courage to ask my father about my mother's death, why he couldn't seem to let her go. It was the only time I ever recalled my father having yelled at me in a way that felt as if he'd cast me right out of his heart. From that day on, a cold distance had lingered between us–detachment that'd left me feeling like a stranger around him.

Although Jericho hadn't raised his voice, I could feel it stirring again. The panic of becoming strangers.

"Distance?" The word left a bitter sting on my tongue, as I forced it out of my mouth. My muscles tightened while the all-too-familiar ache snaked behind my ribs like the first sign of frost. It warned that my heart was going into lockdown mode--that the walls which had once encapsulated the fragile little organ, ones I'd spent years trying to deconstruct, would once again fortify into an impenetrable barrier. Against anyone, including Jericho.

I turned to leave before that icy cold feeling had a chance to harden and prod my mouth to say something regretful, but a tight grip of my arm pulled me back.

"Farryn …"

The logical side of my brain told me he was right, because he knew himself better than I did. All these strange things meant something that I couldn't begin to understand. But my heart didn't think rationally, or logically. It craved what it had been denied in his absence. The very thing it had been starving for most of my life. "For months, I prayed for your return. Begged that you would come back to me. And now you want distance. I understand your need to protect, but I'm not afraid."

"If you knew the depraved things that have crossed my mind since my return, you would *volunteer* to keep your distance, I can assure you."

"Perhaps I'm naive for saying so, but I know you won't hurt me. I know the very thought torments you."

The way his brows came together told me I'd hit a sensitive spot, but then his jaw hardened. "You're right. It does torment me. But that means nothing when that blackness slips over me and something else takes over. It has happened before. I have awakened from a dreamless slumber to blood on my tongue and death on my hands. Do not doubt the full scope of my potential to harm." With my arm still trapped in his grip, he rose up from the edge of the tub until towering over me. "If I am concerned, you should be, too."

I stared him dead in the eye. "If you're so capable of hurting me, then why keep me?"

With a steely expression, he cupped my face, gaze riveted on my lips while he ran a thumb over my cheek. "Because I'm selfish. Giving you up would destroy me." Fingers curled around the nape of my neck, he pulled me in for a kiss. "I'm asking you to play along, just until I know what's going on."

My head toyed with the impossible calculation of how long that could've possibly been. An hour, a day, a week, *months*? And to what extent? Would he become like my father had, avoiding hugs and kisses? Waving at me when we passed in the hallway? The ache from before pulsed inside my chest again. *Get a grip, Farryn.* "If that's what you think is best."

"It is." He lowered his hand from my face and backed up a step. Just like that, an unsettling chill slid between us like a jealous lover. "I need to leave the cathedral for some business with an old acquaintance." He stepped past me, out of the bathroom and into his bedroom, where he rummaged through his armoire for a shirt and pants.

"Business? At this hour?"

After slipping the shirt over his head, he smirked. "Demons do not follow the regular business hours of humans."

It wasn't my intent to pry, but given both of us were essentially wanted *criminals*, I at least wanted to know where to start if he didn't happen to return. "Where?"

"In the corpse of a forest that is now Misty Hollow. I intend to summon him, but I don't want him here."

"Right."

"Get some rest. It's been an eventful night, and I'm sure you're quite tired."

With a sharp nod, I turned away from him, and when tears sprang into my eyes, I hurried from the room so he wouldn't see just how much this request to remain separate had crushed my heart. As I made my way to my own bedroom, that cold chill in my chest stirred again.

7

JERICHO

*A*fter fastening the cape over my shoulders, I slipped a black eyepatch over my ruined eye and stared off at the door through which Farryn had just walked. Every muscle in my body urged me to go to her, to swipe her up into my arms and fuck every ounce of doubt out of that overthinking brain of hers. Except, I'd had enough experience to know the subtle changes going on inside of me were just the beginning.

Screams. Wide eyes. Blood.

I trailed my gaze to the marking on my arm, running my fingers over its surface, which burned at the touch. A hazy memory filtered through my mind, of holding Farryn underwater, hands clawing at that very spot. I flinched, screwing my good eye shut.

"Liar," a familiar, detached voice whispered.

When I opened my eyes again, I strode out of the bedroom and took the staircase toward the foyer. As I did so, long-forgotten memories swirled inside my head, taunting me to unlock one of the many compartments in which I'd stored them away. It was wrong of me to keep Farryn, knowing what I was capable of, what I had the potential to do if the demon inside of me were given the opportunity to take over.

I couldn't let her go, though. As selfish and cruel as that made me, such a thing would ensure not only my own destruction, but that of others, as well. The silvery tattoos were a stark reminder of what happened when I sank into that kind of madness.

As I exited the cathedral, I was greeted by all three dogs, who practically tackled me to the ground, their tails wagging incessantly while they clustered around me, vying for my attention. I let out a chuckle and petted Cerberus, and Fenrir pawed at my other arm.

"What is it? You want attention, too?" I turned to pet him and felt a nudge from Nero in a refusal to be left out. "I must admit, I missed you mongrels." Cerberus licked my arm, and all three dogs trotted after me toward the stables.

As I prepped Onyx, my black Friesian, with a saddle, I glanced back at where the clingy canines stood to attention behind me. "You're to watch over her while I'm gone. No one comes near this cathedral. Understand?"

Cerberus barked, and as I led the horse from the stable, I patted him on the head.

Wind whipped past me as Onxy galloped me toward the Misty Hollow Forest. I'd decided to summon an old friend of mine, Trezhyr, one I knew from centuries ago. A very prestigious ally to the Noxerians, who were a corrupt breed of demon lords–the most powerful below Lucifer himself. It was they who facilitated claim over damned souls, like Farryn's, and only those in their tight circle would be privy to such information. If anyone would've had any insight into which demon had been given rein over Farryn's soul, however, it was Trezhyr.

In my early days in Nightshade, I'd been swiped up by the

Noxerians, kidnapped, essentially, seeing as I was just shy of nineteen when the Sentinels had banished me for burning down Praecepsia. The prestigious lords had recruited me into their Knights of the Infernal Order—a group of warriors trained by the ancients to carry out the mission of wiping out the A'ryakai, angels who'd disguised themselves as demons and whose sole purpose was to purify the angel race by killing off mixed breeds and pure-born demons. Far from the righteous morals of their celestial brethren, they were ruthless in their mission and connected to powerful archangels.

I, alongside eleven other hand-picked demons and half-breeds, had been tasked with hunting down the corrupt angels in Nightshade. It was Trezhyr who'd served as an informant for the Noxerians, and had always been a trusted friend. Even when I eventually left the Order to seek out Farryn, he'd always made a point to pass along information that had kept me one step ahead of the Noxerians. Even so, despite his sincerity, he was too connected politically for me to divulge where I slept, which was why I found myself on my current journey.

I finally reached the Misty Hollow woods and brought Onyx to a halt beside a half-charred oak with an exceptionally large trunk. Dusk settled over broken and burned husks of trees whose vibrant green canopies had once shaded the sky. From my pocket, I pulled a silver stick of *cret'calatięsz,* a summoning chalk that created small portals in Nightshade.

On the dead tree's trunk, I drew a circle and scrawled Trezhyr's name in its center. Placing my hand against the bark, I spoke his name, and the area inside the circle wavered with heat. As a figure drew toward me on the other side of the blurred bark, I edged backward. A boot stepped through first, followed by a leather-clad leg, and finally the familiar white and silvery hair I remembered from nearly a quarter century ago.

When he emerged fully from the tree, he stood upright, only a hair shorter than me, and his lips stretched to a crooked smile as he shook his head. "Jericho Van Croix." Clasping forearms, we gave each other a quick pat on the back. "Been a long time, my friend." Eyes trailing over the surroundings, he frowned. "You could've at least summoned me to a nice tavern with maidens in busty dresses. What is this shit?"

Folding my arms, I chuckled. "A tavern is far too crowded for what I need to discuss. I do not mean to trouble you with a summons, but I am not entirely in the position of showing my face in public these days."

His frown deepened. "Am I to assume the rumors of your return are true, then? That you were drawn back from Ex Nihilo?"

"Word spreads quickly, it seems."

"It does. How can I help?"

I leaned against one of the nearby trees and stroked a hand over my jaw. "I need to know the fate of a particular human soul."

"Ahhh, Jericho. Much as I would love to help you get a leg up on your business, I cannot divulge information like that."

"This is not about brokering souls, I'm afraid. Were it that simple, I would not have called you out here. It's about my female."

Groaning, he took three paces to the right. "Her soul is damned? By your claiming?"

"No. She beat me to it. She is the human who brought me back from Ex Nihilo."

Exhaling a sharp breath, he lowered his gaze and paced three steps in the other direction. "What is her name?"

"Farryn Ravenshaw."

With arms akimbo, he shook his head. "Fuck."

I didn't like the expression on his face, which told me whoever owned Farryn's soul was unfavorable. "Who is it?"

"Telling you puts me at tremendous risk."

"I would not ask, were it not her."

Rubbing a hand down his face, he groaned again.

"Tell me. I'm losing my mind over it. You recognize her name, correct?"

"Oh, I recognize it, all right." He let out a mirthless laugh and resumed his pacing back and forth. "The council spent all evening discussing her name."

My pulse pounded in my throat, the anticipation scratching at my lungs as I waited for him to reveal the name.

"The one who's laid claim to her soul is your father."

The words repeated on an endless loop inside my head, their meaning lost to the rage simmering in the very depths of my bones. I balled my hands into fists at my sides, my muscles hardening, breaths hastening with every increased thud of my heart. "My father," I said past the tight clench of my jaw.

"I'm sorry, my friend."

"Is there nothing that can be done?"

His brow flickered, and he turned away. "If we weren't talking of your father? Yes. But the council's hands are tied on this. He *specifically* requested her, Jericho."

Body shaking with fury, I turned away from him and hammered my fist into the nearby tree. The impact sent it crashing to the ground on a thunderous crack of splintered wood, and a plume of black ash rose into the air. "I will hunt him and kill him."

"You know you can't do that."

I did know the consequences. I'd been told my whole life that killing him was not an option, due to the power he wielded. Unfortunately, the detriment of all five realms wasn't enough of a deterrent to keep me from doing it, anyway. Not when Farryn stood to become his slave. Every creature could perish, as far as I was concerned, so long as Claudius Van Croix failed to get his filthy hands on her.

Of course, I had no intentions of voicing those thoughts to Trezhyr. Instead, I forced myself to calm, in spite of every muscle in my body spoiling for blood. My father's blood.

In my current state, he would be far too powerful to overcome.

I needed to restore my wings, replenish the vitaeilem that my body could no longer produce, and begin my hunt before the baby arrived. "So, I have no other option. You, for example, couldn't claim her soul on my behalf?" I, of course, already knew the answer to that. It was only for the sake of making him believe I had lost all hope that I bothered to ask.

"While I may be a respected member of the council, I am, by no means, an ancient lord, like your father. I would be inviting war upon my name to even suggest such a thing."

"And there is no other option."

He snorted, turning away from me. "Of course there is. Close the portal to Eradyę, and everyone's problems will be solved."

I was glad that he stood with his back to me, so he couldn't see the flicker of intrigue he'd just lit within my mind. Closing the portal to Eradyę was no easy task. Centuries of angels and demons alike perishing under the weight of the barren realm had proven as such.

But I possessed something other angels did not—the ability to walk through that hell without succumbing to its insatiable hunger to feed on my vitaeilem. Only my father and I were capable of surviving the realm long-term, due to the creatures inhabiting it. Ones that could infect any breed of demon, or angel, outside of our kind and wreak havoc.

But again, it would've required far more power than I had at my disposal right then. So the task of tracking down Farryn's father to help restore my wings had just become paramount.

"Aside from pulling a miracle out of my ass, let me know if there's anything I can do."

Reaching out my hand, I shook my head. "You've done enough for me by telling me this. I appreciate it more than you know."

After a quick handshake and sharp nod, he stepped back through the portal, which sealed behind him, leaving me standing there alone and filled with fury.

But although the rage burned like hellfire inside of me, at least I had direction. Purpose.

A single-minded goal to destroy my father at all costs.

8

THE BARON

*M*orning sunlight beat down on the baron's face, and he opened his eyes to the sound of a quiet knock.

"My Lord, I've come to check on your wounds," Drystan spoke low, as if he did not want anyone to hear. "May I come in?"

"My wounds are just fine."

"Of course, but I am afraid I cannot go about my day without first checking."

"I insist that you go about your day and leave me to sleep."

"It is your mother who has asked that I fetch you, My Lord. I only want to ensure that you are in a state to accept her invitation."

Groaning into his pillow, the baron stretched and flexed his muscles, the absence of pain reminding him of what had happened the night before with his wounds. "Yes, I will meet with my mother. I do not require your examinations. Allow me to dress first."

"Very well. I will let her know."

Running his hand over his head, the baron yawned,

before he sat up from his bed. He rubbed his hands together, smiling at the warmth stirring between his palms. The cold floor met the soles of his feet, as he slid from his bed and hooked his fingers beneath the hem of his tunic, pulling the garment over his head. As he tossed it aside, a strange sensation hit the back of his neck, and he turned in time to catch Drystan staring wide-eyed.

His cousin pointed at him, finger trembling as he held it outward. "M-M-My L-L-Lord ... your back! It is .... There is .... The wounds ... gone! All of them are gone!"

"Just like a rat, you snooping vermin." The baron swiped a fresh tunic from his armoire and covered himself. "Perhaps you would fancy a spyglass for closer examination."

"I saw your wounds just yesternight. They were ... horrific. Grotesque! I do not believe it possible they could heal in a single night."

"And yet, I stand before you as living proof."

Drystan shook his head, taking a step toward him and back again. "It is not possible. Not. Possible."

"Who exactly determines what is considered possible, or not, hmmm? You may want to speak to this person with regard to your lack of companionship."

The surprise on his face withered to an unamused expression. "Do not patronize me. I know what I saw, and I have worked closely enough with the church's infirmary to know what manner of healing is possible."

"Drystan." Yanking a pair of breeches up over his leg, the baron hopped on one foot, trying to keep from toppling over. "I will not ask you to make sense of what seems to deceive your eyes, but should you speak of it ... well, I am afraid we will share the same fate."

His cousin's brows came together in a tight frown. "Of course I will not speak of it. Are you mad? I have watched their methods of drawing out bad spirits from the Ravers."

Ravers was a term used by the Pentacrux to describe those whose mental faculties had declined. Ones they had deemed suffered from insanity due to a demon's curse. "It is more unpleasant than having watched your punishment."

"Good. Then, we have no more to discuss on the matter."

Fingers lodged into the mop of red hair atop his head, Drystan paced. "How? How did .... How is it possible?"

"I am afraid that is a question I cannot answer. Now, if you will excuse me, I would like to finish dressing. Without prying eyes."

"Of course, My Lord. I did not intend to spy. I was merely concerned for you."

"I do not require your concern, nor your examination."

"My apologies for the intrusion." With a nod, his cousin backed himself out of the room and closed the door behind him.

After dressing, the baron made his way to his mother's drawing room, where she often spent her afternoons working on embroidery, or painting. She stood with her back to him, as he entered, a paintbrush in hand while she stared off toward a blank canvas propped on its easel.

"You called for me, Mother?"

"Come. Sit." She did not bother to look at him, as he strode across the room and took a seat on the empty chair beside her. "Ahhhh, there it is. My inspiration."

"If I am a source of inspiration, perhaps you should seek a new hobby."

She chuckled, dragging her brush through one of the many colors smudged across her palette. "You make for a handsome muse, my love."

"You flatter me, Mother. Might I ask if that is the purpose of our meeting?" he asked with a smile in his voice.

Her smile faded to something more serious. "Drystan tells me you were taken to the undercroft."

"Drystan could use a bit of embroidery work across his lips."

Tipping her head, she set a freshly dipped paintbrush to the canvas and moved her arm in long strokes. "What was the nature of this meeting?"

"Why else does the bishop call upon young boys, but to exorcize the evil inside of them?"

"So, your father was behind this?" She kept on with her painting, her strokes becoming more aggressive at the mention of Lord Praecepsia.

"When is he not? Bishop Venable heels to his every command."

"While such conversations are safe with me, I caution you to speak so candidly, Son. And what took place at this meeting?"

Images from days ago, when he'd first been taken to the undercroft, flashed through his mind. When he'd refused simple questioning, and the bishop had resorted to more physical means of coaxing out his confession.

"Tell me. I demand to know," his mother urged.

"I was thoroughly flogged."

Eyes wide, she dropped her palette and rushed toward the baron, pawing at the hem of his tunic. "I want to see."

"Mother, please. I am not in pain."

"Show me!"

The baron lifted the garment he wore and sighed. "Not so much as a scratch."

"You were, in fact, flogged."

"Yes."

"Why do you not bear the wounds of such punishment?"

"I would prefer not to say." Biting back a smile, he lowered the garment and sat back in his chair.

"I insist that you do."

"They were quick to heal." The amusement in his voice failed to appease his mother, whose frown deepened.

"No. Floggings are only quick to heal in child's play. Not when you are at the mercy of Claudius Van Croix. You were not taken to that undercroft for a ruse. You healed them yourself. Tell me, is this true?"

"To speak such things would label me a *Raver*. Is that what you want?"

"I am your mother." Warm hands gripped tight to his jaw, drawing his attention to the sincerity in her eyes. "I would sooner take every secret to the grave. Now, tell me."

"Fine. I placed my hand upon my abused flesh and had only to imagine it healed. And it was so."

The corners of her lips flinched, as if she wanted to smile but the anger inside of her refused such a thing. "Does anyone else know about this?"

"Drystan."

Eyes screwed shut, she groaned and looked away. "Jericho …"

On the table between the two chairs sat a teapot and empty cups, alongside slices of barley bread. The baron ordinarily loathed tea, but he hadn't had a bite to eat in days, so he poured a cup and shoved the bread into his mouth. "He will not speak a word of it, lest he prefers a sizable hole drilled into his skull," he said around a mouthful of food.

"Drystan has always been favored by the bishop. Do not doubt the possibility of betrayal with that boy."

"I am the only friend he has, Mother. The others look upon him as a bastard child, in spite of what Bishop Venable says about his mother being *pure* and *wholesome*."

Frustration colored her expression when she stared back at him. "Should he tell them about your healing, they will surely send you back to the undercroft for more punishment."

"It is already decided. I am to return once my wounds have healed."

"What do they believe warranted this punishment?" She lowered to her knees, taking his hand in hers. "Tell me, Jericho."

"I followed Father into the woods. And what I saw there was–"

With a shake of her head, she raised her hand. "Say no more. I know all too well what you saw."

"You do?"

"Listen to me." She gave his hand a squeeze. "This punishment is a test. While I find relief in your healing, it is unfortunate. They will consider it aberrant. Impossible. There are things in this world that you do not yet understand. Truth cloaked in lies. You must prove to them that you feel pain as they do. That you heal as they do. That you are what they are."

As he swallowed another bite of bread, he focused on her cryptic words, puzzling them in his head. "I do not understand. Do you ask that I not heal my wounds, when I am capable of such a thing?"

"That is precisely what I ask of you."

"They will kill me. I have heard of other boys subjected to such punishments, never to be seen again. Have you not heard their mothers calling for them in the village?"

"I have. Which is why I am warning you to do as I say."

Frowning, he slid his hand from his mother's. Had she truly just asked him to suffer his punishment without question? "Do you not think those other boys screamed and bled and pleaded for mercy? That their skin did not bear the marks of their punishment, as expected?"

"You are quite different. Your father treats you this way because he knows what you are capable of, and he fears it. They should all fear you, Jericho." The earnest glint in her eyes sent a snaking feeling crawling beneath his skin. "It is your wrath which frightens me more than the possibility of death."

"You have no concern for my death?"

"If I thought them capable of causing it, yes. I would."

Although he was young, the baron understood the implication in her words.

"But reckless violence is not in your heart." Eyes softened with a smile, she reached out to cup his face. "That is not what I want for you, my beautiful son. Through guidance, you will understand. You are of age now."

"Of age for what?"

Her smile widened, alight with the kind of spark he'd not seen in years. "Very exciting things, my love. Wonderful things. And I have the perfect mentor for you. He will show you how to use these magnificent gifts and to suppress the urges."

"What urges?"

The smile from before withered to a worrisome expression, and she ran her thumb over his cheek in a gentle stroke. "There is darkness inside of you, Jericho. An animal that claws at you. Tell me you do not feel it inside your belly every time you are faced with the notion of right and wrong. Tell me you do not crave certain … sensations."

He could not deny any of that. The night before had proven to be the most horrific in all his life.

"Your life is a test."

"What kind of test?"

Both hands cupped his face, and she planted a kiss to his forehead. "Someday, I will speak more freely. Someday, you will better understand. Solomon will help guide you in the meantime."

"Solomon? The church organist?"

"Yes. He is much more knowledgeable than you can imagine."

"Why would you trust someone so closely associated with the Pentacrux?"

"I promise you, someday, when you are ready, truly ready, I will tell you everything."

He gripped both her wrists, desperate for the answers he'd spent his entire life pondering. The oddities that had never made sense to him. He wanted to know everything. Every peculiar detail about himself. "I am ready now."

"No, my son. Your journey has only just begun." It was strange, the way she could look both sad and happy at the same time.

"Do you love my father?"

Lowering her hands from his face, she pushed to her feet. "I have certainly tried."

"I have no love for him. If that holds true for both of us, then, why do we stay? Let us leave this place. Leave him."

"It would certainly be easier." A small and wistful smile withered to a frown. "I am here for reasons you cannot understand quite yet."

He lurched forward in his chair, the dismissal in her tone grating on him. "You are ill. He has made you ill, and tomorrow you will be more ill than today."

"As difficult as the coming days will be, I am asking for your trust. Know that, if I thought for one moment that I could escape freely with you, and that I could keep you forever, I would not hesitate. But that is not what my path demands of me. Our fate lies here. *Your* journey begins here. And so you must promise me, no matter what, you will surrender your will to faith."

With a resigned huff, the baron slouched back in his chair. "I promise."

9

JERICHO

*F*uck.
  Fuck!
Drink in hand, I paced my office, ignoring the bone-splitting visuals of Farryn at the mercy of my father. I wanted to crush something. Kill it and bring it back to life, so I could kill it again. The rage moved through me like an electric storm. I threw back the entire glass of absinthe and, deciding it wasn't strong enough, reached for the chthoniac. The urge to drive my fist into every wall had my knuckles tingling.

I had to stop thinking about it. Farryn was just shy of four months into her pregnancy. There was still a bit of time to figure something out, yet I knew all too well the way time could torment. Friend one moment, foe the next. At the very least, I would bind myself to her, which would give me the legal right to destroy any overlord who laid a hand on her, including my father.

I'd have claimed her right then. Dragged her out of bed for our own little binding ritual. Except, the physical changes she'd undergo might've put the baby in harm's way. It wasn't just that my blood would merge with hers, that our hearts would sync together, or that our skin would be primed to crave each other's touch. It was that she would also become immortal. All the cells in her body would harden and calcify to sustain life for eternity. While it wasn't entirely painful, it was exhausting, and potentially dangerous for a growing baby, so I'd have to wait until after she gave birth. Which left me a ball of nerves.

Combing my surroundings for some distraction, I found it in a newspaper article lying on my desk. In the bottom corner of its folded edge, I could just make out *Condemned For Death*.

Every week, the neighboring towns collectively put out a list of prisoners sentenced to punishment or exile to Ex Nihilo. I unfolded the paper to view a list of headshots for all of the prisoners. A quick skim through the list, and I paused on a familiar face.

"Well, I'll be damned."

Vaszhago.

It had to have been a couple decades since I'd last seen him.

Vaszhago had once been one of the Noxerians most savage sell-swords. One whose talents in tracking I'd come to know of firsthand, when he'd been sent to assassinate me after I learned of Farryn's rebirth and abandoned my knighthood to seek passage back to the earthly realm. As a Knight of the Infernal Order himself, he'd made for one hell of a rival, not only possessing the skills to fight, but the proficiency to wield the unique powers that had secured his place within the Order. My own, of course, was the very power that I now lacked.

According to the newspaper's accompanying article, Vaszhago had brutally murdered an overlord, which was a no-no in Nightshade. Bold, really, as it was unlikely that anyone who murdered a lord got away with it, seeing as the tribunal never offered mercy and went out of their way to hunt the killers down. His punishment was Ex Nihilo, scheduled to be carried out the following day at dusk, in the neighboring city of Velthrock.

Still holding the paper in hand, I fell into my chair and leaned in toward one of the cabinets on my desk. Placing a hand against its surface unlocked it, and opening it showed a few trinkets stored inside, one of which was a black leather box with the Knights silvery emblem–serpents entwined around a dagger, with wings at either side. I set the box out on the desktop and opened it to one of the most finely crafted daggers ever to exist in the five realms. Holding it in my hand brought back memories of having fought side by side with Vaszhago–a history that spanned centuries, and worlds apart from where I'd eventually ended up. From warrior to the demon equivalent of a Wall Street grinder, brokering souls between Heaven and Hell.

And now, nearly as powerless as a mortal.

What a waste to see a warrior, with gifts and abilities like those Vaszhago possessed, be sent to the eternal darkness of Ex Nihilo.

A crawling sensation fingered its way down my spine, a blackness settling over my mind. Sharp pain struck my skull, the blare of metal on metal scraping over my eardrum with such intensity, I screwed my eye shut, jaw clenched. The base of my glass clattered against the desktop, as I blindly slammed it down, and fingers pressed to my temples, I tried to calm the storm raging inside my skull. Jagged bolts of lightning flashed behind my shuttered lid, while thoughts took me back to my time in the nothingness. In the pitch blackness, I could hear the familiar maniacal laughter of my father. A sound that infected my ears like a thousand tiny parasites crawling around inside my head. In my mind's eye, I saw things. Long black appendages extending out from my body that longed to hook themselves into flesh. I felt urges that I'd long suppressed. Ones that craved blood and screams and violence.

And Farryn.

But I wanted her in a way that sent a shudder down my spine. A way that unraveled every romantic notion and bastardized it into something depraved.

In the very core of my thoughts was that day in the woods, when I'd happened upon my father and his sister, and the cold sensation which had coiled up my spine while watching him defile her. As if she were nothing more than an object. A toy he obsessively longed to keep at his disposal.

I breathed hard through my nose until the pain subsided, and I opened my eye to a too-bright blurry scene that left me flinching. I groaned and reached for my drink, setting the dagger aside.

Another long sip, and I shook my head of the visuals. The headaches weren't new, and neither were my degenerate thoughts. I'd been plagued by unbidden visuals all throughout my time in Ex Nihilo, and the moment I'd returned to the mortal realm, the first thing I'd craved was Farryn. Not my beautiful, feisty Farryn, but the quiet, subdued version that cowered before me. It wasn't right. Yes, I'd always wanted to possess her. I'd even developed an obsession for her—one that bordered on criminal--but it was her spark, her fire, which had always drawn me. The warmth of her.

And if things continued to progress, if I failed to control this beastly side of me, one slip could enslave her for eternity. Even then, having her enslaved to me wouldn't spare her from my father. It'd only make for a miserable eternity.

I needed to track down Farryn's father, because each day

without my wings drew me deeper into the darker half of my soul.

Throughout the course of my life, I'd had moments of having been depleted of vitaeilem, had felt the darkness consume me, which was how I'd come to rely so heavily on a highly forbidden drug, known as seraphica.

It so happened the Noxerians had taken an interest in, and made exceptional coin from, selling the potent tonic made from the blood of angels, so their motives in hunting the A'ryakai were two-fold: eliminate the angels *and* harvest their precious vitaeilem to synthesize a watered-down version, which could be consumed by both angels and demons.

A little over a century ago, I'd developed something of an addiction to it. Craved it in the same manner one might fiend for modern day cocaine. Although it was a watered-down version of pure vitaeilem, it kept the malevolence inside of me dormant. Particularly during the years when I'd found myself in the bowels of depravity. It was Farryn's birth which had forced me to kick the addiction. To heal and replenish my vitaeilem, so that I might be strong enough to protect her.

I surely didn't want to go back to sucking down vials of it. To become so glutted on the high of feeling good again that I could forsake what was most important to me.

And I surely couldn't bring myself to murder an angel again.

As I stared out the window of my office, a shadowy form in the distance caught my eye. I sensed him before I could even make out what it was, and I smiled as Cicatrix neared the cathedral. I unlatched the window, allowing the black raven to fly into my office, and he landed on my desk with an obnoxious flap of his wings, rustling the papers strewn there.

Any news on Farryn's father? I asked through the vinculum bond we shared.

Not yet. We have eyes across the realm, watching for him. We will find him.

With a nod, I stroked my hand along his wings and reached into the drawer of my desk to offer him a piece of dried meat from those I kept in a jar. *I thank you for your persistence. Just as well, I may join you in the search. It's only a matter of time before the Infernal Ones come sniffing around here for Farryn. I need my wings, as I'm sure you understand.*

Yes, of course. I will not fail you, Master.

The bird gulped back the proffered treat and hopped along the desk, back toward the window. He flapped his wings as a sign of excitement. *"Let us go now!"*

"I'm afraid I can't do that yet, my friend," I said, aloud that time. "I can't bring Farryn with me, it's far too dangerous a trek." Should The Fallen catch sight of her, they could've very well tried to swipe her up and hand her over to their overlord, who would then have died at my hands without question.

Which would've left me at the same mercy as Vaszhago, having killed a prominent figure.

The article on the desk caught my eye again.

Vaszhago.

Dangerous as he might've been, he was an unrivaled and merciless killer who could've potentially served as a bodyguard to Farryn in my absence. And my presence. One gnawing concern of mine was that if Farryn's father failed to remember anything about the Omni, and journeying to find him proved to be a dead end, my weakening angel powers could become more of a threat to her and the baby than any other. In that case, I'd need someone bold enough to put a blade to my throat, and Vaszhago was undoubtedly the demon for that. In fact, the bastard would probably glean some enjoyment out of it.

Assigning him the task would require a *ba'nixium*, a curse which would bind him to Farryn's life. Meaning, if she died or suffered, in turn, he would suffer the most horrific pain known to a demon. And if he was foolish enough to touch her in a sexual manner, he'd suffer more than that at my amusement.

Undoubtedly, Farryn would surely hate the idea of having a babysitter shadowing her all hours of the day, but I could see no other option. To properly protect her myself and *from* myself, I needed to restore my wings.

In the meantime, I needed a safety net. A means of ensuring that I wouldn't be the one to harm her--which meant I'd be traveling to Velthrock to barter for the freedom of a demon who'd once tried to kill me.

The dreary sound of *Nocturnis* filled the room, as I played from memory--a song I'd learned many years ago. I found solace in the music, a moment of quiet reflection, when my world felt as if it had been thrown into utter chaos. To have returned from the pitch blackness of Ex Nihilo, into the hell of having found out Farryn had damned her soul to bring me back, it was as if everything around me had caught flames.

The ornate dagger of the knighthood sat on the organ console above the drawknobs, and beside it, a glass of half-sipped chthoniac. The blade, I'd planned to slip into Farryn's nightstand later--a means of protection, as it tended to be very effective against all breeds of demon. Including my less favorable form. It would give her a fighting chance in the event I couldn't control myself around her.

As I played on, the hair on the back of my neck stood. On

my next breath, a wave of something thrilling pulsed through me, the pull of craving, and as I caught her delicious scent on the air, my body hardened.

In spite of the urge to smile at Farryn's presence, I tamped it down.

Devil's blood, staying away from her was going to be impossible.

10

FARRYN

*T*he forlorn music echoed down the hallway, as I approached the organ room. It'd been months since I last heard Jericho play, and a warm, nostalgic feeling swept over me as I recalled that first evening when he'd caught me spying on him.

As massive as the cathedral was, the music reached the farthest corners through the vents, so when I heard it, I instantly felt a pattering in my heart. With a candlestick in hand, I hid behind one of the pillars, watching the way his body moved with every haunting note. He was mesmerizing. Perhaps the most complicated man I'd ever met in my life. So many different facets made up his personality, like a scintillating black diamond with endless planes, that he was anything but predictable, or boring.

Having watched him for about five minutes, I mentally urged myself to approach, but hesitated. Debating. I wasn't sure why. Perhaps because, even after all we'd been through, what we'd become to one another, the man still carried an air of dominance and authority in this place. An ominous undercurrent that seemed much more pronounced since his return from Ex Nihilo.

And yeah, the suggestion to remain separated sucked. It'd broken my heart, and I'd spent the last hour soaking in a bathtub sobbing over it. After which, I'd attempted to relax in bed awhile, but my heart still felt too unsettled. I'd spent months in bed, and all I wanted was to see him.

Honestly, I'd planned to pay him a chaste visit, but just in case he'd changed his mind about the separation, I made a point to wear one of the oddball dresses I'd found tucked at the back of my armoire. As if the universe wanted me to wear it. With a laced-up bodice that tapered at the waist, and long, flared sleeves with a flowing skirt, it reminded me of something out of a gothic renaissance festival. A far cry from the simple Blackwater uniform.

The music ended, and my muscles lurched with the longing to step out from behind my hiding spot. Palms sweating, I pressed myself against the pillar, as if it would somehow stop me from going to him. *Just go to him already!*

"Do you intend to stand there all evening?" The deep timbre of his voice carried on the air, as darkly euphonious as the song he'd just played.

Of course he sensed me there. Nothing got by the man.

With a sheepish smile, I rounded the pillar, and my pulse hammered as he turned to look at me. It didn't matter that the man had seen me naked a dozen times before. Whenever that nefarious gaze of his landed on me, butterflies shot to my stomach. "I wasn't sure if you were going to tell me to get lost."

"Does that sound like something I would say?" Beneath the appreciative glint in his eye, there lay a shadow of something darker. More carnal. "New dress?"

I lifted the hem of it, which exposed more of my thigh. "This old thing? No, I found it in my closet." His gaze tracked me like a predator, as I made my way toward a pew across from him and plopped down, ungraciously, not bothering to cross my legs as I sagged back into the wood and sat the candle holder beside me. Watching his fingers curl around the edge of the organ had me inwardly smiling. "You look mad. Am I in trouble?"

"Frequently, it seems." He lowered his gaze to my thighs, which stuck out from the raised hem of my dress.

I brought my knees together, squirming under the weight of his attention. "Well, I don't mean to break the rules of separation, I just wondered if there was any news on my father."

A gaze of winter blue met mine and the appreciative sparkle from before sharpened with austerity. "Cicatrix informs me they've not tracked him yet. But I will be joining them in the search."

I straightened in my seat, giving up on the silly flirtations. "Oh. Okay. When do we leave? I'll probably need to change out of this dress into something warmer."

"I'm not taking you with me, Farryn. The only thing keeping you out of the Infernal Realm, at the moment, is the baby growing inside of you. *My* child," he said with an air of possession. "Should you suffer some injury, or worse, every demon that falls under the purview of the one who seeks your soul will be summoned to hunt you down."

I caught the flinch of his eye, and the way he turned his gaze away, jaw clenched, made it perfectly clear how much that thought bothered him. "That can happen any time, Jericho. Climbing the stairs. Taking a shower. Sleeping. You think it's wise to leave me here alone, instead?"

"I will make arrangements for that, as well. As much as I would love to watch you reunite with your father, I won't risk you becoming a fallen overlord's slave." The words rolled off his tongue like a bitter taste he wanted to spit from his mouth.

"I'll disguise myself."

"I could smell you from down the hall. Your vitality would attract them like flies."

"To shit."

Rubbing a hand down his face, he reached for his glass of what I guessed to be absinthe, given its bright green color. "Your scent is intoxicating. You couldn't evade them if you tried. This entire realm is infested with malevolent types who wouldn't bother to honor the rules of the ancient elders. The kind who would carve the child out of your belly while they fed on your soul." His gaze landed on my thighs again, just before he tipped back his drink.

"Fine. I'll stay put like a good, pregnant, little human. But promise me, if you find him, you will bring him to me."

"If I can track him down, I will do my best to bring him back."

"Promise." Brow raised, I crossed my arms over my chest, which seemed to draw his gaze to my breasts.

"What is a promise to you humans? I could promise you the world, then set it aflame, and nothing changes."

"I've not seen him in years. I've not heard his voice. Looked into his eyes. Heard him say my name. All I have are infinity symbols made of twine, and a lifetime of sadness and confusion." I sighed. In truth, I'd grown pessimistic about seeing him again. The daughter inside of me clung to a small sliver of hope, but the adult who'd already lived through years of pain and emptiness had come to accept that I might never see him again. "If you manage to find him, if he's here, I need to see him."

"I understand. I will bring him home."

With a nod, I glanced around the room, trying not to look

at him, for fear I'd crack and start sobbing again. "So, these arrangements you made for me. What are they?"

"I intend to hire something of a bodyguard for you."

"A bodyguard?" The thought was so ridiculous, I accidentally snorted a laugh.

"It's necessary if we're apart."

"So, where does this *bodyguard* come from? Another save from death row, like the dog caretakers you hire?"

His lips curved to a smile. "Actually, yes."

"Seriously? I'm assuming he's on death row for a reason?"

"He's a very skilled killer who happened to eliminate the wrong demon."

Eyes narrowed on him, I waited for the punchline for what had to be a joke. "And you trust him to watch over *me*? Because that doesn't sound like you."

"He will be bound to you through a curse that, if broken, would essentially be eternal pain and suffering."

On an exasperated huff, I slouched back in the pew. "Well, you certainly cover your bases. Do you trust him not to harm Anya when she retrieves him?"

"She won't be retrieving him. I will."

Frowning, I crossed my arms again. "So, you're okay leaving me to go off and buy a *bodyguard*, but heaven forbid you leave me here to search for my father? This isn't just about leaving me alone, is it? This bodyguard is another barrier between us, too."

He buried his gaze in his drink. "A precaution."

"A killer. And just how do you know him?"

"He tried to assassinate me once."

All I could do was nod, because not a damned lick of it made any sense. "I think something happened in the crossing over from Ex Nihilo. Something isn't right with you."

"Something did happen. It's why I'm doing this. Vaszhago won't hesitate to kill me, if I attempt to harm you."

Vaszhago. Of course he'd have a name that reminded me of a musketeer. "And who's to say he won't try to kill you because he's having a bad day? Or because his coffee got cold too quickly?"

His lips twitched with a smile that he buried in another sip of his absinthe. "It's hard to explain, but we have something of a moral code between us."

"Oh, well, never mind my apprehensions. You have a *moral code* between you." The irritation inside of me flared, and I turned away, scowling. Having essentially taken care of myself since I was old enough to make my own pot of coffee–which was about age nine–the thought of someone shadowing me sat like a barrel of rotten animosity in my gut. "Look, I get it. You're worried. You're insanely overprotective. To a fault, really. A bit obsessive. And maybe even slightly unhinged. But I don't need all this, Jericho. I don't need a bodyguard, and I don't need you acting like I'm fragile, or like you have to stay away from me. I'm a big girl. I can take care of myself."

His chest rose and fell with a heavy sigh. "Farryn, please trust me on this."

I drummed my fingers on the pew's glossy wood, still keeping my irritated gaze from his. "Fine. But don't expect me to be nice and sweet."

"I wouldn't dream of that." In my periphery, I caught sight of him reaching behind him. "I have something for you."

"Oh?" I swung my attention back around.

"Don't get too excited." He lifted a black, leather case from a small ledge, stirring my curiosity as he turned toward me. On the case was an emblem--serpents entwined around a dagger, with wings at each of its sides.

"You were in a fraternity?"

"Something like that." Lips cracked to a smile, he ran his

finger over the emblem, before his smile faded to a frown. "Knights of the Infernal Order."

"That sounds very medieval."

"They go back a long way. The ancients fought in the great war against the heavens."

"Are you talking *the* war? As in, *Book of Revelation* variety of war?"

"Yes."

Jesus. Literally. I wondered if he'd actually met the guy all of a sudden. "You aren't that old, are you?"

"No, smartass. I was *trained* by the ancients. I didn't say I *was* one."

"As a Knight of the *Infernal* Order? So like, Hell? The *bad* guys?"

"The bad guys. In fact, the leather of this case is made from flesh."

I grimaced, wondering if he meant human flesh, but I didn't have the balls to ask. "How did I not know this about you?"

"It's not exactly dating conversation." Pulling back the sleeve of his shirt revealed the veins in his forearm, where the silvery tattoos gleamed. He pointed to a faint white outline embedded beneath the tattoos. The same emblem embossed in the leather had been branded on his arm.

"How did I miss that?"

"It's not something I'm proud to show off. I've done very bad things in my lifetime."

I knew that about him. Jericho was a bad man. Essentially the villain in my story, who killed without mercy and gave little-to-no thought about morals and virtue. I'd come to terms with it, because good men didn't scare away the monsters that were inevitably coming for me. "You've also done some good, Jericho, which makes you complicated. Bad, but complicated."

From inside the case, he lifted a beautiful and elaborately carved object made of silver. Or so it appeared, anyway. As he removed a blade, it made a satisfying melodic swish sound.

"A knife?"

"A dagger is what we like to call it. Made of celestial steel and reinforced with a curse."

"Curse? Like the one Drystan used?"

"Not quite." He held up the dagger, twisting it around as if admiring it. "This blade, you must strike a certain way to send someone to Ex Nihilo. It'll be safer for you to sleep with."

"Sleep with … as in under my pillow?"

"Yes."

"Why?"

"Precaution."

"Look, I know I just gave you the '*I'm not a child*' lecture," I said in air quotes, "but I'm also not the bad-ass you seem to think I am. The most impressive thing I've ever done with a knife is manage to *not* get peanut butter on my sleeve."

Only a hint of a smile played over his lips as he stood up from the organ bench and stepped toward me. Damn the flutter in my heart, as he approached in his black button-down shirt, which showed off just a hint of silver tattoo beneath the sleeves. "Any *bad-ass* training taught in your realm would fail to work here, anyway. What is vital to humans is not the case with demons." He flicked his fingers, urging me to stand up. "Come. I'll show you."

"Sure that's a good idea? It could be dangerous, getting too close."

"You're mocking me."

"Damn right." With a huff, I stood up from my seat, and the moment I was upright, he dragged me close to him. My body mourned the heat given off by his, and I craved that proprietary grip of his against my hip. It hadn't been more than a couple hours of staying away from each other, and it already felt like an eternity.

He turned me just enough to let a cold detachment slip between us and tapped at my elbow. "Arm out."

While disenchanted by all of this, I did as he commanded and held my arm out like an aloof teenager.

"There are two positions with this blade. Outward and chambered." Cold steel kissed my palm, as he placed the hilt there and curled my fingers around it. "Tip toward the elbow is chambered. You use your fingers to quickly flip it outward, when needed." He slid my fingers over the hilt to position them a different way, but all I could feel was his strong arms around me and his solid chest pressed at my back. "Do you feel how nicely that slips across your palm?"

"Yes." I didn't bother to mention what else felt nice slipping across my palm.

"Good. Now try by yourself."

In the same quick movements, I repeated what he'd taught me, flipping the blade around in my hand. Strangely enough, the motion felt completely natural. So much so, I frowned as I watched my hand perform as if it belonged to someone else.

"Seems you're a natural." Jericho's voice, tinged with confusion, matched the confusion swirling in my own head. "You've never taken a self-defense class?"

"Does volleyball in gym class count as self-defense?"

"No."

"Then, no. Maybe I just want to hurry up and get to the cutting part." I hated the way the sound of his chuckle tickled my chest and sprang goosebumps across my arms. "What's next?"

"Impatient." Gripping my arm again, he guided the blade

outward. "There is a three-strike rule when fighting a demon, or angel. Stun. Silence. Sever."

"You've killed many angels?"

"Enough of them. Unbeknownst to many, there is a nerve that runs beneath a demon's skin, across his chest like a shield, up to the back of his neck. A very sensitive one. It helps him pick up on certain vibrations, like your increased pulse rate." As he ran his thumb over my wrist, I momentarily lost focus on his words. "The tiny change in temperature. The hitch of your breath." Warm licorice-scented breath hit my neck, and I closed my eyes, tamping down the urge to turn around and kiss him, whether he wanted me to, or not. "When struck, it's like hitting an open nerve." He came around from behind, standing before me like a wall I wanted to climb. With my wrist gripped in his hand, he guided the blade up over his chest. "Up and across. Then flip the blade to chambered, as I showed you."

As commanded, I did as he told me, again slightly flabbergasted how easily it moved in my hand. As if I'd done it a thousand times before. I just caught the flicker of confusion on Jericho's face, which told me I wasn't the only one surprised.

"At the throat is an organ." When he tipped his head back, I watched his Adams apple bob with a swallow. "There are clicks, made by a different vocal chord to those of a human, which create curses and power. If given the chance, they will hold you in a trance, harm you with their chants. Unless you silence them by dragging the blade deep enough to puncture that organ." He gently led my hand across his own throat to demonstrate. "And finally ..." He tapped at his temple. "Unlike humans, we have a very strong psychic power that originates here. It allows us to transport between realms as easily as walking through a door. One quick strike severs that ability. The execution of all three activates the curse, and your victim bursts into flames."

I flinched at that and turned away from him, taken back to that night on the grounds of Blackwater, when his wings had been sliced clean off and he had burst into flames in the same manner he'd just described.

"I'm sorry. It's not my intent to upset you. I only want you and the baby safe."

Eyes screwed shut to banish the visuals from before, I nodded. "I know. I hope I never have to see that up close again."

"As do I. But it's best for both of us if you can defend yourself."

"If you think that I'm going to use this on you, you're wrong. I don't care what you turn into."

"Do not be under the impression that I'd have any modicum of control or that I would recognize you enough to stop myself if it got to that point." Fingers dug into my hips one last time before he released me.

"You speak as if you have been to that point."

"I have."

"How?"

Brows knitted, he lowered his gaze. "Pain is very powerful. At times, more powerful than anything else. There is a place in the deepest, darkest depths of the mind, where all hope is lost. The point at which you realize that nothing is going to save you. Had you found yourself in the mouth of that serpent, you would know the creeping blackness that lies in wait. And there was a time I surrendered myself to it."

Staring off, I tried to imagine the utter hopelessness he was trying to convey, but as if my head refused to sink that deep into darkness, I couldn't. "I don't know that feeling. Even when you were gone, I couldn't accept it. As impossible as it was, I knew you'd come back."

"For humans, hope is innate. An essential part of your being. For me? It is a fragile thread that can snap at a moment's notice. That thick and suffocating blackness is a matter of breathing a different kind of air, regardless of my pedigree. I'm not immune to it, Farryn."

Eyeing the blade still caught in my palm, I shook my head and stepped past him, placing it back on the small ledge of the organ. "You can teach me how to use this. But you can't teach my heart to follow through, if it's you at the end of my blade. That's just the way it is."

Expelling a huff, he turned to face me, and my eyes darted straight to the muscles that stretched the fabric around his biceps. Strong arms I longed to capture me. "You are perhaps the most stubborn human I've ever met."

"You say that like it's a bad thing."

"Tell me you've gleaned something from this little lesson."

"I have. Stun. Silence. And sever. I won't forget."

"Good," he said, and I found myself trapped under the weight of his stare as it trailed down the length of my dress. "I'll make a point to teach you each day. Vaszhago can teach you, as well."

"I don't want *Vaszhago* teaching me."

Gaze on me as he passed, he took a seat back on the bench and leaned against the organ with his drink in hand, his shirt undone, body relaxed and delicious enough to eat. "What do you want, Farryn?"

The question came as a surprise, but when I caught a glimpse of his eye, the need sparkling there, it was the first time I believed that he truly felt some torment in staying apart, as well. "What do you think I want?"

His cheek flinched as if he might smile, his focus on his drink. "Tell me."

He was playing with me again, taunting me with that sexy

smirk and vicious gaze. God, I missed the cat and mouse game with him.

Instead of answering, I sauntered around the edge of the organ and stole his drink, which I set back down, and before he could stop me, or protest, I slid my leg between him and the keys, lowering down on his lap. Straddled over his legs, I watched his chest rise and fall, felt the tension in his muscles as he gripped the edge of the bench. Resisting me.

It didn't matter how his body responded, his hungry gaze told me everything.

"I want *you*." I circled my hips against him, noting that placid facade of his slowly cracking.

Bowing my head to kiss the base of his throat, I ran my palm over the impressive bulge sticking out from his slacks. The man was hard as stone. A growl rumbled deep in his chest, and he slid a hand across my throat, giving a warning squeeze.

"Given my voracious appetite when it comes to you, Miss Ravenshaw, I'd advise against touching me that way." His voice carried a husky rasp of desperation. "Unless you'd prefer this pretty dress of yours in shreds on the floor."

A quick glance toward the pillars showed no one there, and I sucked my lip between my teeth as I stared down at him, wanting him so badly my thighs ached and trembled. "I would, Mister Van Croix."

War raged across his face, like a battle between what he wanted and what he needed. "Devil's blood, you are my Heaven and Hell." His sharp jaw hardened with stubborn opposition, the veins of his neck popping to the surface, but he didn't push me away.

I slid my arms back around his neck, fingers in his hair, and kissed him, feeling his tongue slip past my teeth, his growl vibrating over my lips. "Then, I should appeal to both your angel *and* demon side."

"You appeal to every fiber of my being. Every vile and wanton cell in my body."

"Play me a song," I whispered, and I kissed one of the hammering veins, feeling his sharp exhale scatter over my skin.

His arms wrapped around me, and he wedged me closer against his chest, my legs dangling around the back of him. A despondent chord filled the room, and he tipped his head just enough to take my mouth. I wrapped my arms around him and slid my fingers through his hair, sucking the bitter anise flavor from his tongue. In slow circles, I ground myself against his slacks, lazily dry humping him. Through the fabric, tiny vibrations beat against my exceptionally sensitive cleft, traveling up inside me, and I held him tighter, letting out a shuddered breath.

The strokes across the keys became fast and erratic, every sonorous note dancing around us, the vibrations pounding a rhythm of desire. My body felt small against his, pliant, as his arms moved around me, while he kept on with his dreary song.

"Fuck." The music stopped abruptly on a dissonant note, and he reached up beneath my dress, rough hands gripping tight to my ass and pressing me against his bulge. "You tempt and tease me incessantly."

"Then tell me to leave."

He growled again, teeth clenched, as he dragged my pussy over his groin like a threat. "This is what you do to me. Your scent. Your touch. There is no madness more insufferable than trying to keep my hands off you." It was clear he didn't *want* me to leave. Head lowered, he guided me over his rigid length still tucked inside his pants, and groaned. "I can't properly express how badly I want to defile you right now." Fingers slid inside the back of my panties, over my ass, and down over my aching hole.

I'd been touched by him a number of times in the last few days, but the feel of his finger taunting me, gliding over my hungry and swollen flesh, had me biting my lip again. Desperate for his touch. "I promise I won't stop you," I said.

Gaze on mine, he watched me as he pushed two fingers up inside of me. The feel of them moving within me wound my stomach muscles tight, and a potent combination of relief and victory swam through me, as he played along, giving me what I wanted. Of course, anyone could've walked in on us, but I was too lost and intoxicated. Drunk with the lust that pulsed through me in waves.

A memory slipped through my mind–*his hand gripping my wrist, tugging me toward the woods, the fear of being caught.* Lustina's memories. Mine. Innocent and forbidden love.

Breathtaking.

"You feel so good," I whispered, circling my hips, stirring his fingers inside of me.

While his merciless digits curved deeper, his thumb slipped between the cheeks of my ass to that tight forbidden ring, the pressure threatening to breach it. "Fuck them. I want to feel how much you want me."

As he asked, I backed myself to his knuckles, then back up to his fingertips, and down again, plunging his fingers in and out of me.

"What a greedy little Vixen you are," he whispered at my ear. "So hungry."

I upped the pace, letting out a quiet moan as the hum of electricity tickled me from the inside out. Tiny trembles vibrated my thighs, and I shuddered a breath, gripping the nape of his neck as I rode his fingers.

It wasn't enough, though. Not nearly enough. My body remembered all too well what the man felt like inside of me, and it yearned for something bigger. The kind of pressure that would fill me completely.

I gave a hard squeeze to his bulge, inciting another groan. "You're playing with fire right now."

"Are you going to deny me?" Not long ago, he'd told me that he'd never deny me. That all I had to do was take what I wanted from him. Bottom lip caught between my teeth, I moaned again as I backed myself down his fingers and ground myself against his knuckles.

"You know I can't say no to you." His jaw hardened like he was angry that I'd challenged him. Before I knew what was happening, he shot to his feet and laid me across the long bench, looming over me like a raging storm. The way he shoved his fingers into his mouth, sucking the wet shine from them, sent a flutter to my stomach, and when he let out a masculine sound of satisfaction, I felt my arousal spill into the silk of my panties.

He unlatched his belt with one hand, pushing the hem of my dress up over my knees with the other. Bending forward, he lowered his head between my legs, and his nostrils flared as he inhaled deeply. "The smell of your need is mouth-watering."

Once free of the loops, the belt hung from his palm like a threat, and he wrapped it around my wrists, securing them tightly, before pushing my arms above my head. He swiped up the blade he'd used during our lesson and twisted it in front of me.

Something thrilling moved deep inside of me, coiling in my stomach, and I swallowed hard, imagining the thoughts in his head right then. Never taking his eye off me, he lowered the blade to my thigh, drawing a faint and gentle path upward, toward my panties. In one swift slash, he sliced the flimsy fabric away, and I gasped when the cool air kissed my bare flesh.

Another clean glide of the blade up from the hem of my dress cleaved it in half, and he pushed the tattered cloth to either side of my body. A tremble ran through me. I'd never felt more vulnerable and exposed. Jericho had always taken such care to keep me shielded from prying eyes, but right then, it seemed he couldn't have cared less.

The clench of his jaw told me he was tense. Angry. At me? "You are mine." He yanked me down the bench, the fabric scratching over my back, until my ass met the edge of it. "You belong to no one else."

I nodded back at him, a sliver of confusion cutting through me, as his scarred lip curved into a slight snarl.

"If another should dare so much as a chaste kiss to your cheek, there isn't a corner of this world, or any other, that could shield him from my violence."

Strong fingers bruised my hips. Something had gotten into him. I could feel the heat burning his skin. The way his muscles bunched and hardened around me. He'd worked himself up. Over what? I didn't know. Perhaps the meeting in the woods. I wanted to ask, but I was too greedy for him to risk bringing it all to a screeching halt.

"I'm yours." I whispered. "Only yours."

As if my words had diffused him, the malice from before diminished, his gaze a winter blue that held me captive, and he bent forward, seizing my lips in a kiss.

He lifted himself away, attention trailing down my body. Lying naked before him, I watched as he licked his lips, his unpatched eye swallowing every inch of my flesh. I'd had men look at me before. Desire me. But never with so much reverence and appreciation and something I couldn't quite pinpoint. It was a look unique to Jericho. The same way I'd imagine him gazing at a sky full of stars. With the blade's hilt still caught in his palm, he ran his hands over my body, and pulses of electricity snaked beneath my skin.

He placed the hilt of the blade against my exposed clit.

Hot vibrations felt like the warm popping of champagne bubbles, and I arched on a gasp.

"Ah!" The metal conducted the current from his hand, and a humiliating sound escaped me as it hummed against my flesh.

"Which do you prefer? The blade, or my cock?"

"Your cock. Please."

Wearing a wolfish grin, he circled the hilt faster, and I squirmed beneath him on a quiet moan. My fingers grasped at his unyielding belt still binding my hands, desperate to hold onto something.

He ran his tongue along my collarbone and bit down at the crook of my neck. A strange euphoric high swept through my senses, dizzying and pleasurable at the same time.

I closed my eyes and let out an utterly pathetic sound, a cross between a whimper and a giggle. At the prod of my fingertips, I opened my eyes and felt cold steel against my palm, as he slid the blade between my clasped hands. "Do not hesitate. Do you understand?"

I didn't answer at first, too caught up in his deadly gaze, but when his brow winged up over the top of the eyepatch, I nodded.

"Good girl. And when it becomes too much?"

"Mercy."

Without warning, he gave my ass a smack, and a sharp sting followed. He pushed my legs to either side of the bench, spreading me before him, and lowered to his knees. "You are the only creature in all five realms who will ever bring me to my knees." The moment his tongue hit my bare seam, I let out a hiss and jerked my hips forward. His hands cuffed my knees, holding me to the bench, in an uncompromising grip, and he dragged his tongue over my clit in rapid little flicks that had me crying out, back arched. Desperate.

My fingers squeezed the hilt of the blade still trapped in my bound hands as I writhed against his unforgiving face. Tiny pulses of lightning danced over my flesh, the vibrations carrying up into my womb. The man feasted on my pussy, sucking and licking, the wet sounds and moaning telling me he was enjoying his meal.

As he shook his head between my thighs, a wave of turbulent pleasure swept through me, and I curled my toes, desperate. Wanting. "Jericho, please!"

He inserted two fingers again, fucking me with them, and licked his bottom lip as he stared down at me, watching me in that concentrated and calculated way. Always studying me. A look of pure dominance that turned my willpower to mush. "Tell me what you need, Tu'Nazhja."

"I need you."

"You have me for eternity." His finger curled inside of me, just enough pressure that a soft grunt ticked in my throat. "If it's relief you crave, though, you need only to ask."

"Please. Oh, God, please."

The sound of his dark chuckle thrummed my libido, sending a shiver across my skin. "Look at you. So polite." He licked the arousal he'd worked up from his fingers. "So delicious," he said, slowly unbuttoning his shirt, which he peeled from broad shoulders and tossed aside. His body, ravaged by scars and tattoos, and carved in deep lines of muscle, was a perfectly crafted machine, honed for sex. The sound of his zipper had me looking down my body to where he sprung himself free. The size of his erection threatened a whole lot of soreness the next day, but I didn't care. He directed the tip of his cock along my seam, and the electrical pulses had me spreading my legs wider for him. The vibrations traveled up inside me so deep, my knees trembled against him.

Hands gripping the bench at either side of me, he pushed

into me on small teasing thrusts, only so far before pulling back out.

"More, please," I whispered, my voice pathetically needy. It wasn't just the sex I craved, but the closeness. To know that we were still okay, even if things had taken a strange turn since coming back to Nightshade.

"I'll fuck you tonight, Farryn, hard and as mercilessly as you've worked me up right now, but we remain separate until I have a better grasp on what's happening with me. And I swear to Christ, if this goes south, you better act first and think later."

I didn't want to admit how much the thought of the distance hurt me, because even if I'd let some of my vulnerability shine through for Jericho, I still kept my heart on guard. It didn't make sense why, given the way he'd poured his obsession over me. Part of me still didn't believe that I deserved him, that I was worthy of the sacrifices he was willing to make on my behalf.

But I had sacrificed, too. A lot. *Everything.*

And even as nothing but a mere mortal, I had saved him.

Lying to his face, I nodded while swallowing back the tears that itched to break free.

At that, he drove into me, all the way to the hilt, and I tipped my head back, imagining another time, another place, where things weren't so complicated.

"Fucking hell, you feel so good. There is nothing in the world so divine as your tight little *saericasz.*" The word was one he'd taught me back at Aunt Nelle's—some kind of fruit that demons called a woman's pussy. He stared down between us, as if to watch his cock sliding in and out of me. As he drove in again, he circled his hips, and I tilted my head back on a moan. A rough hand fisted my hair, and he pressed his forehead to mine, breathing hard through his nose, his mood changing to something fierce. *"Imolz era'da amreloc,"* he said, his rasped voice in an accent that appealed to some deep-seated part of me.

"What did you say?"

He didn't answer. His powerful body moved over me like a dark and furious thunderstorm. "I will crush whatever forces threaten to harm you. No matter who, or what, they are."

"I love you." My words faltered on the twinge of sadness simmering in my chest. How could I possibly feel this loved and desired, while still, something wedged itself between us. An invisible force that kept us apart, even when we were the closest we'd ever been.

As my mind mulled those unnerving thoughts, he railed his body into me, his skin hot and damp, muscles flexed and tense. Warm breaths scattered over my neck, his exhales shaky, fervent. He slid his palm across my throat, squeezing with just enough pressure to part my lips.

I arched into him, feeling his steel chest against my breasts.

He took a nipple into his mouth, sucking, licking, pulling between his teeth, and at a sharp sting, I flinched and moaned. Hot coils of need burned in my belly, the cusp of climax riding the edges of every frantic breath that escaped me. Sex with him was never just sex. We made love as war, a battle of giving and taking.

As if he could taste the desperation on the air, he sealed my mouth with his lips, eating the mewling little sounds trapped in my throat. The rhythm of our slapping skin echoed through the room as a reminder that the man was relentless in his pursuit for climax. Determined. He released my mouth, tipping his head as he studied me some more.

The intensity of his stare had me turning away, closing my eyes, but in the darkness, I imagined the look on his face, that concentrated expression of his, and a tickle of excitement fluttered in my stomach. The grip at my throat tightened, his pace aggressive, jostling my body with every hard thrust. Deep guttural grunts reached my ears, like the sounds of a rutting beast, both feral and foreign.

I opened my eyes.

With his one visible eye a glowing red, he jerked against my body, pounding into me with bared fangs and two small bumps protruding from his forehead.

The distant sounds of screams echoed inside my head.

A door.

777.

A gnawing fear expanded inside my chest like a crushing grip over my lungs. I couldn't move. Could scarcely draw in a breath. Mumbled words, spoken too fast, crackled in my ear as a heavy whisper. I didn't understand them.

The air turned winter cold. The mumbling grew louder. A thick and heavy weight claimed my limbs.

I opened my mouth to scream, but nothing came out.

A long, serpent tongue slid past Jericho's lips and into my mouth, tasting of bitter cinnamon and fire. All I could do was let him invade my mouth, my body too caught up in a tingling state of paralysis.

My muscles slackened, and what felt like a thousand shocks of pleasure moved through me. I shook and convulsed, panting so fast I couldn't fill my lungs.

His skin turned a deep black, and as he pistoned in and out of my weakened and useless body, I could feel something growing inside of me. Twisting and tightening. Clawing from inside. A whispered scream grew louder. Louder. Louder. It struck like a hammer against my skull in a powerful crack of thunder. I'd heard the sound a number of times before. One so piercing, it shot through me like a bolt of lightning.

Fluids trickled down my ass, my head too caught up in

the moment to care whether it was blood or arousal, but whatever it was made for an even slicker glide, as he continued to fuck me, ignoring the distress that had to have been written all over my face.

"Stop, please! Stop!"

Why wasn't he stopping? Why did he keep going?

I was trapped within my own body. Suffocating. Drowning. The pleasure winding through me pulled on every muscle like a marionette. How could that be? How could I be terrified and aroused at the same time?

The blade fell out of my hands on a clang.

Volatile exhilaration burned in my muscles, heightening to such a level, I was certain I would ignite into flames. Every nerve ending flared, raw and vibrating.

The screaming in my head reached a deafening pitch that exploded in my ears.

Everything turned black.

"Farryn," a deep but soft voice whispered. "Wake up. Please."

I opened my eyes to find Jericho staring down at me, his expression twisted with agony. Confused, I looked about my surroundings, noting the tall organ pipes, the stone pillars, the scent of aged wood and something heady on the air.

Sex.

I wriggled my arms and craned my neck to see my wrists were still bound by the leather belt.

Realization trickled in. *Hands shackled. The blade that sliced my dress open. Intense pleasure.*

Red eye. Fangs. Terror.

Blackness.

On a gasp, I shot my gaze back to his, a tremble of fear

moving through me. "You. I saw you. A monster. F-f-f-fangs and a red eye, and …"

His expression turned even more grim than before, and he pushed away from me, stumbling backward into the pew.

It occurred to me what I'd just done by confessing what I'd seen–put an even thicker wedge between us. I wished I could've taken the words back, to hold them in so he wouldn't do what I suspected was coming next.

"You screamed. Screamed as if I'd hurt you."

I sat up, resting my bound hands in my lap. "You didn't hurt me. I swear it."

"I could've. And the damned thing about it is, I have no recollection. One minute I was tearing your dress away, the next I was tearing my hand from your throat."

"Don't do this, okay? Please. I can't bear the thought of something coming between us."

"And I can't bear the thought of strangling you to death. So, what the fuck am I supposed to do!" His voice thundered around me, bouncing off the walls, his words like a hard slap across my face. "I told you this was a bad idea. I told you to stay away from me. To keep your distance."

"So, you're blaming me now? For what? Because I wanted you? Wanted to be close to you?"

Brows lowering in obvious frustration, he looked away, his hand balled to a tight fist.

"Look, I know something has changed. How could it not? You were trapped in a black void for months. But, in spite of what you say, your true self remains at the core, Jericho. It's there. And I know you won't hurt me."

"Then, why do you look terrified?"

"Because you're a little terrifying when you look like that. I mean, I know giant moths aren't going to hurt me, but it'd scare the shit out of me if one got tangled in my hair. You see what I'm saying?"

Without a word, he pushed up from his seat and unlatched the belt from my wrists, then looped it back through his slacks. His muscles still held a shine of sweat that had his tattoos glistening. He swiped up his discarded dress shirt, which he tossed to me. With a beat of hesitation, he gripped the back of my neck and planted a chaste kiss to my forehead. "I'll return soon."

"You're leaving again?" I slipped my arms into the shirt that was twice my size and buttoned it up.

"Yes. I need to find a Band-aid to put on a gaping hole that's going to be a serious infection before we know it."

"I don't understand. How are you so sure this is going to turn into such a huge problem?"

Granted, I'd never seen the more demonic side to him, but it was Jericho. The same crazy, obsessed man who would've stabbed his own heart out, rather than raise so much as a finger to harm me.

"Because I've been down this path before. I've had my vitaeilem depleted to the point of violent thoughts. And believe me when I say, it gets worse. Much worse."

Even so, despite his words, I couldn't imagine him harming me. Ever. "So, what's the Band-aid?"

"I need vitaeilem. Desperately."

"The angels' lifeblood? Isn't that what I felt earlier? When you ... you know ..."

"Yes." The way he ran his hand back and forth over his skull, I knew he was stressed. Upset. "I want to give you love and pleasure, Farryn. But unlike humans, who can give love and receive it in return, a demon cannot. It's consumed as light fare, but it doesn't fill. Therefore, what is given depletes. And that's when the taking becomes greedier. More violent. I no longer have the capacity to replenish vitaeilem. There's an imbalance in me that needs rescaling."

"How?"

"You ask so many questions."

"I wouldn't, if you weren't so mysterious all the time. I'm just curious to know how it works, is all."

He rubbed his jaw. "There are two ways: I slaughter an angel and consume his vitaeilem, watching him die a slow and painful death. Or I find a shady dealer in town willing to sell the generic and watered-down version."

"A drug?" I wanted to ask him how it was made, but I was afraid he'd actually tell me.

"It isn't my first choice. But neither is murder. For the moment, anyway. I'm in a bit of an impasse." Eye screwed shut, he stroked back and forth over his head. "I can't be without you. The desire and craving I have for you are like lodged hooks pulling at my chest. At the same time, I can't be near you. My body wants to claim you, and at the moment, I'd risk *enchainsz*. I need something to bridge the two. Vitaeilem is the bridge."

"What is *enchainsz*?" My accent was nowhere near as clear as his when I spoke the word.

"Sexual slavery, essentially. Fucking you damn near to death."

A terrifying thought. I could hardly walk after one night with Jericho. Several nights in a row would've probably put me into paralysis.

"This drug … does it have side effects?"

"Of course it does. What drug is taken without consequence? It won't be enough, though, it never is. But it's better than the alternative." He shook his head slowly. "I will not suffer another eternity without you."

Lowering my gaze, I nodded, not entirely understanding the repercussions, but I trusted him to do what he needed to for himself. And I was selfish enough to want him to feel better for us. "Whatever you do, please just be careful. Because I won't be without you, either."

11

THE BARON

*A*cross from where his mother sat, the baron peered through the carriage window, staring out at the thick patches of trees and open fields slipping past. For weeks, his mother had spoken of the mentor she had arranged for him, and it was only when Lord Praecepsia decided to travel to Rome that she'd informed the baron of a scheduled meeting.

According to her, the boy would meet in secret with this mentor every time his father went out of town, which seemed much more frequently as of late.

"What was the nature of your union with my father?" he asked his mother on the journey.

She sighed and frowned. "As long ago as it was, I can scarcely recall."

"Did you love him?"

"In so much as one could love a flower before tasting its poison. He was handsome. Charming. All things necessary to lure the unwitting. I was naive."

Poison was right. He'd proven to be toxic to his mother's health over the years. The very thought churned a sick

138

gurgling in the baron's gut. "He never cared for me, either. Why? If I am his heir. Born of his blood. Why does he shun me?"

Her expression didn't soften with sympathy, but remained impassive and cold. "He does not look upon you as a son, but a threat. Perhaps the only true threat he will ever know."

"What kept him from killing me? What keeps him from killing me now?"

"He can't. His blood runs through you and is cursed. *That which is made to suffer, so too, shall suffer in return.* If he kills you, he kills himself."

"Cursed?" It was strange, the way his mother spoke the word so freely, when the idea was too closely associated with witchcraft--a charge punishable by death, according to the church.

"Yes. Nature has a way of protecting life." A devilish glint in her eyes told him nature had little to do with it.

Just like that, all made sense. The baron could never quite grasp what had kept his father, who'd made it perfectly clear his entire life how much he loathed him, from ultimately driving a blade through his flesh. "Does that go both ways?"

"No. It is only passed from father to child. In addition, you are not yet in tune to the fact that you have instincts, my son." She reached forward and set her hand over his, where it rested against his knee. "They are *unique* instincts that I have gifted you, and so long as my blood runs through you, they will protect you. With them, you pose the most significant threat to your father. But you must learn to control your compulsions, or you will put others at risk."

"Why are you opposed to destroying him? If I am capable, why not rid the world of such evil?"

With what the baron surmised as a look of intrigue, she sat back on the bench. "You would kill your own father?"

"If it meant saving you, yes."

"The evil in this world does not end with one man. It is constant and ever-changing."

Groaning, he slouched back in his seat. "It is as if you speak to me in another language, Mother. I do not understand what you are telling me."

"I am telling you that it is not your place to kill your father, no matter how tempted you may be."

"What is the purpose of having me mentored if I cannot kill what threatens me? Of forcing me to endure punishment without healing?" He lifted his arm, yanking back the sleeve of his tunic from a scar he could've easily healed with his own hands.

The way she merely glanced at the vestiges of his wound left the baron wondering if seeing them affected her, at all. "It is only flesh. Your punishments serve to keep them blinded to what you are and what you are capable of."

"Why?" He pushed his sleeve back in place, finding it useless as a point of argument. "If I truly possess the ability to destroy them, why hide what I am?"

"Because your gifts serve to guard and protect human life. Not destroy it. By exposing what you are, you cast fear into their hearts, and they will try to destroy you, as a result. Which would put you in a very precarious position." Still, her words remained cryptic to the boy, as if she longed to keep him in a state of confusion. "Abandon the notion of killing your father. For it puts far too many at risk."

Sneering, he looked away, but turned back at a rough shake of his arm.

"Promise me you will banish such thoughts. Promise me!"

"I promise. But only because it is you who asks. At least tell me why."

"Your father has debts." She flinched, her gaze falling

away from his. "Horrible debts. And should he perish, those debts would fall in your hands."

"I would gladly take the burden of a few debts to know that he—"

"Enough! You do not know of what you speak, and I ask you to remain silent because of it. I am not foolish enough to suffer his torment, nor to watch you suffer the same over something so insignificant as coin." It was rare that his mother had ever gotten so nettled over something he'd said, and the way her stern brow softened told him she regretted having raised her voice. "I know it frustrates you to be left in the dark. All will make sense in time. I promise."

The carriage slowed along a dirt path that wound through the trees toward a thatched roof hut. In the open yard, a well-kept Andalusian horse stood penned in a makeshift corral connected to an unimpressive stable. A goat, pigs, and sheep had their own separate pens about the clearing, while chickens roamed freely.

Arms behind his back, chin tipped high, Solomon, his supposed mentor, waited beside a young blond boy, who looked to be slightly older than the baron and built with more stock. When the carriage finally rolled to a stop, both approached before the coachman even had the opportunity to dismount.

The door swung open, and the blond reached a hand for the baron's mother. "Lady Praecepsia," he said with a respectful nod, as she exited the carriage.

After a moment's hesitation, the baron followed after her, waving off the blond's offer to help him, as well.

Wearing an easy smile, his mother sauntered toward Solomon, who promptly bent forward to kiss the back of her hand.

"Lady Praecepsia," he said on an air of reverence. "It is

both an honor and a pleasure to have you grace us with a visit."

"No need for formalities." Chuckling, she patted his shoulder, urging him upright. The baron had never seen his mother act so casually, as if the two were longtime friends, and he frowned at the strangeness of it.

"It is my best effort to show respect where respect is due." A dark spot in the whites of the old man's eyes caught the baron's attention, and his focus zeroed in on a tiny star shape there. One that seemed deliberately placed, with its perfect edges. So unusual, he found himself staring at it for far longer than he should have. However, the unnerving white, almost *glowing*, of the old man's eyes as he stared back at the baron forced the boy to look away. He'd been around the blind before, but the way Solomon carried himself, the way his eyes seemed to fall on the baron, gave the unsettling impression that he could somehow see him.

"And you, Lord Van Croix, I am honored to officially make your acquaintance."

"Perhaps you can enlighten me, seeing as my mother chooses to keep secrets. What *exactly* is the nature of our meetings?"

His cracked lips stretched to a smile. "You have much to learn, and I have much to teach. That is the nature of our meetings."

"Teach what? To play an organ?"

"Jericho!" his mother snapped beside him, her eyes angry and accusing, which left him feeling a small bit of remorse for having upset her twice.

Solomon only chuckled and gently tapped her arm, their interactions proving to be a distraction. "I can certainly teach you that, as well. How are you with a sword?"

"I've been training with Pentacrux soldiers since I was a boy."

"That is quite an education." He reached both hands behind his back, and the slice of sharp steel was the only warning before he produced two long and unusually curved swords made of the finest-looking steel the baron had ever seen. "I much prefer two at a time."

The baron just caught the smile his mother tried to hide as she lowered her gaze. "Were you a soldier?"

"A very long time ago."

"You can fight with both swords at once?"

"As I said, young baron, I have much to teach."

"Teach what? If I am not permitted to fight my *true* enemy," the baron said, glancing back at his mother as he made a subtle reference to his father, "then, what is the point?"

"Is it only fighting that you think makes a great warrior?" Solomon asked, and damn the man and his milky-colored eyes that seemed to be looking right through him and sent a nervous thrumming through the boy's muscles.

"What else is there to being a warrior? Teach me, *wise* one." An air of thick sarcasm clung to the baron's words.

"I intend to do just that."

"Well, then, I will let you get on with your lessons here." The baron's mother turned to him, resting her hands on his shoulders. "Do not underestimate him, son. He will surprise you. I shall send a carriage to retrieve you at dusk."

"Dusk? You intend to have me stay until then?"

"As Solomon said, you have much to learn."

"I can walk back to the manor. It is not all that far."

"I do not think you will be in a condition to walk at any significant length." She chuckled and pressed a kiss to his forehead. "I will speak with you more this evening."

On those parting words, she left the young baron and, with the help of the blond, climbed back into the carriage.

"Well, then, let us not delay. Dusk will arrive before we

know it," Solomon said behind him, and the baron turned to see him stuffing his swords back into some unseen scabbard at his back. He nodded toward something beyond the baron. "Grab those tools."

The baron glanced toward a hammer, hatchet, and saw lying beside the horse corral, again as if the older man could see them. "What for?"

"Your first lesson, young lord, is never question me. I give an order, you follow the order. No questions."

"How dare you speak to me that way. I am Lord Praecepsia's son and—"

"I would not care any more if you were the king's son. Grab the tools and follow me." With that, Solomon hobbled off toward the hut, and with a quick glimpse over his shoulder, the blond sneered back at the baron as he followed after the older man.

Were it not his mother's insistence that he be there, he would have taken the opportunity to leave right then. To dart off into the woods without ever looking back. Unfortunately, he had seen his mother's ordinarily docile nature turn feral before and thought better than to inspire that side of her again.

After gathering up the tools, he found Solomon and the blond standing at the back of the hut. He tossed the tools to a clamor onto the ground, the sound only startling the blond into a flinch.

Solomon rested his palms on the blunt end of an upturned ax. "You will begin your lesson by chopping wood."

"Chopping wood?" The boy didn't bother to hide the repulsion in his voice. "What does that have to do with wielding a sword?"

"You question me again."

"I question an absurd request that seems to have no

logical purpose, other than to assist in the completion of your chores."

"You haven't the strength to wield two swords at once. It is no wonder you dropped the tools. Your arms are weak."

The old man's words grated on him. "You are blind. You cannot see my arms, let alone judge their strength."

"I do not have to see to know your weaknesses, young baron. You wear them like a child in a grown man's armored suit."

Hands balled to tight fists, the baron bit back the urge to knock the old man backward. "You insult me again."

"And I will insult you frequently. Until you learn not to question my intent."

"I will speak with my mother. This will be our last meeting, I can assure you."

The sound of the elder's mocking chuckle sent a tremble of rage through the boy. "Of course. Now, as I was saying, you will chop the wood there. When you are finished, you will climb that ladder to the roof and patch a hole that has made for a terrible leak. The incessant dripping into a pot keeps me from sleep."

"Repair your roof. Would you like me to wash your breeches? Cook your supper for you, perhaps?"

Solomon let out another quiet chuckle and shook his head. "That will depend on how quickly and efficiently you complete the other chores."

"Do not mock me! I did not come here to be some ... slave to a blind old man and ... whatever in Hades he is to you!" The baron pointed toward the blond.

"Soreth? Soreth is my apprentice. An academic, for the most part, but he was no different than you when we began our lessons a few years back. Sounded like you, as well." The old man hobbled over to a pile of wood stacked beside a tree stump. He patted around for one of the pieces, and the baron watched him awkwardly place it on the stump. A second later, he brought the ax down on a perfect strike, splitting the log clean down the center. "Unlike you, Soreth listened without question. And while you insist that the skill of a Pentacrux soldier is unmatched, I can assure you, Soreth would be the exception."

"Him?" While the baron had no love for the Pentacrux, he had witnessed their rigorous trainings, had taken part in them, and knew his claims were ridiculous. "I should like a demonstration of such skill."

"Against whom? You? I would not advise such a challenge. You are not ready."

"I may not wield two swords at once, but I can surely handle one."

With a heavy sigh, the old man shook his head. "Perhaps it is necessary. And after this match, you agree to begin the task of chopping wood?"

"Only on the condition that, should I prove to be victorious, he will do the chopping instead."

"Agreed. And should he prove victorious, you will not question me again. Or the next match will be against *my* sword."

"Agreed."

With a nod, Solomon handed off one of the swords to the baron, the other to Soreth. "These swords are equal in length, weight, and bite. It is only skill that will put one of you at an advantage over the other."

In the yard behind the small hovel, the baron took his stance with the sword in hand, just as he had been trained since he was old enough to wield a weapon. Not for the glory and victory of his country, or the Pentacrux, but to one day defeat his father. To slice his blade across the elder Van Croix's throat and watch him choke on his own blood.

The boy across from him, though bigger in stature, held

his sword loosely in his hands. His terrible form was far more casual. Mocking, perhaps. An observation which sent a prickle of irritation through the young baron.

At first, the two circled each other, and as Master Tennyson had instructed him years ago, the baron did not take his eyes off his opponent. He watched his footing, his grip, where the blond's gaze slid over him as he undoubtedly surveyed where to land the first strike. An unnerving tickle climbed over the baron's neck, but he ignored it. Concentrating. Studying.

What felt like a thousand small centipedes scampering across his neck intensified. He slapped his hand against his nape.

Soreth struck out.

The baron's reflexes shot forth, and he blocked the intended hit on a clang of steel against steel. Sparks flew on impact, and a tiny vibration rumbled across his palm. The blond drew back again and swung out. The baron met his blade with a counter cut and parried a swing aimed at his shoulder.

Soreth blocked it, his movements weak and sloppy, but effective.

The sensation from before returned, the pattering so unnerving that the baron stepped back from his opponent to scratch at his neck and shoulders. It was not long before the scuttling felt as if it'd moved from his neck to his arms, and he broke his attention to stare down at his hand, where something seemed to move beneath his skin, poking at his flesh as if it would break through his skin at any moment. On a gasp, he dropped his sword. Not a second later, he felt the bite of cold steel propped beneath his chin. The sensation withered ,and he lifted his gaze to Soreth, who stood at the opposite end of the blade wearing a wicked smile.

"It was you. You … did that."

Brows upturned, Soreth tipped his head. "Did what?"

"You cheated. I do not know the manner in which you did it, but you did not fight fair."

"As I said, your swords posed equal threat. It was your skill which set you apart." Solomon tapped on the flat of the blade, encouraging Soreth to lower it from the baron's throat.

"Had he not used trickery, he would not have won."

"I cannot argue. Soreth is not a properly trained swordsman. However, I suspect he could comfortably challenge four or more Pentacrux soldiers at once and prove victorious."

"What is he? A warlock?"

Solomon chuckled, shaking his head. "Come now. That is a human term. One that suggests all things which defy the laws of this world are evil. And yet, you have seen such aberrations, have you not?"

He'd have been a fool to admit such a thing. "I have seen nothing."

"I will not *force* you to see truth. You must see it on your own."

"And I suppose that's why I am here? You are the great and wise master who will reveal all truths to me."

With a sigh, he shook his head. "I am a blind, old man who has simply grown weary of the lies."

"Is it not you there, every Sunday Mass without fail, playing their hymns and singing of their god. What would you know of truths?"

"You know as well as I do of what truths lay hidden among the lies." Solomon lifted the baron's discarded sword and sheathed it back into the scabbard. "Surely, it was not chance itself that led you to your father in the woods."

"How do you know of that?"

"I know many things. Now, if memory serves me, I believe you have wood to chop and a roof to repair."

∿

Grumbling, the baron tossed aside the extra reeds, after having replaced those which had been damaged by the accumulation of heavy snowfall. Every muscle in his body ached, and as he stared down the rickety ladder, he wondered if he even had the strength to make it down. Dusk had settled over the land, and it was the sight of the approaching carriage that would return him to the manor which lifted his spirits enough to make the climb down.

Once the baron had dropped to the ground, Solomon hobbled up to him, his mere presence twisting the baron's lip into a snarl. "You did well today, young lord."

"You are fortunate to have stolen a day's worth of work out of me. It shall not happen again."

"You are not the least bit curious?"

"About what? The best herbs to season your supper? Which tool might repair a broken carriage wheel? I am not interested in what you offer to teach."

Brow quirked, the old man sighed. "That is unfortunate. It is such simple tasks which offer fortitude and strength."

"And yet, based on my sparring with Soreth, I see your lessons do not promise any more than mind tricks."

"Soreth proved victorious because you've not explored your own strengths. Your own mind tricks."

The comment gave the boy pause. "You are saying I can make others feel as if bugs are crawling over them."

"I am saying you are capable of more than that, young baron. But you are arrogant, impatient, and excessively untrusting. So go on back to your great master swordsman who will continue to train you in mediocrity."

Once again, the urge to clobber the old man had the boy grinding his teeth. "It is far better and more noble to train toward something, than to act as your personal servant.

What exactly did patching a roof teach me, hmmm?" The baron only caught the older man's subtle smile, before the carriage came to a stop. As the boy stepped in the direction of it, he heard Solomon call out to Fenwick, the coachman, his eyes staring off.

"You there. Kind sir, would you do me a favor?"

Frowning, the coachman rolled his shoulders back and glanced around the carriage, returning his attention back toward Solomon. "You ask a favor of me, Sir?"

"Yes. If it is not too much trouble."

"Of course not." The coachman clambered down from the carriage and ambled across the short stretch of yard toward them. "What would you have me do?" he asked on his approach.

"Do you see the walking stick I've left there?"

The baron twisted around, knowing the man's walking stick was lying on the ground at the hut's rear where the coachman could not have possibly seen it.

"Mind tricks." Sneering, the baron spoke low, so as not to rouse the coachman's attention.

"Ah, yes, would you like me to fetch it for you?"

"If it's not too much trouble."

"Not at all."

Confused, the baron watched as the portly man strode toward the hut. Directly toward it. The boy's jaw gaped so wide with shock, it practically unhinged itself, when Fenwick strode through the walls of the structure itself, disappearing into the mud plaster and logs which made up its outer appearance. Within seconds, he strode back through, as if the barrier were not there, at all.

"Who are you, that you see and know these things?" the baron asked with an air of panic in his voice.

"There is much to understand. Return again, and I will tell you."

12

JERICHO

*T*he monotonous clop of horse hooves marked the seemingly endless path ahead, as Onyx cantered toward the village.

I loathed having to get about like a human, either by horse, or foot. What would've been a fairly quick flight would now take me half the night to get there and back, but while losing my wings had felt like giving up a part of myself, it'd been a small price to pay to save Farryn. Even at the cost of the heavens hunting me, for having broken their rules to stay away from the girl, for evading my fate to Ex Nihilo, and perhaps worst of all, for offering up my wings. One did not hand over his celestial power without consequence.

Those were simply the crimes *I'd* committed, never mind all the ways Farryn had pissed them off.

I needed to fix what was broken within me, for her sake. To offer her some form of protection, particularly now that I knew what awaited her on the other side of the pregnancy. The heavens would be hard pressed to seek her out in Nightshade, if they had any thought that she might be here, so she might've been safe in that respect. But the bastardly creature to whom she owed her soul would surely come to collect once the baby had arrived. While the demon inside of me might've made a more formidable opponent, I feared what that might mean for Farryn. The rage that my father had incited in me stoked the beast I'd buried long ago.

I thought I'd seen the last of Claudius Van Croix after he'd fled Blackwater Cathedral. I'd even gone so far as to hunt him down in Eradyę, except the barren world had begun to eat away too much of my vitaeilem. I was fortunate back then to have been able to replenish the lifeblood inside of me. Took a couple weeks for my body to recover from depletion, and those weeks were probably my darkest. Suffering hallucinations. Craving depravity. Blood. There'd always been a light at the end of the tunnel, though. A promise that I'd recover, if I could just get through the rejuvenation process.

There would be no rejuvenation this time. No light in the darkness.

Seraphica was the only solution. A temporary one, I hoped.

Unfortunately, the drugs to which I'd once been addicted would only add to the growing shit-pile of problems we faced, but at least they'd help stave off the urge to consume Farryn's soul. To enslave her to my sexual cravings. The vitality of her was what called to me. Even before I'd slipped out of consciousness and into the state of my demon, I knew I wanted it. Her. Taking it, though, would mean ending her life. Ensuring that she could never return to the mortal realm.

I loved her too damn much to risk it. Even if staying away from her was the worst kind of torture, I'd do it for eternity if it meant protecting her.

The once-lush forest of Misty Hollow, which had burned

to the ground after I'd set it aflame, passed on my right. The scene brought to mind that night, the look in Farryn's eyes as she stared down at me seconds before that white hot blaze engulfed me. The horror and pain, confusion and betrayal. It was a look I'd taken into the void, one that would haunt me for months after. I'd wanted so badly to tell her how sorry I'd been. How much I loved her.

All I'd been able to do in that moment was hope Barchiel held up his part of the deal. I'd added a *contiszha* to our agreement, meaning that, even if I got trapped in Ex Nihilo, breaking his promise would mean he'd be subjected to *casmal'zhation*. Essentially, being turned inside out. A soul, like Barchiel's, reborn into immortality would've survived the excruciating pain for mere seconds before dying absolute death. Unlike banishment to Ex Nihilo, there was no coming back from that.

What seemed like ages later, I finally reached the small village of Stygian Falls. A hum of anticipation simmered in my blood, as if my body knew what I'd come for. The streets were quiet on the surface, but I knew where to go to find what had been essentially banned in an agreement between the heavens and infernal realm.

Seraphica, though mostly synthetic, still required blood of an angel, and the task of procuring it was something I was all too familiar with. When I wasn't reaping souls for the Noxerians, I was betraying my fellow angels by handing them over to be drained, in exchange for my own personal supply. And because I hadn't technically carried out the slaughter myself, I went unpunished for a number of years. A fact which pissed off Adimus, the leader of the Sentinels, who petitioned the heavens to have me banished to Ex Nihilo after I'd handed over an old friend of his to the Noxerians.

The bastard was the first who'd come to mind when Barchiel had told me one of the Sentinels had made a deal with Drystan, to take Farryn in exchange for safe passage to Nightshade on the night of the blood moon. The night I'd broken their rules and crossed over to the earthly realm, sacrificing my wings. He wouldn't have gotten far, anyway. The moment Drystan crossed the Vale into Nightshade, I'd have been there, waiting for him.

If any of the Sentinels were so inclined to cross over for Farryn into Nightshade, it'd be Adimus, and if I had to guess, it would be he who'd wanted to impregnate her. A thought that struck a murderous chord in me, and all the more reason I needed to keep my wits.

I needed the drugs.

At the opposite side of the village, I dismounted my horse and tied him to a post outside of a butcher's shop whose lights were off with it being after hours. Alongside the shop stood a long, skinny door, through which one would have to turn sideways to pass. It wasn't a particularly noticeable door, just a dirty brown that hardly stood out, where it was wedged between the butcher and apothecary. Tugging my hood up, I gave one furtive glance around, then knocked on the thick, wooden panel where the translucent glimmer of a ward ensured no unwanted visitors were given entry without their heads imploding as a consequence. Seconds passed, then a small square in the center of the door shifted and two eyes peeked out at me through the created window.

"*Sang àysh'la cin'tchinez,*" I said as a low whisper. *Blood of five blades.* Five blades referred to the five brothers who ran the joint, and the promise of blood against anyone who ratted them out. With the power of the Noxerians behind them, it certainly wasn't an idle threat.

The small peeping window slid shut, and at the click of the lock, the door opened on a creak to reveal a tall, skinny man with a gaunt face and black circles under his eyes. The band on his throat told me he was dojzra.

I followed him inside the narrow corridor that opened to a wider passage, dimly lit only by flickering sconces. The sound of feminine moans carried on the air. Though fairly mild when compared to some of the places found in Kilenshire–the neighboring town run by The Fallen–this place had a seedy atmosphere, the kind that crawled over the back of the neck. It was a place of sin and debauchery, where unsuspecting innocence was swiped up and corrupted.

A place I would never bring Farryn.

The path ahead was familiar to me, one I'd walked half-dazed while slipping in and out of blackness. We finally reached a thick, iron door at the end of the hallway, through which we descended a stone stairwell into the bowels of the building.

There, the moans turned to screams. A sickening cold swept over me as distant memories filtered in. The kind I'd hoped to put well behind me, but such was life to bring everything swinging back around like a goddamned wrecking ball. One last door at the bottom of the stairs opened up to an arena, a space which spanned nearly the entire village of Stygian Falls, hidden from the human souls. Nearly every town and village in Nightshade had an underground scene where bad things went down. A sort of Nexus, which linked the ancients in somewhat of an inverse world to the one aboveground.

If the dark web were a physical place, it'd be the underground scene.

The scent of blood and death carried on the air, and something warm tingled across the back of my neck. The form of the man who led me along blurred, turning shadowy and undefined. The surroundings pulled on something inside of me. A force that clawed the back of my ribs for escape. Flickers drew my attention toward a flame dancer at the opposite side of the arena, the orange streaks playing on the air around her, moving in slow motion. I could hear the flame crackle even across the arena. The sound of her breath. My skin crawled.

I came to a halt, and as if sensing it, the gaunt man turned toward me, his eyes quizzical.

Leave. Leave now.

I couldn't tell who was speaking inside my head–the demon, the voices who'd abandoned me decades ago. Farryn?

It had no feminine or masculine tone, no sense of authority, or supplication. Yet, I couldn't ignore it.

The heated tingles from before slithered over me, and I lifted my arms to find my skin blackening at my fingertips. Like ink dripping down my hand, the raven tone stretched toward my wrists. A panic settled over me.

I needed seraphica. Immediately.

I kept on, toward the room I'd visited so many times before it'd become a second home. The tall man waved me through a door, and I took the lead into a room where apothecary bottles sat lined on old, crooked shelves, their labels dark and ominous. An aged male, with straggly white hair and spectacles, hobbled toward me, his nails long and yellowing.

"Seraphica," I said, the bitter sting of the word making me grimace.

"Angels' blood is illegal, my friend."

"Don't fuck with me. You've sold it to me before."

"It's getting harder to come by. A rare concoction, indeed."

"I will not leave this place without it."

The old man looked me up and down and chuckled darkly. "And how do you wish to pay?"

Reaching into my pocket, I kept my gaze on the locked

cabinet where I knew he kept the mystical drug and tossed a coin onto the countertop. One well worth his trouble.

"I would ask how you came about this coin." He clamped his bony fingers over it, sliding it toward the edge of the counter and depositing it into his palm. "But I don't care. I've got one tincture left. I'm afraid that's all."

It'd last me no more than a few days, but it was better than nothing. "I'll take it."

"Very well." He twisted away from me and slid open that cabinet, from where he pulled out a small black apothecary jar and handed it over. "I knew you'd be back, by the way. The angels' blood … it never leaves you entirely."

"I am half angel." I swiped it out of his hands more abruptly than I'd intended and squeezed a small bit of the black fluid into the dropper, which I deposited onto my tongue. Within seconds, warmth shot through my veins, the familiar exhilaration bubbling up from the depths of my memories. Disgusted with myself, I shoved the dropper back into the bottle and stuffed it into my pocket.

The old man chuckled again. "And I'm the holy savior."

Showing no amusement, I strode out of the room and back through the arena. Pure angels' blood would've had me feeling energized, alert, essentially myself. Seraphica was mixed with a few other bedeviled ingredients, ones that had my stomach twisting, and the scene before me stretched far too wide, the fringes blurring out of focus.

The cool, nighttime air stole my breath as I exited the building, and as I passed an alley on my way back to Onyx, an unsettling sensation crawled over the back of my neck. I turned to see that I had stopped at the mouth of the alley and stared toward its dead end hidden by the shadows.

"Liar," a distant voice echoed inside my head, and in that exact moment, I caught sight of a soft glow toward the center of the dark passage. With hesitation, I walked toward it, and

came to an abrupt halt before a tiny Nightshade flower which had grown up through the cobblestones.

Screams hammered inside my skull. Then laughter. Vicious, mocking laughter.

I screwed my eyes shut, rubbing the ache at my temples, and in doing so, I invited the unbidden visual of a brunette lying beneath me, her face pale white. Eyes vacant. Shaking my head snapped me out of the memory, and I backed myself toward the alley's entrance, pushing away memories I couldn't stand to think about. The flower sat glowing, unmoving.

Silent.

Back at the cathedral, I strode down the hallway toward my chambers, and paused at Farryn's ajar bedroom door. Through the crack, the room stood dark and still, but I could see her, *sense* her lying in bed. That sweet scent of vitality carried on the air, and I entered with quiet steps, coming to a stop alongside her bed. Whatever tension I'd felt before eased as I dragged a featherlight touch across her cheek, and long, black eyelashes, which rested against rosy cheeks, fluttered in dreams.

How utterly perfect humans looked while sleeping. Angelic.

Alive.

I wanted more than anything to climb into bed beside her and feel the life pulsing through her. To slip into a blissful slumber with her body pressed against mine, so perfect in my arms.

Without the violence and darkness that had consumed my head.

The small bit of seraphica wasn't enough, though. As if

my body had remembered the way I'd abused it all those years ago, the tonic wouldn't be sufficient to keep me from hurting Farryn, as I'd hoped. I needed a guarantee that she and my child would be protected at all costs.

I would head out at first light for Vaszhago.

13

FARRYN

*S*ave him, a detached voice whispered.

My eyes shot open, and on a gasped breath, I jolted upright, searching the dimly lit bedroom. The empty chair. The curtain, which hung motionless against the window, beyond which an overcast sky loomed. Movement drew my attention to the left of me, and I just caught the shadow of something disappearing beneath the armoire.

I kicked back, the headboard crashing into my spine.

At a knock on the door, I let out a scream.

"Miss Ravenshaw, are you all right?" Anya asked from the other side.

When staring at the bottom of the armoire showed no further movement, I cleared my throat. "Yes. I'm okay."

"May I enter?"

"Sure."

The door clicked and swung open, and Anya entered carrying a silver tray. Her face pinched to a frown as she crossed the room toward me, and she tipped her head while setting the tray on the adjacent nightstand. "What is it, dear? You look like you've seen a ghost."

"Under the armoire. I saw something."

Anya twisted toward the furniture and frowned harder. "Under that clunky thing?" She stepped toward it, but I reached out and grabbed her arm.

"No, wait! What if it's ... what if it's ..."

"What if it's what?" Her frown softened to a warm smile, and she unlatched my fingers from her arm. "You're just having bad dreams, is all. Here, I'll show you."

"No, Anya! Come back."

Instead, she kept on toward the armoire and knelt down, peering beneath it. "Nothing, except a few horrific dust bunnies. Good grief, I'll have one of the girls take care of that."

I let out a sigh of relief, the tension in my muscles easing. Maybe it had been nothing more than a lingering nightmare.

"Perhaps you could do with a bit of light in here." She strode toward the curtains and threw them back, letting in bright beams of light that had me shielding my eyes.

"I don't know what my problem is. I keep hearing voices, and my dreams are *awful*. Jericho seems to think it's normal pregnancy stuff."

Silence hovered between us as I realized what had just slipped out of my mouth.

"Pregnancy?" At the air of intrigue in Anya's voice, I lifted my gaze to see her brow winged up. "You are with child, Miss?"

Nerves still rattled, I feigned a smile for Anya's sake. "Um. Yes. Just under four months."

"Well." Anya clasped her hands together and chuckled. "Oh, my. You and the Master. This is ... this is wonderful!"

"Thank you, Anya. If you could keep it between us for now, though, that'd be great. I just don't want any–"

Raising a hand in the air, Anya shook her head. "Say no more. Your secret will not pass these walls, Miss. But what a secret indeed! The Master as a father?" She slapped a hand over her mouth, wearing an incredulous expression. "Well, it sounds so strange to say! I never thought I'd see the day."

That made two of us. I hadn't really planned on a pregnancy at any point in my life. Had never fantasized about being a mother, or pictured myself capable of keeping something other than a cactus alive. And that was pushing it. "Do you remember pregnancy, at all?"

Brows lowering, the older woman sighed and clasped her hands. "No. Not a single moment. I remember our last conversation about Aurelia, and some vague memories of her, but ... that's all, I'm afraid." Anya frowned, as though trying harder to remember. "Seems it was just too long ago for me."

Perhaps the most frustrating part of the pregnancy was the loneliness of it. I had no sage advice, not that anyone would've been able to offer much about a child whose father happened to be half angel.

Except ...

I did know *one* person, if I could call her a person. Lustina's mother, Catriona, who I'd stumbled upon in the bookstore.

Gabriel had been Lustina's father, an archangel, and if anyone might've had a clue about all these strange symptoms, it was her. If by chance she was still there, and still remembered me, perhaps I could bounce the millions of questions I had off her. At least find out if what I was feeling was normal. I'd read about headaches during pregnancy, but nothing like the odd dreams, hallucinations, the screaming, and black vomit.

Jesus, what had my life become that I was hopeful for a centuries-old ghost to be the afterlife version of Doctor Spock?

An intense shifting in my stomach had me snapping

upright, and I set my hand against my belly, feeling some-thing snake beneath my skin.

"Is everything all right?" Anya tipped her head, drawing my attention to her.

With a sheepish smile, I nodded. "It's the baby." I bit my lip, contemplating the next question. "Wanna feel?" Although I smiled through the offer, I hoped she'd decline. It all still felt kind of weird to me, and I vowed never to be the crazy, pregnant woman who shoved her belly in everyone's face for a grope.

Her brows pinched together, a dubious expression claiming her face. "How far along did you say you were?"

I shrugged. "A little over thirteen weeks, give, or take."

"And you feel movement already?"

"Yes." Much as I wanted to tell her that I was pregnant with a sentinel who clearly didn't follow the rules of human pregnancies, I didn't want to leave her questioning my sanity.

"That seems unusual. I may not remember anything about my own pregnancy, Miss, but I certainly recall that one does not feel a baby move so early."

With a nervous chuckle, I lowered my gaze to hide a frown. "You're welcome to feel for yourself." At that point, it was a matter of defending myself.

With what I perceived as reluctance, she reached toward my mostly flat belly and rested her palm there.

A couple of seconds passed before I felt a punch so intense, I flinched. "Ah! Jeez. Did you feel that?"

Anya peered up at me from beneath lowered brows. "Feel what, Miss?"

Weird.

Eyes narrowed, I shook my head. "You didn't feel that kick just now? I'm surprised it didn't punt you across the room."

"I felt nothing, except your fingers squeezing mine."

"Wow, okay." I shifted a little and moved her hand slightly left. Another kick, more intense than the first, had me bending over myself, and I let out a small cough. "You had to have felt that one."

Anya lowered her hand, the concern etched in her brow telling me she hadn't felt it that time either. "You're feeling okay, Farryn?"

She rarely called me Farryn, and the implication that I *wasn't* feeling okay struck me like a slap to the face.

Clearing my throat, I pushed myself back, wanting some distance between us. "I'm fine. Maybe it's just a bit deeper inside of me and only I can sense it right now."

Her lips stretched to a pitying smile, her eyes holding a motherly sympathy. "Perhaps. Could be hunger, you know. You look a little on the light side."

"It's not hunger, Anya. I have a pretty good idea what a rumbly tummy feels like." The quick snap of my tone left me feeling remorseful, and I softened my voice. "This is something *moving* inside of me."

"Of course, dear." She reached toward me and gave my hand a light pat. "You know your body better than anyone. Don't mind me. These aging hands probably couldn't feel a thornbush." The dismissive tone to her voice bothered me, though. The kind of polite reassurance that carried a back-handed slap. "I do think you could use a bite ... or two ... to eat, though. And if you need anything else, I want you to tell me. Anything at all. Master Van Croix insisted that you be comfortable and cared for."

"You really don't have to go through the trouble, Anya." A new discomfort settled over me, and I pushed a strand of hair behind my ear. "Seriously. I'm not one for being babied." It was true. With the kind of distracted parents I'd had growing up, I hadn't even been babied when I was an actual baby. Aunt Nelle certainly hadn't gone out of her way.

"I hardly think bringing you a few meals every so often is babying, Miss. The Master simply wants to ensure that you're comfortable."

"He left this morning?" I only assumed after the conversation we'd had the night before when he'd told me about Vaszhago.

With a huff that I took as disapproval, she sat back and crossed her fingers in her lap. "Yes. Said he had to look into acquiring new staff. Strange, he usually has me take care of that for him."

He didn't want to risk that the murderer he bought to babysit his pregnant girlfriend would decide to kill you on the ride back.

Even in my head that sounded wrong.

"Maybe he just wanted some fresh air. Get out of the cathedral for a bit," I offered with a smile.

The moment her eyes narrowed on me, I knew an uncomfortable question was about to fly out. "What happened to the two of you, Miss? Where on earth did you go for all those weeks?"

Well, Earth.

Don't slip, Farryn.

"We thought you might've gotten caught up in those wildfires that spread through the forest," she prattled on, while I contemplated how to answer the question without spilling the beans about her existence in Nightshade. "Nearly lost all of Misty Hollow." She must've been referring to the fires Jericho had set. "So many carcasses of what looked to be a strange breed of animals. I feared finding human remains in the aftermath of it all."

The Alatum, no doubt. The creepy looking creatures that resulted when The Fallen had had their wings severed by a cursed blade. My heart ached a little at the memory of having watched Remy turning into one.

"We truly thought–well, I don't even want to say aloud what we thought."

I didn't know what to say to her. I couldn't come out and lie to her face–I just couldn't. Telling her the truth, though, would've meant a conversation that would've either made me look like a lunatic, or sent her into cardiac arrest, if she hadn't already died once.

Nibbling on my lip, I contemplated what exactly I could live with, wishing to all the gods in the universe that she hadn't asked me that question. "We were …" I swallowed hard and cleared my throat, my palms sweating all of a sudden. "Um. I was–"

"No need, dear." Brows winged up, she glanced down at my stomach. "*Clearly*, the two of you were looking for some time alone."

"I wouldn't say that was *the reason* we left, but it's certainly been an eventful few months."

"No doubt. Anyway, I know three mongrels who are chomping at the bit to see you. They've been whining at the back door for the last two and half hours."

The visual of that made me chuckle. "I'll get dressed."

"Mmm. Cerberus has been particularly affected by your and the Master's absence. Wouldn't eat much for the first week. The connection he has with you, Miss. It's uncanny to me."

At her words, images flashed in my head.

Sitting in a clearing of the woods. Playing with three small, black, roly-poly puppies. Hearing a distant whistle, and the puppies running off into the woods.

Lustina's memories, no doubt. Cerberus had met her, *me*, before.

"We go way back."

Anya tipped her head and frowned.

"It's just a saying where I'm from."

"Ah. Well, I'll let you get back to it."

I stepped out of the back door of the cathedral to find Cerberus, Nero, and Fenrir off sniffing around in the yard. As soon as I stepped down the stone stairwell, all three enormous dogs ran toward me, and the sight of them tearing across the yard made me chuckle. As they neared, their steps slowed, and Cerberus took what appeared to be a cautious stance, hackles raised, body hunched. He sniffed the air, as if he was unsure of who I was all of a sudden.

Frowning, I patted my leg, urging him closer. "Hey, Cerberus, come here. It's just me."

The dog's lips peeled back into a vicious looking snarl, and my spine snapped to attention. The collective growl of all three dogs sent a wild tremor through me.

Bigger than an English mastiff, they made an intimidating trio when calm, but when growling and snarling, they were downright terrifying.

"Cerberus? What is it?" I turned to see if there was someone standing behind me, and on finding no one there, I swung my gaze back toward the dogs, panicked to find they'd lurched closer.

Saliva dripped from their maws, their eyes burning with something that sent a shudder down my spine.

What the hell was wrong with them? They acted as if they'd never seen me before. As if I was a complete stranger to them.

A glance over my shoulder showed the door about fifteen feet behind me, and the gesture seemed to prompt Cerberus to lurch again. The other dogs followed suit.

"Shhhh," I said, holding up a trembling hand. "Stay. Cerberus, stay."

He barked back at me, the kind of barking I'd heard when the Alatum were attacking. The kind of barking meant as a warning before they would attack.

With urgency pounding against my ribs, I backed myself slowly away, keeping my eyes shifting between all three dogs. Every nerve in my body screamed for me to run, but I knew better. I'd watched how quickly these dogs sprang into action and mauled their victims without mercy.

Slow and easy, I inched toward the door, and I swallowed back a lump of horror in my throat when all three of them prowled toward me.

Attention zeroed on Cerberus, in particular, I stretched a shaky hand behind me, desperate to feel for the doorknob I'd yet to reach. A bloodthirsty fury burned in Cerberus's eyes, and as if sensing my intent, he charged forward.

Breath held, I spun on my heel and dashed for the door. I swung it open just as Fenrir leaped for me, and on a gasped scream, I slammed the door behind me, hearing the dogs clawing and snarling on the other side.

Through panting breaths, I sagged with relief and blinked back the tears in my eyes.

Something was wrong. Something had changed.

They were no longer my protectors.

14

THE BARON

The Baron reached the manor, his thoughts lost in the old man's words. Who was Solomon, if not merely the blind organist?

Human?

If that was the case, how did he become privy to these unusual circumstances that failed to make sense in the human world?

The carriage stopped in the semicircular drive of the manor, and as the baron prepared to exit, he heard voices on the other side of the door. Peering through the window showed the coachman, Fenwick, speaking with his father's henchman, Alaric.

"Now?" Fenwick asked, his brows pinched to a confused frown. "But we've just returned, and I'm certain the young lord is exhausted after a long day."

"Yes. Immediately."

"Very well." The carriage door opened, and Fenwick cleared his throat. "My lord, your father has returned early from his travels and asked that I take you to the monastery."

"The monastery? At this hour? For what purpose?"

"I am afraid I do not know."

The henchman merely tipped his chin up, the refusal to say clear on his face.

"My mother asked that I meet with her first."

"You will do no such thing." Alaric rested his hand on the hilt of the dagger at his hip, the gesture telling the boy that he'd use force, if necessary. "I was tasked to fetch you immediately. Your father will meet you in the undercroft."

"I was told that I would not be required to return until my wounds healed."

"I suppose you will have to learn for yourself the reason for which he summoned you." He twisted toward Fenwick, towering over the portly coachman. "Perhaps you will step back so that I may join Lord Van Croix in the carriage."

After an unsure glance toward the baron, Fenwick did as Alaric asked.

As the larger man climbed inside, the baron scooted away from him, keeping as much distance between them as possible. The door closed, and only moments later, they were off.

Silence carried for an exceptionally long time, the baron stealing glances every so often and catching the subtle stroke of Alaric's hand over the blade on his lap. A marking on his thumb caught the boy's attention. Some sort of strange branding that'd been burned into his flesh. Not like the mark of the Pentacrux, which the baron easily recognized. Something he'd never seen before.

"You would spare yourself immense pain with a simple confession," Alaric said, finally breaking the silence between them.

"You are either foolish, or ill-informed. Confession does not free oneself from pain. Surely, you have made note of those who've gone missing."

"And what are your theories about that?"

Saying them aloud to his father's righthand would have

been as incriminating as if he'd sprouted wings before the bishop. No one spoke ill of his father, and particularly not the Pentacrux, so instead, the baron turned his attention back toward the window. "Tell me, Alaric. Would you kill me on my father's command?"

"Yes," the man answered without a single hitch.

The baron's lips twitched, his suspicions confirmed. "If it is loyalty that compels you, know that he would slide a blade across your throat with little more remorse than for the dirt on his boots."

"And still, twice the regard he has for you."

The baron kept his gaze locked on the passing landscape, puzzling over why his mother opposed the murdering of her husband, considering Alaric spoke the truth. He did not say another word for the rest of the ride to the monastery, and when the cart breached the gates of the building, coming to a stop in the clearing, a sickness twisted in the baron's stomach. "You know what he does in these meetings, yet you say and do nothing."

"My loyalty extends only to your father."

"Like a lame dog who has only to limp once before getting put down."

"Come, young lord, I am certain there is much to be discussed between you and the good bishop." Alaric's mocking tone grated on the baron, and he ground his teeth, holding back the ire burning inside of him.

He followed after Alaric into the grounds of the monastery and toward the infirmary. Makeshift beds lay scattered about an open room, where the pentashes scurried between them, offering ladles of water from wooden buckets. At the opposite side of the room, Bishop Venable stood beside one of the sick, his hand waving in the distinct gesture of the cross.

With a jerk of his head, Alaric urged him to follow, and as

they passed one particular bed, a hand reached out to grab his wrist. The baron turned toward a frail-looking, older woman, whose eyes bulged wide, gray hair in disarray about her head. A Raver, as the Pentacrux would have labeled her. She pulled at his arm, lifting her upper body from the bed, where shadows of stains on the blankets below her indicated she'd been there a while. An awful stench crinkled his nose, and he fought the urge to gag. "Your Grace," she rasped. "Save us."

"I am not a holy man," the baron responded, tugging back his own arm, but her clutch tightened.

"He vowed to deliver my soul this eve. I've a young daughter. I will give you her hand, if you'll take me from this evil place."

"Quiet, you crazy old loon!" Alaric snapped beside the baron, and he swatted the older woman's hand away.

The woman fell back against her bed in despair and turned into her pillow, where she buried a sob.

"Should I require your interventions, I will ask," the baron said, as Alaric gave the boy's elbow a nudge.

"And know that I do not require your invitation," the guardsman said to the back of the boy's head. "The bishop is waiting."

They finally reached the bishop, who had moved on to another bed, offering prayers to a younger man who stared off, eyes a white void. The baron would've thought him dead, if not for the steady rise and fall of his chest.

"It is our duty to take in the sick of mind," the older man said, as he dipped a ladle into the bucket held by the pentash who stood beside him. He deposited the water into the supine man's opened mouth, dribbling it down the seemingly unconscious man's chin. "The world casts them out as lost and broken souls, but they can be saved by the Holy Light and exorcized of the demons which plague them."

"How do you know it is demons who plague them?" The boy's bold inquiry earned him a narrow-eyed stare from the bishop.

"The Holy Father does not create imperfect souls. How could He when we are made in his image?"

"And you say it is your duty to offer them compassion and mercy?"

"Yes. We are the servants."

"And did you offer mercy to the young Lord Fletcher?" The boy Drystan had told him about, who'd been taken to the undercroft for having seen something unusual crawl out of an apple. None had heard from him since.

"Of course. Would you like to pay him a visit?"

The question caught the baron off guard, as he'd not expected the boy to be alive, much less permitted to have a visitor. "Yes. I would."

"Very well. Come with me, young baron."

The bishop took the lead beyond the infirmary to the staircase, which the baron knew led to the undercroft below the monastery. Once in its cold and damp depths, they followed a path toward the all-too-familiar rooms, but turned down a different corridor, one in which the baron had not yet seen. The bishop came to a stop before a door and pulled out a long skeleton key. The baron's heart pounded in his chest, as he stood. Waiting. Wondering what he'd see on the other side.

The door swung open to a small room lit only by the waning light of dusk that poured in through a nearby window. On a rickety old cot lay the young Lord Fletcher in a simple white nightshirt.

Stepping inside the room, the baron kept his gaze on the boy, who did not move, nor acknowledge his presence. Yet movement of the other boy's chest told him the young lord still lived. "What ails him?" the baron asked, coming to a stop alongside the boy's bed.

"Possession. Lucifer sank his willful claws into the boy's mind and has not let go."

Eyes a vacant white, like those of the man's in the infirmary, the young lord stared up at the ceiling with unflinching constancy.

The baron reached out, running his finger over the boy's arm and noting the ice-cold temperature of his skin.

As if he were already dead.

When the baron drew his arm back, the boy reached out and clutched him with long, claw-like nails that dug into his skin. A jolt of alarm rattled the baron, and he tugged against the boy's hold. The young lord's white eyes rolled over to black, and he snarled back at him. "They want to eat me! The demons! They will come for you! And feast! Feast on our flesh, and our soul will be gifted to the Infernal Lord! Hail to the Infernal Lord!"

With a hard yank, Jericho wrenched his arm away and took a step back, frowning down at the boy. He was the second to speak of demons coming for him.

The first having been the elderly woman.

"Poor young man," the bishop said beside him. "'Tis a shame when they succumb to evil. The boy had such an incredible life ahead of him."

"Is this not a holy establishment? Do the demons not cower in the presence of the *Holy* Father?" The baron could not help the sneer in his voice, recalling that it was a mere worm in an apple that had brought Lord Fletcher to that place to begin. The other boy had not always been that way, which led the baron to believe something had happened in his time there.

"By taking in the possessed, we invite the infernal darkness into our sacred monastery, but I am far too merciful to turn my back to those who need help."

"Lies. Lord Fletcher was no more afflicted by evil than the shoes upon your feet."

The bishop's eyes narrowed on him, and the baron could have only imagined what thoughts swirled inside his head right then. "You do not believe in the inherent evil of men?"

He did. His own father was an example, though the baron had since learned of his true nature which made him so. Not human flesh and blood, but that of something which derived from the infernal places he had only read about in Bible study.

"My mother says humans are born inherently good."

The bishop's lips twitched. "Come with me."

As much as he wanted to ignore the bishop's request, he followed after him, if only out of curiosity. Two rooms down from Lord Fletcher's, the bishop came to a stop at another door and opened it to a man who lay on the center of the floor. His arms and legs had been removed, leaving horridly severed stumps oozing blood that pooled beneath him. The pallor of his face told the baron he did not have much longer to live.

"This is Ivan Danesh." The bishop's voice broke through the baron's thoughts. "He was an infamous criminal who terrorized neighboring towns. Pamphlets were distributed all over Praecepsia. In a satchel he wore while traveling, the guardsmen found relics of black magic."

"*Relics* of black magic? And you removed his arms for that?"

"We removed his arms as they were instrumental in cutting fetuses from the bellies of young mothers. He believed they made the perfect food for the devil."

"Why not just kill him, then? Why torture?"

"Evil does not die. We must expel it, or it will spread

through this community like a wild flame. Perhaps you view these procedures as a source of amusement, young baron, to which I take a most grievous offense. But they are designed to save the souls of the innocent. Come. We've one more soul to see."

As before, the baron followed the bishop out of the room and down a more familiar corridor–the same one which held the room where the baron had suffered the whipping to his back. At the memory of those lashings, his skin flared with a phantom pain, and when the bishop opened the door, the baron scarcely breathed.

Strapped to an X-shaped cross in the center of the room, a stark-naked Drystan sobbed, tugging at the binds which held him. "Please! I beg your mercy!"

His cries became a distant sound to the rushing of blood in the baron's ears. For there could only be one reason they'd chosen to punish his cousin.

15

JERICHO

I lifted the hood of my leather coat to conceal my face as I strode up the stone stairwell to the Velthrock prison tower. One of the oldest in all of Nightshade, the tower boasted fifteen levels of cells lined around the perimeter of the giant cylinder structure. Overlords and nobility were imprisoned in the higher levels, and those rooms were far more comfortable than the ones below them. Prisoners there were allowed conjugal visits, often with more than one female, which they were also permitted to consume later. Sometimes, lower-level human prisoners were given to them in lieu of the unappetizing slop of discarded carcasses provided by the local butcher. Ground-up entrails, or bone water. While demons could certainly survive on it, it was the human soul, in particular, that offered the most sustenance.

The dungeons housed the most dangerous criminals, and in most cases, they were the ones executed for what were deemed as horrific crimes, such as killing an overlord, or even the unsanctioned hoarding of souls.

Bigger towns, like Velthrock, had certain groups, such as

the Mortal Collective, made up of cambions who fought against the illicit consumption of innocent human souls. They protected children, mostly, who were the most vulnerable, allowing them to be redeemed. Comprised of powerful half-breeds, the Mortal Collective were effective at keeping the peace and delivering souls to the angels. Human prisoners bound for consumption were thoroughly inspected by them for any opportunity for redemption. If they found nothing, the prison was given the green light to offer a sacrifice.

I entered through the iron doors, making my way toward a small, elven-looking man with pointed ears and a slightly elongated nose. He wore spectacles over which he peered down at me, as I approached the tall desk that stretched to about twice my height. Two beastly guards, with faces that looked like a cross between a human and a wild boar, flanked him at either side. Androgidez demons, I supposed. The brutes of Nightshade who often carried out punishment and public executions. I didn't bother to lower the hood from my face, as I came to a stop before the desk that towered above me.

"Can I help you?" the clerk asked.

"I would like to see one of the prisoners you have housed."

"Name."

"Vaszhago Kemoran."

He cracked open a book and made a sighing sound in his throat as he flipped through the pages. "Vaszhago. Vaszhago. Ah. Oh. Um."

"Is there a problem?"

"Well, yes. This prisoner is due to be exiled in less than an hour."

"I understand."

With a long claw-like nail, he pushed his spectacles higher

up the bridge of his pointy nose. "What is the nature of your visit?"

"I might like to buy his freedom."

"His freedom? Well, fat chance of that, considering who he sent to Voltusz." Another term for absolute death. Unlike Ex Nihilo, it was the only place from which a demon, or angel, absolutely couldn't return. He let out a snorty chuckle and slammed the book closed on a plume of dust. Waving it away, he coughed.

"Perhaps you can run it by Warden Noth'ra. He owes me a favor."

Years ago, when I'd first started out as a broker of souls, I'd happened to be meeting with the warden, a pompous and arrogant man, to negotiate a fairly sought-out soul on behalf of a client. One of the more violent prisoners had gotten loose and plowed through the office door toward him. The crazed-looking demon had somehow gotten his hand on celestial steel, and as he'd made a beeline, charging straight for the warden, I'd intercepted and sent the poor sap to Ex Nihilo hours before his scheduled extradition.

As a show of gratitude, the warden had offered a fair trade for the soul I'd been negotiating, and an I.O.U. of sorts, provided in the form of an *Empyreal Debenture*, which sat tucked inside my coat pocket. I reached inside, drawing the attention of the two Androgidez who watched me warily. Scroll in hand, I unrolled the document down to the official seal at the bottom. The man at the desk peered down over his spectacles, his eyeballs moving back and forth, as if reading it.

"Well, I stand corrected. My apologies, Mister Van Croix." A door concealed in the smooth surface of the towering desk opened to reveal a dark corridor beneath the man. "Take the platform to the dungeon level. Mister Kemoran is at the end of the hall. Inform the guard that you have *Gratisz li'brunok.*" Which meant I had my choice of any prisoner, on death row, or not. Not even powerful overlords were offered such a thing, which left me wondering why in the Infernal I'd use such a rare and useful gift on Vaszhago, of all demons.

I breached the doorway, and a frigid air hit me like a curtain as I made my way toward a platform at the end of the hallway. Another guard met me there and opened the platform's door, allowing me to step into the circular cage. "Dungeon," I said to the guard, who closed the door behind me, and the cage set into motion, lowering via pulleys and cables that creaked as I descended.

The level below, arranged in a circle around the cage, comprised of cells with long corridors in between that ran perpendicular to the platform and held more cells and prisoners. Angry hollers and curses echoed around me. An object sailed out between the bars of one cell door, hitting the grated cage wall, and I casually peered down to see a bone falling into the depths below. Ten levels down, the cage finally came to a stop on a hard thud at the bottom. Only a small amount of light made the tunnel ahead somewhat visible, and I waited for the guard to open the door, before pulling out the scroll again. "*Gratisz li'brunok.*"

The guard gave a nod, allowing me passage. "Just let me know which one."

"Vaszhago."

"End of the hall. Would you like him to go with you now?"

"Let me talk to him first."

"Very well."

Not that my old nemesis had much choice. The alternative was Ex Nihilo, and even a hardened killer like Vaszhago had to be pissing his pants at the thought of that. The guard directed me toward a corridor between two cells which faced the platform. I strode down the dimly lit hallway, ignoring the moans and calls.

"Hey. Hey!" A strong scent invaded my nose, the familiar aroma of vitality, life, emanating from the cell to the left of me. A petite woman with shoulder-length-straggly purple hair reached through the bars of her cell for me. "Can you do me a favor? I'm not supposed to be here. It's a mistake. Can you get the guard for me? He's been ignoring me for the last three hours."

"How are you here?" I asked only out of curiosity. I had no intention of speaking to the guard on her behalf.

"So, funny story ..."

At that, I kept on. I had no time for long drawn-out stories. My curiosity wasn't that strong.

"Hey!" she called after me. "Hey, asshole! You asked! I was just–where are you going? Hey!"

Her voice faded as I reached the end of the hallway and peered in on a pathetic lump of meat slouched against the stone wall. Long, unkempt hair hid his face from me, and the scent on the air told me he hadn't bathed in weeks. Threadbare clothing merely clung to his oversized body, and the bottoms of his bare feet were black with dirt.

I came to a stop before his cell, casting a shadow over him, but he didn't turn his gaze to me.

"If you've come to offer me redemption, I refuse."

"There isn't an angel in existence that could save your foul soul."

When he finally turned, fiery amber eyes rolled back, and he groaned. "Well, this is awkward. Have they asked *you* to carry out my exile?"

"I'm here to break you out."

With a snort, he rested the crown of his head against the wall, drawing my eyes to the silvery band at his throat, which not only subdued his powers, but if he tried to remove it, would detonate and blow his skull all over the prison cell. "Ah, yes. And the cherubim will escort me to the Heavenly Isles, singing my praises of a righteous life."

"You've been hitting the angels' blood, I see."

"You'd be a whole lot prettier if I was."

"I have a proposition."

"The answer is no. I will not bind with you, nor enslave myself as your concubine bitch dojzra. No offense, but I'd rather burn in the infernal fires eternally than go anywhere near your cock."

"And I'd wish the same. This isn't about me. It's about my female."

His brows winged up, and with his crown still resting against the wall, he rolled his head toward me. "Ah, well, depending on how pretty–"

"You'd do well to bite your tongue, unless you'd like it severed from your mouth."

"Touchy."

"I need someone to watch her closely."

"How close? As in watching her bathe?" Undoubtedly trying to get a rise out of me, he grinned, the sight of his teeth urging me to knock an unsightly hole in them with my fist.

"This is your last warning, or I will petition the guard to speed up your exile and carry out the task with the dullest blade."

On a chuckle, he rolled his eyes again and shook his head. "How many centuries must a man live to become as vapid and miserable as you?" He waved his hand in dismissal. "You mixed breeds have no sense of humor. So, what *exactly* is the job?"

"You will be bound to her as a guard for a period of time. After which, in exchange, you will walk a free man."

As if mulling it over, he stared off toward the darker half of his cell. "Guard her against whom?"

"I suppose I should first ask where you stand on killing me these days."

"I fuck my own hand to thoughts of running my blade through you."

Releasing a heavy sigh, I stuffed my hands into my pockets. "Glad to know you still think about me after all these years. You will protect her against anyone who might be a threat." I loathed having to say what would surely put a smile on the smug prick's face. "Including me."

As expected, he grinned again. "And what's to keep me from taking your head either way?"

"I am the only one who can grant your freedom. And let's not forget, of all the times you've tried to kill me, I am the only one who did not fall victim to your blade."

"Yes." Grumbling to himself, he lifted his knee and rested his elbow there. "It pisses me off that you've spoiled an otherwise perfect record. These threats to her ... who are they?"

Glancing around for anyone who might've been listening, I leaned closer and lowered my voice. "She is wanted by both the Infernal Lands and the Sentinels, for crimes against the heavens."

"Fuck me sideways. Do you have any idea what the heavens would do to me, if they happened to get their hands on me?"

"It's that, or sit here counting down the seconds to Ex Nihilo. As someone who's been there, I can tell you, death at the hands of a Shee'vai would be less torment."

His body jerked with a snorted laugh. "I'd take your cock over one of those crazy banshees. And just how, pray tell, did you escape Ex Nihilo?"

"I'll tell you on the journey back. Do we have a deal, or not?"

"How long am I indebted to you? Just gauging whether, or not, exile would be worse."

"She is due to begin transition to cambion after the baby is born."

"Baby?" The amusement on his face twisted to repulsion. "What sick world would grant you spawn?" He didn't give me a chance to answer before he rubbed a hand down his face and said, "All right. Fine. I'm in. If you'd kindly get me the fuck out of here now, I'd appreciate it."

With a half-smile, I nodded. "Guard!"

The burly guard from before strode toward us, and as he passed the purple-haired girl who called out for him, he smacked a baton against her cell, the clatter of iron echoing down the hallway. On arriving at Vaszhago's cell, he pulled a set of keys, and the moment the door opened, Vaszhago jumped to his feet in a defensive stance.

As if he'd suddenly not trusted the guard.

Once he was upright, I could see thick black chains binding him to the walls, shackled to his arms and legs. Not the typical iron, I guessed, as they wouldn't have properly held a savvy escape artist like Vaszhago. Scattered about the bits of skin visible through the holes in his clothes were cuts and bruises, obviously left by weapons hearty enough to leave scars. The kind of metal to which I'd grown quite familiar, as the same kind of weapons had been used on me as a boy. With a smirk, the guard yanked on one of his chains, and the demon stumbled toward him. Vaszhago rolled his shoulders back, gaining his composure, and looked the beastly guard in the eye. "When I'm free, I'll return to this place for your head."

The guard let out a chuckle, unlocking the cuffs from around Vaszhago's wrists. The moment both were free, the demon swiped the blade from the guard's pocket before he even had the chance to gasp, and not a second later, he stood behind the guard with the weapon propped at his throat.

"Don't be foolish," I warned. "Not when you're mere steps from freedom."

"Freedom? No. What makes you think that I would choose to be enslaved by you."

"You kill him, and you'll place me in the very precarious position of protecting my innocence. In other words, I'll kill you myself."

In my current state, I couldn't even say if that was possible, but he didn't need to know that.

Vaszhago lowered the blade and patted the guard on the arm, earning a snarl from the clearly humiliated demon. "We'll resume our play some other time. My freedom awaits." He dropped the knife, which scraped against the cement floor, and made a casual stroll toward the door, coming to a stop alongside me. "You're shorter than I remember."

We stood at equal height.

"You certainly smell worse," I volleyed back.

"Well, now. Let us get on with this, shall we?"

The guard trailed our steps, giving Vaszhago the evil eye as we kept on down the corridor. Once again, the purple-haired female called out to us.

Vaszhago came to a screeching halt and lifted his nose in the air, undoubtedly smelling her.

As I passed her cell, I felt the sharp tug of my coat and looked down to where she had managed to take hold of it.

"Please take me with you! They plan to send me to Infernium after the sick bastards in the penthouse are finished with me. I'm begging you."

I pried her fingers loose from my coat, noting her hands were ice cold. "Infernium?"

"A ridiculous misunderstanding."

Vaszhago sighed and shook his head. "Sorry, love, you'll have to wait for the next crazy train. Heard you talking in here and … clearly you don't have a roommate."

"Yeah? I heard you talking, too. Insisting the guards use lube."

Vaszhago only chuckled in response, but the guard growled beside me, lurching toward her, but I threw out a hand to stop his advance.

She turned her attention back to me, her hands curled around the bars of her cell. "Look, I'll do whatever you want. I heard you talking about a lady. A baby. I know lots about babies. I can be her attendant!"

"I got a better idea," Vaszhago interrupted. "We'll come back in a week, when you're settled in Infernium, and throw popcorn through the bars at you."

"I get it." Her lips stretched to what I surmised was a fake smile. "It's hard coming to terms with the fact that you couldn't turn on the knobs of a sink, let alone a woman, but that's no reason to be an asshole."

With a groan, I pinched the bridge of my nose, growing weary of their bickering. "Enough of whatever this is. I'm sorry, but no. I'm not here for charity."

"And I'm not asking for your damn pity, jerk. Okay, I am. But with *dignity* in my voice."

"I'm sorry." I took a step in the direction of the platform, just as she backed away from the bars, shoulders sagging in defeat.

"You slay the demons who tormented you as a child, and this is the thanks you get. A lifetime sentence with all the catatonics. Brilliant."

I halted midstride. "You're human. Are you not?"

"Yeah. So?"

"You know of demons and how to slay them."

"One was a lord. Dirty prick liked kids. Look, you really

186

can't leave me here after admitting all of this." She jerked her head toward the guard. "Noodle dick is gonna tell all his friends, and then I'll be *whore d'oeuvre* to the assholes upstairs."

I narrowed my eyes on her, searching for any sign that she might've been something other than human. "You're aware of what all of this is?"

"What? Your little Purgatory wannabe world? Yeah. I may look dumb, but I ain't dumb."

"These demons you supposedly slayed--how'd you do it?"

"There ain't no supposed about it. I ran my blade through their chests and popped them in the skull." Using her thumb, she demonstrated each move.

It was then I focused on her eye and caught sight of the tiny, black star just outside of her iris. The telling mark of her kind. "You're a *Dra'Akon*." Not that she would've admitted it. They were humans with certain abilities, capable of slaying demons. Most times, they worked as spies for the angels, alerting them to crimes against the heavens, predominantly in the mortal realm.

"I have no idea what that is. Why are you asking me all these questions?"

She was a horrible liar, too. But if still connected to the heavens, she might be a means of negotiations for Farryn. "What is your name?"

"Vespyr."

"Guard. I'd like this one, as well."

"You're bringing her?" Vaszhago groaned beside me. "Promise me I don't have to share quarters with this one."

Watching the guard reluctantly unshackle her from the wall, I chuckled. "I've a feeling she'd sever your nuts, if you went anywhere near her."

"It's true," she said. "I actually have a collection of demon nuts. Wanna see it?"

~

Once back at the front of the building, the clerk had me sign the Empyreal Debenture and hand it off to him. He gave me Vaszhago's belongings—a hooded cape, dagger, and a small bag of coin.

"What happened to my boots?" Vaszhago growled.

The clerk shrugged, lips stretched to a foxy smile. "I've no idea. What you see is what we have."

"Bunch of lying thieves," the demon grumbled and snarled back at the guards.

Nothing was handed off for the girl, and I turned to see her shrug. "Didn't bring much."

The clerk turned his attention back on me. "Would you like their bands unlocked now?"

"If I may have the keys, I'll wait until after I'm in the safety of my own home."

"Of course." The clerk handed off a set of two keys—one for each prisoner—to the beastly guard beside him, who then passed them down to me.

With that, all three of us exited the building to the awaiting coach.

"What? No coachman?" As the son of an Infernal Duke, Vaszhago was no stranger to royal customs, but he'd long given up that life when he was recruited as a Knight.

"Good labor is hard to find," I joked and turned to face him. Although ordinarily, my powers would've surpassed his, in their absence, he'd have made a much more intimidating opponent without that band at his throat. I flicked my fingers for his hand. "I'm certain the band would make for an uncomfortable ride back to the manor."

Vaszhago let out an exasperated huff, offering up his hand.

"I believe you know the words," I said, reaching beneath

the carriage bench for the satchel I'd tucked there and the dagger held within it. Taking it into the prison would've been futile, as they would have confiscated it.

After muttering a string of curses, he cleared his throat. "I. Vaszhago Kemoran of Netherium do solemnly swear to uphold the integrity of the five realms or be at the mercy of my *lord*." He garbled the words as if they left a bitter taste on his tongue. "For the span of eternity."

Dagger held over his palm, I drew an X inside a circle with three dots, the glyph symbolizing the *ba'nixium* curse, which would prevent him from harming Farryn. "Your life is bound to Farryn's life. If she should die, so then will you suffer for eternity." Inky-black blood oozed up from the marking on his palm and quickly sealed into a raised scar. "And let me add that if you lay so much as a finger on her, I will shove your hand so far up your own ass, you'll be able to scratch the back of your throat." At that, I slipped the key into the band at his neck and, with one click, removed it from over a bright red ligature.

Vaszhago rubbed the inflamed skin, as I handed off his cloak and dagger which bore the emblem of the Knights.

With a flick of my fingers, I urged Vespyr to come forward so I could remove her band, as well. As I reached to shove the key into the lock, she knocked my hand away, frowning. "Aren't you forgetting something?"

"Forgetting what, exactly?"

"The weird blood ritual thing you just did to him?"

Vaszhago sneered and climbed onto the carriage bench.

"I don't feel the need to–"

"Because I'm a woman?" Arms crossed, she glared back at me. "Sexist asshole. You don't think I'm capable of killing the two of you right now, if I wanted to?"

"I don't have a history of mistrust with you."

"Well, I insist." She shoved her hand into my chest.

"C'mon, pretty boy. Carve me up."

I stared at her, suddenly understanding why she was bound for Infernium versus one of the work camps. "Do pacts not go against your vow as a Dra'Akon?"

"I told you, I have no idea what that is. But if I did, no. It wouldn't."

"If something were to happen to Farryn, you would suffer incredible pain with this curse. Unimaginable pain."

"I took a class on econometrics once. Your little blood curse ain't got nothing on that." She nodded toward Vaszhago. "Besides, if he's worth a damn, I shouldn't have anything to worry about, right?"

"Do we have time for this?" Vaszhago said in a bored tone. "With my balls now tied to your female, I'm a little anxious about who's guarding her at the moment."

"The next time you mention your balls and my female in the same sentence, I will sever said balls and feed them to you." I turned back to the woman and, with impatience, took her palm. "You know the words?"

"I. Vespyr St. James from Dade City, Florida, do solemnly swear to uphold the integrity of the five realms or be at the mercy of my lord for a span of eternity."

"You remembered all of that?"

Smile stretching her lips, she tapped at her temple. "Photographic memory."

I carved the same symbol into her palm and bound her to Farryn, just as I had with Vaszhago. As the black fluid oozed out of her cut, she gasped. "That is wild." She held up her hand and turned to her side. "Is that not wild, Osiris?"

I frowned, observing nothing beside her, except her own shadow. "Yes, well, let's be off."

We climbed into the carriage, and as I took a seat beside Vaszhago, he snorted. "Told you."

"Cap it."

16

FARRYN

*A*t the sound of barking, I pushed out of bed and scurried across my room toward the window, watching the dogs chase after the carriage where Jericho sat beside a man literally dressed in rags. Through the window, I could see his dirty bare feet, the sight of which made me shiver, given how cold it was outside.

I felt Anya's presence beside me. "This should be interesting," she said with an air of amusement. "I wish I knew what it was that made the Master so sympathetic to criminals."

"How many do you think this one has killed?"

"In a place like Velthrock prison? My goodness, he'd have to be quite dangerous."

Great. My babysitter, the serial killing demon.

The carriage rolled to a stop, and after Jericho dismounted, he glanced up toward me, flicking his fingers in a gesture for me to come down.

An uneasy sensation twisted in my stomach, but I gave a nod, and with Anya trailing after me, I made my way out of the bedroom and down the stairwell to the first floor foyer, where Jericho had just stepped inside.

Behind him, followed the prisoner.

And behind the prisoner, came a petite young woman, perhaps twenty, or so, with bright purple hair that stuck up in all directions.

The sight of her brought me to a screeching halt, and confused, I looked back to Jericho.

"This is Vaszhago." He gestured toward the male first, whose face was hidden behind bedraggled black hair that reached his shoulders. "He has agreed to serve as a guard to you and offers his life, if necessary."

In an act that seemed so utterly strange, I didn't know how to respond, Vaszhago knelt down, head bowed. He spoke in a language that I didn't understand, but given the nod of approval from Jericho, I assumed it was respectful.

"You don't have to—" I started to say and was quickly cut off, when Jericho added, "And this is Vespyr. She has agreed to assist you through the pregnancy."

The girl followed the same gesture as Vaszhago, kneeling to the floor. Only, she spoke plain English. "It's an honor to be your attendant, my lady."

My lady?

Everything about the introduction felt awkward, but I sent her a warm smile and looked back to Jericho. "Can I speak with you for a second?"

Nodding, he turned toward Anya. "Would you be so kind as to get both of them settled. And see to it they have what they need for a proper bath."

"Of course, Master Van Croix." With a jerk of her head, Anya led the two strangers up the staircase, and I trailed my gaze after the young girl, who smiled as she eyed me warily on passing.

Once they had ascended to the upper level, Jericho jerked his head for me to accompany him and took the lead toward his office. We rounded the corner, and he pushed through the door, heading straight for the liquor tray. He tossed his cape over his chair and poured himself a glass of a strange, glowing red liquor with white bubbles and thick white steam gathered inside the glass, reminding me of something found in a mad scientist's lab.

With a confused frown, I studied the unusual liquid as I took my seat, momentarily distracted from my earlier irritation. It wasn't until he sank half the drink back in one swig and gave his head a rough shake, as though it'd burned going down, that I finally broke from my spell.

He held up the glass, tipping it a bit, and I noticed the bubbles intensifying, as if the drink were boiling hot. "Chthoniac. The most infernal liquor that ever existed. One sip would probably kill a human."

Jesus. He'd just downed half of it in one gulp. I shook my head of the thought. "What is this? You said a bodyguard. And now an attendant? Jericho, I don't need an attendant."

"They were going to have her sent to the higher-ranking demons to be raped and consumed."

"What?" I blurted out and cleared my throat. "Are you serious?"

"She's a living soul, much like you. Which means, they would've made sport of it and reveled in the spoils."

"How? I mean, I wasn't supposed to have survived the tea that Xhiphias gave me, right? That was some weird, reincarnation special deal, wasn't it? How is she living?"

He swallowed back another sip of his drink, that time without so much as a twitch of his nose. "I suspect that she has the ability to astral project."

"Astral project?"

"Her body remains on earth, while her consciousness crosses planes."

"So, she's not physically here?"

"No one is *physically* here, except you, me and Vaszhago."

"So, can't she go back across planes?"

"Theoretically, yes. I'm not sure why she'd choose to stay and face the punishment of becoming an imprisoned lord's plaything. And meal."

Something seemed off. The man had thrown a fit when I'd first arrived at the cathedral begging to be taken in. Suddenly, he was okay with a shady criminal girl?

With a slow shake of my head, I watched him pour another drink. "You're careful. Too careful. What makes you trust her?"

He sighed, taking another swill of the red bubbly. "Only that I know the integrity of her kind. She was willing to bind herself to you through blood."

"What? Why would she do that?"

"I'd imagine to save her ass from Infernium, to where she was bound. I believe she's Dra'Akon. They're demon slayers whose bloodline goes back centuries."

The longer I stayed in Nightshade, the more I began to realize my father had only just scratched the surface of this world and all its complexities that went beyond simply angels and demons. Demon *slayers*? That sounded like something out of a video game.

"I was trained by one as a young boy. Though I suppose we won't know the extent of her skills until she actually slays a demon."

"This doesn't make sense. You and Vaszhago are demons. Why would she go with you? Or trust you, for that matter?"

With a slight shrug, he slid his empty glass onto the desk. "It's possible she could be here to kill me, or Vaszhago. But whether that's true, or not, I know for certain that above all else, she would protect *you*. Her calling is to guard humans. And that's all that matters to me."

There it was—exactly as I suspected. The man wouldn't have brought a stranger into the house, unless it meant yet another layer of protection to the thick shield he'd begun to build around me. "You think she would try to kill you?"

"Technically, the blood binding won't allow it, unless I attempt to harm you."

The man had an answer for everything. "You really bought the whole entourage, huh?"

With his hands shoved into the pockets of his black slacks, in a casual but somewhat arrogant stance, black shirt buttoned down to mid-chest and clinging to his biceps, he reminded me of a mafia boss, which seemed fitting at the moment. "It's not every day you piss off the heavens *and* Hell. I figured it's better to be prepared for war." The worry on my face must've been a marquis with flashing lights, the way his brows came together in concern. "What is it?"

"You think they'll come for us? Here?"

"I am preparing for any possibility." He rounded his desk, slowing to a stop before me, and leaned back against the polished wood behind him. The feel of his warm palm against my cheek was a balm to my growing fears. Eyes riveted on my lips, he stroked a finger over them, perhaps wanting to kiss me, and God, I wanted him to. I wanted him to lift me up into his arms, set me down on that desk, and fuck me with the same reckless passion as when we'd started the night before.

Before my head had effectively ruined everything.

"You make it hard not to love you, you know that?" I asked.

"As do you."

In spite of his words, a sadness filled the space between us. An emptiness that I wanted to cleave through with a chainsaw. "Well, I should probably get back to staying completely separate. It seems everyone is keeping their distance."

"What does that mean?"

"Earlier, I went outside to see the dogs. They went berserk. Tried to attack."

Brows pinching to a tight frown, he lowered his hand from my face. "Cerberus tried to attack you?"

"Yes. I don't know what I did. He acted like he didn't recognize me, at all."

"You carry my sigil. He would essentially be going against *me*, if he were to attack you." He shook his head, running his hand over his jaw. "I've never seen disloyalty out of him in all the time I've had him."

"Well, I'm not putting his loyalty toward you to the test. I'm already tied to an ex-convict, who I'm not convinced won't try to cut his losses."

"I'll see what's going on with Cerberus. And I'll not begin the search for your father for a couple days, so you might feel more comfortable with Vespyr and Vaszhago." He returned to his chair and eased back into it, looking casually lethal and utterly delectable, as usual.

Again, I found myself mourning the times I could take what I wanted, as he'd encouraged me to do, without the look of suspicion in his eye, like I was some kind of criminal breaking the law.

Everything was different, and I hated that even the dogs— the first to lower their vicious guard around me when I'd arrived in Nightshade, now looked at me as an enemy. "To be honest, it bothered me. Cerberus and I had such a great connection. More so than Camael, even."

"You did. It doesn't make sense that he, in particular, would behave that way toward you. I'll command they stay away from you. If necessary, I can have the dogs penned during the day so you can get outside, have some fresh air."

Waving my hand in dismissal, I shook my head. "No. I'm not going to have you pen them because of me. That would be wrong. This has been their home longer than mine. I'll be fine. Really. Just makes me sad to have to keep my distance, but I certainly don't want to be their next meal." My days at the cathedral were going to look different now that I couldn't go out and frolic around with the dogs, like I once did. "And don't worry about sticking around for a couple of days. The sooner you set out, the faster we find my father, and this ridiculous need to separate will be over."

"Come here." Leaning back in his chair, he patted his knee, and though I wanted to be incredibly stubborn and deny him, I did as he asked, taking a seat on his muscled thigh. Hands threading through my hair, he pulled me in for a kiss, for which I closed my eyes and savored, relishing the smoky, hot cinnamon flavor of his drink on my tongue, before he broke free. "Do not make the mistake of thinking I enjoy having to keep my hands off you. There is no greater torment."

"I know it has to be this way. I know it's not your fault."

"When my wings are restored, and the baby is born, I intend to claim you."

At that, I drew back, frowning. "*Claim* me? The sexual slavery thing you were telling me about?"

His lips twitched for a smile he seemed to resist. "No. It's a different kind of bonding ritual. It's called *con'jeszis*. Essentially, making you my mate, so that no one else can lay claim to you. Not even an overlord." A lock of my hair slipped between his fingers as he toyed with it. "It's forbidden with a mortal, which is why I abstained before, as phenomenal as it would've felt. Your body becomes immortal in the process. It would've damned your soul." Grief flickered in his gaze as he draped the lock of hair over my shoulder. "But you beat me to the punch on that front."

His mate? While I'd never really dreamed much about a wedding and marriage as a child, certainly not *mating* a man, it wouldn't exactly be torture to be bound to Jericho. Unless, of course, we remained separate for eternity.

"Will this keep me from becoming cambion?"

"No. It'll mean that if anyone dares to penetrate you, he will suffer intense pain. And I will have the legal and recognized right to destroy him. Including an overlord."

I caught the tic of his jaw when he said that. If that was the demon equivalent of a wedding proposal just then, it certainly wasn't the most romantic, but so what. My heart had already decided on Jericho. Anyone after him would've just been horribly sloppy seconds with mold on top. "Then, yes. I say we do it. How does it work?"

Huffing, he turned away from me. "That's the part you might not like so much."

I shifted on his lap and let out a nervous chuckle. "What do you mean?"

"In order to be recognized, the ritual must take place before the council."

"Oh. What, are you afraid of getting blood on the floor when you bite me, or something?"

"Not quite." His brows lowered to a mantle of vexation. "The ritual requires that I fuck you in front of them."

A cough sputtered out of me, as I choked on my own saliva. "I'm sorry," I said, beating my palm against my chest. "What?"

"The binding is a sexual experience in the demon realm, as there really is no closer connection between two individuals. In order for the binding to be recognized by the tribunal, it must take place publicly."

My heart pounded inside my throat, and I swallowed past the lump there. "I ... I don't know ... *Mister Overprotective* is suddenly okay with everyone and his grandma seeing me completely nude?" Another nervous chuckle slipped out of me.

"No. I'm not. In fact, it enrages me to think of anyone laying eyes on you. But if it means the demon who touches you suffers unimaginable pain, then yes. I will fuck you in front of a stadium of demons and angels, if I have to."

Skin burning with humiliation at the thought of such a thing, I mindlessly scratched at my neck. That was not Jericho. He was a man who made his own rules. Who defied Heaven and Hell. Something had gotten into him in the last couple of days. A shift that had him saying and doing things that weren't aligned with who he was. "Why is this so important to you, all of a sudden?"

His muscles tensed around me, as if I'd hit a sore spot. "This isn't *all of a sudden*. I've dreamed of claiming you for centuries."

"Look, I was completely on board with the bonding, up until you mentioned public sex. You guys don't have a demonic justice of the peace, or something? Maybe an Elvis drive-thru chapel?"

His frown deepened.

"What is the point?"

"It is a long-standing tradition that goes back centuries. They watch and determine whether we are worthy of their blessing."

"Worthy? So, it's not enough that we humiliate ourselves, we're to be judged?" I scratched harder at my neck, not realizing how hard, until he swiped up my wrist and a burn streaked across my skin where I'd dug my nails. "This is like webcam porn. I can't. I can't do that. No shame to those who can. The whole voyeur thing is just not *my* kink." I turned away from him, but when I tried to push up from his lap, he tightened his grip in a way that told me his thoughts on the matter were non-negotiable. As much as I understood his position of wanting to protect me, there was no negotiating. "I just feel like a bonding should be a bit more natural. Not because you don't want someone else to lay claim to me." I'd taken on an argument that wasn't even mine, grasping at anything, just to get him to change his mind about the ceremony.

"I don't think you understand the consequences, if that should happen. The very thought of another touching you, kissing you, *fucking* you," he said through clenched teeth, and his grip dug tighter into my thigh. "A public claiming is far less degrading than what you could ultimately be exposed to under the rule of an overlord."

I couldn't even believe I was hearing that from him. Jealous and possessive Jericho suddenly all for the prying eyes of others who would be doing God knew what while watching us. It wasn't even the risky, adrenaline-rush variety of voyeurism. The forbidden touches under the dinner table, or make out sessions in a dressing room. It was full-on sex in plain view. In front of those who were judging to determine the worthiness of our love. The most ridiculous thing I'd ever heard. "What happened to the man who would destroy anything that came for me? *Legions* of angels and demons?"

"In case you've forgotten, I no longer possess the power to fight so much as a fucking *dzilagion* dragon."

The serpent creature that had tried to pull me under when we first arrived in Nightshade. "Is that what this is about?"

"No."

"Then, what? Because you've been acting strange. Not yourself."

He smirked and reached around me for his glass again, pouring himself another drink. "I suppose the impending damnation of my unborn's mother will do that."

Unborn's mother? Why did he make it sound so detached, like something out of a sci-fi movie?

"I guess I have more faith that you'll restore your wings and get your mojo back."

Staring down into his drink, he let out a humorless laugh and kicked back a swill of it. "Do you not understand that there are forces out there, powerful entities, that can crush an entire realm at the wave of a hand?"

"Not to sound self-deprecating, but I doubt a powerful entity capable of destroying realms is interested in the soul of a hormonal mom-to-be."

"Damn it, Farryn! Stop being a naive human for once!" He slammed his fist on the desk beside us, startling my muscles, and I turned to see a crack he'd left in the wood. "For some, you are desirable simply because you belong to me, and the very thought of that strikes a murderous chord. I would sooner watch every miserable creature in every realm burn to the ground than hand you over." A spike of pain struck my skull, as he curled his hand into a fist and pulled my hair back, exposing my neck. "You are mine." He licked his lips, eyes directed at my throat, as if he were about to bite into a juicy steak.

It was then a thought occurred to me. One that explained his strange behaviors. His hot to cold possession. The only thing that made sense.

He knew the demon who had laid claim to me.

I only just threw my hands out, palms hitting his chest, as he yanked me to his mouth. Breathing hard through my nose, I waited for him to sink his teeth into my neck. "You know, don't you? You know who has claim to my soul. That's why you met in the woods."

Releasing me, he looked away, not bothering to answer, but the ire in his expression confirmed my suspicions.

"Tell me."

"Telling you will only put undue stress on you."

Which was undoubtedly why he'd kept it from me. A

thought that failed to make me feel any better. "Tell me, Jericho. I want to know. It's someone you know. Someone who wants to hurt you."

His lips screwed up to a snarl as he stared down into his drink. "There is only one who has ever endeavored to destroy every piece of my life."

"Who?"

"My father."

A dizzying shock swept over me. I could've thought of a number of shady individuals, including Barchiel--or Bishop Venable, as he was once known. But my God, his father? That had to be the most screwed up family drama I'd ever heard. "And is he the one?"

"Yes."

My heart shriveled with his response, and I clutched the edge of the desk to keep from swaying with the waves of nausea pulsing through me. "And your father would try to–"

"He absolutely would. He would tear that child out of you with his bare hands, knowing it would kill me."

"And there's no way you can stop this."

"He is untouchable. The council fears him and the consequences of pissing him off." His hand resting beside me on the desk balled into a tight fist. "I still intend to barter for your freedom, and I *will* claim you. Publicly, so that every ancient lord on the council knows you are mine."

I felt stripped bare already. As if all my choices, everything I wanted, had been torn from my grasp. Caught between father and son. It was hard for me to swallow, considering the only crime I'd committed was bringing someone I loved back. Even if, in my heart, I knew I'd do it again, I began to wonder if coming to Nightshade, falling in love with Jericho, had been a mistake. If things would have been better had he never gained back his memories of me. It broke my heart to even imagine such a thing, but the way things were playing out felt like impending doom. "The claiming. What's stopping you from doing it now?"

"Only the baby. The ritual would deplete your energy and nutrients and potentially kill the child."

"And is that all? The only reason?" Perhaps it was ridiculous of me to expect it, but I only wanted him to ask. Ask me if I wanted to be claimed. Even if the choices were slim and not in my favor, I wanted to know that he was willing to offer me that much dignity, at least.

"Yes."

I snorted a mirthless laugh. "And I thought I was naive when it came to love."

"That is because you're accustomed to words that have grown meaningless for your language. What I feel for you is a word that does not exist in human vocabulary. Stronger than *love*."

"Are you implying that what I feel for you isn't real?"

"What you feel is nothing more than a fleeting human emotion. When I claim you, you will understand."

I pushed his hand away and stood up from his lap, straightening my dress, and as I rounded the corner of his desk, holding back tears was futile. For the first time since I'd met him, I felt adrift. Alone. Instead of taking a seat in the chair, as before, I walked past it toward the door.

The sound of chasing footfalls told me he was not about to let me walk out of this office.

The truth was, I didn't know how to process the emotions bouncing wildly inside of me. My heart was a fragile vessel of entropy, an unsteady beat of chaos.

Jericho was my first love, and I kind of felt as if I'd just been slapped with invalidation. I needed to chew on it. To untangle the confusion in my head and decide whether, or not, I was just overthinking. I needed to dissect his words a bit without the pressure of having to look him in the eye and respond.

Just as I reached the door, an arm shot out from behind me and slammed it shut. He pressed his body to my back, trapping me between himself and the door.

"Jericho, let me go." My voice wobbled with the tears in my eyes. I was on the verge of cracking.

A possessive grip of my hip yanked me back to him, and I felt him bury his face in the back of my neck, inhaling deeply. "There is not a single thought in my day that doesn't involve you. I want you in a thousand different ways, and at the moment, I'm losing my mind. I wish I could say it was the demon inside of me who longs to take you this way. To claim you, with or without your blessing. I will not come to my senses, though. Even before Ex Nihilo, before I lost my wings, I longed to make you mine. Officially."

"I am yours. Officially. I do not need a bunch of old men watching me prove that I love you."

"And as much as I appreciate and agree with those sentiments, I am determined to keep you protected from the one conniving bastard who would take from you without an ounce of mercy or remorse." His hand slid around my neck, and he cupped my jaw, pressed his lips to the other side of my face. The hand he'd thrown against the wall to slam the door shut slid down the hem of my skirt to my thigh. "I will give you pleasure and everything you desire, but I will never give you up. To anyone. In the end, you will be *mine* eternally. Not his."

I wanted to tell him that I loved him. That after months without him, I understood his burgeoning obsession, his need to protect me, which seemed to shadow everything else. Something had settled over me, though. This place, the one to which I'd longed to return, had become foreign all over again. It didn't feel like home to me anymore.

"Let me go," I whispered. Tears slipped down my cheeks, and he pushed off me, allowing me to open the door. Without a glance back toward him, I scurried out of the office and back to my room.

~

I splashed cool water on my face, which took down the swelling heat in my eyes after having cried. I'd come to the conclusion that my hormones must've been completely out of whack. The Farryn from before would've just told him to go to hell if she didn't like, or agree with, what he was offering. She would've demanded that he meet her halfway instead of steamrolling over her. As I suspected, a bit of time to think had set my head straight.

I'd eventually revisit the conversation with Jericho, but for right then, it wasn't necessary, so I forced my stubborn, argumentative-loving self to drop it.

A hard thump pounded inside my stomach, and I bent over on a sharp exhale, resting a hand there. What felt like a thousand serpents beneath my skin sent a shock of terror through me, and I lifted my dress, turning myself in the mirror, where I watched black markings move across my belly. As if there were little snakes running beneath my skin. My breaths hastened, pulse raced. Dizziness claimed my balance on seeing my skin move like that, and I stumbled to the side.

"*Save him,*" a voice whispered, and I glanced up to see the woman I'd seen in dreams, the blonde with dark eyes, standing behind me.

I spun around to find nothing there and turned back to the mirror. The figure had disappeared.

At a hard knock at the door, I let out an involuntary scream.

"Miss Ravenshaw? I'm sorry to bother you … it's Vespyr. Um. Your attendant."

Screwing my eyes shut, I took deep, calming breaths through my nose.

Just an illusion.

Resting my hand against my stomach proved that nothing snaked beneath my skin, and I sagged with relief.

It was just an illusion.

I strode across the room, out of the bathroom, and opened the door to find a slightly shorter girl with wet purple hair standing in the hallway, wearing one of the signature Blackwater dresses. The same dress I happened to be wearing. "Hi."

"Sorry, um. Anya?" She hiked a thumb over her shoulder, as if Anya was standing behind her right then. "She thought I should come say hello. Introduce myself properly."

The brief meeting in the foyer hadn't given much insight into the girl, but Jericho had mentioned the integrity of her kind. And with as protective, and obsessed, as the man was, I doubt he'd have invited someone into his home that he didn't have a good sense about. He surely wouldn't have allowed such a person around me, if the conversation we'd had earlier in his office was anything to go by.

Mentally dismissing the hallucination with a shake of my head, I smiled. "Sure. Come in." While a part of me thought it weird to invite someone into my bedroom as if it was an apartment, or something, in truth, the room was about as big as an apartment, with a fireplace and chairs, which was where I led Vespyr. I gestured for her to sit, and I took the other seat across from her. From the carafe that Anya had brought up to me earlier, I poured a glass of water, my hands shaking all the while. "Would you like some water?"

Her eyes shifted from my hands to me and back to my hands. "I'm good. Hey, is everything okay?"

"Yeah. I just. I'm always shaky." A nervous chuckle escaped me, and I drowned it in a long sip of water. An uncomfortable silence lingered between us, broken only by the sound of my gulps. I set the glass down and cleared my throat. "So, Jericho told me you were imprisoned?"

"Yeah, well, wrongfully so." With a roll of her eyes, she sagged into her chair and toyed with the embroidered pattern of the upholstery. "It was self-defense, really."

"What happened? If you don't mind me asking."

Shrugging, she folded her legs up onto the chair, as if to get cozy. "Nah. I don't mind. I killed some … thing."

"Thing?" Given what Jericho had told me about her being a demon slayer, I felt comfortable asking the next question. "A demon?"

Smiling, she rubbed a hand down her face. "What a relief. It's weird that no one around here sees them like we do. 'Course, no one where I'm from sees them either. They think I'm crazy." She pulled her legs tighter, brows knitting to a frown.

"You can astral project."

"Yes."

I couldn't help studying her, wondering how exactly astral projection resulted in what seemed to be a physical body in Nightshade. But that was the case with all the souls there. "So, why stay imprisoned here, if you can just come and go at will?"

Another smile played on her lips as she lowered her gaze. "So, what did you do in the human world?" she asked in an obvious diversion.

No way I was letting that question slide, but I answered her anyway. "I was a student."

"Of what?"

"How about you answer my question first?"

Her chest rose with a deep breath, and she huffed. "I don't

have the best situation at home. Sometimes, somewhere else is better, even if it's not all that great. No doubt, if they would've actually sent me to be some slave, or to Infernium of all hellish places, I guess I would've gone back. I'm not glutton for misery, you know. And look." She waved her arm, gesturing toward the room. "I'm living it up in a creepy, gothic cathedral now. How cool is that?"

"Infernium … you've heard of it?"

She toyed with the hem of the dress, pulling at a loose string. "Everyone here has heard of it. I think they're more afraid of that place than the possibility of winding up in Hell."

"Why?"

"I've only ever heard stories. *The place the angels fear to tread.*"

"Why do they say that?"

"No angel has ever come out alive, I guess. Humans, either. I sure as hell wasn't going to let them send me there."

"It sounds terrifying."

"Yeah." She stared off for a moment, eyes unfocused, as if in thought, then shook her head. "So, are you going to tell me what you studied, or is it going to remain one of the great mysteries of the universe?"

"Iconology. Symbols."

"How'd you get into that?"

"My dad. He was a professor of religious studies and did a lot of language studying. Ancient languages. Trying to decipher codes and whatnot. I was always into puzzles and the challenge of solving them. I was fascinated by his work."

"That's cool. I did three semesters at Caltech, but dropped out."

"What was your field of study?"

"Astrophysics." She lowered her gaze, as she sat picking at

her fingers. "I guess I needed my world to feel bigger than it was. Sometimes, it's suffocating."

"It is."

"Guess that's why I come here. It reminds me that as big as earth is, it's nothing at all."

"You've been coming here a while, then?"

"Since my mother died." Lips flattened, she lowered her gaze, keeping with the fidgeting of her loose string, which had grown twice in length. "She was the only one who ... saw me. *Really* saw me. When she died, I felt like the world stole from me. Just ... ripped her right out of my hands without apology. No remorse. That was the first time I learned that prayers were useless. I thought maybe I might find her here." Her words struck a chord, given it was my mother's death which had prompted my father to seek out Nightshade, and ultimately what drove me to come after him.

"How old were you when you first came to Nightshade?"

"Eleven. I thought I was dreaming one night. I saw one of my classmates from school, Sebastian, standing in my bedroom. I had no idea what he was doing there, so I followed him out of my house and into the nearby woods. On the other side was this weird village I'd never seen before. I spent the whole night hanging out with this kid. Running through the streets. Laughing. Living." Eyes unfocused, she seemed lost in her reminiscing, smiling as she told the story. "I felt so free. And when I returned back home, I crashed onto my bed. What felt like minutes later, I woke up." Her smile faded to something more serious. "My mom told me that she'd gotten a call from another classmate's mom, telling her that Sebastian had been hit by a car while riding his bike the day before. He died instantly." Running her finger across her bottom lip, she stared off. "Night after night, he came to my room, and we would run through those woods to the village. And it wasn't long before I realized, it wasn't a village. It was another realm." Strange, how utterly different her story was from mine. Two completely different experiences, and yet, there we both were, sitting by the fire in purgatory together. "What brought you here?" she asked.

"Fate, I guess you could say. My mother died, as well."

"Huh. So, we have something in common, then."

I hesitated to tell her that in just a few months I'd become half demon. Perhaps the very thing she slayed. I'd be enslaved to a man who, according to Jericho, would do whatever he could to make my life miserable as a means of vengeance. And unlike her, the chances of Jericho pulling me out of that prison were slim. So, instead, I nodded. "I suppose we do."

17

THE BARON

Standing before Drystan, the baron studied the markings made to his cousin's flesh. Strips of glistening gashes marked fresh wounds, and the scent of seared meat on the air told him the other boy had been burned as torment.

Beside one of the pentroshes, the baron's father wore a bored expression, and if to to add insult, he yawned. The mere sight of him had the baron's muscles bunched in anger, and when the older Van Croix sent him a smirk, the younger lord wished he could have ripped it clean off his face.

One of the pentroshes slipped a blacksmith's glove over his hand and lifted a long piece of iron from a small brazier at the corner of the room, which glowed an ominous bright orange. As he strode toward Drystan, the boy wriggled in his binds, his eyes wide with fear.

"No! Please! I'm begging you! Please!"

"Tell us what you saw, boy," the bishop's voice dripped with malice, a sound which twisted the baron's stomach. "Tell us now and avoid further punishment."

Through tears, Drystan turned toward the baron, his eyes

pleading, but they had no effect on him. Should he tell them, the baron stood to suffer more than a few burns to his flesh. A long and tense silence followed, and the way Drystan squirmed told the baron his secret was not safe with his cousin. Except, to his surprise, Drystan clenched his jaw, eyes hardened with stubborn tenacity. "I saw nothing, Your Grace."

The sound of sizzling flesh crackled beneath the over-powering scream that bounced off the walls. Drystan shook and jerked against his binds as the iron seared his naked belly. Skin tore from his body as the pentrosh lifted the iron away from him.

"You speak with the tongue of the devil, boy." The tenuous clip in Bishop Venable's tone spoke of no mercy and little patience. The older man nodded toward the pentrosh who strode back toward the brazier and warmed the iron rod again. "If it is the threat of consequence that keeps you from speaking the truth, know that I will pardon you on this occasion."

The baron's eyes shot to his cousin's once again, only that time, Drystan didn't look back at him. He kept his gaze cast toward the floor as he breathed heavy and fast through his nose. A minute later, the pentrosh strode up to him again with a freshly warmed iron and lowered it toward Drystan's thigh.

"He can heal his own wounds! He has the power to heal his own wounds!" As the confession flew from Drystan's lips, a tight grip of alarm squeezed the baron's chest, and he backed himself away. "I swear I would not think it possible myself, Your Excellency, but I saw it with my own eyes. Wounds that should have taken weeks to heal had done so by the morning after his punishment."

The bishop jerked his head toward the pentrosh who placed the iron back into the brazier and removed his glove.

Drystan sagged against his binds, his obvious relief nearly palpable.

"Remove the good baron's clothing."

The pentroshes rushed toward him, but the baron pushed them away and threw a fist toward the jaw of the older one. The man stumbled backward, knocking over the brazier on a scintillating plume of embers. The second pentrosh lurched toward him again, but the baron gave one hard kick to his chest, knocking him backward, as well.

He spun on his heel to head back toward the door, but the tip of a blade met his throat, the steel pinching against his Adam's apple. Alaric stood with a smile, casually holding his blade. "These holy men are far too polite to remove your head. But I'm not."

The baron bit back the urge to punch the guardsman in his smug face, and felt the harsh jerk of his arms as the pentroshes yanked him backward. At either side of him, they removed his vest and tunic, until his upper half was as naked as Drystan's.

A collective gasp filled the room. A cold finger dragged across the flesh he'd healed himself, and the baron sank his teeth into his tongue, swallowing back the disgust trapped at the back of his throat.

"It is true. Not a scar mars his flesh," the bishop said, his voice tinged in what the baron took as a cross between awe and revulsion. "Strap him to the cross."

Hands jerked him around, and the baron watched as a pentrosh released Drystan from his binds, catching the boy before he fell to a slump on the floor. "See to it that his wounds are looked after," Bishop Venable said, as they dragged the other boy from the room.

The smile on Lord Praecepsia's face grated on the baron, when the pentroshes dragged him toward the cross and secured him facing the opposite direction as Drystan had, so that his stomach rested against the wood and his back was exposed. With the last of the bindings locked in place, the baron braced himself for what would inevitably come next. There'd been too much venom in Venable's voice for him to believe they would grant him any level of pity. And if he were being honest, he did not want their pity, particularly that of his father. The baron lifted his gaze toward the elder Lord Van Croix, and when the first tendrils of heat brushed over his unbroken flesh, the boy gritted his teeth, waiting for that hot iron to kiss his spine. He willed his mind to the dark mind-space, where nothing existed. Nothing could touch him.

A white-hot burn crackled throughout the room when the pentrosh held the iron to the baron's back. A jagged light flashed behind his eyes, his body trembling with the agonizing pain that speared through his detachment, clawing at his attention. He did not cry out, though, nor did he make the same pathetic mewling sounds that Drystan had moments before. Instead, the baron clenched his teeth and curled his fingers around the binds. The intensity of the burn eased and the wet sticky sound that chased the lifting of the rod could have only been his flesh tearing away.

In the reprieve that followed, he found his father staring back at him, the look of disappointment bringing a smile to the baron's face.

"We will see after tonight if these wounds heal. And we will know the truth, young baron."

The bishop's voice grew distant to the thoughts in the baron's head. Strange that, when one was accused of devilry, the parents who'd borne the child failed to face any punishment. Of course, the elder Lord Van Croix could have easily blamed such an aberration on the baron's mother. His father had been far too entrenched in the Pentacrux, held too high a position, to be seen as anything but holy and righteous.

Had they only seen what he had seen in the woods.

In the boy's periphery, he caught sight of the pentrosh striding toward him with the hot iron once again, and the words of his mother echoed inside his head.

"They should all fear you."

They were the only words that kept him grounded. That gave him the confidence to know these men couldn't truly hurt him, if what his mother had said was true. When the pentrosh placed the iron to his flesh, he feigned a tortured outcry. Not because that particular torment hurt any more than the last.

He did it for his mother, and the promise he'd made to her.

Wet concrete scraped across the baron's cheek, the unyielding surface smashing against his shoulder as the two pentroshes tossed him into a dark cell. The cool, dirt floor of the cell offered only a small measure of relief, while the torment he had suffered wreaked havoc on his body.

"You will stay here overnight for observation." The bishop stood over him, the hem of his robes dancing over the baron's wounds as if to tease his pain. "A pentrosh will be on guard to watch for any sign of trickery, or magic. We will check your wounds in the morning, and by the Holy Father's grace, if they have healed, so will begin your exorcism."

Exorcism. The baron had heard rumors of the ritual. Bloodletting. Floggings. Tongue burning. Inversion therapies, all designed to banish evil from one's soul.

After another sweep of his hem over an open wound, all of them left the cell, closing the iron door behind them with a heavy thud.

Shuttering his eyes, the baron rested his forehead against

the dirt and breathed through his nose, focusing on the raw and open gashes scattered across his back. In the silence of his mind, he felt a strange sense brush over his skin, and he opened his eyes to find two deep green orbs staring back at him. A boy, perhaps only slightly younger, crouched beside him, wearing a dirty nightshirt that hung over his grimy feet.

The baron lifted his head, only to get a clearer view of his cellmate, and realization struck him. Willem. He'd seen the boy before, wandering the village. The townsfolk had called him mute. Feral.

His mother had died years before, leaving him at the mercy of his father, whose closest companion was a tankard of ale. It only occurred to the baron in that moment that the last time he'd seen the boy scampering about the village, begging for scraps of food had been months ago.

The baron did not bother to strike conversation, as he neither had the inclination, nor energy, given the pain that scratched for his attention.

Instead, he lowered his head and closed his eyes again.

Through the dark void of dreamless sleep, a crackling noise reached the baron's ears, and he opened his eyes to the dark cell. Movement in his periphery drew his attention to the walls, where shadows seemed to crawl toward the opposite corner of the room. The bricks of the wall darkened and cracked in their wake, as if unseen forces punched at them. A bone-penetrating chill washed over the baron, the air carrying something more than winter's cold. Though the boy had never known the feeling of death, he was certain whatever moved through the room held no vitality.

A glance down at his hands showed the shadows crawling over him, turning his skin an inky black. He lifted his hands into the air, frowning as he examined the strangeness. An incessant hum beneath his skin sent a shiver down his spine. As the shadow crawled up his arm, past his elbow to his shoulder, panic seized his breath. His skin turned a scaly black wherever the darkness touched him.

Through panting breaths, he kicked himself back, as if he could escape it, and the moment his spine hit the brick wall behind him, he flinched at the burn where his wounds festered. Still, the shadow followed, undeterred, and the baron looked toward the door, where he knew the pentrosh was just on the other side of it.

He couldn't call for help, though. If the pentrosh saw him that way, he'd alert the bishop. They would call him evil, and even if the strange event had never happened to him before, Jericho knew all too well what had taken over him. The same wicked beast which overtook his father. The same black, scaly flesh which he'd seen back at that cabin in the woods.

An ache flared at his forehead, and with shaking hands, the baron reached up to palpate two small bumps protruding through his skin.

He let out a gasp, and when he slapped his hand over his mouth, thinking the pentrosh might hear him, he noticed claws where recently trimmed nailbeds once were.

"No," he whispered. "This cannot be so."

A scream jolted his muscles, and he shot his attention toward the corner of the room, where Willem lay on his back twitching in a violent fit. Shaking his head, the baron scrambled on all fours toward him, and as he neared, he noticed something he had not before. Black curling smoke in the shape of an arm crammed down the boy's throat, the rest of the attacker's body concealed by the shadows.

The boy let out another gurgled scream, his limbs stretched out and trembling. Jericho reached out for the smoke, but when a palpable sensation smacked his palm, he drew back on a gasp. Red glowing eyes turned toward him, and in the next breath, the shadows lifted along with the chill. A paralyzing burn washed over his flesh, and when he looked down at himself, the black scaly flesh from before had disappeared, returning to his usual skin tone.

The boy stilled, before he opened his eyes and kicked back away from Jericho. "It's you!"

Jericho did not know what struck him most–his accusation, or hearing the boy speak. "No, I saw you in distress. I came to help."

"Y-y-you your eyes! They're b-b-black as night!"

A quick glance back at the door, and the baron pressed his finger to his lips, urging the boy to remain quiet. "I mean you no harm." He leaned in and spoke low, "Something attacked you."

"Spirits. They come for me every night. Sometimes, only for a moment. Others, it seems to last hours."

"What do they want from you?"

"My soul. I will not give it. So they torment me."

"Your soul. They're demons, then."

"Yes. The longer I stay, the more they torture. I cannot tell between dreams and reality." He pulled his knees tight to his chest, hugging them.

"Why does the bishop keep you?"

"I refuse to speak. To tell them of these nightly visits. The moment I do, my fate is sealed."

"They will not let you leave this place if you speak of evil entities tormenting you."

"And so, I am damned either way. This eve, I thought it best if I let the demon have my soul." A look of shame claimed his face as he lowered his gaze. "Perhaps it would end this misery."

"I do not think that is so."

"Why do your eyes change color? They were red and now they are blue."

The baron could not answer that himself, but he did not want the boy to view him in the same light as the shadow which had attacked him. "They change when I am scared."

"I would not make them privy to such a thing. It might prove to be an amusement for them. I am Willem, by the way."

"And I am Jericho."

"The young Lord Van Croix. You are quite different from your father."

The sound of that relieved him. "Forgive me for saying so, but I believed the rumors that you were mute. You speak rather eloquently."

"I engage in conversation when necessary. Otherwise, I find silence to be the most effective means to avoid others."

"What is the noise in here!"

The harsh voice of the pentrosh startled the boy, whose eyes went wide with fear.

Jericho turned to where the pentrosh had stepped inside the room and shielded his eyes against the intrusive light from his lantern. "I heard sounds of pain. I was just checking on my cellmate."

"Get away from him. The two of you are to remain separate in this cell, per order of the good bishop."

"If we are to remain separate, why place us in the same cell?"

"I have neither time, nor inclination, to answer your questions. Now, move back to your corner."

Biting back the stubborn urge to disobey, the baron did as ordered and slid himself back to the other corner of the room.

"Know that if it is trickery, or black magic up your sleeve, young lord, the name and title you bear will be meaningless."

"And when you find there is no black magic, or trickery, I'll expect an apology."

"Bite your tongue. Evil always reveals itself." The pentrosh left the room, closing the door behind him and shutting out the light.

On a sigh, the baron leaned back against the bricks, careful not to scrape his wounds on the rough surface. At first, he stared into the darkness of the room, wondering what had lived inside those shadows. Or not, as the case might've been. He pondered the crackling sounds and the chipped bricks, which had returned to their unbroken state. What was the strange aura that had crept over the cell? Why had some of those who suffered afflictions been kept in the infirmary, while others were imprisoned in cells? Had Willem been tortured, as well?

So many thoughts and questions ran through his mind, agitated and swirling, like a boiling cauldron of unknowns. The answers to which he would not likely find there.

He closed his eyes, once again, returning to dreamless sleep.

It was not long before light trickled into the cell, and the door swung open. The bishop entered, flanked by his holy coterie of rabid dogs in robes. They seized the baron at both sides and yanked him to his feet. Spun around, he faced the barred window, with his back, still bearing the unrelenting burn of unhealed gashes, to the bishop.

Footsteps closed in on him. In the dead quiet, Bishop Venable let out an exasperated breath through his nose. He poked the end of his crosier into one of the boy's still unhealed wounds, and the baron let out a growl of agony. "The boy heals at will. There is no other explanation. And he will be broken to learn the truth."

A heavy weight of despair sank to the pit of the baron's stomach.

18

FARRYN

On a small ledge that I'd taken for a bench, beside the library's window, I stared down at where the dogs nosed around the yard, while Anya and another of the cleaning staff took laundry off the clothesline. A twinge of jealousy stabbed my heart on seeing the young maid reach out to pet Cerberus, who didn't snarl, or bark, or bite. He'd come to trust them in my absence, and even though Jericho would've credited me as being the human who'd allowed others to gain that trust, it didn't make me feel better, knowing I'd lost it somehow.

The bonding conversation I'd had with Jericho still sat heavy in my chest. I hated that everything had to be so complicated in the demon realm. It couldn't just be that we'd bond together and that was that. They had to throw in some weird voyeur kink and judgment on top of it.

On a wistful sigh, I turned my attention back to the book in my hands–*Angel Numerology*.

It was no coincidence that I'd been seeing 777 repetitively in dreams, and thanks to my father's maniacal interest in angels, as well as to my own studies, I knew there was more to it. I just didn't know what it had to do with me, in particular.

Most of the human references described a divine symbolism–luck, success, the path toward something good. Typical of our species, always looking for a way to hit the jackpot in life.

I'd come to know better. The universe didn't hand out freebies for nothing. Even the good required an exchange, and leave it to text written by an *actual* angel to clarify that point.

According to the book, 777 wasn't necessarily something positive. It served as a warning of change and, once seen or experienced, meant no return to the before.

No undoing what was already set in motion.

Which could've meant a myriad of things, but seeing as the worst of my worries happened to be changing into a soul-collecting demon soon, it seemed pretty obvious what the heavens were trying to tell me.

I was Hell-bound, no matter what.

Flipping the pages, I searched for the next concerning number–the one I'd been seeing a few times. 137. The time on the clock when I'd wake from nightmares, and every time I suffered a strange hallucination in the middle of the day.

Again, from my own repertoire on religious numerology, I recognized it as either a sign of the angels, or some biblical reference. All I'd found in the Bible was an excerpt reassuring me that God was with me.

Pretty sure that ship had sailed when I'd had sex with a half demon.

And again, in spite of humans turning every combination into a lottery pick, I knew there was more to it.

Unfortunately, the book confirmed my suspicions.

Frowning, I lowered the book and stared down at the words I'd just read.

From death brings life.

It wasn't a single number, but two separate meanings combined. A duality. Thirteen represented death and seven was creation. Perfection.

A new beginning.

Perhaps it meant my soul was damned upon the birth of the baby. I accepted that, even if the thought scared the shit out of me. But what if it meant something else?

Something darker? More obscure.

In that case, what would have to die to bring forth life?

The plan to venture into town and speak with Catriona had been cut short by storms that were expected to pass through soon. Anya had thought it best to wait it out and consider going the following day. With all the questions swirling in my head—more so than before—I'd need some kind of distraction between now and then, or I'd end up going nuts having to wait.

A smudge of black slipped past my periphery, and I looked out the window to see the flick of a long and skinny black tail. Confused, I leaned into the pane, peering out along the wall of the cathedral, where a black cat pranced along the narrow ledge.

Not just any cat. A Sphynx with a very sassy saunter.

"Camael?"

With the number of times I'd hallucinated something, I didn't entirely trust my eyes, though.

Barking snapped my attention to the dogs in the yard below. Anya and the maid had left, and all three of the animals jumped and snarled, their attention on my window.

Holy shit.

Tossing the book aside, I unhooked the window latch and pushed up the heavy frame, my arms trembling with the effort. The barking sharpened, louder than before. Once cracked enough, I stuck my head through the opening.

"Camael? Here, kitty-kitty!" At the kissing noise I made, she twisted toward me, bringing into sight familiar multicolored eyes–one deep brown and one blue–which was unusual for her breed.

Confirming that it was, in fact, Camael.

On the ledge of the cathedral.

In a completely different realm.

I'd ponder the *how* of it all later, but right then, I needed to get her off that ledge.

The dogs barking grew frantic below, all of them sounding like they'd rip her to shreds if she happened to fall. Reaching a hand through the window, I tapped the concrete, urging her to come to me. "Come on, kitty. Come here."

Instead of doing what she was told, the ridiculous cat sat back and lifted her paws, which she proceeded to lick in my face. Camael's way of telling me to fuck off.

"This is why I left you in the mortal realm, you know," I said, removing my shoes and lifting up my skirt. I slipped my leg through the window until straddling the frame, and the cold stony ledge met the tip of my toes. "Don't make me do this, Camael. I really don't want to do this."

The dogs barking had become so wild and intense, it was surely only a matter of time before someone would come to investigate and catch me half hanging out of the window.

The annoying cat stopped licking her paws and sat watching me with pointed interest, as if entertained by the idiot human who was about to fall to her death. "Camael! Come here now!"

Reaching out a hand, I flicked my finger toward her, to which she made a sport of by swatting at me.

"You're going to fall and die, stupid cat! And if by some miracle you don't *die*, those dogs are going to carve you like a Tuesday roast! Now, get over here!" I thrust my arm out farther and, in doing so, teetered forward.

I lost my balance.

"Oh, shit! Oh, shit!" A scream ripped from my throat as my body swung through the window toward the snarling dogs below.

Something yanked on my arm, bringing me to a screeching halt. I looked up to find myself clutched in Vaszhago's unyielding grip. On a growl, he yanked me back, and I shot up like a geyser, the rough concrete scraping across my chest as he pulled me back inside. On an ungracious tumble, I fell to the floor.

Rubbing my arm, I frowned. "You didn't have to yank so hard."

He snarled back at me, his eyes a glowing orange. "What the hell were you doing out there?"

"I saw my cat on the ledge. I didn't want her to become a meaty morsel, so I tried to call her in. Unfortunately, cats don't listen. Ever."

Peering through the window, he looked both right and left. "I see nothing."

Snorting, I awkwardly pushed to my feet and straightened out my dress, noting a snag in the fabric of the bodice. "Yeah, well, I'm sure you ruined all the fun by saving me from a gruesome death. She's probably sulking somewhere."

Jaw shifting and undoubtedly pissed off, he twisted around, shoulders square and battle-ready. With his hair clean and pulled back from his face, black leather pants beneath a long black hooded tabard, black leather belts secured at his waist, and a pawn shop's worth of weaponry hanging off him, he looked like something out of a Mortal Kombat cosplay kink. A far cry from the rags he'd worn the first day he'd arrived. "Are you aware that you and I share a curse? That if you would have fallen off that ledge and died, I would've spent all of eternity feeling the exact moment when a man's balls are ripped from his body. Every minute of every day. For eternity."

"Do your balls actually get ripped off? I'm just asking."

His jaw shifted again with his obvious irritation. "I was tasked to keep an eye on you. Nobody said I couldn't chain you to a chair all day long."

"Well, don't worry, because I'm going to have a talk with Jericho, and soon, you'll be on your merry little, murder-loving way."

"Trust me, if there was a way to break ba'nixium, I would have done it the moment I saw you dangling out that window. Unfortunately, it doesn't work that way. I'm tied to you until your change to cambion."

"What?" Eyes narrowed, I crossed my arms, trying to wrap my head around what he'd just said. "Are you telling me I have to deal with a grumpy-ass shadow until after this baby is born? That's months away. I thought he hired you to watch me while he searched for my father?"

"Congratulations. Your first misunderstanding as a couple."

It wasn't our first, but *irrelevant*. "I don't need someone watching me."

"Did you happen to slip into unconsciousness a moment ago when you nearly plummeted to your death?"

"That kind of thing rarely happens. It was a freak moment."

He lifted his nose, his nostrils flaring as if sniffing the air. "Do you smell that?"

My arm twitched with the urge to sniff myself. "Smell what?"

"Bullshit. You are, by far, the most accident-prone female in all five realms. In fact, it wouldn't surprise me if you tripped and tumbled into Nightshade."

"Does the first time count?"

"I suddenly have an overwhelming sense of regret."

Raising my hand in the air, I shook my head. "I didn't pick you. And remind me when the baby is born never to let Jericho pick the sitter. And, for the record, I was only trying to save my cat."

"I wouldn't worry so much about your cat. She seems to have better survival skills than you."

Clearly. The poor thing had suffered emotional drought and famine all those months that I had fallen into depression over Jericho's death. It was a wonder she'd never tried to steal my breath at night while I slept. "So, what is this curse, anyway? You're not allowed to harm me, right?"

He expelled a growly sounding sigh. "Unfortunately not."

"What happens if you do?"

"The same thing that happens if you stupidly hang out of a window and fall to your death."

Noted. "You can't harm Jericho, either?"

"I can, actually." He grabbed one of the chairs from the table, which he turned around and hiked his boot up onto, setting his elbow atop his knee. "Though it must be deemed necessary. As in, if he endangers your life. Otherwise, I'll just be bound to you until you die of natural causes."

This guy. If there was an award for absolutely zero social skills, he'd have a trophy room. "Jericho said you once tried to kill him. Why was that?"

At first, he only stared back at me, and one thing about the guy–he'd perfected the scary poker face. Whatever thought was running through his head was as mysterious as the ingredients of a hot dog. After a good minute, he dropped the statue play and rolled his shoulders back. "There was a time I would've killed you simply for asking." From a holster clipped to his pants, he tugged a dagger that looked similar to the one Jericho had given me, with its metallic hilt and ornate blade. He nabbed an apple from the table, one I'd grabbed from the kitchen earlier but hadn't bothered to eat, and carved a chunk of it. "I was hired to kill him," he said, and popped the bit of apple into his mouth.

"Who hired you?"

Huffing, he carved his next piece of apple in a way that had me wondering if he was imagining my eyeballs beneath his blade. "I'm not required to answer these questions."

"Then, don't. I'll just go back to doing something reckless, like hanging out the window."

If he could've shot laser beams from his eyes, I was pretty sure I would've been a pile of ash right then. With an unamused expression, he slid the chunk of apple into his mouth, chewing it slowly. "Zorreth. The Founder of the Knights is who hired me."

"The Knights ... you're talking about your little demon fraternity? Knights of some order ..."

"Knights of the Infernal Order."

"Right. So, this founder guy ... why did he want him dead?"

"One does not leave the Infernal Order when one wishes."

In spite of the fact he sounded a little *Game of Thrones*, his words sent a chill across the back of my neck. "So what then, you couldn't kill him?"

"I could have."

"Why didn't you?"

He placed the half-carved apple back on the table and wiped his blade across his leathers. "He saved my life."

"So ... you let him go."

"Letting him go would have resulted in my own death," he said, sliding the dagger back into one of a half-dozen holsters clipped to his body. "I killed Zorreth instead."

Just like that, it clicked. "That's how you ended up in prison."

"It is."

Okay, so Vaszhago earned a small modicum of respect for that. "And considering he left because of my birth, you've been in prison over twenty-two years?"

"Give or take."

It made me wonder if immortals viewed time the same way we did. If those years had felt like an eternity, or if they slipped by in a blink. "He seems to think you'll wholeheartedly kill him without question."

"I will."

Frowning, I leaned back against the windowsill. "You would kill him. After he saved your life, after you killed a lord and was sentenced to Ex Nihilo on his behalf? Why?"

"Because that is what he asked of me."

Groaning, I shook my head. "You honestly think there's nothing inside of him, not a speck of goodness, that would keep him from harming me?"

He shrugged and rubbed a hand across his jaw. "I cannot answer that, except to say, he has buried his needs for far too long. A demon who has been trampled by the weight of virtue will inevitably become resentful. Violent. Unpredictable." His eyes flickered like a flame on that last word.

"So, why hasn't anyone come for him if *one does not leave* the knighthood?"

"The Noxerians forbade Zorreth's crusade. They thought him a fool."

"Noxerians?" I asked, trying to recall if Jericho might've mentioned them.

"The most powerful demons in the infernal realm."

"And they were against Zorreth because …?"

"A half-breed with too much power at his fingertips becomes a threat. There were twelve knights of the order at his beck and call. Each one with a rare and unusual gift."

In other words, the Noxerians probably wanted Zorreth

dead. So why they would arrest Vaszhago for having carried out his murder was a mystery. "Jericho controls lightning."

"A *rod* can control lightning. He can harness the power inside him through vitaeilem."

"What does that mean?"

His lips curved to a half-smile. "If he were so inclined, he could destroy all of Nightshade as easily as waving his hand."

"Jericho said there were others like him. Half demon and half angel. Do they have that power?"

"No."

"And what is your rare and unusual gift?"

On a huff, he lowered his boot and twisted the chair back around, pushing it back beneath the table. "I have shared enough for today. You have company."

"What?"

"Miss Ravenshaw?" The sound of Vespyr's voice was a distant echo, and I guessed her to be in the organ room.

"Up here!" Eyes locked on Vaszhago, I called out to her and, a minute later, caught sight of her purple hair as she made her way up the stairs toward the library. It was once she'd fully ascended that I noticed what lay snuggled in her arms.

"Camael?" I pushed off my window perch and met her at the top of the staircase.

"Found her in my room. Snoopy thing was pawing at something under my bed. Have you been here all morning?"

"Yeah. Vaszhago and I were just–" I glanced over my shoulder to find he was no longer standing there. Frowning, I turned further, not catching so much as a wisp of his tabard. Weird. "Well, he was there a minute ago."

"Careful around that one." Her warning had me twisting back to face her, and she dumped my annoying little death trap into my arms. The cat meowed, seemingly happy to see me, like she hadn't almost lured me to a concrete nosedive just minutes before. "Heard the guards talking about him at the prison. Seems he has an appetite for humans. I know you have that whole curse thing, but ... he's tricky."

Hopefully, his balls being torn off for eternity was enough of a deterrent. "Thanks for the heads up. And by the way, you don't have to call me Miss Ravenshaw."

"Oh. Okay." The smile on her face withered to a frown. "Enough of that, Osiris. She was definitely not being paternalistic."

"What?"

With a sheepish smile, she stuck out her elbow, as if to prod something that wasn't there. "He likes to use big words. Doesn't often get their meaning right, though."

"Who?"

"My shadow. Osiris."

I made a subtle lean to the side, finding nothing or no one behind her.

"Oh. You can't see him right now, silly. Stairwell is too dark. He likes to hide."

After some of the hallucinations I'd suffered over the last few weeks, I'd have been calling the kettle black telling her she was crazy. I certainly had no room to talk. "Well, so we're clear, I was not trying to be paternalistic."

"Oh, I know. You're a genuine person, I can tell." She snapped her head to the side again. "She is genuine. Stop being so mean, Osiris. There is no blonde."

My thoughts skidded to a halt, and ice-cold fingers of shock slid over the back of my neck. "What did you just say?"

"He keeps calling you two-faced. Asked who the blonde is."

The hairs on my neck stood up, and I turned to find no one standing behind me. "You can see a blonde?"

She strode past me toward the table, where she swiped up the half-carved apple that Vaszhago had left there. "I can't, no. But apparently Osiris can. He said she's scary-looking," she said around a mouthful of apple.

"So, you and Osiris are not the same person, then."

Frowning, she shook her head. "I told you. He's my shadow."

"And he sees a blonde somewhere."

"He says she's with you."

A shiver spiraled down my neck, and I resisted the urge to look over my shoulder again.

"When you say *with me*, what exactly do you mean?"

"Did you hear that Osiris?" She looked past me, toward the shadowy staircase where she'd stood just moments before. "She asked a question. Osiris?" With a dismissive shrug, she took another bite of the apple.

While her imaginary friend failed to answer, I sat pondering the possibility that Vespyr and I might've both had a ticket on the same crazy train. A cold and hollow sensation filled my chest and tickled my stomach, as I watched her smile, biting into her apple without a care in the world.

"He's fickle sometimes. Some days, he doesn't shut up, and others, he's silent. To be honest, those are the worst days." Chewing slowly, she stared off, then broke from her silent musings. "Is everything okay? You look like you've seen a ghost, or something."

"Yeah. I think I just need to get some rest."

"Sure. Can I bring you anything? I kind of feel useless."

"Maybe later? If you want to just keep an eye on Camael for me, that'd be great. She has a tendency to wander where she shouldn't." Acids gurgled in my throat, like I might throw up any second, and in spite of the food in her hands, I turned to dump Camael back into her arms.

"I can do that. Hey, don't worry too much about what

Osiris said." The sympathetic smile on her face only had me feeling worse. "He likes to make stuff up."

Which might've eased my worries, except that I'd seen the blonde myself.

And given the information I'd just read about the numbers I'd been seeing, perhaps she wasn't entirely harmless.

19

THE BARON

*W*ith his wounds only just healed, the baron exited the carriage just outside of Solomon's hovel. The old man stood leaning against a shovel, chin tipped up as if he were listening intently. The baron suspected he'd have had little success ever sneaking up on him, given his keen senses.

Likewise, the baron also suffered from overly keen senses, and he winced at the strong stench of the manure pile outside the horse stable where Solomon stood. "I would like to walk home this evening," the boy said to the coachman, who gave a sharp nod in response.

As the young lord strode up to his mentor, the corner of Solomon's lips lifted to a smile.

"Ah, the good baron returns."

"Had I the choice, you'd still be shoveling shit."

Solomon chuckled, placing the shovel against the wooden fence. "Have you given any thought to our last conversation?"

The last being when Fenwick had walked straight through the old man's hovel. Perhaps the baron would have been inclined to answer, but the pain of the scars on his back told him to bite his tongue. "An illusion."

Brow winged up, Solomon jerked his head and nabbed a walking stick from against the fence alongside the shovel. "Come with me."

On a groan, the baron followed after the hobbling older man who led him beyond the stretch of his yard and into the woods. "Where's Soreth?"

"Tending to his studies."

"As in arithmetic, philosophy, that sort?"

"A bit more involved, but yes. That sort. He longs to be an academic."

The baron sneered. "Better that than a soldier."

"It is true, he prefers books over swords." Solomon stopped before a tree whose branches, laden with bright red apples, hovered well above their heads. "And perhaps that will serve him well someday."

Still distracted by the tree, the baron tipped back his head, studying its height. "Why is this tree so unusually tall?"

"It is an unusual tree. Now, help me gather up some apples for my horse."

Frowning, Jericho stared down at the mostly rotten apples which had long fallen. "No *lesson* today?"

"Every moment of your life is a lesson, young Lord. A test." Solomon bent down, sniffing the air, and by some miracle, he reached for one of the lesser bruised and battered fruits on the ground.

Jericho followed suit, bending to his knee, and he lifted an apple so decayed, his finger pushed through mush. Revolted, he tossed the fruit away from him and caught sight of a perfect apple. "A test of what?" he asked.

"Your virtue, of course," Solomon said, picking through a small pile and depositing another into his coat pocket.

With a quick glance over his shoulder to make sure the

older man was still occupied, the baron pushed to his feet and strode across the patchy grass, the mushy fruit squishing under his boots. He knelt alongside the shiny apple, noticing the perfect gleam of its bright red skin. With no intentions of offering up such a magnificent specimen, he polished the fruit on his coat and lifted it to his mouth for a bite.

A hard smack to his cheek knocked the boy to the side, and the apple fell out of his hands onto the ground. Hand covering the harsh sting of Solomon's palm, the baron looked back at the old man, who stood over him with milky eyes that stared off. "Devil's teeth! Are you mad? What was that for?"

Instead of answering, Solomon drew one of the swords from its scabbard on his back. In one whoosh of a slice, the apple split in two, revealing a rotted black core that pulsed with movement.

Disgusted, the baron swallowed a harsh gulp, and when a black serpentine creature slid from the apple's flesh, tendrils of horror washed over him. The creature bore eyes and fangs and slithered toward him with a kind of determination that sent a shiver down his spine. The sound of metal sliced through the air, and seconds later, the creature lay split in two.

As the baron leaned forward to examine it closer, the cleaved remains shriveled into nothing more than black curls of smoke. "What in God's name was that?" he asked through chattering teeth.

"God had nothing to do with that creature." Solomon sheathed his sword and reached down, offering the baron a hand. As the boy reached back for him, the older man asked, "Now, do we wish to speak freely? No silly games or mind tricks?"

"To speak of what I just witnessed would be my execution."

"Not likely. Inquisition and torment, however? Perhaps."

"It exists. The creature that Lord Fletcher saw. The one Drystan saw but refused to say." The black pile of ash where the creature had fizzled to dust scattered in a passing breeze, and it wasn't long before it dispersed entirely, as if it'd never existed at all.

"Yes. They exist. In every corner and crevice of this world, you will find demons and spirits longing to claim your soul by any fiendish means."

The baron imagined himself biting into that apple, only to discover its mushy center and the creature which surely would have slipped down his throat. He swallowed a harsh gulp at the thought. "Had I eaten the apple, what would have happened?"

"Eating the apple itself is something of an agreement."

"An agreement? What kind of agreement?"

"Passage of evil." Solomon reached down for another slightly imperfect apple, stuffing it into his coat pocket. "By biting the apple, you invite it into your body. You offer permission to do its bidding."

"You're telling me that, by eating the fruit, I'd have been offering my soul?"

"Not entirely. You'd have allowed the creature the ability to possess you. You would have committed atrocities at its command, and ultimately damned yourself."

The boy glanced back to the cleaved apple still lying on the ground, frowning at its luring outer perfection. How unsuspecting amongst the rotting fruit. "That doesn't seem fair."

"No one said the devil played fair, young baron."

Perhaps the things he'd seen were not merely illusions, or delusions. Maybe they were real. And maybe evil didn't always present as perfection to lure. Perhaps it hid in shadows on walls, seen only by those who happened to notice the deviant flicker of movement. "I do wish to speak candidly, if I may."

"Yes, of course. I am here to answer whatever questions you may have."

"While in the undercroft of the monastery, I ..." The boy hesitated, never having spoken so openly about such a thing. "I saw a shadow. With eyes. It moved across the cell and somehow the cell changed. I changed. It attacked my cellmate, rather violently."

"What you saw was Eradyę. It is the shadow of the Infernal Lands, which exists as a separate plane."

"Separate plane? I do not understand."

Solomon stretched out his arms to either side. "All of this that you see, the trees, the sky, the clouds, the apples, the birds. They are all part of your world. The mortal realm. But imagine for a moment that you could peel back what lies before your eyes like a painting's canvas. The other side would be a new plane. Another world."

Another world? The baron had studied enough to know more educated scholars would have called the old man a Raver for having suggested such a thing. Yet, Solomon spoke about the other worlds with ease, as if he'd actually seen them firsthand.

"There are multiple planes. The shadow world, which is much like Purgatory, is called Noc'tu umbraj" he went on. "Etheriana--or what you perceive as Heaven. There are the Infernal Lands of eternal suffering, which most humans refer to as Hell. And then there is Eradyę, ruled by an ancient who goes by the name Letifer. The latter is the only one which can move and co-exist inside the other planes. Does this make sense?"

"You're saying that what I saw in that undercroft was another world?"

"It is a darker version. A complete inverse to this one. A

barren land of starving souls, which was never meant to be opened."

Much as the baron hesitated to entertain these ludicrous conversations, he couldn't help himself. "Who opened it?"

"Letifer." Solomon scratched the back of his neck. "However, it is your father who keeps it open."

"So ... why did I change, and not the boy?"

"What resides inside of you is something which is capable of surviving in that world."

"What resides within me?"

The older man's expression turned grim. "You have seen what your father is."

At first, the baron did not answer, but lowered his gaze, contemplating the consequences of such a question.

"Is it not why you were punished?"

With a hesitant nod, the baron chewed on the inside of his cheek.

"Your father is a very rare breed."

"Breed of what?"

"Need I say it aloud?"

In truth, it wasn't necessary, for he had seen firsthand the evil that lived inside his father. He didn't need to give it a name to know it was everything the baron didn't want to be. "And what I saw is what grows inside of me?"

"You are more fortunate than your father. For you also carry the untainted purity of your mother's blood."

"And this affords me some exception."

"It does."

That brought the baron a small measure of relief. "My mother is kind and generous. Nothing like my father."

"It is true, her benevolence knows no bounds. But in the presence of something as evil as Eradyę, such benevolence can be consumed. *Overcome*." Brow quirked, the older man's lips curved to a slight smile. "Would you believe me if I told you that your father did not always carry darkness in his heart?"

Struck by his words, the baron frowned. He could not imagine such a thing, for his entire life, he had only known his father to be cruel and unreasonable. "You're saying he was a good man?"

"There was a time he might have been worthy of your mother's love."

No. Impossible. The man's heart had always been impenetrable. Stony and cold. "When was this?" the baron asked on a mirthless laugh. "In another life, perhaps?"

"Well before you were born. He was a warrior. One who commanded great respect. Even I held him in high regard."

Shaking his head, the baron held back the hysterical laughter begging for escape. "What happened to this renowned and respected creature?"

Solomon's brows pinched to a frown, his pale eyes seeming to stare right through him. "That, I do not know."

No matter what the older man said, the baron could not bring himself to believe it. Surely, even a small glimmer of goodness would have remained in him, and given Lord Praecepsia's comfort when watching his own son's torment, he found the blind man's words difficult to swallow. "When I changed in the undercroft, it was into my father's true form."

"Yes. And the longer you stay inside of that realm, the easier it is to wear that skin."

"How do I avoid it? How do I stay out of Eradyę?"

"You remember what you are at your core. Do not give in to selfish temptations and pursuits. Like the apple." Solomon's lips curved to a grin, as he tapped his stick along the path and jerked his head for the boy to follow.

The baron fell into step after him. "How was I to know the apple held such a rotted core?"

"Did it not seem unusual how perfect it was, when every other fruit bore bruises and cuts?"

How foolish of him not to have seen for himself. "It did, yes."

"The evil in this world does not always present itself as a monster, but as a thing you find most beautiful. Take your father, for example. Why would a man who is capable of such destruction in his true form bother with social graces and royal etiquette? Why would an otherworldly creature attend Sunday Mass and feign the role of a doting husband and father?"

Why, indeed. Had the others in Praecepsia known what lurked beneath his flesh, he wondered if they'd shun him, given the way so many were fond of him. "I ask myself frequently. I don't know why."

"The answer is trust. The surface of the apple into which you almost bit down led you to believe it was just as pristine on the inside. Had you known the truth, you would have avoided, or destroyed, it. Humans are not weak, and they are surely not incapable of defeating evil. It is often that they simply do not know how to recognize its true form." He came to a stop on the edge of the forest, where his property met the trees. "We all play our part. To many, I am merely the simple and harmless blind organist. Even if my charge in this lifetime is to protect humankind, to them I would be deemed evil."

"And what of me? Am I not half evil? The monster?"

"That is your trial in life, Jericho. To determine what draws you most. It is not the darkness itself which makes men evil, but what compels them. Learn to control your impulses, to recognize malevolence cloaked in virtue."

"Like Bishop Venable."

The old man smirked. "You see? It is not as difficult as you think."

~

On his way back to the manor, the baron took the footpath through the woods, one worn down by travelers. The same woods where he had last seen the unusual girl with stardust eyes and raven hair.

Years of hiding away in forests had taught him to move carefully and with caution. The dagger at his hip served as his only weapon against anyone he should meet on the path, but the baron was not concerned about marauders, so much as the possibility of Alaric trailing his steps. Should his father's guard take notice of anything that drew the baron's attention, he would surely report back to Lord Praecepsia.

Only the sound of birds chirping and the light wind through the treetops filled the otherwise quiet and peaceful forest. One of the many reasons he enjoyed his time in the woods. The trail kept on, curving through trees and brush, until he left the main path and headed through a patch of knobby holm oaks, their twisted trunks so thick, one could carve out a small cave inside. Their sprawling branches made an enormous canopy overhead, and the baron had always thought that if faeries ever existed, they would surely make that patch of trees their home.

Past the grove, he reached the familiar woods from before, and when the sound of singing carried through the trees, a smile teased his lips as he recognized the flawless pitch and tone. He followed the music through the forest to a clearing, where the girl sat twisting flower stems into a sort of crown.

So beautiful, the way the dusky sunlight struck her hair, adding a shine to her long locks. And her eyes. Gods, he'd never seen eyes like hers before. Even as far away as he stood, he had the keen eyesight to pick up the many flecks of color. The way her long dark lashes batted when she smiled.

Enamored with her, the baron watched silently, feeling as predatory as a wolf.

Something about her sent warmth through his veins. For a brief moment, he'd considered Solomon's words, about evil being cloaked in beauty, but surely a creature whose innocence perfumed the air the way hers did could not harbor an ounce of darkness.

"She is a curious one, is she not?"

The unfamiliar, feminine voice hardened the baron's muscles, and he spun around, dagger drawn to face a redhead standing behind him. The woman must have been twice his age, judging by the lines in her face and the scattered strands of gray amid the red, and wearing a smile, she did not break her attention for the knife pointed at her.

He glanced toward the girl and back again. "Do you know her?"

Brow raised, she looked past his shoulder toward where the girl sat and smiled. "I'd say so. Carried her for months inside my belly. Stubborn child, that one. Did not want to come into the world with any ease, I can tell you that much."

The baron lowered his dagger, tucking it back into its sheath. "Forgive me. I did not mean to draw a weapon upon her mother. You merely startled me."

"Mmm. And might I ask what brings you to these part of the woods?"

He twisted toward the girl again, feeling that full sensation in his chest as he caught sight of her smiling while she fitted her handmade crown atop her head. "I merely heard her singing. Her voice is quite lovely."

"Like an angel's."

"Yes. Precisely. May I ask her name, My Lady?"

The sound of the woman's quiet chuckle drew his attention to hers again. "Oh, I can assure you, I am no lady. A thief. A sinner. Trouble to some. But no lady." Her laughter died to a wistful smile as she continued to stare off toward the young girl. "To answer your question, though. Her name is Lustina. Born of the light."

Lustina. He'd never heard the name before in his life. Girls from the village had common names, such as Edith, Agnes and Miriam. Her name echoed in his ears like a song.

The baron realized he'd forgotten his manners and had failed to introduce himself, so caught up in the girl. "My apologies. I am–"

"I know who you are, young lord. It was I who brought you into this world. And if I catch you spying on my daughter again, I shall gladly take you out of it." Her cheeks dimpled with a smile that matched the girl's. With a raise of her brow, she lifted her skirt just enough to keep from dragging on the brush and stepped past him. "Good day, My Lord."

He smiled after her and stole one more glimpse of the girl. Lustina. In that moment, the baron was certain of three things.

First, he had no intentions of staying away from her, as her mother had requested of him.

Second, the feeling in his chest was the undeniable proof that something still beat inside of him.

And third, Lustina, born of the light, would one day belong to him.

20

JERICHO

*A*t my desk, I flipped through the pages of the grimoire I'd picked up the last time I'd ventured to the bookstore with Farryn. The book was so thick, it'd taken me an hour to scan through it, and I hadn't even reached the end yet. I turned the page to an illustration of three women, standing around whom I presumed to be the messiah after his death, given the wounds on his palms and feet and the blood on his forehead. The text beside it described ancient healers known as the Met'Lazan. Humans, hand-picked by the heavens who were bestowed powers beyond the confines of mortal medicine. And they were believed to have been the ones instrumental in the resurrection of Messiah.

Apparently, they possessed the power to invoke angels and demons, but could not use their abilities to heal other mortals. I read on to learn that they spoke a language known only to the highest order of angels. One so innate, most didn't even realize their fluency in speaking it, until called upon by the heavens.

Interesting.

I skimmed the text faster, hoping to learn what language

it was that they spoke, but the ink toward the bottom of the page blurred, as if it'd gotten wet and had become completely illegible.

Frowning, I turned the page and found the Pentacrux described in the next insertion–a completely different topic from the Met'Lazan. I turned the page back and the ink had somehow blurred even more than before. I watched as the beginning of the text, which I'd already read, bled into the paper, until the only thing I could make out on the page was the illustration.

What in Lucifer's name?

I flipped to other pages. The text there remained perfectly intact, but when I returned to the page describing the Met'Lazan, it had almost entirely turned into nothing more than an enormous, smudged ink spot.

"Splendid," I muttered, flipping through more pages in the book.

An image caught my attention, and I paused on a realistic looking drawing of a black-winged demon in chains, body arched on the ground as if in agony. Just looking at it echoed a throbbing pain in my groin. It was paired with a description of Rur'axze, an incredibly agonizing sensation, exceptionally worse than the human equivalent of blue balls, which happened when a male existed in the same timeframe as a particular female or male--his mate, essentially. Even separated by realms, they could sense the other, and he would fall into Rur'axze, needing to be sated only by him, or her.

According to the article, the symptoms predominantly struck at night as the hormone that caused it had ties to lunar phases, and like with fucking werewolves, that piqued on a full moon. It was a condition known only to affect demons, which made sense, as my vitaeilem had lessened and the demon half of me had become more dominant in recent weeks. The consequence of Rur'axze was accidental soul consumption, or a type of bonding known as *enchainsz*. Unlike a true mating bond, enchainsz was a purely sexual form of slavery.

Much of the information provided, I already knew. The bit I was looking for was revealed in the next paragraph, which suggested diablisz steel as a means of preventing harm to the other person. Forged by the heavens, it was the only steel strong enough to restrain a demon from going after what he craved.

"Wonderful. I'll be sleeping in chains every night."

At a knock on the door, I closed the book and grabbed my drink, easing back into my chair. "Come in."

The door cracked open to show Vaszhago, and I gestured toward one of the two chairs in front of me. From my desk, I grabbed a silver case, opening it up to a dozen black cigarettes. Unlike the human variety, these didn't produce the godawful scent of tobacco, nor leave the yellow stains of nicotine behind. They gave off a much richer aroma, a pleasant one.

The demon plucked one of them and set the end of it to his tongue to light it up. "I don't think she likes me very much," he said, taking a drag as he fell into his seat.

"You're not very likable." I lifted a decanter of chthoniac with a raised brow, to which he nodded, and I poured him a glass.

"Maids seem to like me just fine." After raising the glass like a toast, the crazy bastard tipped it back, and within seconds the bubbly red was gone. He slammed it onto my desk, and I filled it again.

"That had to burn."

Jaw clenched, he shook his head. "Been a long time since I had straight chthoniac."

"As for my staff, given the nature of your kind, I'll caution you. If any of them go missing, you'll be at the top of my shit-list."

He chuckled and eased back into his chair, taking a much smaller sip of his drink. "If I decide to feed, it'll be on something more substantial than a poor unclaimed soul."

"No crossing The Vale to the mortal realm until the job is finished."

He took another drag and blew it off. "You'd watch an old friend starve?"

"Were we ever friends?"

"Did I kill you?"

"Well, whatever conscience you may have magically sprouted back then no longer applies. Particularly now."

"Why is that?"

I rubbed a hand down my face, dreading the thought of having to ask the favor. "I need you to chain me at night. And if I attempt to harm Farryn in any way, you're to end me without hesitation."

Vaszhago's eyes shuttered, and he tipped his head back smiling. "Do you know how many times I've dreamed of hearing you say those words? What a strange turn of events." Canting his head forward, he stared back at me, his eyes flickering orange. "The Jericho I once knew would not lay down his life for anyone. *Anyone.*"

The truth in his words took me back to that time before Farryn had been born, when I was nothing more than a walking corpse with violence in my heart. "She is the exception."

"And of all the wonderfully skilled creatures in this world, you chose a human girl."

"She fascinates me." I buried my smile in another sip of my drink.

"If I ever achieve being in the presence of one without wanting to consume its soul entirely, perhaps I'll sample what fascination you glean from mortals." After polishing off the remains of his drink, he pushed his glass onto the desk and held up his hand when I offered another. "What exactly is causing all of this *concern?*"

"I'm in Rur'axze. The only thing that can temper it is the one thing I happen to be low on at the moment." I'd been low on vitaeilem before, while submerged in parts of the demon world that had drained my angel energy. The worst had been when I'd stumbled upon the portal to Eradyę in the underground scene. The shadowed world where my father had hidden away.

"Vitaeilem? Have you not considered seraphica?"

"Seraphica for a Sentinel is the equivalent of getting a hand-job from a wraith."

Vaszhago snorted, running his hand over his jaw. "Surely, you feel something more significant than that."

"Not much."

"And so, now, you are at the mercy of your demon half." After blowing off another plume of smoke, his lips curved to a cunning grin. "If not for the binder which prevents me from doing so, testing the strength of your bond with Farryn would certainly make for good sport."

"Know that I would kill you. Painfully so."

"If she doesn't first." Groaning, Vaszhago shook his head. "You have me follow after a female who invites death with every bumbling step."

I smirked at that, watching him push up from his chair and stamp out his cigarette in the ashtray on my desk. "I've some diablisz steel cuffs and chains in one of the rooms of the undercroft." Left over from the times prior to Farryn's arrival, when the maids, particularly Evie, would indulge my occasional craving for pain. With my memories of Farryn lost, I'd had no understanding for why I'd woken from dreams needing to fuck something like my life depended on it. Had I known it was her the whole time, inciting those urges within me, I'd have probably ended up a dead man for tearing through planes to get to her. Perhaps losing my memories had been more merciful than anything. "I'll ask you to confine me each night."

He gave a tip of his head and turned toward the door before exiting my office.

One small detail still troubled me, however, as I stared down at the grimoire once more. Rur'axze held enough power to affect a mated couple across planes. The book had described demons tearing through one world to the next to satiate the incessant drive which burned inside of them. Aside from Cicatrix and the other birds, I would be alone in my search for Farryn's father.

I would need to find a way to restrain myself while scouring neighboring towns and villages, or risk abandoning the expedition to come after her.

Or worse, seek relief in other ways.

I exited the back of the house to find all three dogs waiting at attention for me. Cerberus stood as still as a statue, ears twitching for the first command to leave my mouth. "Come," I said in a stern voice, and he broke his stiff stance, lowering his head as he trotted toward me.

Lowering to one knee, I ran my hand over his shiny, black coat and lifted his muzzle, looking him straight in the eye. Black orbs stared back at me without a hint of tension, or betrayal.

"I hear you tried to attack Farryn."

With his jaw still caught in my palm, Cerberus diverted his eyes from mine on a whine.

"She is not a threat to you. She carries my child inside of her."

No sooner had I spoken the words than his lips peeled back into a quiet snarl. His eyes shifted to mine, flickering orange, as they did when the dogs felt threatened, or angry. A low and steady growl rumbled in his throat, echoed by the two dogs still standing to attention behind him.

"Enough!" As curious as I was to know what it was that he'd found threatening about her, I didn't like the look in his eyes. The murderous gaze I'd seen on a few occasions, moments before he'd torn an animal, or demon, apart with his teeth. The thought of him tearing into Farryn that way had me squeezing tighter to his jaw, affirming the warning from before. "You have been a loyal friend to me my whole life, but you threaten to harm what I love most, when she has caused you no harm in return. She has shown you the kind of love and acceptance most do not, and you would approach her as a mindless beast? You are better than this."

The orange glow dimmed to the black from before, and Cerberus whined again.

"You're to stay away from her. All of you. Do not go near her." I pushed to my feet and stared down at the dog, who sat with his head lowered, as he did when he was in trouble. "Dismissed."

Whining again, Cerberus reluctantly turned away, looking back at me with sadness in his eyes before he trotted off with the other two.

21

FARRYN

*T*he waning light of dusk trickled through the curtains into my room, as I lay in bed staring out at a soft glow that shimmered over the treetops, from the Nightshade flowers somewhere below my window.

Four days had passed since the arrival of both Vespyr and Vaszhago. In that time, I'd kept to myself mostly. Reading. Exploring the cathedral and rooms where I'd not before ventured. Always shadowed by the two of them.

While Vespyr tended not to hover, she checked on me frequently, always inquiring whether, or not, I was in need of something, and often, I wasn't. Much as I'd come to enjoy her company, I didn't need an attendant. It felt ridiculous. While my energy and appetite had certainly waned in recent days, I was still perfectly capable of doing things myself.

Vaszhago, on the other hand, remained a silent watcher. Even the times I didn't see him, I could sense he was there. Maybe one of the weird side effects of the binder, or something.

As much as I could appreciate Jericho's reasons for hiring the demon, I hated the lack of privacy. It was only a matter of time before Jericho would leave to search for my father, and I prayed not only for their safe return, but that my father could help Jericho and I return to some semblance of normal again. The separation between us had worsened in the last couple of days, with him constantly in his office, his face always buried in a book. Studying. Constantly. Obsessing over his lost power and whatever else had begun to consume his thoughts. At night, I'd catch of peek of him staring in on me, before he'd stride off down the hallway.

I avoided approaching him myself, for fear he'd bring up the bonding issue again, but my body mourned his heat, his touch. The absence of it, of him, overwhelmed me sometimes. Like he'd never left Ex Nihilo and only his ghost roamed Blackwater Cathedral.

Each day, I lived the tortuous reality of having him so close, yet being oceans apart. As his baby grew inside me, I felt as if I were withering on the outside, though not quite slipping back into the same dark headspace as before.

He was still alive, after all.

Earlier that afternoon, I'd watched him swim in the grotto room, the place I'd first seen him half-naked when I'd arrived at the cathedral. Though still impressively well-honed, he'd looked slimmer than before, his body undoubtedly suffering under the weight of his stress. Something I knew of all too well, as I had begun to notice the prominence of bones in my own figure as of late.

When not lamenting over Jericho and myself, I'd attempted distraction by inquiring about Osiris, Vespyr's supposed shadow friend, but she claimed he'd stopped speaking with her since the day in the library. Convenient. Seemed everyone was suffering whatever inexplicable silence had fallen over Blackwater. I suspected there had been more to Osiris, though. Perhaps more than Vespyr even realized, because I hadn't mentioned the blonde to anyone, aside from that night back at Aunt Nelle's, when I'd told Jericho about my dream. Since then, I'd suffered another nightmare of the strange woman standing in my room here, staring at me. I'd woken up screaming, and only Vaszhago came plowing through the door asking if I was all right.

As if Jericho hadn't heard me, at all.

While I appreciated Vaszhago's quick response, I hated that it was him. As childish as it sounded, I wanted Jericho to burst through that door and lift me into his arms. I wanted his words of comfort. His touch.

The light dimmed in the bedroom as night gradually fell over the cathedral, and in spite of knowing I'd never fall asleep, I closed my eyes. I'd come to learn that if I didn't shutter out the cathedral by a certain time, it would begin playing tricks on my mind. Sending shadows across the wall, or a creaking sound that'd have me feeling like someone was in the room. It was better to be asleep.

Through a dark haze, a different sound reached my ears. Not the creaking of wood, nor howling of wind against the windowpane. Loud. Tormented. It reached down inside my chest and squeezed my heart.

"Jericho?" I whispered, sitting up from the bed.

Wearing only my thin nightgown, I slid from the mattress, the cold, hardwood floor kissing my feet as I padded toward the door. Through a small crack, I heard the sound echo down the dark hallway, an outcry as if he were in intense pain. Panic stabbed my chest at the thought he might've been hurt, and I slipped out, following it around the corner toward Jericho's room.

As I neared, he bellowed a sound that urged me to break his separation rules, and I opened the door just enough to see him lying in bed, his arms and legs bound by chains to the posts of his bed.

Grunting and moaning in pain, he writhed against his

shackles. Pangs of agony speared my heart on hearing him suffer so miserably, and I stepped closer.

An unyielding grip of my arm pulled me back into the hallway. I swung out as I spun around, and my fist landed hard against a crushing palm. I looked up to see Vaszhago wearing an unamused expression.

"Where do you think you're going?" he asked in a flat, but threatening, voice.

"He's in pain."

"Of course he is."

I frowned and glanced back to Jericho. "What is wrong with him? And why is he in chains."

"The chains were his idea. Seems I forgot the gag in his mouth." On a sigh, Vaszhago released me and tucked a blade I hadn't noticed back into a holster at his hip. "He literally aches for you. Pathetic, really," he said, crossing his arms as he leaned against the wall.

A gag in his mouth? Chained? He'd essentially been imprisoning himself every night?

As though finally sensing our presence, Jericho raised his head from the bed, and I studied the sheen of sweat coating his body, the exhaustion in his eyes behind a shadow of something that sent a shiver down my spine. Need. A deep, primal hunger that I'd never seen in him before. Not even the night at the bell tower, when he'd made it clear that he was going to take me. No, the look he shot back at me right then was nothing short of ruthless and uncompromising. The way a killer might look upon its next victim–an inexplicable cross between thrill and malice.

"Farryn!" he rasped, giving a hard yank of the chains. "Come here, Farryn. Come to me."

The yelling he'd done earlier seemed to have affected his voice, giving it a deep, guttural tone that titillated every cell in my body and sent goosebumps across my skin. In spite of the fear hammering through me, a fevered hum of excitement pulsed beneath my skin.

"How can I help him?"

Vaszhago sighed. "Let him enchainsz and fuck you for the next three months straight. It'll burn off his pent-up energy, and he'll be right as rain."

"Enchainsz?" I frowned, keeping my attention on Jericho, who grunted as he pulled on his binds. "Jericho said that's basically sexual enslavement."

Shrugging, Vaszhago pushed off the wall, and when he came to a stand behind me, Jericho bucked and growled even more. "What's the harm, really? You'd be a hell of a lot easier to keep track of, and I'd know exactly where you were at all times."

I pondered what he was saying, and while I craved being close to Jericho, I certainly didn't want to become his walking sex toy for the next three months. "Jericho said it was dangerous."

A tickle at my scalp alerted me to him lifting a lock of my hair and pulling it through his fingers. "A bit dramatic. He wouldn't kill you. Outwardly. You might go a little hungry. Battle constant exhaustion, depending on your stamina. Perhaps numb–"

I swatted his hand away, frowning. "That's not love. It's sex and nothing more."

Vaszhago let out a groan and resumed his leaning against the wall. "You humans and your obsession with love …. Such a frivolous and complicated emotion. Useless, really."

"You've never loved?"

"I live by a simple regimen. Eat. Fuck. Kill. Repeat. A demon has no appetite for love."

"That sounds incredibly boring."

"As does your *love* life."

I sneered at that, ignoring the ache between my thighs as

I watched the way Jericho moved his hips in the slow thrusting motions of sex.

Dear God.

On an agonized howl, he arched up off the bed, his arms trembling as he pulled the binds taut. The silvery tattoos scattered across his body glowed in the surrounding darkness, so beautiful and mesmerizing. He looked like an angry male stripper, his glistening body both hard and pliant at the same time. Somewhere in the back of my mind, *Pony* by Ginuwine played in time to his slow and maddening thrusts. Need curled in my belly just watching him.

"Farryn!"

"Are the chains really necessary?"

Vaszhago smirked and peeked into the room. "If you had any idea what things he really wanted to do to you, it'd probably terrify the good and righteous baroness."

Baroness. I'd hated when Remy called me Princess, but somehow baroness didn't bother as much.

"I've had to send away three maids wanting to give him release."

I snapped my attention back to Vaszhago. "Who?"

"Does it matter? He'd have rejected all of them. He wants you. Anyone else is … generic."

Perhaps it should've terrified me to think of what he'd might do to me without those chains, but a much deeper instinct had taken over. One that urged me to ease him. "The chains are tied to a wooden bedpost? Seems he could break that pretty easily."

"Diablisz steel has its own tensile strength. It doesn't rely on the object to which it is tethered. Every link creates its own resistance. The longer the chain, the stronger it is."

Strange, how many rules of this world defied the laws of physics in mine. "Is there nothing else besides enslavement?"

"You could give him some relief, and perhaps he might settle. It is your scent and your touch he craves."

"You're certain he won't hurt me?"

"I'm certain he could. But would he with you?" He gave an insouciant shrug. "That would be an interesting hypothesis to test, wouldn't you agree?"

A gut-wrenching moan bounced off the walls, and I flinched at the intense pitch of it, as guttural as if Jericho had just been stabbed. "Farryn! Come to me!"

"I can't watch him in pain. If he were to try to enchainsz me, how would he do it?"

"He would bite the artery which supplies blood to the brain." He touched a finger to the carotid artery in my neck, which had to have been hammering right then. "It's the venom he produces right now that will make you complacent. Once it's in your blood, you are nothing but a helpless little moth in a spider's web."

"Okay, so avoid putting my neck by his mouth."

Lowering his finger from my neck, Vaszhago chuckled. "We would not be demons if it were that easy. In his state, he produces a particular pheromone, the effect of which is so strong, even you may find yourself less concerned about *love*."

"You make him sound like a sexual weapon of mass destruction."

"For you, he could be quite dangerous. But should he try anything–"

"I don't need you standing outside the door."

"I don't need to stand outside the door to know when you are in distress."

I recoiled, frowning back at the demon. "What? Why?"

"I'm bound to you."

Stupid binding. Not only did the guy shadow me, but he

could feel my distress? For a split second, I wondered if he could feel everything else going on inside of me.

"Fine. But I don't need an audience, so whatever little perception thing you have going, you need to shut it off for a little while." The truth was, sometimes Jericho did scare me during sex. Not in a bad way. Ordinarily, it sent a strange thrill through me, but even as savage as he could be, he'd always maintained a small bit of chivalry about him. However, that gentleman charm had clearly exited his body, the way he thrusted his hips and moaned my name.

"As you wish," Vaszhago said beside me. With that, he strode back down the hallway, and once he rounded the corner, I swung my attention back toward Jericho.

Avoid the teeth.

With a nervous step inside the room, I closed the door behind me on a quiet click. Light from the hallway withered to the soft glow coming in through the window. The tired creak of floorboards marked my cautious steps, as I crossed the room toward him.

His bellows died to heavy panting and grunts, and the rattle of chains told me he hadn't given up his fight for escape. "Farryn." Over the course of months, he'd said my name a number of times, but there was a deep, provocative quality to the way he said it right then that rolled off his tongue like a command.

I came to a stop at the end of the bed. The light from the window illuminated every carved line of muscle in his body, and the frantic pulse of blood which created a map of veins across his arms and legs. The silk pants he wore stuck up at his groin in a bulge, the size of which I'd not seen before. Twice as big as the last time we'd had sex, which sent another shudder down my spine.

"Come to me," he urged.

A delicious scent hung on the air. Masculine and heady,

with a hint of spice. It hit the back of my throat and saliva pooled on my tongue. Eyes rolling back, I gripped the bedpost as a wave of dizziness swept over me.

"Come here, Tu'Nazhja. I need to feel you."

The deep timbre of his voice struck a sensitive chord that shot from somewhere deep inside my ears straight down to my core, and a warm, toasty sensation settled over me like a cozy blanket.

In some distant part of my mind, Vaszhago's words from earlier echoed: *In his state, he produces a particular pheromone.* It must've been the scent in the air that had me feeling like I'd just sipped warm cocoa spiked with a shot of potent rum.

Stay away from his teeth, I mentally warned myself again as my feet compelled me closer. Standing alongside him, I could see his body trembling, and I rested my palm on his naked stomach, feeling his muscles twitch and flex beneath it.

"Yes." His voice carried a violent edge of need that innervated a tremble through my muscles. "I want to feel your hands on me."

I rested my second palm beside the first and ran my hands over his tightly coiled abs, my fingers dipping into the deep ridges of well-honed muscles. Lower and lower, until I brushed my fingers over the band of his pants, and when I glanced back at him, he lifted his head, his unpatched eye seemingly riveted on the path of my movement. As much as it troubled me to see him chained up, the sight of his big, intimidating body restrained to the bed sent another rush of arousal soaking my already damp panties.

Watching him, I snaked my hand beneath the band, and at the first palpation of his cock, a knot formed in my throat. Its girth made wrapping my fingers around him impossible, and its length had to be on par with his forearm, which I found myself staring at, as I ran a finger along his shaft. Jesus, the man was huge!

Tingles hummed over my fingertips as his vitaeilem traveled into my hand and up my wrist. Those tiny wicked sparks vibrated across my nerves and, like the sound of his voice, gathered between my thighs, fluttering like delicate wings low in my belly. I let out a soft grunt, mindlessly squeezing his shaft, while the electricity played between my thighs.

"Take it out," he said in a husky tone, his voice oozing with a dark and wicked threat. "I want you to see what your touch does to me."

Peeling back his pants set the beastly appendage free, and the sight of it resting against his stomach had me swallowing a gulp. For reasons I couldn't understand, though, I wanted it in my mouth. I wanted to feel the thick veins against my tongue, feel the blood pulsing as it hardened his cock. My lips tingled at the thought of his skin moving between them, those tiny electrical shocks tickling my tongue.

Yes, I wanted it.

I climbed onto the bed and straddled his legs, and the taut hum of his body silently professed his need. With his thick cock in hand, I bent forward, and that spicy scent hit me again, my mouth watering for his taste. The moment my tongue pressed to the slick head, he bucked his hips on a hiss. I took him into my mouth, only just past his tip, before it hit the back of my throat, not even halfway down his shaft when the pressure jerked me forward on a gag. Pulling back up on a string of saliva, I tried again, forcing myself a little further than before, but choked a second time.

He bucked again, clearly anxious.

Taking him into my mouth a third time, I only reached a quarter of the way down his length before I gagged yet again with the threat of acids shooting up my throat.

Damn it, he was too big! It was clear I wouldn't be able to pleasure him that way, and a quiet, mocking laughter echoed inside my head. A feeling of failure wormed its way beneath my skin, and my cheeks burned with the humiliation of it.

"Farryn, please. Gods, you're killing me." Jericho writhed beneath me, and he bit into one of his bound arms as he ground his cock against my palm still wrapped around his shaft.

"Jericho, I want to give you some relief, but–"

"That isn't what I crave. I want to taste you. Give me your saericasz," he said in a rough voice that sent another fluttery wave to my stomach.

Still feeling like a talentless slug, I slid off his body to the floor and slipped out of my panties, tossing them aside. The wild glint in his eye stoked tremors in my muscles, as I climbed back onto him, that time straddling his stomach and his cock, which rested against it.

He let out a sound of satisfaction, circling his hips beneath me. The wet glide of skin against my flesh mingled my arousal with his sweat, as he spread my juices over him.

"Sit on my face."

The warmth of embarrassment heated my cheeks, but I crawled up his hard body. The stretch of his arms at either side of his head made straddling his face seem impossible, so I stopped at his chest. From there, he had to lift his head and could just barely reach the apex of my thighs.

"Closer," he growled.

Swallowing past the lump in my throat, I scooted closer and rested my shins over his outstretched arms, my face only inches from the wall, which put my dreadfully weeping pussy right where he wanted it. "Am I hurting you?"

"Lift your gown," he said, ignoring my question, and the shaky impatience of his voice sent another shiver down my spine.

I did as he asked lifting the white gown up to reveal my bare sex positioned directly over his mouth.

His unpatched eye shuttered, and when he prodded his nose over my clit, I jerked forward. Breathing deeply, he dragged his face over my sensitive flesh and let out a deep, rumbling sound of approval. "You smell fucking divine."

The moment his lips clamped over me, I shot my hands out, gripping the top of the headboard, and let out a whimper. His hands curled into tight fists in the binds, and he lifted his head, kissing and sucking. Eating me like he was devouring a ripe, juicy peach with his lips. My stomach curled tight, my thighs squeezed his head, holding him there, and my jaw turned slack with a moan that wouldn't come out.

The wet warmth of his tongue prodded my entrance, before he flicked across my clit, the sensation tightening my belly even more, as I rested my chin on the top of the headboard. Lip caught between my teeth, I circled my hips, desperate, needy. The slickness of my arousal made for a wet sound as he ate at my pussy, and I cried out, grinding against his face.

The sensation fell away, and I looked to see him turning his head to the side, kissing my inner thigh. From that angle, I watched a protrusion at his forehead break the skin there, without bleeding. Two small nubs sharpened to a point as they pushed through, thickening with their growth. They curled back toward his hairline, their ribbed surface twinkling with silvery tattoos that matched the ones across his skin. When he tipped his chin down, one of them dragged over my slit, its rigid surface sending a flutter to my stomach as it vibrated with electricity, the same way his cock had moments before.

I reached down to grab a handful of his hair and rubbed myself against the horn's surface, humping it like an animal. What had I become that I could fuck a demon's horn? The mere thought of what I was doing sent a shiver of humiliation through me, but it felt too good to stop. The horn glistened with my fluids, every ridge of it teasing out more of my arousal.

At the tickle of my thigh, I released the horn and looked down to see his tongue sweeping over my flesh while growing longer.

Longer.

The length of it lashed out like a serpent's tongue, and before I could process what I was seeing, it slid up inside of me. I arched up, fingers cramping where they gripped tight to the headboard, as it curled up into me. Every muscle in my body stiffened with the sensation of tiny painless hooks rooting me in place for him, and eyes rolled back, I surrendered to the unnerving paralysis sweeping through me, as he fucked me with that abnormally elongated muscle. The tip of it curved just enough to hit a spot that sent a pulsing throb down into my thighs, and resting my forehead against the headboard again, I let out shallow, shuddering breaths, every muscle taut, coiled, boiling. A humiliating sound left my throat, a cross between a sob and a moan, while his tongue snaked in and out of me in perfect cadence.

"God!" I cried out, and I anchored my teeth over the smooth, unforgiving curve of the wooden headboard, desperate to bite down on something.

A dark chuckle echoed all around me, and he flicked his tongue faster, teasing that wicked ball of nerves. Pressure mounted across my abdomen, like a desperate, hollow ache needing to be filled. It heightened, burning in my belly like I was going to pee all over him. Tighter. Tighter. So tight!

An explosion of pleasure shot through my veins, and I cried out, grinding my sex in his face as the orgasm crashed over and into me. So powerful, it vibrated my bones.

"Release me from the binds, Tu'Nazhja. I need to fuck you. Now."

His voice carried a feral edge that sliced through my euphoric high like a poison-dipped blade. The long serpent tongue seemed to have shrunk to normal size, as it no longer stuck out past his lips.

Muscles weak and trembling, I crawled back down his body. "I can't ... Jericho ..." I panted, trying to catch my breath. "I don't have a key." The terrifying reality was, I probably would have if I did.

"Release me! Now!" He tugged on the chains, which rattled against the bed's frame. Snarling and flexing his arms, he watched me slide lower. "Make no mistake, these chains will not keep me from you."

Still glutton for more, I positioned my soaking entrance to his tip, and when I circled it over the bulbous head, he stilled.

"Yes, that's it. I want to feel your wet cunt. Let me fill you."

I wanted to lick the intoxicating words from his lips and swallow them. Whatever had come over me had rendered me completely obedient to the man and his demands. I couldn't stop myself if I wanted to. It was as if every need which blazed through him burned inside of me, too. As though his body silently communicated through mine, I knew what he wanted, what he craved, and I wanted to feed it to him.

At the first prod of his cock, I sucked in a sharp breath and shook my head. "Wait. It's too big."

"It'll fit." He raised his hips, the tip breaching my entrance and threatening pain. "Relax and let me inside of you."

Swallowing a gulp, I slowly eased myself down his thick shaft. Once seated as far as I could, about halfway down his shaft, I let out gasp as he filled me in a way that sent a swell of panic rushing over me. "No, I can't. It's too big." Shaking my head, I lifted my hips to pull myself off, and a sharp pain brought me to a halt.

Eyes wide with fear, I shot my gaze to his and noticed the single black orb, once a warm blue, staring back at me. His horns had fully extended, curling back over his head to long, spiraled points. An inky blackness traveled down his arms, turning his skin to the same color as his hair. Terror coiled up my spine as I watched him transform before my eyes.

Raising my hips a second time sent another sharp pain up inside of me, and I cried out, still impaled on his cock.

His lips stretched to a wicked grin. "You're mine."

I shook my head, my muscles trembling with fear. "No, no! Jericho! It's too big."

The scent of spice perfumed the air as before, and that warm, toasty sensation settled over me again. My muscles relented and the tension fizzled, my head caught in that space between waking and dreaming. The dark silence just before sleep. The same sensation I'd experienced when drunk, just before passing out.

Slipping in and out of it, I opened my eyes and found myself rocking against him, slow and easy.

"That's it. Fuck me." The sound of his voice wrapped itself around my senses, until all I could hear, feel and smell was Jericho.

In that blank, rayless place, he consumed me, and enraptured, I clenched around him, focused on every stroke in and out of me. I upped the pace and closed my eyes.

What had felt painful quickly turned pleasurable, and weak with appetence, I lowered myself to his chest, as he pistoned himself in and out of me.

"How does it feel, *mę amreloc?*"

I didn't understand the last part, but the accent and the way he spoke, coupled to the feel of him rocking beneath me, damn near sent me over the edge right then. "So good," I whispered, clawing into his chest, as he drove his hips into me again.

"Take all of it. Deeper."

All of it? It already felt as if he were on a mission to drill himself up into my belly. A whimper escaped me as I lowered my hips with his next thrust, fingers digging into his muscles as I stretched around him. "Ah! Jericho!"

"Fuck, that's a good girl," he said roughly, kicking his head back. "Now circle your hips. Feel me inside of you."

With trembling muscles, I moved my hips as he'd commanded, and felt the tiny electrical impulses dance over my flesh, marking his depth. A shudder rippled over me, and I let out a shaky breath. "Oh, God."

"Say His name again, and I will fuck it out of your vocabulary."

Ohgodohgodohgodohgod.

"There was a time you called me your lord, and as a young boy, I felt it was wrong to hold you beneath me." His tone carried a dark malicious snip, and while that wasn't entirely unusual for Jericho, the edge of domination and control sent a tremble of fear through me. The pressure inside of me eased as he backed out, then swelled with the slow drive of his hips. "But the truth is, I quite enjoyed the sound of it on your lips." In and out, he pumped his cock, the pain from before twisting into a strange comfort. A need. Calm settled over me, my body soft and pliant to his steady thrusts. "Say it. Tell me what I want to hear."

"My Lord, you feel so good." Much as I wanted to deny it, calling him lord prodded a submissive part of me that I didn't realize was buried until that moment. I'd always been in control of my life, and was never one to take orders from anyone, let alone a man. But right then, I wanted to be his supplicant. I wanted to fall to my knees and follow every filthy, depraved command he gave me.

"Let me claim you. Lift your head." He pistoned faster, my body jostling and weak with whatever odd, cozy sensation had come over me. "We can do this every hour of every day. I will bring you to climax over and over, fucking you until you are so full of my cum, you won't be able so much as exhale without it dripping down your thighs. Would you like that, Tu'Nazhja?"

"Mmmm." I smiled, biting my lip as the obnoxious wet sounds left little doubt that his dirty words turned me on.

"Then, give yourself to me. Let me claim you now."

With flaccid arms, I pushed off him and tilted my head, willingly offering myself. I wanted it for reasons I couldn't understand. Imagining his teeth in my flesh, the bite of pain mingling with the pleasure, sent another titillating rush of fluids down my thigh. "Yes. I want you to claim me," I whispered.

"Come closer, my love. Give yourself to me."

22

FARRYN

a loud screeching sound hammered through my skull, the same high-pitched scream I'd heard so many times before. As it pierced through my senses, I screwed my eyes shut, and at the first scratch against my throat, I shot upright and slapped a hand to my neck. Opening my eyes showed Jericho snapping his teeth, his incisors elongated to sharp fangs that dripped with a black substance.

"Jericho!"

His hips relentlessly drove into me, becoming painful as his cock swelled inside of me.

"Jericho, please!"

He didn't stop.

The black in his eye turned red, and panic exploded inside of me. Was this real, or just a dream? Surely, he would've stopped if it were real. He wouldn't have kept going after I'd begged him to stop.

As words floated through my mind, I reached up to his hand caught in the binds, pressing my palm to his. "*Strę vera'tu!*"

He slowed his thrusts, and the look in his unpatched eye held a shadow of betrayal.

The horns at his forehead retracted back into his skin, sealing to a smooth surface.

The black of his skin faded, returning to his usual tone, and I once again stared into a sea of blue. Confusion swirled in his gaze, his brows pinching to a frown as he glanced up at his bound hands then back to me.

"Farryn? What are you doing?"

I lifted my hips, and just as before, what felt like a jolt of electricity shot up into me. "Ah! God!"

"Fuck." Jericho buried his face against his arm and groaned.

"What's happening?"

"It happens before a claiming. The head of my dick swells up. It's to keep you from getting away, which is why I specifically told you to *stay* away."

No wonder it felt like something had expanded inside of me. "You're saying we're stuck like this? For how long?"

"However long it takes my body to realize I'm not claiming you."

"Are we talking hours?"

His chest expanded and contracted beneath me on a heavy sigh. "Farryn, when I ask you to do something for your own good, please just do as I say."

An awkward humiliation washed over me, as I lay across his body with his dick still firmly lodged inside of me. "You were in pain. I wasn't going to stand by and watch you suffer."

"And here we are."

I peered down between us, to where we were joined at our hips. "Should I let you finish?"

"As much as I *need* to fuck you right now, that might not be a good idea. You could incite it all over again."

"So, we just … stay like this?" Not that I minded. After nearly a week of distance, I'd begun to crave the feel of his skin against mine. Unfortunately, the longer he stayed inside of me, the more my body stretched around him and the urge to stir into motion tugged at my belly.

"Yes. My absolute hell. Feeling you. Smelling you. Wanting you so badly, I'd chew my own fucking arm off to touch you right now." His comment made me chuckle, and I glanced up at his bound hands.

"I'd call for Vaszhago to release you, but no."

"Absolutely not," he agreed.

"Should I massage your arms, or something? Keep the blood flowing?"

"Doing so is going to send the blood somewhere else, and I don't want to risk it. In fact, try not to move too much if you can."

On a deep sigh, I breathed in the delicious masculine scent that was entirely Jericho. "This was stupid of me, huh?"

"Asinine is the word that comes to mind."

"I'm sorry." I lifted my gaze to find him twisting his arm, as if studying a way to slip out of his binds. "Maybe I should've just let you–"

"Don't even say it." His brows lowered to a frown. "Come to think of it, how did I stop? I've been told it's impossible to stop."

"*Strę vera'tu.*"

"I'm surprised that worked."

I rested my head against his chest, and the steady beat of his heart sent a calm through me. Eyes closed, I focused on the soothing rhythm that had lulled me to sleep so many times before. "I've missed this sound. I've missed you."

"I'd have preferred Ex Nihilo over being this close to you and having to keep my distance. I hoped to begin the search for your–"

I reached up and pressed my finger to his lips. "Please. Let's not talk about him when I'm … you know. It's weird." The sound of Jericho's chuckle was music to my ears and brought a smile to my face. "This isn't so bad, really. We should make a point to do this when you're not so … monstery. I like lying with you like this."

"Yes, but I insist that you be completely naked the next time. Preferably moving."

I opened my eyes as a thought struck me. "Wait--what if I have to pee?"

"Seems I'll have to suffer the consequences of your weak human bladder."

"You'd seriously let me do that?"

"Know that you're the only one in five realms that I'd ever allow to piss on me."

"I feel so honored by that, in a strange way." The mortifying thought had me inwardly cringing, though. Only slightly less humiliating than the time I'd given a guy a blow job and threw up all over his stomach. A fear I'd had with Jericho's monster cock halfway down my throat. "Don't worry, I won't put it to the test. If I can help it."

"I appreciate that." He jerked his head for me to kiss him, which I did, then rested my head back against his chest.

Contentment settled over me. A feeling of utter bliss, as I lay atop of him, with the sound of his heart in my ear, and his long, easy breaths.

Until at last, I drifted into the void.

Movement jostled me, my cheek sliding across something warm and wet. I opened my eyes to portraits slipping past my periphery, and the unsettling sensation of the world moving too fast for my brain to process. I lifted my head from bare skin, drool stringing from my lips, and stared up at Jericho's perfectly precise jawline.

The scenery switched to the familiar surroundings of my bedroom, and as he carefully laid me down, realization finally crept in. Memories from the night before. Jericho in pain. Chains. Pleasure. Pain. *Contentment.*

At what must've been a look of absolute confusion on my face, Jericho smiled down at me, dragging a finger across my cheek. "Vaszhago unchained me early this morning."

I sucked in a sharp breath, recalling the state in which I'd fallen asleep.

"No worries, darling. You were lying beside me. Your gown covered us both."

Thank goodness for that. "What time is it?"

"Three in the morning." He leaned forward, planting a kiss to my lips. "Rest."

"Last night was the first time I slept without nightmares, or hallucinations, in a long time."

His eye crinkled with concern. "You're still having them? Here?"

"Yes."

"Of what?"

"It's nothing, Jericho."

"Tell me."

I didn't want to say, for fear that he'd worry over me and do something crazy like have someone watch me sleep, but I was drowning in my confusion and fear. I needed to talk to someone who could help me decide if it was a pregnancy thing, or a trick of the mind. "The blonde. I keep seeing visions of her. And then …"

"And then what?"

"Did you happen to say anything to Vespyr about my dreams?"

"Not at all," he answered without hesitation. "In fact, I

think I've said maybe two words to Vespyr since she arrived. Why?"

"It's stupid, and I'm going to feel stupid telling you this."

"Tell me."

"Apparently, Vespyr has an imaginary friend named Osiris."

"Yes." With a quirk of his brow, he crossed his arms over his chest. "So I've been made aware."

"I didn't say anything about my hallucinations to her. But nearly a week ago, Vespyr told me Osiris saw me with a blonde." Studying his reaction for any sign that he might've thought I was crazy had me nibbling the inside of my lip.

"With?"

"She keeps appearing around me. I see her standing behind me, or see her in the mirror's reflection. Unfortunately, Vespyr hasn't spoken to Osiris since, so I couldn't ask him any questions, and she swears that she herself can't see it." Each time I'd thought to dismiss the comment, I found myself calculating the possibilities of her, or him, seeing the strange woman standing in close proximity to me.

"You've not said anything about the blonde to anyone? Perhaps Anya?"

"No one but you."

With the back of his finger, he pushed a strand of hair from my face and bent forward, planting a kiss on my temple. "I don't want you to worry over this. I'm sure there's an explanation. I'll speak with Vespyr. In the meantime, get some sleep."

Nodding, I snuggled myself into the thick blankets, which he tucked around my body.

He bent forward to kiss me again, on my lips that time, and all the days of worrying over the two of us melted away.

23

THE BARON

The crunch of autumn leaves announced the baron's approach, as he strode toward the spot where Solomon had instructed him to meet, deep in the woods. The old man stood with his back to him, and the baron could not help but wonder how unsettling it would be to lose one's sight. Yet, Solomon did not so much as stir, seemingly confident that it was the baron who approached.

In the clearing ahead, what had to be fifty black birds poked around in the grass, in search of worms. He'd not seen so many gathered in one place since the day at Mount Helios, when he'd fallen off the rock and watched them circling overhead.

"Are you not tempted to ask who approaches? What if I were someone else?"

Solomon craned his neck toward the boy, revealing a smile, and turned back toward the birds. "I knew immediately."

"How?"

"The cadence of your walk. The scent of castile soap." He nodded toward the clearing. "And the birds."

The baron glanced toward the unruffled creatures, who seemed to have no awareness of him. "The birds? How would the birds offer any awareness?"

"They know you, young lord."

"How?"

"Ask them."

The baron slid his gaze toward the old man, studying him before he let out an incredulous laugh. "You're mad. I had suspected as much, but now I am convinced."

"It is not madness. Close your eyes and speak with them in your mind."

"I will not make a fool of myself by attempting what is impossible."

"Have you tried to speak to them before?"

"Of course not. I have no cause to speak to birds."

The older man's brow quirked up. "Then, how are you so sure that it is impossible? Humor me. I will not speak a word if you are to look a fool. Doing so would have me locked up with the Ravers, yes?"

"Absolutely."

"Well, then. Your secret is quite safe with me." He turned back toward the birds, tipped his chin back, and raised his hands into the air. "Now, close your eyes and speak to them in the silence of your mind. And do not question my sanity again. It is disrespectful."

Frowning, the baron stared back at the birds, who ignorantly went about their pecking, not sparing so much as a glance in his direction.

The man is a fool, he thought to himself. *A raving fool.*

I've always thought so, too, but he does make a good point.

The baron heard the words in his head as if someone had spoken them aloud, and on a gasp, he jerked and tumbled backward, stumbling over the exposed roots of the tree behind him. The hard ground smashed against his backside, pain shooting up into his spine, but he ignored it. Only a few feet away from him, a blackbird stared back at him, head tipped to the side.

Are you all right? the strange voice spoke again, and the baron looked to Solomon, who stared out over the field, seemingly oblivious to what was happening.

"Did you just speak to me?" the baron whispered, not wanting to draw the old man's attention.

Yes, the voice answered.

"I have gone completely mad." Running his hand over his head, he broke eye contact with the bird, fearing the creeping sensation that crawled up his spine.

"I can assure you, it is not madness." Solomon hobbled toward him, his walking stick tapping against the ground as he approached. "It is a bond you share called *vinculum*."

"How did you know we shared a bond?"

"I didn't for certain, until just now."

"Vinculum. What is that, exactly?"

"There are certain animals of this world who have an awareness, so to speak. They are familiars. Birds and cats are most prominent, and ravens, in particular, have the ability to slip into the world of the dead."

The birds stole the baron's focus again, as he sat mentally calculating the many ways he must have lost his mind. In his world, only Heaven and Hell existed, and those who spoke of Heaven were spared suspicion of madness, while those who spoke of Hell were subjected to torment and exorcism.

Where, then, did these creatures go to walk alongside the dead? And why had the baron been able to speak with them?

"What is the purpose of this bond?" the boy asked.

"The birds are the eyes and ears. Servants of your kind."

"Servants? You mean I can command them to do something."

"See for yourself."

Confusion clouded him, but the baron pushed to his feet and stared out over the field of seemingly oblivious birds. *I command you to take flight.*

Not a breath later, every bird shot up into the air as if a predator approached and circled overhead.

On a shock of laughter, the baron raised his hand in the air. *Now swoop!* He brought his arm down to emphasize the order, and every bird did as commanded, swooping down across the open field before taking to the sky. He raised his hands again, this time without saying a word, and as if compelled by strings, the birds followed his every movement, swooping and darting toward the sky, circling and scattering. Arm in the air, he mentally ordered one of them to land on his outstretched arm, and he smiled when a bird broke free to perch there.

A tremble of fear washed over him, feeling the weight of the large bird and its claws digging into his flesh. He imagined its beak could've torn holes in him as easily as a well-sharpened blade, if the bird desired. Instead, it sat preening its feathers, entirely comfortable to perch there.

"This has to be one of the most fantastic days of my life," the baron said, running his fingers over one of its soft feathers, and he lifted his arm to send the bird into flight. Not wanting to exhaust the poor creatures still flying overhead, he directed them to land in the field and go back to their aimless pecking in the grass.

"Still think I'm mad?" Solomon asked beside him.

"Yes. But I suppose that makes two of us." Still struck with awe, he broke his stare to turn toward the older man. "What are you, that you have an awareness of such things?"

"I am a mere mortal."

The star shape the boy had noticed before, in the corner of Solomon's eye, caught his attention again. "Surely, there is more to you than that. Tell me. I swear I will not say a word."

"I speak the truth. Nothing more than a mortal. I am from an ancient line of the Dra'Akon."

"Who are they?"

"Hunters, borne of the gods, but fated to suffer pain and die as any human."

The baron could not imagine one so knowledgeable and open to the impossible. Every human in his life would've surely shunned such things as speaking with birds and talk of other worlds outside of Heaven and Hell. "What do you hunt?"

"Whatever seeks to harm mankind. It is our duty to protect."

Thoughts took him back to that night in the woods, when he'd seen evil in the flesh. "Are there others like my father?"

"There are others, though not entirely like him. His kind is rare."

The baron had gleaned that much from his mother, though she did not entirely elaborate. "Are you here to kill him?"

"No. As much as I would enjoy such a task, it is not my place."

"Why?" It pleased the boy to know he was not the only one who could see through the Lord Praecepsia's façade.

"Because as I said, it is our duty to protect. And there are forces far more threatening than your father."

More threatening than the creature he'd seen in the woods? "What forces?"

"You."

24

JERICHO

*R*ubbing a hand across the back of my neck, I paced my office, my thoughts still stuck on the night before, with Farryn. One bite. That's all it would have taken to claim her. One bite would have turned her into a mindless, sex-hungry zombie for all of eternity. Though she would have craved it most from me, such a transformation would have put her at risk once she'd transitioned to cambion. And my bastard father would've surely tried to exploit that. A thought which compelled a lethal rage inside of me.

I could've punched a fucking hole in the wall because of it.

A knock interrupted my thoughts, and I paused my pacing to see Anya peeking in through the cracked door. "Master, you asked me to fetch Vespyr, and I've searched the grounds, along with the dogs and other staff. We cannot find her anywhere."

"When was the last time anyone saw her?"

"Well," she said, stepping into the office and closing the door behind her, "I suppose that would be yesterday afternoon in the atrium. She was talking to herself quite a bit. Concerning, but I felt no need to interrupt her."

It was possible she had returned to the mortal realm. My only issue with that was the information she would take with her, and whether, or not, she might feed that information to the wrong angel, who might then send the Sentinels after me.

"If she returns, I want to be notified the moment she sets foot in Blackwater, and bring her to my office immediately."

"Yes, Master. Is … everything all right? You seem rather stressed this morning."

Snapping away my gaze from hers, I strode around to the other side of my desk. "I'm fine, thank you."

"Very well. Oh, I forgot to say, congratulations to you." Her lips stretched to that wily, gossip-filled expression of Anya's. Clearly, Farryn had said something to her, and although it wasn't my first choice for everyone to know, I suspected she'd needed the support. "I hear you're to become a father."

Considering I'd insisted on impregnating Farryn, congratulations didn't feel entirely in order. I felt bastardly for pushing it on her, but to spare her from the same fate as Lustina, in her previous life, I would have done just about anything the universe commanded of me. If sparing her soul would've meant killing three hundred people whose names started with the letter T, I'd have pulled out a directory and gotten to work.

"Yes. Thank you."

"I never thought I'd see the day! You must be so excited."

The arrogant side of me loved the idea of an heir. The logical side knew Fate must've been drunk off her ass to grant me spawn. "We're looking forward to it."

"As am I. And don't worry, your secret is safe with me." She ran her pinched fingers across her lips as if to zip them shut. "I shall not tell so much as a soul."

"I appreciate that."

"I'll let you return to your work, Master." On those parting words, she exited the office, and I stared at the decanter of liquor set out on my desk.

"To hell with it." I poured myself a drink and flipped the pages of the grimoire to where I'd left off the day before.

In the last few days, I'd come to learn that the black scratches that had been left on my arm the day Farryn and I had returned from the mortal realm, when she'd clawed at me while I'd held her underwater, were the markings of an unbound soul. One removed from the body, usually in a traumatic way, like soul-stripping, leaving it with no physical host. They often hovered in close proximity to the *ję'untis*, those whose souls remained attached to their bodies, in an effort to compel them. The unbound couldn't commandeer a body, like demons whose souls had a physical form, not without permission from the host. But through scare tactics and a dark aura they carried, they could be quite persuasive.

According to the text, the streaks that had been left behind on my arm were the imprint of the stripped soul's dark energy, or *tę nebrisz*. The burning of the wound was a physical sensation of evil. The sharing of their pain.

Seeing as a stripped soul remained invisible to all entities, except the host or individual they wished inhabit, it was often overlooked as a culprit in hauntings and possession. Essentially powerless, the unbound soul could do no more than compel and haunt. While it probably scared the shit out of Farryn, the likelihood of it harming her was slim.

I had only ever witnessed a soul-stripping once, wherein it had been removed from its host. A torture so horrific, there was no mortal equivalent.

Burning. Flaying. Amputation.

Nothing compared to the agony of being unnaturally

ripped from one's physical self. Yet, I had watched it firsthand.

Syrisa.

My father's prisoner. The one whose name Farryn had spoken in dreams.

'Liar,' a voice echoed in my memories, and my muscles tensed.

As I understood, a stripped soul lacked the ability to ever return to its former body. It roamed aimlessly, dormant. Invisible and lonely, until starvation sent it fading into the void. Without the ability to fully attach itself to a physical body, it languished over time.

Memories of a naked woman with a shaved head, stretched by rope between two posts, flickered through my thoughts, and I sipped the drink in my hand.

I hadn't told Farryn the entirety of my encounters with Syrisa. What she'd done to me, *wanted* from me, and what I'd failed to deliver, but with the dreams and hallucinations Farryn had been suffering from as of late, specifically mentioning a malevolent blonde, I wondered precisely how powerless an unbound soul could be. Was it possible she had somehow made a connection to Farryn? It seemed unlikely, given how many centuries had passed since her soul had been stripped. Surely, she would have starved to death.

A vision flashed through my head, interrupting my thoughts, and I closed my eye and focused on the unbidden scene, a literal birds-eye view of a wall I recognized a few villages to the north. It surrounded the seedy town housed within called Dreadmire, a place overrun by The Fallen. Crime ran rampant there, and any human soul unlucky enough to be taken in was never heard from again.

Along the outer surface of the wall, carved into its chipped and weather-worn stone, stood an alcove, butted up to the adjacent woods. Within the alcove hung various objects on strings–symbols I recognized to provide protection and defense. The space contained a makeshift bed and blanket, which sat outside of a small firepit. I could hear Cicatrix caw in the vision, and a figure lying on the bed, bundled in blankets, shifted abruptly as though irritated by the noise, then turned over. Frowning, I mentally focused on the face of the old man, which was covered in dirt and grime. His hair had grown out, white and unkempt. One of his eyes had turned milky white, as if he'd gone half-blind. If not for the fact that Cicatrix could sense him in a way no human ever could–a sense I could feel as I watched through the bird's eyes, which essentially confirmed his identity–I wouldn't have recognized the old man.

Farryn's father.

The view drew closer, as if Cicatrix had swooped toward him, and the old man shooed him off.

He swooped again, and Farryn's father sat upright, the blanket falling away to reveal filthy and threadbare clothes barely clinging to a body that hadn't been properly nourished in quite some time, given the sharp protrusion of his bones.

Cicatrix had found him.

I eased back into my chair, exhaling a sigh of relief while the vision fizzled away. Part of me felt a burning need to pour a drink and celebrate. The other part of me knew better. Finding him didn't guarantee the restoration of my wings. The fact that he'd been tracked down in Nightshade was cause enough to cast aside celebration, because any human who resided here long enough could scarcely recall their own name, let alone the meaning of an ancient sigil. The trek to get to him could prove fruitless and nothing more than a reunion between father and daughter. I had to accept the very real possibility that my wings would be lost to me forever, but damn that sliver of hope burning inside of me. One would almost think me human, the way it titillated me to hop on my horse and seek him out right then.

I planned to leave for Dreadmire under the cover of night, however, to avoid being seen--which unfortunately meant having to leave Farryn at the mercy of Vaszhago. Though he'd proven watchful and trustworthy, I didn't trust anyone entirely when it came to her.

Yet, given the events of the night before, perhaps it was better I left.

25

THE BARON

The baron swung his dagger to chop a path through the thick web of thorns slowing his pace, as he and Soreth trekked up the mountainside. "What are we looking for?"

"Wolfsbane." Soreth stepped through a particularly dense cluster of thorns and jumped back. "Devils blood!" Red drops spilled from a small scratch on his forearm where a thorn must have caught him. "I've grown weary of this already."

"Is Wolfsbane not poisonous?"

"To humans? Yes. Extremely."

"What does Solomon want with it?"

The blond cast a scowl over his shoulder and snorted. "Offer one good reason why I should tell you?"

Swinging his blade over another ratted entanglement of thorns, the baron shrugged. "Because I may know exactly where to find it."

A moment of silence hung between them, Soreth undoubtedly contemplating the consequences of telling the boy his master's intent. On a huff, he glanced over his shoulder, his expression resigned. "When mixed with Nightshade, it is a very potent elixir known as *la'ruajh.*"

The ruse. He knew the language Soreth had spoken, as it was one his mother had taught him since he was a child. A language his father did not understand, and therefore, it had served as a secret language between them. "What is it?"

"It masks the scent of vitality by making you appear as one of the dead."

"But you are not dead?"

Soreth's top lip curled back as if repulsed by the question. "No. Of course not. Simple earthly flowers cannot kill my kind."

"What exactly is your kind?"

"Pure-blooded Elysiumerian," he said with a haughty tip of his chin. "Our ancestors are Seraphs."

Seraphs. Elysiumerians. All these words meant nothing to the boy. "In what part of the world were you born?"

"I was not born in the mortal realm."

"I thought you might have been from the place of my mother's birth. You speak her language."

The other boy let out a humorless laugh, shaking his head. "You are, perhaps, the most ignorant half-breed I've seen yet." On a growl of frustration, he took to the sky on a whooshing sound. Enormous white wings trimmed in glistening gold spread from either side of him, holding him up into the air as if strings tethered his back to the sky.

"How!" The baron pointed a trembling finger at him. "How did you command them?"

"Do you not know how to control your own wings?" the other boy asked in a derisive tone.

"I can summon them, and make them disappear, but I cannot make them carry me up into the sky and hold my position there, as you are."

"Tell me where to find the wolfsbane, and I will tell you how to command your wings."

He considered the question for a moment, then nodded. "Do you see that plateau up there?" Jericho pointed to a stone ledge sticking out from the side of the mountain. "There is a cave there. It is just inside the cave. Now, tell me."

"Call forth your wings."

"My wings … right. Uh, give me just a moment. I cannot always summon them quickly. Or at will." Clearing his throat, the baron rolled his shoulders back and closed his eyes. He imagined his own wings, black and silver, sprouting from his shoulder blades. When he opened his eyes, he glanced to either side of himself, finding nothing but a stretch of thorny bushes.

Cheeks warm with embarrassment, he closed his eyes again, really concentrating on the detail in his wings. The raven-colored feathers that bore a slight hint of blue, and the needle-thin lines of silvery metal. Yet, when he looked again, all he took in was the bored and unimpressed expression that twisted Soreth's face.

"Mary and Joseph, it'll be nightfall before you manage the task."

The other boy's words goaded the baron's frustration, and a growl rumbled in his throat as he closed his eyes and focused again. At a sharp whoosh, he loosed a sigh of relief. Opening his eyes showed the glorious black wings stretched out to either side of him.

Soreth rolled his eyes. "How did I know you'd have black wings. All right, now flex the muscle in your arm, as if you would lift your arm into the air. But do not actually lift it into the air."

Jericho attempted what he'd described and flexed his wings. His body shot up, but no higher than the top of a carriage, before he came crashing back down into the thorn-bushes. "Ah!"

The other boy chuckled, his mocking sending a dark rage through the baron. "Oh. I forgot. Once you're in the air, you must continue to flex the muscle to keep you up. And to fly, you essentially roll your shoulders back." Demonstrating, he flew off, and leaving the baron to untangle himself from the painful prickly bush.

Once free of it, he brushed a few lodged thorns from his breeches, pushed to his feet, and glanced to either side where his wings stretched out from his body. "Up and hold." He flexed the muscle in his arm again and he arrowed upward, that time beyond a carriage height, to the top of the trees. "Hold," he grunted, squeezing the muscle again. His body dipped with a sharp drop, and he let out a gasp, clenching the muscle tighter. Breathing hard through his nose, he eyed Soreth landing gracefully on the ledge a short way off from where he hovered in the sky. As instructed, the baron rolled his shoulders back, and his body sprang forward, the wind cutting at his face as he flew to where the other boy waited.

As he neared, panic gripped the baron's throat. His body hurled toward the jagged rock, and no amount of flexing could divert his path. He let out a guttural scream and closed his eyes, contracting his muscles. Both wings coiled back, and the baron hit the rocky wall on a hard *thunk* before falling to the ledge below.

Soreth chuckled again, the sound of it stoking the anger and humiliation burning inside of the baron. "That had to be the most pathetic display of flight I've ever seen."

"Sorry I'm not as perfect as you."

"That is a shame," the boy said, striding toward the mouth of the cave.

Grumbling to himself, the baron pushed to his feet and

followed Soreth into the cave's entrance, where the tall purple flowers stood up from a small patch of grass.

"Strange how it grows here." Soreth knelt to the ground, running his hand over the grass that had grown out from the rock. He plucked one of the blades, studying its end, which even the baron had noticed bore no roots.

"Solomon tells me you are a scholar. Where do you study?"

"Here."

"In Praecepsia? There is no university here. The closest would be Rome."

"Your universities are mediocre at best. I am only here to observe."

"What university do you attend?"

A high-pitched noise echoed over the surrounding stony walls, like that of an animal, and both boys turned in the direction of the cave's depths.

Soreth nodded toward the darkness beyond them. "Go have a look, while I gather the flowers."

"Why me? And why bother? Let's just gather the flowers and go."

"Are you not curious to know what made that sound?"

"No."

"Well, I am." He turned back to the flowers and waved the baron off. "And as the eldest, I am ordering you to look. Now, go."

"I do not take orders from you."

Soreth didn't bother to look back as he plucked up one of the flowers, holding it up to the light. "Do it, and I will tell you how to land properly."

"What good is landing properly, if I am mauled by a vicious beast?"

"You are like a terrified girl. No, in fact, I know girls who are far braver than you."

The baron's mother had taught him that a number of women had a power worthy of respect, so the boy's comment was not received as intended. "And?"

"Just. Go. Look."

"Fine. But if I am attacked and killed, I will haunt you for an eternity." Teeth grinding in his skull, the baron turned toward the back end of the cave.

The sound, which reminded him of squealing, arrived again, louder that time. After sending an angry scowl back at Soreth, he strode toward it, his body taut and wired and ready to swing out at whatever came at him. The light faded behind him, the deeper he ventured, and his eyes adjusted, as they always had since he was a child. A trait he'd once feared amongst other children, thinking something had been wrong with him. As was the case, there *had* been something wrong with him, after all.

In the darkness of the cave, his eyes could make out a soft glow around shapes, which essentially allowed him to see. With cautious steps, he scanned the interior of the cave, his hand set to the dagger at his hip.

The squeal echoed a third time, much louder than before, and the baron frowned. It almost sounded like … "Puppies?" he muttered, as the tension in his muscles eased. Only a little though, considering a mother wolf--or worse, a bear-- could've been nearby. Devil's teeth! If a mother bear caught sight of him, he'd have surely been mauled. And if that were the case, no matter his condition, he would've been sure to lead the beast back to Soreth.

He rounded a wall of rock, and the squealing heightened to yelps. Multiple yelps.

Tucked beneath an overhanging rock, he found a tiny black puppy. Its tail wagged as he approached, and cracking a reluctant smile, he reached out toward the small beast.

It snarled and barked back at him, its eyes turning a

glowing orange, like flames. What mongrel had eyes that turned such an unusual shade? The sight of its pathetic attempt to look vicious only made the baron chuckle, though, and he reached for it anyway, scooping the rolly ball of fur up into his arms. Wriggling in his grasp, the puppy snapped its teeth and snarled, but the moment the baron rubbed its belly, the wicked little creature calmed.

A putrid scent carried on the air, and the baron crinkled his nose. Gods, what was that stench? More yelps and barks drew him farther into the little nook, and there, he found more of the tiny black mongrels running and hopping around.

Still holding the one in his arms, he counted five more. Six in total. They whined and yelped and made their little squealing noises, which failed to let him know what was wrong. The scent grew stronger until it was thick in his throat, and he gagged, nearly dropping the first puppy.

A black mass sat in his periphery, and on a startled breath, he turned to see an exceptionally larger version of the puppies lying on its side. A pool of purple-colored fluids lay just outside of her mouth. *Wolfsbane.* Their mother, no doubt. Why on earth she had consumed it didn't make any sense, considering most of the animals knew to stay away from the notoriously poisonous flower.

The puppies gathered at his feet, their tails wagging frantically. As he reached to pet another, it bit his finger.

"Hey!" The baron drew back his hand, squeezing out the small bit of blood the puppy had drawn. The pup hopped in a circle and leaned back on its haunches, letting out a playful bark. The spry little mongrel then lurched toward a spilled drop of blood, licking it clean off the rocky floor.

All five of them gathered beneath him, lapping at the specks of blood on the rocky floor. The beast tucked in his arm sprang forward and licked the blood off his finger.

Frowning he sat the puppy on the ground with its siblings and held out his hand, squeezing out more of his blood. All six puppies gathered at his hand.

They must have been starving, waiting by their dead mother for who knew how long.

Another bit his hand, but that time, he only flinched, allowing them to feed off his blood.

"What are you doing?" Soreth's voice carried an air of repulsion as he stood over him.

"I found the dangerous beasts making all the noise."

"Do you not know what those are, you fool?"

"I do. They're called puppies. The most vicious puppies I've ever seen in my life." He chuckled as one lapped up more of his blood, tickling his finger with its tongue.

"Those are hellhounds. Demons."

The baron snorted at that. "Well, don't get too close, their puppy teeth aren't exactly feathers, but their tongues will surely be your demise."

A high-pitched yelp snapped the baron's attention back toward Soreth, where three of the puppies had wandered toward the other boy. On the ground lay one of the pups, his head severed from his body and blood oozing from its wound.

Mouth gaped in shock, the baron stared down at the mutilated puppy whose body still twitched. "Why did you do that?"

Collective growls erupted inside the cave as all the puppies set their attention on Soreth.

"We are not here to pity evil, but to banish it."

Hands balled to fists at his side, the baron snarled as viciously as the little beasts gathered around him. "They are harmless!"

"To one who is half demon, I'm certain they seem that way."

He swung his sword again, and another yelp signaled a second severing.

The baron shot up from the ground, turning to face the boy. "Enough of this! They've done nothing!"

"Do you not know what hellhounds do? What their *bitch* mother did while alive?" He pointed to the carcass lying off to the side. "They eat children because they are the easiest prey. Have you not heard of young ones going missing in the woods?"

"These are only puppies, Soreth. They've not done any wrong." As one of the puppies behind him lurched forward, the baron swiped him up and held him to his chest, then knelt down, keeping the other two back. "Let them go. We will go."

"I will not allow them to grow into the evil beasts that they will surely become." Before the baron could stop him, Soreth swung his sword again and lobbed off the head of the third puppy who'd kept on with its growling.

Fury exploded inside the baron, and he reached out for the other boy's sword. A flickering bolt of lightning shot up the steel from where he'd gripped the business end of the weapon, and the moment it reached Soreth's hand clutched to the hilt, it knocked the other boy backward onto the ground.

Snarling, Soreth shot back to his feet, and the baron flipped the sword around in his hand and pointed the blade at him. "If you come near them, by the gods, it will be your head on the ground next."

The older boy's lip trembled with his obvious anger. As if he had any right to be angry. "Keep them, if you are so inclined. But know that they will turn on you. Evil has no regard for loyalty. Which is why I do not understand why Solomon wastes his time on you."

With that, he turned and strode toward the entrance of the cave.

Sighing, the baron knelt to the ground, watching the three remaining puppies cautiously sniff around their fallen siblings. They whined and lay beside them, the sight of which had the baron scowling after Soreth.

"Not everything must follow the uncharted path of fate," he muttered, and reached out to pet one of the pups, who made a pained noise in its throat before kicking back its head and howling.

The other two joined in the song, the sound so miserable it hurt his chest to hear it.

After another few minutes, their howling died down, and he scooped one of the puppies into his arms. "I will call you Cerberus. The alpha and leader. And you are Fenrir," he said to the one that had nipped him first. The last trotted over to him on its own, and he awkwardly reached down to lift it up, piling him in with his siblings. "You will be Nero, since you are so willing to leap toward the sword. And though all three of you may be fierce, you will be loyal to me. But only me. And in turn, I will protect you."

Cerberus licked his face as the baron carried them out of the cave.

26

FARRYN

I ran a warm cloth over my arm, the scent of jasmine thick on the air. So long as I kept the water level below my breasts, I could stave off the panic attacks I'd suffered since my father's attempt to drown me. Unfortunately, the eerie blackness of the water still roused an unsettling feeling, as my head conjured images of *Nightmare on Elm Street* and Freddy's hands coming up out of the surface. Fortunately, I'd gotten more than enough sleep the night before, which seemed to have kept my nightmares and hallucinations at bay. Strange, how much better I felt, having slept most of the night, even while tethered to Jericho. But perhaps that was *why* I'd slept so soundly.

A clang from my adjacent bedroom sent a wire of tension through my muscles, and I sat up in the water. "Hello?" Through the bathroom door, I could only make out the bed and the window beyond it, where nothing moved.

With a dismissive shrug, I lowered myself back to the water and resumed my washing. Another clang sent me upright again, the bathwater spilling over the edge of the tub with my abruptness. "Who's there?"

A flare of anxiety shot through my nerves, and standing up from the warmth of the water, I was struck by a blanket of bone-chilling air as I reached for the towel I'd sat out on the edge of the tub earlier. After a quick pat down, I stepped out onto the cold tiles and, with cautious steps, made my way into my bedroom.

At the sight of a figure near the window, I let out a screech and jumped backward, my spine crashing into the wall behind me. A regal looking woman who wore an ornamental wrap around her head sat perfectly poised on the chair next to the window. Large bangle earrings and bracelets dangled from flawless dark skin, and when she smiled, a strange feeling of warmth and familiarity came over me.

"May I ask what you're doing in my room?" I glanced back at the door I swore I'd locked earlier. "And ... how did you get in here?"

A brightness shined in her eyes as she smiled. "I've been here a few days. Haven't you noticed?"

I studied her expression, trying to gauge whether, or not, she was of sound mind. "Who are you?"

"Come now, Farryn. You know who I am." She spoke in a beautifully articulate accent, a sound so melodic and crisp, it struck a chord of satisfaction.

"I've met you before?" In spite of the overwhelming familiarity, I couldn't recall where, or when.

"I may not always take the same form, but yes. In another life."

The moment she spoke the words, a vision of a cabin slipped through my mind. One set in the woods, with the delicious scent of broth and meat on the air. A cozy warmth burrowed in my bones at the memory. "Lustina met you. The cabin in the woods. Camael?"

"Excellent guess!"

"Camael. You … share the same name as my cat."

"Of course I do. Your Aunt Nelle was a good friend of mine."

"She named the cat after you?"

"No." A devilish humor flickered in her eyes. "I take many forms. Temporarily, of course. Sometimes, it's a cat. Other times a bird." With a graceful wave of her hand, she gestured to herself. "Or a human."

I schooled my face to keep from revealing my disbelief. "So, you're one of those shifters, like in a romance novel?"

A trill of laughter filled the room, every sound from her mouth like a song. "No, no. I am something of a free soul. I move from one form to the next. And when I leave that vessel, it returns to whatever it was before."

"Uh-huh." A quick glance toward the clock on my night-stand showed one thirty-seven. Of course it did. Which meant this probably wasn't real. "How did you get here? Like, from the neighbor lady's to Purgatory."

"I come and go here." She adjusted her skirt, an elabo-rately printed fabric that somehow seemed fitting for Camael. "Have done so for quite some time."

"Am I … am I hallucinating you right now?"

The flicker of her brow sent a tickle of distress through my bones. "Perhaps."

"That sucks." A downward glance, and I cleared my throat. "Can you excuse me for one moment. I'd just really like to put on some underwear."

"Of course."

I darted back into the bathroom, slamming the door behind me, and tossed off the towel. Tumbling into the coun-tertop, I hopped on one foot, hustling to slip on panties and the nightgown I'd set out. Even though it was still fairly early in the afternoon, I saw no point in throwing on a dress.

A sense of urgency goaded me as I wrestled my still-damp

skin into the tight sleeves of the gown, which sought to trap my arm halfway. "Damn it!" I pushed through on a hard thrust, cringing at the screech of torn fabric. Lifting my arm showed a slight tear in the armpit. "Oops."

I dashed back into the room, where Camael still sat in the chair, prim and proper and reminding me of a queen, the way her presence filled the room.

Which made sense, considering she'd always behaved that way in her cat form, like she didn't have to answer to anyone.

"Can I get you some water, or tea? Do you drink anything in this form?"

She tilted her head forward and smiled. "I'm fine, thank you."

"So, what brings you to Nightshade? The neighbor lady didn't kick you out, did she?"

A hearty laugh jostled her body, clattering the many bangles and necklaces she wore. "No, no. She is always very accommodating. I came here to check on you. And to pass on a warning to you."

"Uh-oh. Warnings are never good."

The humor from before withered into an earnest expression that had my pulse rate climbing. "I have seen a dark aura in your future. Although it is not entirely clear, I sense you are alone, but divided."

Divided? "As in, uncertain about something?"

"There is a duality that I can feel. On one shoulder sits revenge. On the other is love."

I thought back to the angel numerology I'd read about. Thirteen and seven. A glance at the clock again showed it was still stuck on the same time. "Revenge? Against whom?"

She tipped her head back, waving her hand through the air as if there was something flying around her head. "There is a dark smoke through which I cannot see as clearly as I once could. But I will caution you to tread carefully. And trust in your heart."

Why the hell were the warnings always so vague? Trust in my heart? What the hell was that supposed to mean? The last time I'd spoken with Camael, as Lustina, she'd cautioned me *not* to trust or follow my heart. Memories of the conversation filtered into my mind:

"Some fates cannot be changed, child. But yours can. You do not have to bear the burden that has been placed on your shoulders. Walk away from him. Urge him to sacrifice his love."

"I remember you told me in a past life of stories about *The Dark-Winged One*. You said he demanded a sacrifice. It was Jericho, wasn't it? You urged me to stay away from him."

"And you did not."

"Well, to be fair, your stories failed to mention vibrating feathers, so here we are." I waved my hand toward my stomach and watched her brow kick up.

"You are with child?"

"You didn't see that in a vision?"

"No. But as I said, my visions haven't been entirely clear. As for what I warned you about before, it seems you have temporarily broken the curse. Congratulations."

Except, her congratulations didn't seem all that celebratory. Unless I was mistaken, she almost sounded disappointed. "The Blood Moon Curse, where did it come from? Why me?"

"No one knows exactly where it came from, as it is as old as the origins of human beings."

"As old as the origins of human beings. You're saying, every pentad blood moon, a young girl has died."

"Unless she breaks the curse. As far as I know, only you and one other has accomplished that."

Catriona. Lustina's mother. She'd gotten pregnant by the

angel Gabriel, and according to what I did happen to know about the curse, only an angel's baby could break it.

"Then, the Dark-Winged One isn't Jericho. As far as I know, he isn't *that* old."

"In your story, it is. In stories before you, it was another."

"Who?"

"He goes by the name Letifer, bringer of death. An ancestor of Jericho who rules a barren land of hungry souls. Another realm called Eradyę."

I remembered Jericho telling me about Eradyę, but he never mentioned any ancestors there.

"So, this Letifer, he was the source of this legend about a sacrifice."

"Yes. Up until he fell into slumber. During which time there has been balance between good and evil. But should he wake from his slumber, it is you he will seek."

"Me? Why?"

She sighed and toyed with one of the bangles on her arm, spinning it over her wrist. "He has always sought out the cursed for reasons to which I am not privy."

"But I'm not cursed, remember? Jericho and I … you know." I circled my hand over my yet-to-swell stomach. "Bun in the oven."

"Your kind is chosen for a reason, Farryn. You suffered the Blood Moon Curse for a reason. Just as there was a reason you were reborn from Lustina, and she was born of another before her, and countless others before that person. Whatever that reason is, it still puts you at risk."

Wonderful. So, pregnancy hadn't been the magic cure all. "What keeps Letifer in slumber?"

"Souls. He feeds on life. And should he go hungry, he will wake and hunt."

A mirthless laugh escaped me. "And I'm his food? Like, what the hell am I supposed to do about that?"

"That is a mystery of the heavens, and I wish I knew, for your sake."

A cold stab of nausea curled in the pit of my stomach. "So, when you said that I didn't have to bear the burden … when you told me to urge Jericho to give up his love for me. You weren't actually trying to save me."

The bleak shadow behind her stare stoked a feeling of dread. "Those who have perished before you are the fortunate ones. The Dark-Winged One's fate is like crystal. I can see every detail of his future, and he will wake from his slumber. Unless his path can be diverted, there will be much suffering and death. Truly, the fate of the five realms has been greatly jeopardized by the love you share with this Sentinel. For, if Letifer learns that you are alive, he will certainly seek you out."

Hand lodged in my wet hair, I paced, because what else did one do when a Nostradamus bomb had just been dropped in her lap? Back and forth, I tried to make sense of everything she'd said to me, and after another minute, I paused, rubbing my hands together as thoughts arrived too fast.

"So, let me get this straight. I just want to clarify. You're telling me that, for centuries, this curse has existed–girls dying on a pentad blood moon, except for me and one other, who broke the curse by getting knocked up. And even though I'm still *alive*, I *survived* the curse, I *won The Hunger Games*, Jericho's great-great grandpa Dark One might wake up from the grave and come after me, anyway. Because I'm some Mary Sue who's *special* enough to be hunted by a freaking legendary baddie for reasons you can't even tell me."

"You've a very creative way of wording it, but yes. Essentially."

"Uh-huh." I resumed my pacing, biting my lip as the pounding of my heart told me a panic attack was about to make an appearance any second. "Did I happen to mention that I'm currently on the shit-list of both Heaven and Hell, too?" Skidding to a halt again, I set my hands on my hips, still chewing the shit out of my lips. "Yeah, for whatever reason, I'm Miss Freaking Popularity right now. It seems everyone wants to throw me on a spit and feed me to the gods."

"Well, considering not many of the cursed survive, I suppose the ones who do lead exciting lives."

"Exciting ... I'm about to turn cambion when this baby is born. Apparently, that's the angels cue to begin the hunt, and right now? That seems to be the lesser evil."

"You are not the average human being. You'd do well to avoid the comparison. Of course the heavens and Hell are watching you. If the stories are true, and I believe in them, your very existence is a threat." Rolling her shoulders back, she maintained her poised posture, studying me in a way that wasn't prodding an answer. "Although my vision is not entirely clear, I see no animosity from the heavens. The vision tends to be far more chaotic when darkness and light are at odds."

"But that's just it. They're not at odds if they're both hunting the same thing, right? As a matter of fact, the angels and demons are probably giving high fives on their way to come get me."

"I do not sense the wrath of the heavens in you."

Weird, considering I'd apparently pissed them off by bringing Jericho back. And I'd probably double-down the resentment the moment I turned cambion.

Still, I did feel a small bit of comfort in her words, even if I didn't entirely believe them.

Until she added, "The darkness I see is the strongest I've ever envisioned. Meaning, you are at great risk."

Fantastic.

Eyes narrowed on hers, I crossed my arms and surrendered my logic to the irrational anger rising up in me. "Why now? Why didn't you stop me from going to Nightshade in the first place? Why didn't you impart this sage advice when I was barely able to get out of bed all those months? Why wait until I'm confused and freaking out."

"Would anything I've said have changed your mind? Has it? If I told you to walk away from him now, would you?"

"No." It was the truth. Not even the prospect of becoming his eternal sex slave would deter me at that point. Particularly after she'd just told me that all of Hell still had it in for me.

"As I suspected. You are with child now. And regardless of whose *shit-list* you've landed on, you have a duty as a mother. So, my advice to you is this: Stay alive." Resting her hands atop her knees, she pushed up from the chair and twisted to the window behind her, unlatching its lock.

"What are you doing?"

"Leaving," she said over her shoulder.

"Through the window?"

"Yes."

"Okay ..." Biting my lip again, I nodded. I'd just had a twenty minute conversation with my cat. If she wanted to leave through the window, who was I to say what was weird. "Speaking of which ... back in the library. I almost died trying to get you off that ledge. What's up with that? What kind of prophetess godmother lets someone fall to their death?"

With a fiendish smile, she shrugged. "I saw Vaszhago coming for you. Suppose I wanted to test his reflexes."

Of course she did.

Cinderella got a fairy godmother who spun out a beautiful dress and sent her off to a ball to meet Prince Charming. I got a cat who tried to kill me and pin the doom of the five realms on my love life.

At a quiet knock on the door, I only glanced over my shoulder, and when I turned back, Camael was gone. Frowning, I strode across the room and peered out of the window, finding the crazy, black cat sat on the ledge licking her paws. A niggling thought sat at the back of my mind, one I didn't want to acknowledge, but the way it clawed at me, I couldn't help but wonder—had I just imagined an entire conversation with my cat?

Let it go, Farryn.

The unsettled feeling at the back of my head flashed a warning of what I couldn't bear to admit—that maybe the conversation hadn't happened, at all.

Cerberus strolled by, and the moment he looked up and caught sight of her, or me, and barked, I took that as my cue to duck back inside.

When I turned back around, Jericho had stepped into my room wearing black leather pants, boots, a vest with a white shirt beneath, and had a black, hooded cloak draped over his arm. I'd seen him wear something similar to the costume party we'd attended a while ago, but holy hell, he looked good. Real good. Too good.

"Going out?"

"Cicatrix has found your father."

I didn't entirely absorb his words at first, after the conversation with Camael that still had me questioning whether I'd spent the whole time talking to myself. "My father? You're certain …" Knots of anxiety swelled in my stomach, and I swallowed past the sudden dryness in my throat. "It's him?"

"Quite." Jericho's lips curved into a slight smile.

The knots tightened and unfurled into a wave of strange giddiness that had me caught between smiling and frowning in an expression that must've looked ridiculous. "My father is here?"

"Just outside of Dreadmire. If I leave now, I can make it there by morning."

Dizziness swept over me, and as if sensing that I was about to pass out, Jericho shot across the room before I even realized my knees were giving out, and with a grip on my arm, he pulled me upright. Too many emotions battled inside of me at once—fear, excitement, uncertainty—all clashing inside my head in a tumultuous brew of panic that threatened to explode any moment. Tears stung my eyes, and I let out an unattractive chortle.

He wrapped his thick arms around me, caging me against him, and when he kissed the top of my head, a peaceful calm settled over me.

"Please let me come with you," I whispered.

"It would be dangerous for you to travel there. Dreadmire is overrun by The Fallen, and there is no semblance of order. They are under the rule of an overlord who would turn you into a slave." His hand slid down to my stomach as he leaned forward and pressed a kiss to my lips. "The mere thought of one touching you sends a murderous rage through my bones."

"Isn't it dangerous for you, then?"

His lips twitched as if he might smile at that. "Do not worry about me. I've not survived centuries in anticipation of your return to fall victim to a bunch of ruffians. They've no interest in me, particularly now that I am essentially powerless. But you … I don't even want to imagine what they'd do if you fell into their hands."

"And what about my father?"

"He's staying outside the walls. They seem to have left him alone, but I wouldn't presume he's safe."

Nodding, I pressed my palms to his chest. "We shouldn't waste any more time, then." On tiptoes, I tipped my head back and kissed him. "Please, come back safe. Both of you."

He cupped my face in his palms and sighed. "Please stay out of trouble while I'm gone."

His comment brought a much-needed smile to my face. "You know I can't do that."

With a chuckle, he ran his thumb over my cheek. "Do not think I'm above chaining you to the bed."

"Pretty sure you already have. And if you promise to come back safely, I might let you do it again."

His brow quirked. "That's a promise I'll be sure to keep, then."

Sighing, I nodded, taking him in one more time. "Do you have to wear that, though?" I said, gesturing to his outfit, which had him looking like something out of a dark fantasy.

A quick downward glance, and he frowned. "You expect me to ride horseback in a suit?"

"No. Of course not. I just didn't expect you to look like every girl's wet-dream demon assassin."

"Human females dream of demon assassins?"

"You'd be surprised."

"We'll explore that conversation, as well, upon my return. As much as I would love to have you elaborate the details, I want to arrive by morning." Hooking a finger beneath my chin, he lifted my gaze to his. "We will also revisit the discussion of bonding. The possibility of doing it sooner than later."

A feeling of dread sank to the pit of my stomach all over again. "You said it would hurt the baby, though."

"I said that it could. If my search for information proves otherwise, I will claim you before the birth." He planted a chaste kiss to my forehead. "But again, to be discussed when I return."

With a reluctant nod, I feigned a smile. "Go. And I love you."

"And I, you." One more kiss, and he strode out of the room.

As tormenting as the thought of public claiming might've been, something else clawed for my attention right then as the realization of everything finally sank its teeth into me.

My father, a man I hadn't seen since I was a teenager, was here in Nightshade.

And Jericho was bringing him home to me.

27

FARRYN

*O*f course I couldn't sleep.

Huffing, I turned to my side as I lay in bed, staring out the window. Every time I closed my eyes, my mind wandered to Jericho galloping through the dark woods on his black horse, his cape flying behind him, as wolves and demons chased after him. Like something out of a dark fairy-tale, except I didn't want to be the damsel in distress, locked in the tower, waiting for his return. I wanted to be on my own horse alongside him, fighting them off like some badass fae queen defending her kingdom.

The sad and pathetic reality was, I'd have probably fallen off my horse hours before and gotten mauled by a pack of wolves, leaving him to fight off demons while he buried my half-eaten carcass.

Yeah. Probably better that he didn't drag me along.

As I lay counting stars in the sky, a shadow outside of my window caught my attention. Muscles stiff, I watched for it again, slowly lifting my head from the pillow.

Bigger than a bird, it left me contemplating impossible theories, like maybe Jericho had miraculously grown his wings and had already returned. Or maybe Remy had risen from the dead. Certainly nothing more plausible, like perhaps an intruder outside my window.

The shadow hovered toward the edge of the frame, as if peering in on me, but the soft glow behind him only created the silhouette of a man whose features I couldn't make out.

In a subtle move, I buried my face beneath the sheets and left one small gap to see out through. I slid my hand under the pillow for the dagger that Jericho insisted I keep there, even though I originally had no intentions of following his orders. Cold metal hit the tip of my finger, while I scoured my brain for the three words he told me to remember.

Stare. Strike. Stab.

No.

Slap. Stab. Stick.

No.

Stun. Sob. Sting.

What the hell did he say!

The window slid open, and I slapped a hand over my mouth to contain the scream begging for escape.

The dogs barked below, and the figure paused, as if assessing the situation, before he set back into motion, sticking one leg through the window opening. Swallowing hard, I breathed through my nose, mentally willing my muscles to stop their trembling.

Scream.

Scream, you idiot!

I opened my mouth to do just that, but could summon nothing more than a whispered sound. As if my voice had been cut. Frowning, I pushed again, but only a scratchy noise came out, one the intruder would've undoubtedly taken as a snore.

The figure still cloaked in shadows tiptoed across my room toward me.

Stun. Sever. Strip.

No!

Stun. Slice. Sever.

Stun. Silence. Sever! Stun. Silence. Sever.

My hands shook as he neared. Closer. Closer.

Oh, God, I couldn't do it. I didn't trust myself enough.

Shadows moved behind the stranger, and in the next breath, a flash of steel marked the path of a blade, and I shot up in bed, just as Vaszhago grabbed the intruder from behind, holding his dagger at the man's throat. How the demon even got into my room without my knowing was a mystery I'd ponder later. Right then, I was just relieved as hell to see him.

"I am a friend! I am a friend!" the man shouted, holding his hands into the air. "I don't come to harm. I know Jericho Van Croix."

"Well, unfortunately for you, he isn't here." The dark threat in Vaszhago's voice was as unsettling as the orange glow of his eyes. "But I'm sure that's why you snuck inside, isn't it?"

"I only chose the window because of the dogs."

"And what luck that you chose that of the lady of the house."

"Hers was the only one open."

"You say you're a friend of Jericho's," I interrupted, the curiosity burning inside of me as they argued back and forth. "Who are you?"

"I am Soreth. I knew him as a boy."

A boy? Then, perhaps Lustina had met him before, though his voice and presence didn't summon a single memory right then.

"You are an angel." Vaszhago spat the word as if it burned in his mouth. "I can smell your kind from a mile away."

In my sleep-deprived mental fog, I shook my head. "An angel?"

"I am, yes. But as I said, I do not wish any harm."

An angel! Oh, God. I scooted back onto the bed, the urgency to run from the room pulling my attention toward the door. Had he come for me in Jericho's absence?

Perhaps Camael was wrong in her vision about not sensing the wrath of Heaven in my future. Maybe that whole conversation had really just been a figment of my brain trying to make me feel better. Except, that it didn't really make me feel better.

Swallowing past the sudden dryness in my throat, I dared myself to ask, "Is it me you're after? Are the angels coming for me?"

"I am alone."

"And just what brings you for a visit so late at night, *Soreth*? Do all angels sneak into the rooms of human females, or is it just the exceptionally horny ones?" The way Vaszhago held the angel to the blade, taunting him, I couldn't help but wonder how close he was to sliding that metal across the intruder's throat.

Angel's throat, rather.

"I've come only to deliver a message."

"From whom?" Vaszhago asked.

"Forgive me, but that is none of your business."

"My blade says it is." The demon lifted the weapon higher, an ominous glint of the metal flickering in the dim light as he held it propped at the crook of the angel's neck. "In fact, it's getting thirsty for blood."

"Vaszhago," I pleaded. "It might be important." I turned my attention back to the angel. "I can pass the message onto him. We're ... kind of dating."

Soreth shook his head as much as the sharp steel would allow. "I must speak with him directly."

"Well, then, congratulations. You just won an overnight stay in the dungeon." With a rough kick to the back of the intruder's legs, Vaszhago urged him toward the door.

Soreth somehow spun out of Vaszhago's grasp and drew his own sword. Judging by the smile on the demon's face, I had to believe he'd released him intentionally. The two stood face to face, and after a good few seconds of staring, Vaszhago's grin stretched wider.

"That's cute. Crawling bugs." The demon's eyes flared a bright orange, and Soreth cried out, his back bowed and eyes screwed up in pain. "If you're going to play mind games, go for the gusto." With ease, he gripped Soreth by the neck and guided him out of my room. "If it's bugs you like so much, you'll find plenty down in the cells. Nasty bastards who like to burrow under the skin."

"Vaszhago," I said, as he slipped out of the door with Soreth. I wanted to ask if the cell would hold an angel. If it was strong enough to keep him from sneaking out and swiping me up in the middle of the night, because I sure as hell didn't trust the man who'd just snuck through my window like a seasoned thief. But then I remembered, Vaszhago wouldn't have chanced putting him in the cell if he thought he'd escape and come after me. "Thanks."

He gave a slow nod and closed the door behind himself.

I exhaled a relieved breath, hating to admit that Jericho had chosen wisely with him. He'd proven to be exceptionally stealthy and skilled, a loyal protector, even in Jericho's absence.

Still mildly shaken, I lay back in bed, covering myself in the thick blankets. I closed my eyes, focusing on my breathing.

Calm.

Chilled air breezed across my face, and remembering the

window hadn't been closed from the break-in, I opened my eyes just in time to see a shadow move across the wall.

Oh, shit! Another one!

I shot up in bed, eyes searching the dark room.

No movement.

Gaze trailing the walls, I watched for even the slightest flicker.

Nothing.

I scampered out of bed, crossing the room for the window, which I clicked shut and locked, then hurried back to the bed.

Probably just my brain trying to settle down. *Vaszhago would've likely caught whoever it was.* I had no idea what kind of awful punishment Vaszhago stood to suffer if he failed in protecting me, but it kept the demon on his toes. And again, I hated to admit how much I appreciated that. Jericho had always made me feel safe like that, too, and I was thankful he'd sought out someone comparable in his absence. I lay back against the pillow, and resumed my easy breathing.

A rough kick inside my stomach had me grunting, and I placed my hand against my belly. A hard surface slipped beneath my palm. Something that felt like the broad side of a fully formed arm with an elbow.

An adult arm.

On a startled breath, I removed my hand, and a cold, nauseating gurgle in my chest had me swallowing back the urge to throw up. My hand hovered over my belly as I taunted myself to touch it again.

God, please. Let me feel nothing.

Trembling, I rested my hand there again, and breathed a sigh of relief when there was no movement. A creeping sensation crawled over the back of my neck, as I recalled the conversation with Anya the other day, when she'd rested her hand on my stomach and felt nothing. How much of what I was feeling was real, and how much was in my head? Was anything normal?

I needed to talk to Catriona. *Tomorrow.* Storms, coupled to my concerns over Jericho, had kept me from venturing into town, but unless I wanted to drive myself crazy with questions, I needed answers.

28

JERICHO

*S**tay the course.*

I clutched the jagged bark of the tree trunk, pressing my forehead against the scratchy surface as a wave of agony tore through me. Onyx stood tied to a second tree, the poor horse probably wondering what the hell was going on since I'd diverted from the trail. The pain had struck just after nightfall, and I should have reached the Vendaris River by that point, which would've taken me straight to the wall of Dreadmire.

Unfortunately, my Rur'axze had other plans.

Sweat beaded my forehead, the ache throbbing deep. I breathed hard through my nose, my body trembling, shaking, *needing*. What I craved was miles from me right then and, if I had to guess, probably fast asleep in dreams.

Farryn.

Gods, even her name sent a new pulse of pleasure, as my mind conjured unbidden images of the night before. Her face glutted in passion as she sat atop of me, her throat so close to my teeth I could almost taste the salt of her skin on the sliver of air between us.

I curled my fingers into the bark, my stomach coiling with the urgency that beat through my muscles.

Go to her. Take her. Claim her.

No. I screwed my eye shut, willing myself not to move. If given reign over me, my cravings would have me returning to Blackwater and tearing through her bedroom, where hopefully, Vaszhago would have a blade ready for my throat. My obsession with the woman made me a greater threat than the infernal creatures who craved her soul.

I just needed the worst of it to pass. At some point, the ache would reach its peak, and so long as I stayed away from her, it would begin to fizzle away. Unfortunately, I was at the upward slope, where every step hammered against my willpower like a diabolical hailstorm.

In a small act of mercy, the pain eased for a moment, nothing more than a brief respite, if past experiences were anything to go by. I'd removed my coat and tunic, desperate to cool the flames burning inside of me, and still, my body shivered, in spite of the intense heat which consumed me. I fell to my knees, stealing every second before the next wave hit.

I needed release.

Even if by my own hands.

Though the effects would pale in comparison to fucking Farryn and claiming her, it might be enough to let me get back on the road.

I gripped the aching bulge in my trousers and shivered at the image of Farryn's soft hands touching me. Her nails digging into my back and those slender thighs wrapped around me.

"Well, what have we here?"

The sultry voice reached my ears, and I turned to find three women—one blonde, one redhead, and one brunette, all standing off about fifty feet from where I was bent over. In spite of the frigid temperatures, each wore a light, flowy dress that clung to their curvy forms.

Fuck.

Succubi.

They probably smelled me from a mile away.

"Leave me. I do not require your assistance." Often times, when demons would fall into Rur'axze, they'd seek out a succubus, the only creature who could withstand the constant need for sex, the only one that fed on it. They gleaned energy from fucking and claiming souls, the same way some demons did by eating human flesh. It was a mutually beneficial relationship, if the demon didn't happen to know where to find his mate.

I did, though. And I surely didn't crave the females who inched closer to me.

"You are clearly in need. We could smell it across the forest." The redhead stepped ahead of the other two, her erect nipples practically leading the way. "You look and smell utterly delectable. What delicious depravity the four of us could share. Tell me, handsome, how does a warm, wet pussy sound to you right now?"

A stab of pain struck my groin as visuals of Farryn taunted me again, and I let out a grunt, cupping myself harder.

"I think you hit the nail on his *head*." The blonde chuckled from behind her. "Speaking of which, I bet yours is stunning, isn't it?" Lip caught between her teeth, she rubbed her finger over the surface of her dress at where I guessed to be the apex of her thighs. "I want to feel it across my lips as I suck the cum from your cock."

"I get him first!" The brunette sauntered forward, ahead of the other two, the three of them altogether too close for my comfort. "Sweet Mother Lilith, look at his tattoos and muscles. And the eyepatch! He's a warrior, for sure. The sight of him makes me wetter than a Meridian monsoon."

"Enough! Leave now, or I will not be held responsible for my actions."

"What will you do? Fuck us to death?" The redhead tipped her head and chuckled. "One taste, handsome, and you will glut on the three of us like a wolf on sheep. You can hardly stand upright, you're so horny right now."

"Leave me, and I will be on my way."

"Stay," she volleyed back. "And you can watch my sisters eat each other's wet little cunt while I suck your cock dry. How does that sound?"

"Please," the blonde urged. "It's been ages since we had one so virile. Travelers are scarce through here as it is, and none are so ... rousing." She squeezed her dress, and as she lifted the hem of it to her thighs, I turned away, breathing hard through my nose. "You're in pain. Come, we've a cabin not far from here. We'll take care of you, however long you need. We will feed you and fuck you until the pain subsides."

Pain.

Pain had always offered some release, even in the absence of a female.

I could get them to attack me. It'd take something really shitty to say to them, though--as roused as they were by my scent, it would have to be truly insulting.

Unpatched eye closed, I cleared my throat. *"Mortesz ul' Lilith."* *Death to Lilith.* For a succubus, there was no greater insult than wishing the void upon their mother.

The redhead's eyes flared orange, her hands balling into fists at her side. "What did you say?"

"Was it not loud and clear enough for you?" I chuckled through another stab of pain. *"Mortesz ul' Lilith!"* My voice echoed all around us in mocking, and before I could react, all three of them were on me, their claws tearing into my neck and arms, teeth in my muscles. Ear-piercing screams had me flinching as I let them take their anger out on my flesh, my muscles burning with every poison-tipped scratch of their nails.

"I will rip your flesh from your bones!" The blonde screamed and lashed at my throat. "May the infernal gods feed on your remains!"

I wanted to laugh at that, to tell her the infernal creatures would get no enjoyment from my cursed bones, but instead, I focused on the scorching flames that snaked beneath my skin, as the venom in her nails sank its teeth in me.

The brunette scored a line down my back and bit down into my shoulder. Red sailed a hard kick to my groin. A jolt of agony shot up into my throat, and I coughed, choking on the intense pain that had me bent over myself. My muscles shook with the urge to throttle her, but instead, I forced myself to concentrate on the numbing ache of her attack. "Fuck!" Blackness seeped into my periphery, my balls throbbing and burning as if they might explode.

Another few minutes, and they seemed to grow tired of the attack, each one of them dropping away.

I could only imagine what I must've looked like then. Bleeding. Trembling. Torn apart.

"You will get no release. May you suffer through the night," Red said, and she shot into the darkness, her flowy dress trailing after her.

The blonde spat on my back, then followed behind her.

The other must've left ahead of them, as I didn't see her anywhere.

Once they were out of sight, I exhaled a shaky breath, taking in the extent of my wounds. Fire blazed over my skin, crackling and hissing as their poison burrowed deeper.

At a flash of Farryn's face tipped back in ecstasy, I groaned. "No, no!" I didn't want to make the association with her and the pain I felt then, but somehow my mind mingled the two. As the ache spread across my back and neck and arms, I rested my forehead against the dirt, knees bent beneath me, my thoughts anchored to Farryn. Her moans. The feel of her soft body around my cock.

I shoved my hand down into my leathers, and a shudder of pleasure coiled in my stomach. Frantic, I unlatched my pants and sprang myself free, releasing a held breath when I found relief in the pressure against my shaft. Up and down, I stroked myself, and at a flare of pain, I grunted and worked my hips to the imagined thrusts into Farryn's tight hole. Gods, she had every muscle burning, every breath stuttering out of me, as I fucked my own palm.

I bit down on my bicep, outstretched beside me, while stroking myself harder. Faster. Imagining how good she'd feel right then.

The sounds and sights and smells danced through my memories like lust grenades. The pressure heightened, pulling tight. So fucking tight. Until it finally snapped and hot jets of release spilled out onto my hand. Pulse after pulse, I came so hard, tiny jolts of lightning hummed over my skin, rendering me lightheaded. I grunted, stomach twitching, as I pumped out every drop of cum into a pool beneath me. A relieved smile teased my lips, while I remained bent over myself, breathing, savoring the intense pleasure still coursing through me.

Something dark moved in my periphery.

Weak with rapture, I turned my head to find the brunette from before stepping out from behind a tree, her eyes alight with something that fucking destroyed the euphoria still crashing over me.

"You're a Sentinel!" she whisper-yelled, tiptoeing toward me.

"Close enough." I just needed a moment to catch my

breath, and I'd get back on the road. Eye screwed shut, I groaned at the poison still working itself over me. The effect would last a couple of hours, which would make for a miserable ride to Dreadmire, unless I had enough vitaeilem in me to heal some of it.

"Please, Jericho. I'm starving."

Frowning, I turned toward where the brunette had stood moments before. In her place was a face I recognized, one so ill-fitted there, I wondered if I'd fallen into dreams.

"This is who you fantasize, isn't it? Her?" Long, black hair framed the soft glow of her face. No, not her face. Farryn's. Down to the stardust eyes and the smattering of tiny freckles over the bridge of her nose.

Fuck. "You're not her."

"I am. Do you not feel it?"

My stomach turned at that. The ache from before rising up into my throat once again. The sight of her must've incited a new wave. A new craving.

No.

No!

With renewed confidence, she stepped closer. "You want me. I know you do. I can smell it on you. Claim me. Fuck me, Jericho," she said in a voice that sounded too much like Farryn's. Too much.

I cast my gaze toward the ground, refusing to look at her, and shook my head. A cramping knot of pain twisted in my groin, sending a shudder through my muscles.

"She is your only weakness, isn't she? You would suffer eternal hell for her. I saw it in your thoughts. Oh, I've yearned for that my whole life."

I rested my head against my forearm, breathing hard as my cock filled with new blood and my hips begged to thrust into something warm and inviting. "Please, leave me. If there is any ounce of mercy in you, leave me now."

"No. You're going to make love to me, Jericho. Filthy, passionate love. Whether you want to, or not. I'm going to feed off you, and you're going to take from me and ease your pain." A scratching sound drew my attention to her once more, and her dress crumpled at her feet.

Panic hammered through me, as I took in her naked form.

Every inch of it familiar.

Beautiful and perfect.

Everything I desired and craved.

Farryn.

29

FARRYN

 y eyes snapped open on a gasped breath, and I shot up in bed, my head still caught up in the last minute of my nightmare.

A cold hollow burned inside my chest as I recalled Jericho in the woods, his body glistening with sweat, as he held another woman, a brunette, pinned to the tree while he took her roughly from behind. So real, the overwhelming scent of sex and the sounds of her moaning over their slapping skin still invaded my senses. My muscles tensed and twisted as I watched his ass flexing into her, but the worst was when he'd turned toward me, as the watcher in my dream, and the look of absolute intoxication written on his face as he'd glutted on her body.

Throwing back the covers, I scrambled out of bed and rushed toward the bathroom, only making it in time to expel the frothy, black liquid that shot out into the toilet bowl. My throat wobbled as I stared down at the unnatural-colored vomit, burning with the acids that sizzled in my mouth. The sadness and shock that'd pounded through me moments before spooled in my gut, pulling tension through my muscles. Irrational anger wound tight inside of me.

He wouldn't.

Would he have, though? I'd seen him the night before, writhing with the need to screw something. Vaszhago had told me that he would've rejected the maids, wanting only me, but what if it had gotten bad enough? What if his pain had become so unbearable that he had no choice but to seek out another?

Was I the type of woman who could cast my dignity aside for that?

No.

Unfortunately, I was a selfish devourer of jealousy, and though I hated the thought of him suffering, particularly alone in the woods, I couldn't forgive him for seeking out another. Especially after having pushed me away all week.

The rigidity in my muscles pulled tighter, and I pushed myself to my feet, taking in the tired, frail look of my face in the mirror. At a flash of the beautiful brunette from the dream, one with a pale curvy body whose bones didn't peek from beneath her skin, I looked away from myself.

After a quick rinse of my mouth, I returned to my bed, from where I stared out at the stars in the sky, wishing they could tell me where he was, what he was doing.

Stop it, Farryn. Stop this!

It wasn't like me to let my emotions hook themselves so deeply. I'd have blamed hormones, but at just under four months of pregnancy?

I needed to get out of the cathedral, to breathe in fresh air and loosen myself of these silly thoughts and worries. I'd make a point to visit Catriona the following day, come Hell, or hailstorm. Chatting with her would surely ease some of the uncertainties swirling inside my head.

After all, I knew in my heart that Jericho wouldn't have indulged in another woman.

Not if it was me he coveted.

30

THE BARON

Fresh wounds flared in protest as the baron removed his tunic and tossed it on the sandy shore along the river. Ordinarily, he'd have washed himself in the elaborate bath house back at the manor, where one of the servants would have attended to him, but he did not care to put the bishop's harsh punishment on display.

Muscles tense and trembling, he stepped carefully down into the icy water, dreading the moment he'd submerge his whole body. Drawing in a tight breath, he sank below the surface on one quick dip, and though the frigid water was enough to jar his heart, the numbing bliss of it kept him immersed in its watery cage. The fire which had blazed across his back, where Bishop Venable had torn open old scars with a new whipping toy, sizzled away in the wintry depths, and the baron was hard-pressed to emerge.

His lungs pounded for one sip of air, though, and the boy pushed up out of the water, eyes opening on Drystan, who stood at the shoreline, his expression downcast.

"You are the last I wish to lay eyes on," the baron grumbled, wiping water from his face. The chilled air bit at his wet skin, his bones and muscles stiff and thick. He hadn't spoken to his cousin since the day in the undercroft, when Drystan had confessed to seeing him heal his own wounds.

"I did not want to tell him. You saw what he did. What he was doing."

"And did I not suffer every day since? Where are your fresh wounds, Cousin?"

Drystan winced, his hands knotting the hem of his tunic as he fidgeted. "My punishment is your silence."

The baron let out a mirthless chuckle as he cupped himself and emerged from the water, swiping up his own discarded tunic. "Then, I shall keep with the torment."

Drystan's hands balled into fists as he lurched forward. "Please. You are my only friend. It is not my intent to remain at odds with you."

"And it is not my intent to remain friends with one who would betray me. One who would break for such meager punishment." He slipped his tunic over his wet torso and reached for his breeches next, yanking one leg over his damp skin.

"Forgive me, but I am not like you, My Lord. Whatever fondness and tolerance you seem to have for pain is not one we share."

"No. You are not like me, at all, I suppose." Gaze cast downward, he fastened the laces of his leather breeches and yanked on his boots. "Because were that you, I would not have uttered so much as a breath." The baron lifted his gaze to find Drystan's brows pinched together, his eyes brimming with torment. "I was your friend. But friends, we are no more." He strode past Drystan, leaving the other boy there by the river.

Once far enough into the woods, the baron hid behind the thick trunk of a nearby tree, watching for the moment when the other boy would tire of standing there and leave.

An exceptionally long time passed while his cousin seemed to stare off toward the water, before Drystan gave a glance around, and the baron ducked back when his eyes scanned over the trees. Not a moment later, a flash of movement at Drystan's back drew the baron's eyes toward the unfurling of two brown wings that spanned either side of his cousin.

A beat of shock tore through the baron, his eyes fixed on the wings, which appeared smaller than either his, or Soreth's. Could they even carry his lanky body into the air? His question was met with quiet grunts and growls of frustration, as Drystan hopped, seemingly desperate to take flight.

Given the baron's certainty that they shared the same father, he'd suspected that Drystan likely harbored similar traits as himself, though he would not dare question the boy. Not after what had happened in the undercroft. Instead, he watched with amusement, as Drystan struggled to get off the ground, and after another few tries, he let out a bellow of anger that echoed through the trees. Birds scattered overhead, momentarily distracting the baron, and when his gaze landed on Drystan again, the wings had tucked themselves back into his flesh.

The sight left a bitter taste in his mouth, not so much the secrecy of what he'd seen, but the hypocrisy and denial. What conversations they could have shared, if only his cousin had not proven to be a conspirator to Bishop Venable. They could have been the best of friends, but the baron had never felt more distant to his cousin than right then.

When Drystan finally set on the path back toward the manor, the baron headed in the opposite direction, deeper into the woods. It was not long before he neared an abandoned homestead, one thought to be haunted by the family who had been brutally murdered by what rumor had described as a pack of wolves, given the state of their remains.

Of course, he had never believed such nonsense.

It had seemed the perfect place to hide his new pets, seeing as the baron was certain his father would have had them destroyed back at the manor. Twice a day, he made a point to visit them, bringing them scraps of food and water. For the most part, they slept, but sometimes he'd come upon the cabin hearing them growl in play, or howl in loneliness. Those were the times he feared someone might find them and destroy them, as Soreth had done to their siblings.

As he approached the clearing where the cabin sat, however, the sound of giggling carried on the air, and frowning, he slowed his steps.

"My, aren't you a frisky little beast!"

The melodic voice he recognized instantly prompted the baron to duck behind a thicket, and he followed the sound to the east side of the cabin, where the giggles grew louder and danced over the back of his neck like silk ribbons. There, sitting in the high weeds, he found the raven-haired girl, and at her feet, tromping the weed stalks, the three puppies pounced at each other in play.

Panic wound through his muscles, the uncertainty of whether, or not, the dogs might attack her still prodding the back of his mind. But as he watched them play and bark, it became clear the little mongrels meant her no harm.

Fenrir's tiny tail wagged as he barked and nipped at the hem of her dress, but instead of growing angry with him, she chuckled and tapped at his tail, inciting a game of chase with it, as the puppy spun around in circles.

The baron snickered, his attention focused on the locks of hair that slid over her shoulders when she bent forward to pet Cerberus. She lifted his small body up into the air and planted a kiss atop his head, and the baron wondered what it would feel like to be the object of her affection. To have her look upon him in that adoring way that made him want to grab her face and bite her perfect heart-shaped lips. Tension wound inside of him, and he licked his own lips imagining such a thing.

After watching them play a bit longer, he whistled for the dogs while still tucked behind the brush. The girl jumped to her feet, eyes scanning the surrounding trees.

All three dogs trotted away from her, toward where he knelt to keep out of her line of view. Gaze to the ground, he contemplated what to do next.

Should I make myself known to her? It would've been rude, otherwise.

What would he say, though? Only those with perverse intentions spied on young girls that way, even if she was only slightly younger than himself. However, the woods were a perfect opportunity, without prying eyes and the pressure of formality, and he most certainly wanted the opportunity to talk to her.

To hear his name on her lips and watch her bow in deference, once she learned his stature.

When he lifted his gaze toward the house again, though, the girl had disappeared.

31

JERICHO

"Do not come any closer." Palm crushing the tree bark, I remained bent over myself, clutching my groin with my other hand.

"Look at me, Jericho," the brunette spoke in a stolen voice that sent a shudder through me--the perfect pitch and tone belonging to Farryn. "Tell me you do not want what you see."

"I do not–" A stab of pain struck low in my gut, the ache traveling straight to my balls.

The succubus chuckled, and though I refused to look in her direction, the strong scent on the air told me she was closer than before. "I do admire a man so taken by a woman that he would suffer unimaginable pain. Do you know I once watched a demon in Rur'axze have sex with a deer carcass? Surely, I am far more appealing than that."

"I do not want to hurt you, and I am urging you to leave me."

"Hurt me? I quite welcome the pain with pleasure. Tell me, lover. Does she like it when you bind her arms? When you spank her red?"

Breaths stuttering, I rested my forehead against the dirt,

wheezing as the pain took hold. An ache at my skull marked the protrusion of bone, as my horns pushed through flesh, and I lifted my head as the pleasure of feeling them harden and grow struck as painfully erotic as my hardening cock.

Thoughts of Farryn rubbing herself against their surface the night before had me dragging them against the dirt, desperate for that sensation, and the tips of my fingers turned an inky black, which crawled up my arm, illuminating tattoos across my skin.

Fuck. *Fuck*!

I couldn't stop it. Part of me didn't want to, the ecstasy of taking my demon form drawing me further away from my resistance.

"I would let you do all manner of things to me. Willingly. Or not, if you'd prefer a bit of force. I'll put up a chase, if you like."

Gods in Hell, the thought of that sent a new rush of blood to my cock, the ache in my balls a testament of my predatory desires.

"Stop talking!" I barked out in a voice that wasn't mine. It belonged to something dark and wicked, and the more it took hold of me, the less certain I was that I could resist her.

The brush of her finger across my wounds had me clawing at the dirt, forcing myself away from her.

Don't look at her. It's not Farryn. Not Farryn.

"Look at me, Jericho," she battled back in a voice that I wanted to eat from the air. "I want you. So badly. Gods, you are beautiful. Look at you."

Deep heaving breaths, and I could feel a blaze of heat consume me. I turned toward her, taking in the perfect form of Farryn. She'd taken every detail from my memories, down to the tiny scar just above her hip that I recalled from when she was a child and had fallen off her bike. Gods be damned, I wanted her. Now.

Take.

"If I were you ..." Another stab of pain struck my groin, and I let out a pained grunt. *"Run."*

Twisting on her heel, the succubus darted off in the opposite direction. The sight of her naked ass, *Farryn's* ass, triggered something inside of me. A deep seated, primal instinct to chase.

I took off after her, my speed twice as fast as before. Lust burned inside of me, as I watched her hair trail behind her, her body jiggle with every hard step.

Closer. Closer. So close, I could smell her arousal on the air.

Blackness settled over me.

In the dark void, screams pierced my ears.

My eye shot open.

A naked body dangled in my grasp, pinned to the trunk of a tree. When I trailed my gaze upward, horror rippled through me on finding the succubus staring back at me, head cocked to the side of my palm, her eyes glazed over in the telling vacancy of death.

On a sharp exhale, I released her, letting her body fall to a slump, and as I stared down at her discarded form, an unbidden memory took hold. Of another time.

Another woman.

I'd killed her the same way. In the alley back in the town of Stygian Falls, where a single Nightshade flower now marked her eternal rest. That was, after all, how they came to be. When life was taken without permission, the soul could not be claimed, and so it became one of the many glowing flowers that gave the realm its name.

What have you done?

'You know it wasn't her. We know her scent. The way she feels,' An inner voice answered back. The beast inside of me had rejected her, and the only small measure of relief was the

persistent ache in my groin, telling me I hadn't taken her sexually.

"You didn't have to kill her!" My voice thundered as the frustration gripped my lungs, and I stepped away from the fallen succubus.

The sound of agony carried through the trees, a loud piercing screech of moans, multiple moans, which signaled that her sisters had sensed her death.

I backed farther away and spun around, before dashing back through the dark woods toward where I'd left Onyx tied to the tree. After swiping up my tabard and sword, I hopped onto the horse and took off into the night.

32

FARRYN

I stared down at the poached egg and toast, and roasted sweet potatoes on my plate, beside a glass of orange juice. All of it looked delicious. Smelled delicious, too, but I couldn't stand the thought of eating. Not after the dream I'd had, or the nightmarish experience of watching someone climb into my window.

Palm to my stomach, I tried to settle the gurgling of nausea, and recoiled at the thought of that unsettling snaking sensation. My mind also remained wrapped up in Jericho and whoever the hell that woman was, and then the intruder who'd had me wired most of the night, jumping at every sound. In spite of what the angel had said, I couldn't help the paranoid thoughts of more of his kind coming for me. Dragging me out of my bed and doing whatever it was angels did to punish the wicked.

Exhaustion weighed like an anchor on my muscles, and the burn of my eyeballs was the desperate pull of sleep. How silly of me to think that Jericho's return from Ex Nihilo was the end of the dark circles and baggy eyes.

A figure moved in my periphery, catching my attention when she took a seat across from me.

Frowning, I tipped my head. "Vespyr? What …. Where have you been?"

Her cheek dimpled with a smile, and she shrugged. "Around."

"Everyone has been looking for you."

The smile on her face faded to surprise. "Really? Well, I was … visiting my sister."

"Your sister." Tone flat, I studied her while picking at my eggs. "As I understand, Jericho is planning to have a chat with you at some point about you coming and going." Not that any of the conversation really mattered to me. I'd had someone break into my room the night before and dreamed that Jericho had had sex with a woman in the woods. Vespyr coming and going wasn't exactly the most pressing issue at hand, but seemed to be a welcomed distraction.

"What's the big deal with me coming and going?"

I was inclined to tell her that Jericho and I were both on Heaven and Hell's shit-list, but instead, I kept it simple. "He tends to be a private person."

"It's just my sister. Not like I'm working as a spy, or anything." Snorting a laugh, she reached for my toast and took a bite. "Food is so weird here. Obviously, we're not really eating it. It's just what our brains remember tasting. But I feel like I'm actually eating it. Like, texture, flavor, dryness. Wonder if that's why the rest of them don't bother to eat much. They forgot how it tasted."

"So, your sister," I said, pulling her back to the conversation. "You never mentioned her before."

"You never asked about her."

"She's not here in Nightshade?"

"Nope. She's living her best life in suburbia USA." She reached for my juice and took a sip.

"But she visits you."

"Yep. Every Wednesday she visits me."

"Where?"

"At the hospital." An obnoxious crunch announced another bite of toast, which she drowned in another, long sip of orange juice.

The eating was somewhat of a nuisance that I had to ignore for the moment. "You're in the hospital, right now?"

"Well, yeah. I've kinda been there for a while." Another obnoxious crunch followed a slurp of juice.

I wondered how much of what she was telling me was true. "How long?"

She jerked her head toward the rest of my food. "Hey, are you going to eat that?"

Without bothering to answer, I pushed my plate toward her. "How long have you been hospitalized?"

Sliding the plate in front of her, she took hold of the fork and shoveled in a bite of sweet potatoes. "Two years," she said, her words garbled around a mouthful. "Give, or take."

I let out a little cough and cleared my throat, my head trying to wrap itself around what could have possibly been the reason she'd have been hospitalized that long. The other thing was, did I even believe it? "You've been in a hospital for two years?"

"Yep."

"And you're how old?"

"Twenty-three."

"If you don't mind me asking, why?"

Lowering her gaze, she seemed to fidget with her food, moving it around the plate and stabbing the tip of the fork into her potatoes. Her actions reminded me of a child trying to avoid having to answer. "I do kinda mind, but ... you seem okay to talk to." She shoveled in another bite and let out an appreciative moan. "It's been so long since I had real food. The shit they put in feeding tubes is nasty."

"You're ill, then?"

"I suppose you could say that. The docs call it *catatonia associated with schizoaffective disorder*. Or something like that."

Just like that, the burning question of why she'd choose to remain in Nightshade at the risk of imprisonment made sense. "I'm sorry."

"Don't be. Not your fault." She rubbed the back of her hand across her nose and sniffed. "Where we come from, they don't know what we know. I killed, which sucks, but I didn't have a choice. He was evil cloaked as a human, and it looked like I'd murdered a good and innocent man. An upstanding citizen. I was the one who looked crazy." Snorting a laugh, she shook her head. "Turns out, he was an overlord here, too."

"So, was it killing him that put you in a catatonic state?"

"No. I was arrested, and thanks to a longstanding history of psychiatric evaluations, I was deemed unfit for trial and admitted to a psychiatric hospital for treatment. So happens, one of the overlord's little minions posed as an orderly there and put a hex on me." She pushed the food away from her. "He basically keeps me prisoner inside my head. Can't really move my body, unless someone is lifting me up. Can't talk, or make any facial expression. I just feel trapped there."

"That's why you come here. These demons, you hunted them?"

Gaze still cast downward, she nodded. "This was personal."

"Is there no one who can help you? Did they even bother to question what made you turn unresponsive?"

Shrugging, she shook her head. "What could they possibly imagine, Farryn? They have to believe what their eyes see.

What their human tests tell them. It's not like they scan me for demon hexes, you know? I'm basically screwed."

"There's got to be a way to set you free from this."

"Maybe." She waved her hands dismissively and popped another sweet potato in her mouth. "But enough about that. You've got enough on your plate with the baby. I just … didn't want you to think I was out to mess things up. Van Croix was cool to let me stay here. It's nice. I like this place."

Maybe it was something in her eyes, a deep sincerity I'd rarely seen in other human beings, but I believed her. Not that I'd been the best judge of character my whole life, but Vespyr didn't strike me as ingenuine. On the contrary, I felt an odd sense of comfort around her. "It's nice having you here, too. It's been a long time since I've had someone to talk to. Besides Anya, of course."

"Humans here have no idea about demons and angels, though. So weird, right?"

"Sometimes, I wonder if Anya questions it." I leaned forward, lowering my voice. "But she'd probably never admit it."

"Probably better, anyway. Getting people to see things for what they are is exhausting."

I snorted at the truth in that. "It is. I spent my whole life questioning what was real and not. Sometimes you just have to stop questioning and let things be what they are. Even if it goes against what you've been taught to believe. You know what I mean?"

Again, she cast her gaze from mine and smiled. "Yeah. I know exactly what you mean. You're really easy to talk to. It's nice having conversations again." She ran her finger over an embroidered pattern in the table cloth, seemingly lost in thought. "What's it like? Pregnancy?"

Expelling a breath, I stared down at my stomach, which bore no evidence that a baby lived inside there. "It's weird,

sometimes I feel something there, and other times, not at all."
I didn't bother to mention that it was the times when I didn't
feel anything at all that I felt most relieved. Because I wasn't
reminded that there was something very wrong with this
pregnancy.

"I think it's beautiful. Life growing inside of you. Must be
the most incredible feeling in the world."

Lips flattened, I nodded and, for whatever reason, felt the
telling sting of tears. Hormones, I guessed. Or guilt, as
nothing she said was entirely tear-worthy. Because I felt
shitty for not having the same thoughts about the baby that
everyone else seemed to have. Once it was born, I'd be separated from it, after all. Forced to leave and face whatever
punishment awaited me in Hell.

Vespyr reached for one of the daisies in the vase and
snapped off the bit of the stem which had been submerged.
Leaning to the side of the plate of food, she stretched toward
me, and on instinct, I sat back from her, but realizing her
intent, I bowed my head, allowing her to slip the flower
behind my ear.

"What was that for?"

"You just looked like you needed a dose of daisies." Smiling, she sat back in her chair. "Whenever I was sad, growing
up, my momma would always say to me, *'You know what you
need? A dose of daisies.'* So we'd go to this little shack of an
ice cream shop, called *Daisy's*, not far from our house. It
was off the side of the road, surrounded by this massive
field of wildflowers. Just as far as you could see. So beautiful and bright. So many colors, blended together." A
sparkle shined in her eyes. "I remember I always felt so
warm and free. Like nothing bad could ever touch me
there."

There was something about Vespyr that she wasn't telling
me. A secret about her, but I didn't get a sense it was some-

thing threatening. On the contrary, I got a sense that someone had hurt *her*.

Touching my finger to the flower, I smiled. "Thank you. I did need it."

She offered a small smile. "Where the hell do they get daisies from this time of year, anyway? It's freezing outside."

I chuckled and reached to twirl one in the vase. "There's a greenhouse off the back of the cathedral. Used to be tended to by Garic--he was kind of the grounds-person here."

"He's not anymore?"

A sadness swelled inside my chest, recalling the day I'd found his ashes in the woods, where he'd taken his own life. "No. Not anymore." With a sigh, I stared off. "Hey, I don't suppose you know how to drive a horse and carriage?" I asked, trying to lighten the somber mood.

"Yeah."

"Really?"

Shaking her head, she chuckled. "No. Sorry. What the hell is up with that, anyway? I feel like I'm living in a Jack The Ripper era here."

"Well, considering most here have wings, I suppose cars aren't all that necessary."

"True. Why do you ask? About the carriage?"

"It seems Anya can't take me into town." Sitting back in my chair, I sighed. "And I really need to go."

"I don't think so." A deep, annoying masculine voice responded that time, and I turned to see Vaszhago standing at the entrance to the dining room, arms crossed where he leaned against the wall.

"I need to talk to someone. It's important."

"Our definitions of importance clearly differ. Therefore, you can wait until Jericho returns."

A stubborn flare of defiance rose up in me. "I am not waiting another day. I have waited long enough to speak with her, and so help me God, if you try to keep me from going, I will–"

"Look, Vas," Vespyr interrupted. "She's pregnant. Needs fresh air. When was the last time you carried a bundle of joy?" Brows winged up, she tipped her head and, before he could respond, kept on. "Exactly. Women have been known to die of boredom. You wouldn't want that to happen, would you?"

His expression remained stoic, completely void of humor, interest, life. "What is the dire nature of this meeting?"

"I have questions."

"What questions?"

"The kind that can't be answered in books, or by nosey demons who've never spat a whole baby out of their asses. I am going crazy. I can't sleep. I'm not hungry. Ever. And I'd really like to know why the hell I'm vomiting black."

In my periphery, I could see Vespyr's head snap in my direction. "Seriously?" she whispered. "That's messed up."

Vaszhago's lips twisted with a look of repulsion. "Humans are such disgusting creatures."

"So, will you take me to see this woman in town?" I asked, ignoring his comment.

"Where?"

"The bookstore."

"Did you not just say the answers can't be found in books?"

"I'm not going there for a book. I'm going for a person. Er, ghost. Whatever you call them."

"Wraith." Groaning, he rolled his eyes and pushed off the wall. "Very well. What harm could you conjure in a bookstore with a wraith?"

"Well, you'd be surprised. But, I promise, I'll go in, ask her some questions, and leave."

Vespyr shot up out of her seat, knocking it backward into

the wall behind her and tipping over the vase of flowers. Water scattered across the tablecloth, and I lurched to place the daisies back with what little water remained. "I'm coming with you."

"Absolutely not. Being accompanied by one bumbling human is humiliating enough."

I glared back at him. "That's mean."

"Yeah. And all the more reason I'm coming along." Vespyr wore an exaggerated smile. "Post haste, Vas."

"You call me that again, and I will carve out your tongue with a dull blade."

"Damn, you are moody," she said, righting her chair. "Don't they have a pill for that here?"

"Yes. It's called celestial steel." Glancing over my shoulder, I smiled back at Vaszhago as I stacked my breakfast plates to return to the kitchen, and he cocked a brow as I passed him.

"Look who's mean now?"

The horse plodded along the stony path, as I sat beside Vaszhago, who halfheartedly held the reins. "Why human transportation isn't utilized as a means of torture amongst demons, I'll never understand." He'd originally insisted that I sit in the carriage with Vespyr, but I had some questions that needed answering, so like the stubborn human I was, I chose the seat beside him.

"I take it you have wings, as well?"

"Yes."

"Are they feathers, like Jericho's?"

"No. Mine are skin."

For some reason the thought of that sent a shudder of disgust through me. "Like a bat?"

"I suppose. But exceptionally larger."

Vaszhago was a fairly decent looking guy, indisputably handsome, but the thought of skin wings had me gagging a little in my throat. "So, the angel that you imprisoned last night. Do you think he came for me?"

"I do not presume to know the intentions of an angel," he said in his usual bored tone.

"You didn't interrogate him?"

"Why should I? He can rot in that cell, for all I care." The hate practically radiated off the guy while he kept his attention on the path ahead.

"And he can't get out?"

"No. He cannot."

"How are you so sure?"

The slight curve of his lips was the first hint of reaction I'd seen on his face all day. "Because I chained him to the wall with Diablisz steel and put him into paralysis."

"Paralysis. Is that one of your demon tricks?"

"Tricks?"

"Oh, I'm sorry. *Gifts?*"

"One of them."

"What's another?"

He rolled his shoulders back, straightening his posture. "As you are off limits, sexually, I'll refrain from answering."

"Ah, yeah. Please do." Jesus, did every creature in Nightshade have some weird kink trait? A memory of Jericho dragging one of his feathers across my breast left me shifting in the seat, and I cleared my throat, desperate to banish the visual in case Vaszhago picked up on any odd body changes. "Well, anyway, thanks again for coming to my aid. I tried to scream, but for some reason, I couldn't."

"You couldn't because I paralyzed your vocal chords."

I snapped my attention back to him. "That was you? Why would you do that?"

With a dismissive shrug, he answered, "I didn't want you to scare him off."

"Well, that was … kind of dicky."

"I rather enjoyed it. The silence."

Narrowing my eyes on him, I turned back toward the road, mentally noting the barren-looking trees where Misty Hollow once stood. How sad to see so many burned to blackened stumps. "So, if he's an angel, couldn't he sense you there?"

"No. I stripped his senses."

"What? How?"

"That is my rare and unique gift." The one he'd hesitated to tell me of that day in the library, when we were chatting about the Knights of the Infernal Order. He'd told me they had chosen Jericho for his ability to control lightning, but had refused to reveal his own.

"So, that's why the Knights chose you.

"Yes. I hunted angels."

"Jericho did, as well."

"Yes."

"For angel's blood, right?"

A sound of disapproval gurgled in his throat. "You humans and your endless inquiries."

"What else are we going to do? It's a long ride." Another glance at the surroundings showed a small village off in a distant valley.

"Yes. We hunted them for blood, and to eliminate the A'ryakai."

"What are they? The A'ryakai?"

"Angels who believe in a pure race, and that half-breeds and demons should be wiped from existence."

Strange to think we weren't the only beings who shunned others. I'd always chalked that up to ignorance of our species.

Turned out, angels could be just as ignorant. "So, they're like the white supremacists of angels?"

"In its crudest definition, I suppose."

"What about humans? Do they believe the same about us?"

He quirked a brow, and his lips curved to a half-smile. "They believe you are inferior in every way. But they are forbidden by the heavens to kill you."

"Why?"

"Only certain angels are permitted to kill humans, and only when necessary. Outside of them, anyone else would suffer the wrath of the Elysian Council."

It amazed me how little we humans knew about angels, in general. So many rules and laws and groups to regulate them.

"Of course, that doesn't mean the A'ryakai wouldn't try to find equally creative ways for disposing of humans anyway. They are exceptionally conniving."

"They sound like assholes."

Vaszhago snorted at that. "They are."

"For a demon, you speak eloquently." The last demon I'd met was Remy, who was actually a fallen angel, and he spoke about as regally as a drunken frat boy.

"I am of noble blood. My father was a duke."

"A duke. Wow. In the mortal realm?"

"No. The Infernal Lands."

"Oh. That makes sense." I couldn't quite wrap my head around what Hell must've been like, but Vaszhago almost made it sound disturbingly romantic. Like castles made of human skulls, but elegant at the same time.

As the scenery changed to the familiar buildings and shops of the downtown area, Vaszhago turned the carriage alongside a cobblestone curb, where he hopped off and tied the horses to a post there. While he rounded the horses, presumably to help me down, I jumped off the carriage myself, boots landing against the cobblestone with a thud. Vespyr followed suit, exiting the back of the carriage, and strode up alongside me.

"I'll wait here for you," Vaszhago said, hiking his boot onto the carriage step. From his pocket, he pulled a shiny silver case and opened it to show what looked like cigarettes, except they were black with intricate gold metallic designs on them. He pulled one out and ran his tongue over one end of it, which lit with a bright orange glow.

I should've already headed in, but the shiny golden ribbons that rose into the air like smoke when he exhaled had me mesmerized.

Vaszhago took another long drag of the weird cigarette, and blew it off, his eyes on mine. "Are you going to stand there, or go inside?"

Blinking away my fascination, I shook my head, cheeks burning with embarrassment. "Yeah. Right. Be right back."

Vespyr trailed after me, as we made our way into the book store. Although the lady I recognized from my last visit waved from behind the counter, I didn't bother to ask her about Catriona. She'd told me there *was* no Catriona, and I suspected things hadn't changed much in that regard since then.

Instead, I followed the same path up the stairwell. When we arrived at the wall that had moved on its own, I scanned over its surface for a button, or means of opening it.

Running my hands over it, I glanced to the side to find Vespyr mimicking my movements.

"What are we doing?" she asked, and the question made me want to laugh, given how intently searched the wall, apparently having no idea what she searched *for*.

"Trying to find a way to open it."

"A wall?"

"It's not just a wall. It's a secret passage." Sweep after sweep produced nothing, though. And, in fact, the wall really didn't look like it had the ability to move, at all. No cracks, or such, to suggest it sat on any sort of track.

"I don't think this wall opens."

"I know it does, though. I was here last time, and it did." I rose up on my tiptoes, palpating a faint black line that proved to be nothing more than a tiny gap in the wallpaper.

"Okay, well, while you're looking for it, do you mind if I check out the romance section?"

"Sure."

"Cool." The sound of her footsteps faded around the corner, and I groaned, still not finding a way to open the damn wall.

"Are you looking for something?"

The familiar voice brought a smile to my face, and abandoning my search, I turned to find Catriona standing behind me. With long, fiery locks of red hair and a youthful glow to her face, she reminded me of a princess out of a Disney flick.

"You, actually."

"How are you, Miss Ravenshaw?"

"That's actually why I've come to speak with you. I don't know, exactly."

"Come. Let us find a quiet place to talk." She rested her palm against the wall, and lo and behold, the damn thing moved on its own. Just like I said.

I glanced off toward the direction where Vespyr had gone, and on not seeing her anywhere, I followed Catriona up into the dark stairwell. The door slid shut behind me, and even though I'd taken the same path before, it still felt unnerving being closed off from Vespyr and Vaszhago. Flickering lanterns marked the path, and Catriona nabbed one from its bracket as she passed.

"You read the book I gave you?" she asked over her shoulder.

"Yes. The story was beautiful."

"It was, wasn't it? However short-lived."

The dark stairwell opened to a different room than before. Gone was the strange glass case which housed the books on shelves, replaced instead by a beautiful garden room overflowing with unusual plants and flowers in magnificent, vibrant colors. Breathtaking.

I followed her toward a bench set beneath an arbor that was adorned in vine-like purple and green flowers with red speckles near their centers. Flowers I'd never seen in my life. Across from the bench stood an ornate coffee table, where a teapot sat beside two cups, as if she'd been expecting company. "You're Lustina's mother."

"I am." She ushered me toward the cushioned bench and took a seat beside me.

I studied the way the cushion dipped as she sat down, and the fact that I *felt* the presence of another beside me. "The lady in the bookstore downstairs, she had no awareness of you the last time I was here. You're a wraith?"

Clasping her hands in her lap, she nodded. "Merely an apparition."

"Catriona, the reason I'm here is ... well, I'm pregnant."

"I figured as such." She reached forward for the teakettle and poured what appeared to be a strange rainbow-colored fluid into one of the cups. Steam rose over the top of it, and though I wasn't the biggest fan of tea in general, I sipped it, delighted by the ginger citrus flavor. "One does not avoid the cursed blood moon prophecy otherwise," she kept on, pouring a cup for herself. "My poor Lustina did not." Wearing a wistful expression, she held the small teacup to her lips and took a sip. "Of course, if she had, you would not necessarily be here."

"Do you know how it works? What happens to those who *actually* perish on the blood moon?"

"That is a secret only the sacrificed are privy to." She took another sip of her tea, her movements slow and gracious and mannerisms like that of a noblewoman, the way she held her posture straight. "My hope is that they find peace, as well."

"Do you remember being pregnant with Lustina?" I straightened my back, too, noticing the ache of having had horrible posture my whole life.

"Yes."

"How? I just mean ... I thought everyone loses their memories here." Holding the teacup in the same delicate manner, I attempted to be as gracious, but failed when I dribbled the fluid down my lip. Embarrassed, I set the cup back onto its plate and cleared my throat.

"Some do. Some of us do not. I still carry quite a few memories of my past. There are some dark patches. A void here and there. But I've remembered important moments. Perhaps due to being cursed-born."

"So, do you recall in your pregnancy any unusual symptoms?"

"Unusual?"

I hesitated to say at first, for fear of her answer. "Loud sounds in your ear. Hallucinations. Really vivid nightmares. Black vomit."

"Goodness, no. Nothing like that."

Not even the slight smile could hide the disappointment of hearing her say that. "And Lustina's father. He was an angel, correct?"

Her cheeks dimpled with a demure smile, and she pushed a strand of hair behind her ear. "Ah, well. An angel with a bit of the devil in him. That one .... Few men had the power to make me shiver in their presence. Ceallach. Now, he was something."

"I actually met him. He goes by the name Gabriel now."

"Gabriel. Hmmm." Gaze lowered, she ran a thumb over her lips as if his name lingered there.

"Seems he remembers you fondly, too."

Clearing her throat, she straightened even tighter than before, the sight of her making my back muscles ache. "Yes, well, 'twas a very long time ago."

"He helped me bring Jericho back from Ex Nihilo."

"Did he now?" The look of surprise on her face faded for something more thoughtful.

"I'm … fated to become cambion. So it's possible, I suppose, that these symptoms might be related to that." I toyed with the hem of my dress, hoping she didn't catch the slight tremble in my hands. Happened every time I thought about what would happen after the baby was born. "When the baby is born, that's when they'll come for me. I'm just really scared." Saying the words brought tears to my eyes, which surely must've been hormones.

"Don't be." A slight twinge of embarrassment washed over me, as she rested her hand on mine and tipped her head, drawing my attention to her. "I brought young Lord Van Croix into the world. and I will say, given the blood that runs through his veins, he is quite exceptional. There are few who could rival the pure evil in this world. Van Croix is perhaps the only one who would stand to be victorious. And he is *fiercely* protective, as I recall." She gave my hand a gentle squeeze, the humor on her face fading to an earnest stare. "So do not fear the infernal who wish to lay claim to your soul. Fear *for* them." Her words cast a chill down my spine.

I didn't want to tell her that he had lost all of his power because of me. Had sacrificed his wings and abilities in order to save my life.

My mind slipped into thoughts of Camael and the conversation we'd had. "A friend told me that those cursed to die on a blood moon were chosen. And that the curse itself goes back to the beginning of mankind. Do you know what it is that subjected us to this?"

She slid her hand from mine and sighed. "I am afraid not. And for the sake of your child, I pray that the gods will tire of toying with us."

"Me, too."

"As for the symptoms you've been suffering ... there is a healer that you might inquire about." Stuffing her hand down into the cushion of the bench, she pulled out a card, which she handed off to me.

Frowning, I examined the crack of the cushion, wondering what else was stuffed there, then glanced at the name on the card, embossed in red ink. "Kezhurah?"

"She is quite knowledgeable."

"How do I contact her?"

"A scrying mirror is one way. However, if you don't have a scrying mirror, some *cret'calatięsz* will do."

I didn't even want to attempt what she'd said, seeing as I'd have surely butchered the word. "What is that?"

"Summoning chalk. Draw a circle on the wall, write her name in the circle. Place your hand over her name and speak it aloud."

"Wow. Like the supernatural version of Facetiming."

Wearing a confused expression, she tipped her head. "I'm sorry?"

"Nothing." I lifted the card between us. "Okay, I'll look into her. Thank you for this. For everything really."

Her eyes softened with a smile. "You are my Lustina reborn. I would do anything for you, dear. Come see me when that baby arrives."

"I will." I pushed up from my seat and followed the same path down the creepy stairwell, to the wall that moved on its own. On opening, I caught a flash of purple as Vespyr jumped around on a sharp exhale. "Holy shit! It does move!"

"Told you." Tucking the card into my dress pocket, I took the lead back down the rickety staircase to the main floor, with Vespyr at my heels.

When I pushed through the entrance, I was greeted by a thick, white fog. One so dense, I couldn't see past my own hand, while I held it outstretched. Tiny white and gray flecks of what appeared to be ash settled onto my palm, and when I looked up, the sky had disappeared behind the obscure vapor. I turned back toward the bookstore to find nothing but fog. Even as I reached out my hand for the door that I recalled being no more than two steps away, my fingertips met nothing but air.

"Vaszhago!" I called out, having clearly lost my bearings. "Where are you?"

"Farryn?" The sound of Vespyr's voice had grown alarmingly distant, and I spun around, scanning for her purple hair.

An intense burn flared in my eyes, and the mist in them made it nearly impossible to see. "Vespyr! Vaszhago!"

No one answered back.

A shadowy figure moved toward me. One I couldn't quite make out. "Vaszhago?" I backed myself away, unsure of who it was, but it advanced faster than I could escape it. Two wrinkled hands reached out, their palms resting against my belly, and a breath later, I was staring into the black eyes of an old woman. She wore a ratted hood over straggly, white hair that framed a face I somehow vaguely recognized. From where?

Eyes, black and soulless. Lips peeled back to a wicked smile over yellowing teeth. Before I could react, the sound of a *whoosh* hit the air. A flash of metal slipped between us. And I didn't so much as utter a word, before the old woman let out a deep guttural scream that sent a chill down the back of my spine. She held up two bloody stumps where her hands were a moment before, the sight of them making my knees weak and my chest cold with queasiness.

As she lurched toward me, I jumped back seconds before her body burst into flames.

A cold sensation swept over me. I panted hard through my nose in a failed attempt to stave off the panic rising up in my throat.

The fog lifted to reveal Vaszhago standing alongside me, holding the sword that'd severed her hands like a hot blade through silk. I stumbled backward, but he caught me before I hit the ground. Another set of arms wrapped around me, those ones belonged to Vespyr, and she and Vaszhago both carried me back toward the carriage.

"What the hell was that?" I asked, gently pushing their hands away to regain my composure as I climbed onto the carriage bench.

"Not human," Vaszhago answered.

33

JERICHO

I'd followed along the Vendaris River for most of the night, my thoughts wound up in the succubus, which I had brutally slain and left for dead. Voices in my head had argued that she was not Farryn and deserving of her fate as an imposter, but it didn't matter. I had taken another life. While I felt relief in not having fucked her, as much as she looked, sounded, and smelled like Farryn, having killed the woman didn't sit well with me.

My skin burned where the new, silvery tattoo marked the burden of her soul. I wanted to believe that had it not been me, some other would have come along and killed her just as viciously as I had. The truth was, my obsession over Farryn had reached an alarming peak. Even the demon that tore at my conscience refused to settle for anyone else.

Thankfully, I was able to cast aside those cravings and stay the path throughout the night into morning.

The gray, ominous mass of Dreadmire's wall stood off in the distance. On the other side of it, The Fallen reigned in a conundrum of anarchy and violence. Anyone unfortunate enough to land themselves within those walls would've likely been subjected to slavery of the worst kind. Why Farryn's father chose the outskirts of such a place remained a mystery to me.

Onyx ambled over the thick brush parallel to the wall, and I scanned for the small alcove where Augustus, Farryn's father, had taken shelter. A caw overhead signaled Cicatrix had located my position and guided me toward the spot where he'd seen the old man.

Through the barren trees, I spotted the notch in the rock where Augustus had made a disturbing little home. Talisman relics hung from the ceiling of it, and the old man sat at a small bonfire, warming his hands against the early morning frost.

A good distance away, I dismounted, not wanting to scare him off, and hid behind trees as I made my way closer to the cave. It was only when I was near enough to make out the weathered texture of his skin that I emerged from my hiding place behind an oak tree and strode toward him.

He scrambled for what I presumed to be a weapon, but I held up my hands.

"I mean you no harm."

A trembling hand held a blade toward me, his good eye wide with a crazed fear. "Do not come any closer!"

"Do you remember me, Augustus?"

The old man's brows lowered, as he seemed to study me, his faulty gaze sweeping over me. "Van Croix."

"Yes. You came to me a while back, regarding your daughter, Farryn."

He lowered the weapon and set a finger to his lips, obnoxiously shushing me. "Do not say her name." Tucking the blade away, he leaned forward, peering up at the trees in a paranoid way, then settled back against the cave wall.

I appreciated his protective nature and strode just a bit closer, still keeping my distance so he wouldn't dart off in thinking I might be a threat. "She came to me, as you anticipated."

A flicker of a smile danced across his face, and he nodded. "She is safe, then."

"For now."

"I am grateful."

"I can take you to her."

The man's eyes shuttered, and gaze cast downward, he shook his head. "No."

"Forgive me, but I made a promise to your daughter, and I intend to keep it."

"As much as it pains me to say so, I must refuse. I am a danger to her. *They* are searching for me." He glanced around again, as if something had flown overhead, which prompted me to look upward.

Only Cicatrix circled above us.

"Who?"

"To say their names would summon them. I do not speak their names." He nabbed one of the objects hanging from the ceiling and held it tight to his chest.

"Very well. I've come to ask you a question. About the Omni."

With hands fitted with ragged, fingerless gloves, he scratched the back of his neck. "The Omni?"

"Yes. Tell me what you know about it."

Again, he peered up at the sky and back down to the bonfire. He rocked in place, quiet. Contemplative. "I found the Omni in a print left behind from centuries ago. It was the approximate location to where I believe Praecepsia once stood before it burned."

I kept my lips zipped on the fact that I had been the one to burn Praecepsia down.

"A colleague of mine," he prattled on. "He had traveled there and found the print. He was the one who sent it to me.

For months, years, I studied it. I tried to tie it to one of our existing languages, and then when that proved fruitless, I studied the symbols against Enochian. Utilizing every resource available to mankind, I searched for its translation. There was nothing. Nothing!" His body shook as he spoke. "When I arrived here, I sought out your texts for some meaning. And still, I found nothing. I came to the conclusion that the Omni was useless, unless spoken by a particular group skilled in its language, known as the Met'Lazan. Only they know its translation."

I'd read about them in the grimoire before the pages had faded. "So, the Omni must be translated by them and no one else?" For Farryn's sake, I hoped that wasn't the case, because the events with the succubus the night before assured that things were getting worse with me.

"As I said, I attempted to translate the words, myself. I utilized rituals known to conjure. Nothing came of it. So, yes, I believe it is a language meant only for them."

"Who are these Met'Lazan, exactly?"

"Healers. They are believed to have raised Jesus from his tomb. Powerful healers who have access to the vitaeilem that exists in Etheriusz."

"I don't understand. How does one gain access to Heaven?"

He leaned forward, and in spite of the uneasy gestures, him looking around once again, his gaze held a glint of excitement. It was a topic he seemed to be enthusiastic about. "The exact means is unclear to me, as well, but as I understand, when an angel or celestial being dies, its lifeblood must go somewhere, right? That somewhere is an atmosphere that surrounds the heavens, known as Etheriusz. It is a powerful glow, comprised of thousands upon thousands of angels who've perished." He held up his hands, as if emphasizing his point. "And it is their lifeblood which provides the protection of the heavens. Should it be broken, it would render them vulnerable. In essence, the Met'Lazan serves as a conduit for this lifeblood."

"You're saying the Met'Lazan can tap into the accumulating lifeblood of dead angels?"

"Yes!" His hands balled into fists, and he shifted with fervor. "The Omni is a sigil designed to tap into that energy. Whether for good, or evil, it depends on the Met'Lazan. Unfortunately, I don't know much about them, as every text I've read turned illegible before my very eyes."

Which likely meant some unseen force was protecting their identity. "The Met'Lazan is an individual."

"A human. Ancient gods decided that neither Heaven, nor Hell, should hold such power. So, they granted it to a neutral source." Like it was a nervous tic of his, he leaned forward again, searching the sky overhead. "Unfortunately, most Met'Lazan don't even know they possess the power of the Omni. It isn't apparent to them until they are summoned to speak."

"So, you do not know how to translate it. You don't know how to access its power."

"No. I am essentially useless. But that doesn't stop the evil from seeking me out."

Fuck. Despite already having considered the possibility that he might not know, his admission still struck a crushing blow to what little hope I'd harbored. "How do you remember all of this? Many in Nightshade lose their memories."

"A rather generous creature, a fallen angel, was willing to reverse time and send me back to the mortal realm. There, I was able to retrieve what I could from my journal. He brought me back to Nightshade, and I have been hiding here ever since."

"Cassiel?"

"Yes, that was his name."

I leaned against the tree beside me and crossed my arms as I pieced everything together. "And when you came to me. How did you know of mine and Farryn's history?"

"There was nothing in the mortal realm, admittedly. I found a woman in the bookstore who offered an illuminating text when I inquired about Praecepsia."

"Catriona."

"Yes. Quite beautiful. And through her, I learned of your fate through a story I read. I thought it absurd at first, until I began to notice a few subtle similarities between Lustina and my Farryn, most notably the eyes. And then there was the image tucked inside of it. A painting with a girl who looked undeniably like my Farryn." He paused, nostalgia swirling in his gaze as he stared off with a smile. "The woman at the bookstore offered to pass the book along to Farryn, should she inquire."

"The woman you spoke to was Lustina's mother. A wraith, from what I understand." I glanced around the interior of his cave again, noticing the few makeshift tools he must've used for hunting, and the erratic scribbles of languages and symbols—signs of loneliness and madness of being out in the woods on his own for too long. "Come back with me. Farryn is quite anxious to see you."

He winced and lowered his gaze. "Countless days have passed thinking about her. Every moment. But something hunts me here. Something evil."

"I can offer you protection."

"You can't. It is a debt which must be paid. I have delayed the inevitable, but perhaps it is time."

"She has waited years to reunite with you. Was it not her mother who compelled *you* to seek out Nightshade? Surely you can understand her desperation."

Gaze still lowered, he offered a solemn smile. "It's true.

Her mother fueled my obsessions in the beginning. However, I've since come to learn, fate is cruel to those who love with unflinching devotion."

In the time that I watched over Farryn, I'd had my suspicions that his wife had been unfaithful. Unfortunately, I hadn't cared enough to investigate, as my attention remained solely on his daughter and nothing else. "Still, my home is secure. It is protected by hellhounds. You would be safe there."

Shaking his head, he reached into his pocket and I stepped forward to accept the object, the shape of it recognizable as a ward. "Give this to her. Tell her I'm sorry. I'm sorry for everything, but I owe Netherium." One of the larger kingdoms in the Infernal Lands. The same place where Vaszhago's father lorded as duke. "It doesn't matter where I am. They will come to collect. I'd prefer Farryn not bear witness to that. So you tell her whatever you need to tell her. And don't come back here. Don't ever come back here."

"Augustus–"

"Please!" His body shook with frustration and what I gathered to be a bit of pain.

Nodding, I stepped away from him. "If that is your wish."

"It is. Go now." His lips trembled, and his eyes held the shine of tears. "Take care of her for me."

With a sharp nod, I strode back toward Onyx, and as I held the reins to mount the horse, an unsettling sensation struck the back of my neck.

Turning back around showed Augustus still warming his hands at the fire. But even as far as I stood, I could see something stirring in the flame.

Fire demons.

"Augustus!" I called out, spinning back toward the cave. "Get out! Now!"

The old man shot to his feet, but not fast enough.

Nowhere near fast enough for the fiery hands that reached out from the flames and dragged him in. The sound of his painful outcry sent a shudder down my spine. Hellsfire was known to feel like one's skin being slowly peeled from its bones.

"No!" I darted toward him, and as I leaped toward the bonfire, I only just touched the tip of his hand before he slipped into the blazing depths. Out of reach.

The flame fizzled to smoke, and only the reverberating echo of the old man's screams carried through the trees.

34

THE BARON

*F*ire spread across the baron's flesh as he lay on the cold floor of the cell. The torment was nothing new. He had endured such pain for months since the first whipping at Bishop Venable's hands, and he'd grown accustomed to the agony of torture. Forehead resting against the dirt, he knew to breathe in deeply through his nose. To lay perfectly still so that his wounds did not stretch and break open. He knew to moan and cry, as if in pain, so Bishop Venable would not become wise to his ruse. And he knew, above all else, never to heal his own wounds.

From the corner of his eye, a flicker of movement drew his attention toward the shadowy half of his cell. It'd been weeks since he'd last been placed into a room with another prisoner. Or patient, rather. Most times, he had been left alone to face the breadth of his injuries in silence.

He lifted his head, not entirely certain that he had, in fact, seen movement at all.

Until the shadows shifted across the wall.

"Who is there?"

The shadows gave way to slender legs and arms, and the

long, blonde locks of a woman. "I do not mean to interrupt your healing, My Lord."

"Who are you?"

"My name is Syrisa. Syrisa of Soldethaire."

Soldethaire. A northern village he'd heard about, whose inhabitants had been taken by the Pentacrux, many of them as prisoners for the way they lived almost savagely, well before the baron had been born. She pushed forward, crawling toward him like an animal on hands and knees, into the light shining through the window. Across her skin were the telling and familiar marks of abuse—bruises, cuts, the glisten of burn marks and new skin. The shine of metal drew his eyes to her throat, where a gold band dug into the flesh of her neck. The woman had been tormented, that much he could tell.

"I did not take notice of you before. How did you find your way inside this cell?" the baron asked, curious about her. He would've surely noticed her, even in the darkest corners of the small space, given that his eyesight allowed him to see through shadows.

"It so happens that I don't like the dark much. Does it trouble you?" She still hadn't answered his question, as if she didn't want to say.

"No." He studied her closer, and at the first spark of recognition, his eyes widened. "You are the Widow of the Woods. The woman who lures young boys to her cabin."

"Widow of the Woods, you say. Is that what they call me these days?" With a roll of her eyes, she chuckled. "Jesus, Mary and Joseph. They will inevitably find something to make a woman out to be a predator."

"You do not seduce young boys into your cabin, then?"

"Should a boy find his way into my cabin, I can assure you, it is his own free will which compels him. Have you never taken a fancy to older women before?"

He tightened his lips to hide his repulsion. "Not usually."

"Really? Ah, well. To each his own."

"Why are you here?"

She gave a wistful sigh. "Love. I loved someone deeply. And he was stolen from me. Cursed."

"And how old was this love of yours?"

"Your age, thereabouts."

The woman had to have been at least two times the baron's age, given the maturity in her features, perhaps even older. "I am only sixteen. You laid with him?"

Lips stretched to a grin, she dragged her hand over her arm in a way that the baron wondered if it was meant to be seductive. "Many times. We did far more than lay together. And he enjoyed it."

"That doesn't excuse that you took advantage of him."

The smile on her face faded, and her eyes stared into his, shadowed by a darkness that made his skin crawl. "Men take advantage all the time. I was married to a man thrice my age. He took me when I was only twelve years old."

"He's a monster, then, not a man."

"Oh, the chivalry in this one!" She threw her head back on a laugh. "Well, this man taught me things. Things I ultimately taught my young lover."

"Do not say that. It is not love you seek."

"What is it, then, young baron?"

"Power. Yours was stolen at a young age, so you wish to steal from others."

Brows winged up, she scratched at her chin. "You're quite astute for your age. But you're wrong. I did love him. He was delicious. Enjoyed the darker pleasures."

The baron hung on that word, curious as to its meaning when related to laying with her. "What darker pleasures?"

"Tell me, young baron, have you ever found yourself aroused at the sight of blood? Have you ever held your breath underwater and denied yourself a single sip of air until your hand brought you to climax?" She sucked her bottom lip between her teeth and widened her knees, drawing his eyes to the shadows that hid her indecency. "Have you ever wanted to fuck something after a whipping?"

His eyes shot to hers, the stark nature of her words striking him like a slap across the face. "Get out. Get out of here now."

"I meant no ill intent." Smiling, she drew her knees together again.

"I no longer wish to speak with you, and I ask you kindly to leave, however you managed to find your way into this cell."

"As you wish. My apologies for disturbing you." Rocking forward to her knees, she backed herself toward the shadows again, until he no longer saw movement from that corner.

Once he was certain that no one was there, the baron pushed to his feet, flinching at the agonizing burn of his wounds as his skin stretched with the movement. He hobbled toward the shadows, his eyes adjusting to the dark as he neared the stone wall there.

He found nothing. No door. No passage. No way to exit the cell from that corner. Only a lingering chill, which climbed the back of his neck as he stepped away from it.

35

JERICHO

The news I had of Farryn's father hung like a heavy albatross around my neck, as Onyx trotted up the driveway toward the cathedral. To avoid the succubi, I'd taken a different route home, a longer one that had taken an extra day to return to Blackwater, giving me plenty of time to relive the scene over and over in my head.

I was only glad Farryn hadn't been there to see it. Even having witnessed fire demons before, it still made for a troubling visual.

While I'd had to break a promise to bring her father back, out of respect for his interest in protecting her, given the timing, I had to believe the old man had waited for the possibility that he might hear news of Farryn, for the chance to be able to pass the ward onto his daughter. Perhaps it was enough for him, to know she was safe.

Not that the ward itself would've done Farryn much good. The particular demon who would own her soul, my father, happened to be immune to wards. Even so, I believed anything was worth a try.

Early embers of dusk settled over the trees, and all three

dogs chased after me, Fenrir nipping at the other two as if to rile them into play. As Onyx trotted to a stop, I hopped off, meeting Anya at the foot of the staircase and handing over the reins.

"Master Van Croix, I'll take care of the horse. You might want to go check on Farryn."

Her words had my muscles tensing with alarm. "Is everything okay?"

"She seems to be a bit ill. Taking a nap. As I understand, she returned with Vaszhago and Vespyr from the bookstore the day before yesterday, and has been feeling out of sorts since."

I strode up the staircase into the cathedral, and up the second staircase toward the bedroom corridor. When I reached Farryn's door, I gave a soft knock before entering. A mound of blankets on the bed had me quietly prowling toward it, not wanting to wake her if she was asleep. I came to a stop alongside the bed and ran a gentle palm over the long, raven locks scattered over her pillow.

She rolled onto her back, her face a pale and ghostly white, but her lips stretched to a welcoming smile. "Hi."

"Hi. You're not feeling well?"

"Just my stomach." A hearty cough jerked her body, and she twisted back around, curling into herself as she gripped her stomach with a grunt, then shivering as if she were freezing.

Slipping my arms beneath her, I lifted her up off the bed and carried her into the bathroom, her body trembling in my arms. On the edge of the tub, I sat down with her in my lap, and pressing my palm to the surface of the tub, I whispered, "*Inflodiusz.*"

Water poured in from the stone's edges, filling the exceptionally large basin, the black surface emitting a soft glow that gave just enough light to see by. When I stuck my hand in, the temperature felt as inviting as the hot springs I used to enjoy when I was younger.

Farryn still shivered in my arms as I undressed her, and I imagined she must've been quite ill not to have mentioned a word about her father up until that point. She lifted herself up off my lap just enough to remove her panties, and once completely unclothed, I helped her down into the bathtub.

After she'd seated herself, I grabbed a washcloth from the linen cabinet and dipped it into the water, before dragging the soft cotton over her brow.

"Tell me how this happened?"

"I don't know. It struck pretty fast." She sat up, her eyes wide as she glanced around. "My father. Where is he?"

The dreaded question. I couldn't bring myself to lie, but at the same time, I didn't want to upset her and risk the consequences of stress. "Would you have him visit you while indisposed?" I asked with a feigned air of amusement.

"No, but I can get dressed." Pushing up sent her backwards as if wave of dizziness had swept over her.

"I beg to differ." I caught her by the back of her neck before her head could hit the stone and gently laid her back down into the tub. "Relax. Did anything precipitate this?"

"I went with Vaszhago and Vespyr into town. We st-stopped at th'bookstore, th'one you took me to, so that I could speak w'Catriona." As if a sudden sleepiness weighed on her, her words carried a slight slur. "When I exit'd th's-tore, th'was a thick, white fog of ash." She shifted in the water, flinching with the movement. "I cou'n't see pas'it. Los' sigh'of Vaszhago an' Vespyr. And then ou'of th'blue, th'was a woman. Dressed 'na hooded cloak. But 'er eyes were black 's'night. Only jus'touched m'stomach 'fore Vaszhago found me an' sliced her han's off. Burst 'nto flames afterward."

"She put her hands on your stomach?"

"Yeah."

On a forced exhale, I rubbed a hand over my jaw. "She could've been vocatori."

"Wha'sat?"

"A summoner. Fuck." I pinched the bridge of my nose, doing my best to reel in the vexation brewing beneath my skin. "Did Vaszhago leave you at any time?"

"Wasn' his fault, Jericho. Why're you mad? Wha's it mean?" She rolled her head against the surface of the tub, and I brushed away the wet hair plastered to her face.

"I don't know. It depends on what she was trying to invoke. We'll have you checked by a doctor immediately."

"There's a healer Catriona tol'me 'bout. Her card's in m'dress pocket. Maybe call her? Or ... chalk 'er. Wha'ever y'call it."

Her slurring seemed to get worse by the minute, and I pressed a hand to her forehead, noting the intense heat that radiated against my palm. Stuffing my hand down into the water, I whispered, *"Fri'guse."* The temperature cooled just enough to keep her warm without heightening her burgeoning fever. "I'll take care of the summoning. I want you to rest." I leaned forward and kissed her, the scent and taste of her drawing me out of the thoughts that had plagued my head the whole ride back to the cathedral.

"On'more thing ... 'n angel broke 'nto m'bedroom."

"An angel?" I couldn't tell if she was serious or delirious.

"Vasz'go got 'em. Down'na dungeons."

Something dark moved through me, twisting my insides. "An angel here?"

"Yeah. Said he ha'da'm'sage for you." A sliver of fear shined in her eyes as she stared up at me. "Jer'cho," she whispered. "Y'think th're c'ming f'me?"

With a gentle grip of her chin, I held her attention. "You don't worry about that. I'll take care of this angel. No one is going to touch you."

"'Kay. 'M'so happy y'back."

She let out a wet bark of a cough, and when I retracted my hand, I frowned on seeing black fluids splashed over my skin. Examining closer, I noticed strange movement in each black drop, as if something lived inside of it. Sliding my attention back to her showed a spark of panic, before her eyes rolled back, and I lurched forward, grabbing her before she sank below the water's surface.

I lifted her out of the tub and, with her wet, naked body limp in my arms, carried her across the room to the bed, where I lay her down on the mattress and covered her with blankets. Back in the bathroom, I found her dress crumpled on the floor and fished out the card from its pocket. After one more check to be sure she still breathed, I made my way down to my office and rifled through my desk drawer for the *cret'calatięsz* summoning chalk.

On my way back to Farryn's room, I passed Vaszhago, who must've sensed my urgency because, without a word, he followed after me, but came to a stop at Farryn's doorway.

"Don't let anyone in." I ordered, to which he gave a nod and stood guard outside the door. "I'll speak with you about the angel afterward."

Once back inside her room, I drew a circle on the wall with the chalk and, within it, wrote the name embossed on the card. *Kezhurah*. Hand pressed to her name, I spoke it aloud.

Moments later, the edge of the circle lit with a bright light, and the form of a tall, curvy woman appeared in a loose, white tunic and brown leather pants. A long, white braid lay draped over her slender shoulders, and against her hip, a brown, bulging satchel rested. A tattered, off-white cloth hung from the belt that cinched the tunic at her waist, and she carried an intricately carved black staff which she tapped against the floor.

Without introduction, she sauntered over to Farryn, and even though I was the one who'd summoned her, my muscles twitched with tension as she dragged a finger down Farryn's damp brow.

"I stay one night." The accent on her tongue was one I didn't quite recognize. "After, she will be well again. And what will you offer in exchange?"

"Whatever you ask, it is done."

"A *septier* of celestial steel." A septier was a gift of seven. A rather gracious gift, as it related to the coveted celestial steel. In her case, what amounted to about seven pounds of it.

"Would you accept a dagger?"

"That will suffice, yes." From the satchel at her hip, she pulled out long fibery strands, which I deemed to be kestle root, and a small vial labeled blood of aenge. An aenge was a somewhat rare and uncommon flower, which grew mostly along rivers. Its center carried a red nectar that, when squeezed, made the flower appear to bleed out. The nectar itself was said to be particularly potent and effective in drawing out bad spirits.

"What is wrong with her?"

The woman threw back the covers from over her, showing Farryn's naked body curled into a ball. All over her skin were newly made black markings, like the one she'd left on my arm weeks ago when we'd crossed over into Nightshade. So many of them, all of which must've appeared after I'd left the room as she didn't have them when I'd given her a bath. "She harbors the unbound."

I knew that much from my reading. "I was under the impression that the unbound starved to death. That they couldn't inhabit a body."

She ran her fingers over a particularly dark marking along Farryn's ribcage. "That is the case with most. Seemed this one found a way."

Aside from her trembling, Farryn didn't so much as stir beneath the woman's touch.

A tingle across my skin diverted my attention toward the dark coloring of my fingertips, and a glance through the window confirmed what I feared. The sky had darkened significantly since my return, and my preoccupations with Farryn had kept me from noticing the moon was already high and bright. Fuck. My Rur'axze would be kicking in soon. "And what of the baby?"

"Baby?"

The scent of Farryn carried on the air, invading my senses. Trying to ignore it proved impossible, as the sweet aroma hit the back of my throat and watered my mouth. "She is pregnant."

The woman's face held a sobering expression, and she glanced momentarily toward Farryn.

I blinked hard, trying to ignore the sight of Farryn's naked form, because Hades in winter, only a rotten bastard would notice such a thing while she lay sick and suffering. "Can you remove this soul from her?"

"I will try." After unlatching the satchel from her hip, she set it out on the nightstand beside the vial and root, then removed a small crucible from its depths. "It will depend on the will of the soul."

"They are relatively harmless, these unbound souls." It was coming, my Rur'axze, and hellsfire, I couldn't stop it. No matter how much I wanted to, my body could not tamp down the urges rising up inside of me. And when it occurred to me why that might've been the case, a unbridled rage burned beneath my skin. Aside from another woman present in the room, I suspected my body recognized the weak nature in Farryn. The fucking predator in me knew she'd be easy to claim in her condition.

"For the most part, they are," the woman said in answer.

"But if they were malevolent in life, it is possible they can carry that malevolence with them. This one appears to have been with her for quite some time." With a pair of scissors, which she'd also retrieved from her bag, she snipped a small lock of Farryn's hair and deposited it into the crucible. Over that, she poured the blood of aenge and broke small pieces of the root.

"*With* her, you say?"

"Yes. Inside of her."

Inside of her? Damn it. They typically hung close to the living, rarely given the opportunity to enter the body. "For how long?" Fortunately, Kezhurah kept herself busy, perhaps not noticing the storm brewing inside of me. I'd need to get out of there soon, or risk harming both of them.

"I cannot say. Long enough that I can sense a restless nature in it." Covering the crucible with both hands, she spoke whispers in a language with which I was not familiar, and beneath her hand flickered a soft, orange glow.

"It is my understanding that they are invisible. That they cannot be seen, or sensed, by anyone outside the host. How then do you sense its restlessness?"

She removed her palms from over a tiny flame inside the crucible, which instantly fed on the root and Farryn's hair. "I do not read the presence of the spirit. It is Farryn's body which tells me these things. Her pulse is unusually high. The erratic marks over her flesh and frailty of her body tell me whatever is inside of her wants out." A bit concerning, when she'd seemed surprised to know Farryn carried a baby inside of her, as well.

"Why doesn't it leave her, then?" I kept my attention anchored on the flame as it grew taller, as Kezhurah pried Farryn from her curled position and stretched her flat onto her back.

I shook away the vile shiver of need pulsing through me on seeing her laid out. Even in her sleeping state.

Especially in her sleeping state.

"I would venture to say it wants something from her."

"The baby?"

"What misery to inhabit a baby!" Kezhurah chuckled, running her hands over Farryn's belly. "What could a soul compel an infant to do? No. I do not believe it wants the child. They do not typically inhabit without some agreement. They may compel outside of the body, but to be invited inside, Farryn must have given permission, at some point."

"I can't imagine she would have done such a thing knowingly."

"You know as well as I do, Mr. Van Croix, that evil can be quite cunning. She may not have even realized at the time that she was offering her body as a vessel."

I stared down at Farryn's face, the seemingly peaceful sleep into which she'd fallen. *Go now,* my head urged. The small sliver of decency left in me. "I'll inquire when she's feeling better again. In the meantime, I will leave you to do your work. Should you need anything, let Vaszhago know."

Kezhurah looked over her shoulder toward the closed door where Vaszhago stood guard on the other side, her stare lingering there for a long moment. "She may shake and whine a bit, but I promise, I am not out to harm her."

A thunderous boom bounced off the walls, and my attention shot toward the crucible, where a blast of a flame rose up, licking the air.

"Seven witches! I've never seen that before." Kezhurah waved her hand to blow away the thick plume of smoke. She lifted the crucible to reveal a black marking left behind on the porcelain.

"What does this mean?" I asked.

"I do not know. Ordinarily, the mixture of root, hair, and

blood of aenge would burn for most of the night. I've never seen it burn all at once like that."

Farryn's limp body jerked upright, her eyes still closed, as if something had yanked her by the chest. From her mouth, a black curling smoke rose up from between her parted lips, and I watched as it hovered at the ceiling for a moment before dissipating. Her body slammed back to the pillow, and moments later, she moaned and shifted on the bed, but it seemed to be more in dreams than in pain.

"The unbound?" I asked, glancing upward to see a black, shadowy residue on the ceiling above us.

"Not entirely. It is a negative energy given off. As you know, demons can sometimes give off smoke that way, but in this case, the soul is angry about something. But do not worry. She seems to be okay." The woman dragged her palm over Farryn's forehead. "The fever has gone down significantly already."

When she removed her hand, I touched Farryn's skin to confirm for myself. "Good." The blackness on my skin had crawled up to the level of my elbows, and without another word, I strode from the room. I hated having to leave Farryn in that state, but there wasn't enough seraphica to stave off the urges coming over me. Damn this!

At the door, I spoke low to Vaszhago. "She comes recommended by a friend, but watch."

Nodding, he gave a downward glance, undoubtedly noticing my arms. "Should I secure your chains?"

"No. Do not leave this spot. I'll have one of the others do the honors." I'd had the housekeeping staff chain me before, just under entirely different circumstances. "Keep me advised if anything goes awry. And what of the angel?"

His lips curved to a wicked smirk. "Paralyzed and chained."

"Good. Anyone we know?"

"Calls himself Soreth. Beyond that, I didn't ask any questions. As far as I'm concerned, the only good angel is a dead one. Unfortunately, he claimed to have a message for you."

Soreth. Not the most threatening in the heavens, at least. "Once this shit-storm passes, I'll head down. In the meantime, do not let Farryn out of your sight."

On the way toward my room, I passed Vespyr, who shuffled down the hallway toward Farryn's room. "Walk with me," I said, bringing her to a skidding halt.

"Am I in trouble?"

"Where've you been?" We rounded the corner to the corridor where my bedroom stood at the end of the hallway.

"I spoke with Farryn, and she gave me the lowdown on your need for privacy." She chatted quickly as she trailed my steps. "I went to visit my sister, is all. It won't happen again, I swear."

"The next time you decide to venture to the mortal realm, don't bother to return here."

"Got it. What's going on with Farryn?"

"She's not feeling well." I gave a quick glance over my shoulder, noting a look of genuine concern on the girl's face. "As I understand, you had an eventful day in town."

"Yeah. Weird. She told you about the old lady?"

"Yes. What were your senses about her?" I pushed through the door and jerked my head for her to follow me inside.

Frowning, she looked around the room. "That's the messed up thing. I didn't sense anything. It was like, nothing there, but I saw her. Well, about two seconds before Vas chopped her limbs like carrots. Hey, is this your bedroom?"

"Yes," I said, peeling away my shirt. For her sake, I left my pants on, though it was going to make for a miserable night.

Still frowning, she cleared her throat and stood just inside the room, as though uncertain whether, or not, to keep following. "You think her not feeling well is related to the old hag?"

"I'm not sure. In the meantime, I need you to do me a favor."

"Um. What do you need?"

I lifted the chain attached to the wall above my bed. "I need you to chain me to my bed."

Her mouth slackened. "Why?"

I rubbed a hand down my face, irritated that I had to have the conversation at all with her.

36

FARRYN

 I opened my eyes to the darkness of my room, the soft tickle of sheets across my legs tightening my thighs. Lip caught between my teeth, I squirmed on the bed, an ache blooming at my core.

Jericho.

Only a sheet covered my naked body, and I arched my back, dragging my sensitive nipples across the fabric. The ache throbbed and pulsed, the need pulling like a thread, and I held the sheet to my breasts as I sat up in bed.

Wind blew in through the opened window, fluttering the white curtains. On the wall across from me, a circle had been drawn with the name *Kezhurah* in the center of it.

Kezhurah. The healer. I looked down at myself, recalling a sickness which had churned in my stomach earlier, and I placed my hand there. Not so much as a gurgle. In fact, I felt fantastic. Fantastic and needy. As if I'd slept for hours and had awakened from an explicit dream. When I glanced over, the clock read one thirty-seven in the morning. Was it a dream, then?

Jericho. Something in my body compelled me. Wanting him.

I climbed out of bed, taking the sheet with me. The sound of voices bled through the door, and I paused, listening. One of them was Vaszhago. Another belonged to a woman whose voice I only vaguely recognized. Flirtatious conversation, and when I swung the door open, Vaszhago was leaning into a woman who reminded me of something out of a pirate movie.

"Farryn?" she asked, stepping out of Vaszhago's arm cage. The concern on her face told me that my presence was unexpected. "Are you all right?"

"Yeah. I feel great. Really great, actually. I was just … going to see Jericho."

"Farryn," Vaszhago warned. "Not a good idea."

"Why?"

"Do you recall the last time you visited?"

"Yes. I also recall that I was fine." The need burned so intensely, I didn't even care if I ended up stuck like last time. I'd slept like a baby that night and enjoyed feeling him so close to me. After all, I'd figured out my safe word for him.

Brows pulled together, he tipped his chin back, staring down at me. "You're no longer feeling ill?"

The woman reached for me, but hesitated, her brows winging up as if to ask if it was all right, to which I nodded. She pressed her palm to my forehead and closed her eyes. The tension written across her face softened. "It seems your fever has subsided. You have a slight increase in pulse, but nothing like earlier. I do not sense the distress of before."

"I told you. I'm fine. I just *really* want to see Jericho." The ache gnawed at the apex of my thighs, desperate for that tickly vibration that always sent me over the edge.

"Except that he specifically asked me not to let you do that."

On a exasperated huff, I crossed my arms. "It's either that, or I stand here staring at you all night." I shifted my gaze from her and back to him. "My death stare is unrivaled."

"Fine. I'll be right here if you need me."

"I promise I won't. By the way, did you happen to see my father return with Jericho?"

When the demon shook his head, I frowned, wondering if I'd been in a delirious state when I'd asked Jericho about him. I could've sworn he'd given me the impression that my father was here. Unless I misunderstood. Entirely possible in my state of mind at the time.

"You did see him return, though?"

"Of course."

With a nod, I stepped past the two of them, feeling Vaszhago's stare burning the back of my head as I shuffled in my sheet down to Jericho's bedroom. Through the door, I could only make out moaning and grunting, not the loud outcry of pain from before. Hopefully, he wasn't on the cusp of settling.

"Farryn," he rasped, before I even set my hand to the knob.

I opened the door only a crack and peeked in on him. Across the room, just as before, he lay writhing, his body glistening with sweat. "Come here."

Any other time, I would've hesitated, but as horny as I felt right then, he could've been in full-on demon mode, and I'd have still pranced up to him like a naive kitten on a lion.

His chest rose and fell as I neared, his eye riveted on the sheet covering my body, and when I loosed my grip of it, letting it fall to the floor, a sparkle of appreciation danced across his face. He licked his lips, shifting his body as if excited. The tattoos on his skin glowed and moved with the flexing of his muscles. The sight of him sent a shot of arousal to my core.

The same cozy feeling of before settled deep into my bones, softening me.

"Come closer, Tu'Nazhja. Climb onto me."

I took a step toward him, and paused when I caught sight of a bent link in his chain. As if he'd caught on to what had captured my attention, his lips stretched to a cagey grin. One hard yank broke the chain from the bedpost, freeing one of his arms. Another set his other arm free. He lifted both hands in the air, twisting them in taunting.

My blood turned to ice. An alarm blared inside my head, and I spun around on my heel for the door.

A force slammed into me from behind, pinning me to the wall, and as I opened my mouth to scream, he sealed it with his hand. I slinked a hand down across my stomach, wondering if the baby had been jostled too much with the hit to my belly. "Jericho, wait—" My words were nothing more than mumbled noise behind his palm.

"Shhhhh." He pressed his hard body into me, his arm banded around my waist. "I've already waited centuries for you." The voice which spoke only held a hint of the man I recognized, grated by the feral tone of a beast.

I bucked against him, slamming my ass against what must've been incredibly swollen balls.

The shadow of malice when he groaned in my ear told me it'd hurt. "You shouldn't have done that," he growled, and spun me around to face him.

Every muscle in my body quaked in fear. Surely, Vaszhago should've felt it. Surely, he'd come pounding through the door any second.

Eye black as night, horns protruding, skin darkening, Jericho was shifting into demon mode before my eyes. "The only thing that would make this more thrilling," he said, dragging his nose over my throat. "Is if I were given the opportunity to chase you through the woods first."

I squeezed my eyes shut. "Strę vera'tu!"

Jericho pulled away from me, and for a split second he wore the same look of betrayal as the last time I'd brought his fun to a screeching halt with the word. Except, his eye didn't turn back to the familiar blue as it had before. It remained black.

An unsettling fear spiraled down the back of my neck. It didn't work. *Shit!*

"No safe words." Fangs bared and dripping with black, he shot toward my neck, and I let out a scream.

Panting, I stood there, waiting for him to bite down.

An angry growl rumbled in his throat as light bled into the bedroom from the hallway.

"Lucifer's left tit, a demon can't even get his dick stroked without having to come separate the two of you." The sound of Vaszhago's voice was both a relief and an annoyance.

Something wet hit my shoulder, and I turned just enough to see black fluid drip from Jericho's fang, his body held suspended. Paralyzed.

"Honestly, you make me want to reconsider Ex Nihilo."

"Release me!" Jericho growled, his body frantically jerking against mine as I slipped out from between him and the wall. "She is mine! Release me at once!"

Absolutely mortified and covering as much of my body as I could, I scrambled for the sheet still lying crumpled by his bed and wrapped it around me.

"No. But come to think of it, perhaps I should. Perhaps we should just get this over with so everyone can go on their merry little fucking way." Vaszhago's scornful eyes were on me, as I approached the door. "And just how did you manage to get him free?"

"I didn't. He broke the chain."

He strode toward the bed and lifted the broken chain from the mattress. On a growl, he tossed it back down. "This is what happens when someone else does the chaining. I always double it up." He nodded toward me. "Go."

Frowning, I stared back at him. "Why? What will you do to him?"

"Haven't decided yet."

"He didn't hurt me, Vaszhago. I'm fine. He just … scared me."

Jericho wriggled only so much as the paralysis Vaszhago had clearly placed on him would allow. "Had I full powers, you would be dead!"

"I'm aware," the demon answered in a bored tone before setting his attention back on me. "Tonight, it was a simple scare. Tomorrow, he could full-on claim you, or worse. Remember, it's not you I'm worried about. It's me."

Always the asshole. "I will stay away from him, then. I swear it."

"Humans have no true means of binding their words. They're just words. Meaningless," he hissed. "Now, go. Or I will snap his spine as you watch."

"You hurt him, and I will stab myself in the throat."

"You'd have to have access to knives."

"I'll hold my breath. Drown myself in the bath. Spit on a freaking papercut!"

"No, you won't." He rubbed a hand down his face. "I've got an idea. But if you don't go back to your room, I'll put you into paralysis and drag you there myself."

"Fine. I'll go. But just know? I'm watching you, demon." I pointed two fingers toward his eyes, then mine.

"A basket of kittens is more of a threat."

Grinding my teeth, I turned and left the room, tromping back toward my own bedroom. Halfway there, something struck my belly, and I skidded to a halt, placing my hand on it. A snaking sensation against my palm had me recoiling.

"Farryn? Are you all right?" The voice belonged to Kezhurah, who tilted her head, staring back at me.

"Yeah. I'm fine," I lied. "Thanks again, for everything."

"My pleasure."

A strange sensation burned in my stomach, a deep cramping nausea, but I held my smile as I stepped past her and back into my room. Crossing toward the bed, I felt the ache intensify, just as it had the night before.

Lie down, Farryn. A little rest is all you need.

I climbed into the bed and wrapped the sheet around me. While my mind anchored itself to thoughts of what Vaszhago might do with Jericho, the stabbing sensation in my belly clawed for my attention.

A strange sound reached my ears. Crying.

A baby crying.

I sat up in bed, staring across the room at the circle where Kezhurah's name was still drawn on my wall. A dark thought chimed inside my head. Babies. What if she stole them? What if she planned to steal mine?

Shaking my head of it, I lay back down, chiding myself for being so irrationally ridiculous.

Stop being paranoid.

The baby wailed again, and again, I found myself staring at the circle.

Was it so farfetched to think the woman stole babies in Purgatory?

Groaning, I turned into my pillow, burying my face. "You're not even far enough along," I muttered into the cotton. "Stop it."

What the hell was wrong with me? Where were these thoughts even coming from?

Blowing out an exasperated breath, I closed my eyes, figuring I needed the sleep. Didn't matter that I had felt better for a short jaunt there, something still didn't feel right inside of me. I forced myself to relent the thoughts of Jericho and Vaszhago, and to allow myself to slip into dreams.

The baby cried again.

37

THE BARON

The baron trembled as he lay stretched over a bench in one of the undercroft cells, his back bloodied and torn apart by the whipping he'd endured. His arms lay limp at his sides, useless and weak from having hung from chains for hours. When the bishop could no longer prod him to reveal his ability to heal, he'd resigned himself to keeping the baron in line, performing *necessary* exorcisms, which had included whippings, burnings, whatever pain he'd deemed vital to cleansing his soul.

He would've given anything to place his hand on his skin, to feel the tickle of energy as the wounds sealed themselves. Instead, he focused on breathing and ignoring the searing agony every time he stretched too far.

"You are in pain," a familiar voice spoke softly, and he turned his head to find the light-haired woman from before staring back at him. Blood stained her lip, which appeared to have been split open, and she'd had twice the bruises of before. Her shins bore the telling gashes of fire clamps, metallic clamps fixed to a part of the skin and heated until burning hot. They were then cranked to pull the skin apart, tearing it open like a ripe fig.

"Seems you suffer quite a bit, as well."

Her lips stretched to a smile, and she crawled across the floor, her ragged gown dragging behind her as she made her way toward the barred window. There, she pushed up on tiptoes, only just fitting her small hand through the bars to gather what looked like mud. Carrying it on her fingers, she shuffled toward him. "I've learned ways to soothe the pain. Let me show you."

The baron shifted away from her, but winced at the flare of a wound. "Does it heal?"

"Well, no. It only cools the burn of it."

He settled back over the bench and allowed her to spread the mud over the worst of his wounds, judging by their pain. His skin practically sizzled as she painted his back, and he let out a sigh of relief when the ache lessened there.

"Better?"

He gave a nod, breathing easier than before. "Why are you here?"

"Did we not discuss this matter the last time, Baron? When you effectively cast me out?" Her tone carried a bitter bite, as if he'd hurt her feelings.

"Where did you go? I saw no entrance. No means of exit."

"You were looking for the obvious."

"Do not toy with me. Bishop Venable has branded you a witch. Why haven't they executed you?"

She snorted, sitting back in a way that wasn't like that of a lady, at all, with her elbows resting atop spread thighs, between which her gown draped to hide her privates. "Why haven't they executed *you*?"

"It is obviously because I am the son of Lord Praecepsia."

"Well, it is obvious that I harbor a secret."

"What secret?"

Eyes narrowed on his, she tipped her head. "Now, why would I tell the son of Lord Praecepsia?"

"I have neither patience, nor care, for your games."

"My, you are an ornery one." She chuckled, shaking her head. "It so happens that I know what your father searches for when he sets off on his little journeys abroad."

"What is it?"

"Not what. *Who*."

"Who is it?"

"A girl."

While he knew his father had set off on many journeys, he'd never been made privy as to the purpose. "My father searches for a girl?"

"Not just any girl. The one who stands to set him free."

"Free? From what?"

"Do you see this cut upon my lip?" She tapped it with her grimy finger. "Do you think I suffered this much torment to turn around and spill my secrets to you?"

"Why not just tell him your secrets, then?"

"Secrets are power. The more you have, the more powerful you become. That, and I don't particularly care to die."

The baron stared at her longer, puzzling over the woman who seemed as much an oddity as any unearthly creature he'd witnessed over the last few months. "Tell me how you exit the cell without a door."

"Tell me why you refuse to heal your own wounds when you are perfectly capable of doing so." Her brow winged up in a knowing way, and she smiled. "I have many powers which are subdued by the horrible little piece of jewelry at my throat." Her comment drew his eyes there, where the metal gave off an ominous glint.

"The band. Can you not pry it off?"

"No. The only way to free myself of it, is to kill the man who put it there."

"Who?"

"Your father. He cursed the only one I've ever truly loved. And he shall pay for it. *Gravely.*"

He snapped his gaze to hers, curious as to what level of madness a person would have to succumb to confess such a thing. He glanced toward the door, finding it odd that the pentrosh who typically stood guard outside of it had not yet come crashing through, accusing her of treachery. "You wish to kill my father?"

"I cannot, as I am not powerful enough at the moment. But you are, young lord. You are quite capable of it."

"And I would acquire tremendous debt for my effort."

"Debt easily paid, for a man of your talents. I would help you. And you will be spared when the Dark-Winged One awakens again."

The Dark-Winged One? Again, he found himself glancing back at the door for the pentrosh who would've surely called her a Raver for such talk of dark forces.

Something told him not to trust the woman. Perhaps she was merely a test. The bishop's attempt to teach him another lesson. "I do not want your help. Hire a sell-sword to do your bidding."

"A sell-sword will inevitably fail. They always have. Your father is a very powerful man. Untouchable to most. But you … you can walk where others can't."

"Walk where?"

"Eradyę. It is where your father is most powerful."

The other plane about which Solomon had told him. Had he entertained her reasoning, he'd be branded a Raver. "If that were true, why does he stay here?

"He would starve in Eradyę. There are no viable souls to feed off, and the angels cannot tread there, for their powers would be depleted. Fed on by the realm itself. Free me, and you will never suffer punishment by his hands again."

"Such words would get you killed. In fact, I'm of a mind to think you are nothing more than a test. I do not believe in such fantasies as Eradyę. Nor do I believe that you have powers."

"Then, you are a fool."

"Leave me." The baron turned away from her, and new pain blazed across his back. He let out a grunt and clutched the edge of the bench.

"Do not resist the pain, young lord. Embrace it." The tickle of his shoulder shot his attention to the woman who had moved in too close. "Enjoy it." She ran her finger over his skin, and the baron shivered, the blood running straight to his cock.

"Do not touch me!"

The soft caress of her finger hardened into the vicious bite of her nails, as she scored her finger across one of his wounds. The baron cried out, and as he turned to smack her hand away, she gripped his wrist. Eyes on his, she guided his hands down past the laces of his breeches and forced his hand over his cock.

In his mind, he wanted to tell her to stop. To push her away. His voice wouldn't produce a single sound. His muscles locked into a painful state of paralysis, as she guided his hand up and down the erect flesh. He had never been touched by a woman her age, and his chest tightened with a cold, hollow feeling.

"Pain can be beautiful when mixed with pleasure," she whispered. "Do not deny your darkness. Embrace it."

Tears formed in his eyes, the anger rising inside of him while his body responded to her touch in a way that made him want to vomit. His whole body shook with both fear and disgust, as he remained bent over the bench, his hand limp to her will. Just as he had back in his room, he succumbed to the orgasm that sprung forth on their joined hands. Humiliation burned inside of him, as he buried his face in his arm.

"How was it, young lord?" When he dared to glance over at her, she had begun to lick his release from her own palm, and, the sight of her turning his stomach, he looked away again.

What had he done?

Why had he allowed such a thing?

Worst of all, why had he climaxed?

His body shook with rage and shame.

"My Lord?" At the first brush of her finger across his arm, he leaped toward the woman, knocking her back against the dirt. Wounds across his back screamed in angry protest, but he ignored the agony burning across his skin for the rage that seethed in his blood.

"Do not touch me! Do not ever lay your hands on me again!" A red haze clouded his vision. He wrapped his hands around her throat, tears slipping down his cheek.

Eyes wide, she stared up at him, and he could feel her tremble beneath his palm. "Would you hurt me, as your father does?"

Every muscle in his body shook with the urge to throttle her neck until the life drained from her eyes. Instead, he released her and sat back on his heels, his mind agonizing over the last few minutes. "I am nothing like my father."

She reached to touch her neck and flinched, before her lips stretched to a smile. "*Liar*," she whispered.

38

JERICHO

*H*ead pounding, I pressed a palm to my temple and opened my eye to Vaszhago standing over me.

"Welcome back."

Confused, I sat up from my bed and noticed the chains broken, lying in a heap. Mind rewinding to what I could remember, I stared off, sketching mental images of Farryn being ill, summoning the woman, Kezhura. Vespyr chaining me for the night. Everything afterward was a blackness I couldn't see past, but as I peered down at the broken chains, a sickening thought came to mind.

"Farryn?"

"Is fine. The vixen came looking for attention, and it seems she received it tenfold."

"I didn't hurt her?"

"No. I stopped it."

My muscles sagged with relief, and I fell back against the pillows behind me. "I'm surprised you didn't steal the opportunity to end me right then."

"Thought about it." He held up a vial in which a red film,

flecked in sparkles, clung to the glass.

"Vitaeilem?" I asked.

"Had to cut your angel friend. If he is a friend, I'm sure he'll forgive."

Rubbing a hand down my face, I shook my head. "You're certain I did not harm Farryn."

"You did not. Not so much as a nick to her skin."

"I appreciate your vigilance."

"The two of you are exhausting." On an irritated huff, he stepped back from the bed. "Truly, a human toddler would be less troublesome."

I sneered at that and pushed up from the bed. "Is she asleep now?"

"It seems. She hasn't emerged from her room, but Kezhura has checked on her."

"So, is she well. Well enough to come looking for trouble with me."

"Presumably. She is perhaps the most stubborn woman I have met in the entirety of my existence."

"Isn't that the truth." Throwing on the black robe I'd draped over the chaise earlier, I headed toward the door with Vaszhago in tow. "I'm going to have a chat with our guest."

"Should I accompany you?"

"No. I wouldn't exactly consider Soreth much of a threat."

Vaszhago snorted. "He certainly did not put up much of a fight."

Once we reached Farryn's door, I cracked it open and strode across the room, coming to a stop alongside her bed. Staring down at her, I took comfort in seeing her easy breaths, the way her lashes fluttered in dreams, and the lines of worry softened to peace. Gods, even the small dose of pure vitaeilem felt good, and I longed for the day when my power would be restored and I could touch her without the threat of my demon half. If not for Vaszhago's intervention, who the hell knew what I'd have done to her.

While my conscience begged to give her up and set her free, I wouldn't. Not then. Not ever. And perhaps I should've loathed that about myself, but I had never professed to be a good man.

Good men didn't burn down cities for the woman they loved.

After pressing a kiss to her cheek, I exited the room and headed back down the stairwell, through the back of the cathedral, and down to the enclosed staircase which led to the dungeons below. Chilled air cooled the burn of my skin as the effects of the vitaeilem took hold. In one of the empty cells, I found Soreth curled up into a strange ball on the floor, his body contorted in such a way that his nose was touching the sole of his foot.

"Is this how he's kept you imprisoned?"

Only Soreth's eyes tracked upward. "Yes. He told me that, were I not a friend of yours, he'd have had me sniffing my own ass."

The comment had me chuckling, and I leaned against the bars of the cell, arms crossed, marveling the demon's downright cruelty. "I'll have him release the paralysis spell on the condition that you don't hand me a line of bullshit about why you've come."

"I come with news." His voice was slightly muffled by his position, and I continued to fight the urge to laugh. "We are old friends, are we not?"

"I don't even trust friends these days."

"I must admit, it is quite impossible to have a serious conversation this way."

I ran a hand over my mouth in a poor attempt to stave off the laughter begging to escape. "I will try to ignore it. Now keep on with your explanation."

"That contemptible demon didn't even ask before he cut me and stole my blood."

I didn't bother to mention that he'd taken it for me. Doing so would've alerted him to my weakened state, and though I'd known Soreth for many years, I would not have admitted such a thing to him.

He groaned, his body hardly moving but remaining stiff and rigid. Poor bastard would undoubtedly be miserable once Vaszhago lifted the spell. It was no mystery how much the demon hated angels. He probably prayed for one good reason to send Soreth to absolute death. "The Sentinels are aware that you've returned from Ex Nihilo."

"You've crossed The Vale, putting your life at great risk to inform me of this?"

"Have I not been your harbinger for centuries now?"

"What else brings you here, and bear in mind, I can have Vaszhago leave you smelling your own ass."

Soreth huffed, undoubtedly tired of the paralysis. "I need asylum. It is not safe for me in the mortal realm, nor the heavens. And here, I'll be hunted by the Noxerians and their band of jolly sell-swords."

"I was once a jolly sell-sword for the Noxerians. What makes you think you're safe here?"

"I would like to think that you did look upon me as friend."

Soreth and I had never truly been what I'd have considered friends. He'd always carried an arrogance about him that clashed with my own. "Why are the mortal realm and the heavens not safe for a pure blood like yourself?"

"I have had a vision. One of a man who cracked the Omni."

Farryn's father, undoubtedly.

"I wish to speak with him as he is in grave danger. I believe he knows where to find the Met'Lazan."

From what I'd read, the identity of the Met'Lazan remained a mystery, even to the angels. "Unfortunately, you're too late. Fire demons came for him already."

He let out a forced exhale that I took for disappointment. "That is unfortunate."

"Take comfort in knowing he did not know the identity of the Met'Lazan. He spent a number of years studying the sigil, to no avail. My question is, what do you want with this Met'Lazan?"

"It is our duty to protect the human who possesses such power." In spite of his cramped position, his voice held the fervor of urgency. "Do you know that the Omni grants full use of all the vitaeilem stored in Etheriusz? Do you have any idea how dangerous that would be if the individual sided with the Infernal? We would be powerless against attack."

Suddenly, my reasoning for tracking down the Met'Lazan felt a bit selfish, but *c'est la vie.*

"Every angel and half-breed would be turned into slaves, or worse," he prattled on. As if I gave a damn about any other angel, or half-breed. "It is our duty to protect the precious sigil."

The only thing I cared about lay sleeping in her bed, and I'd fuck over every angel and demon in all five realms to keep her safe. "Something isn't adding up. Why would the heavens hunt you for that?"

"The Met'Lazan is typically human. Only the higher power angels know the identity. Those of us in contact with humans are forbidden to know. They feel we would corrupt that power to our own gain. But I cannot help the visions. And I cannot subdue the fear of knowing our realm would be destroyed should any creature, other than the angels, get their hands on this human."

All the more reason for me to find it first. Knowing Soreth, he'd probably squander the Omni for the good of the whole, or whatever pathetic mission the angels used to protect their power. "You said the Met'Lazan is a human soul. What else can you tell me?"

"Not much, I'm afraid. Just that they tend to be female. And that they are born in times when evil stands to threaten the realms." He let out a groan, his leg twitching. "Perfect! I've a damn itch on my leg."

"And you do not know who this Met'Lazan is?" I asked, ignoring his complaint.

"No. I only know that she was born in this time." More twitching signaled that the itch had gotten worse. "For Heaven's sake, can you please scratch my leg for me?"

"I'm afraid I forgot the key to your cell," I answered in a dismissive tone. "You are certain that this female was born in our time?"

"I am an academic, Jericho. Reading scriptures and scrolls is my life, unlike some. It's all I do, day in and out, for centuries at a time."

"And there is only one Met'Lazan?"

"Some time ago, there were many. Perhaps a dozen, or more, who walked the mortal realm. Now, their numbers have dwindled. We do not know why, entirely. I have a theory that she resides here in Nightshade."

My interest piqued at that. "How can you be sure?"

"In my vision, I saw a place. At the foot of Obsidian Mountain. The gates. The awful door knocker. The rooms there."

Infernium. The place he described was the asylum. *Where angels feared to tread.* Meaning, if Soreth planned to seek out the Met'Lazan, he surely had no intentions of going there himself.

"Then, you didn't just come here seeking asylum."

"The place is believed to be haunted by the souls of Eradyę." The barren land of souls that my father had called home. The realm capable of seeping into other realms to feed off the poor souls there.

"That's why you're here. To recruit me."

"You are half angel, and perhaps the only one capable of walking Eradyę for any great length of time. In my pocket, I have a vial of *la'ruajh* to help mask my vitaeilem for a short time. But it doesn't keep my powers from depleting there. It would be a slow and miserable death if I were to get trapped. But you've walked Eradyę before.

"Eradyę depletes me, as well." I had fought wars for the Knights of the Infernal Order, which had subjected me to that cold and barren world and the soulless creatures which inhabited it.

"Yes, but you can survive it. You can find your way out."

"I almost didn't the last time." I willed my head not to think about my time spent in that realm, how it had drained my vitaeilem and turned me into something that would've made my father proud. "And those who manage to escape are starving for souls."

"You would not, though. With the Omni, you could fully restore your vitaeilem."

"Except that we have no certainties. We do not know who the Met'Lazan is, let alone whether, or not, she would know the Omni if she saw it."

"It is innate for them. Somehow passed from one Met'Lazan to the next. It is as natural as speaking Pri'Scucian is for us." Much of what he said corroborated that which Farryn's father had told me.

"Us. Since when did you ever include me in your little angel entourage of Elysiumerian."

"You are the exception to most half-breeds."

"And yet, it is only demons who keep a realm like Eradyę in check." Centuries ago, Eradyę had once tried to spread through all of Nightshade, claiming its souls and invading other demon territories. It had been the Knights of the Infernal Order which had conquered them, sending them back into their own realm. It made sense that the barren realm had confined itself to Infernium—a place of vulnerable souls whose minds tended to be more open to the existence of demons. Spreading out from there would have resulted in war.

"Demons were only victorious because Letifer remains in slumber. Should he awaken, the full breadth of the Mortunath army would be at his disposal. They would infect every creature in all five realms. *Including demons.*"

"And it is this Met'Lazan, this human, who can bring down the heavens." It wasn't a question, seeing as I'd already gleaned that much from Farryn's father.

"Yes. By crumbling our only defenses. Should a realm such as Eradyę gain access to the vitaeilem in Etheriusz, the angels would be vulnerable. Sitting ducks for the starving Mortunath."

"Then, it seems the heavens would have this human Met'Lazan killed. She would be a threat, after all."

"She could also be instrumental. By having access to vitaeilem, she can grant incredible powers with nothing more than a whisper."

Which was all the more reason why I needed to find her myself. To restore my wings. My power.

Because if war was on the horizon, as he claimed, I would be defenseless without it.

"I will have Vaszhago lift the paralysis, and you will be permitted to walk freely in your cell. As a courtesy to an old friend, I will allow you to remain here. But you will be confined to this cell. The bars are reinforced with Diablisz steel, which means you cannot get out, no matter what powers you possess." After the night before, I questioned the strength of the steel, although a demon in Rur'axze was known to be creative and determined when it came to his female. "If you should disagree with that arrangement, you're welcome to leave."

"I thank you. Very much. I would like to stay, so long as I'm not contorted this way."

I snorted at that. "I'll have the staff bring you some food. Don't go anywhere."

"Asshole."

39

THE BARON

"What troubles you, Son?" The sweet lilt of his mother's voice struck the baron's heart, as he stared out of the carriage window on his way to Solomon's cabin.

He'd have preferred to walk the distance, as usual, but his mother had insisted on accompanying him that time. Wearing a feigned smile, he glanced back at the older woman. "All is well, Mother."

She made a sound of disapproval in her throat and cocked a brow. "Perhaps that worked with your nursemaid, but I can assure you that I am not so easily fooled."

He loved his mother, and trusted her above all others, but he would sooner die than speak of the wretched woman, Syrisa, and the vile ways she'd touched him in that undercroft. Although Lady Praecepsia was kind and gentle, she had always been fiercely protective of him. Even if he thought such a creature as Syrisa deserved punishment, he could not bring himself to be the reason for her execution.

Still, he couldn't shake the shame that had gnawed at him all hours of the day since that night. If evil existed, it lived inside of the sensation that crawled over his skin whenever the memory came to mind. He could feel its claws digging into him, tearing away at his conscience.

"I'm simply curious as to why you chose to accompany me this time. I am not troubled by it, only curious"

She sat back on the bench, her slim shoulders aligned with her perfect posture. "Sometimes, I enjoy the visits with Solomon."

"How did you come to know him?"

"Through your father, actually. A very long time ago, they were friends." A hint of a smile played on her lips as she seemed to recall the memory with fondness.

He remembered a conversation he'd had with Solomon, about his father having been a much different person at one time. "Was father good back then?"

She ran her hand over the silken sleeves of her dress, her gaze cast from his as if she contemplated the question. "Yes. There was a time he was. He had a rather dark sort of charm, much like yours." The slightest smile flashed across her face. "Uncommon, yet genuine."

"What happened to him?"

Her chest rose and fell with a forced exhale. "What happens to a man who chooses glory over love?"

"Do you think he could possibly change back?"

Brows flickering, she stared off. "I have certainly dreamed of it. But dreams only last for so long before you are forced to face the reality of waking from them." Attention diverted toward the window, she kept on with the fidgeting of her silk sleeve. "You have not spoken of your visits with Bishop Venable in some time. They seemed to have lessened a bit, have they not?"

"They have."

"I suppose it is their newest prisoner keeping them so captivated, and I am grateful for that."

"Which prisoner?"

"Syrisa of Soldethaire. I'm sure her name is fairly known at this point."

The sound of her name spoken aloud, on his mother's lips, stirred a sick sensation in his gut. He shifted on the bench with his sudden discomfort, and at a flash of memory, of the woman's hand guiding his along his cock, he felt acids gurgling in his throat. "You are often quick to defend a woman. What makes her the exception?"

"Many women find themselves wrongfully accused, and you are correct, even those thought to be irredeemable are worthy of forgiveness."

"You are saying she is not?"

She rolled her shoulders back and cleared her throat. "When you were not quite a full year, your father attempted to smother you with a pillow." Though the story was one he hadn't heard before, it did not come as a surprise to the baron. For he always knew his father had despised him, from the moment of birth. "Syrisa had informed him that his own son would one day be his demise. It didn't take long, however, for him to realize that he could not kill his own son without suffering equal injury, and so he failed in his attempt." She shook her head, as she continued on. "And despite her warning to him, I did not look upon her with any ill will, or malice in my heart. Not until the day those boys were pulled from beneath the floor of her cabin." Brows tight, his mother looked away and held a kerchief to her face, as if she suddenly felt ill. "I wanted to believe in her, and not your father. For I knew the evil inside of him." Fingers wringing the kerchief, she sat staring down at her lap. "How many times are women unjustly labeled, after all. But I had yet to discover the darkness in *her*." She lifted her gaze to his again, her eyes a sobering reflection of solemnity. "Just as there are dangerous men, there are also dangerous women."

"What happened to the boys?"

"What happens to a rabbit in a wolf's den?" She let out a long exhale. "Your father and I will never see eye to eye on any matter. Except for Syrisa of Soldethaire."

The baron's mother had agreed to let him walk home through the woods after his session with Solomon. Although he'd wanted to tell her about his pets, he feared their appearance might cause alarm. The puppies certainly had their darker moments–such as the day he'd found them feeding on a nest of baby rabbits–but he knew in his heart that they weren't evil. Certainly not deserving of being slain for merely being hellhounds.

On a prior visit, he'd stolen freshly discarded scraps of meat from the venator's butchery and stored them away in one of the old barrels at the cabin. Over the course of the week, it'd begun to rot, and the barrel itself was a nauseating task to open, but the little mongrels didn't seem to mind. In fact, they seemed to eat more fervently when it'd sat out for a while. As if they enjoyed the stench of rot.

Hopefully, his pets would provide some much-needed distraction.

His mind had been consumed during his training with Solomon. The disturbing revelations made by his mother, coupled to his encounters with the woman, Syrisa, had made it difficult to focus on the lesson that afternoon, which happened to be healing a bird struck by a stray arrow. A weapon made of infernal steel, according to Solomon, given the scar that remained on the bird's broad side. The raven, who he'd playfully named Cicatrix, had thanked him for healing his wound a number of times through the vinculum bond they shared.

Glancing upward, the baron found the bird flying overhead, following him into the woods. Blasted thing would not leave him alone, and the last thing he needed was another pet.

Master, someone sits in the clearing ahead, it said--perhaps the first useful bit it had said in all of its prattling—and the baron froze in place, wondering, hoping. Could it be *her*, the raven-haired girl, Lustina, returning to play with the puppies?

He dashed through the trees toward the abandoned cabin and, on reaching the clearing, found the girl sitting in the same place as the time before.

All three puppies bounced around her legs, nipping at her dress in play. Late afternoon sun bathed her in a warm, golden light, giving her skin a mesmerizing glow. She giggled as the puppies barked and pounced, and she allowed Cerberus to hop up into her lap.

Resigned to make himself known, the baron stepped forward, but halted when a cold sensation crawled over the back of his neck.

The image of Syrisa licking her fingers after what she'd done to him sent a shudder of shame through him, and he stepped back. He wanted to carve those thoughts from his mind with a sharp blade and burn them out of existence. But such a thing was impossible, for it had already seared itself and taken a monstrous shape inside his conscience.

Stomach tight with tension, he ground his teeth at the thought, unable to lift his gaze to the beautiful Lustina. Like a devil looking upon an angel.

His hand tingled with a phantom memory of the older woman's palm clutched over top of his knuckles, guiding him. Lips peeled back, he clenched his hands into tight fists. He should have fought her. Why hadn't he pushed her away?

You enjoyed it, he could hear her whisper in the darkness of his mind. *Do not deny your darkness. Embrace it.*

His gaze lifted to the girl again. The beautiful girl, whose pure and innocent scent carried on the air like that of a garden of white roses and gardenias.

Too innocent.

Regardless that she was poor and carried far less status, the baron thought himself unworthy of such a virtuous creature.

He stared down at his hands and grimaced, wishing he could cut them away from his arms. Hands that had brought him to climax under the most vile of circumstances.

Hands that were no longer clean enough to touch a girl like Lustina.

40

FARRYN

*S*till unable to sleep through the achiness in my belly and the sound of a baby crying in the wall, I snuck out of my bedroom and rounded the corner to Jericho's room. I needed to know that he was okay. That whatever Vaszhago's little plan was didn't include some twisted demon torture, or worse, though I didn't entirely have a bad sense about the demon. For reasons that didn't make sense, given their history and what he was, I trusted Vaszhago.

Even so, I needed to know.

Peering into Jericho's room showed his massive bed empty. I strode across the room to the bathroom to find it empty, as well. Had Vaszhago locked him in the dungeon?

And what about my father? I hadn't had the chance to confirm with Jericho that he'd returned him, as Vaszhago had said.

On the way back down the hallway, I gave a quick knock to the door of an adjacent bedroom, listened for an answer, and cracked it open, snooping inside to find it completely dark, save for the moonlight pouring in. Squinting, I scanned over the furniture, not finding anyone there.

I couldn't remember much of the conversation I'd had with Jericho while in the tub, my head had been in a constant fog then, but I could've sworn he'd told me that my father was there, at the cathedral. Surely, Jericho wouldn't have lied.

Unless he hadn't wanted to stress me out at the time—which was most likely.

The truth was, I wasn't all that hopeful about seeing my father again. Perhaps that was the skepticism in me rising to the surface, but I just had a sense that Jericho would return solo. So, while I made the effort to search for him, it was a bit halfhearted.

Quietly, I closed the door and moved down to the next bedroom, performing another quick sweep. As I passed a third door, the sounds of thumping and moans brought me to a screeching halt.

"Fuck me, Vaszhago. Harder!" What sounded like Kezhurah's accent bled through the wooden panels, and I tiptoed back from it, not wanting to have him shadow me while I continued my search.

As I stepped quietly past, though, gnarled coils of pain twisted in my belly, and I rested my hand there on a grunt as the crampy sensation moved through me. I froze in place, breathing hard through my nose, focusing on the sudden quiet from inside the room. *Shit.*

After a harrowing moment of keeping perfectly still through what felt like the kind of pains I'd get after food poisoning, the bed went back to thumping. I kept on through the hallway, skipping over Vespyr's room, down the staircase to the foyer. A light in Jericho's office caught my attention, where it shined under the door, and I stopped there. Hand poised to knock, I hesitated for some reason.

I carried the man's baby, but for some reason, my head still viewed him as my employer every time I approached his office.

"Farryn?" he asked in a voice that didn't hold the demonic rasp to it like before.

The achiness turned to fluttering in my stomach, as I pushed open the door to find him sitting at his desk, a shadow of anger behind his eye.

Wearing a sheepish smile, I stepped inside, closing the door behind me. "Hey. You're alive."

"As are you."

"Was I not supposed to be?"

"You weren't supposed to be in my room."

Huffing a breath, I crossed the office and took a seat in one of the chairs. "Separation is getting old."

"Do you know how easily I could've snapped your neck?"

I smirked, not wanting to admit it was the fear that excited me most about him. It always had been with Jericho. Made me feel like an adrenaline junky sometimes, the way I toyed with his restraint. And while it might've been slightly terrifying to see his chains broken earlier, I couldn't deny the small thrill that'd curled my spine. "You don't scare me," I lied.

A feral glint flickered in his eye, his cheek twitching as if he might smile. "Regardless, you shouldn't come into my room at night. It's dangerous."

"Then, I suppose you shouldn't entice me as much as you do."

Leaning back in his chair, a half-sipped drink in his hand, he looked utterly delectable with his shirt unbuttoned, showing off those silvery tattoos. "How are you feeling?"

"Great, actually." A partial lie. While I wasn't on the verge of death, the pain still had my stomach twisted up.

"Why are you awake at this hour?"

"I was hoping you'd tell me what happened with my father."

His chest rose with a deep breath, and he leaned forward

and filled his glass with the red fluid he'd claimed would kill a human. The way he refused to look at me told me Vaszhago was right–he hadn't returned with him. "How much do you want to know, Farryn? And I'd advise you consider that question carefully."

"Everything," I said without hesitation, and caught a flicker of his brow before he tipped back the drink and shook it off. "Is he alive?"

"If you're asking if he's capable of returning to the mortal realm at any point, as a fully functioning human being, the answer is no."

I tried not to let the worry consume me yet, because he didn't actually say he was *dead*-dead. Or what they, in the afterlife, considered absolute death, anyway. "You saw him?"

"Yes." In one swill, he finished off a second drink. "Fire demons came for him. Dragged him down into the flames."

Alarm shot to my throat, and I sat forward in my chair. A stab of pain struck my belly, but I bit back the urge to grimace and only held my hand against it, mentally willing the ache to go away. "What does that mean?"

"It means he dabbled in some bad deals. They came to claim his soul."

"Didn't you stop them?"

"There is no stopping a fire demon, Farryn. It's why I've been exceptionally careful with you. To piss off the infernal realm could bring horrific consequences." He lowered his gaze, setting the glass onto the desktop beside an ornate envelope opener. "I urged him to come with me. I offered him the protection of my home. But he refused."

A sting of tears hit the rims of my eyes. Though the flicker of hope had been dim, I hadn't anticipated the possibility of it being snuffed entirely. "Why? Why would he refuse?"

"Because he was resigned. And he didn't want you to see

him that way. Whatever memories you have of your father are much better thought upon than watching him succumb to hellfire. Trust me. He was doing it for you."

"And now he's gone. Gone completely." The reality of that failed to penetrate my skull, though, and I sat staring off, my mind blank to everything. Another sting of tears hit my eyes and I blinked to stave them off, as in my periphery, Jericho reached into his desk for something.

He pulled out an odd-looking object made of twigs. "He wanted you to have this."

"What is it?" I asked, accepting it and running my finger over the twists of wood and thin pieces of bark tying them together.

"A ward. I suspect the one that kept the fire demons away for a while."

Staring down at the strange, little symbol, I was taken back into memories of my father hanging similar objects around our house. "Is there nothing we can do? Anything to save him? Or bring him back?"

"No." He huffed, drumming his fingers against the desk. "Once the soul is claimed, there are few options."

My poor father. How horrible was it that a man who had never done anything more than chase after silly symbols could have been subjected to eternal suffering? He'd never murdered, nor abused a creature in his life, aside from the time he'd almost drowned me, but of course, he'd had no control as I'd since learned that a demon had possessed him. "So, what happens to him?"

If possible, Jericho's expression turned even graver than before. "He's punished. Eternally. Unless the Infernal Lands can find some use of him."

Find some use. I didn't even want to think of what that could mean.

As I held the ward to my chest, the pain broke over me.

The tiniest beam of hope I'd chased like the flitting strings of a balloon carried too far out of reach.

Arms wrapped around me, and Jericho lifted me up from the chair, carrying me to the other side of the desk, where he sat down and held me like a child. "Forgive me for not telling you earlier," he whispered and kissed my temple.

Face buried in his neck, I surrendered myself to the misery. For years, I'd been made to believe that my father had committed suicide, but somewhere deep inside my heart, I never truly believed that. I'd seen too much as a child to think a man as knowledgeable in the afterlife as he was would succumb to something so simple as death. However small and unlikely, fate had given me a sliver of hope, a small shred of mercy when I'd learned of Nightshade, and the possibility that I might've seen him again.

But then it was lost, and I supposed that I never fully believed in it, anyway. Nothing was ever given back--I learned that lesson long ago with my mother.

For what seemed like an hour, Jericho held me as I sobbed into his chest until I cried myself dry. I sat up from him, slightly embarrassed of the wet shine of his skin where I'd leaked tears all over him. "I understand why you didn't tell me at first. I'm just glad you were there. I'm glad he wasn't alone when they came for him." I opened my palm from around the ward, its edges bent a little from where I'd clutched it. "And I'm glad I have this. These fire demons, is it possible they'd come for me?"

Cupping my jaw, he tipped my head back to meet his fiery, dauntless gaze. "I will tell you this. Nothing would stop me from diving into that flame alongside you. What-ever fate awaited you would be mine." A chaste kiss to my lips left me craving that burnt cinnamon flavor on his tongue.

When he pulled away, my body mourned his attention,

which spurred a thought. "How are you not turning into a demon right now? I thought I brought that out in you."

"The angel in the dungeons, Soreth, provided a hefty dose of much needed vitaeilem." Thumb running across my bottom lip, he seemed riveted, as if he yearned for more, as well. "I'm intoxicated."

"Intoxicated?" I lifted my chin to kiss his jaw and felt him tense beneath me. "I should take advantage of you then."

"Farryn, you were lying in a bed with a deadly fever not very long ago."

"I'm feeling better."

"And your fath–"

I pressed a finger to his lips to silence him. "Please. I could really use the distraction right now."

He gripped my wrist, pulling my finger away from his mouth, as if insulted that I'd silenced him. Seconds passed while he stared back at me with that predatory gaze of his, then with his palm at the back of my head, he finally crushed me against his lips.

For the first time in weeks, I felt like I was kissing Jericho again. My Jericho. He gripped my face, holding me to him, his greedy mouth devouring my breath.

I let out a hard exhale through my nose and pushed up from him. In frantic movements, I hopped off his lap only long enough to slide my panties down my thighs and kick them away, before I was straddling his thighs again. The moment his lips found mine, his hand was up my gown, and he ran his finger over my sensitive flesh. The humming vibration beneath his skin was twice as powerful as before, and my thighs shook as the tickle against my clit had me gasping against his face. When he shoved two fingers inside of me, I clenched around him, not surprised when his fingers slickened in a few quick pumps.

"So wet already." A deep guttural sound purred in his

chest when he shoved those two glistening fingers into his mouth. "So divine."

"It's been a while since we've done this without your hands bound in chains."

I reached down between us, fumbled with his belt buckle, and sprung him free.

He let out a hiss as I stroked him. "I'm going to fuck you so raw, you'll have to be carried back to your room."

His words sent a shiver down my spine. I hadn't been properly fucked in weeks, not without some strange interruption that kept us both from climaxing. I prayed this time would be different. That I would experience the glorious moment of release.

Positioning myself over him, I impaled myself on his cock in one painful glide, the thickness of him filling me as I slowly worked myself down his shaft. The pressure had me biting my lip, while tiny electrical impulses scattered over my sensitive flesh. God, he felt so fucking good, I wanted to cry and smile at the same time. Like a snug-fitting key.

He rested his hands at my hips and groaned. "If ever I longed for Heaven, I have surely found it buried in the depths of your tight, wet cunt."

I licked my lips and smiled, circling my hips, grinding myself against his groin. "I quite like when you talk like a dirty renaissance man."

We fell into perfect cadence with each other, just as it had been before everything changed. Slick arousal lubricated every glide of his cock, creating the perfect friction.

The chair squealed as it rocked with our movements. The vibrations jittered over my ass and thighs each time I came down hard on him, and the masculine sounds in his voice left me craving more. *More*. Wrapping my arms around his neck, I upped my pace and felt his palms squeezing my ass, as he guided me up and down his rock-hard cock.

"Hell's flame, you feel so fucking good, Tu'Nazhja," he said in a husky voice that sent a shudder through me.

Faster and faster, he pumped in and out of me. Our bodies moving like a single machine. I closed my eyes and lost myself to the sensation, drifting into the dark subspace of my mind. Only the sound of Jericho's panting breaths, his grunts and moans, tickled my imagination there. A beautiful, black void, where nothing could touch me.

He let out a vicious growl, and when I snapped my eyes open, the sight that greeted me churned a sickness in my gut.

My fist rested against his bicep, and in its grip was the envelope opener I'd seen earlier. Panic filled me when I realized the object sat lodged in his flesh, and I released it. "Oh, my God! What have I done?" I couldn't even remember having reached for it, let alone stabbing him.

Gaze wild with a dark and wicked expression, Jericho swiped up my wrist and licked the blood trickling down my palm. He shot up out of the chair, taking me with him, and with the metal still sticking out of him, he laid me back on his desk.

In one hard thrust, he was inside of me again, his body moving over me like a dark storm ready to strike me down with lightning. I recalled the times I'd once feared that ominous thunder and its ruthless destruction. Not anymore. I embraced it. Surrendered to its power and let it ravage me from the inside out.

A jarring bolt of electricity moved through me, an exquisite shock to my muscles that had me crying out. Without mercy, he railed into me, his muscles damp with sweat and hard as stone. I held onto him, taking each punishing blow of his cock. He burned like the hottest part of a flame, and I wanted to be consumed by him.

My muscles tightened.

If there was still pain in my belly, I could no longer feel it at that point. Everything inside of me had gone numb. Numb for all but Jericho. His scent. His voice. His unremitting drive toward climax. I clenched around him, my thighs shaking.

Breaths stuttered out of me and warmth heated my cheeks. I tipped my head back on a jolt of pure ecstasy and shivered out a rush of pleasure that had my toes curling into his back. God, it'd felt like forever since I'd climaxed, and every cell in my body rejoiced, humming and buzzing with the lingering high.

An agonized groan, like the quiet rumble of thunder, warned of his release. His body shuddered out jets of warm fluid that dribbled down my ass. He pulled out and shoved my hand to his cock where more of his release spilled over my palm. "For weeks, I've dreamed of filling you," he rasped. "This is what you've done to me." Yet another jet shot across my forearm, as he worked my palm over his slick shaft, breaths stuttering.

Until he finally stilled.

It was only then that I let the reality of what I'd done to him crash over me. Releasing him, I let loose another shocked exhale. "Jericho ... I ... I don't know what happened. What came over me."

With his body still blanketed over mine, that shiny piece of metal glinted in my periphery. "It's all right," he said, breathless and trembling, the tiny shocks still rocking over his flesh.

"It's not! I s-s-s-stabbed you!"

A dark chuckle served as a momentary distraction, the sound of it stirring inside of my chest. "I enjoy a little pain with my pleasure." He took hold of the metal and yanked it out of himself on a sickening sound of wet meat that had my stomach twisting.

"Which is fine. I don't judge you for that, but ... I don't even remember grabbing the thing."

"At all?"

"No. I fell into this black space inside my head."

"Fuck." He pushed up off me, fluids dripping from the head of his still erect cock, and he stuffed himself back into his pants.

I sat up from the desk, my legs dangling over the edge of it as I attempted to daub some of the spilled release from my hands and thighs with my gown. The fluids seeped into the dress, creating a massive wet spot there. His balls must've weighed two pounds each with all that pent-up tension, given what I'd just cleaned. Instead of relief, though, his face held a troublesome expression.

"What's wrong?" I asked.

"We'd hoped to have banished it."

"Banished what?"

He reached back and rubbed the back of his neck, the concern on his face darkening with every second. "Was there any time that you encountered someone who may have persuaded you into doing something?" He reached around me and poured himself another drink, while I pondered the reason for his cryptic question.

"I mean, Aunt Nelle always made me eat my peas. I freaking hate peas."

"I'm not talking about peas. I'm saying you may have unwittingly given an unbound soul permission to use your body."

A cough flew out of me, and I cleared my throat. "I'm sorry, what?"

"An unbound soul. Essentially unattached."

"Are we talking demon possession?"

"Not quite as traumatic, but yes."

My mind spun back to the times when I'd felt something moving in my belly that didn't quite feel like a baby, per se, and queasiness stirred in my gut. "And this soul is in me?"

"I believe so."

"What makes you believe so?" Acids burned the back of my throat as vomit threatened to add more fluids to my dress, but I swallowed it back.

"The marking left on my arm after we arrived in Nightshade. I did a small bit of research, and it seemed consistent with an unbound soul."

"And you're just now telling me this?"

"It's only been a theory of mine. Up until earlier, when Kezhurah sensed something inside of you."

"Oh, God, I think I'm going to puke." I slid to my feet and turned around, bending over the edge of the desk to rest my forehead against my arms. "Oh, God, this is … this is bad."

"It isn't like a body inside of your body, Farryn." He ran his palm over my back.

"Um. I beg to differ. I have felt some weird shit moving inside of me."

"And *you're* just now telling *me* this?"

"Touché." I pushed up from the desk, taking deep breaths through my nose to calm the churning in my gut. "What do you mean when you say I gave it permission? I never gave permission to anything to possess my body."

"It's the only way they can inhabit. They aren't like normal demons who can possess at will."

"How?"

He leaned against the desk beside me, arms folded. "They're crafty. Have you bitten into anything–fruit, for example, which may have looked rotted on the inside?"

The visual of that had me crinkling my nose. "Ugh. No. The sight of rotted fruit would sicken me. I'd have spit it out."

"Anything you might've signed recently?"

"No, I don't think–" I slapped a hand over my mouth, my mind reeling back to the day in the gynecologist's office.

"When I visited the doctor a couple months ago." I fluttered my hands, the nervous energy pulsing through me as it occurred to me what I may have inadvertently done. "T-t-t-there was a weird document they asked me to sign."

"What kind of document?"

"It was printed on a really thin paper. Almost translucent. It was supposed to be some kind of waiver for the ultrasound. But … it was worded so weird, I almost didn't sign it."

"What did it say?"

"Something about allowing my body to be entered with a transducer. Oh, God." The sickness from before reared its ugly head, and I jerked forward as if to spew all over his desk. Slapping a hand to my mouth, I choked it back, as Jericho reached under his desk for a silver trash can and set it down beside me. After more deep breaths, until the acids subsided, I continued. "There was a weird … glitchy moment when he inserted that thing. The electricity went out, and they couldn't get a good view of the baby. He said there was something there, but he couldn't see what it was."

Jericho fell back into the seat and pinched the bridge of his nose. "Fuck."

"You're not helping my urge to puke. What does this mean?"

"It means it found a way to stick with its host. And I suspect whatever is living inside of you has learned how to send you away."

"What? Send me away, how?"

"When you say you went into a black subspace, that was the soul putting yours to sleep, so to speak."

I didn't want to admit that what he'd said made sense, as that was exactly what it'd felt like. "But … I was aware of things around me. I could hear you, but I didn't have any awareness of picking up that opener."

"It's an unnerving feeling when something takes over your body."

"How do I get rid of the damn thing?"

"I thought we already had, but perhaps we need to consider another method." He ran his thumb over his bottom lip, his good eye staring off, contemplative.

"What method?"

"I don't know in the case of a soul *wanting* to remain. I've taken over a body before, but the last thing I cared to do was stay in it. Unbound souls are different, though. They need a physical body in order to truly exist." He let out a huff and rubbed a hand down his face. "Soreth is fairly well-educated on the topic of souls. I can inquire and see what he knows. Are you in pain, at all?"

"At the moment? No." Still a little queasy, but I couldn't sense any pain anywhere, aside from the ache of having had him fully erect inside of me.

"I'm going to see if he has anything to offer."

"Will this entity hurt me? The baby?"

The way his brows came together certainly failed to put me at ease. "According to Kezhurah, it depends on the malevolence of it. She said this one has been with you a while, so I would imagine not, but after what happened to you outside of the bookstore, I won't take any chances."

Wringing my fingers together, I tried to ignore how many times it'd felt like something had punched me from inside. How many times I'd felt a stabbing ache of pain, or queasiness. The black vomit I couldn't explain and the hallucinations. All of it made sense when possibly tied to this disturbing revelation. "I want it out of me. Whatever I have to do, I want this damn thing out of my body. God, can you even imagine, Jericho? I stabbed you with a freaking envelope opener?" I couldn't even say aloud the visual that'd slipped behind my eyes, of this entity compelling me to harm the baby after it was born.

"Let me speak with Soreth. And don't worry, I'm going to remove this soul if I have to rip it out of you with my bare hands."

"Is that possible?"

"It is." His frown deepened, and he stroked his jaw. "But at the risk of incredible pain to you. I will not subject you to that unless absolutely necessary."

At a knock at the door, I cleared my throat and took a step back from Jericho, hoping the office didn't smell like he'd just railed the hell out of me. I slipped the trash can back under the desk and crossed my hands over the wet spot on my gown.

At the quirk of Jericho's brow, I gave a nod.

"Come in." His voice carried a tone of authority that never failed to send a flutter to my stomach, and he eased back into his seat. Surprise rose up into my throat when he gripped my waist and yanked me onto his lap. He gave a possessive squeeze of my thigh, as Vaszhago entered the office and strode toward us.

"How did I know I'd find you here?" the demon asked with a not-so-enthusiastic tone in his voice.

"I would've informed you first, but, uh … sounded like you were *engrossed*." I kept my tone flat and crossed my arms.

The demon's cheek twitched with a smirk as he rolled his shoulders back.

"Is Kezhurah still here?" Jericho's question grew distant to the thoughts of my father and the freeloading soul taking up residence inside of me.

"No. She seemed satisfied with Farryn's progress, so she returned."

"I'd like you to retrieve Soreth for me. Bring him to my office. I've a matter to discuss with him."

"Very well." He gave a nod and swung his attention to me. "For the record, I heard you tiptoeing outside my room. Your footfalls are obnoxious."

"Yeah? Well, you two were pretty obnoxious, too."

His lips curved to a smirk as he turned and exited the office, closing the door behind him.

"My footfalls aren't obnoxious, are they?" When Jericho didn't answer right away, I turned to see him staring off, his thumb mindlessly rubbing over mine, not a trace of humor in his expression. "Are you all right?"

He broke his stare and lifted his gaze to mine, his expression quizzical.

"You just look really concerned." I ran a thumb over the deep crease in his forehead.

"I'm fine." He snatched up my wrist and kissed my fingers. "I just want some answers. Now."

"Should I go to my room?"

"No. I want you here. Right here."

"Why?"

"Because I want to see his reaction when you're in the room. If I sense anything is off, I'll know to leave him locked in the dungeons."

I shook my head and pressed my shoulder against his chest. "You really don't trust anyone, do you?"

"Not where you're concerned."

"Except Vaszhago."

"I only trust Vaszhago because I know what harm will come to him. No one who intends to hurt you is safe around me."

A smarter woman would've surely taken his words as a sign of crazy possession and probably run for the hills. Given my fears, which simmered just below the surface, his words wrapped around me like a security blanket and gave just enough of a squeeze to make me feel safe.

The door clicked open to admit Vaszhago and Soreth, and in the light of the office, I could see the guy more clearly. He reminded me of a blond Clark Kent, with the sharp angles of his face, which must've been an angel thing, because Jericho had the most impressive jawline I'd ever seen. Vaszhago gave a hard shove from behind, and the angel stumbled forward, shooting the demon a glare over his shoulder. The two of them strode toward Jericho and me, the angel's eyes on me the whole time. Something about him gave me the creeps. Probably the fact that the asshole had climbed in through my bedroom window.

Once the angel had taken his seat, an uncomfortable silence hung in the air. Vaszhago stood off to the side, his shoulder propped against the wall in a casual stance. The complete opposite to the tension running through me right then.

Jericho didn't bother with any formal introductions, before he started in with, "Soreth, I brought you to my office to pick your brain."

Lowering his gaze, the angel shifted in his chair and cleared his throat. "Of course. How can I help?"

"Tell me what you know about unbound souls."

He rolled his shoulders back and sat up in his chair. "Very well, um. They are souls without a physical body–"

Jericho raised his hand, interrupting him. "Specifically, I want to know how one gets rid of an unbound after inadvertently allowing it inside the body."

Soreth jerked, his eyes flitting from me to Jericho, and back to me again. "Would you be asking me this question for any particular reason?"

"Yes. I want to know the answer."

The angel swallowed a harsh gulp and shifted again. "Once the soul establishes a connection with the physical body, assuming it doesn't starve and perish beforehand, it will gradually begin to take over. Could take days, weeks, months if it can find a sustainable source of nourishment."

"Souls?"

"Not necessarily. It depends on what fed it in its natural form." He cleared his throat again, and I caught a subtle glance toward me. "A succubus, for example, feeds on sexual energy. Therefore, it may compel its host to sleep with a number of partners. In that case, if successful, it might exist inside the body for months."

Jericho moved beneath me, his fingers curling into my hips in a possessive way. "And what banishes a soul from the body."

"Well, there is only one way to banish an unbound soul. Surely, you recall the last time we witnessed such a thing."

A sudden, cold sensation stirred inside my chest, like the first pangs of nausea settling over me. Not wanting to draw attention to it, I swallowed hard and breathed through my nose. The chill expanded and pulsed, pushing against my ribs.

Their conversation became a distant sound over the blood thudding in my ear. I pushed up from Jericho's lap and felt a tight grip of my arm. I twisted to see Jericho's face pinched to a look of concern. Sending what had to be an unconvincing smile, I shook my head. "I'm just feeling tired. I'm going to return to my room."

He nodded at the demon across the room, and when my gaze landed on Vaszhago, I caught him pointing to Soreth, brow winged up, as if to ask if he'd be fine left with the angel.

Jericho nodded again and tugged me to his face for a kiss. "I'll come check on you."

"I'm fine. Truly. Just a little tired from earlier."

With a slow nod, he released me, and as I walked toward the door, I heard Vaszhago fall in after me. Good grief, I'd need to hurry back to my room, or he'd surely make something out of it.

As I stepped out into the foyer, the walls shifted around me,.

Don't pass out. Don't pass out. Don't pass out.

Blinking away the wooziness, I climbed the staircase and let out a sigh of relief when I arrived at my door.

"You're all right?" Vaszhago asked, tipping his head as he studied me.

"Fine. I didn't eat much today, so it's just a little light-headedness."

"Do you need to eat?"

"No. Not this late. I'll end up puking all over the place."

Lip curled to a look of utter disgust, he backed himself away. "Very well. I'll wait outside your room."

Ugh. I hated the way he'd taken the guard thing so seriously. "Cool."

41

THE BARON

"*W*hat's so important back at the village?" the baron asked, quickening his pace to keep after Soreth, who remained two steps ahead of him. He'd been on his way to Solomon's when Soreth had crossed paths with him, scuttling through the forest as if he'd been chased by a horde of bees. He'd told the baron to follow after, though he hadn't told him the reason.

"A soul stripping. I've only read of them. Never saw one in person."

"What is it exactly?"

"Precisely as its name suggests," the angel said over his shoulder, as he stepped over a toppled log. "A soul being stripped from the body."

The baron followed over the log he'd already encountered once that afternoon. "Do demons not consume souls all the time?"

"This is not the same thing. It is a physical separation of body and soul." Soreth used his hands to demonstrate, clasped together, then quickly unclasped. "A demon can feed on a soul, perhaps even consume it, but certainly not all at once. It's a terribly painful procedure."

"And so, why would we want to witness such a thing?"

"Because it is rare. And I am here to study such things. Therefore, I want to see."

The baron glanced back toward the other direction and stumbled, catching himself before he fell. "Well, I suppose Solomon won't mind if I come with you. If it is rare, as you say."

They reached the edge of the forest and took the narrow footpath leading down into the village square. Most public executions took place on the grounds of the monastery, specifically in its courtyard, an area teeming with flowers around a small fountain, which the baron always thought added such an odd contrast to what took place there.

Once at the monastery wall, Soreth flattened himself against the stone and peered in on the courtyard. "Stay out of sight," he whispered. "This one prefers young boys. Should she see you, she may try to feed on you."

"Young boys? Whose soul is getting stripped?"

"Syrisa of Soldethaire."

Syrisa.

Her name echoed inside his head. The baron's stomach lurched, and he stepped back against the stones, where the gates to the monastery had been left open, as they often were during public executions. "Soreth, what exactly–"

His question was cut short by the sound of a gut-wrenching scream, and the baron turned to find horses approaching the monastery, galloping at an unusual speed. He remained off to the side to avoid a trampling, and when the carriage passed, he caught sight of an unclothed body, covered in dirt and grime and blood, being dragged behind it. Her blonde hair had been shorn down to her skin, making her nearly unrecognizable. If not for the familiar wounds on her shins, and the band at her throat which glistened in the afternoon sunlight, he'd have thought her to be someone else.

She screamed as the gravel tore at her naked flesh, while the carriage entered the square, circling the platform and the villagers. Tension wound in his stomach, his eyes riveted on the scene. Aside from the clacking of horse hooves, not a sound rose from the spectators who'd gathered to witness her execution.

The horses came to a stop, and the screams died to sobbing.

Tethered by her ankles, she clawed at the dirt, as if she could get away from the two Pentacrux soldiers who approached her.

"No! No!" Her outcry echoed through the mostly quiet square, smothering the sounds of the few who whispered amongst themselves.

One guard untied her feet, while the other yanked her upright. Seemingly weak and injured, she hung defenseless in their arms, as the two guardsmen carried her up onto the platform. The moment they climbed the staircase, a collective gasp filled the air as the wounds on her back where the gravel had torn at her skin became visible.

She had changed since the baron had last seen her in that undercroft, which must have been nearly a fortnight ago. Her body had grown thinner and frail, seemingly starved in that period of time, her bones sticking out through her mutilated skin.

The soldiers cuffed her to chains which hung from an ominous wooden contraption that had her legs spread, her arms stretched above her head. The starkness of her naked body—the light patch of hair between her legs and breasts, which carried horrific marks of torture--sent a queasy feeling to the baron's gut. Unable to look upon her that way, he turned to find that Soreth remained fixated.

What kind of angel found such a thing so riveting was beyond his imagination.

From the crowd, Bishop Venable stepped forward, dressed in his ceremonial garb with elaborate embroidery and the Pentacrux symbol sewn into his mitre and lapels. "My good people, this woman stands before you as both a criminal and heretic. She has tainted our faith in humanity with despicable acts against mere children. She is a thief and witch who threatens our community. And so it is written in scripture that such atrocities be punished in a most grievous way, so that we may cleanse the evil which has descended upon us, and send a message to likeminded individuals that such wickedness will not be tolerated."

The crowd erupted into shouts and screams. The baron could just make out the words *heretic* and *whore*.

Hands outstretched, the bishop quieted them once more and turned toward Syrisa. "Have you any final words?"

Laughter rose up from the stillness, and it took a moment for the baron to realize it had come from the woman on the platform. She lifted her head, staring out over the crowd. "You are all going to die. Every last one of you. By the flames of The Infernal, you will all perish when my beloved, Letifer, awakens!" Her laughter turned obnoxious, and the crowd broke into more shouts and screams. Beneath their raucousness arrived another familiar sound, and Jericho turned to where the crowd parted for four massive dogs. His father's dogs, which were kept in kennels back at the manor. On a few occasions, he'd heard the vicious beasts feeding on a prisoner, the screams carrying through the night.

His stomach twisted, as their caregiver struggled to keep the dogs from pulling on leashes stretched so tight, it was a wonder they didn't snap. The baron looked around the crowd that was made up of mothers and fathers and children, all of them shouting, pining for the blood of the woman.

While the baron certainly had no love for her, he could not help but wonder what compelled them to bear witness to such a thing.

Again, he turned his attention to Soreth. "Will they know?"

"Know what?"

"Do they see the soul being stripped?"

"No. That is the reason for the dogs. To mask the effects."

"Effects?"

"Sometimes, the skin splits away."

He snapped his attention back to Syrisa, imagining the visual of such a thing. "That is horrible."

"Most times, they explain it as the evil tearing through the body, but such a thing can be disturbing and cause a frenzy. So they bring in an animal to feed off it."

"You believe her to be evil. Guilty of the crimes of which she is accused."

"Yes." There wasn't a hint of doubt in Soreth's voice, as he continued to stare in on the woman. "There is no opportunity for redemption. Her soul is as black as they come."

"Because of what she did to those boys?"

"That. And because she once served Letifer."

The baron could not recall whether, or not, he'd heard the name before. Perhaps Solomon had mentioned him once. "Who is he?"

"The bringer of death. He resides in Eradyę and, at the moment, remains in slumber there."

"How do you know she served him, if he remains in slumber?"

"Because, as I understand, that is what she screamed

during her torments. She referred to him as her lover, who would wreak havoc on all five realms."

"Is that what happens if he wakes from slumb–"

Screams tore through the monastery, and the baron snapped his attention toward Syrisa, whose eyes appeared to be fixed on the dogs that growled and snarled, pulling at their leashes. A chill rippled down his neck, the way she watched the animals approach.

"Unleash the hounds!" the bishop commanded, and the moment they were cut loose, the baron's heart pounded in his throat.

In one split second, Syrisa turned, just enough that it seemed her gaze had landed on his.

He caught the slight lift of her lips, a hint of a smile.

The dogs barreled into her. Her body jostled with the assault, but she did not let out a single scream. Instead, she tipped her head back, eyes closed, while the beasts fed on her flesh.

The baron's father, Lord Praecepsia approached the woman from behind and whispered in her ear.

Her face contorted, twisting to a look of sheer agony, and only then did she release a scream. One that carried on the air and rattled the baron's bones.

42

JERICHO

*M*y mind rewound back to that day at the monastery and watching Syrisa succumb to the pain. She'd had dogs mauling her without so much as a whine, but the moment my father had whispered in her ear, she was no longer silent.

I paced back and forth, drink in hand, as Soreth sat at a small table, reviewing texts he'd taken from my library, along with the grimoire I'd studied for weeks.

Letting out an exasperated huff, he sat back in his chair. "There is truly little known about the unbound."

"Makes sense, considering they're invisible most times." I tipped back a sip of my drink to drown the frustration sitting heavy at the back of my throat.

"This text says that, in time, it can cast the host's soul into subspace permanently."

Fuck. Exactly what I didn't want to hear. "What is it that allows it to become increasingly powerful over the host?"

"Nourishment. It grows stronger with nourishment."

"Which it relies on the host for."

"Correct." He leaned forward over one of the books and

ran his finger over its pages, as if skimming the text. "According to what I've read, there are two ways to banish the unbound. The first is as we've seen with the soul stripping. Incredibly painful and possibly risky for the host, as it could cause damage."

"And the second?"

Brows knitted, he lowered his gaze. "By killing the host. The unbound doesn't care to be stuck inside a lifeless body, and so they exit rather willingly. It compromises the host, of course, but it, at least, releases their soul from subspace and allows for redemption."

"Oh, well, we wouldn't want the soul to be unredeemed, would we?" The bitter sarcasm in my voice was the result of too many hours spent studying. Bargaining in my mind what I'd be willing to do for Farryn. "Is there no reasoning with this entity? Perhaps striking a deal of some sort?"

"I suppose it's worth a try, but if it is contented inside its host, it certainly won't be inclined to leave."

I stared down into my drink, swirling the dark, bubbly, red liquid around the glass. "You remember Syrisa of Solde-thaire, not just the soul stripping, but who she was?"

"Of course I do. I was there when they pulled those boys from her cabin in the woods. The village had asked me to evaluate their wounds, as I'd studied a small bit of human medicine."

"What happened?" My mother had refused to give me the details, fearing that speaking such evil aloud would invite it into our home. And so I was left bereft, curious, but I'd never bothered to inquire about her further.

"The rumor going around was that she had molested the boys for some time and tortured them. And certainly, when their bodies were pulled from the cabin and laid out on the grass, it was clear that torment had, in fact, been carried out." He exhaled a long breath, rubbing his hand over his forehead. "Aside from bite marks all over their flesh, their torsos were concave, as if something had been drawn out of them. Entirely disturbing. But the worst of it was their eyes. Often times, with bodies, you see what we now know is corneal clouding. Back then, they believed it was a sign that the soul had left the body." He circled his hand by his own eyes, staring off in thought. "*Their* eyes were a deep red. Blood red. Beyond petechial, or subconjunctival hemorrhaging, which can affect the whites of the eyes. That's often associated with asphyxia." Eyes still fixated, as if reliving the moment, he shook his head. "The entire cornea, including the iris and pupil were red. Absolutely disturbing to look at."

"And so, what did she ultimately do to the boys?"

"She was known to take boys in, to entertain them sexually, but in this case, it appears that she consumed them."

"Consumed the souls? Their flesh?"

His throat bobbed with a swallow, and he cleared his throat. "When I opened the boys' bodies, I found their torsos to be completely hollow. No organs, no blood, no bones. Their torsos had essentially been carved empty. Yet, they bore no evidence of having been previously cut. No stitched wounds. Nothing that could possibly explain the oddity."

"I've not heard of this story. No one ever spoke of it, and surely such a thing would've sparked rumor."

"Of course it would've. That is precisely why I never shared my findings. With anyone. Until now."

I rubbed my hand across my neck so incessantly, it burned there. "So, what you're telling me is that Syrisa was an entity that fed on human organs."

"Not entirely. She fed strictly on the organs of children. And I believe she chose those boys for a reason. Young boys were how she managed to remain youthful."

The knock that interrupted held a frantic beat, and I swung my gaze around. "Come in."

Anya pushed through, breathing hard through her nose. The sight of urgency in her eyes wound my muscles tight.

"What is it?" I asked, already striding toward her.

"Master Van Croix, I ... It's Farryn–"

Alarm pummeled at my muscles, and I didn't wait for her to finish. I shot past her and up the staircase to Farryn's bedroom.

43

FARRYN

Thirty minutes before ...

*W*hispers reached my ears in the dark. So many whispers. They spoke so fast, I couldn't hear what they were saying. Slamming my hand over my ears proved futile. They were in my head, deep inside my skull. Over and over, the same sound, but the words lacked clarity.

I sat up from my bed and the room shifted, like a glitch. The whispers grew louder, the wisps of the voices crackling inside my head. The sound vibrated down my spine, stirring a queasy sensation in my stomach.

Pressure swelled and throbbed in my ear, and I opened my jaw in a poor attempt to release it.

Shadows moved over the walls, taking the form of bodies dancing around a bonfire. The bodies came together in pairs, at first, then as one big group. They pulsed in sync, in a way that reminded me of a heartbeat. Over the incessant whispers, the sounds of moans filled my room. Not of pleasure, but agony.

"Stop it," I muttered. "Stop it!"

The bodies pulsed faster, in the telling movements of sex, and I scanned my room, finding nothing more than furniture, which stood quiet and still.

A strange sensation crawled over the back of my neck, and I lifted my gaze toward the ceiling.

A black residue overhead quivered like a festering wound. An object the shape of a limb pushed through, like a rubbery skin, as if an elastic barrier kept it trapped. I could feel a mirrored movement inside my belly, and I rested a hand there, my stomach twisting and turning in knots. The limb pulled back into the ceiling, and what looked like the shape of a face pushed against the black elastic, its mouth agape.

Breaths panting, I ran my hand over my belly and let out a quiet sob on feeling the same gaping mouth and teeth beneath my palm.

"No, no, no," I said on a stuttering breath.

The face slipped back into my stomach.

The grunting and moaning sounds heightened. The whispers converged into a single voice.

The shadows turned erratic, violent in their abrupt jerks and thrusts.

'Banish the innocent from thy womb! Banish the innocent from thy womb!'

Pressing my palms over my ears, I squeezed my eyes. The whispers arrived faster, louder. Until they reached a deafening sound. I opened my mouth to scream, and a high-pitched ringing pierced my head.

Jagged flashes of light flared behind my eyelids in the same shape as the shadows on the wall.

The ringing faded.

The shadowy flashes of light merged into the darkness and disappeared.

Blissful quiet hung on the air again, and I opened my eyes to find the strange blonde, the one from my nightmares, standing alongside the bed staring down at me. She reached out a hand, and when she touched my stomach, I kicked away from her, the headboard behind me knocking into my spine. An intense, cramping ache struck my belly, and I cried out.

"This will only hurt a little," she whispered.

A wet sensation drew my eyes to the white sheets, where dark red fluid pooled out from beneath me. My chest tightened with panic, the air too thick to breathe.

"No! No!" Another rush of fluid gushed from between my thighs, and I tipped my head back on a scream.

44

THE BARON

*B*ending forward to lace his boots, the baron paused on hearing a quiet knock at his door. "May I enter, Your Lordship? I have your breakfast."

Groaning at the sound of Drystan's voice, the baron went back to his tying. "Very well."

Drystan took careful steps and set a tray of food down on a table across from the bed. He lingered there, watching.

An irritating sliver of impatience prodded the baron, and he sat back on his mattress to face the other boy. "Well, what is it? Why are you still here?"

"Forgive me, I was only curious to know if you planned to attend the execution later."

"Execution of whom?"

"A witch is to be burned at the monastery."

Sneering at that, the baron shook his head and rounded the bed for his breakfast, knocking Drystan in the shoulder as he passed. "No. I will not be attending the bishop's ridiculous display of power."

"But … she is a witch, My Lord. She has prophesied terrible things."

"Oh, Heaven forbid. Not the prophesies. And is the *good and virtuous* Bishop Venable not equally prophetic for speaking of war. Did you not hear his sermon? The Parable of the Weeds." He held out his hand, the way the bishop had while delivering his homily. *"Let both grow together until the harvest: and in the time of harvest I will say to the reapers, 'Gather ye together first the tares, and bind them in bundles to burn them: but gather the wheat into my barn.'"* The baron bit down into the bread, glowering at his cousin while he chewed. "I suppose you, dear Cousin, shall be invited into the barn, while I burn with all the other injurious weeds of the field."

"I do not believe you to be a sinner. Misguided perhaps, but not a sinner."

The baron let out a dark chuckle. "You are quite qualified to make such an assessment, I am certain."

Brows pinched, he lowered his head in that pathetic gesture that always reminded the baron of a scorned child. "I do not intend to come off as arrogant. I simply mean, I believe it is wrong what happens to you in the undercroft."

"Oh, *I* am sure of that." He turned away from the boy and spread the jellied fruit onto his bread.

"If it is not the monastery, where are you going, if I may ask?"

"You may not."

"I just thought I might accompany you, is all."

The baron let out an ungracious snort and took another bite. "And miss the burning of a witch?" he asked around a mouthful. "Perish the thought."

"I have tried, desperately, to regain your friendship, My Lord, and you consistently reject my kindness."

"And I will continue to do so. For I will never look upon you as a friend for as long as I live. Now leave."

Lips pressed to a hard line, Drystan gave a sharp nod. "As

you wish." He spun around on his heel and tromped toward the door.

"Give my regards to the good bishop," the baron said, as the boy exited his room.

After finishing his breakfast, the baron headed down the familiar path toward his dogs. The plan was to feed them more meat scraps, then head to Solomon's for an afternoon session, seeing as his father wasn't expected to return until the following day. As he entered the forest, his mind clung to the conversation with Drystan. Not specifically what had transpired between them, but the witch.

Another accused.

He'd not attended a public execution since the soul stripping of Syrisa, nearly three months prior, an experience which would be forever seared into his mind. He could not banish the small bit of curiosity over who the bishop might have deemed heretic that time. Seemed any woman who demonstrated even the smallest manifestation of independence was struck down by the church as being wild and lacking proper discipline. Possessed by demons.

'*A woman's heart bears the fire of warmth or scorn,*' his mother had always said to him, and as a result, the baron had grown to appreciate and respect the feisty ones. He admired their strength and tenacity and had never felt intimidated by them.

As he approached the dilapidated cabin carrying a satchel of heavy meat, he smiled on hearing the dogs barking. They'd grown significantly in the last few months, alarmingly fast. All three of them stood at the level of his chest, and he was certain they could swallow his head whole, if they were so inclined.

Cerberus came bounding toward him, tongue lobbed off to the side, with Fenrir and Nero at his rear. The dogs managed to tackle him to the ground, and the baron let out a hearty laugh as they mauled him with their tongues.

"All right! All right!" He batted them away, catching just a scratch of Fenrir's teeth across his arm. "Sit, or I will not feed you so much as a crumb!" All at once, the dogs sat back in a perfect line, just as the baron had taught them in prior visits.

A detestable rotted scent carried on the air, and he followed after it, crossing the yard toward a large, brown mass that lay at the edge of the adjacent woods. A bear, he guessed, though it was difficult to discern, given its state. The dogs had clearly consumed it, leaving nothing but bones and fur.

He couldn't blame the dogs, really. Their appetite had grown in recent months, and the baron simply couldn't haul that much meat without someone noticing. His only worry was that someone would happen upon the carcass, and who knew how many more littered the forest. The venators would begin to take notice eventually and stir up stories of monsters in the woods, and it would only be a matter of time before they'd come hunting the dogs. He'd need to find a new hiding place for them soon.

As he lifted his gaze, he noticed the patch of weeds off in the distance, where he'd often found the girl, Lustina, playing with the dogs. He hadn't seen her in quite some time. Not at the cabin, nor in the clearing deeper in the woods where he'd first stumbled upon her. As if she had suddenly disappeared. An emptiness filled him, seeing as he often looked forward to laying eyes on her, quietly watching her as she went about her day. Sometimes, she would play with the dogs. Other times, she would sit quietly, weaving crowns of flowers and sticks. He never approached her, though, perfectly content to watch. At night, he would think of her as he brought himself to climax, and sometimes, the urge would hit him in the day, as well. On a few occasions, he would have to find a place absent of prying eyes and relieve the ache in his groin. Not seeing her anymore troubled him, and had he not been due to arrive at Solomon's that afternoon, he'd have wandered the forest in search of her.

Instead, he returned to the dogs, who still waited on their haunches for his next command. He quickly fed them the gift of meat, then started on the path toward Solomon's.

The bright blue sky overhead darkened with an abruptness that slowed the baron's steps. He glanced upward, watching a black overcast swallow the blue. The sound of crinkling drew his attention to the trees, where summer's green foliage withered before his eyes, and the crumpled black leaves fell from the trees, producing barren limbs that seemed to desiccate, turning white.

A faint mist drifted from the sky, and the baron held out his palm, capturing what looked to be bits of ash raining down on him. He felt a strange twisting in his gut and he stared down at his hands to find a black discoloration crawling up his arm. Just like the time in the undercroft.

Eradyę was what Solomon had called it.

The barren world.

"Well, look what we have here." The voice that spoke to him felt like ice-cold fingers down the back of his neck, and he turned to find his father standing off a few yards away. Dressed in a long, black, hooded tabard, he somehow blended into the scenery that surrounded them. "On your way somewhere?"

The baron didn't answer him, and instead watched warily. It was rare he traveled anywhere alone, and the fact that he did not have Alaric at his side sent alarm through the baron. His father hadn't been expected to return for two more days.

When the boy glanced down at himself again, the blackness had climbed to his elbows and seemed to be working its way up to his neck. A hollow ache in his stomach felt like something clawing itself out of a hole, scraping the inside of him. "What is happening to me? What is this?"

"You are becoming."

"Becoming what?" he dared to ask, not truly wanting to hear his father's response.

With a skyward glance he looked around, before his gaze landed back on the baron. "This world, it feeds off your vitaeilem. The moment you step inside of it, do you not sense something consuming you? A feeling of gnawing in your belly?"

He *had* felt that. A disturbing sensation of teeth and nails deep inside his gut. He rested his hand there, the panic rising up in his throat.

The sound of crackling branches drew his attention toward the trees, where shadows moved in a way that seemed unnatural. As if many objects were casting them, yet there was nothing but trees when he glanced around. "You do not change in this world?"

"I change at will. You see, I've learned how to control the hunger which feeds on me. I've learned how to keep it from consuming me."

"How?"

Instead of answering, he smiled and crossed his hands behind his back, pacing between the two trees ahead. "Why have you not tried to kill me yet?"

"You're my father."

"And that means so very much to you. I'm touched."

The blackness spread farther than before, over his arms and he could feel the tingly sensation at his neck. Dread stirred a cold sensation in his chest. "Am I dying? Withering like the forest?"

A loud screeching echoed through the trees, and the baron turned around, eyes trailing over the ghost-white tree trunks for what could have made such an awful sound.

His father's chuckle sent a shudder of fear down his spine. "You will not perish here, because my blood runs through you. The blood of Letifer. I cursed him, and in turn, he cursed me. And you. We are one of few who can walk this plane freely without being *infected* by what lives here."

Still searching for the source of the sound he'd heard, he asked, "What lives here?"

"Would you like to see?"

The ruckus of ferocious barks and snarls echoed behind the boy, and he twisted to find all three of his dogs bounding through the forest, toward him. Dread sank to the pit of his stomach. For months, he'd tried to keep the dogs away from his father, who he feared would destroy them. When they reached the baron, they stood at either side of him, guarding him. Cerberus paced in front of him in a way that reminded him of a lion guarding its pride.

Lord Praecepsia's brows winged up. "And what is this? You've found yourself a pack of guardians. How lovely."

"They do not belong to me."

"It seems they beg to differ."

The screeching echoed again, and the dogs turned their attention from the boy's father to the woods, seeming to take a sudden interest in it.

"Stay, boy," I whispered to Cerberus. "Stay."

Whining, the dog sat back on its haunches.

The gnawing sensation in the baron's belly intensified, and he placed his hand there, trying to settle the strange feeling that'd come over him.

"It craves, even if you don't want it to." His father's voice had grown distant to the thoughts inside his head. Horrible thoughts.

As if manifesting themselves, he glanced to the side to see Syrisa standing there, her long, blonde hair draped over bare shoulders, as her thin gown clung to her full breasts.

She isn't real, he told himself. *Not real*. Yet, he could feel her phantom hands on him, as if she stood beside him, stroking him. Agony stabbed his belly, and the baron fell to his knees, grimacing as it moved through him. The dogs shifted around him and whined, clearly nervous. His groin throbbed as the ghostly stroking sensation heightened.

"Tell me that you do not find gratification in pain," his father kept on, still standing off from him and watching him writhe in pain. "Tell me you didn't enjoy when Syrisa put her hands on you."

A burst of anger exploded inside of him. "No! Do not speak another word!"

"Tell me you didn't find relief by her hand."

"No!" The boy slammed his palms to his ears, and in the silence of his mind, a soft feminine voice rose up from the darkness. *Lustina's. 'Pain in pleasure is beautiful,'* she said in that calming sing-song voice.

When he opened his eyes, the girl stood before him, wearing the white gown that revealed her much smaller breasts. She stroked a gentle hand down Cerberus's back, and the dog stilled alongside her as if suddenly contented, no longer fussing over the baron.

"Do you not touch yourself to thoughts of me, My Lord? When you are in pain, do you not bring yourself to climax?"

Shame and humiliation beat through him, and he lowered his gaze from hers, unable to look her in the eyes.

"Would you like me to relieve you now, Your Lordship?"

Another stab of pain struck his groin, and he bent forward, cupping himself. The girl knelt to the ground beside him and reached down, resting her hand over his.

"Please. Let me touch you."

"You are not real." Somewhere beyond him stood his father, watching. Undoubtedly ridiculing, though he could only hear Lustina's sweet voice.

The innocent and demure smile on her face sharpened, and not a moment later, he was no longer peering back at Lustina, but Syrisa.

Repulsed, he shoved her away from him, and her body exploded into a white dust.

"We have needs," his father said. "Needs that are subdued under the iron fist of virtue. I am not your enemy, Son. I am your father, and I love you."

"You do not love," the baron gritted out past clenched teeth. His body vibrated with the anger that moved through him like a storm. "You do not know its meaning. You are weak!"

"Weak? Allow me to show you what true weakness looks like. Tell me, have you ever gazed upon a creature and wondered what it looked like when it suffered?"

The sound of agony drew the boy's attention to his right, where Solomon sat on his knees, wincing. "He is not real," the baron said aloud, his voice carrying an edge of uncertainty.

"Isn't he?"

Screams slashed their conversation, and the baron's muscles twisted up as he watched Solomon's body bend backward into an unnatural and grotesque arc of his body, trembling as if in intense pain.

Cerberus barked, but kept his distance.

The baron shot to his feet, his hands balled to tight fists at his side. "Stop this! Stop it now!"

"Did you honestly think I would not find out about your little meetings."

"He has nothing to do with this! Let him go!"

"Has he not taught you how to properly destroy my kind?

He cannot do it himself, so he has employed you to do the honors."

The sight of Solomon stirred a surge of something else inside the baron. He looked down to see tiny jagged lights dancing across his palm. The same bits of lightning he'd noticed when he'd healed himself.

"Yes, look how magnificent!"

The rage simmered inside the boy as he stared back at his father. He imagined a bolt of lightning straight through the elder man's chest. Could feel the heat burning inside of him. Urging him.

Kill him. Kill him now.

"It is calling to you, Son. The darkness in your belly longs for blood and carnage."

"Jericho!" Solomon shouted back at him, his body still twisted and trembling. "Do not … kill him!"

The sound of his name struck the boy, as Solomon had always referred to him as young lord, or baron. He lurched toward the older man, but stopped when Lord Praecepsia raised his hand.

"I would not get too close."

The screeching sound of before reached his ears, closer that time. The dogs leaped into a frenzy of barking and snarling. That horrible sound echoed all around him, coming from all directions. And he twisted around as it grew louder and louder, trying to determine its direction. It was only at the sound of Solomon's tortured cry that he snapped his attention back that way, and the dogs lurched forward.

Four grotesque creatures with oversized limbs and balding heads scampered around the old man. Their eyes were a blood red, their bodies thin and wiry. Dark skin that reminded Jericho of a rotting corpse stretched over sharp protrusions of bone. He'd never seen anything so terrifying in his life.

Cerberus reared back on his haunches as if to charge toward them, and as the baron rested a hand on the dog to settle him, drawing his attention to the sparks dancing across his fingers, a thought sprung to mind. Could he cast the energy as easily as he could draw it in?

He threw back his arm and thrusted forward, sending a bolt of lightning toward one of the creatures, hitting it square in the flank.

It shriveled under the flash of light and crumbled to dust.

He sent another. And another. And another still, until all four of the monsters lay as ash on the ground. Once destroyed, he dashed toward Solomon, whose flesh bore the vicious tears of fangs, spilling blood and gore onto the ground around him.

Lord Praecepsia chuckled, the sound of his amusement grating on the baron as he held his mentor's head. Rage burned inside of him. Feeling a grip on his arm, he peered down at Solomon, who shook his head, his milky, unseeing eyes staring off somewhere beyond the baron.

"Do not ... seek vengeance. Do not ... kill him, young lord." The older man convulsed in his arms, until, at last, he stilled.

"No. No!" Jericho lowered Solomon's head to the ground and stroked the short-cropped hair on his head.

"He was your friend!" He stood, the old man's final words chiming inside his head as he strode toward his father. *Damn the debts.*

"That was long ago. He is no friend of mine now."

The sound of screeching from behind brought him to a halt. He turned to see Solomon jerk on the ground. The old man arched up, as he was before, contorted in a strange arc that hurt to gaze upon. Red bled into the milky white of his eyes, giving him an unnerving appearance that had the baron backing farther away.

Solomon reached out a hand, and his arm extended well past the length of a normal arm.

Cerberus and the other two broke into a barking frenzy, the incessant sound pounding against the baron's skull as he desperately tried to make sense of what he was seeing. Elongated arms and legs and skin that mottled before his eyes. By the time Solomon pushed to his feet, his back hunched, knuckles dragging on the ground, what stood before him was no longer his mentor. It was the very thing that had attacked the older man mere minutes before.

"What have you done?" The words hardly broke free of the baron's stiff jaw.

Lord Praecepsia chuckled again, but the baron's attention remained fixed on Solomon, whose eyes locked on his, as if the blindness had lifted. "He is what is known as a Mortunath and while he cannot infect you and turn you into his kind, he *will* consume you, if given the chance. On the contrary, if he should sink his teeth into one of your hounds, he *will* turn them into one of his kind. And what beautiful creatures they would make!"

"Cerberus!" I shouted over his barking. "Quiet!"

The dog whined and sat back on his haunches.

"Home, Cerberus. Home!"

The dog whined again and made a sound in his throat, which the baron took for disappointment.

"Home! Now!"

On a growl, all three dogs trotted off in the direction from which they'd come, though the baron did not bother to watch as he kept his attention fixed on Solomon.

"He will not cease to consume you entirely. You will have to kill him."

With another screech, and the old man bounded toward him. Jericho felt the tingle in his palms from before and shot a bolt of lightning between the two of them, intentionally avoiding a strike to Solomon. The bolt hit the ground on a blast of blazing foliage that caught flame and fizzled to curling black smoke.

"Stay back! I do not want to kill you! Stay back, Solomon!"

But the old man charged after him, and the baron had no choice but to spin around and run. He darted through the trees ahead, which opened to the clearing of the cabin.

A blast of light nearly blinded him as he leaped toward a patch of grass, and when he glanced over his shoulder, Solomon stood in the shadows. He did not advance toward him. As if he had abandoned his chase.

The baron slowed his steps and studied the stark contrast of light and shadow, where it seemed an invisible barrier existed between the two of them. The intersection of two realms, through which Solomon apparently could not breach.

Lord Praecepsia strode toward the edge of it, straddling the two. "I cannot control the Mortunath. I can only control the realm which holds them. Their master slumbers, and thank heavens for that. Or all five realms would be consumed."

"What do you want? What do you want from me!"

"If I cannot kill you, as you carry my blood, then perhaps the best solution is to utilize your talents. You see, war is coming." His father walked the precarious line between sunlight and darkness, hands behind his back. "I have made countless enemies who would love nothing more than to watch me bleed out. Should that happen, hell will literally break loose."

"I will not defend you. I will not become your slave."

On a huff of disappointment, Lord Praecepsia came to a stop. "I had a feeling you would say that."

The line of darkness consumed the light, until the baron

looked up to see the same blackened sky looming over himself. His gaze snapped to Solomon.

The old man charged toward him.

Dread filled his chest, as he raised his hand and shot a bolt into Solomon's heart. Not a moment later, his mentor collapsed into ash.

The darkness lifted to light again, and the baron sank to his knees.

45

FARRYN

"*S ave him.*"

I opened my eyes. A deep, cramping ache pulsed in my stomach, and I let out a quiet moan, breathing through it.

Jericho sat alongside the bed, my hand clutched in his, my fingers pressed to his lips. What swirled in his eye took me back to the night he'd fallen to his knees while staring up at me, moments before his wings were severed. A cross between pain, sadness, and utter remorse. A look so intimately familiar, one I'd dreamed about incessantly, that my muscles twitched with the urge to reach out for him, before the flames could engulf him.

Confusion hung at the back of my mind like a black cloud while I studied him. The way he didn't speak a word, but there was so much agony brimming in his expression.

The ache intensified, and I grunted, squirming against the cool sheets.

Pain. Screams. Blood.

On a gasp, I squeezed his hand. "The baby!" Twisting on

the bed, I lifted myself enough to see there was no blood beneath me. For only a split second, a sense of relief came over me.

Only a dream. Only a horrible and cruel dream.

"Farryn." A calm, but cold darkness in his voice embraced me like a winter's night.

Before I could ask him what had happened, a sharp stabbing pain radiated across my abdomen, knocking the breath from my lungs.

"Shhh, just relax. Breathe." Pressure across my stomach drew my attention to where Jericho rested his hand, as if to settle me.

Something was wrong. Very wrong. "The baby?"

When his brows pinched tighter and he shook his head, I felt a strange tingle at the back of my neck. He lifted my hand to his mouth and kissed my palm then lowered his head, looking the way one might in prayer.

The tingle intensified, branching across my skin like snow crystals, expanding outward, down my arms and to my fingertips. It reached my lungs and wrapped itself there like a tight fist.

Say something. Please!

Panic rose up into my throat as I waited for him to say the words. "Jericho? The baby ..." My voice faltered, my throat thick with tears that I refused to unleash. Everything was fine. It was just a dream. "The baby is okay, right?"

Gaze still lowered from mine, he squeezed my hand and shook his head. "No, Tu'Nazhja," his voice carried an agonized weight of despair, and the fist over my lungs clenched tighter.

Words floated on the air between us, as meaningless as the questions that swirled in my head. *Why? How?* I couldn't absorb them because I didn't believe him.

I shook my head and slid my hand from his. "No. Nope. It was a dream."

As if confirming his words, warmth oozed from between my legs, and it was when I felt the thickness of a pad beneath my bottom that a dark void washed over me, a blackness through which I couldn't see, or remember. But I knew somewhere on the other side of it was a weight I couldn't bear. A pain so heavy, it would crush me if I dared to acknowledge it.

"I still feel the baby inside of me. I still feel it moving. I know the baby is there." The rims of my eyes burned with the threat of tears, which blurred his form as I stared back at him.

Gaze cast from mine, he cocked his head to the side and cleared his throat, undoubtedly trying to stave off tears of his own. "Farryn ..."

A thick dread filled my lungs, every breath toxic and greasy with the misery of unspoken words. Dead. Gone. No more.

The black void of before fizzled inside my head, to the moment when I looked down at myself and saw the blood. Too much of it, pooling onto the mattress. The blonde standing beside me. The ringing in my ears.

"No," I whispered. "No, no, no." Gripping my stomach, I curled into myself.

"I'm so sorry, my love."

Jericho's words were a distant sound to the pounding of blood in my ears. Agony tore through me like a hot blade, and the sound that ripped from my chest was foreign. So desolate and hopeless. A suffocating vapor of misery hung on the air, and my lungs locked. I couldn't breathe.

I buried my face into the pillow and screamed. Screamed for the baby I would never cradle in my arms. The clean and innocent scent I would never breathe in. I screamed for the smiles and giggles and tiny handprints drawn on walls. I cried for the quiet nights whispering to Jericho as the baby slept between us. For never seeing him hold his child for the first time. I cried for every lost moment fate had stolen from me.

"I'm sorry," I said. "I'm so, so sorry."

"Sorry for what? This isn't your fault."

"It is. I should've ... I should've eaten better. I should've taken better care. I did so many things wrong."

"You did *nothing* wrong."

I had. And now the baby was gone.

Forever.

Eyes swollen and burning, I stared off toward the open space of my room that my head had convinced me would never see the likes of a cradle. Deep in my heart, I knew. Knew that the baby was just not meant to be. It felt as if I'd cried every tear left in me, but I knew there was more to come. I'd lived through months of pain after I'd lost Jericho. Except, he'd come back to me.

Strong arms wrapped tightly around me, as Jericho held me against him, his chest to my back. Just breathing.

My chest felt like a roomful of butterflies catching fire, leaving me to choke on the delicate ashes. Everything hurt. Everything burned. And yet, at the same time, I felt nothing at all. Numb. "Was any of this real? The baby? Was the baby even real?"

At that, he took my hand and pressed his palm to mine. "*Strę vera'tu,*" he whispered in my ear. *As real as the stars.*

Anger twisted in my stomach, stoking the pain there. The pain of an empty womb. How cruel was it that we not only suffered loss, but the agony of our bodies slowly coming to terms with the hollow, the ache of emptiness. "Then, God must be cruel. Why would He give something real--something mine, and then take it away?"

"I wish I could take this pain away from you. I would take it all."

An idea struck then, one I hadn't even considered before. "Could we ... could we reverse time? Like I did when Remy and I returned to the mortal realm. I could go back to just before we arrived in Nightshade. We could stay in the mortal realm. Can we do that? Can we go back?"

He planted a gentle kiss to my shoulder. "I can't bring back the baby, Tu'Nazhja."

"But you're not. You'd just be reversing time." My words were frantic. Desperate. Pathetic. "I promise I'll do it better next time. I'll do everything better."

"Farryn, listen to my words. Reversing time will not put the baby back inside you. You would return as you are now.

"That can't be true. I can't be pregnant one day, then not pregnant the next."

"The universe will adjust for discrepancies. You would suffer as you are now on the eve before your return."

There it was again, the small pinprick of hope fading off in the distance. "This is my punishment, isn't it? This is what I deserve. I defied Him by bringing you back. And so He took from me. Eye for an eye, right?"

Arms wrapped tighter around me, his muscles damn near suffocating me. "Don't do this, Farryn."

"I will do this. I *need* to do this. Because pain is, and will always be, the consequence of love." My voice broke, and more tears, endless tears, welled in my eyes. "I never wanted a baby. Never saw myself as a mom. When you told me pregnancy was the only way to break the curse, for a split moment, I felt imprisoned by that." The tears slipped over the bridge of my nose and down my cheek. "I hate myself for that."

Jericho didn't say anything, only stroked his fingers over my arm in a slow and calming pace.

"I didn't want to fall in love with this baby as much as I did. And I hate myself for that, too." Voice thick with tears, I closed my eyes to a visual of first holding him in my arms, feeling the weight of a tiny bundle against me. "I am a coveter of pain, who loves most when something is taken away. My mother. My father. You. And now the baby."

"Perhaps it isn't that you love most when it's gone, but that you recognize it was love all along."

"Even if I didn't want it in the beginning?"

"The world has taken too much from you, Farryn. In an effort to avoid the pain, you convince yourself that you don't want, or need, love. The human heart is nothing short of tenacious in the way it protects its most vulnerable parts. It will literally starve itself of the very thing it craves most, to the point of decay."

It was true, every word.

For too many years of my life, I avoided the inevitable pain that came with love, and in turn, I invited a new kind of suffering. The emptiness of a lonely heart. I'd become addicted to the aftermath of love's torment, its darker half, poking needles into hollow and unhealed wounds to remind myself that misery could be eternal. Because my ascetic-loving heart believed the chronic ache of isolation was far better than the stab of loss.

"I am capable. I do love."

"Of course you do. Humans have an innate masochistic pleasure in pain. If you didn't, you wouldn't dare to love at all. And what hell that would be."

His comment brought to mind a new torment. "Hell is coming for me now, isn't it?" I didn't want to ask the question aloud, for fear the demons would hear me, but it was inevitable. As strong and determined as Jericho was, I didn't even know if he could stop what was coming for me. "Now that the baby is gone, I'm going to owe my soul."

"You're not going anywhere. Not without me and not without war against my father. Don't even think about that right now. You've got enough on your plate."

"How did you do it? How did you survive Bishop Venable and your father? Their torment all those years?"

He looked thoughtful for a moment. "I learned to embrace the pain."

"Weren't you terrified of your fate? How far they'd take it?"

"I'd be lying if I said no. But when you force yourself to face what you fear most, you become impervious to its pain. Inviolable." On a slow blink, he seemed to snap out of his thoughts. "But I don't want you consuming yourself with those thoughts. Should my father so much as touch you, I will make him suffer an agony worse than hellsfire."

"Won't they send the fire demons after me, like they did my father?"

"I'm going to see if I can strike a deal with the Noxerians. I'll barter your soul for something they may find more valuable."

On a shock of distress, I turned over to face him. "Promise me you won't hand yourself over. Promise me now."

When he didn't answer at first, I gripped his bicep, digging my nails into him. "Promise, Jericho! Losing you will be worse than any hell I stand to face."

"I promise. I'll think of something. For now, I want you to relax and rest. And if you need anything, Vespyr is chomping at the bit to do something for you." He stroked a finger down my temple and pushed a strand of hair behind my ear. "I'm going to have to leave for a couple of days, to travel to Ariochbury. That's where the Noxerians' fortress stands."

"And you swear you will return. You won't barter yourself?"

His brow flickered, as if he didn't want to answer. "I swear it."

Though not entirely at ease, I let out a calmer breath. "A fortress, you say?"

"It was an elaborate castle they had constructed centuries ago, to defend themselves against attack."

"In Nightshade?"

"Yes, though they have ties to the Infernal Lands. Nightshade is neutral ground for negotiation with the heavens, which was how they came to be."

It was strange, there was so much history in Nightshade that we didn't even know about in the earthly realm.

"How did you become a Knight?" I asked, desperate for distraction. I needed it. I needed to push away every soul-crushing thought, because things were about to get worse, and I couldn't afford to slip into the quicksand of emotions that threatened to pull me under.

"Is now the right time for stories?"

"Yes. It's the perfect time. Tell me."

A quiet pause lingered heavy on the air before he continued. "Very well. When I arrived in Nightshade, Eradyę had gained a significant foothold here, led by my father, of course. The Knights kidnapped me, thinking I could be made a pawn against him. They didn't anticipate how much of a bastard he was, or how willing I was to see him fail." He entwined his fingers in mine and lifted my hand for a kiss. "Once I understood their reasoning behind my capture, I was all too willing to fight alongside them. With significant success in conquering the creatures that inhabited the realm, the Noxerians created a treaty with my father, which confined him to the Obsidian Mountain."

Frowning, I stared off. "Obsidian Mountain?"

"It is a stretch of black-sooted mountains on the southern border, also called Obsidia. It happens to be the location of Infernium."

"The asylum you spoke of. The one from my dreams."

"Yes."

Which made absolutely no sense why I would've dreamed of such a place. "What stopped them from imprisoning, or killing, your father?"

"Because doing so would unleash hell. My father is the only thing that keeps Letifer in slumber."

Letifer. I remembered the conversation with Camael, and how she had spoken of the end of the world. "And if he wakes, we're all doomed."

"If he wakes, every creature in every realm stands to become one of his Mortunath. And yes, we'd basically be fucked."

It didn't seem real. It seemed like the kind of talk found in fantasy novels, with doom and gloom and the big bad guy who would destroy everything to his own gain. I kept waiting for the moment when I would wake up, and I'd be lying in bed back at Aunt Nelle's, all curled up into Jericho, whispering about the awful nightmare I'd just had. As much as I yearned for distraction, tried to cast my stress aside, as he'd told me, I found myself right back to worrying about my fate. "Do you anticipate the Noxerians to be receptive to making a deal?"

"It's hard to say, with my father being the one to have claimed your soul. Of course, it doesn't matter *who* has laid their claim. I've no intentions of turning you over."

Panic and frustration mingled together inside me in a

turbulent mix that had me feeling like I could throw up. "But you said that was bad. That the fire demons would come."

"They would. Unless the Noxerians refused to grant claim to your soul."

I could feel my pulse hasten with the burgeoning anxiety. "But the likelihood of them making a deal is slim."

"Yes. Denying my father what he wants will only make him more determined."

The panic exploded in a flash of light that sent a shuddering ache to my skull. "God, this is too much! Too much!"

So many unknowns floated around my head, my muscles bunched with the distress pounding through me. I couldn't even mourn my baby because of it, and the thought of that tore at me. I didn't want to think about this. About what some fucking demon planned to do with me. I'd lost! I'd lost so much between my father and my baby, and now the universe wanted more. Why wasn't it enough! "I just want to hit something. I want to hit something so hard it hurts. Until it feels as helpless and pummeled as I do right now!"

"Then, hit me. Right now." His words caught me off guard, and I frowned up at him to find no hint of amusement. Only the cold and austere gaze of a man who refused to be swayed.

"No."

"Do it. Show me your pain."

With gentle hands, he rolled me on top of his body, and I straddled his stomach, feeling a hint of humiliation from the pad I wore. The pad soaked in the blood of my baby. A baby that I was robbed of.

"Hit me, Farryn. As hard as you can."

The anger swelled inside of me all over again. "Stop it. Stop it!"

"Think of what was taken from you!" He grabbed tight to my wrists and gave a slight jerk. "Come on! Pretend I'm the thief. Your thieving God who took from you. I am the one who has forsaken you. Hit me!"

"No!"

"Do it!"

"Stop it!" Irritated by his insistence, I gave a hard smack to his jaw.

He didn't so much as flinch. Instead, he clenched his teeth, his lip curved to a snarl. "That's it. Harder."

Harder. The words beat through my chest like a war drum. The idea that he could've been twisting my pain into some sick masochistic torture of his own enraged me, and something took over me. I snapped. In a fit of fists and nails, I punched, scratched, and smacked him.

Every hit, I waited for him to haul off and hit me back, but he didn't. He took it all. Every miserable and pathetic thought about myself, I pummeled into his chest and jaw and stomach and arms.

I knew he was goading me, maybe because he really was hurting, and this was his way of dealing with the anger and disappointment. By accepting pain. Punishing himself the same way my thoughts punished me. It was wrong of me to respond, but I wanted it out of me. The anger. The hate. The bitterness. It felt so good, I slipped into a blind haze of violence. Punching, punching, punching.

Until exhaustion weighted my muscles, and I collapsed forward. Breathing. Just breathing.

The haze lifted.

I tipped my gaze to him and took in the horror of what I'd just done. The scratches down his cheek. The split of his otherwise perfect lips. The blood from my nails smeared across his chest. Trembling, I sat up from him, my body numb and cold with shock. "What have I done?"

He grabbed my wrists again and pulled me into him. "Don't you dare feel remorse. You just showed me the pain inside of you. Your pain is my pain. When you suffer, I suffer. These hits are nothing to the ache in my heart." He tipped his face to mine, and his kiss was so gentle. Gentle in a way that made me feel undeserving.

A sob shook my body as I lay forward, pressing my ear to his chest. And with the sound of his steady heartbeat, I closed my eyes.

46

JERICHO

On my way to the dungeon, so many thoughts swirled inside my head.

The baby. My father. Vengeance.

Memories took me back to the night when Lustina had passed and I lay at her side, hoping to spend just a few more moments before the Sentinels would come for me.

A frail old woman had hobbled up to us as we lay on the ground.

"My Lord, you have lost so much," the strange, elderly woman says, standing off just a short distance away.

I've never seen her before in my life, and given the state of Praecepsia after having burned it to the ground, I was hard-pressed to believe she was from here.

"If only you had helped me, I could have saved her."

I frown, and raise my head, studying the old woman with white, straggly hair and weather-worn skin, bent over herself where she leans into a cane. The audacity of her words strike me like a slap to the face. "Who are you?"

"You do not recognize me?"

"I would not have asked, if I had."

Her wrinkled lips stretch to a smile. "Liar," she hisses.

The creeping tendrils of familiarity dance over the back of my neck, and a cold chill climbs my spine. "Syrisa."

"I know this pain. For it was your father who cursed the only one I've ever truly loved. He banished me to this world, and now he's stripped my soul and forced me into this frail and tired body. Allow me into yours, as I have taken this one, young lord, and I will exact vengeance upon your father. For he is the one to blame for this atrocity. For all your pain and suffering."

"I would sooner swallow flames than let you anywhere near my body."

She lets out a dark chuckle and points a long-nailed finger at me. "I have seen the future. And you will be punished. All will be punished." Her gaze falls on Lustina beside me. "But she will return. And when she does, I will be waiting."

Had murdering my child been her vengeance against me? Could she have possibly survived all those centuries to punish me for not having helped her?

Vaszhago called out to me from behind, interrupting the memory. He strode up to me, his face carrying what little remorse the demon was capable of showing. "I'm sorry to hear the news."

I gave a sharp nod, the sting of loss still burning in my throat.

He reached into his pocket and retrieved an object. "Kezhurah left this in the event that anything might've changed with Farryn. I only hesitated to pass it on because, well, see for yourself." He deposited the cold object into my hand–a glassy black stone that reflected the frown on my face.

"Witch's Call." The stone was said to have belonged to a witch named Venefica, who resided so deep within the mountains of Obsidia, her existence remained questionable. She was rumored to have lived in the time of the ancients as their most prized alchemist, who concocted elixirs said to have enhanced their powers. Demonic powers, as she could not harness that of vitaeilem, as desperately as she'd been known to try. The stone was a free pass, of sorts, to request a favor from her. Again, all of it was rumor, as the stories about her were hearsay. "I do not wish to enhance the powers of my demon half, seeing as that is what she's most renowned for, though I appreciate the gesture."

"She has been known to practice a darker form of medicine. One Kezhurah wasn't comfortable with, to lure a soul from the body. However, there was the issue of the baby. She would have surely demanded it in trade."

Soulless creature. "And what would be the cost without the child?"

"I wouldn't begin to know. It is why I did not feel compelled to pass it along. But I did not want to keep it from you, in case you found it useful."

Glancing down at the stone once more, I ran my thumb over its smooth, glassy surface. "I appreciate it. Perhaps I'll inquire a bit more. At the moment, I've a much bigger issue on my plate. Now that the baby is lost, she will begin her transition. It is my father who has laid claim to her soul."

Vaszhago blew out a harsh breath and shook his head. "Seven devils, that is a dirty move on the Noxerians' part to grant him claim. Perhaps it's punishment for your having abandoned the Knights."

"Undoubtedly so. I intend to meet with the Noxerians, to see if I can offer a trade."

"It'd have to be a damn enticing one."

"Perhaps an Elysiumerian angel?"

Vaszhago's lips stretched to a grin. "I don't know why I ever tried to kill you. Seems we would've gotten along swimmingly."

"Yeah, well. I didn't have a woman I was willing to curse

my soul for back then. Seems there isn't much I wouldn't be willing to do."

"Make sure you fill another vial of vitaeilem before you offer the arrogant prick up." With a pat on my shoulder, he stepped past me and continued on up the corridor.

I stared down at the stone still clutched in my palm, trying to imagine what Venefica would require in trade to remove the unbound from Farryn. I'd heard stories, ranging from slavery to deplorable deeds, and there really wasn't anything I wouldn't have given, or carried out, for Farryn. Once I'd secured the trade for Farryn's soul with the Noxerians, I'd look into it, because Syrisa's lust for vengeance against my father could've proven to be yet another complication to the shitshow.

Stuffing the stone into my pocket, I kept on toward the dungeons.

Even if Soreth had proven to be somewhat helpful, I still didn't trust him. One of the reasons I'd allowed him to stay, though, was the possibility that he might still be of some use. The Noxerians wouldn't be so quick to risk denying my father claim to a soul, unless the trade was worth it. Had I not lost my wings and power, I might've been able to barter my services. To restore my position as a Knight and agree to fight on their behalf in the event of invasion.

Unfortunately, I didn't even know where to begin tracking down the Met'Lazan who could help me get my wings back, and it seemed no one besides the high-ranking angels had any knowledge of who she was. Angels who wouldn't lend a piss if I was on fire. It might've been a possibility to track the female down, eventually, but I'd run out of time with the loss of the baby.

As an Elysiumerian scholar, Soreth was the next enticing consideration. His knowledge on all things angels would've secured his life, so offering him up wouldn't have necessarily been a death sentence. If he cooperated, they might have even been willing to make him comfortable.

Yes, it was a bastardly thing to do to an old friend, but when it came to Farryn, my loyalties went out the window. I had no problem with serving him up on a spit with an apple in his mouth.

I headed down into the dungeons, where, unlike last time, he was free to at least walk around his cell, and judging by the excess of empty plates outside the bars, my staff were all too happy to keep him comfortable.

Soreth stood facing slightly away from me, studying a grape, which he popped into his mouth and chewed slowly. "Do you remember the days when grapes were associated with status, which the noblemen and monasteries enjoyed?"

"I do, yes."

"Nowadays, any Tom, or Dick can grow a grape vine, and it means absolutely nothing for status."

"Your point?"

"Humans place such ridiculous importance on things." He finally turned to face me, and his brows came together. "She lost the baby."

"I figured you knew she was pregnant."

"Well, admittedly, it's much more difficult to sense it when said child is half Sentinel."

"She wasn't very far along, but it's devastating just the same. Much was lost." Hands rubbing together, I silently mulled through the thoughts that'd hammered my skull for the last hour. "What if I told you that I believe the unbound soul which resides in Farryn is Syrisa of Soldethaire?"

"Syrisa?" Soreth shook his head, staring off in his usual thoughtful way. "I don't think so. It's been centuries, Jericho. Without power, it's difficult to compel a host to feed. It isn't like a demon possession."

"I believe Syrisa has found a way to not only feed, but to

471

control the host. By sending them off into a dark-space inside their minds."

"She fed on children. I've not seen anything like what happened to those boys in centuries. And trust me, I've studied. I've watched for it."

I stared down at my hands, which had begun to tremble with rage the moment the thought had crossed my mind. The moment all the pieces had come together, painting a grotesque and fucked-up picture in my head. What I wouldn't have given right then to wrap my hands around the woman's throat and squeeze until her neck snapped. "I think she feeds on pregnant women. The fetus, to be exact. There is no compelling in that case."

The way he stared off for a moment, gaze swirling in thought, told me it wasn't entirely implausible. "Jericho, I understand you are incredibly upset, but understand that humans are often not physically equipped to carry one of our kind."

"I don't believe that was the case with Farryn. And she has seen Syrisa in nightmares and hallucinations."

He lowered his gaze in the contemplative manner I grew accustomed to seeing as a boy, and I could plainly see that he was trying to choose his words carefully. "While that is unusual and something to consider, the chances that Syrisa was able to bounce from one pregnant host to the next for centuries is a bit of a stretch."

"Why? Think about how many women have suffered loss? Over and over. They try and try. It is a constant food source for a *parasite* like that." I could hardly push the words past my teeth. "I want her out of Farryn's body, and I'd like you to accompany me on a bit of a journey."

"Journey to where?"

"The Obsidian Mountains."

"Is that not in the same vicinity as the Noxerians? Are you

serious? I set one foot on their territory, and they'll string me up and cook me alive."

"You said you have a way to mask your vitaeilem."

"Yes, but I am ... *exceptionally* good looking. They're going to know I'm Elysiumerian in one glance."

Arrogant prick. "I'm happy to rearrange a few features, if you'd like."

"Why do you require company on this trek?"

"I intend to meet with Venefica there," I lied, lifting the stone from my pocket.

The intrigue in Soreth's eyes damn near lit up his entire cell. Should've known something rumored to be nothing more than a myth would entice him. "The black witch?" His voice held an annoying pitch of awe.

"It's possible she might have a way to release the soul from Farryn. But I am unfamiliar with her alchemy. I thought you might be able to assist. Her lair is said to sit on the edge of Eradyę, and will require your *la'ruajh.*"

"It's quite risky."

"It is. But what's a little risk, to say that you are the only scholar in the heavens to lay eyes upon Venefica." Without a doubt, I had to have been the most manipulative bastard in all five realms.

The plan was to make the trek toward Ariochbury, which happened to be just east of Obsidia, which meant Soreth would be none the wiser, up until we reached the castle. At that point, I would slip him *feleszunguiz,* or cat's claw. A very potent knock-out drug, to which angels just happened to be susceptible. I'd used it a number of times back in the day, when I hunted the A'ryakai. Odorless, colorless. He'd never know, until the point when he'd eventually wake up in the Noxerians clutches. And by that time, I expected to be on my way back to Farryn.

"Very well. I will accompany you."

47

JERICHO

"May I ask why we're traveling by horse, when we've perfectly capable wings that would not only get us there faster, but would be far less painful to endure?"

I climbed up onto Onyx's saddle and waited for Soreth to mount his steed. "A set of white wings in the air would draw every fallen angel out of his burrow. They'd easily capture you, of course, seeing as you're so unfamiliar with the lay of the land, and they hunt in packs, meaning that, after you're in their clutches, they'd subject you to unspeakable humiliation and sexual acts, before draining all of your vitaeilem and ultimately sending you off to absolute death, or Ex Nihilo. But if you're up for a chase, I'm happy to accommodate."

"Horse is fine," he grumbled and awkwardly climbed up onto his like a haughty angel with a full set of perfectly functional wings. "How do you manage to keep your balls from getting smashed?"

"Learn to embrace the pain," I said, glancing up to see Farryn staring down at me from her bedroom window.

I'd visited her earlier that morning, after a final dose

vitaeilem from Soreth, to say my goodbyes. Her cramping had lessened from the day before, but her spirits remained downcast. It killed me having to leave her again in such a state, to risk that my father might come after her in my absence, but I had to get her out of his clutches, and the only way to do that officially was through the Noxerians. As much as I'd wanted to claim her, to ensure that my father would never touch her, doing so that soon after having lost the baby might've brought harm to her.

While the idea of leaving her weighed heavy on me, fortunately, I knew firsthand how skilled Vaszhago was at killing Mortunath, having fought alongside him as a Knight, and I trusted he'd keep her safe, as the agreement bound him until she turned cambion.

With sadness still shadowing her eyes, she waved at me.

I waved back, and my gaze caught on movement to my right, where Cerberus trotted around the corner of the cathedral. Once the hound laid eyes on Soreth, a deadly glow rose to their surface, and his lips peeled back into a vicious snarl. Seconds later, Fenrir and Nero prowled up alongside him, snarling in the same threatening manner. Without a doubt, they'd remembered the angel and what had happened to their siblings by his hand.

"Do you recall the hellhounds I salvaged from that day in the cave? The ones you told me would never remain loyal to me?"

He snorted, sliding around on his saddle in what I guessed to be a poor attempt to adjust his groin. "Vicious little mongrels."

"It seems they remember you." I canted my head toward the hounds, and not a moment later, all three of them lurched into a dead run.

"What in God's name!" Soreth frantically jerked his body back and forth. "How do you get this damned beast to move?" Panic laced his voice, and I couldn't help but chuckle.

I trotted up next to him and gave the steed a slap to the ass, which sent it into a gallop toward the gate. "I wouldn't loosen your grip!"

I nudged Onyx into a gallop after him and whistled to the dogs to stay back. Not that I'd have minded watching them mete out their vengeance.

After all, Soreth was a prick for having slaughtered puppies.

~

"For God's sake, man. I need to get off this blasted thing before my groin explodes." Soreth cupped himself with a moan, as we brought the horses to a stop along the tree line of a forest. "Honestly, you must have iron balls."

We'd traveled most of the day, and the waning light told me it'd be dark in the next couple of hours. The castle was only about a league away, and I'd hoped to lessen the distance, but perhaps it was best to get the dastardly deed of drugging him over with then.

"Fine, we'll stop for a quick respite."

"How much longer until we reach Obsidia?"

Had I said another few miles, assuming he had any basic lay of the land, he'd have been suspicious. "About another two hours."

"Thank goodness, then. I need to rest. I could not tolerate two more hours of this. Truly, humans are such masochists."

As I hopped off my horse, I grabbed the vial of cat's claw from my pocket in as subtle a movement as I could muster and poured a capful onto a kerchief. It only took a miniscule amount of the elixir to knock an angel out. I popped the cap off the water sack, and with my back still turned to Soreth, who moaned and complained as he walked off the pain, I coated the outer rim of the water sack's neck. Twisting around, I handed it to him for a sip. "Drink?"

Soreth stopped his pacing and accepted the sack. "You didn't poison it, did you?" As he raised it to his lips, he paused halfway, then lowered it. "You first," he said, handing it back to me.

With a snort, I took the water sack from him. "Have ye so little faith?" I tipped the sack back, close enough to my lips to look as if they'd touched, but far enough not to expose myself to the drug, and poured a long swill down my throat. I opened my mouth to show him the water pooled there, before swallowing it back. "Satisfied?"

"Yes." He flicked his fingers for the water. Not that angels required water, like humans. After a day of travel, the cool sensation of the liquid simply felt good against the back of the throat. It was refreshing without being a necessity.

I watched as he pressed the water sack to his lips, and waited.

And waited.

And waited.

He handed the water sack back, before returning to his pacing, and for a brief moment, I wondered if he'd caught on. If he'd seen that I hadn't actually put my lips to the thing and followed suit.

He stumbled.

Stumbled again.

"What in the unholy …? I think … I'm no' feelin' s'good." He staggered to the side, rubbing his forehead, and swayed. "Wha's'ron' w'me?"

A second later, he crashed on a hard thud into the dirt.

I couldn't help but smile as I stood over him, staring down at his gaping mouth as an obnoxious snore flew out of him.

So much for angels being perfect.

I lifted his upper half up off the ground and carried him toward his horse. With one heft, I hoisted his body over the saddle, his abdomen teetering across the center, arms and legs dangling at either side of the beast. After grabbing the reins and mounting my own horse, I headed toward Ariochbury.

Stone walls stood the height of the skyscrapers found in the mortal realm, their stones fortified by a dark magic that prevented anyone from entering without permission. I tugged the cloak over my head, hoping the guards would not recognize me in the darkness, and set Onyx on an easy pace toward the gate.

Once there, a guard I'd never seen before looked me over, before setting his attention on Soreth, and jerked his head toward him. "What's this?"

"A gift for the Noxerians." I flashed him the pin bearing the Knights of the Infernal Order emblem, praying he wouldn't suddenly study my face.

Ordinarily, he would've collected my weapons, but the emblem implied loyalty to the highest degree, and so he did not bother to ask for them.

Unlike in the earthly realm, demons held business hours at night, which made our arrival timely. The guard smirked and strode toward Soreth. Kneeling to the ground just below Soreth's head, he took a drag of his *fumoszh*, which resembled a black, earthly cigarette but carried a toxic fume that only a demon could resist choking on. He blew the smoke into Soreth's face, and the angel didn't move. Didn't so much as twitch. Seemingly satisfied, he waved me on, and the heavy iron gates lifted, beyond which lay a massive courtyard that teemed with all sorts of high-ranking demons.

Once inside, another guard guided my horse to a tie-up and offered to carry Soreth inside for me. Denying him would've roused suspicion, so I nodded, and the demon hoisted the angel from the saddle and led me through ornate wooden doors. It seemed we walked through at least a half-dozen corridors adorned in rich ornate tapestries and detailed portraits of past Noxerian council members, before we reached the grand room. The place where the Noxerians conducted business.

A long table at the back of the room seated fifteen ancient nobles, some of them old enough to remember the Great War. They looked on over a small crowd of disciples wearing unenthused expressions, as if bored.

I strode up to them, keeping my head low until I was standing before them. With a nod toward the guard who'd carried Soreth in, I waited for him to deposit the angel onto the floor, then removed my cloak.

Nearly every noble lifted his head, some wearing expressions of contempt, while others appeared shocked.

Here we fucking go.

"Either you are foolish, or charmed by the prospect of execution." The one who spoke in a raspy voice, laden with age, was Korgeerasz, the chairman of the Noxerians. "Which is it?"

"Perhaps a bit of both, Your Grace."

"It has been years since your betrayal, but surely you did not think we would forget?"

"I did not." Saying anything else would only anger them, so I kept my responses brief.

"Then, why have you returned?"

"I wish to make a bargain."

"A bargain." He echoed the words in a sneering tone that implied such a request was a slap to the face. "For what?"

"There is a female whose soul you've granted claim."

"Who is this female?"

"Farryn Ravenshaw."

The elder looked to his left, toward one of the other nobles, who cracked open an oversized leatherbound book and thumbed through it. He gave a nod and whispered into the ear of the nobleman beside him, who whispered to the next, and the next and the next, until it reached Korgeerasz.

The old man let out a deep guttural chuckle, his sharp, black eyes on mine. "It seems your father has already laid claim to her."

"He has. I would like to make a trade. Her soul for another."

"And what is this trade you offer?"

I reached for Soreth's shoulder and turned the limp angel onto his back. "Pure Elysiumerian. He's a scholar."

The noblemen shifted in their seats, undoubtedly enticed by such an offer. One of the men a few seats down, wearing an embellished *galeruszha*--traditional attire for his breed of demon--lifted his nose into the air and sniffed. "I do not smell vitaeilem on this one."

"He has masked the scent, Your Grace. I can assure you his wings are white as snow and his eyes blue sapphires." Perhaps the most telling features of the Elysiumerians.

Korgeerasz looked thoughtful for a moment, then leaned into one of the men closest to him. They seemed to exchange whispers, spoken so low, I couldn't make them out.

Soreth was a hard bargain. One worth contemplating. A scholar could've given them an edge against the angels in the event of attack. I was essentially handing over a guaranteed win for the Noxerians, in the event of war.

Yet still, they deliberated.

"While your offering is quite generous, we are in no position to bargain."

Shock wound down the back of my neck, a tight fist squeezing my lungs. "Might I remind Your Grace, that such an offering is quite rare."

"Perhaps, yes. And it pains us to decline. But the treaty states that your father is entitled to souls rightfully claimed through the council. To accept this bargain would break such a treaty and risk war with Eradyę."

"Have you forgotten that I am the only creature in all five realms capable of destroying him?"

"We've not. Surely, you are not that ignorant."

I lowered my gaze, breathing deeply to calm the rage simmering in my blood, because the last thing I needed to do right then was kill an ancient elder. "I am asking you to reconsider. For the good of the whole."

"We uphold our decision," Korgeerasz responded.

Jaw tight with rage, I rolled my shoulders back, desperate to maintain my composure. "Then, I would like to bond with this female, with witness, to ensure that he does not also lay claim to her womb."

A long pause followed, and when I glanced up, I caught the wicked grin stretched across the face of the elder. "We would not be in a position to grant you such a request as that, either."

Hands balled to fists, I lurched forward. "I fought alongside you! Against my own blood!"

"You did, yes. And it is only out of gratitude for your loyal service all those years that I will allow you to walk freely from this meeting without imprisonment for your abandonment. You are owed nothing, Van Croix. Leave immediately, before we decide to confiscate the angel, anyway."

Fuck.

Fuck!

They'd called my bluff about killing my father, a threat they'd feared while I was in their clutches. Knowing that I was capable of murdering him, of setting Letifer free and dooming all five realms, they'd always been careful with me. Their response didn't make sense, until I turned around and caught sight of Bishop Venable, or Barchiel as he went by those days, crossing the court. Without a doubt, the bastard had told them of my lost powers.

After hoisting Soreth up onto my shoulder, I strode toward where he stood passing out his drug, Rapture, to the nobles like candy.

When he looked back at me, the appraisal in his eyes turned to shock. "Van Croix?"

"I'm sure you're quite surprised."

"I did not expect your return from Ex Nihilo."

"And you made a point to speak of what happened. What did you do, Barchiel, tell them you were the one who'd smited me?"

"It does not bode well for me that you've returned. Through your death, I've gained stature. And now, they will look upon me as a liar."

"You are a liar. And if the prospect of killing you twice didn't bore me to tears, I would surely make a point to do it now, in front of all your new friends. Luckily for you, I've got somewhere to be." Burning with rage, I strode past him, ignoring whatever he shouted after me as I made my way back through the corridors, to the courtyard, where the horses awaited us. I threw Soreth's still-unconscious body up onto the saddle and guided the horses out through the gates.

48

THE BARON

The carriage slowed to a stop in front of the manor. Home.

It had been two years since the baron had last seen the place, or his mother, for that matter. After Solomon's death, she'd sent him away to Cavendale, a university just outside of Rome. Much as the baron had detested and fought against leaving her, to pursue something as trivial as academics had seemed at the time, she had insisted, assuring him of the great relief it would bring her. For, while he was away at school, his father's attention was directed elsewhere, and the baron only hoped it hadn't been set on his mother during that time.

She stood before the entrance at the top of the staircase in a finely crafted, blue gown, which effectively hid the frail state of her body beneath.

For two years, the baron had immersed himself in his studies at Cavendale, until the day a courier had sent word that Lady Praecepsia had begun to deteriorate. At which point, he had been called home.

The vibrance of her smile showed no hint of suffering,

but there remained shadows behind her eyes that the baron noticed as he stepped out of the carriage to meet her.

"My son," she said, arms wide, as he strode up to her and fell into her embrace. "You've returned a man!"

"I have missed you, Mother. How have you been?"

"I am better now that you are here. Tell me of your studies at Cavendale."

"I could regale you with stories of watching the grass grow, which would be a far more interesting topic than Cavendale."

His mother let out a chuckle, guiding him up the staircase with her arm hooked into his. "As I understand, you did quite well there."

"Is nothing a secret anymore?" he asked, his voice pitched in amusement.

"No. Mother knows *all.*"

"Where is Father?"

"In his chambers. He has arranged a visit from Bishop Venable."

"For what purpose?"

"It is for me. The bishop seems to think he can cure what ails me with his useless prayer and magic tricks."

"And what is it that ails you, Mother?"

Wearing a solemn smile, she lifted their clasped hands to her lips for a kiss. "Let us not talk of this now. I want to bask in the joy of your return, my son."

As they entered the foyer, Lord Praecepsia stood just outside of his library, his eyes scrutinizing and emotionless, as the baron had expected. "I would like a word. *Son.*"

Although her expression pulled to a concerned frown, his mother patted the baron's arm and gave a nod. She unhooked her arm from his and planted a kiss to his cheek. "I shall see you at suppertime."

Two years of being away from his father had momentarily caused the baron to forget the unnerving tensing of his muscles whenever his father paid him any attention. As the older man turned his back and entered the library, the boy felt a tightness in his neck on trailing after him.

Once inside, Lord Praecepsia closed the door and took a seat at a wooden table, where a number of books lay strewn about its surface. "Welcome home," his father said in an unwelcoming tone. "I was not aware that you were due to return. And what illuminating things have you learned while away?"

"Is that why you called me in here, Father? To inquire of my studies?"

The mirthless smile on his face faded. "Of course not." From a pitcher on the table, he poured a red, bubbly fluid into a golden goblet and pushed it toward the boy, who kept his hands at his side, away from the proffered drink. "Do you not trust me?"

Of course he didn't.

The older man poured himself a drink, and tipped back a sip. Brows quirked, he held up the goblet for the baron to see it was empty. "You see? It is not poisoned."

The baron reached for the drink and, keeping his eyes on his father, took a sip. A sharp burn hit the back of his throat like a blast of flames, and the baron coughed, splashing red fluid across the tabletop in front of him.

Lord Praecepsia let out a hearty laugh and poured himself another glass. "And I thought you'd have returned from Cavendale a man."

Rubbing his throat where the burn still lingered, the baron coughed again. "Perhaps you might enlighten me as to the nature of this meeting."

Drumming his fingers against the desk, the elder man stared back at him. "Since you've returned to my domain, you will resume your sessions with Bishop Venable once a week in the undercroft."

"What for? What purpose do these sessions with the bishop serve, aside from your own amusement?"

He slammed his fist on the table, his lips curled in contempt. "You will not speak to me that way! And you will certainly not question Bishop Venable, or his methods." Face red with anger, he unfurled his fist for another sip of drink and cleared his throat. "Further, you will train with the Pentacrux, as before. There will be no more frivolous studies. There are forces moving against us, and you will fight for Praecepsia, as well as Eradyę."

"The barren lands?"

"Yes. You have no awareness of threats, beyond this realm, which would love nothing more than to enslave me and turn me into a pawn. While you may be contented with such a thought, know that there are others, far worse, who have no care for humans."

"If you wish to make me an ally, to fight on your behalf, then why subject me to Bishop Venable?"

His father's lips curved to a grin. "You were correct when you said that I gleaned amusement from your punishments. I enjoy watching you suffer, for no other reason than I cannot stand to look upon you."

Rage simmered beneath the baron's skin, and choking back tears, he shot up from the table. "What loyalties would you ask of a son you seek to harm."

Lord Praecepsia smirked up at him. "I did not *ask* for your loyalty. You will fight on my behalf simply because you have no choice."

The baron strode from the library, out of the manor, and across the yard toward the forest, where he'd often hidden away since the time he was a boy.

Deep into the forest, he came upon the abandoned cabin,

where he'd left his dogs to fend for themselves while away at Cavendale. The cabin appeared even more dilapidated than before, the weathered clay and wood scarcely holding the walls together. The roof had caved in. Grass grown nearly as tall as the boy.

He whistled, hoping the three of them might have stayed in what had become their home for a number of years. There was no movement. No stirring.

They'd either moved on, or had been hunted as a threat.

An ache stabbed his chest, as he recalled days he would play with the dogs and train them to follow his commands. Times when he'd found some semblance of peace, watching them carelessly frolic about. And of course, the times when the girl would come to play with them. It'd been quite some time since he'd seen her. The baron had assumed she and her mother had moved on to another village. Perhaps one that did not force her to remain on the outskirts.

He plopped down in the grass and tore away chunks of long, green blades, thinking of his mother and what little he had learned of her condition. According to the courier, she had experienced frequent moments of weakness, oftentimes fainting for no apparent reason.

Of course the bishop assumed something vile had taken over her. The baron could only imagine what his little elixirs had been designed to do.

Voices reached his ear, and frowning, he turned toward their direction. He followed the path beyond, along the river. At the bank, he found his cousin Drystan sat beside a girl whose back was turned to him. A long black braid draped over her shoulder, and the simple white shift she wore told him she was a servant of some sort.

Drystan noticed him first, his eyes wide with surprise. It was when the girl turned around that the baron's heart leaped inside his chest.

Her.

Her. The raven-haired beauty. Only, she no longer carried the features of a child. She had grown more beautiful, and although the glint in her eyes had faded slightly, he instantly recognized the scintillating stardust colors.

"My Lord, I was just fetching water with the girl," Drystan said behind her.

The baron glanced down to his cousin's empty hands, and a twinge of jealousy struck his throat at the thought of the two of them alone together. "With no bucket. How clever."

"We lost the bucket by accident."

He stepped closer to the two of them, his eyes searching for any sign of affection between them. Had he begun to court her in his absence? If it were true, that she was a servant, Drystan would have certainly been better suited, based on his lack of title. The bastard son of his father. Of course, no one else in Praecepsia knew that little secret. "I see you have found a proper escort for the woods," the baron snipped, his irritation since returning home only growing by the minute.

Brows tight, Drystan lowered his head, undoubtedly angered by the remark. "She came with Bishop Venable. She is assisting him with your mother."

Assisting the bishop? In essence, helping to poison his mother with whatever elixirs the bishop was feeding her. The overwhelming disappointment clenched his stomach.

His gaze shifted to the girl again, appraising her dress, which matched those of the other servant girls he had seen back at the monastery. Ones who hoped to become a pentash for the church. "Assisting him," he spat. "Then, she is as equally useless."

"I beg you not to speak about the bishop that way, My Lord. He is a good man, and such words have consequences."

"Yes, I suppose they do." Amusement colored his expression for only a moment before his cold eyes found the girl again. *Lustina*.

No longer the girl he remembered from the woods, but a disciple of the *good and holy* bishop. The fact that she could participate so willingly in Bishop Venable's unscrupulous methods of trying to cure his mother only churned the anger and disgust in his gut.

The girl stepped forward to curtsy. "Baron Van Croix, it is a pleasure to meet you."

"It is *Lord* Van Croix," he corrected, eyeing her dress. "Seems your righteous and holy upbringing has failed you in proper etiquette. And dress, for that matter." He scanned over the outfit meant to symbolize purity and chastity. "The kitchen rags would make finer material." He sniffed the air and scowled. "And smell better."

"My Lord, she meant no insult."

The sound of Drystan's voice only exacerbated the baron's ire, and the way he came to her defense sent another bolt of jealousy through him. "Do the two of you share the same mind?"

"She is no more than a servant."

"I do not need your observations. I know exactly what she is."

"I apologize for my ignorance, My Lord." Gaze still cast from his, Lustina interrupted their bickering. "I am not yet accustomed to all the rules of nobility. I come from a much simpler way of life."

"Indeed."

She lifted her gaze to his, the flicker of defiance in them spiking his blood with excitement. "Are you rude to all ladies, or only those deemed beneath you?"

He'd not expected her to speak with such insolence, and the baron found himself caught between intrigue and shock.

489

"Again, my apologies, My Lord," she added in a much more acquiescent tone.

"I would mind your *tongue*, girl. Our way of life dictates that such lack of respect is just cause for removing it. And as for the *ladies* who find themselves beneath me, I can assure you, they tend to think of me as quite charming."

"Is it so charming to speak of your conquests in front of the girl?"

The hint of spite in Drystan's tone amused the baron. "At least I have conquests of which to speak. Must be difficult around all those stable boys and small animals."

Jaw clenched, Drystan lurched toward the baron. "I am no sodomite! Such a thing is a sin! A despicable and repulsive sin!"

Sin. On two occasions, while away at Cavendale, the baron had caught glimpses of men together, enjoying each other's company in a way he'd deemed romantic. Although the nature of their relationship was foreign to him, given he had never witnessed such a thing before, the sight had not troubled him. The idea that their affections for each other had been scorned by those who would ruthlessly burn women on stakes for heresy was a sickening hypocrisy, and the baron found amusement in Drystan's revulsion. "Only in the eyes of your beloved church, but do not be afraid. I won't speak a word of it."

"Lies! Your words are lies!"

"If they are lies, as you said, why do you blush so, *Cousin?*" The baron grinned, his goading only stirring more ire in the other boy, made clear in the bright red of his cheeks.

"Enough! The bishop was right--you speak with a forked tongue! Your mother should've disposed of you like a bastard child!"

The baron's muscles snapped with tension, the fury inside of him burning like a hot flame. Had the girl not been present, he may have risked sending a bolt of lightning straight through his cousin's heart right then. Instead, he lifted a gem clipped to his shirt and held it up, twisting it in front of Drystan and Lustina.

Once, when the baron was young, his father had made the mistake of striking him at a formal dinner held at the manor. His mother had stolen the opportunity to draw attention to it, which prompted one of the noblemen in attendance to inquire if he employed a whipping boy to mete out the baron's punishments. From that day on, Drystan had been assigned to the task, as he had been the baron's closest friend at the time. On only a few occasions did the baron subject his cousin to such punishments carried out by Tothyll, one of his father's guards who also participated in executions. And he'd always felt remorse afterward.

Given the boy's ruthless comments, the baron hoped that Tothyll was feeling particularly vicious that day.

Drystan gasped and dropped to his knees. "Forgive me, My Lord. Forgive my blasphemous words."

The moment the words were spoken, bits of dust fell from the baron's palm that enveloped the gem.

The girl's eyes widened, and he stared back at her as a warning, that if she spoke a word, he would make her life hell.

"Tothyll will take pleasure in meting out your punishment."

Head bowed, Drystan's shoulders sagged as he rose to his feet. "My Lord, your mother asked me to fetch you. Perhaps you should not keep her waiting."

Staring out the window of his mother's chambers, he watched the carriage off in the far distance, the dust from its wheels flying up over the trees.

"What has you so riveted, Son?" His mother spoke in a weak voice, from where she lay in bed.

"I see the bishop has found himself a new pet to replace Drystan."

"Extend the girl your grace. The world has not been kind to her."

He snorted at that. "Not been kind to a girl who accompanies the most powerful man in Praecepsia?"

"While I do not know the nature, or purpose, of Bishop Venable's affections toward her, it was at his orders that her mother was burned as a heretic."

A stab of shock struck his chest, as he recalled having met her mother in the woods the day he had spied on the girl. How wild and vibrant she was with her red hair and the same flicker of defiance he'd seen in Lustina that afternoon. "Burned?"

"Yes." She coughed, and the baron shuddered at the wet barky sound of it.

He turned and strode back alongside her bed, taking a seat on the mattress beside his mother. "What are these treatments?"

She groaned and rolled her head against the pillow. "Their ridiculous rituals."

"It is not rituals which make you this way. Tell me."

"The bishop feeds me elixirs he swears will heal."

"And why do you accept?"

"The moment I decline, he will assume that I do not want to be well. That I harbor something inside of me that wishes to remain sick. And oh, what fun he would glean from an exorcism, or worse."

"What is it that makes you sick, Mother?"

"I am dying. It is why I had Alaric summon you back."

Had he heard her correctly? Surely not.

"A little every day, I suppose," she added, and still, he could not bring himself to absorb the words. "But it has taken its toll over time."

He shook his head in disbelief. "How can you be sure of this?"

"Because what your father takes from me is what I need to survive, and I can feel myself growing weaker and weaker by the day."

"What does he take?"

"My lifeblood. He feeds on it."

Her blood? What sick and disgusting creature would feed off another's blood? He'd only ever seen animals, like bats, do such a thing. "You lay dying. And tell me, does he still run off to the woods for his little trysts?"

"Yes, I am certain of it."

Rage tore at his muscles as he shot up from the bed and paced the room, back and forth. "What is so special about her? Why does he choose her over you! Why not take her blood!"

"She and I are not the same. And she does not threaten him, Jericho."

"And you do? You can hardly lift your head, Mother." It was then a thought struck him. "Earlier, did you say Alaric summoned me?"

"Yes." She pushed herself higher up onto the pillow, her hand slipping with her weakness, and the baron lurched to lift her.

With caring and gentle hands, he assisted his mother to a sitting position, noting the frailty, the sharp protrusion of bones in her arms. "My father mentioned that he had not been made aware of my return. How can that be?"

"Alaric did not tell your father, on my command."

"What?"

She flicked her fingers, urging him closer, and the baron bent down, turning his ear to her. "He is not loyal to your father. He is a spy."

The boy nearly tumbled backward on hearing her words. He frowned, shaking his head as he straightened. "For whom?"

"Your father has made many enemies. Including those of the place where I come from. War is coming. And you will have to decide which side you intend to fight for."

"Where is it that you come from, Mother?"

A knock at the door interrupted the two, and one of the maids entered the chambers, busying herself with cleaning the rags that had been left scattered on the floor.

"We will talk more, Son. Allow me some rest now."

"Of course." So many things had already come to light in the short time since the baron had arrived back. He needed to process them himself.

49

JERICHO

I stared up at the wall of the Obsidian Mountains, the summit of which disappeared into the dark clouds overhead. The moon sat high in the sky, shining down on a dark and ominous entrance just off in the distance. The mouth of a cave few were brave enough to breach.

It was at the foot of the Obsidian Mountains where I'd been reunited with my three hellhounds, nearly two decades after my banishment to Nightshade. They'd apparently crossed the portal when a manhunt had ensued, after one of the venators had spotted Fenrir and was quick to falsely claim he'd slain the beastly dog. Cicatrix had been the one to tell me of their location, as the raven had kept watch over them in the mortal realm, and I'd found them holed up in a cave here, feeding on scraps and carcasses, before bringing them back to Blackwater Cathedral.

Soreth groaned beside me, where I had lain him down on the gravelly bed of dirt. "Oh, heavens," he said, turning over in time to expel a torrent of vomit.

I kept my attention on that entrance, wondering if it had

been worth the change in direction from Ariochbury. "You passed out," I lied.

"Why do I feel like something plowed over me?"

"Been riding a while, slung over the saddle."

Huffing a deep breath, he finally rolled back to face the mountain, and his eyes widened. "We're here?"

"Yes. Obsidia," I answered, as if that'd been the plan all along. The calling practically burned in my pocket, as I turned it over and over in my palm. "I suppose we should get on with it."

"Wait." The angel swallowed a gulp, his gaze still directed toward the cave. "You're certain this witch will be any help?"

"No. I'm not certain of anything anymore. I only know that I am willing to walk through Hell for Farryn, if necessary. And if you are suddenly too fearful, then you are welcome to stay here."

Grumbling, the angel pushed to his feet. "Fearful. I am not fearful. Elysiumerians are not afraid."

I rolled my good eye at that and checked the dagger at my hip. "We are on the edge of Eradyę. I don't know how many creatures inhabit the cave of this mountain. All I will say is, should you come upon a creature that looks more animal than anything, do not waste your time studying it. Run."

"Noted."

The two of us strode toward the mouth of the cave, and I looked up to see the sky darkening, the moon disappearing behind the blackness of a clouded and starless sky. We breached the cave, and my sight adjusted to the tenebrous surroundings. Shiny black stalactites hung from the ceiling, which looked like teeth hanging over the stalagmites. An ice-cold chill clung to the air, creating mists of breath every time I exhaled.

Poised for a threat, I held my dagger clutched in my fist

and took careful steps. Sounds echoed through the cave, like the long creak of an old rocking chair.

"This place is pure evil. I can feel it deep in my bones." Soreth spoke low, trailing behind me.

"Perhaps it's just that fear you claim not to feel," I said over my shoulder.

The narrow cave opened to a pool of water, the black surface of which reflected the teeth overhead, and I caught a flicker of movement on the rocky ledge behind us. Pausing my steps, I scanned the surroundings, to find no further movement, at first.

A shadowy figure prowled behind Soreth in the water's reflection, while the angel unwittingly glanced around as if unaware of its presence. As it neared, creeping up behind him, with no eyes and ghost white skin, it bared its fangs. As subtly as I could muster, I tightened my grip of the blade's hilt, muscles poised for attack. The creature advanced, crawling over the rock toward the angel.

"Are we just going to stand he–"

I threw out my dagger, inches from Soreth's cheek, and pierced the open maw of the creature that appeared seconds from biting into the unwitting fool.

Soreth's gaze followed the path of the blade, and on a gasp, he jumped back when he caught sight of what had tried to attack him. "What in the unholy scriptures was that abomination!"

"There are times when the Lord grants acceptance of the word *fuck*, and I'm certain this is one of them." I slid my blade from the creature's throat, and it fell into a pile of white flesh onto the cave floor.

"I believe you're right. What in the *fuck* was that?"

"Must you scholarly types give everything a label? It's ugly, and it likes to bite. What more do you need to know?" I twisted back toward the pool, scanning the surroundings for any more of them.

"Quite a bit more, in fact," Soreth argued. "This could be a completely unknown species."

"Well, then, feel free to stay and study it." I sheathed my blade and stepped in the opposite direction.

"I think not."

We kept on, rounding the water to the other side, where black moss hung draped over an entrance that, on closer examination, appeared to be the underside of an enormous jaw. I stepped back further to see actual teeth, confirming that it was some sort of colossal-sized animal which must have died there centuries before, given the decay of bone and the way the rocks had begun to form around it. The entrance was no more than long strands of black moss, through which I took the lead. As I pushed the moss to the side, it hissed, and I turned in time to see tiny insect-like creatures scampering up its leaves, making the moss appear to move.

The interior of the skull opened onto an illuminated room that hugged a colossal pyre, which burned black at its base. Crudely carved, stone furniture decorated the inside, where a number of objects hung about from the ceiling, tethered by strings, reminding me of those used by Farryn's father to ward off The Infernal.

I turned to see Soreth's wide eyes trailing over the room, his mouth gaping with what I imagined was horrified awe.

"Who goes there?" a raspy voice called out, but when I scanned over the interior, I saw nothing but broken dolls hanging from twine, their limbs removed, alongside small pots filled with gods knew what, and symbols chalked into the stone. Drawings that stood out in stark clarity against the black surface of the wall.

"I wish to speak to Venefica." I held up the Calling and

caught only a flash of black in my periphery, as something swiped it out of my fingertips.

When I turned back to face the flame, a hunched figure stood before it. Long white, straggly hair framed a wrinkled face and long nose, beneath a black hood.

"What is it you seek?"

"The means to remove an unbound soul."

She hobbled around the fire toward a table, which held apothecary jars and strange specimens suspended in larger jars filled with liquid. On closer examination, I noticed a tiny foot in one of the jars and frowned. "Is that all you came for, *Lord* Van Croix?"

"This entity stands to harm someone I care about."

The sound of her dark chuckle sent a shudder down my spine. "You sought me out for *love*. How precious." Her unnerving gaze landed on Soreth. "And is this your love?"

A glance at Soreth showed his face twisted into a scowl. "Absolutely not," he said.

The older woman sneered, keeping her gaze on him. "You should never trust an angel, Lord Van Croix. The righteous are rarely right, at all."

Pressed with impatience, I ignored her comment, the desire to return to Farryn clawing at my insides. "The woman I speak of is ill."

"I am aware. It was I who summoned a doppelganger to Miss Ravenshaw, as she stepped out of that bookstore."

My muscles tensed, fist gripped tight to the hilt of my dagger. "You murdered my child?"

"No. I think you are quite aware of what murdered your child. She is why you're here. The one who feeds on the young to remain youthful."

"Who?"

"Syrisa of Soldethaire."

I shot Soreth a glance before returning my attention to the woman. "And why would she choose Farryn's body?"

"Because only you have the power to destroy your father. To carry out Syrisa's vengeance."

Smart, really. Of course she would choose the only woman for whom I'd doom all five realms by killing my father. "Was this doppelganger sent on behalf of a favor you entertained?"

"Yes. Your father's, to be exact. He wanted the unborn murdered. Imagine my surprise on finding something else had laid claim."

I swallowed back the black, poisonous fury that climbed my throat. "I want her out. Out of Farryn's body."

"You are aware every Calling bears a price."

"I am."

"For vengeance against the woman who murdered your firstborn, I demand a rather generous payment." She tapped excessively long and crooked nails against the table, as if impatient for my reaction.

"Name your price."

"Fate calls you back to Eradyę. And when it does, I want Letifer's heart."

The literal heartbeat of the barren world, rumored to have been impossible to find. "Are you mad?"

"Why, yes, Lord Van Croix. I am." She poured apothecary jars into a black, stone mortar and pestle, her whole body moving with the toil. She blew over top of it, and a flame caught, the sound of crackling echoing over that of the bonfire in the center of the room. "I expect payment in kind. You desire vengeance and the destruction of Syrisa. I desire vengeance in return."

"That is what my father promised you, isn't it? Letifer's heart?"

"No. Your father promised me the first child he would

bear with Miss Ravenshaw. Now, Lord Van Croix, do you wish to strike a bargain?"

The words cut like a blade down my spine, and the rage from before bubbled to the surface again. What little vitaeilem was left in me vibrated across my skin, the electricity tingling my fingertips. I wanted to kill him so badly, my palms burned with the fantasy of throttling his neck until his eyeballs popped out of their sockets.

"Do not do this, Jer–" Soreth grabbed his throat, his mouth gaping as if something invisible had wrapped itself around his neck. He dropped to his knees, gasping, choking, clawing at the dirt.

"You were saying?" Venefica asked, pouring the black fluid she'd concocted into a vial.

"How do I go about retrieving this heart?"

"It is encased in a glass sphere at the center of Infernium. The *heart* of the labyrinth. It is what feeds Eradyę, by absorbing the energy of souls and vitaeilem. So long as it beats, Letifer lives."

"And what happens afterwards?"

"The world collapses and the portal closes. You will have merely minutes to find your way back out. If you don't, you will remain trapped inside Eradyę with the Mortunath."

Trapped inside that dark and lifeless world seemed worse than Ex Nihilo. "And if I close the portal, Eradyę no longer poses a threat to the other realms."

"Until it's opened again, yes. Now, what say you?"

"Yes," I said without hesitation. "I wish to make a deal."

"Very well." From the table, she lifted the vial that carried the black substance. "You will administer this to Miss Ravenshaw, after which the soul will be released. She will remain in a deathlike state for a period of three nights. If you fail to deliver Letifer's heart, she will remain that way eternally.

Three nights from when you administer the elixir. Remember this."

"I understand."

"I hope so, My Lord. For your sake, I do."

An unsettling feeling stirred in my gut, as we followed the path up Blackwater Mountain toward the cathedral. The words of Venefica spun inside my head, over and over and over in the hours it took to ride all through the night, at a much faster clip than when we'd left. Sunrise was still another couple of hours away, and by then, I'd have to make the decision. Feed the drink to Farryn and leave her alone, yet again, to retrieve Letifer's heart …

Or face the consequences of my father violating her for an eternity and Syrisa keeping her imprisoned in subspace.

If I could close the portal, though, I could kill him.

Damn the glimmer of hope that stirred in my chest.

"I know you think this is the solution, Jericho, but you asked me to come along for a reason." If Soreth had had any awareness of the actual reason, he'd have surely felt foolish right then. "I have mulled over what that substance could possibly contain to put Farryn in a deathlike state. All I can come up with is Nightshade. How she intends to reverse those effects seems impossible to me."

"Farryn has defied the impossible before."

"And you are perfectly willing to accept the conse-quences, if you're wrong." The urgency in his voice seemed uncharacteristic for an arrogant prick. "If the witch can't be trusted."

"Why are you so against the idea? What do you care? She is a mortal to you. Below you."

"While I may not harbor much love for mortals …. Never

mind. I've nothing to say about this. Except that I find it reckless."

"Recklessness is a necessity, at times. I will not stand by and hand her over to my father."

"Why is he so hellbent on having her, anyway?"

A question I'd asked myself a number of times, with only one explanation that made sense after all these years. "He blames me for what happened to his sister."

"I didn't know your father had a sister."

"Yes. So happened he was fucking her. Apparently, when I burned down Praecepsia, they fled to Eradyę. She was bitten by a Mortunath, and so he returned here with her. To Blackwater Cathedral. He kept her in the dungeons for centuries, feeding her souls in Nightshade, which earned him a very dark reputation that I somehow inherited from him."

A long pause followed, the quiet filled only by the clop of horse hooves. "That is why there are so many Nightshade flowers outside of Blackwater," Soreth said from behind. "Unclaimed souls."

"Yes. My father was a butcher. Some would say for love, but I don't believe he's capable of such emotion. The Knights arrived to push him out of Blackwater, and he fled. I personally ended my aunt's life."

"So, this is revenge."

"Yes."

"Certainly complicates things."

When we arrived at the gates of Blackwater, Soreth hopped down off the horse. "If you don't mind, I'd prefer not to be chased by hellhounds. I'll use my wings."

"Very well. But should you fly into Farryn's room, I will happily clip those wings of yours."

"Of course," he said, handing me the reins to his horse.

As I watched his wings unfurl, I couldn't help a small spark of jealousy. How I missed the feeling of the bones pushing through my skin, the wind catching on my fathers, the energy dancing over me. Perhaps one day I would know that feeling again.

My priority for then was keeping Farryn safe.

I cantered up the driveway, with all three dogs chasing after me, and brought the horses to a stop at the cathedral staircase. All three of them barked and snarled, and an upward glance showed Soreth climbing into the library window. A reminder that I needed to fortify some of the entry points.

Once inside the foyer, I took the staircase up to the second floor, noting how quiet it was at that hour. With no sign of Vaszhago outside her door, I peeked into Farryn's room and crossed the floor to find her snoozing away. Although her eyes remained shut, I could see the swelling around them seemed to have gone down since the day prior. I brushed a finger over her cheek, and she let out a quiet moan, shifting on the bed.

Eyes heavy with sleep, she peered up at me. "Y'home." She blinked slowly, as if still caught up in dreams. "How'd it go?"

Smiling, I bent forward and planted a kiss to her cheek. "Shhh. Sleep. We'll talk tomorrow."

"'Kay. L'you." She rolled back over, and within seconds was snoring.

"And I you." I quietly backed out of her room and found Vaszhago standing just outside of her door.

Wearing a confused expression, he hiked a thumb over his shoulder. "Wanna tell me why I just caught Soreth climbing in through a window?" he asked, telling me why I hadn't found him guarding Farryn's room.

Groaning, I rubbed a hand down my face. "Things didn't exactly go as planned."

"They rejected an Elysiumerian?"

"Yeah. Seems they don't want to piss off my father."

Hands planted on his hips, he shook his head. "Bunch of pussies. All of them."

"I did visit Venefica."

"And?"

"She gave me this." I retrieved the vial of liquid from my coat pocket. "It apparently puts Farryn in a deathlike state, which will force Syrisa out."

"But …"

"She requires Letifer's heart as payment."

Vaszhago shook his head a second time. "Devils blood. That is quite a trade."

"It is. But if I am successful, I can close the portal to Eradyę."

"And kill your father."

I cocked a brow, still enticed by the prospect of that. "Exactly."

"And what of my balls while she's in this deathlike state?"

"I can't say. I suspect she'll begin transitioning to cambion soon." I glanced back toward the bedroom, catching the slow rise and fall of her chest. "How was she today?"

"Ate a bit, according to Vespyr. Seemed in slightly better spirits."

"Here's hoping it stays that way. I'm going to head down to my office to do a bit of reading on what this elixir might contain. I appreciate you passing along the Calling."

"Of course. I'll get Soreth locked away in the dungeon."

"Where is he now?"

"In his cell, apparently. He went there rather willingly."

"I still don't trust him wandering. Not with Farryn."

"I understand. I'll lock him up now."

With a pat on Vaszhago's back, I gave a sharp nod. "Good man."

50

FARRYN

"*Save him.*"

I opened my eyes to see a faint light shining over me.

The ward my father had given me dangled over my head from where I'd secured it to my headboard, and swung back and forth as if something had knocked it. The wood sticks creaked as they bent on their own to form a new shape, and I frowned as it morphed before my own eyes into something I didn't recognize.

The sound of a baby crying had me sitting up in bed, and I looked across my room to find a dark hallway there, lit only by a single lantern, leaving its end shadowed. A glance around showed all of the furniture of my bedroom in its proper place, but for some strange reason, the hallway still stood across from me, where the empty wall would've been.

Was I dreaming? I must've been.

It wouldn't have made sense otherwise.

The baby cried again, the sound piercing my heart. A sense of familiarity crawled over me, and even if I'd never had the chance to meet my own baby, had never held it, nor heard it cry, something about the sound compelled me closer.

Pausing as I climbed from the bed, I stared down at the pillow, beneath which hid the dagger Jericho had given me. The one from the Knighthood. After another glance toward the corridor, I slipped it from beneath the pillow, holding it in a trembling hand, as I tiptoed forward.

"*Save him,*" the detached voice whispered again.

"Who?" I asked. "Who do you want me to save? Is it my baby?"

No one answered.

A dizziness swept over me, the view ahead flickering before my eyes, and I stumbled to the side. A blackness closed in, shrinking the view. As I lifted my arm to rub my temple, I stared down at my hands, one of which still held the dagger, but they didn't look like my own. They looked like someone else's–bonier and softer skin with pointier nails. Twisting them in front of me, I felt a sickness stirring in my gut.

"*Save him,*" the voice said again.

A distraction.

Heavy exhaustion settled over me like a lead blanket, my eyes so drowsy and burning, I couldn't keep them open.

Blackness.

When I opened them again, I was standing at the entrance of the corridor, staring in on the long hallway ahead. Without much direction from my head, I walked toward it.

As I passed the armoire, a strange tickling danced over my body, and the moment I stepped into the corridor, a chill burrowed deep inside my bones.

Gray walls matched a gray floor, where shadows from the lantern flickered over it.

I looked back to my room and the empty bed there, noticing a small red patch on the sheets.

My baby.

Blackness again.

The sound of an infant crying breached the endless void.

I opened my eyes and swung my attention toward it, staring off into the shadowy darkness. "My baby," I whispered. Was it possible it'd been taken from me? Perhaps I didn't lose it, at all. Perhaps it was stolen.

"Is someone there?" I called out.

No one answered.

An uneasy feeling swept over me, and I closed my eyes. "If I am dreaming, wake up now."

"Farryn?" Snapping my attention back the other way showed Vespyr standing just inside the corridor. She scanned over her surroundings, brows pulled tight. "What is this?"

A knock at a door sounded distant, almost muffled and I lifted my gaze toward the bedroom beyond Vespyr. "Farryn?" I could hear Vaszhago's voice on the other side.

The baby cried again, the sound tugging at my heart.

A feeling of elation wrapped around me, the relief of knowing I might hold it in my arms, and I smiled back at Vespyr. "Do you hear him?"

The pounding on the door in my room grew louder.

Head tilted to the side as if listening, Vespyr frowned. "Who?"

"My baby. He's crying for me."

"Farryn …" The color seemed to drain from her face. "I think we should go. Let's go back. Now." Vespyr twisted back around, but just as she took a step toward the bedroom, the scene shimmered and wavered, as if an invisible and translucent wall stood before her.

Every muscle in my body stiffened, yet I couldn't bring myself to move, as if I was glued to the floor where I stood.

What a strange dream, I thought to myself.

"Farryn!" My bedroom door flew open and Vaszhago

rushed forward, as if he would step right into the corridor
with us. His arm slammed into something, knocking him
back a step, and the scene shimmered again. He jumped to
his feet and charged again, pounding his fist into the translucent barrier that only wavered with his abuse. "Farryn!"

A loud crackling sound echoed down the hallway I'd
passed through, and as graying darkness crawled over the
view of my bedroom, I watched in panic as everything disappeared behind a gray, stone wall.

Vespyr banged against the stone with both hands. "Hey!
Hey! Let us out! Vaszhago!"

Pound, pound, pound.

Pound, pound, pound.

The sound reverberated inside my skull, and I squeezed
my eyes shut. When I opened them again, the scenery didn't
lift.

I blinked hard, shaking my head.

Wake up. Wake up.

Still, it persisted. Everything went silent, muting around
me. I watched Vespyr pound her fist against the wall, but
could not hear the sounds of it, nor whatever she spoke
when she glanced over her shoulder at me. The scene fizzled,
a blackness clinging to the fringes, as if I might pass out. I
rubbed my temples against the ache throbbing there.

The sound returned in clarity again.

Vespyr looked over her shoulder, back at me. "Farryn!
Help me find a way to open this!"

I glanced back toward the shadows, then, on a jolt of realization, dashed toward the other side of her, pounding
against the concrete as she had. "Vaszhago! Jericho! Help!"

Blowing an exasperated breath, Vespyr rested her forehead against the stone. "I don't think it's going to open." She
turned around, eyes trailing over the ceiling and walls again.
"What the hell is this place?"

"I pray it's not what I think it is."

"What?"

"In my dreams, there are dark corridors and doors. Like some kind of enormous labyrinth."

Vespyr stepped forward, her gaze ahead. "Okay, well, there's usually a way out in a labyrinth, right?"

"A maze. A labyrinth only leads to the center."

Tipping her head back, she ran a hand down her face. "Why do I get the feeling the center of this place is really bad?"

Running my hand over the wall's surface one more time, I turned around to face the dark corridor ahead. "Assuming this isn't just a dream, this wall isn't going to open. So, we might as well move forward."

On a weary groan, she yanked a knife from a holster at her hip. "Weapon check."

I stared down at the dagger still clutched in my palm and held it up. "Check?"

"Jesus, anything we encounter here is going to have to be fought close up. That sucks," she said, shoving her blade back in its holder. "Any practice using that blade?"

"A little. Jericho gave me a lesson."

Her brows winged up to a look of concern. "One?"

"Well, yeah."

"Let's keep it simple, then. If anything comes at us, I'll do the fighting, and you watch my back. Got it?"

"Sounds like a good plan."

"'Kay. Let's get this bitch over with. I drank about a gallon of water before bed, and I'm going to have to piss soon. Not sure I trust the bathrooms here." She stepped ahead of me, her blade leading the way, and after shooting one more glance toward the blank, gray wall behind us, I followed after her, nabbing a lantern from its bracket on the way.

~

The wall through which we'd walked had long disappeared into the shadows behind us, as we kept on through the labyrinth, and I held the lantern up over my shoulder to find an empty corridor.

"There's a room ahead," Vespyr said, nodding toward a door on the right side of the hallway. "Osiris says we should check it out."

"Osiris? He just decided to show up?"

"Well, yeah. He usually does when I'm in trouble."

"Wonderful."

A screeching echoed from behind, the shrill sound sending a chill down the back of my neck, and both of us came to a halt. It reminded me of a cat being tortured, high-pitched and threatening at the same time.

I spun around, holding up the lantern, though the light only stretched so far. It shook as it dangled from my trembling hands. "What the hell was that?" I asked, staring off toward the shadows.

"I'm not really sure I want to know."

Another screeching sound, louder than the first, reverberated around us.

On a strangled breath, I swung the lantern toward the door we'd reached. Room 137. "I say we head for the room," I whispered, and at a glimpse of Vespyr's wide eyes, I slowly turned back toward the shadowy corridor.

My heart caught in my throat, as I watched one dark limb step into the halo of light. Another limb followed the first, and then a skull. The figure that emerged reminded me of a long-decayed corpse. It lifted its head to show two, blood red eyes fixed on the two of us. Its jaw unhinged to a horrifically wide gape, and the screeching sound echoed again.

All at the same time, the two of us spun around and

dashed toward the door and the creature sprung forward, bounding toward us on all fours. I grabbed hold of the door's handle.

"Open the door!" Vespyr screamed beside me.

A quick sideways glance showed the creature mere yards from us.

I pressed the lock and slammed my shoulder into it. The door swung open, and we toppled inside, the concrete floor crashing into my hip and sending a shattering pain to my abdomen.

"Ah!" I cried out, as the lantern tumbled out of my grip, and I twisted to see Vespyr scramble to slam the door shut. A hard *thunk* knocked her back a step, the creature's hand sliding in through the crack in the door, and she pulled her blade. Without a hint of hesitation, she stabbed the creature's long, bony hand, sounding off another of those godawful screeches, and it retracted its limb. A streak of blood, so dark it looked black, stained the wall.

I pushed to my feet, ignoring the pain in my abdomen, and pressed myself into the door alongside her. Another hard *thunk* knocked both of us backward, but we charged forward, plowing into the steel panel, until it finally clicked shut.

The thudding stopped.

Palm pressed to the door's surface, I closed my eyes and breathed hard, resting a hand against my stomach that hadn't quite healed yet. When I opened my eyes again, Vespyr wasn't standing beside me. I spun around to see her looking out through a window, which cast a small ray of light into the room where we stood, brighter than that of the lantern I'd dropped.

"Vespyr?" I whispered as I approached her from behind, but she didn't answer. It wasn't until I stood alongside her that I noticed a look of distress coloring her face, breaths stuttering out of her.

I followed the path of her fixed gaze to a room on the other side of the window, where a young boy, perhaps nine or ten years old, stood fidgeting before a group of other boys. About the same age as him, they all sat cross-legged on the floor, and a shine of tears streaked down his cheeks as he stood there, his lips curved downward, as if on the verge of crying.

I hadn't worked out why he stood before them, or what had upset him, but another glance at Vespyr showed tears wobbling in her eyes, as if she somehow knew.

Behind the boy stood a man dressed in the telling robes of a priest, and I caught the all-too-familiar Pentacrux symbol embroidered into his vestments. He held a long ornate crosier in one hand, and a thick book of scriptures in the other.

A woman stood alongside the boy, wearing a simple A-line dress that reached past her knees. The cross around her neck bore the same symbol as that on the priest's robe.

The children, too. All of them were dressed in the same uniform. Gray shorts, a button-down shirt and burgundy tie, and over that a jacket bearing the same Pentacrux sign.

"Children of the Holy Father." The clergyman stepped toward the seated children, whose attention was directed toward the boy. "Is this the outfit worn by a girl, or a boy?"

"Boy," the children all said in unison.

"Yes. These are the clothes worn by a son of the Holy Father. Not a *daughter*." The clergyman waved the woman on, and she stepped toward the boy, removing his jacket, his tie, his shirt, his shorts, and his underwear, until he stood completely naked in front of them. When he tried to cup his groin, the woman smacked his hand away, forcing him on display.

The urge to smack her face had my palms tingling, and I curled my hands to fists.

Bruises and cuts marred his body, obvious signs of suffered torture, and he jerked with his sobbing as he stood before the other children. The sight had me turning away, and in doing so, I caught a glimpse of Vespyr beside me, whose cheeks were wet with fallen tears.

Frowning, I turned back toward the boy, and it was then, I noticed his features. Similar features. The eyes. The same nose. The same lips and jawline.

"Children, does James have a girl's body, or a boy's?" the Pentacrux clergyman asked.

James? A brother?

"Boy's," they answered again.

And then it hit me.

Oh, God.

A deep, hollow ache stirred in my chest as I looked back at the child who stood naked and crying in front of them.

I covered my mouth with my hand, the tears in my eyes blurring the scene.

Vespyr.

"Say your name, *boy*."

Head lowered, the child didn't say a word.

"Say your name!" One hard whack sent the child forward, tumbling to already bruised and scraped knees.

"Vespyr!" she cried out, and the clergyman cracked the crosier over her back.

Once. Twice. Three times.

"That is not your God-given name!" the elder man roared in a thunderous voice that bounced off the walls. "Say your name! Say your name! Say your name!"

The other children chimed in, as well. "Say your name! Say your name! Say your name!"

The tears fell down my cheek when I closed my eyes on

the horrific scene. Once again, I found myself questioning if I was asleep and merely in a nightmare.

"You will learn to respond to a woman's touch," I heard the clergyman say, before a loud sob broke free from the child.

I couldn't bring myself to watch, the sickness in my gut rising up to my throat as I imagined the woman in there violating her.

Beside me, Vespyr let out a whine of panic and covered her ears, before screaming, "Stop it! Stop it! Stop it!"

I wrapped my arms around her, feeling her body tremble with sobs against me. Tears fell down my cheeks as she broke in my embrace.

"Say your name!" The clergyman's voice crackled around us.

"Vespyr," I whispered. "Your name is Vespyr."

I felt her fingers digging into me, clutching me so tight and confirming my thoughts of whether, or not, this was simply a nightmare for her, or real.

The room darkened, the light of the lantern flickering to blackness. A sudden emptiness in my arms sent a wave of panic through me. "Vespyr?"

A new light filtered in behind me, and Vespyr was gone.

Spinning around brought me peering through the window, where she lay in a chair that looked like something found at a dentist's office. Her arms and legs had been strapped. A leather band strapped at her throat. Her eyes shifted frantically over the men who surrounded her, dressed in white uniforms that made them look like orderlies. All of them bearing the Pentacrux symbol.

But off to the side stood the clergyman, holding his black book, his eyes an unholy red. "This child harbors a demon! We must banish it! Banish this lust for lying with men! Men dressing as women! It is a sin!"

Eyes wide, I lurched forward and banged on the glass. "Hey! Hey!" I slammed it harder, frantic. "Leave her alone, you fucking prick!"

"Farryn!" Vespyr cried out through clenched teeth. She broke into another sob, shifting and squirming in her binds, to no avail.

"Quiet, demon! You will no longer find safe harbor in this body! I banish you! Banish you to Hell!"

The hum of electricity had my heart pounding against my ribs when one of the orderlies flipped a switch connected to one of many cables that fed the leather straps.

No. Please not this.

Vespyr's screams bounced off the walls, stoking the hysteria already hammering through me. I twisted around, searching for something. Anything I could throw through the glass. The room on my side of the window was completely empty of furniture, or any objects large enough to break it. There was no door to the other room. No other means of getting to her.

Her screams rose up again, and I lifted my bare foot, slamming my heel into the pane.

It didn't give.

I banged again, thumping my palm so hard against the glass, pain shot up through my wrist. "Stop! Stop this! Get the fuck away from her!"

Vespyr's screams reached a deafening pitch, and I slapped my hands to my ears. A darkness flashed over me, dragging me into it. In the black space, the screams vibrated all around me. Deep inside my ears. Not her screams. My screams. Impossibly high-pitched screams.

I opened my eyes to the glass shattering and falling around my bare feet.

Vespyr lay shaking on the bed. Neither the Pentacrux priest, nor the orderlies were anywhere in sight. I climbed through the window, careful not to cut myself on the shards of glass sticking up from the frame. Once clear of it, I scampered toward her and went to work unlatching her binds. I removed the bit that had been shoved between her teeth, and she whispered in rapid succession: "Say your name. Say your name. Say your name. Say your name." Over and over.

As gentle as I could, I slid my arm beneath her back, and helped her to a sitting position, but her eyes remained staring, as if she were looking at something past me, the sight so chilling, I turned to look, and found nothing there. "C'mon, Vespyr. Let's get the hell out of here."

51

JERICHO

I held the vial up to the light, studying the way the liquid moved, as if in slow motion. Definitely not Nightshade, as Soreth had presumed.

The door to my office slammed open, and Vaszhago burst through, breathing hard. "She went into the wall."

Shooting up out of my seat, I nearly dropped the vial, and tucked it into my pocket. "Farryn?"

"And Vespyr."

Not bothering to wait for any further details, I shot like a bullet of rage up the staircase toward Farryn's room.

The wall across from her bed held a circle where the wallpaper had curled away and shriveled, the plaster beneath browned and stained, like the decay found in abandoned buildings. I touched my hand to it, noticing the ice-cold surface.

My father.

Fury cut through me like a sharp blade, and on a growl, I slammed my fist into the wall. Over and over, I punched it, rattling the armoire. A picture popped off somewhere to the left of me. All that stood on the other side of the gaping hole

I'd created was the next bedroom. Muscles still burning with rage, I set my palms to the unruined parts of the wall, trying to catch my breath and calm the relentless pounding of my pulse.

"You saw them?" I asked, as Vaszhago strode up behind me.

"Only just. The entrance was shielded by a ward I couldn't break through. There was a gray corridor on the other side."

"Corridor." My thoughts wound back to Farryn's dream. The corridors. The devil knocker. "Infernium. They're in the labyrinth."

Vaszhago groaned and rubbed a hand down his face. "Fuck me."

"I'll need blood from Soreth, if I'm to walk there. The place feeds on vitaeilem. I'll need my armors to slow it." As a Knight, I'd been given black, steel armor, forged from the Obsidian Mountains. It was known to slow the osmotic way that Eradyę fed on vitaeilem. Not strong enough to prevent depletion, but enough to stave it off so that I might have time to retrieve Farryn. "I just need enough to get in and get Farryn."

"I'll take care of that. And I'll come with you."

"I do not know what awaits us in this labyrinth."

"Given the fact that my balls are on the line, here, I do not rightly care."

With a nod, I headed toward my chambers, as Vaszhago made his way to the dungeons. Once inside my room, I pushed the armoire to the side to reveal a door hidden there. I opened it on a small chamber, where the armored suit hung from a bracket inside. The material was thinner than that of most armor, lighter to wear. In the center of the chest the emblem of the Knighthood, made of silver, stood out against the black.

I donned the suit quickly–the chest armor, pauldrons, bracers, and gloves, then pulled the hood of its attached black cape up over my head.

It'd been years since I'd worn the suit. Centuries since I'd faced the darkest of creatures in all five realms.

As I strode from my chambers, Vaszhago met me in the corridor, his jaw clenched in frustration. "The angel is gone."

"Gone? You secured him last night, correct?"

"Yes. There's no sign that he escaped through the bars, or any part of the cell. It's as if he disappeared."

Fuck. I'd gotten a decent dose of vitaeilem from Soreth, but probably not enough to make it through to Farryn. I only hoped a greater instinct to protect her, even in my demonic form, would tamp down any urge to snap her neck like I had the succubus. "I'll deal with that later. For now, we need to get to the asylum."

Vaszhago and I exited the cathedral, when an unsettling cold brushed over the back of my neck. An unnerving sensation, and I looked to the sky to see a black-winged figure flying toward us.

"The last thing I need right now," I muttered, keeping on toward the horses.

"Sentinel?"

"Yes," I said through clenched teeth, as Adimus touched down on the cathedral lawn.

Cerberus and the other dogs charged at him. With a raise of his hand, Adimus sent all three dogs flying backward on a yelp and strode toward us.

"Going somewhere?" he asked without a trace of humor in his voice.

"If you've come for her, she's not here."

"I've not come for her, specifically."

Frowning, I steeled my muscles and turned to face him.

"Know that if you've come for me, I will kill you before I go willingly."

Adimus rolled his shoulders back, the insult undoubtedly a slap to his face. "I've not come for you, either. I'm here for Soreth."

I breathed a small sigh of relief. "Well, you've just missed him, as well. With all due respect, I don't have time to inquire anything more. I have to leave. Now."

"I'm coming with you."

Vaszhago and I exchanged a quick look, and I turned back toward Adimus again.

Perhaps sensing our confusion, Adimus let out a sigh. "Soreth has gone astray. He's gotten himself involved in the A'ryakai, and I'm sure I don't need to tell you the danger in that." The angel had always been a bit arrogant, but the A'ryakai took their prejudices to the extreme. "If he is anywhere near Farryn at the moment, that could be very bad."

"Why?"

Brows lowered, he rubbed a hand over his jaw, looking contemplative for a moment. "It puts me at great risk to tell you this, but perhaps it will make you less suspicious of me."

Something told me I already knew what he was about to tell me, something I'd suspected earlier, but dismissed.

"Farryn is the Met'Lazan."

A cold chill spiraled down the back of my neck as I stared back at him. Of course, it was Farryn. Because the universe loved to fuck with me. And while I'd suspected Farryn for a brief moment, I'd just as quickly thought it too fucking convenient.

"Those born to the Blood Moon Curse are descendants of the Met'Lazan. It is why they're made to perish and be reborn. So that the knowledge is passed."

I scratched the back of my neck where that damn tickling

sensation persisted and shook my head. "That's impossible," I said, but I knew better. It made sense, and I had been too wound up to see what was right in front of me the whole time. "She's *the* human. The one who can access the vitaeilem in Etheriusz?"

"Yes."

Laughter burst forth from my chest on a cough. "All this time, I have searched every bit of information possible so that I could protect her, and ... it was her?"

It made sense, then, why Soreth had sought me out for asylum. Something had felt off about it from the beginning, which was why I'd kept him locked in a cell.

"Every morsel of information you might've been able to scrounge would've left you at a dead end. The universe goes through great lengths to keep the identity a mystery, it's known only to the highest order of angels. The ancient gods chose a human. A neutral and fragile force to carry the power of the heavens."

"Then, how did Soreth become privy?"

With an unenthused expression, Adimus growled. "By stealing files he was forbidden to touch, on behalf of the A'ryakai."

Urgency goaded my muscles, but as I twisted back toward the stables, Adimus lurched toward me.

"Where are you going?"

"To retrieve my horse. I don't have time for any more lessons in history. My woman is in danger."

"Ah, yes. I forgot. You sacrificed your wings and power."

"To save her life. You certainly weren't doing me any favors. And she damned her soul to bring me back."

Huffing, he lowered his gaze. "I've only recently become privy to what she is."

"And was she not worth the effort when she was nothing more than a human?" My muscles clenched as I fought the urge to throw a fist in his face right then. "You, and the good of the whole."

"Still, when this is over, knowing what she is, you will keep your distance from her, as she is now protected by the heavens. As for damning her soul, The Infernal cannot lay claim to the Met'Lazan."

"If she was truly protected, you wouldn't be here now. You cannot set foot inside of Infernium. That is why you sought me out. Why didn't you come for her sooner? Why are you only trying to save her now?"

"In order to protect her fully, she would have to be taken to the Heavenly Isles. Unfortunately, she was pregnant with a half demon. As you are well aware, half demon breeds are forbidden there. Your love for her has essentially placed all five realms in peril."

"So, my father cannot claim her soul? He does not own it?"

"No. He can, however, keep her imprisoned, so I suggest we get to Infernium posthaste."

"I'd love to. Unfortunately, I have to travel like humans."

He pulled an object from his tabard and held it up. It was similar to the *cret'calatięsz* summoning chalk, but bright blue–the kind only granted by the heavens. "I can get you there, but unfortunately, I cannot open the portal inside the labyrinth. I can only take you to the entrance of Infernium."

"Good enough."

52

FARRYN

*V*espyr hobbled along, as we made our way slowly through the corridor. Arm wrapped around her, I lifted the lantern up to the door we'd just exited–the room where Vespyr had been tortured to find it no longer read 137, but 220. Somehow, we'd gotten farther along in the labyrinth.

The screeches echoed again, farther back than before, but close enough that I didn't want to be out in the open. "I think it wants us to go into the rooms. It pushes us deeper into the labyrinth."

"I can't …. I can't do that again," Vespyr said through tears, and I hugged her closer.

"I promise you won't go through that again."

The creatures sounded off again, somewhere behind. Closer than before. With urgency, I looked ahead to find another door, and we shuffled inside, quietly closing the door behind us.

I turned to see the room was a forest, with tall trees that loomed over us, and a starless sky above them. While I was anxious to see if we had somehow inadvertently found a way out, I needed to give Vespyr a minute to rest. Her body still shook against me, as I sat her down at the trunk of a tree, eyes scanning for any sign of priests, or orderlies. Once lowered onto her butt, she closed her eyes and took deep breaths, while I kept watch, trailing my gaze over the surrounding trees, but all seemed peaceful. No sign of a single creature.

"What is this place?" The moment Vespyr spoke, I turned my attention back to her, and took a seat beside her. "Is this Hell?"

"I don't know, but … these corridors are familiar to me. I dreamed them. And when I told Jericho of my dream, he was certain the place was Infernium."

"Oh, no." Face twisted up in agony again, she pulled her knees up and buried her face into her arms. "We're fucked. We're so fucked!"

Resting my hand on her arm, I gave a gentle stroke. After another minute, she lifted her head, the distress from before only slightly less apparent. "Are you okay?"

At first, she didn't answer, and I didn't press. Instead, I just sat beside her, threaded my fingers together, and let her breathe.

"I was eight when I was adopted. My mother was hit by a drunk driver, died suddenly, and I didn't really have any other family who could take me. So, I ended up with an excessively religious family who were involved in this cult-like church."

"The Pentacrux?" I asked, interrupting her story. Lifting up the arm of my gown, I showed her the branding on my skin beneath. "Did their symbol look like this?"

"Yes." She frowned at the marking on my arm and looked up to me.

"They are a cult. A very dangerous one that dates back centuries." I didn't bother to elaborate how I'd been born with the branding, and to my relief, she didn't ask.

"I knew who I was from very early on," she said, continuing her story. "I'd always been drawn to delicate lines and softness. My mom, when she was alive, knew it. She would buy me dresses and let me borrow her fancy high heels. And we'd have tea parties in the backyard together. It was never weird. It never troubled her to see me that way." Gaze lowered, she dragged the back of her arm over her eyes, wiping at tears there. "My adopted family was vehemently against what they considered *aberrations*. They always questioned my upbringing with my mother. Trying to look for reasons why I might've been fucked in the head, or something. Forget that I had perfect grades, and my home life with my true mother was art and music and books." As she stared off, more tears wobbled in her eyes. "So, one day, when I was about eleven years old, they told me we were all going on a camping trip with friends of the church. I didn't want to go, but my adopted mom told me that if I did, if I went willingly, she would take me to buy whatever clothes I wanted. So I went. I trusted her." A streak of tears fell down her cheek, and Vespyr sniffled and swallowed hard. "Imagine having to barter to wear what makes you feel comfortable." She shook her head and wiped the tears away. "They beat me. Kept me in a cage and fed me oats with water in a dog's bowl. They electrocuted me while showing me pictures of two men together, or a man wearing makeup. They cut me to bleed out the demons in me. And they watched as one of the elder women of the congregation …" She shook with a sob, and I squeezed her hand, resting my other palm over it. "As she fondled me and put her mouth on me. They told me I had to respond to her, or I'd be whipped. The fucked-up thing was? I was eleven. Eleven! It wasn't even about sex for me."

"Vespyr, I am so sorry." I pulled her into me and let her cry more tears, until she settled again.

"During my tortures, I sensed something off with two of them. Something that wasn't human. Something evil. Their eyes would change, and sometimes, they would speak in tongues." Eyes lost to what must've been memories, she toyed with a lock of her hair. "I ran away from home when I was fifteen, and that's when I met Donovan on the streets. It seemed he was looking for me. He told me that I was born Dra'Akon. An ancient group of demon killers. I thought he was nuts at first." She chuckled, running her sleeve across her nose. "But he trained me to see them. And there were so many. Walking among us. It was a terrifying awakening." Sitting up from me, she took a deep breath and cleared her throat. "I tried to do the 'normal' life for a while," she said, raising her hands to air quote the word. "Which just meant I wasn't actually killing anything. Oddly enough, considering what he taught me, what we hunted, life was fairly *boring* with him. We basically just tried to keep a low profile, so no one would get wise to what we were. What we were doing. During the day, he worked construction, and at night, he dragged home demons to interrogate and kill. He lived in a modest house of a quiet suburb. He insisted that I stay in school to keep a normal outward appearance. Let me wear whatever the fuck I wanted," she said on a laugh. The humor faded from her eyes. "But I couldn't let it go. I dreamed of what'd happened to me at that camp every night. And after a couple of years, I went back for the two demons who tortured me, and I killed them, just as Donovan had taught me."

"That's how you ended up in the psychiatric hospital."

Another brush across her nose and she nodded. "Thanks to my adopted mother, I had a long history of hospital stays, because the Pentacrux ran those facilities, too. Here, I rid the world of two dangerous demons, who would've gone on to hurt countless others. And they thought I was crazy."

"They don't know what we know."

A tear slipped down her cheek, as she sat twirling a loose string on her uniform. "My whole life, I just wanted to be seen for what I was. Just see me for who I am. How messed up is it that I had to come to fucking Purgatory to feel accepted."

I squeezed her hand, tipping my head to guide her eyes to mine. "Vespyr, if this place becomes too much, go." A thought came to mind just then. "Wait. Can you astral project out of here? You could go back to Blackwater and tell Jericho where I am. They can come for us."

"I'm not leaving you."

"You'd be saving us. Please. Just try."

"Farryn. I don't want to leave you here alone in this place. What if I can't come back? What if Jericho doesn't find you?"

Tears blurred my eyes, and I forced a smile. "I don't want you to leave, either. This place scares the shit out of me. But if there's a chance, I think we should try."

The agony sketched across her face told me she was conflicted, but after another minute, she nodded. "I'll try." She closed her eyes and let out an easy breath. After only a few seconds, she opened them, cleared her throat, then followed the same routine as before.

Nothing.

"I can't. I can't leave." A hint of panic laced her voice, as she closed her eyes and tried a third time.

Still nothing.

Slouching back against the tree, she huffed. "It's no use. I can't even return to the mortal realm."

Wracked with disappointment, I sighed. "Why on earth would you follow me in here?"

"It's not like that corridor screamed Disneyland. Why on earth would you step into it?"

"I heard a baby crying. And someone kept telling me to save him. I couldn't really stop myself. I kind of blacked out, and when I woke up, truly woke up, that's when the wall closed."

"I hate to say it, but I wish that fucker Vaszhago was here. Do you think they'll find us?"

"I don't know. I hope so. In the meantime, we'll stick together. I think if we go back out the door, we'll be farther along in the labyrinth."

Vespyr twisted around, looking behind the trunk of the tree. "Farryn ... the door is gone."

"What?" I scrambled onto hands and knees and looked for myself, finding nothing but trees. "What the hell? That's where we came in."

"I get the feeling whatever it is *wants* us to venture into all of these rooms."

"I think you're right. There's something to it. Like a puzzle. The first room we came to was 137. I saw that number repeatedly in dreams and hallucinations I've had throughout the day."

"What does 137 mean?"

"I believe they're separate. Thirteen and seven. Death and creation. When we exited, there was 220 on the door. It's possible it could be references to the Bible."

"Or the two could mean duality." Vespyr nibbled on her lip, her eyes contemplative. "Could be tarot?"

"Maybe. Whatever it is, I think it's guiding us toward something. And I think we need to keep our eyes open." A shine flickered in my eyes, and I looked up, to see a gossamer thread stretched between the trees just over my head. I followed its path toward darker, more shadowy parts of the woods ahead of us. "Looks like the only way out is through the woods."

"I don't know about you? But I've read plenty of fairy tales to know that never ends well."

53

THE BARON

The baron stepped inside the dark room, staring across to where his mother lay, weak and still. He did his best to reel in the tears, but as he gazed upon her frail form, he felt the sting of tears hit the rims of his eyes.

"Will you stand there all evening?" she asked in a breathy voice.

Head down, he crossed the room and came to a stop alongside her bed. He couldn't speak a word, as if his voice had been cut right out of his throat.

"I am dying."

He looked away, breathing hard through his nose to stave off tears, and felt the gentle touch of his mother's fingers guiding his face back to hers.

"Do not cry for me. For I am not in pain. Cry for those who suffer."

"Why, Mother? Why did we not leave? Why did you choose to stay and suffer his abuse?"

She brought his hand to her lips and kissed the back of his palm. "If I am to be honest, I dreamed of that very thing so many times. When you were first born, I found myself torn between duty and motherhood. How badly I wanted to steal you away, but I could not."

"Why? What duty? As his *wife*?" He couldn't help the repulsion on his lips as he spoke the word.

"My sweet son, I have kept you in the dark for far too long, and it's time you know the truth."

"What truth?"

Her eyes softened with the kind of warmth that made him want to curl up beside her. "You have agonized for so long about what you are and what you are to become. You have seen the evil that resides within your father, but do not fret. For you carry goodness. *My* blood. The blood of the Elysiumeria."

He studied her face, searching for any sign of delirium. What he'd learned from Soreth over the last few weeks was the nature of Elysiumerians, and how they were perceived as supreme. "I am half Elysiumerian?"

"Yes. You come from a very powerful bloodline."

He let that sink into his thoughts. "So, I am not entirely evil?"

"No. You are what is known as a Sentinel. The guardians of the heavens. And one day, they will come for you. Because you are a rare breed. A rare and wonderful breed."

"And what happens to me, when they do?"

"You will be taken away from here. Protected. And you will no longer suffer at the hands of your father." She gripped his arm, her nails digging into him. "But you must remain good, Jericho. You must follow the path of righteousness and not give in to the tempting darkness that resides within you."

"What would happen then?"

"The Sentinels will become your enemy. And you cannot afford to be at their mercy while your father remains a threat."

So many things seemed clearer in that moment. Questions that had swirled inside his head for far too long had finally begun to make sense. "Will they come for you? Will they take you home?"

Tears filled her eyes, and she shook her head. "My time is done. I chose this fate."

"Why? Why would you choose to stay? I would have gone with you."

"It is not only you that I stay for."

Confusion flickered over him, and he frowned back at her. "Is there another?"

Her eyes grew heavy, her grip of his arm faltering. "You've become quite fond of her," she said in a weak voice. "Lu ... stina."

"Lustina?" She stayed to protect Lustina? From what? "Why?"

Her lips stretched to a feeble smile. "She is ... strong. But ... vulnerable. You must ... choose goodness ... for her." Stuttered breaths interrupted her words, and sweat beaded over her brow. "Protect her ... at all ... costs. And ..."

He stared down at her, as she seemed to focus on breathing, her brows pinching together as if in pain. "And what, mother? Tell me."

She swallowed hard. "Do not ... give in to evil. Never tell them ... what you are."

His mind from refused to move from the girl she'd asked him to protect. "Mother, is it Bishop Venable who threatens her?"

She didn't answer.

Didn't move.

Panic swelled in the boy's chest, as he stared down at his beautiful mother and her sweet, angelic face. "Mother?"

Tears welled in his eyes.

He rested his forehead against her temple, breathing in her floral scent.

And he wept.

~

A cold chill raked over his skin, as the baron followed Bishop Venable down to the undercroft. Remorse churned in his gut for the way he'd spoken to Lustina after his mother's services, and he'd wanted the chance to apologize to her, if not for the pentash having interrupted them, informing him to meet with his father and the bishop.

While the girl had only tried to comfort him, the words of his mother echoed inside his head with a bitter ache. Over the weeks, he'd grown feelings for the girl. Terrifying feelings that compelled him to sink his claws into her, to possess her before she, too, could be stolen away, like everything else he'd come to love.

The route the bishop took to the undercroft was all too familiar to the boy, and if it was pain his tormentor longed to exact, the baron had already suffered too much to care.

They reached the room where his *exorcisms*, as the bishop often referred to them, had taken place. The pentrosh who followed behind him stepped ahead, as they approached, and opened the door without a hint of guilt in his expression.

The baron entered the room, too preoccupied to put up a fight, but came to a halt as he stepped inside. Tethered to the very chains from which he normally hung, his father's right-hand, Alaric, stood naked, his body marred by burns, cuts, and marks of other, unspeakable torments. One of his eyes had been cut from its socket, leaving a blooded, gaping hole in its place.

Lord Praecepsia stood behind the man, wearing his usual cold and detached expression.

As the door slammed behind the baron, he flinched, his

nerves on edge, never having seen the man before him looking so vulnerable. So weak.

He'd come to despise Alaric, up until he'd learned the man's true identity. A spy and ally to his mother. For years, the man had tormented him, which, he had come to realize, was nothing more than a ruse for his father.

"It has come to my attention that my most trusted right-hand deceives me," Lord Praecepsia said, arms crossed as he circled the man. "He has been gathering information on me to feed back to my enemies, to use against me."

"He is as Judas was to the Messiah!" Bishop Venable said beside the baron, smacking his crosier against the dirt floor.

"The penalty for treason is death." The baron's father turned to face him, his eyes dark and brimming with enmity. He strode toward the boy and pulled a dagger from the sheath at his hip.

On instinct, the baron jumped back, expecting him to lash out and cut him. Instead, the elder Van Croix lifted his hand and set the blade in his palm. "It is time you learn a lesson, boy. To protect your land, your name, your family."

The baron stared down at the blade in his hand, taking in the weight of the cold steel.

"Run the blade through him, and you shall be exempt from any punishment this evening. Prove yourself loyal to me."

The boy wished more than anything that he had the courage to run the blade through the man standing alongside of him. He shook his head. "I cannot."

"Do it. Or I shall string you up by your ankles and bleed you to near death."

The baron knew all too well it was not an idle threat, and hands trembling, he stared down at the blade, studying it's perfectly sharpened tip that would slice through the man's flesh with ease.

"Think of how many times he's subjected you to torment. How unrepentantly he has carried out offenses against you."

It was true, but the baron had come to realize that any other behavior would have planted a seed of suspicion in his father's mind. Still, he shook his head and handed the blade back to him.

Lord Praecepsia glanced down to the weapon and back to his son, his brow quirked. "Imagine, for a moment, that is the young, raven-haired girl strung up by her wrists."

The baron's muscles tensed, his jaw tight with the rage that moved through him. Rage he would not dare show, for fear his father might follow through with such a visual. The older man's lips stretched to a smile. "Run this blade through him, or I can promise that she will be the next to find herself strung up in this very room."

He steeled his muscles and curled his fingers around the hilt of the blade. Gaze lifted to Alaric's, he took in the tilt of the man's chin, as if he welcomed death. As if there was more honor in dying. Without a hint of hesitation, the baron crossed the small space separating him from Alaric and stabbed the blade into the man's exposed abdomen. He gave one hard twist, and Alaric let out a grunt.

Head lowered, he stepped back and let the blade fall to the floor with a clang that climbed up the back of his spine. The dark chuckle that reached his ears had his lips curling with repulsion.

A deep penetrating burn lit across his forearm, and the baron peeled back his sleeve to find a silvery marking etched into his skin. He ran his finger over it, drawing back when the heat of it met his fingertip.

"Your first kill. And, by the gods, it will not be your last," his father whispered.

54

FARRYN

"I feel like I know these woods," I said over my shoulder, as Vespyr followed behind. Something about the trees and the narrow footpath curving through them struck me as strangely familiar, though I couldn't summon a single memory.

Perhaps they were Lustina's.

"So, then, tell me you know the way out, because I hate the woods about as much as I hate pineapple on pizza."

Vespyr's comment brought a smile to my face, as I stepped cautiously over the brush. "You're a sick woman."

She snorted, and something up ahead made a loud crackling sound that brought both of us to a halt. "Shit," she whispered.

A flicker of light drew my eyes to a gossamer strand overhead, which bounced and stirred the leaves of the trees through which it was threaded.

Twisting back toward her, I raised the dagger up and pressed a finger to my lips to quiet her. When she nodded, I kept on through the trees, until we reached a small, straw hovel that reminded me of something out of a dark fairytale.

From its thatched roof, the thin translucent strings stretched out in all directions of the forest around it. As if they all converged there.

"Jesus, that's creepy as fuck." Vespyr ran her finger over one of the threads, and I watched as it vibrated all the way to the hovel.

"*Save him,*" a detached voice whispered in my ear, and I twisted around toward Vespyr.

"Did you say something?"

"Yes, I said that's creepy as fu–"

"Not that. Something else."

Frowning, she shook her head, and I turned back toward the hovel.

"I know this place. I've seen it before." My mind stretched to centuries before as I dipped into Lustina's memories. "The widow in the woods."

"What?"

"It was what they called the woman who murdered the boys. They called her the widow in the woods."

Vespyr let out a mirthless laugh. "Well, that sounds absolutely inviting, doesn't it?"

Something urged me forward, in spite of my guts telling me to get out of there. The only thing was, my guts had apparently forgotten that there was no exit the other way, and I suspected our only escape lay within that hovel.

Heart beating against my ribs like it wanted out, I crossed the clearing, and as we approached the open entrance, that lacked a proper door, I squeezed the hilt of Jericho's dagger so tightly my knuckles burned. A candle flickered inside the hut, and as the two of us stepped through, my throat thickened, every cell in my body quivering, when I took in what sat in the center of the room.

The strands did converge within the hovel, creating a weblike structure throughout the interior. The strings were attached to the body of a woman clothed in a white dress made of cloth strips. Atop her head was a cone-shaped hennin, wrapped in the same cloth that covered her eyes. Blackened fingers, as if dipped in tar, swept over the nothingness in front of her, and she tipped her head back, as though listening.

Movement out of the corner of my eye drew my attention toward what looked like a mummified body, about the size of a child, completely cocooned in the threads. A muffled scream sent a shock of panic through me, and I snapped my attention back toward the woman, who settled again, her head lowered, as if she'd fallen asleep. With careful steps, I looked down to avoid stepping on the strands, which I was certain would rattle her awake. Using the dagger, I gently sawed into the cocoon, careful not to cut too deeply, and nodded at Vespyr, then to the woman, signaling for her to keep an eye out.

She nodded back and twisted toward the woman, as I continued to saw, loosening the threads of the cocoon to reveal a small hand. A torso. And finally the face of a little boy. Not just any little boy, but the one from my dreams. The one I'd so often chased through the corridors.

Wiping away tears, he sat up from the web, and eyes wide, he threw his arms around me, as though he somehow recognized me from the dream. The motion vibrated the strands, and I gripped his arms to make him still. Vespyr tugged at my arm, and I turned to see the woman sitting upright, her head sweeping back and forth, as if she sensed us there. She opened her mouth to reveal a mouthful of pointed fangs and let out a scream that carried a deep, guttural, demonic sound.

"Run!" Grabbing the boy's hand, I yanked him from the webbing, and we hustled back toward the entrance.

It was no longer there.

Frantic, I scanned over the hovel, catching sight of a door behind the woman. "Fuck!" I pointed toward it, and Vespyr took the lead, chopping away at a strand that blocked our path.

The moment it was loose, more strands wrapped themselves around her arms and ankles, yanking her feet out from under her.

Vespyr let out a scream as the strands tangled around her.

I lurched forward, cutting them away from her body. Pain radiated over my abdomen, and I glanced down to see one of the strands coiled around my waist, so tight the thread cinched my gown and burned my skin. Still, I kept on with my sawing.

The woman let out another terrifying howl, and a second strand wrapped around my throat.

Tight bands dug into my neck, and I dropped the blade, clawing at them. My lungs burned for a sip of air, and I opened my mouth, desperately trying to capture one small drag of it.

Vespyr wriggled and screamed.

The boy clawed at strands digging into his legs.

Darkness closed in from my periphery. I was passing out. I needed air. Air!

The scene shrank to nothing more than a pinprick.

The sound of a woman crying out in pain reached the black void, and I opened my eyes to the floor of the hovel, where pools of blood lay scattered. Confused, I lifted my hands and found blood staining my palms.

The scent of carnage clung to the air, and I turned to find the woman writhing on the floor, blood pouring out of small tube-like structures sticking out from her skin, which must've been where the strands had been attached. They lay completely severed from her on the ground. The cloth dress she wore was saturated in dark red blood, clinging to her figure.

Behind me, Vespyr hung from the webs, eyes closed, head cocked to the side. On a jolt of panic, I swiped up my fallen blade and went to work, slicing her binds.

The movement seemed to wake her, and she startled on a gasp, but let out a long exhale. "Oh, God. What the hell did you do?"

I set her arms free, and then her ankles, and glanced back at the woman, still twitching and writhing. "I did this?"

"Yeah. You kind of went crazy." Vespyr rubbed her wrist where a ligature mark remained. "Thought you were going to kill me, for a second there."

Behind me, the boy still clawed at the strands that had worked their way up to his knees. I knelt down, and began slicing away at them, careful not to cut his legs.

Once he was free, I pulled him to his feet, and the three of us made a run for the door.

55

JERICHO

*T*he closest Adimus could get us through the portal, without the Noxerians detecting him from the sky, was about a mile from the asylum. A mile I'd had to walk, thanks to not having my fucking wings. A thought that grated on me.

We strode through the sandy stretch of land toward Mount Obsidia, the late morning sun beating down on the black armor I wore and creating an infernal heat that had me damn near panting.

"So, what does Soreth intend with her, exactly?" I asked, the words like bitter acid in my mouth.

"He intends to turn her over to the A'ryakai, which will propel his status amongst them. I suspect he will keep her for himself, to ensure his position."

"Is it not forbidden for an *angel* to take from a human?"

Adimus glanced back at me and forward. "It is. As you're aware, the A'ryakai do not play by the rules."

"And yet, many an angel has turned Fallen for such an offense."

"It is their bloodline which affords them certain privileges, yes."

Which meant Soreth would suffer no more than a slap to the wrist, if he violated Farryn. "Hypocritical cunts. All of you."

Vaszhago snorted beside me.

"Tell me what happens to the Met'Lazan after they perish. Their souls do not end up in Heaven, or Hell."

"No. They do not." Brows furrowed, Adimus shook his head. "Come, Jericho. Why do this to yourself?"

The question only set fire to my curiosity and goaded my need to know . "I want to know what happened to her. After the day Lustina drowned. What happened to her soul?"

"For centuries, the Met'Lazan returned here, to the ancient temple of the gods. To be cleansed of their knowledge of the Omni. It was a means of safeguarding the sigil. However, the gods fled this realm, forsaking the Met'Lazan. Eventually, the temple crumbled. And Infernium now stands in its place."

I skidded to a halt. "Are you telling me Lustina was sent to Infernium after her death?"

"I believe she was, yes. But it was not the blood moon prophecy which killed her. It was Bishop Venable."

"Yet, she died on the night of the blood moon."

"Merely coincidence." He lowered his gaze from mine, the sight of his sudden discomfort setting off alarms inside my head. "She was with child."

Pregnant? A cold sensation snaked through my veins, while a fist of agony squeezed my chest. "Pregnant? Then, she would have survived. She would have survived that night."

"Yes. Just because the prophecy exists, doesn't mean the cursed cannot be murdered."

Air expelled from my lungs, my knees wobbling with

weakness, while I stared off. A baby?

The shock faded for the black, toxic rage that exploded through my muscles. I turned and slammed my fist square into Adimus's jaw, knocking the angel back onto his ass. "You sent her there!" Before he could push to his feet, I scrambled over top of him and pounded another punch to his face. And another. "You rotten motherfucker! You sent her straight to my father! To be tormented!" Another punch. And another.

As I drew back my fist again, a force held it upright, keeping me from launching it into that fucking nose of his.

"It is not our decision to send the Met'Lazan there! It is as it has been for centuries! Your father was a fool for seeking her out. The purpose of the temple is to erase all memory of the Omni upon death. Chances are, Lustina remembered nothing." Daubing the blood from his lip and eye, Adimus pushed me off himself, and I fell to the side, finally released of whatever spell he had placed on me. He turned to Vaszhago, sneering. "Thanks for the help."

With a grin, Vaszhago pulled the black cigarette he'd lit from between his lips. "Was hoping I'd get to see him finish you off, to be honest. I'm a bit disappointed."

Every muscle in my body shook with rage, my chest locked up with the tension as I stared back at Adimus. "You never once tried to save her."

"To enter Infernium now would be a death sentence for an angel."

"Why did you not tell me? I would have gone after her. Why did you not let me save her from that hell?" It explained the nightmares Farryn kept having about the place. She was remembering Lustina's time there.

He hiked a knee up, resting his elbow atop it. "They die here. Their souls are cleansed, and they fade into the black abyss until they are reborn. Your time with her would've been cut short."

"At the time, I'd have traded my soul for a single minute more with her. I would do so for Farryn now. Clearly, you've not loved, if you cannot understand that." I pushed to my feet and strode past Vaszhago in the direction of Infernium.

"I have loved," Adimus said from behind. "I happened to love your mother very much."

The urge to throw another fist in his face tugged at me, but I didn't want to waste any more time than I already had. "Not enough," I said over my shoulder.

"She stayed to protect her. Lustina." Adimus spoke at my back, as I didn't slow my pace, and his words took me back to that day, knelt at my mother's bedside, as she lay dying. She'd told me to *protect the girl at all costs*. At the time, I'd thought it was simply her affection toward Lustina which had prompted her to say so.

"She knew she was Met'Lazan," I said, looking ahead to see the mountain not far from where we strode.

"Yes. For years, your father tormented her to get her to confess. He fed off her vitaeilem and subjected her to unspeakable acts of cruelty, and still, she refused to divulge the name of the girl she'd been sent to protect."

The confession stabbed my heart, knowing my mother had given her life to protect Lustina, and I couldn't save neither her, nor Lustina, in the end.

"Lustina would have lost the memory when she passed, only to remember it when she was reborn." Adimus trailed after me, his words fading for the rage simmering in my head.

"Farryn now carries this memory and is at risk because she *lives*. The odds of her remembering the Omni are frighteningly good so long as her heart still beats"

"You better pray that it still beats if you're so holy. Because if anything should happen to her, I will bring Hell to the heavens."

~

It wasn't long before we arrived at the gates of Infernium. The decayed asylum sat at the base of the mountain, the mere appearance of it a threat, with its gargoyle statues and dark vines climbing the outside of it. A darkness loomed over the building, separated by a wavering wall that shimmered where the light from where we stood hit it.

The very edge of Eradyę's border.

"This is as far as I go," Adimus said, staring up at the ominous building. "I cannot stay long in Nightshade, as I'm sure The Fallen have already sensed my presence here. The entrance to the labyrinth lies in the tunnels beneath the asylum." He reached into his pocket and pulled out a vial, which he handed off to me. "This should be enough vitaeilem for you to summon a bolt straight through the heart of Letifer, which resides in the center of the labyrinth. Retrieve Farryn and exit quickly, for once the portal is closed, you cannot escape."

"This is why my father sought Farryn out. If she can access vitaeilem, she can power Eradyę."

"Up until she dies. Then Letifer will seek out the next Met'Lazan. And the next. And the next. Until all of Etheriusz is drained."

"I will not let that happen."

"Godspeed."

"I do not need your holy well wishes. They mean nothing in Infernium." On those parting words, Vaszhago and I strode through the gates toward the staircase. I took small comfort in knowing that Farryn was likely alive, given that Vaszhago showed no sign of pain.

Passing the gargoyles whose eyes were a glowing red, I jogged up the staircase to the door where the devil door knockers stared back at me. Three knocks opened the door, and the two of us entered the asylum. A chill hung on the air, creating mists of breath as I made my way into the lobby. Old stone walls, stained with age and decay, gave an unkempt look to the inside.

A nurse, donned in a white uniform and nursing cap, watched us as we passed, her youthful face flickering to that of a skeleton with decayed flesh, and back to the youthful appearance again.

"I think she likes me," Vaszhago said quietly beside me.

I'd have laughed, if my muscles weren't so wound up over the thought of Farryn being in this place. How terrifying it must've been for her, particularly with as little fighting skills as she possessed. I was glad to know Vespyr had gone after her, so she wasn't alone, at least. But given my father's intent, Vespyr surely didn't stand to survive.

Past the desk, the asylum opened to something of an old, decayed atrium, with its glass dome overhead and levels upon levels of what must've been over a couple thousand patient rooms, or more. We kept on ahead, toward the hallway where an exit sign flickered in the distance.

Rooms lined the hallway, where patients sat out in wheelchairs. An old man in nothing but what appeared to be a cloth diaper sat facing toward the exit. As we passed, I turned to see his eyes were glazed over white, his hands shaking incessantly. He whispered unintelligible words to himself.

We kept on, passing a woman who rocked back and forth in her chair. "There is no God." She reached out for the two of us as we passed, just missing my arm. "Help me, angel. Help me. Please!"

We finally reached the end of the hallway and pushed through the old, medieval-looking door to a stairwell. I peered over the edge of the railing to find the staircase wound for levels below us and glanced back at Vaszhago. "Ready for this."

"Ready as I'll ever be, I suppose."

We jogged down the staircase, the sound of our heavy boots echoing off the walls, until we reached the bottom. Someone had painted *HELL* on the door, and I knew we'd found it.

The entrance to the labyrinth.

With a deep breath, I pushed into a gray corridor, with gray walls, gray floors, gray ceilings. As I stepped over the threshold with Vaszhago following behind, the sound of grinding stone from behind had me twisting around to find the wall closing behind us.

"Well, I suppose we're committed now," Vaszhago said.

A door up ahead on the right caught my attention, and I strode toward it. I swung it open to find a quiet winter forest on the other side.

Vaszhago chuckled behind me. "You've got to be fucking kidding me."

Huffing, I stepped inside, the ice-cold air invading my lungs as I trudged through the snow.

"Want to tell me why we're entertaining what is clearly bait?"

"I do not intend to leave any part of this labyrinth unchecked for Farryn. If I have to search every room, every corner, it's what I will do."

"Surely, she's got to be farther along in this thing than this."

The flicker of lights up ahead brought me to a stop. With slow and careful steps, I prowled toward the cabin, the sight of which sent a chill across my flesh. It looked uncannily like the one my father's mistress had lived in.

"Do you recognize it?" Vaszhago asked.

"Unfortunately, yes."

Something compelled me closer, even with my head telling me to turn around and go back. Blade in hand, I approached the window, beyond which two figures appeared to be fucking. The familiar face of my father spurred a sick twisting of my stomach. His mistress was bent over a wooden table, her long brown hair draped over the side of it.

She turned to face me, and I zeroed in on stardust eyes and the familiarity of her young face.

Lustina.

Eyes panicked and ablaze with fear, she let out a distressed scream. "Help me! Please!"

On a roar of anger, I charged toward the window and hammered my fist against the glass. When it wouldn't break, I strode toward the door, pushing against the handle to open it.

The door wouldn't budge. I rammed it with my shoulder, slamming myself into the seemingly feeble wood. Still, it wouldn't move. I could hear Lustina crying on the other side, begging, and the sound of it tore at me. Frantic, I pounded my fists against the barrier, and noticed the blackness crawling up my hands.

Vaszhago grabbed one of my arms, but I threw his hand off, hammering my palms into his chest and knocking him backward. He pushed to his feet and charged at me again, slamming me back into the walls of the cabin. "It's not her! Remember you are here for Farryn!"

I stilled at that and noticed I no longer heard Lustina screaming.

"Drink some of the vitaeilem. Just a small bit, yeah?"

Breathless, I nodded and reached down into the satchel at my hip, and pulled out the vial. After uncapping it, I tipped back just enough of the angel's blood to send a tingle through me. When I lifted my hands again, the blackness moved back toward my fingertips.

56

FARRYN

$\mathcal{W}$e exited through the door, and I grabbed another lantern hanging from its bracket. Holding it up to the door showed 445.

"We've moved farther." I twisted around to Vespyr and the boy, who I just noticed wore threadbare clothes, his bones sticking out through his skin. "What's your name?" I asked, marveling how much he looked like a young Jericho to me, perhaps only eight years old. It troubled me to think that he was trapped inside the labyrinth alone. And for how long?

Gaze lowered, he shook his head.

Perhaps he couldn't speak. "It's okay, you don't have to tell me." I turned toward the corridor again, searching for the next door.

"Elyon," he whispered.

Something struck me as familiar about the name, about him, and I twisted back, marveling at the bright blue of his eyes and the black raven hair. "How did you get here?"

He looked around and lowered his gaze, shrugging.

"Is your mommy or daddy here?"

The look he shot me, chock with confusion, made me

wonder if he had parents, at all. Perhaps he wasn't real outside of this place. A dream, like everything else. One that would crumble to dust, a thought which saddened me. "It's okay." I smiled, stroking a hand down his hair.

We began our trek down another stretch of gray walls and floors, my head spinning with all the possibilities of what could've possibly happened back at that hovel. How I managed to single-handedly, according to Vespyr, mutilate the widow.

"Did you know that there's a word that exists specifically for ants?"

Frowning at Vespyr's interruption, I glanced back at her. "What?"

"Osiris taught me the word. It's the positive interaction that ants have with other species. Like butterflies. Beetles. Plants. It's called *myrmecophily.*"

"Why are you telling me this?"

Smiling, she shrugged. "Because I'm still a little rattled from having been at the mercy of the spider woman. But also, it's kinda cool when you think about it. They have these relationships with others that help them thrive. Wouldn't it be cool if humans were more myrmecophilous? With other humans, I mean. Not ants."

"I think the word for human myrmecophilia is compassion," I said over my shoulder, watching for another door. "And by the way, this is a little weird to have this conversation right now. No offense, but I'm not appreciating ants very much at the moment."

"What if there's something that's helping us in this place, though? Like a force that ensures that we survive?"

I glanced back and smirked. "It's surely not sparing us much, is it?"

"No, but we could've died back there. Yet, we didn't. Because something wants us to survive. To succeed. It's like a myrmecophilous aura. Gah! Could you imagine? If more humans were that way, abuse wouldn't exist. Because we would all want one another to succeed. So we would tend to each other. And be kind to each other."

"Yeah, and unicorns would prance across the skies, shitting rainbows down on us." The moment I said the words, I regretted it, as I glanced back and took in the disappointed expression on her face.

"Are you always so cynical?" she asked.

The answer was *no*, I hadn't always been. There'd always been a glimmer of hope inside me somewhere, but life had gotten heavy and complicated in recent months. Hope had begun to feel silly, a frivolous luxury that I no longer had the energy to entertain.

I paused my strides, allowing her to catch up, and slipped my arm in hers. "I'm sorry. I'll be your *myrmeco-whatever* ant." I reached my hand back for the boy's, and lowering his gaze, he stared toward my fingers as if reluctant to take it. With a shaky hand, he finally grabbed mine, and a shiver ran up the back of my neck on feeling his soft skin, which somehow carried the overwhelming familiarity of having threaded my hand in his before.

"I want to be a butterfly," Vespyr prattled on beside me. "They're my favorite." Smiling, she glanced over her shoulder, and my stomach twisted, watching the mirth drain from her expression. "F-F-F-Farryn?"

I turned, swinging the lantern around to the direction from which we'd come, and I nearly dropped it.

My heart leapt into my throat on seeing at least a dozen of the creatures in the hallway, eyes glowing red, their bodies shifting with impatience. "Oh, fuck."

The boy released my hand on a whimper and scampered off behind us, rounding the corridor, out of sight.

A beastly, dog-like creature, with bloody, matted fur and

bones sticking out, stepped ahead of the other creatures. My heart sank as I studied the slight familiarity in its eyes. A little too much like those of Cerberus, but decayed and twice as demonic.

Oh, God.

On a screech, they charged toward us. We didn't even get two steps before the first one nabbed Vespyr, yanking her beneath it. In three quick stabs—chest, throat and skull, the creature fizzled into black dust. She scrambled to her feet.

Another one dragged her backward.

"Vespyr!" I set the lantern down and barreled forward, dagger in hand.

I stabbed the creature in its skull, watching in horror, as it rose up to his feet, my blade lodged in its head. "Oh, no. Oh, shit."

It grabbed hold of the hilt with its bony hand and yanked the blade out, tossing it off. As it lurched toward me, Vespyr ran her blade over its chest, across it's throat, and in the skull. The three moves Jericho had taught me. Just as before, the creature exploded.

I swiped up The fallen blade and held it ready for the Cerberus lookalike, who barreled right for me with a malicious glint in his glowing eyes.

Another bounded after Vespyr.

"Chest, throat, skull!" she said, charging toward the second.

"Right!" Chest, throat, skull, chest, throat, skull.

Cerberus prowled slowly, as if taunting me. With trembling hands, I squeezed the blade's hilt. Chest, throat, skull. "H-h-hey, boy," I said, swallowing past the lump in my throat.

I jumped forward and managed a slice to his chest, before I jumped backward, dodging the swipe of his mangled paw. "Fuck!"

He barked with a deep guttural sound that sounded more demon than animal.

A rapid glimpse of Vespyr showed her fighting another one of them.

The frustration of being totally useless sent a bolt of anger through me, and I charged again, managing a slice to the demon dog's throat. My movements were so inexplicably precise, that I glanced at Vespyr again, wondering if I'd actually been the one to administer the slice. The dog let out a demonic yelp and stumbled, while black blood oozed from his throat. I stabbed the blade into its head.

Again, almost effortlessly, as if I'd done it a hundred times before.

Not a second later, the dog exploded into a bright orange flame, just as Jericho had said it would with the cursed blade. "Ha! I did it! I fucking did it!"

"Great! Run!"

I lifted my gaze to see a half-dozen more of the humanoid creatures charging at us. Spinning on my heel, I nabbed up the lantern and headed around the corner, where I spotted Elyon squatted down beside the next door. All three of us piled inside the room, and with us on the other side of the door, I slammed it shut.

Eyes closed, I fell back against the barrier, panting.

Vespyr crouched beside me, also bent forward, breathing hard. "That was intense."

I held up my fist to her. "How was that for fucking myrmecophilous."

Snorting, she stared up at me and bumped her fist against mine. "Pretty sure Van Croix would've been proud of you, too."

"I'll have to tell him I killed my first demonic dog. Assuming I see him again."

"You will. We're getting the fuck out of here."

Closing my eyes again, I took deep breaths to calm the rush of adrenaline that'd pounded through me the moment I saw those things.

Calm. Deep breaths. Calm.

"Farryn!" As the familiar, masculine voice called out to me, I swallowed past the sudden dryness in my throat, and my eyes shot open.

I stood in the foyer of my old house, easily identified by the dark, wooden staircase, the strange paisley-print walls, and the layout, which looked exactly as it had when I was fifteen years old. "Papa?"

"Farryn!" The fear and pain in his voice lit a fire in my veins, and I ran up the staircase, finding him in the bathroom with his back to me, facing the tub.

"Papa?" Tears filled my eyes as I took him in. My father. The man I hadn't seen since I was a teenager. The man I never thought I'd see again.

Was he here? Real?

I stepped inside the small bathroom and glanced down toward the tub to see legs submerged in the water. A terrifying sensation gripped the back of my neck, and when he stepped aside, I jumped back on seeing myself.

Drowned.

I let out a shuddered breath, panic expanding inside my chest on seeing my own lifeless face, and flinching, I looked away to find my father staring back at me, a look of pure agony clouding his gaze.

"I didn't mean to do it," he said, with tears in his voice. "I woke up from a dream … and my hands were wrapped around your throat."

I lurched forward, throwing my arms around him. "It's okay, Papa. I know you didn't mean to hurt me."

His arms held me back, and he shook with a sob. "I never

wanted to hurt you, Farryn. Never." The embrace grew tighter. Tighter.

Cold liquid drew my attention to the floor, where water pooled around my feet as it spilled out of the tub.

The door to the bathroom slammed shut, and I released my father on a gasp. Something held me from stepping away from him, and when I looked down, in place of what I thought were his arms was a long, black tentacle coiled around my waist.

My eyes shot to his, and an ominous red bled over into the once familiar hazel that I remembered. Alarms blared inside my head, and I pushed at his chest. In one hard thrust, he pushed me back against the wall, my spine crashing into the tiles. He pressed his lips to mine, and on a blasted exhale, I screamed into his mouth, pushing at his shoulders.

Something slithered into my mouth, the sensation stirring mayhem in my brain, and I broke into hysterics, trying to get him off me. He pulled away, and it was no longer my father's face, but Jericho's. Patch over his eye. Horns sticking out of his head. Skin black as night and the silvery tattoos glowing over his skin. A serpent's tongue swept over his lips.

It wasn't him, though. I knew it wasn't, because his single eye was a blood red, and even in Jericho's demonic form, his eye turned black.

A numbing cold blanketed my legs, and I looked down to see the water had risen to the level of my thighs.

I opened my mouth to let out a scream, but the imposter Jericho pinned me to the wall with a kiss. He guided my hand down to his erect cock, forcing my hand up and down his shaft.

"Relax, Tu'Nazhja." He kissed me harder, and the slithery sensation from before hit the back of my mouth. Acids shot up my throat, as if I would puke, but he kept on with the assault.

His tongue retracted, and he pulled away from me, still clutching my hand as he forced me to touch him. "I'm going to make you my fucking slave. You are mine." The voice didn't hold the deep, rich tone of Jericho's voice, but something diabolical and possessed.

The water bobbed at my neck. "Help! Help me! Help me!"

He kissed me again, and a wall of cold liquid rose up over my head.

The need for air punched at my chest.

Slam. Slam. Slam.

I screamed into his mouth, wriggling in his grasp.

This is how I'm going to die.

The little bit of air I'd managed waned. My lungs tightened to hold onto the last of the oxygen.

A sudden calm swept over me. My muscles relented their fight.

The wall of water crashed down all around me, and as I tumbled in a sloshy mess to the floor, I sucked in a breath, coughing and sputtering water.

Another round of acids climbed my throat, and black fluids spilled out of my mouth, splashing onto the wet tiles.

"Farryn!" Vespyr rushed through the doorway toward me, and I looked around to find no sign of my father, or the demon.

Rubbing a trembling hand over my forehead, I allowed Vespyr to hook her arm in mine and lift me to my feet. "What happened?" I asked, a woozy sensation claiming my balance.

"I don't know. You were standing next to me and the boy earlier. Then I looked over, and you were gone. I heard you screaming." She handed me Jericho's blade, which still carried the blood from the demon dog I'd killed. "You dropped this."

The boy waited in the hallway, holding up the lantern, and with Vespyr's help, I hobbled along with them, as the three of us hurried down the staircase and out the front door.

Once again, we found ourselves in the corridor. I turned to see 519 on the door and shook my head. "I don't know how much more of this I can take."

57

JERICHO

"*T*here's another door up ahead," I said over my shoulder.

"How lovely." With his sword resting at his shoulder, Vaszhago trailed behind in a bored and casual stroll. We'd walked for what seemed like an hour, through nothing but a long dark stretch of gray concrete, not finding another door until then.

Pushing through it, I found myself staring up at the house Farryn lived in as a child. A simple, white two-story, with a dilapidated brown fence around its perimeter. "Her old home."

"Quaint."

We strode up to the door, and I stepped inside, scanning the interior. Drops of water from the ceiling drew my attention to where a wet spot, the size of a carriage wheel, created a bow in the plaster. I took the stairs to the upper level, and at the bathroom door, opened it enough to see the tub faucet running and water spilled all over the tiles. Water splashed around my boots as I crossed the room and turned the knobs off, noticing the full, but vacant, tub.

Frowning, Vaszhago stood at the door. "I'll check the lower level."

"I'll take the bedrooms."

When he walked off, I exited the bathroom and made my way down to the room at the end of the hallway, one I'd grown intimately familiar with. Farryn's old room. When I arrived at the door, I could hear quiet moans bleeding through the panels.

Goaded by the same fury as before, when I saw my father fucking Lustina, I slammed through the door and found Farryn alone. Young. Perhaps seventeen, or eighteen. She wore the uniform she had always worn to school–cropped skirt and white button-down shirt. The hem of her skirt had been hiked high enough that I could see she wasn't wearing panties, and wedged between her thighs was a pillow, over which she rocked back and forth. Her soft moans sent a chill over my skin, and I snapped my gaze away, backing myself out of her room.

"Wait," she said, and I paused, my hand still on the knob. I couldn't deny the way my palms burned with the urge to touch her.

My Farryn.

"You don't want to watch me?"

"You are young."

"You always watched me. Why do you think I would touch myself? I knew you were there. Watching me. Wanting me."

Gods, had she known what vile thing I'd wanted from her back then, it would've terrified her. Not because she was young, but because she was mine and I was impatient to have her. I'd waited centuries for her, and yet, the years of waiting for her to reach what humans would've considered an acceptable age to be taken that way had felt like an eternity to me.

From her Nightstand, she lifted a sketch that bore a likeness to me. "I stole this from my father's office. Do you want to know what I thought about when I shoved that pillow between my thighs?" She pressed the drawing to her chest, where a few of her buttons were unclasped. "I thought of you. Pinning me face down in my bed. Tearing my panties away. Fucking me until I couldn't remember my own name." Sucking a lip between her teeth, she peered at me through those wily, flirtatious eyes that made me want to throw her down and feast.

My muscles burned with the urge to carry out those very steps. I lifted my hands, which trembled with the intense restraint pulsing through me. Black covered my fingertips, crawling down my hands toward my wrists.

She took my hand and wrapped her lips around one of my blackened fingers, working it in and out of her mouth.

"Farryn …" My voice held a pathetic warning as I pulled my hand away. A black haze moved in on the fringes of my view. The more she talked, the more I risked snapping.

"Will you fuck me, Jericho? So I'll know what you feel like inside of me?" Hand at her thigh, she lifted her skirt. Higher. Higher.

"Lower level is clear," Vaszhago said, the sound of his steps telling me he was trudging back up the staircase.

My gaze remained locked on those thighs. Those familiar thighs I'd felt shaking around me, as she clung to me during climax. Every cell in my body quaked, my muscles begging me to throw her onto the bed.

"Whoa. The fuck is going on?" A hard whack to my arm broke me out of the trance I'd fallen into, and when I turned around to swat Vaszhago for laying a hand on me, something beyond him caught my attention. A bony creature with decayed skin, red eyes, and long limbs.

Mortunath.

I swung back around to find Farryn's eyes had turned blood red. She opened her mouth on a loud screech, revealing a mouthful of fangs.

Fuck.

The chime of steel scraping against its scabbard signaled Vaszhago had pulled his sword, and I nabbed the dagger at my hip.

I couldn't kill her. Even if I knew it wasn't Farryn, I couldn't stab a lookalike. And I'd be damned if I'd let Vaszhago kill her, either. As he charged toward the Mortunath in the hallway, I barreled toward the Farryn imposter, knocking her backward onto the bed. A wild glint lit her eyes as I held her pinned to the mattress, and she wrapped her leg around me, rubbing herself against me. "Tell me you don't want to fuck me right now," she rasped in a tone that held a demonic pitch.

"I do not want to fuck you right now."

Her face morphed before me, and suddenly, I was staring down at the succubus I'd killed back in the woods. The sight of her jolted my muscles, and I pushed away from her.

"Do you prefer this face?" Teeth bared again, she pounced toward me.

I sliced the dagger across the front, along her throat, and jabbed her in the skull. Her body exploded into a cloud of black dust.

Screeching from outside snapped my attention toward the window, and I strode toward it, staring down at the front lawn of the house. About a hundred of the Mortunath crawled over each other to get to the front door.

Vaszhago strode up beside me, wiping his sword on a scrap of cloth he'd collected from somewhere. He tossed it away and groaned. "Fuck me."

58

FARRYN

I squeezed water from the hem of my dress, as we kept on down the corridor. The chill on the air had me shivering, teeth chattering, probably drawing more of those creatures after us.

"Farryn!" The sound of my name brought me to a screeching halt, and I turned around, my chest expanding with a held breath.

I stood frozen in place, part of me not really trusting my sight in a realm that had deceived me so many times already. "Soreth?"

"Where's Jericho?" Vespyr whispered beside me, and I looked past Soreth to find no one else following after him.

"Are you alone?" I curled the blade into my palm, preparing myself for the possibility that he might be a demon. "Is Jericho here?"

"Yeah. He and Vaszhago are looking for you. We broke off and separated."

"Broke off? There's only one path in a fucking labyrinth," Vespyr snapped, clearly not trusting the angel's presence any more than I did.

"They checked a couple rooms. I decided to go ahead of them."

"So, they're behind you?" Again, I looked past him, praying I'd see Jericho striding up out of those shadows.

"No. I think they're ahead of you. Jericho's plan is to meet in the center. That's the way out."

Relief curled through my veins like a shot of warm liquor. "So, there is a way out of this hellhole."

"There is, yes."

I frowned back at him, my suspicions bubbling to the surface again. "How did you get here?"

"I was minding my own business, in my cell, when suddenly, the wall opened to a corridor." He shrugged. "I was curious."

"Curious. Right."

That damned screeching echoed down the hall again, and I let out an exasperated groan. "I am just about tired of that freaking sound."

"Same." Vespyr took the lead toward the door where we were headed before Soreth had interrupted.

"It seems the labyrinth is designed so that each room puts you farther ahead," I said, following after Vespyr.

"I see," Soreth said from behind. "And how many rooms have you entered?"

"Three. This will be our fourth. And let me tell you, it's no picnic on the other side of these doors."

Vespyr slammed into the room, and I followed after her, looking over what appeared to be the inside of a cave. Beyond the mouth of the cave was a beach, where the ocean waves crashed on the shore. And standing at the cave's threshold was a woman with long, brunette hair that I remembered twirling in my fingers as a child.

Tears filled my eyes, my chest burning with the kind of longing I hadn't felt in years.

The woman turned around, and I instantly recognized her face. The brown eyes and dimples in her cheeks that my father had always found so endearing about her. "It's you," she said, smiling, and stretched out her arms.

As I walked toward her, desperate for that embrace, she shuffled past me as if I were invisible, and ran straight to Soreth, wrapping her arms around his neck as she drew him in for a kiss.

What the ... fuck?

"I waited so long," she whispered and kissed him again.

I caught the subtle push of Soreth's hands, but she failed to release him.

"Mother?" I felt weird getting any closer, so I kept my distance from the two of them, but she didn't turn around, at all. In fact, she didn't even acknowledge that I'd called out to her.

"What's wrong?" She held her palms against Soreth's face and tilted her head to get his attention. "Why are you ignoring me?"

"What in the mom kink is going on here?" Vespyr whispered beside me, and I elbowed her, not wanting to admit that I was beginning to think there was something to the scenario playing out.

At first, I'd thought it was *my* hell. My nightmare. But given the look of annoyance on Soreth's face, the way his pale cheeks heated red, it was clear the memory belonged to him.

My mother stepped away from Soreth, turning her back on him, which put her face to face with me, and still, she behaved as if she couldn't see me standing there. "Look, if this is about Farryn, I told you ... I couldn't bring her this time. I feel like there's something watching her. Every time I've gone into her room, there's a shadow there. It's the most unnerving thing."

I stood frozen in shock, my feet glued to the bed of the cave below me. Shuddering breaths sawed in and out of me, as I absorbed the picture that she was painting inside my head.

A dastardly scene of betrayal.

Soreth glanced to me and back to my mother. "Enough of this. I don't know you."

Frowning, my mother spun around, and at that point, I just wanted to know the truth. "Soreth ... what are you doing?" Her voice held a pathetic plea that didn't sound like my mother, at all. "I promise, I'll give her over to you, but you have to give me time, my love." She lurched forward toward him, and he took a step back, avoiding her outstretched arms. "Please. If I can sneak her out of the house without her damn father noticing, I will. I will bring her to you, as we discussed."

My gaze flitted to Soreth and back to my mother, my heart pounding way too fast inside my chest. "What is this? My mother was going to hand me over to you?"

Soreth stepped toward me, and I jumped back away from him. "This isn't real, Farryn. None of this is real."

The boy wrapped his arms around me, clutching me tight. When I glanced down at him, he nodded, which I took to mean that it was, in fact, real. "Did you kill her?"

"Do you want the truth, or his lies?" For the first time, my mother looked me dead in the eyes, her expression holding no warmth for me, or recognition. Only a cold and bitter detachment. "He wanted you, but you were protected. Too protected."

"Did Papa know about this? You and him?"

Her brow flickered, the first sign of any emotion, or remorse. "Of course not. It was not my intent to hurt your father."

"Only me."

"Enough!" Hands balled, Soreth stepped toward her, his teeth clenched. "Do not say another word."

"He told me something was after you. That they wanted to protect you, but I didn't deliver, as promised. And he got angry. So angry," she said on a shaky voice, her eyes glistening with tears. "He wanted to keep you for himself."

"Say another word, and so help me, God, I will strike you down as I did that night!" The moment the words escaped him, he looked away, his body shaking.

My body shook, too, from the rush of anger beating through me. "It was you! The night of the blood moon, Drystan told me that one of the Sentinels had betrayed Jericho. It was you."

"There was a time when angels didn't fuck humans, or demons. A time when they were clean. Pure. *Meracusz.* Jericho doesn't deserve the power he was given. Half-breeds don't deserve that kind of power."

"Are you fucking sick? Jericho's mother was *raped* by his father."

Soreth sneered. "How he came to be is not important. He is an abomination. An insult to our kind."

"You were going to take me on the night of the blood moon in exchange for Drystan's safe passage into Nightshade. That was you."

Soreth chuckled, shaking his head as he paced. "Safe passage. The fool was chasing the wrong piece of the puzzle. He thought your father held the power to restore his wings. Idiot half-breeds."

"Who is it, then? Who has the power to restore an angel's wings?"

Still shaking his head, he let out a mirthless laugh. "Seems humans are just as stupid. You, dear fragile, little human, are what is called the Met'Lazan. A healer appointed by the ancient gods, with the ability to access all of the vitaeilem in

Etheriusz. Tell me that you understand how absolutely insane that sounds to you."

My blood turned cold. *Me?* The whole time? I shook my head, refusing to believe such a thing. "I don't know how the hell to translate the Omni. I've never even seen the sigil! I've only heard of it."

His brows winged up. "Haven't you seen it, though?"

"Do you not recall the episode of drawing on the walls, Farryn?" my mother asked from behind, but when I turned to look back at her, she still didn't hold a single ounce of warmth in her eyes. "Or the time you found the bird lying in the backyard. The one the cats had gotten to, remember?"

I stared back at her, the vague images of picking up the bird who didn't move in my palms. Whispering something to it. Watching it fly off.

I shook my head, more frantically than before. "I ... I don't ..."

"You are." Soreth's flat tone matched the emotionless expression on his face. "That's why you're here. This labyrinth is the design of Jericho's father. He's pulling memories from your head and using them against you. He is searching for the memory that will set him free. The heavens want to protect you, Farryn. I want to protect you."

That made no sense. For months, I'd hidden away from the heavens. "No. I committed a crime against them. I damned my soul."

He shook his head. "The Infernal cannot lay claim to the Met'Lazan. You cannot be claimed by the heavens, either. Which is precisely why a human should not hold all that power. You are pathetic and undeserving. It belongs to the pure. The righteous."

Another piece clicked into place. "You're A'ryakai."

"I am. And I am going to protect you. So come," he said, flicking his fingers for me. "Let's get out of here."

"Do not listen to him, Farryn." My mother's voice held a shaky desperation that set my teeth on edge. "He promised I would go to Heaven. That I would be redeemed by the highest angels! He promised, and he broke that promise. Because of you!"

Before I knew what hit me, she plowed into my side. The gravel floor slammed into my shoulder on a burst of pain that spiraled up into my neck. My mother fell on top of me, wrenching my hair back to expose my throat. Her eyes had turned to scarlet bulbs, and her teeth to sharpened crags that she undoubtedly intended to sink into my throat. She lifted the locket from my neck, the one given to me as a gift from my father that I never took off. In one yank, she ripped it from my neck.

"No! No!" Arms pinned beneath her straddling legs, I couldn't move, couldn't reach my blade. Wriggling beneath her proved futile, as she vised my body with an impossible grip.

Vespyr leapt forward and wrapped her arm around my mother's neck, hauling her backward. She screamed and let go, and my mother bulleted backward into the air, before crashing down into a boulder.

As she scrambled to her feet again, Vespyr drew her blade, holding it in front of her.

I jumped to my feet, nabbing mine, as well.

My mother charged forward, but was, once again, thrown back by an invisible blast.

I turned to see Soreth holding his palms out toward her.

Seemingly unaffected by the knocks against the boulder, my mother climbed to her feet again. Instead of coming for us again, though, she tipped her head back and sniffed the air. Back and forth, her head shifted, as if she were trying to determine the source of whatever had distracted her from attacking us, and her eyes landed on Soreth.

Staring back toward her, he waved us over to him. "We have to go. Now. My disguise is wearing off."

"What disguise?"

"It masks my vitaeilem from the Mortunath."

"Mortunath?"

"The creatures that make that strange screeching sound!" An air of impatience colored his voice. "If they bite you, they will infect you. We have to leave. Now! We're almost to the center of the labyrinth!"

The locket lay just out of reach, and I contemplated scrambling for it again, but my body hoisted up into the air, until my feet were dangling about two yards up from the floor. It felt as if an enormous, invisible hand had lifted me up and squeezed me so tight, it knocked a small bit of air from my lungs. "Put me down! Now!"

My mother opened her mouth impossibly wide and let out one of those spine-tingling screeches, which echoed through the cave. The sound of a stampede had me stilling, listening. A cold sensation brushed the back of my neck, and I turned toward the mouth of the cave, where dozens of Mortunath had gathered. My body flew back in the other direction, toward the door we'd come in through, and I fell, skidding to the dirt. Not a second later, the Mortunath poured in, charging straight toward Soreth. My eyes shot to Vespyr and the boy, who seemed to have gotten lost in the sea of creatures.

"Vespyr! Vespyr!"

Soreth ran toward me and held up his palm again. I flew back another few feet, deeper into the cave. A Mortunath demon leapt onto the angel's back, and he twisted around, throwing it off him with his invisible force. Another barreled toward him. And another. My mother clawed at him and snapped her teeth.

"Vespyr!" I screamed. "Vespyr where are you?"

None of the Mortunath seemed the least bit interested in me, as they cornered Soreth against the cave wall and a boulder.

From the cluster of creatures, I saw a flash of purple hair, and with the boy's hand in hers, Vespyr darted toward me. "Go, Farryn!"

The creatures' bodies flew backward, showing only a brief second of Soreth amid them, where he'd fallen to his knees, his face and palm bloodied, as he reached out for us. The monsters charged again, and his screams hit the air.

I spun around toward the door, but paused. "My locket!"

"Fuck the locket!" Vespyr said, snatching up my arm as she ran past me. She yanked me after her, and the three of us slammed through the door into the corridor.

59

JERICHO

*V*aszhago's arms trembled as he held the Mortunath in a state of paralysis. "Could you be so kind as to hurry it along. I'm getting a fucking cramp. This place is sucking my powers like a ramped-up wraith."

I strode up to the last three Mortunath, stabbing each three times. The last one exploded into black dust, and I looked around the yard of Farryn's old house to find a thick coating of black ash covering the grass.

Vaszhago collapsed to his knees and tipped his head back, taking deep breaths. "I'm getting too old for this shit."

I smirked at that. "You need a minute?"

Shaking his head, the demon kicked one knee up and pushed to his feet. "I'm all right."

We strode toward the door and landed ourselves back out in the labyrinth's corridor, both of us walking with a little less pep in our stride after having killed what must've been a hundred, or more, Mortunath.

"To think that's not even a tiny fraction of his army." Vaszhago said, as I caught sight of another door. "The realms are fucked if he ever wakes up."

"He's going to wake. Because I am going to kill my father."

"Well, if you do, just make sure you have that fucking heart nearby."

Letifer's heart, encased in glass at the center of the labyrinth. Had I wanted to invite his debate, protest, possibly even betrayal against me, I'd have told him that I had no intentions of destroying the heart and closing the portal. Not when Venefica required it as payment to free Farryn's body from Syrisa's grasp. I didn't care that it would wake Letifer. That he would undoubtedly assemble his army against the realms. I'd have fought every Mortunath and Eradyean demon, if it meant saving her soul.

Instead, I held my silence, until we came upon the next door and pushed through to a cave. A sound of agony echoed over the stony walls, and we rounded a boulder to find Soreth. His lower half had been entirely consumed, leaving only stringing bits of viscera, which two Mortunath sat feasting on. As we stepped closer, one of them glanced back at us, but seemed uncaring of our presence, too engrossed in its meal. Soreth's upper half had already turned a dark, corpse color, his eyes the telling blood-red. He made a sound in his throat that still had a small bit of agony beneath the pitched screech.

"Do I put him out of his misery?" Vaszhago asked beside me.

"No. But if you feel so inclined to off the other two, I will not protest." I scanned over the cave, toward the mouth of it, where something shiny on the ground caught my eye. As I strode closer, I recognized the gold locket and lifted it from the gravel. Popping it open confirmed it was Farryn's, when I saw the picture of her father.

I didn't immediately notice my surroundings had darkened, until something moved in my periphery. I turned to find what appeared to be Farryn staring off toward the ocean, her white gown blowing in the wind, hair in a tangled mess as it danced about her shoulders.

So beautiful against the ocean's glassy backdrop.

She turned around, and my heart stalled inside my chest. The youth and innocence in her eyes didn't differ significantly, but enough that I could make out the subtleties between her and Farryn.

"Lustina."

Her lips curved to a warm smile. "Hello, My Lord." Beautiful stardust eyes, Farryn's eyes, trailed over me. "My, you've grown quite handsome."

"Are you real?"

Hands behind her back, she stepped closer. "What was it you always said to me? *Strę vera'tu*? As real as the stars." Her smile faded. "If only there were stars here."

Brows lowered, I turned away, recalling the conversation with Adimus. "I did not realize you'd been sent here. I would have never let you remain in this place. I would have come for you."

"Have you not? I am Farryn. Another life. A *stolen* life."

Her words stabbed my heart, and I shook my head. "I should've stayed to protect you. I should have never left you that night."

"No. I suppose not." The cold detachment in her voice struck like a slap to my face. I'd have preferred the strike. "I should not have perished on that blood moon. For I was with child."

The shock I'd felt from before, when Adimus had told me the same thing, still simmered in my bones, reignited by the words spilling from her lips. "A child. In this place."

"Yes. Your son." A tear slipped down her cheek as she lowered her gaze. "Of course, I did not know at the time."

"How? If you died in the drowning? Your body perished."

"I learned that it was not my physical body which had

nourished him, but my soul. As I lay staring up at that magnificent red moon, knowing I would never breathe again, never look upon your handsome face, nor feel your skin against mine, I heard a voice I'd never heard before. A chanting inside my head, so beautiful, it was like a song." Her eyes sparkled with her sad smile, as though she were hearing it right then. "It brought such a sense of calm, and it was that voice which had told me I was with child, and to save him. Save him. So I spoke the chanted words, aloud and in my mind, until I could no longer remember them." The smile on her face faded for a sorrowful expression which tore at my heart. "I saved him."

"That you suffered alone is a torment which will haunt me eternally. I will never forgive myself for it."

With a shine of tears in her eyes, she trailed her gaze over the surroundings, as if searching for distraction. "Did you know this place was once a temple for the ancient gods?" Before I could answer, she kept on, "Since the dawn of our existence, the Met'Lazan have returned here in preparation of being reborn. Over time, the temple crumbled. The gods retreated into another realm. And Infernium was built on the bones of those who perished. The ancient gods had forsaken us. And this place became my hell." More tears slipped down her pale cheeks. "I was violated. Beaten. Tormented."

Pain stabbed my heart, and I fell to my knees.

"Every night, I called for you. I prayed that you would somehow hear me in this place." She slapped a hand over her mouth and sniffled, pausing, as if to hold back crying. "You never came for me," she said in a shaky voice, her words burning inside my chest like a poisonous vapor I couldn't exhale. "But fear not, my love. For I am only a manifestation of your torment. As unreachable as the stars. For, the ancients were merciful enough to let me fall into the fade. I had to leave our son in this dreadful place alone, so that Farryn would one day come to be."

"Forgive me. I beg you, Lustina. I did not know."

Gaze lowered, she let out a quiet sob and shook her head. "Your son still wanders these corridors alone. And so I ask one favor of you. I ask that you destroy Letifer's heart. Free him from this place."

I let out a shaky breath, my head in chaos. "I have vowed to deliver Letifer's heart intact."

"So, as you left me here to rot, will you also imprison your son!" The tone of her voice was foreign, and I lifted my gaze in time to see her skin desiccate into the lifeless, mottled tone of the Mortunath. Fangs protruded from beneath her top lip, and her eyes shifted from the familiar stardust to a stark and glowing red. The eyes of the undead. It was no longer Lustina who stood before me, but a Mortunath demon. "I cursed your name every night! I despise you! I despise you!"

She charged toward me.

I jumped to my feet and grabbed her by the throat, keeping her at a distance. My heart splintered with every hateful word that spilled past her lips as I stared back at her, wishing I could scoop her up into my arms. To tell her how sorry I was. To express the pain that speared my heart, knowing I couldn't save her, but as she was a demon, my words held no meaning to her. Although the true Lustina would have heard them, she was not there. Only the Mortunath which clawed and snapped its teeth at me.

She screamed and screeched like an animal in my grasp.

I jabbed my blade into her skull.

A moment later, she crumbled to black dust, and I collapsed to my knees and pounded both fists into the dirt, as a roar of anguish and anger exploded out of me, bouncing off the cave walls.

60

FARRYN

The three of us pushed through another door, which opened to a courtyard that seemed oddly familiar to me. An enormous stone building, with chipped and broken concrete bricks and domed roof, held a level made of wide arches that was undoubtedly a cloister hallway. My eyes caught on the belltower, though and the exceptionally large bell housed inside of it.

A monastery.

In the center of the courtyard stood a fountain, and my throat flared at the sight of crystal blue water pouring from one of the stone statues. Beautiful white roses decorated the yard of the monastery, and flowered vines climbed over its weathered stone, giving a romantic decayed look.

"Farryn, I don't feel so good," Vespyr said beside me, and as she lurched forward, as if to fall, I reached out and grabbed her arm.

Wrapping it around my neck, I helped her cross the courtyard and lowered her alongside the stone wall of the fountain.

"It's ... something in my stomach aches. It's like hunger,

but feels like clawing, or something." It was as she lifted her arm that I noticed blood.

"Vespyr, did one of them bite you?"

"I don't know. Maybe." She twisted her arm, and as she examined it, I noticed two clear arcs in the shape of a bite. "Is that bad?"

I turned toward the boy, who sat on the other side of me, and when he lowered his gaze, nodding, an ache blossomed in my chest. He twisted around toward the fountain, scooping water up to drink.

Ignoring her question, I dipped my cupped hands into the flowing stream and scooped as much as I could hold, which I tipped into her mouth. "Drink. It might settle your stomach."

She sucked down the water quickly, and I gathered up more to feed her, until she seemed satisfied, then drank some myself. As I lowered my hands from my face, something caught my attention. Black objects lying scattered all over the monastery yard.

Black birds.

Dead.

I turned around to find more of them behind me. Perhaps hundreds, lying motionless.

"Do you hear that?" Vespyr asked, and when I swung my attention back to her, I noticed sweat beading across her forehead and over her cheeks. "Do you hear them?"

"Who?"

"I can hear them talking." Her eyes filled with tears, lips quivering. "The doctors. They're saying I'm sick. My fever … is too high." She panted in between words, and I pressed my palm to her forehead.

I didn't even need a thermometer to know she was burning up. Too hot. Way too hot. Scooping up more of the cool water, I gently poured it over her head, wetting her hair thoroughly, and over her neck.

Lids heavy, she rolled her head back and forth against the fountain, moaning.

"Vespyr." I gripped her face, forcing her to look at me. "I want you to try to return. Can you do that for me? Try to go back again."

A sob shook her chest. "I can't. I can't go back."

"Please try." The tears in my eyes blurred her form.

"Farryn! It hurts!" She curled into herself, and I scrambled to the other side of her, laying her head in my lap.

"I'm here. I'm right here."

"What's happening to me! Oh, God, I'm scared! I don't want to be alone! I'm scared, Farryn!"

"Shhhh." Stroking a hand down her hair, I kissed her forehead. "I'm right here. I'm right here with you. You're not alone."

"I'm becoming ... one of ... them. Please ... kill me. Please." She clutched my arm, and my muscles twitched with the panic pulsing through me. "I don't want to stay here. I want to go home. Please Farryn. Let me go home." At a tight grip of my wrist, I looked down to see her palm clutched over where I still held the blade.

Through tears, I shook my head, wishing I could wake up. *Wake up!* "I can't."

"I don't want to stay here anymore. Please! I'm begging you." Her grip of my arm tightened, and when she lifted my blade-toting hand higher, I broke. Hands trembling, I held it loosely, as she guided it over her heart. "Chest ... throat ... skull," she said on a shaky breath. "Okay?"

Tears wobbled and spilled down my cheek. "Please try to go back. I can't do this. I can't do this!"

"You have to. Myrmecophily. Remember?" Her lips trembled, the blue of death stripping their natural pink hue.

I hiccupped another sob and nodded. "I remember."

"I get to be the butterfly, right?" She let out a tearful

579

laugh. "I get to fly away. Far, far away." With a deep breath, she released my hand and stared up at the sky above us. "Free as a butterfly. Far away from here." For a while she stared, just breathing, until her eyes widened, and in their reflection, I saw the clergyman standing over her with his crosier and book. Blood trickled in to the whites of her eyes, seeping over her gray irises. "Say your name. Say your name. Say your name. Say your name," she whispered over and over.

I dragged the blade over her chest, across her throat, and as I held it to her temple, I rested my forehead to hers and whispered, "Vespyr. Your name is Vespyr."

I drew back and pierced her skull with it. "Fly away," I said through tears.

Her body went limp in my arms only a second before it burst into a cloud of white dust.

Staring down at my shaky, blood-coated hands, speckled in white, I could scarcely draw in a breath. I'd never taken a human life before. Not with my own bare hands. In one cold thrust of a blade, I stole her laughter, her tears, her memories. I stole everything. Just like that, she was gone.

Bringing my hands up to my face, I wept.

Tugging at my sleeve broke me from my staring, and I looked up to see the boy standing over me, urging me to get up. Muscles heavy with anguish, I pushed to my feet.

He was right, I couldn't stay anywhere for too long in this place. As we exited back the door, I twisted around to see 623 on its surface. The corridor felt colder, more terrifying without Vespyr at my side. The obvious silence skated over the back of my neck, and I kept looking over my shoulder, the fear of seeing one of the creatures keeping my muscles in a constant tremble.

A door stood ahead, and as we approached, the air in my lungs thickened.

777.

I only brushed my fingertip across the handle of it before pulling away, and I shook my head. "I can't. I have a bad feeling about this."

A glance toward the end of the hallway showed no other door in sight. Perhaps it was the last in the labyrinth. The center of it.

The boy tugged on my sleeve, and I let out a sigh.

"I have to, in order to get out, don't I? I have to go inside."

From the other side of the door, I heard a baby crying. The same sound I'd heard back in my room, when I'd been lured into the labyrinth.

The same sound which lured me right then.

61

JERICHO

I felt as if I were in a daze, walking through the corridor that wound and twisted into new dark passages. Uncertain if she'd been telling the truth, or if it was a lie. I focused on the foreign word, which ricocheted through my head. Son.

My son.

One I never knew about. Trapped in these corridors. Alone.

Abandoned.

And if what she'd said was truth, the only way to free him was the one thing I couldn't grant. Doing so would have cast Farryn into the dark subspace of her mind for as long as Syrisa inhabited her body.

"What hell will this one bring?" Vaszhago asked, as we approached a new door.

It opened onto the familiar corridor in the dungeons of Blackwater Cathedral. Dread sank to the pit of my stomach as I imagined the possibilities of what I might find there. Seemed the labyrinth was hellbent on tormenting me with my most troubling guilt, and I imagined the very rooms in which I had engaged in countless hours of my own self-inflicted pain could only mean more of the same.

With slow strides, we made our way down the dungeon's long hallway, and at first, I wondered if we'd gotten by unscathed, as not a single sound, or creature, presented itself.

Moans echoed from the opposite end of the hallway.

"Fuck." I rubbed a hand down my face.

"Sounds like it." Vaszhago strode ahead of me. "Might as well see what cunt has decided to torment you this time."

Sighing, I followed after him. Pointing to one of the doors ahead, he put his ear to the wood and frowned. When I finally reached him, he pushed open the door. His frown deepened, and I followed the path of his gaze toward a bed to which a naked Farryn had been chained. Vaszhago lay on top of her, his hand covering her mouth as he hammered his hips into her.

The sight of him sent pulses of fury through my veins. A fire blazed inside of me, and I balled my hands to tight fists.

"You won't say a word of this," the imposter Vaszhago whispered. "Or I will kill him. I will fucking kill him first chance I get."

"Jericho." The real Vaszhago's voice held a quiet warning. "This is not real. I've no intentions with your female." His words sliced over my bones, and I ground my teeth.

"Haven't you, though? Do you think I don't notice the way you make eyes at her?"

"Making eyes is not fucking her. What you're seeing now is lies."

The imposter Vaszhago shuddered a breath. "Had I known a human felt this good, I'd have fucked you sooner."

Farryn whimpered beneath him, wriggling against her chains.

On a furious roar, I plowed forward, and the scene faded into smoke. The anger inside of me remained, though, and a haze of red clouded my vision as I swung around, grabbing Vaszhago by the throat and pinning him to the wall. "Drink the vitaeilem," Vaszhago said on a rasp.

"I do not need vitaeilem to see the truth!"

A deep, cramping ache hammered at my muscles, and I let out a growl, as Vaszhago's powers took over me, paralyzing me. The demon reached into my pocket and pulled the vial.

I could do nothing, as he poured the last of it down my throat.

"I swear by the gods that I have not touched your female in that way. While you often make me want to run my sword through you, I would not betray you like that."

The vitaeilem took hold, bathing the heat of rage in a cool wash of calm. He was right. The labyrinth played on my own guilt and fears, and the only thing in the world I feared was losing Farryn. Outside of the labyrinth, I trusted the demon, as he'd proven loyal.

I grabbed Vaszhago's arm and gave a sharp nod. "Forgive me."

"Come, let's find Farryn and get the fuck out of this place."

62

FARRYN

I placed my palm to the handle of the door when a figure to my left captured my attention. The blonde stood off from us, and an overwhelming sensation of déjà vu swept over me.

"Farryn." Long, golden spun, almost white hair rested on her bony shoulders. Her eyes, a deep chestnut brown, drew attention to the soft pale glow of her face. In spite of her small and fragile frame, which looked to be wracked by hunger, she carried an ethereal beauty.

The woman from my nightmares. From my hallucinations.

Syrisa.

The boy whimpered and scurried off in the other direction.

"Wait!" I called out for him, but he disappeared into the shadows. An intense pain struck my belly, and I rested my hand against it.

The woman let out an evil chuckle.

Lifting the blade I still carried, with Vespyr's blood

smeared across the metal, I steeled my muscles, preparing myself for whatever this final encounter might've been.

She lunged forward, and I swiped out at her, my blade cutting through nothing but air. Still, she stood there, as if waiting. Smiling in a way that curled my bones.

As she lunged again, I pushed through the door and, once on the other side of it, rested my forehead against the steel panel, breathing hard.

From somewhere behind me, a baby cried. My muscles twitched at the heartbreaking sound, and I squeezed my eyes tighter. I had a feeling this door would be the worst of them.

I can't take anymore. Please. I don't know if I can take anymore.

I turned around to be greeted by my bedroom back at the cathedral.

Back to the beginning.

In the center of the room stood a white cradle, and with cautious steps, I approached. Lying inside was a baby with jet black hair and stardust eyes. With a trembling hand pressed against my mouth, I stared down at it. Not *it*. My baby. There was no doubt in my mind.

"Aside from the eyes, he looks just like his father did as a baby."

At the sound of the unfamiliar voice, I spun around, dagger at the ready, and found a man with blond hair, dressed in regal clothes fitting for another century.

An inexplicable tremble of fear moved through me, though the man certainly didn't look anywhere near as threatening as some of the creatures I'd already encountered. Something about him stirred a cold sensation in my chest.

"Who are you?" I asked, studying his jawline and eyes, which held a hint of recognition.

He glanced quickly down at the blade pointed at him. "You know who I am."

"Lord Van Croix," I answered automatically, though I didn't know what had compelled me to call him Lord, except that it felt somewhat natural.

"Lord Eradyę these days, but no need for formalities, my dear. You're welcome to call me Claudius."

Jericho's father. "You're the one who owns my soul."

Hands behind his back, he strode toward the window. "No. I do not. I cannot possess the soul of the Met'Lazan."

"Then, why am I here?"

He looked around my room and pointed toward the wall through which I'd walked into the corridor. "Did you not come of your own volition?"

"I heard a baby crying."

"Yes." His gaze lowered toward the cradle and back to me. "He cries for you every night."

I forced myself not to look at the baby. *He's not real. Just an illusion.*

"If you can't possess my soul, am I free to go?"

"You're back at the center of the labyrinth. Of course." The smile on his face faded. "The baby cannot, though."

I dared myself to look at the baby again. I wanted to touch him, just to see if he would fade into a dream, but I kept my hands at my sides, blade captured in my palm.

"You could choose to stay, however. I know it's quite drab in this place, but I could make it comfortable for you. And your baby." He stepped closer, and on instinct, I stepped around the cradle, guarding the child. "Go ahead. Pick him up. I know you're dying to see how he feels in your arms."

Tears shimmered in my eyes once again, as I glanced over my shoulder at the tiny version of Jericho lying in the cradle. Bundled in a blanket, I couldn't see much more of him, but he squirmed in his swaddling, and when he cried, the sound tugged at my heart. I curled my hands into a fist, anxious to lift him up, but I knew in my heart it was nothing more than an illusion. He wasn't real.

"He cries for you," Claudius said behind me. "*Hold* him."

I set the blade down at the foot of the cradle's mattress and slid my palms beneath the baby, awkwardly lifting him up into my arms. I'd never held a baby in my life, and nothing about holding that one felt natural to me, but at the same time, it felt right. As I pulled him to my chest, I took in the weight of him, how perfect he felt in the crook of my arm. A tearful laugh escaped as I stared down at him. My baby.

His cries settled, and those curious eyes stared up at me as if studying me.

"Tell me that doesn't feel like heaven."

Tears wavered my view, as I buried my nose into his tiny curled tufts of hair that I imagined one day looking like his father's. Eyes closed, I breathed in the sweet baby scent and kissed his head. "I can only keep him if I stay?"

"I'm afraid that is the only way. Do not leave him alone here."

"What do you want from me?" I whispered, and a tear slid down my cheek.

"The same thing I've yearned for, for centuries."

The sound of his footfalls getting closer shot a nervous shiver down my spine, and I glanced to the dismissed blade.

"Freedom," he continued. "The weight of this place is too much to bear sometimes. It is like chains at my throat. But you--you can loosen those chains. You are the Met'Lazan, and only you can set me free."

"How?"

"By giving me access to the vitaeilem in Etheriusz. With it, I will no longer be bound to my *obligations*."

Clutching the baby to me, I took a step back. "Why would I want to help you? After all you've done? All you've taken?"

"Because I have the power to steal the breath from that child with a snap of my fingers." He lifted his hand into the air, and clicked his fingers.

I locked my attention on the baby, whose eyes were closed, mouth gaping, lips the telling blue of death. Lifting him to my ear confirmed no breaths. No fluttering warmth against my cheek. His face had taken on a bluish shade, the sight of which had me rushing him toward the bed, where I lay him down. Hands trembling, I un-swaddled him and held his tiny hands, taking in the icy cold of them.

My pulse hammered as I pressed my lips to his and sent a puff of air into his body. I could scarcely remember the CPR I'd learned back in high school. Tipping his head back, I gently pinched his nose and pressed my lips to his again for another puff of air.

"Your human tricks don't work to restore life here. But you have a secret, don't you, Farryn? You can bring him back to life. You need only to speak the words."

I swiped up my blade again, holding it out to him with a trembling hand. "I am not what you think I am. I don't possess any power, or ability to translate the sigil. Now, please, save him!"

The warmth I'd seen in the older man's eyes sharpened to something much darker. Threatening. "No."

A piercing, high-pitched sound reached my ears, so painful I clenched my eyes and fell to my knees. A clang of the blade falling to the floor hardly registered over the piercing noise, as the agony of it rattled my skull and teeth.

"Pay me no mind, I'm just crawling through your memories."

"Stop! Stop it!"

"I will find what I'm looking for, Farryn. You cannot hide it."

Nausea gurgled in my stomach, and a dizziness swept

over me. I opened my eyes and turned to find a glass sphere sat atop a pedestal where the cradle had stood moments before. Encased inside the sphere was what appeared to be a black, charred heart that pulsed, as if still alive. Bolts of electricity danced over the sphere, creating enough distraction until the pain slowly began to subside.

"So long as that heart beats and is fed vitaeilem, Letifer sleeps. But should he wake, all hell will break loose. Surely, you don't wish that on those you love."

I pushed back to my knees and scooped up the baby to find it had grown bluer than before, its skin even colder. "God, please! Save him!"

"Your precious God cannot save him. He won't save him. But you can. All you have to do is speak the words, Farryn."

"I don't know! I don't remember!"

"You do remember. Now, speak the words and save him!"

"No!"

The baby burst into a cloud of dust.

I let out a scream, my whole body shaking as I held my arms outstretched in front of me.

Claudius lurched closer, and his palm hit my throat, knocking me down so the unyielding floor smashed against my spine.

Blackness settled over me. Screams reached me in the darkness. Horrible screams.

My screams.

I opened my eyes to find Jericho's father over me, pinning my arms down, his eyes black as night. "You think you can fight me? That you can overcome me?"

My blade stuck out of his shoulder, just like the night I'd pierced Jericho with an envelope opener. I must've fallen into the subspace again.

"There are ways to break you, Farryn. Ways to make you remember."

Unbidden memories surfaced inside my head.

Lying on a cold cell floor. Red hot metal burning my flesh. Bodies moving over me, violating me. Blood. Screams. Pain.

"You ... hurt me before." They were undoubtedly Lustina's memories, given their fogginess.

He lowered his lips to my ear. "I don't have to kill you to make you feel dead inside."

"Help me! Someone, help me! Please!"

The man chuckled and shook his head. "No one can hear your screams."

"Please! Help me!"

The door burst open, and I felt Claudius's muscles jerk in surprise. He turned, just as Elyon jumped onto his back. Claudius bucked, but the boy clutched tight to his throat and bit down into his ear so hard, I heard it crunch.

Claudius let out a roar of anger, and releasing me, he reached back and took hold of the boy. In one swift move, he threw him across the room. Elyon slammed into the wall, his body sliding to the floor.

"No!" Rolling onto my stomach, I scrambled toward him, but a hard hook of my ankle yanked me back, and I slid across the floor toward Claudius.

Pissed, I lifted my foot and kicked him square in the face.

The older man growled and lurched forward, but I squirmed away quickly, just missing his swiping hand.

I reached the boy and, with frantic hands, turned his head to find a horrible gash where he must've hit the wall. He breathed weakly, but said, "Mama. I knew you would come back for me."

More memories slipped through my mind.

Pain. Cries. Holding the baby. Laughter. Singing. Kisses. Dancing.

All in this horrible place. A small ray of sunshine in the darkness.

"*Save him.*"

The memories shook me down to my very soul. Lustina's baby.

My baby.

Through tears, I whisper, "Welcome, Elyon Jericho Van Croix."

"You will remember the Omni," Claudius said from behind me. "And I will enjoy breaking you twice."

Anger stirred inside of me, and I turned to face him, the rage burning my skin and drying my tears. "I would rather die than free you from this hell."

His lips curved to an evil arc. "And so you shall."

63

JERICHO

*T*he stretch of gray walls seemed to go on for eternity.

"I want you to get Farryn out. I'll deal with my father, but get her out of here," I said to Vaszhago, who followed after me.

"How? The door we came through sealed shortly after."

Rummaging through the satchel at my hip, I handed him the summoning chalk. "Get her to Kezhurah. Somewhere safe." I fished again and pulled out the vial that Venefica had given me. "And administer this to her once she is out of harm's way. I will then have three days to deliver the heart."

"And how will you get out?"

"My father comes and goes. I will force him to reveal how."

Vaszhago groaned. "Why do I have a feeling I'll be suffering tremendous pain by the end of this?"

Ignoring him, I nodded toward the path ahead on seeing another door. "Finally."

Screams reached my ear, ones that sounded far too much

like Farryn's. The one time I hoped that what I'd find on the other side of the door wasn't real.

I hastened toward it and pushed through the door, straight into Farryn's bedroom. Caught by her throat, Farryn dangled in the air by a long black tentacle, and I trailed my eye down to where my father had taken his monstrous form.

He snapped his gaze toward me and, as I charged toward him, he released his hold on her.

I tackled him to the floor and scrambled over him. Before he could get one of his tentacles around my throat, I sliced my blade through the one closest to me. He let out roar of anger and, in a frenzy of tentacles and teeth, wriggled and squirmed to get loose.

I wrapped my hands around his throat, but on hearing Farryn scream, I turned to see her fighting Vaszhago, as he dragged her toward the door.

"No! I'm not leaving him! Let me go!"

It was no use. The demon was far more powerful.

At a flash of movement out of the corner of my eye, I caught sight of a dark-haired boy following after them, and distracted, I didn't see the tentacle wrap itself around my arm, until a painful wrenching of my muscles snapped my attention back to my father.

Taking hold of his tentacle, I twisted, damn near ripping it from his socket.

He threw me backward against the wall, which cracked behind me on impact. Tentacles lashed out at me, slicing across my skin like the strike of a whip. As he snapped another across my face, I took hold of it and, using what little vitaeilem was left in me, shot a bolt of hot electricity across the surface of it.

On a curse, he retracted, setting himself free, and an edginess settled over me when he didn't flee after Vaszhago and Farryn. I'd expected it, and the moment he'd have left the room, I'd planned to swipe Letifer's heart from the sphere.

He licked the spot on his tentacle where I'd burned him. "Forgive my lack of proper welcome. Son. This place really sucks the joy out of life."

"You must be incredibly disappointed to have lost your ticket out of here."

His wicked grin only stoked my suspicion. "There is no escape from Infernium. The only way out for your little friend is by destroying the heart of Letifer. That, or stabbing him in the skull."

"What?"

"This labyrinth? He created it in his mind. He has the power to project images. You destroy his mind, you destroy the labyrinth and release the key to Eradyę."

Puzzling that new bit of information, I stared back at him. "What key?"

"The one which ties Letifer's heart to this barren world. Without it, he cannot rule."

So, there was a plan B, after all.

"But good luck with that. I have spent centuries searching for him. This labyrinth was designed to protect him."

"So, why not destroy his heart?"

"Because he so kindly connected me to it. If his heart is destroyed, then I will perish, as well. It's futile. Farryn is like a trapped mouse."

Which meant, at the very least, I'd hold power by possessing that heart. Perhaps enough to barter a way out, if he felt threatened.

I lurched for the sphere.

Something wrapped around my throat, yanking me back. As I raised my hands to loosen it, chains wrapped around my arms. My body flew upward, until I was hanging from the ceiling, chains bound tight at my wrists. Diablisz steel, given the fact that it wouldn't break with my twisting and yanking. An invisible force tore my armor from my body, which landed on the floor with a thud. The tunic I wore beneath shredded into torn bits of fabric.

An immediate gnawing ache churned in my gut, just as when I was a boy and had my first taste of Eradyę's power. It scraped at my insides like claws, desperate for the miniscule amount of vitaeilem left in my body, no longer protected by the armor.

Returned to his human form, my father circled me, coming to a stop to my rear. He could undoubtedly see the grotesque stumps of bone where my wings had been cut away, and his dark chuckle confirmed it. "I see you've made wise choices throughout adulthood."

"Perhaps the wisest was setting flames to your mistress's home."

A streak of pain lashed across my back, and I gritted my teeth.

"Hold your tongue, boy. For that happens to be the very reason you're here, at all."

With a sneer, I anchored my attention on the heart encased in glass across the room from me. "I figured as much."

If I could just stall my father long enough, it would allow Vaszhago to get out of the labyrinth with Farryn. And even if there was no escape, she was out of my father's clutches for the moment. The longer I kept him occupied, the more time I'd have to think of a way out.

"After your little tantrum in Praecepsia, I was forced to feed my sister the pathetic souls of Infernium to keep her from perishing. Until the guard came to Blackwater."

It was a story I was already familiar with, but as he proceeded to bore me with his villainous monologue, my head quietly spun out the possibilities that lay before me.

Find a way to get out of the chains and steal Letifer's heart, risking the possibility of no escape.

Or destroy the heart, kill my father, and close the portal forever. As much as the second option seemed less complicated, it wasn't an option, at all, because if Vaszhago administered the elixir to Farryn, I'd have no choice but to keep the heart intact.

I lifted my gaze toward the chains above me again. Unfortunately, I couldn't just yank them from the ceiling. I'd have to find a way to break the individual links.

"I do have one small welcoming gift for you." He strode toward the door, and opened it to a familiar face, which had me slowly grinding my jaw.

Barchiel.

Or Bishop Venable, as he was known at one time.

"Why am I not surprised to see you here." Muscles burning with the tension from the chains, I rested my forehead against my bicep.

Bishop Venable strolled up in his robes, hands clasped behind his back. He still wore the band at his throat, which indicated his enslavement as a dojzra. "You have been the bane of my existence, Van Croix. An entire lifetime of vengeful thoughts."

"Feeling is mutual, I can assure you."

From the pocket of his robe, he lifted a small, black jar, which he held up to me. "Perhaps you don't recall the elixir we fed your mother. A rather potent concoction which draws out the vitaeilem from the blood, depleting an angel in much the same way Eradyę does. In fact, it is made from the ground-up bones of the Mortunath. To any human, it appears as holy water--a blessing, or exorcism." He uncapped it and held it up to his nose for a sniff. "Colorless. Odorless." He splashed it against my skin, and the moment it touched me, it sizzled and burned.

With the prickling of a thousand needles, the elixir absorbed itself into my flesh. Beads of fluid sucked into my skin and pulsed through my veins, like molten lava. I tipped my head back on a growl of pain, and a silver mist expelled past my lips.

It made sense why my mother had looked beaten and exhausted after every session with Venable. He'd put her body through hell.

The sphere made a crackling sound in the center of the room and jagged bolts of electricity lashed out, lapping at the mist, as if consuming it.

Ignoring the pain, I turned my thoughts inward, to where a question loomed on the fringes there. One I didn't want to ask, for fear of the answer, and as I skated my attention back to my father, my stomach already curled into knots. "How did you know about Lustina?"

The upward curve of his lips tightened those knots, as he exchanged a quick glance with Barchiel. "There were rumors of her curse. Of course, I didn't make the connection with the Met'Lazan until I followed her soul into Nightshade. To Infernium." Hands held out to his side, he trailed his gaze over the room. "The great temple of the ancients. And I learned that *all* Met'Lazan ended up here. To be cleansed and reborn. For years, I sought out their kind, traveling to distant lands, bartering with the darkest souls for her identity. All that time, she was right there. Right under my nose."

My jaw turned rigid with the clenching of my teeth. "What did you do to her?"

Hands behind his back, he paced in front of me. "I've waited centuries for you to ask that question."

A toxic rage slithered through my veins, pulling at every muscle in my body, rousing them into a thin wire of tension. The chains rattled. The air thickened. "What. Did. You. Do!"

His pacing stopped, and when he turned with a smile, his

eyes burned a glowing red. "The question isn't what I did, but, rather, *didn't* do to that poor child."

The poison inside of me boiled over, the pressure rising to the surface. I let it quietly move through me, refusing to give him the satisfaction of my rage. When I got loose from the chains, there would be no mercy for him. "Pray that you kill me."

"Come now, Son. You know I can't kill you, not without suffering the same fate." He circled me, coming to a stop at my back. A long skinny tentacle slid across my neck, tightening over my throat. "But I can make you quite miserable. And I can't tell you how earnestly I've prayed for that."

The fury inside of me swelled and festered like a raw, pulsing wound. I peered up at my fingertips which had begun to darken. The blackness crawled down my hands, to my wrists, from my chest to my abdomen.

"Well, what have we here!" Bishop Venable remarked, dragging his finger across my shoulder. "Seems I was right about you all along."

"Fuck off," I rasped, and he chuckled.

"I've got a new toy to show you, Van Croix." From his hip, he uncoiled a three-pronged whip, its braided tips like the steel fangs of a snake. Undoubtedly designed to hook and tear away flesh. "These will make for wounds you cannot heal."

Fuck.

64

FARRYN

I wriggled my arm, trying to break loose from Vaszhago's unyielding grip. "Let me go! I'm not leaving him here!"

The boy clung to the demon's leg, in a futile attempt to bite through the shields of his suit.

"You will only complicate things and make it harder for him to fight Claudius."

"Vaszhago, I am the Met'Lazan. It's me!"

He finally came to a stop, but didn't bother to release my arm. "Do you remember the Omni? Can you speak it?"

"No, but–"

"Then, until you do, you put him at risk." He dragged me farther down the hallway, away from the room we'd escaped. Still clutching my arm, he paused in front of a long stretch of gray wall and pulled an object from his tabard. Summoning chalk.

"No. No!" I yanked and squirmed and even gnawed at his damn bracers, but the stubborn asshole refused to release me. "I'm not leaving this labyrinth without Jericho!"

Ignoring me, he one-handedly drew an awful circle on

the wall, still keeping me imprisoned against him, and wrote Kezhurah's name in the center of it. After stuffing the chalk back into his tabard, he placed his free hand there.

The boy reached up, hanging from it, and bit at his forearm, but it didn't seem to faze Vaszhago, at all. The wall wavered, as if the circle was filled with smoke, and I caught just a hint of translucent barrier shimmering in the light of a lantern somewhere behind us. Kezhurah stepped through and frowned, looking around where we stood.

A screeching sound drew my attention to the other side of Vaszhago, and I let out an exasperated groan when the corridor filled with Mortunath. One hard yank took me through the invisible barrier, which cast a tickle over my skin as we breached it, and Vaszhago finally released his grip once we were on the other side.

I looked around, mentally noting a slight familiarity to the room, even though I'd never personally been there.

"My room." Vaszhago said, confirming my guess.

The healer approached me, and the boy scampered around Vaszhago, smashing into my hipbone as he wrapped his arms around my waist.

Scared of her?

"You look famished. And exhausted. I will make up a quick concoction for you." Her eyes scanned over me and as she reached out a hand toward me, Vaszhago swiped it up before she made contact.

In a strange gesture, he ran his thumb over her palm then kissed it, and at the subtle nudge of my hip, I frowned, scooting to move behind him, as he apparently wanted.

When she turned away, crossing the room for her satchel at the far side of Vaszhago's bed, the demon leaned into me. "Something isn't right," he whispered, as if he didn't want Kezhurah to hear him.

I watched as his bed coverings turned pink before my

eyes and frowned.

"The labyrinth," he murmured. "It's using my memories to create what it thinks is familiar to me. I questioned whether my bedding was pink, and it turned the bedding pink."

"Then, this isn't real," I whispered. "It's just another door."

"I do not believe there is an exit to the labyrinth without destroying Letifer's heart. I'm going to distract her. Head for the door and find somewhere safe to hide." He reached into his pocket and pulled out a vial of black fluid. "Jericho retrieved this elixir from the black witch, Venefica. According to him, it puts you in a death-like state, which would release you of the unbound soul. But you would remain that way until the curse is broken." His face turned grim. "The curse can only be broken by handing Letifer's heart over to Venefica as payment. But should you find yourself in a hopeless situation in which we cannot escape this place ..." He curled my fingers around the vial. "Your mind will not suffer whatever torment is inflicted upon you."

I couldn't imagine what it must have taken for Jericho to even consider something like that. As malevolent as the unbound soul might've been, it was small potatoes compared to the evil I'd seen up until that point. With a nod, I tucked the vial into the pocket of my nightgown. "So, I find a safe place. What's the plan after that?"

"We need to destroy Letifer's heart. So, do not take that elixir unless *absolutely* necessary. Or you will remain in a death-like state."

Jesus. Why even give it to me? With the boy's hand in mine, I edged toward the door.

"Farryn?" Before I reached the handle, Kezhurah turned around, sipping something from a tiny black jar. She stared down at the bedding and ran her hand over the surface, before her gaze fell on Vaszhago, then on me and the boy.

Vaszhago threw out his hand and frowned, then thrusted it out again, palm out.

Kezhurah chuckled and shook her head, as she held up the small jar she'd just sipped. "I am immune to you, demon."

Mouth gaping impossibly wide, she let out one of those awful and annoying screeches, while her eyes turned a blood red.

"Go, Farryn! Now!" Vaszhago yelled, as she bolted, lightning fast, across the room toward where the boy and I spun for the door.

A hard yank of my hair kicked me backward a step.

Vaszhago came up from behind her, and she released me on a scream.

Tightening my hold on Elyon's hand, I pushed through the door, straight back in the corridor once again. The door closed behind us, and through it, I heard Vaszhago's pained outcry and lurched toward where I'd just exited.

You will only complicate things. Instead, I headed back to the room where I'd left Jericho, because damn it, nowhere in the cursed place was safe without him.

As Elyon and I made our way down the corridor, the scene before me wobbled, and I stumbled to the side. He looked up at me with concern, but I smiled, shaking it off.

"I'm fine." The dizziness struck again, a black fuzzy circle closing in from the edges.

Darkness.

Screams pierced through the void, and I opened my eyes, staring down at the boy who lay on the floor beneath me. Face pale and eyes wide with fear, he trembled, and I looked further down to see his arm just below me with two telling arcs of a bite.

"Oh, my God." I scrambled back from him, releasing his small limb.

Syrisa.

"It's okay, I … I didn't mean to–"

The boy jumped to his feet and took off down the corridor.

"Wait!" I called out for him.

Damn it.

Damn it!

I twisted around to see room 777, but I couldn't bring myself to go in yet. I had to make sure the little boy was okay. I had to find him, because I intended to take him away from this place, if we managed to escape. Pushing to my feet, I headed in the direction he'd gone.

Shadows on the floor brought me to a halt.

Hobbling creatures approached just around the corner. On a shaky breath, I turned to go the other way, but Mortunath stood at the opposite side of the corridor, too.

On a screech, they launched toward me, and I pushed through the door, into the room.

When I turned around, the sight that greeted me sapped the air from my lungs.

Jericho hung from a chain in the center of the room, his skin a scaly black. Against his dark tone, gruesome red wounds marred his chest and abdomen, the flesh torn away in vicious grooves.

The urge to vomit tugged at my throat, and a cold fist gripped my lungs. Until his body twitched, his chest expanding and contracting with breaths, telling me he was still alive. Through panicked tears, I scanned the room for Claudius, and tiptoed toward Jericho, who seemed to be unconscious.

As I passed the sphere with the beating heart inside, I gave another furtive glance around before sending a hard shove against the glass. A shock of electricity snapped at my palms and hit my chest like a fist to my heart. I flew backward, crashing to the floor.

The sound of laughter sent a jarring tension through me, and I twisted around looking for the source of it. "If it were that easy for a mere human to destroy, the portal would've closed a long time ago."

The view shifted, the room tipping just enough to send a wave of nausea through me. Something took hold of my ankles, and I looked down through a haze of dizziness to see tentacles wrapped around them.

My body flew straight upward, into the air, where I dangled upside down for only a moment with unbearable pressure rushing to my sinuses. The wall shot toward me at a speed too fast to stop the impact. I slammed into the surface, and a jagged pain shot into my spine, up to the back of my skull. Drawn away again, I rushed through the air a second time. A crippling blow struck my shoulder, and I cried out. My stomach went light, as my body fell to the floor, crashing in an ungracious slump that shot needles of pain into my shoulder blades.

"The legends have always spoken of a dark-winged creature seeking out the Met'Lazan for love. All a bunch of ridiculous fairytales." Claudius chuckled as he approached me. "Letifer isn't looking for *love*. He's looking to feed. Himself. His army. This realm. Only the Met'Lazan has the ability to access that power."

"I told you before. I have no fucking clue how to access that power!"

"Then, we will have to jog your memories."

One hard yank of my ankles sent me flying onto my back, the floor burning over my spine. A monstrous form crawled toward me, its eyes glowing red, tongue like a serpent's. It wasn't until it was looming over me that I could make out features on the face–the roman nose and lips, and the shape of the eyes that held the familiarity of Claudius. But there was something else, too. A sickening familiarity that burned low in my belly. I'd seen this form before. Not only in my nightmares.

A flash of memory struck the back of my head--w*atching the monster crawl up my body, as I lay bound to a slab of cold concrete. Chill air. The scent of death and misery.*

I knew this monster intimately. The monster from my nightmares.

Fear curled inside my chest, and I kicked out at him, failing to connect with his body. I pushed up onto my elbows to scoot away. "No! No! Stop!"

Another hard yank brought me closer to him.

In his hand, he held the blade that I'd stabbed him with earlier. Jericho's blade. Breath stuttered out of me, as he twisted it in front of me.

"I'm curious to know *your* threshold for pain."

Two more tentacles came up over his shoulders and snapped around my wrists, pinning them to the floor. I squirmed and kicked, but could not loosen his crushing grip that pressed against my bones.

An intense roar echoed through the room, and I turned to see Jericho, awake and shaking as he pulled at his chains. Fangs protruded past his lips, his horns sticking up out of his forehead as he took a full-on demon appearance. Jericho grunted, his body swinging with the wrenching of his arms, as he fought to get loose.

His antics seemed to stall the attack, and Claudius paused and looked that way.

The sound of chuckling drew my attention to another familiar face. One I hadn't seen since the night Jericho's wings were sliced.

Barchiel moved to beside Jericho and ran his finger over one of the wounds on his abdomen. "From the time he was a boy, I used every means of torture to learn his weaknesses and try to break him. And he was quite good at hiding them. Even recently, he took his punishment with very little protest. But it seems you are his greatest weakness of all, my dear. Watching his father torment you so mercilessly will surely break him this time."

Fear gripped my lungs, as Claudius climbed higher. With a blackened hand, he gripped my face, holding me in place.

A hot-cold sensation jolted my muscles, as he dragged the blade across my cheek. Screams punched through my chest, and I convulsed in his grasp, desperate for escape. "Stop! Please stop!"

"We've only just begun," he whispered in my ear. "By the end of it, you will hate everything about yourself. And you will do everything I tell you."

A broken sob hammered against my ribs as I held in the urge to cry. I refused to give him that satisfaction.

Distant words echoed in my head. Ones Jericho had said to me a while back. *'When you force yourself to face what you fear most, you become impervious to its pain. Inviolable.'*

"You cannot hurt me," I whispered in a shaky voice. "I won't let you hurt me."

"We shall see."

Jericho growled and twisted against the chains holding him in the air.

A tickle across my abdomen drew my attention to where one of Claudius's tentacles lifted my gown up, exposing me from just below my ribcage down. Eyes on me, he held the end of the blade in his palm, and a bright orange glow sent a shudder of terror through me. When he opened his palm, the tip of the blade also glowed, as if it'd been dipped into molten flames.

"Please don't," I whispered. "Please don't do this."

"The times I've watched Jericho burned with hot blades,

he scarcely let out so much as a whimper. I'm curious to see what sounds he makes when it's your flesh that bears the burns."

Squirming against the appendages failed to break them, and I let out a scream as the heat from the metal neared my skin.

A roar of fury reverberated through the room, and Jericho fell into a frenzy, the chains clanking with the violent jerking of his body.

Claudius chuckled and lowered the blade.

It hit my skin on a sizzling streak of agony as he dragged it across my abdomen. Flashes of light exploded behind my tightly clamped eyelids. I screamed and writhed under the searing hot metal, my muscles frantic to push it away as they trembled and twitched.

A dangerous blackness settled over me.

"Farryn!" The sound of Jericho's voice pulled at me, grounded me, and I opened my eyes to see him jerk and spasm in my periphery.

Focus on him. Stay with him.

Until, at last, the blade lifted away.

The blistering pain had my lungs locked up, my muscles tense and reeling from the agony still pulsing through me in hot waves.

"Look, dear. Look what I carved into your flesh."

Eyes screwed shut, I shook my head. I couldn't bring myself to look at what he'd done to me. Pain snapped across my scalp, as he grabbed a handful of my hair and lifted me to see. A whimper escaped me, the flex of my stomach muscles pulling at the fresh wounds. I couldn't make out the word, only the lines of blood that stretched across my abdomen.

His fingers tightened in my hair, and he pressed his cold, slimy lips to mine. Exhaling hard through my nose, I screamed against his mouth, and when his tongue dipped past my lips, reaching the back of my throat, I gagged.

He broke the kiss, resting his forehead against mine, forcing me to look down at the carving on my belly.

"*Me'retrixis*," he said with ragged amusement in his voice. "In your world, *whore* would be an insult. In our world, there is no greater insult for a female than this."

A wail of pain broke through my chest as he lowered my head, and I turned away from it, while the burn sank its teeth into my flesh.

Swiping up my arm still bound by his tentacles, he held my palm to his chest. "Say the words. Bestow the power of vitaeilem. Say them!"

"Fuck you!" I screamed, and teeth grinding with furious rebellion, I dug my nails into his flesh.

At the sound of his mocking chuckle, I sobbed. "Let us see what a filthy *me'retrixis* you are," he said, tossing away the blade and rising up to his knees.

Another loud bellow struck the air like the crack of a whip, as Jericho fell into hysterics again, thrashing against his chains.

Tentacles pried my legs apart, and Claudius's intent became clear when a long, black appendage stuck up from between his thighs.

"No! No!" I bent my wrists, clawing at the rubbery tentacles wrapped tightly around them, my nails digging and scraping. I flipped over onto my stomach, tangling in the tentacles still bound to me, and I stilled, forehead pressed to the floor, muscles trembling, while my wounds screamed in protest.

White-hot pain lashed my belly as I was dragged backward, and I let out a scream, feeling the skin split with the friction across the wounds. The hem of my gown rose up past my hips, and I fell into a panicked tantrum, screaming and kicking, while the angry burn across my skin festered and flared.

Chains rattled over the sounds of Jericho's furious roars. Something pressed down on my head, holding me in place. As my body jostled with the tearing of my clothes, I caught sight of the vial with black fluid that must've fallen out of my pocket, and my thoughts reverted back to what Vaszhago had said.

No escape.

I slid a trembling hand closer and curled my fingers around it. A tentacle snapped across the back of my palm while another snaked beneath it, swiping the vial out of my hands.

As I stared back at Jericho, tears slid over my nose, and I closed my eyes. In the darkness, I slipped away.

Running hand in hand through the woods. Laughter. Watching the birds overhead swoop and dance through the sky. Kisses under the stars.

The memories shifted. Darkened to a feeling of dread.

The bite of ice cold water. Pressure inside my chest.

Whispers.

Loud whispers.

A language I somehow understand, spoken in perfect pitch and clarity.

Holding my hands to my belly as the watery grave takes me under.

The Omni.

I remembered it all. Lustina had translated the ancient sigil, mentally spoken the Omni to save her baby's life just before Bishop Venable had drowned her. In those precious moments before death wiped her memory of the sigil, she'd given the baby enough vitaeilem to survive while her body clung to its final breath.

I remembered everything, including the words she'd spoken.

An outcry reached my ears—the sound of pure suffering and pain. At first, I thought it'd come from Jericho, but the pressure against my head eased, and I opened my eyes. I turned, curling my legs up to see Vaszhago holding Claudius suspended in the air in a state of paralysis, his body twisted up with blood pouring profusely out of his groin. Lowering my gaze showed his severed penis lying on the floor beside me. I kicked it away and, with a hand set to the wounds on my stomach, scooted myself to the wall, shaking as I stared down at the blood on my gown. My mind scrambled to piece together what had happened to me. The lack of pain between my thighs told me he hadn't penetrated me, and yet, my body turned cold and numb, every cell shaking. Reeling.

Sounds died to a muted silence in my head. I held my hands up, staring at the blood which had pooled beneath me with Vaszhago's attack against Claudius.

"Farryn! Get out of here!" Vaszhago shouted over the din of my thoughts, his voice affected by whatever effort it must have taken to keep Claudius suspended.

I turned to see Jericho, hanging limp from his chains. Shaking. Broken.

So broken.

On unsteady hands and knees, I stumbled toward him, my stomach in so much pain, I could scarcely breathe. A vague awareness of throbbing in my shoulder told me I'd taken a powerful hit against the wall, but the sensation was smothered beneath the intensity of my ruined flesh.

As I neared Jericho, my hand mindlessly brushed over the blade Claudius had tossed away, and I paused, my head still lost in that dark space as I lifted it from the floor, momentarily mesmerized by it. I caught sight of my reflection in the steel. The tears. Blood. The darkness behind my eyes.

Anger roiled and twisted in my stomach in a toxic fury.

A foot stepped in my periphery, the sway of a black robe brushing over top of it, and I followed the length of the robe to find Barchiel standing over me.

"Farryn!" Vaszhago shouted again, but all sound was lost to the fuming rage burning inside of me, until at last, Barchiel bent forward.

"I told you, Miss Ravenshaw, that if you returned, I would hunt you for eternity." He tipped his head in a pathetic show of fake sympathy that shook my muscles. "I can't wait to find that little boy of yours and acquaint myself with him."

The rage spilled over inside of me. On a scream, I held the blade with both hands and stabbed it into his groin.

Barchiel's outcry bounced off the walls as he bent forward cupping himself, and I pushed to my knees until my lips met his ear, and whispered in an unsteady voice, "You won't fucking touch him now." Laughter, crazed and hysterical burst forth from my chest, needling my wounds.

As he fell to his knees, I pushed to my feet and limped toward Jericho. Pain burned across my belly, tears streaming down my cheeks.

He didn't lift his head to look at me as I approached. Only a pained sound rose up from his throat.

With jerky movements, I reached out to touch him, and his muscles flinched. A sob punched at my throat, and I circled him to find his back completely torn apart. At the stumps where his wings had been mutilated to the bone, skin had been literally shredded, hanging off him in nauseating tatters. The retching of my stomach was the only warning before acids shot up my throat, and I fell to my knees on a flare of pain, expelling black fluids. Another round sent a dark torrent firing past my lips, and I coughed, gagging on the lingering stickiness at the back of my throat. With the back of my hand, I wiped the stringy spit away, breathing hard through my nose to catch my breath. Angry with myself, I ignored the pain across my belly and pushed to unsteady feet.

Hands still covered in Claudius's blood, I held them out in front of me, not knowing where to touch him. There was no part of his flesh that hadn't been serrated. Tears welled in my eyes, as I pressed my chest to his back and ran my hands around him, embracing him. Our trembles mingled together.

Another agonized sound escaped him, and as the tears streamed down my cheeks, I held onto him. I lifted my lips to his ear and whispered the words from my dreams. The same ones I'd whispered to the bird when I was a child. The ones Lustina had whispered for the baby growing inside of her.

The words of the Omni. The most powerful words in the heavens.

Nothing happened.

Dread pulsed through me as I released him and stepped back. Had I said them wrong? Had I forgotten them?

I caught sight of his wounds again, which remained as horrific as moments ago, and shook my head. No. It had to work. Something in this fucking hell had to work!

A beam of impossibly bright light beat down from the ceiling, knocking me backward. My wounds screamed in protest, the burn of my stomach leaving me curled in a ball on the floor.

I lifted my arm, shielding my eyes against the brightness speckled in diamond glints that wrapped around Jericho, lifting him up, as if pulling his chest toward the ceiling. A blast of lightning struck his chest, and I let out a gasp.

Fear strangled my throat, as I looked for any sign of movement, wondering if the bolt had killed him. Another bolt struck his chest, this one beating straight through him, where it danced across the floor like a downed wire. The chains binding him melted into silver steam. From his back, enormous black wings unfurled, and I held my hands to my face, awed by their magnificence, as they stretched to either side of him.

The wounds on his abdomen sealed to fresh skin, and the tattoos that covered him glowed a bright silver as the darkness of his skin faded to his natural color.

"Farryn!" Vaszhago called to me from across the room, his arms shaking as if growing weak from holding Claudius. "Run!"

Jericho tipped forward. Light from within his eye turned it a bright silvery glow. Mesmerizing and terrifying at the same time, I couldn't look away.

It wasn't until I heard Vaszhago's outcry that I swung my attention back that way, watching Claudius throw him backward into the wall, where he shot right through the barrier, as if it was transparent.

Claudius scrambled toward me, and as I turned, my movements limited by the pain at my stomach, one of his tentacles captured my ankle. A blistering agony ripped over my wounds, and I let out a scream as he hauled me backward. A cold hand slid over my lips, muffling my voice.

Jericho's body remained suspended, the light still dancing over him as it repaired and renewed him.

Every muscle in my body hurt, but I kicked and fought, because I hadn't come this far, Jericho did *not* walk through hell for me, just to have the only chance for escape stolen out of my hands. Tentacles wrapped around my throat, and all my fight waned as I tore at the rubbery binding that squeezed so tightly I saw stars.

"There is no escape for you," Claudius whispered, and when he removed his hand from my mouth, a shock of pain lit my scalp with a sharp wrenching of my head.

My scream gurgled in my throat, cut short when he tipped the vial of fluids into my mouth. I choked and sputtered, grappling for his hands that covered both my mouth and my nose. Coughing shot the liquid up my nose on an intense burn that seared my sinuses, and I had no choice but to swallow. The potent liquid created a scorching burn as it slid down my throat.

Once his hands fell away, I slumped forward gagging and gasping for breath.

Frantic, I shoved my finger down my throat to try to expel the fluids from my stomach.

Only clear acids shot free to the floor.

A strange sensation lurched inside my gut, and I rested my hand there. It jetted up, into my throat, and I tipped my head back as a black curling plume of smoke flew past my lips and rose upward. It slithered across the ceiling like a shadow, and fell to the floor beside me, taking a ghostly feminine form with slight, curvy hips and slender shoulders. A gaunt woman with dark eyes stared back at me. While I recognized her face as the woman from my nightmare, she looked different. Gone were the locks of long, white-blonde hair, to be replaced by shorn spikes, nearly bald. Her glowing skin was marred with cuts and bruises.

She held out her hands, twisting them in front of herself, and her angry eyes met mine. "What have you done? Centuries, I've waited to have my vengeance! Inhabiting weak and frail bodies and feeding off the young. What have you done!" She lurched toward me, but paused mid-step. Her skin shriveled from her body, leaving nothing but a skeletal frame, which crumbled to a pile of black dust.

A heavy exhaustion weighed down on me, the likes of which I'd never felt before. My muscles weakened. Breathing slowed. So intense was the urge to sleep that I lay my head against the cool, wooden planks of the floor. The light across from me dimmed as I watched Jericho touch down, with his enormous black wings fully restored.

So beautiful, it didn't seem real.

Tears slipped down my cheek. "Strę vera'tu," I whispered.

An overwhelming sense of calm settled inside of my bones, watching and marveling him, and I slipped into the black abyss.

65

JERICHO

I stood from where I crouched and stared down at myself. Pure energy pulsed through my veins, invigorating every cell in my body. I felt whole. New.

Farryn.

I shot my gaze to where she lay on the floor and strode toward her. My steps slowed as I took in her unmoving form, the empty vial that lay beside her. Frowning, I lowered to my knee and lifted it from the floor to see not a drop of it was left.

Urgency beat through my muscles as I lurched toward her, rolling her onto her back. Her angelic face lolled away from mine, and her eyes remained closed, but not fluttering as if she dreamed. "Farryn." I gave a gentle shake and turned her to face me.

A wet warmth hit my fingertips, and I lifted my hand to find blood. Turning her face toward mine showed a horrific gash down her cheek, and my memories snapped through flashes of my father holding a blade to her face. Another showed him cutting her abdomen, and I lifted her blood-stained gown to find *me'retrixis* carved into her skin.

Angry breaths expelled from my nose like a bull seeing red, kettled rage that sliced through me like a hot knife, and I turned to find my father lifting the sphere away from the heart.

As I charged toward him, he swiped the heart from the pedestal and backed himself away.

Raising my hand, I felt the heat of vitaeilem burning through my palms, and my father shook his head, holding the heart like a barrier. "I wouldn't. You kill me, and Letifer will wake from his slumber. You will have to destroy the heart in order to escape, or perish to his army. And believe me when I say, he is a force that cannot be matched. Farryn will never be saved."

I lowered my palm, eye on the heart, my mind calculating all of the possibilities. The sound of splintering bones sent a tremble of satisfaction through me, as his legs twisted into grotesque angles, and he nearly dropped the heart while fighting to stay upright on them.

"You underestimated my love for Lustina when you and the bishop murdered her. And once again, you underestimate my love for Farryn." I raised my palms together, allowing the bolts of electricity to dance between them.

He whimpered, placing his hand to the wall, precariously balancing on brittle legs.

"There isn't a force in this world that I fear when her life hangs in the balance. I would walk through the very flames of Hell for her."

I held my arms out to my sides, and tiny insect-like creatures poured from my palms, their translucent bodies glowing with the light of vitaeilem. "I could've ended you with a single bolt to your heart. But instead, I'll take pleasure in hearing *your* screams, for once."

The insects scattered across the floor like lightning

streams and, before he could escape them, crawled up over Claudius's body.

Screams filled the room, and I strode toward him, reaching down into the cluster of insects crawling over him to pry the heart from his clutches. Through the melee, I caught sight of his wide blue eyes that matched mine, before the insects crawled over them. Another gut-wrenching scream bellowed from his chest, and when the bugs moved on to another part of his body, only two charred sockets remained, white smoke curling up from them while melted flesh oozed from the holes.

Heart in hand, I strode back across the room and knelt at Farryn's side, stroking a hand down her face. "My love," I said on a shuddered breath. I bent forward and lifted her into my arms, her body limp and cold against mine. "You are not alone. I will come for you in the darkness. And I will bring you back into the light."

For a moment, I held her to me until the sounds of my father's suffering died away, and I turned to see the insects had consumed him to the bone. Only small bits of flesh clung to his skeletal frame.

For a moment, all was still and quiet.

An outcry from the other side of the door snapped my attention to where Vaszhago stumbled into the room, his body bent in pain as he tumbled to the floor. The boy followed in after him, running toward me. His brows winged up as his gaze flitted from me to Farryn and back to me.

"Mama!" He fell to his knees and wrapped his arms around her, as if he'd known her his entire life.

I lowered her to the floor and rested my hand on his shoulder.

He flinched and scrambled to the other side of Farryn, away from me, but I couldn't stop staring at him. *My son.* "I promise I will bring her back."

Vaszhago let out another howl of pain, and I pushed up from them, crossing the room to where he lay convulsing on the floor.

I reached for his hand, where I had carved the *ba'nixium* curse tying him to Farryn's life. Placing my palm over his, I felt the warmth expel from my hands into him, healing the scar made the day I'd retrieved him from the prison and releasing him from the curse.

His outcries died down, and he lay shaking at first, then he exhaled one long breath and stilled. "Thank you."

A thunderous boom shook the room, and I turned to see the heart that I'd left on the floor beside Farryn sparkling with bolts of electricity. A gnawing sensation clawed inside my stomach, just as before. The energy inside of me faded a bit, though not entirely.

Vaszhago sat up from the floor, frowning. "You killed your father." When I didn't answer, his gaze flicked from me and toward the skeletal remains of Claudius Van Croix.

"I'd say so."

He turned toward Farryn, who lay unmoving. "Then, we are doomed."

Another boom of thunder struck like an earthquake, and I threw out my hands to steady myself. A loud, unified screech drew my attention toward the window, and I crossed the room, staring down at a sea of Mortunath gathered in the yard below. Thousands of them, as far as the eye could see.

"Scratch that. We are fucked," Vaszhago said, where he strode up beside me.

"No. We are not. There is one escape from this labyrinth. Destroying Letifer's mind." I ran my hand over the wall. "All of what we see is his making. We run a blade through his skull, and the labyrinth collapses. Once free, I'll return his heart to Venefica and Farryn lives."

"That's your plan? Good grief, man. This is the last time I follow you into a corridor."

I turned to face him. "You're no longer under any obligation to protect Farryn. But if you could get her to a safe place until I am able to free us from this labyrinth, I would be in your debt."

He rubbed a hand over his jaw and shook his head. "It does not require a branding across my palm to remain loyal. It only requires that you get us the fuck out of this mess you created."

I wanted to smile at that, but the agony of Farryn's condition still clawed at me. I nodded. "Keep the heart safe, as well."

With those parting words, he strode back toward Farryn, hoisting her over his shoulder with the heart clutched in his other hand. The boy followed after him, glancing back at me when he reached the door.

At my nod, he kept on after Vaszhago.

"You've killed us all. Every realm will suffer." I turned to find Bishop Venable stumbling out from the other side of the armoire, his hand cupping his bloody groin. "You cannot defeat Letifer."

"Don't you ever just fucking die?" I groaned, turning back toward the window and watching more Mortunath pour in from the horizon.

A few windows down, Venable peered out and let out a whimpering sound in his throat. "They will consume us until there's nothing left."

"If that's so, then I should hope they start with your tongue so that I may be blessed with your silence."

Gripping the wooden frame, I stretched back and shot through the window's pane into the sky. The wind caught my wings, taking me higher into the air. Gods, it felt good. Incredible.

From a bird's eye view, I could see the breadth of the army below. A black sea of moving figures, whose growls and snarls hummed like a dirge. An intense heat gathered at my palms. Electricity danced over them. Silver glowed at the rim of my good eye. I threw back my arm and sent a bolt of electricity down onto the crowd below. Flames erupted like a wildfire. Black dust marked a dead hit, as the Mortunath exploded into a murky plume.

I threw out both hands, sending lightning down in both directions, and flew across the sea of Mortunath, taking out hundreds of them at a time. Giants stood among them, large humanoid creatures with charred flesh who swiped out for me. I dodged their massive palms and set fire at their feet. Like the Mortunath, they exploded into black ash that rained down over the yard. The fires burned in patches, yet the creatures continued to pour in. I flew higher and closed my eye, gathering the energy of vitaeilem to my palms. In one sweeping motion, I blanketed the stretch of Mortunath below me in a wall of flames, taking out several hundred more. Dust polluted the air with a thick fog of ash.

An obscure figure approached from the horizon, donned in a red-tinted, steel armor suit and a helmet with three pointed prongs that curled back over his head. Two menacing eyes glowed bright from the depths of the steel mask concealing his face.

"Hello, Grandfather," I muttered.

Black, horned wings emerged from behind him, and he took flight. A darkness rolled in, swallowing the overcast sky. From the palm of his steel-clad hand, he shot a red flame toward me, and when it grazed my leg, an intense pain struck my shin. I looked down to see a deep gash that'd seared my leather trousers, and as if the flame carried some corrosive acid in it, the pain sank to the level of my bones.

Gritting my teeth, I volleyed a bolt of lightning that

struck his armor. His body convulsed in it, as the electricity danced over the metal, and his eyes glowed redder than before. On a growl, he shot across the sky toward me.

I bolted toward him.

We clashed midair on a blast of white lightning and flames.

I let out a growl as the pain washed over me in the brawl. He dug his metal claws into my flesh, and I shot another jolt of electricity over his suit. The two of us tumbled through the sky, the world spinning in my periphery too fast to discern whether I was up or down. I only knew that to release my hold on him would be my demise.

I threw my palm against his stomach, and a bolt of lightning tore a hole clear through his body. He let out a roar of fury and gripped my skull with both hands. A high-pitched sound rattled inside of my skull, one so debilitating, I fell into convulsions.

My stomach went light, and seconds later, a force slammed into my spine, as I crashed to the ground on a sickening crack. The pitch heightened, and I lay on the ground, curling into myself, writhing from the intensity.

Letifer strode up to me, looming over me like a dark cloud, but the sound had affected my vision and I could only keep focused on his steel boots planted alongside me.

"I will imprison you, just as I did your father. I will tie you to my heart. So that, should it be destroyed, you will perish with it."

66

VASZHAGO

*T*he corridor stretched on in what seemed like an eternity, as Vaszhago strode back toward the beginning with Farryn hoisted over his shoulder and Letifer's heart tucked in his palm. The boy followed behind, carrying a lantern that lit the way, though Vaszhago could've easily seen through the darkness.

Sounds reached his ear. Feet pattering against the concrete. He upped his pace, and came to a stop alongside a door. Figures emerged around the corner ahead of him. Some Mortunath, others creatures he hadn't yet encountered. Ones that had bony legs, like a spider with a skull head and fangs. On a painful shriek, they bounded toward the three of them.

"Fucking hell," he muttered, and ducked into the room beside them, looking around to find they were in the prison that Jericho had sprung him from weeks before.

The platform stood off toward the center of the room and, beyond it, levels upon levels of cells. Ogre-sized demons stepped around the platform, jagged teeth bared in threat.

"Fuck me." After gently lowering Farryn to the floor,

Vaszhago rubbed a hand down his face and shook his head, handing the heart to the boy. "Watch this. Keep it safe. And should anything come near you, scream as loud as you can, okay?"

The boy took the heart into his hands and gave a nod.

"I need you to watch her. Guard her, yeah?"

He nodded again, and Vaszhago rose to his feet, turning to face the demons whose eyes glowed a menacing red. "This shit is getting old." He held out his hands, sending a blast of his paralyzing power toward them, but the place had taken its toll. Weakness consumed his muscles, his powers draining. Blade at the ready, he unfurled his wings and flew up into the air. With quick strikes, he stabbed the giants in the skull, one by one. As each exploded into a crumble of dust, the platform shot upward, and Vaszhago frowned as he watched it slowly lower back down to the ground.

More demons piled out of it.

A scream echoed from behind him, and he snapped his attention toward the boy. Looming over him was the heavyset clergyman he'd seen back in the room where Jericho had been tortured.

"Hey!" Vaszhago yelled, holding out his palm to keep the demons away.

The man wrenched the heart from the boy's hands.

As Vaszhago turned, raising his hand to stop the man from slipping through the door, a force struck him from behind, kicking him forward.

He spun back around to the nearly two-dozen demons practically foaming at the mouth to get to him. With both hands stretched outward, his powers fading fast, he made his way back to Farryn and the boy.

The old man scampered out of the room.

On a roar of frustration, Vaszhago hoisted Farryn over his shoulder and followed after the clergyman, back out into the corridor. The boy stayed at his heels, as Vaszhago rounded the stony-gray corner for the next door. Just past it stood more of the Mortunath, clustered together. He threw out a shaky hand, struggling to hold them back, and followed the boy into the room. A hallway stood lined with tall, open-arched windows, like those found in a church. Beyond the arches, the Mortunath growled and screeched in the court-yard below.

Thousands of them.

Vaszhago laid Farryn down alongside the stone wall, where the boy curled up next to her, and the clergyman backed himself toward the arches, as the demon approached him.

"There is only one way out of this labyrinth, and by the Holy Father, I swear that, if you do not destroy this heart, we will all perish."

"Good thing I don't believe in your god," the demon said, and as he raised his hand to paralyze the bishop, a hard slam of the door swung it open, and a dozen demonic creatures pushed through.

With their excessively long limbs and red eyes, they scampered like spiders toward Farryn and the boy. Vaszhago shot a hand out toward them, paralyzing their movements, and when he swung his attention back the other way, he found the old man had tossed the heart over the edge of the balcony toward the Mortunath below.

"No!" Vaszhago threw out his other hand, stopping the heart from falling, his muscles burning with the effort of holding so many in paralysis at once.

"Let it go," the clergyman threatened, his voice tinged with malice. "Your hands are rather occupied at the moment. And if you do not let the heart fall, I will kill Farryn and steal the boy away for myself."

As the old man edged toward the two, Vaszhago's kept his

eyes on him as he held the heart and the creatures at bay. He'd need a third fucking hand to cast the spell over the bastard.

"Do not toy with me, demon. I stand by my word." The old man pulled a blade from his robes and held it up, twisting it in taunting. "This place … it drains your power. Even demons aren't immune to it. You will crumple under its weight."

Rage seethed in his blood, and he ground his teeth. Releasing his hold of the creatures would have them going after Farryn and the boy. Vaszhago growled out his frustration as the old man slinked closer to the two huddled together.

The boy shot up from the floor and charged toward the clergyman.

"No!" Vaszhago cried out. "Fuck!"

The boy bit onto the old man's arm, and as the clergyman raised his blade, Vaszhago released the heart and paralyzed the old man to keep him from stabbing the child.

Growls echoed up from below. Still keeping his hands held outward, Vaszhago slid toward the balcony and peered down where the Mortunath climbed over each other to reach the heart lying on the ground.

Within seconds, it was consumed.

67

JERICHO

The deafening sound rattled against my skull, as I forced myself to my feet and stumbled toward Letifer. I pulled my blade, knowing too well that I'd never have the opportunity to shove it into his brain.

My father was right. His power was unrivaled.

The agonizing pain brought me to my knees before him, and as I stared upward, memories of Farryn flashed through my mind. Every moment. From the first day I set my sights on her at the cathedral, to the night I finally learned who she was. The first time I took her on the bell tower, up until the night I watched her eyes flicker with pain, seconds before my wings had been severed.

All of it felt like a dream. An impossible dream.

Gathering what power I could summon, I slammed my fist into the ground on a roar, and sent a bolt of lightning that shook the landscape. The yard split down the center in a deep cavernous ridge that divided the Mortunath army, so that only a few hundred remained close to the cathedral's entrance.

Peering down at me, Letifer threw his hand to the side, and the ridge I'd created sealed itself again.

I fell back onto my heels, exhausted.

Farryn's faced flashed through my head again, her eyes closed in eternal dreams, and I gritted my teeth. Through the debilitating pain in my ear, I shot upright and gripped his helmet. I'd explode his head with my bare fucking hands if I had to. Lightning shot from my palms, dancing over the metal, and he released a sound that drowned the ringing in my ear.

As he intensified the pitch, I focused my energy on the mask. His body convulsed, the glow of his red eyes dimming.

My head throbbed, the heat in my hands burning against the metal, and I let out a boisterous growl.

He raised his palm to my chest. The blow to my heart that would kill me, but I held on.

For Farryn.

His gaze shot to the side, and I followed the path of it, where the Mortunath scrambled for something. Releasing me, he turned as if to run in that direction. On a thunderous crack, his body exploded into a cloud of red smoke. It took a moment to realize what had happened, as I stared down at my hands.

An object fell to the ground in front of me, and I frowned, lifting it up to reveal a large skeleton key, the bow of which held the face of a demon with red eyes.

As I rose to my feet, the sound of clacking drew my attention to where the Mortunath lowered to their knees. An endless horizon of undead bowing before me.

Overhead, the dark sky wavered and flickered. Shifting. Dread stirred in my gut.

No.

The heart.

I spun around and dashed back into the cathedral doors, which spat me into the gray corridor.

Carrying Farryn in his arms, Vaszhago strode toward me, the little boy following after him. "The clergyman stole the heart."

"Fucking Venable," I muttered as I scooped Farryn into my arms, pushing aside the fear of what that would mean. "We've no time. We have to get out before the portal closes. Tell me you ended the bastard, at least."

"I had more pressing matters," Vaszhago said as he lifted the boy into his arms, and the two of us jogged through the corridors, away from the center of the labyrinth.

Mortunath clustered in the hallway ahead of us, teeth bared at Vaszhago and the boy.

"Kneel," I growled, and every one of them bent down to one knee. As we passed, one snapped its teeth toward Vaszhago, and before it could bite his flesh, I slammed it with the back of my hand, sending it flying into the stone wall. The wall rippled on impact, and a crack climbed up toward the ceiling. The labyrinth was collapsing. "You so much as touch any one of us, and I will destroy every one of you."

They lowered even more, their bald foreheads touching the concrete as we passed.

A sound echoed from somewhere behind us. Not the screeches of the Mortunath, but something deeper, more threatening. The roar of a beast.

Vaszhago frowned back at me, and both of us turned toward it. A clackity noise steered my attention toward the Mortunath around us, who sat trembling, rocking back and forth as if in fear.

"I don't like this one fucking bit," Vaszhago said beside me.

Shadows flickered down the endless stretch of corridor, lit by the lanterns hanging along the path. One by one, the lanterns flickered off, the darkness edging toward us. I only just caught sight of a humanoid figure with long black goat horns, before the next lantern snuffed out.

I yanked one from its bracket, holding it up. Waiting. A figure emerged from the darkness, beyond the halo of light. About fifty yards away stood a beast whose flesh had decayed, its matted fur clinging to abnormally contorted bones, which protruded at odd angles. A stunted nose and pointed ears, set over a black bearded piece of flesh dangling from its jaw, made up a grotesque face, the eyes of it a deep, almost greenish black.

"What in seven hells is that supposed to be?" Vaszhago shifted the boy in arms, as the kid shook and scratched at the demon, undoubtedly terrified.

"If mythology serves me correctly, I'd say that's the ancient Hellborn. Eradyęan guardians. Two more of the creatures joined the first, followed by three more after that– all of them looking like decrepit goats.

Clutching Farryn tighter, I took a step back. "I'd also say this is our cue to get the fuck out of here."

The lead goat opened his mouth abnormally wide, letting out a vicious sound that fluttered the Mortunath.

The lantern in my hand flicked off.

I spun on my heel and took off down a dark corridor, my unpatched eye navigating the pitch-blackness. The sound of hooves, like a stampede chasing after us, told me the beasts were gaining quickly. Vaszhago kept pace, both of us tearing through the corridors on a mission.

Over the thudding rose another harrowing sound, like an air raid siren going off, tensing my muscles as we made our way toward the labyrinth's only exit. The walls wavered and flickered as if heat climbed over them, skinny threads of electricity dancing over the surface.

The portal was closing.

At the clamor of Vaszhago's outcry, I turned to see one of the goatmen claw at his back. Vaszhago shot out a hand, which failed to stop it. The boy jumped from the demon's arms and cowered against the wall.

Hoisting Farryn over my shoulder, I gathered power into the palm of my hand, the heat and electricity dancing over my skin, as the other goatmen scrambled over the walls toward us. A silvery halo framed my view, as I directed a bolt of lightning toward the goat attacking Vaszhago.

The creature flew backward.

I raised my fist and brought it down hard against the concrete, which sent a bolt of lightning up through the labyrinth's wavering walls. The stone cracked and split. The goat figures shot backward on a shock of force.

Vaszhago swiped up the boy again and jogged ahead of me. A quick glance showed his back bloodied and torn up.

The goat creatures scrambled to their feet.

Gripping the back of Farryn's legs, I spun for the exit and pounded concrete, wishing I could've used my wings, but the corridor was far too narrow for their full span.

The thudding from before trailed after us, as we rounded another corner. Like some kind of sick joke, the exit sign glowed ahead, indicating we'd reached the end. I plowed through the door, up the staircase, and back through the first floor of the asylum.

A roar echoed from behind us. The beasts were closing in.

The air raid alarm grew louder, more intense, warning of the portal's closure.

We passed patients who screamed and stumbled down the hallways, trying to get away from the horned humanoids who raced after us. Over my shoulder, I watched one of the goats swipe up an older man, ripping his head from his body on a tearing sound of wet meat. Still holding the man's torso, the creature crouched beside the wall and chewed at the neck stump.

I swung my attention toward the path ahead.

The edges of the portal shimmered mere yards ahead, growing smaller as we approached, and I unfurled my wings, taking flight.

Vaszhago followed suit, trailing after me.

The two of us shot through the narrow gateway only seconds before it zapped and flickered, as if to seal itself.

The doors to Infernium slammed shut behind us. At the sound of clanking I turned, hovering in the air to see the door knockers bounce with what must've been a hard hit from the other side. Not a soul inside the asylum would have been spared by those things. "Get as far away as you can!" I shouted to Vaszhago, and he shot off into the air, still carrying the boy in his arms.

After shifting Farryn to one arm, I held my other hand out, and an intense heat traveled down my wrist, gathering in my palm. My wings tingled with the power, every feather charged with enough vitaeilem to wipe out all of Nightshade, if I were so ambitious. A silvery glow framed the edge of my eye, and I lifted my hand to bolts of jagged light that flickered through my fingers, primed for destruction.

I drew back my fist and slammed it through the air. Bolts of lightning struck down over the asylum and on a flash of blinding white light, the structure exploded into a mushroom shaped fireball that shook the ground and shot a radiant surge of heat, more intense than that of hellfire. I turned away from it, my wings shielding Farryn from the flames that blasted over us. The blaze quickly retreated, sucked into the ground, as if by some invisible vacuum.

The darkness overhead lifted to the bright overcast of Nightshade. The ash which rained down from the sky disappeared with the last vestiges of Eradyę. Only black dust covered the ground where the asylum once stood, and beyond it, the Obsidian Mountain stood unaffected.

I touched down in the ravaged courtyard of the asylum and strode toward the half-cocked gates whose seared metal gave off white curls off smoke.

Adimus still waited for us on the other side. A look of relief claimed his face, but only for a moment before it turned to concern. "What happened to her?"

"I need you to bring her back. Now."

Adimus looked to Farryn and back to me. "What happened?"

"She sipped the elixir given by Venefica."

The way his shoulders sagged sent a shock of alarm through me. "Do you have the key?"

Suspicion sat thick in my gut. "I closed the portal, didn't I?"

He held out his palm, flicking his fingers. "Give it to me. I will take it to the heavens to keep it safe."

"I will give it to you only when you bring her back."

"I don't know if that's possible."

"Make it possible, or I swear on the ancients, I will open that portal again and unleash hell on all the realms!" I stepped toward him, the tension in my jaw so rigid, my teeth nearly cracked. "Bring her back, or you will know my wrath!"

"We cannot do that! She belongs to the witch now!"

Eye on his, I backed away. "Then, it is the witch who will own the key to the portal."

His gaze widened, and when he lurched toward me, he paused mid-step on a pained outcry.

I turned to see Vaszhago's hand outstretched toward him. His powers must've strengthened on leaving the labyrinth.

"You ... do not ... know ... what this will bring!" Adimus struggled to speak as the paralysis took hold of him.

"I know exactly what it will bring. I just walked through

it." I shot up into the air, carrying Farryn in my arms, and flew over the mountains of Obsidia to where the entrance of the witch's lair stood.

Desperation tightened its hold on my sanity, as I breached the threshold with Farryn in my arms and strode through the cave along the same path Soreth and I had taken before, until I finally reached the archaic skull's hollow. Through the black moss, I entered the room with the enormous pyre, which flickered as I stepped inside, reaching toward the fossilized ceiling.

Venefica stood before it with her back to me.

"Lord Van Croix," she said on a long, raspy drawl. "You do not possess the heart that I requested. Therefore, I do not know what compels you to return."

"You are correct. The heart was destroyed. And I failed to deliver it to you."

"And by failing to deliver, you–"

"But if it pleases you, I do have the key to Eradyę."

The old woman swung around, a look of disbelief coloring her expression. "Show me."

I laid Farryn down on the floor of the cave, planting a quick kiss to her forehead, and pulled the key from my pocket where I'd stuffed it. The metal gleamed in the firelight as I held it up, twisting it in front of her.

"The key to Eradyę." Her voice held a hint of awe as she stared back at it. "I held it for centuries before it was stolen from me."

"Centuries? You never once tried to open the portal?"

She chuckled and hobbled over toward her table of specimens and jars. "What use would I have for that barren land? It was only the power of possessing it that I enjoyed. But then it was taken from me and offered as a gift to Letifer." Her shadowy eyes seemed to sparkle as she looked upon it again. "And now it's returned to me."

I gathered the key into my palm, hiding it away from her. "Only on the condition that you bring Farryn back to me."

Her lips stretched to a smile, and she turned away, busying herself at the table. "I cannot say I've ever met a man so determined as you, Lord Van Croix. You bring new meaning to the word *love.*" She spoke the last word like a bitter taste on her tongue.

I said nothing in return, watching her shoulders jerk with her toil, as she smashed something together with a mortar and pestle.

"Very well. I will awaken her from slumber. But know this: no one returns from the black abyss the same. She will be changed."

"Will she remain human?"

"Of course."

"And her soul?"

"No more claimed than yours."

I nodded. "Bring her back to me, and the key is yours."

A moment later, she turned, holding a small snifter in her hands filled with a white, cloudy fluid, from which steam rose over the rim. She hobbled toward me. "Unsheathe your blade and cut across your palm."

Without a beat of hesitation, I did as she asked, removing my blade and slicing a line across my palm. One handed, she curled my palm into a fist, her hands icy against my skin, and she held the snifter beneath, where drops of blood fell into the cloudy fluid on a hiss. "Heart of your heart. Blood of your blood."

"She is still human, though," I clarified.

"Yes. Albeit a very different *breed.*" As she crossed the room toward Farryn, my muscles twitched with the urge to push her away.

"The vitaeilem will not harm her?" While toxic to

demons, its potency would've sent a human into cardiac arrest.

"No. It won't." She knelt to the floor beside Farryn and poured the substance, which slid into Farryn's mouth like white smoke. "In three days, she will wake."

"Three days?"

"You must give her time to find her way out of the darkness, Lord Van Croix." She stroked a hand down Farryn's hair. "But she will. She has a strong soul." On a sigh, she pushed to her feet and held out her hand.

I placed the key onto her palm. "Who stole it from you?"

Smiling, she curled her bony fingers around it. "My sister. Syrisa of Soldethaire."

The sound of her name twitched my muscles. "Your sister?"

"Yes. Much like you, she was driven by reckless desires. She stole the key to the barren world for one who would never love her in return. A foolish girl, held captive by her unrequited love for Letifer, and imprisoned to Claudius's evil quest for ruling all five realms."

"Why Farryn? Why wait centuries for her?"

"At first, Syrisa sought to kill Claudius in order to awaken Letifer, and Farryn would be the ultimate gift to win her lover's adoration. Delivering a Met'Lazan who hadn't yet passed on to the afterlife? Who still lived and breathed vitality. What a gift indeed! But her revenge would become twofold after Claudius stripped her soul. Your father had to die in order to set her free, as that is the curse of the unbound. And since you were the only being powerful enough to destroy Claudius, Syrisa found asylum in Farryn's body. Your incorruptible love for her served as the catalyst for Syrisa's freedom." She stared down at the key in her palm, stroking a long-nailed thumb over the demon's face etched in its bow. "Unfortunately, my sister underestimated *my* vindictive nature."

"How was Letifer sent into slumber?"

"Your father came to me many centuries ago, on a *noble* quest to banish the evil of Letifer, knowing that I sought vengeance for the stolen key. I concocted a poison, much like the one given to your dear Farryn, which he struck into the beast's skull. In exchange, I asked only that he return the key to me. But his good and righteous heart could not hand such power over to a witch, and therefore, I enslaved him to Eradyę and Letifer for eternity."

"If it was the key you sought all along, why have me retrieve the heart?"

The old woman's smile widened even more. "It seems I miscalculated your love for this woman and your loyalty to the heavens. After all, what kind of hero hands the key to the barren world over to a witch?"

"The kind who does not choose anyone else over the woman he loves."

On a dark chuckle, she backed herself away from me, straight into the flames.

68

FARRYN

"*Farryn.*"

The voice called to me in the darkness, and I opened my eyes to the dim light of a room.

I took in my surroundings. The windows along the wall, the dark and dreary masculine decor, the domed ceiling above, and the armoire across from me.

Jericho's room.

On a gasp, I kicked myself back, my spine knocking into the headboard.

Memories filtered in. *Long gray corridors. Widow in the woods. My father. Vespyr. The little boy. Jericho in chains.*

Frowning, I touched my fingers to my cheek, where the dip of a scar passed beneath them.

"It wouldn't heal completely. I tried." The voice arrived from the shadows, and I lifted my gaze to find Jericho emerging from them.

My heart swelled at the sight of him in his black buttoned-down shirt and slacks, his imposing presence that filled the room. A magnificent relief that sent a ripple of panic across the back of my neck. Was he even real? "Are we … still in the labyrinth?"

"No."

I looked around, a sinking feeling of betrayal settling beneath my skin. "How can you be sure?"

"I closed the portal."

A strange feeling in my gut told me that was bad, but I couldn't pinpoint why at first.

Burning in my throat. Black smoke. Shadowy ghost. Black liquid. "But your father … he gave me the elixir."

Hands in his pockets, he rounded the edge of the bed and took a seat alongside me. "The heart was destroyed. I traded your soul for the key to Eradyę."

I recoiled at that, frowning back at him. "What does that mean? Key to Eradyę? As in, the means of opening it?"

"Yes."

"To whom?"

"Venefica."

I shook my head, trying to wrap my mind around what he'd just said. "Vaszhago called her a black witch. You gave the key to a witch?"

"The key remained in her possession for a number of centuries before it was stolen. She never once tried to open the portal." His jaw hardened, his gaze intense. "Make no mistake, Farryn, I would've handed the fate of all five realms to Lucifer himself, if it meant saving you." The tone of his voice was resolute and unapologetic.

My heart hammered in my chest as I took it in. "So … am I still alive? Oh, God, I'm not a ghost, am I?"

His features softened only a little. "No. You are not a ghost. And yes, you are very much alive, to my great relief."

On a shaky exhale, I nodded. "Okay, so we escaped the labyrinth. You brought me back from death. And the portal closed. And what of the boy?"

"He's here. Safe." Jericho let out a groan. "Playing with the dogs as if they were puppies." His lips twitched as if he might smile. "My son. *Our* son."

I had to wrap my head around it. To embrace the fact that I was his mother reborn. Even if it was a different body which had borne the travail of his birth, he was mine. "Can I see him?"

"Soon, yes. I want you to have some time to adjust." He reached for my hand, raising it to his lips for a kiss to my knuckles. "This is a lot to take in."

An impulsive laugh escaped me, one that turned tearful, and he reached out for my hand, his brows knitted with concern.

"What is it?"

Shaking my head, I wiped away a fallen tear. "It's too much. I don't know what to do with all of this." I looked away from him, and more tears slipped down my cheek. "I had to …" The words refused to come out of my mouth, and I swallowed back a harsh gulp. Shaken, I stared down at my hands–the same hands which had pushed a knife into Vespyr. I killed her. I was her murderer. "Vespyr …"

He squeezed my hand, his gaze an ageless tide of blue that sent a calm through me. "It's going to take some time, Farryn."

Dragging my arm over my cheek, I wiped the tears away. "I wish … I could've … that she could've gotten out." The image of her eyes, tormented by the fear and sadness, echoed inside my head, and an unbearable weight pressed down on me, as all the events I hadn't yet processed came crashing in. And I broke. I fucking broke.

My body slid across the bed with Jericho pulling me into his lap, his impossibly strong arms wrapping tightly around me. While I felt safe there, the guilt expanded inside my chest, banishing the air from my lungs. Another flash of memories, ones which felt sketchier, more undefined, slipped behind my eyes. *Lying next to Elyon on the hard concrete, in the dark. Feeling my body slip away. Holding Elyon as tightly as I could, until the blackness settled.*

Lustina's memories. The night she slipped into the fade and was forced to leave Elyon behind.

In that moment, I let go, and just as when the dark plume of smoke had exited my body, I released all of the dark emotions bottled inside, ones I'd had to bury deep and compartmentalize just to keep going while trapped inside that place.

I wept for my lost baby and the dignity that had been stolen from me with Claudius's assault. For Vespyr. My father. Everything I'd lost. All of it.

I thought of Lustina, how helpless and hopeless she must've felt trapped in that place with her child. For what seemed like an eternity, I cried on Jericho's shoulder, as he held me against him, his arms never seeming to tire.

Until I'd finally cried myself to sleep.

~

"There is no escaping Infernium," the detached masculine voice whispered.

I woke with a start beside Jericho, his body wrapped around mine, muscles caging me against him. As I pushed against his arm to release me, he tightened his grip. Black snaking tentacles wormed through my head, and my insides screamed in a silent panic, but I forced a smile, turning toward him. "I just need to use the bathroom," I whispered, and his grip loosened.

When I slid out of bed, he turned over onto his stomach, his arms tucked beneath the pillow, and he watched me, as I made my way toward the bathroom.

I feared what I'd find staring at myself in the mirror, and my heart kicked up when I entered the small room and turned up the chandelier over the tub to brighten the room. Eyes closed, I stood before the mirror, breathing. In my mind's eye, something moved in my periphery.

In the imagined reflection, I caught sight of a monstrous figure standing behind me. Sunken red eyes and scaly, black skin.

On a gasp, I spun around, knocking over the soap dish on the counter.

Nothing there.

No one.

He's not here. He's gone.

Gone.

I let out a long exhale, and eyes closed once more, I turned back toward the mirror. "You survived literal hell. You can survive this," I murmured.

When I opened my eyes that time, I was greeted by a sight that clenched my stomach.

Aside from the slight pink scar which extended from my cheek down to my jaw, my face was flawless. A healthy shade without the dark circles and lines of worry. With a trembling hand, I reached up to touch it, struck by how smooth it felt against my fingertips. A slight glow in my eyes enhanced the speckles of color there, giving them a brighter shine than before. It almost felt like a caricature version of myself, after so many months of looking like death. I looked youthful.

Revived.

"Beautiful."

At the sound of Jericho's voice, I turned to see him looking in on me from the doorway.

"What happened? Why do I look this way?"

"The witch infused some of my vitaeilem into the elixir she gave you."

I snapped my attention back to the mirror, studying the soft glow to my skin. As I palpated its smoothness, my finger landed on the scar again.

A flash of memory showed a monster with tentacles looming over me, slicing a blade across my face. Panic gurgled in my chest, as I scrambled to lift the hem of my nightgown and, beneath, found the scar of the words he'd carved there.

"I would kill him again, if I could. Over and over. When I heard your screams ..." He shook his head, rubbing the back of his neck, torment and pain darkening his gaze. "There is no corner of Hell I wouldn't cross for you. No severity of pain I wouldn't suffer. But when he hurt you ..." His brow flickered, jaw clenched with anger. "I realized just how weak and vulnerable I could be."

Vulnerable. The word didn't belong to a man like Jericho. It didn't fit with a man so implausibly magnificent. Powerful. "You were the one who gave me strength in that moment." A wobbly shield of tears blurred his form. "You are my safe place. My home."

He stepped into the room, closer to me, his proximity setting off a jittering surge through my muscles.

It didn't make sense. I wanted to push him away and clutch him at the same time. My body felt in chaos, my heart clamoring as if for escape inside my chest. I closed my eyes, breathing through my nose.

Fingertips drew a soft trail over my arm. When I opened my eyes again, I saw black tentacles and red eyes, and that wickedly disturbing grin.

"No!" On a heaving exhale, I jumped backward. "No, no, no."

"Farryn." Jericho's deep voice tugged me out of that dark space, and like an invisible curtain falling before my eyes, the monster fizzled away to his beautiful face, with the patched eye and scar on his lip. Brows furrowed in the telling lines of concern, he stared back at me.

Not Claudius.

Not the monster.

Jericho.

My protector. My love.

I rushed toward him, wrapping trembling arms around him, feeling his embrace tighten around me. Safe in his arms. "I saw him. I heard him in my dreams."

"He's gone, Farryn. He can't hurt you anymore."

"He can, though. I can't get him out of my head. He was my nightmare because of Lustina's memories, and he'll continue to haunt me."

A gentle hand smoothed down my hair, and with a grip of my jaw, Jericho urged my head back. "I will kill him again and again for you. Every time he hurts you. Every minute he haunts you. I will bring you back to me."

"How?"

He curled his fingers into mine. "Strę vera'tu. When you feel lost, you say those words, and I will bring you home again."

A tear slipped down my cheek, and I rested my face against his warm and solid chest. Jericho lifted me into his arms, carrying me like a child, as he made his way back to the bed. After laying me down gently, he climbed in beside me and pulled me into him. For a moment, I just breathed, taking in his calming scent and warmth. "Tell me he suffered for what he did. To me. Lustina."

"I gave him an incredibly painful death, and still, it wasn't enough. I would have punished him for eternity, had we not been trapped in that place." He was quiet for a moment, his fingers tracing featherlight circles over my shoulder. "I've never felt a violence so fierce as seeing him hurt you. I've known pain, and I've seen atrocities in my life, but that moment has seared itself into my mind for eternity. It fucking broke me."

I lifted my gaze to his, watching him blink as if to stave off tears. "We survived. We made it. He didn't. He's gone." Climbing over top of him, I straddled his body and gripped his face, staring intently into the beautiful blue. "We survived hell. Together."

His finger trailed down my temple, and he pushed a stray hair behind my ear. "I shiver when I look at you. Because every cell in my body knows you are the only creature capable of destroying me. The only thing in this world I would die for." His hand gripped the back of my neck, and he pulled me into him for a kiss.

The chaos from before stirred inside of me again. The memory of Claudius's cold, slimy lips pressed to mine had my brain reeling. Part of me wanted to push Jericho away, the disgust so overwhelming that a tickle of nausea stirred in my chest.

It's Jericho. Jericho! Claudius is dead!

Screwing my eyes shut, I breathed hard through my nose and felt a cold detachment slip between the two of us. When I opened my eyes again, Jericho stared up at me.

"Farryn, if you need time—"

"No. No!" Anger pulsed inside of me, the rage of knowing Claudius had gotten so deep inside my head as to worm his way between Jericho and me. I threaded my fingers into his hair, gripping tight. "Make me forget him, Jericho. Fuck him right out of my head," I said through clenched teeth. "Make me forget everything."

Gripping tight to me, he flipped us over, putting him on top, and he loomed over me like a starless night. A nightmare in a dream.

I needed this. I needed him. He was the only thing more terrifying than the monster. The dark angel sent to deliver me from the hell that still burned inside my mind. I needed to distance myself from Infernium and what happened to me. Us. All of us.

I needed distraction from the noise inside my head, the nightmares that were sure to come.

"Are you certain about this, Farryn? I will wait for you. An eternity, if that's what it takes."

'I don't have to kill you to make you feel dead inside.' Claudius's words echoed inside my head, stirring rage in the pit of my stomach.

"Yes, I am certain. Get him out of my head. Please. I don't want to feel branded by what he did to me. Used and worthless." A tear wobbled down my cheek, captured by Jericho's thumb as he wiped it away.

"You are far from worthless, Tu'Nazhja. There is nothing I treasure more in all the realms than you. *Ma' baalirhya diszhra.*"

"What does it mean?"

"My most treasured possession."

In spite of his sweet and loving words, I knew better. There were things inside of me that crawled like slugs. Hatred that would never wither. Loathing that would never die. Deep seated memories of my former life, Lustina's life, and the abuse she suffered, horrific things that I could never tell Jericho for fear of breaking him, shattering him into pieces too small to compartmentalize. I had not only suffered at the hands of a monster, but I'd murdered a friend. There was nothing to redeem me. Neither his words, nor his love could pull me out of that fragmented place inside my head whose sharp edges would poke at me for eternity.

Yet, through tears, I smiled. "I love you."

He cupped my face, stroking his thumb over my cheekbone, his expression wary. "Whatever wretched and vile thing lives beneath this flesh and these bones belongs to you. I am yours eternally. And you are mine."

"Then, take me away from all this darkness."

I lifted my hips, nudging him up to his knees, and he stared down at me as he slid my panties off. The scars from the carving on my stomach caught my attention, and apparently his, as he ran his fingers over it. Tears welled again as I waited for him to say something, to know what thoughts churned inside his head.

"The steel was celestial. I tried to heal it, but it cannot be altered by my powers."

I settled back against the pillow and turned away from him. Toxic and poisonous words snaked their way into my head.

Useless. Dirty. Whore.

Even if it wasn't my language, I knew the intent behind Claudius's malicious carving.

Tipping his head, Jericho guided my attention back, and I closed my eyes to keep from having to look at him.

"Open your eyes, Farryn."

"I can't."

"If you think a few scars on your body changes the way I view you, then allow me to show you how wrong you are." At the first soft touch, my eyes shot open to find him bent over me, his lips pressed to the carved lines. "You." He kissed another of the strange letters. "Are." And another. "So fucking." And still another. "Beautiful." Taking hold of my leg, he draped it over his shoulder and planted a kiss to my inner thigh. "And you are mine. These scars are mine. Your *pain* is mine." He stared down at me with such intensity, I had to look away, but a hook of his finger guided my eyes back to his. "Nothing can change what you are to me. No scar. No curse. Not even death."

My body reeled with the urge to crawl away. Through

tears, I shook my head, his words refusing to lay anchor in the mire of my thoughts.

A tight grip of my jaw held me still. "Does it have to be carved into your flesh to believe? I will burn the fucking words across your skin if that's what it takes for you to see the truth, Farryn. You are beautiful. Unbreakable. And anyone who dares to harm you will suffer my uncompromising violence."

For a moment, I stared up at a sea of endless blue and wondered if I'd ever come to accept his unflinching loyalty for me, if I'd ever accept that he was mine in return.

Or merely drift along in this impossible dream for eternity.

I reached for the band of his trousers, desperate for something I couldn't pinpoint. I craved his touch, but it was more than that. I wanted him inside of me. I wanted to slice myself open to him, to give him every despicable piece of me and seal his protection beneath my ruined flesh.

Gaze never faltering, he pulled his fully erect cock free from his trousers and held himself at my entrance.

In one thrust, he was inside of me.

An odd sensation moved through my veins. More intense than before, the tiny vibrations of electricity shot through my blood, and I immediately arched upward, trembling while paralyzed with a pleasure so utterly divine, it brought new tears to my eyes. An intense, almost violent, hunger pulled at me. I felt restless, overcome with a need that chewed at my bones.

"My blood pulses inside of you. Like a magnet, we are drawn to one another. You will feel as I feel, and I will feel as you do." He drove into me again, and I moaned with the burgeoning ache of never wanting it to end. Fingers threaded to a tight fist of my hair. "You are my threshold for pain. The suffering I cannot bear, and my only true weakness. I will not lose you to anyone."

Every cell in my body stirred into commotion, as if it'd been rocked by something powerful, more powerful than the shame and humiliation grappling for my conscience. Ravenous lips hunted my throat, his fingers tangled in my hair, and he stole my breath with a greedy kiss.

Where there'd been hate and loathing, a pure and incomparable love filled that dark hollow of pain. It surged new life into my body like a shock, awakening my heart.

His muscles contracted and flexed around me with the drive of his hips, powerful enough to cast away the dark thoughts inside my head. I was clinging to the edge of the abyss, dangling over a chasm of guilt, and I hated that he refused to let me fall alone.

I wanted to punch and kick and scream, to tell him to go to hell for wanting me in spite of myself, but all I could do was feel. I felt everything. His hands holding me down, his hips railing into my body. His mouth silencing the vicious words trapped inside of me.

Head tipped back, I surrendered myself to him, letting him pummel the remaining shreds of my deprecation, to drag the fear and self-loathing out of me, conquering the dark corners where the monsters and demons dwelled.

The vibrations heightened, dancing over us in sparks of electricity that snapped out at the air around us. A white halo encased us. Two forces coming together as one. Impenetrable. Untouchable.

I clutched his muscled biceps and sank my teeth into his shoulder. He pounded into me faster. Harder. Together, we moved as a machine, the sweat beading over our skin and making for an easy glide.

An impossibly bright light shimmered in my periphery, but I was too caught up to care what it meant, until a sharp pain struck my neck, and I cried out. An intoxicating euphoria swept over me, the view blurring as a blinding pleasure tickled my belly. I felt drunk. Listless. Helpless.

Jericho let out a muffled growl against my skin, holding me pinned to the bed as he kept on with his relentless pistoning. When he pulled away from me, two fangs hung beneath his top lip, dripping a shimmering silver.

God, he was beautiful, with his dark hair and silvery blue gaze, his tattoos and rough, muscled body. A scintillating ember on a moonless night.

My avenging angel.

Hot and breathless, I could do nothing as he railed into me and took a nipple into his mouth, sucking and licking, as he fucked me into a stupor.

The tension wound inside of me, so tight I felt like it would snap any moment.

My muscles trembled. Stiffened.

Bullets of pleasure shot up from my toes and detonated at the back of my skull. A blast of heat scattered beneath my skin, and I let out a scream, bellowing his name.

He shuddered against me, and pulse after pulse of warmth spilled into me. The vibrations had me clenching around him, and he let out a grunt and a curse, pumping out the last of his release. My belly curled with the sensation, the dizzying ecstasy rendering me weak.

Exhausted.

Utterly boneless.

The merciless god of pleasure and his sacrificial lamb.

When he lifted himself up, I stared up at him and something squeezed my chest. A feeling I'd never felt before, it ached and soothed at the same time. I couldn't breathe, and the sensation was so overwhelming that I teared up again. "What is this? Am I dying right now?"

"No, Tu'Nazhja. Do you remember when I told you that

only when I claimed you would you understand my feelings for you?"

"Yes."

"Now you know. It is a pain deep inside my chest that burns only for you. I feel it every time I look into your eyes. Like the light of a thousand stars. An entire galaxy of love."

The tears slipped down my temples, as I felt exactly as he'd described. So much love, it hurt. "I don't even know what to call this."

"In my language, we call it *amreloc*. It happens with the joining of souls. You are now mine. Officially."

"I'm claimed?" I shook my head. "I thought you had to do that in public?"

"I claim you the way I want to claim you. And anyone who doubts it can fuck off."

Smiling, I raised my hand to his cheek, running my thumb over his ruined lip. "Amreloc?"

He swiped up my hand, and kissed my palm. "Yes. My eternal."

"And you are mine." A strange cold sensation snaked beneath my skin and stiffened my muscles. I tried to lift my arm, but couldn't. "Jericho? I feel strange right now."

He stroked a hand over my hair. "Shhhh. It's okay. Your body is turning."

The cold spiked, like tiny needles pulsing through my veins. Panting, I willed my hand to lift from the bed, yet it wouldn't move as I lay beside him. Helpless and paralyzed. Heart hammering inside my chest, I breathed through the tight fist of panic cinching my lungs. "Turning to what!"

"Immortal, my love. You are becoming immortal. And you will belong to me."

The icy sensation moved from my arms to my legs, my toes, my torso, my chest. "I can't breathe! I can't breathe!"

Lips to my ear, he whispered. "Relax, Farryn. It will pass. Allow it to take you."

"Allow what to take me?"

"Your new soul."

His words sent a fresh wave of panic crashing through me. "A new soul? Like ... I won't be me?"

"You will very much be you. But your aging will slow. Your bones and muscles will strengthen. Your heart will beat stronger. Your lungs will breathe easier."

A tingling sensation warned my body was going numb. My sight dimmed, a blackness settling in on the fringes.

"Let it take you into sleep, Tu'Nazhja. Do not be afraid. When you wake, you will feel fucking fantastic. And I will be here, watching and waiting for that moment."

The blackness closed in like a lid over a box with no air. I gasped and choked for one sip of oxygen.

Until the void pulled me in.

EPILOGUE ONE

BARCHIEL

Three days ago ...

*B*reath sawed in and out of Barchiel as he lay against the wall of the Obsidian Mountain. He had only just made it out of the labyrinth before the portal had closed and the asylum burst into flames, which would have left him at the eternal mercy of being hunted by Mortunath in Eradyę. He thanked the Holy Father for whatever interventions had allowed him to escape such a horrible fate.

His *only* regret was not having killed Farryn when he'd had the chance.

Pain throbbed at his groin where the little harlot had stabbed him. Fortunately, she had not severed it completely, as a life without pleasure seemed like no life, at all.

Sighing, he sat up from the stony ledge, looking around the barren wall of rock where he'd come out of the portal, somewhere along the stretch of Mount Obsidia, though he didn't quite have his bearings about him.

Ariochbury couldn't have been far, though. Perhaps two nights walk from there, and he could find some safety once he was within the Noxerians' castle. As he wobbled to the side, the pain struck him again, shooting up into his skull, and he let out a groan. The view before him wobbled a bit, and he narrowed his eyes on a figure striding toward him.

An enormous figure.

He rubbed his eyes, wondering if he were imagining it, given not a soul was known to inhabit that stretch of mountain. Aside from the witch who lived somewhere in the caves below, anyway.

The figure must've been well over six foot tall, with broad shoulders. He wore a long, black, hooded cloak pulled up over his face, and black gloves. A glint of metal at his hip was undoubtedly a sword sheathed in its scabbard.

The bishop could feel his pulse hasten with every step closer, and when the stranger finally came to a halt, only mere feet from where he sat, his heart nearly galloped right out of his chest. The man blocked out the sun as he stood over him, and squinting, the bishop could just make out the roughhewn features of his face.

"Who are you?" Barchiel asked on a shaky breath.

A toothpick sat at the corner of his lips, as he smoothed his hands over his gloves. "Name's Gabriel."

The intimidating air of power practically crackled around them, setting Barchiel's nerves abuzz. The old man cleared his throat and wobbled to the side again. "Very well, I was just leaving."

He spat the toothpick to land not far from Barchiel. "You're not going anywhere."

A nervous laugh escaped Barchiel on turning back toward the stranger. "Excuse me?"

"Does the name Catriona ring any bells?"

Barchiel studied his features, wondering how he might know him, his mind contemplating a means of negotiating with the stranger. He'd done it before. Many times. When he'd found himself in the grasp of his infernal slaver, he'd convinced the demon to make him his dojzra and set him free. He'd done it again with The Fallen when he arrived in Nightshade. And of course, in Eradyę, when Claudius had summoned him. It was only a matter of learning what the man who stood before him wanted. "I'm afraid I don't know a Catriona."

The stranger's chest rose and fell as he glanced away, and the hint of a smile played on his lips when he brought his attention back to the old man. "Ah, Mr. Barchiel, or perhaps I should call you Bishop Venable?" He didn't wait for an answer. "When I'm done with you, you will remember her. And what you did to her. And I can assure you, whatever pain you brought to her will only be a fraction of what I inflict in return."

Barchiel's body trembled as he spoke, and as the image of a red-haired woman burning on the platform spun through his head, he realized there was no compromise this time. No bargaining with the man.

"H-h-how did you find me?"

"Sweet little thing visited me not long ago. Told me all about you. The *good* and righteous bishop." His eyes flashed a menacing silver and Barchiel pressed himself tighter against the wall. "See, I'd given up hunting souls a long time ago, but when I found out what you did to Catriona, well, I decided to come out of retirement for one last hurrah."

"Who? Who told you this?"

"Her name is Farryn Ravenshaw." From the holster at his hip, he pulled a vicious-looking dagger, with curled serrated edges undoubtedly designed for tearing away flesh. "So when I've had my fill of your screams and decide to run this blade through you one last time, to send you into Voltusz, it's her you can thank for it."

The bishop's blood turned to ice. Why he hadn't killed the

wretched little nuisance when he'd had the chance was the only repetitive thought in his head. He scrambled to get to his feet, and a force slammed into his throat, pinning him to the stony mountain wall behind him.

Enormous white wings unfurled behind the man, spread out at either side of him, and Barchiel shuddered a breath.

"So, this is how it goes from here," the angel said. "No escape. No redemption. And no mercy."

EPILOGUE TWO

FARRYN

One year later ...

a field of multicolored daisies stretched toward the woods, as I sat watching Jericho teach Elyon how to find his vinculum bond with Cicatrix. Over the last few months, Elyon had begun to replenish the powers that had been consumed by Infernium--powers he never even realized he possessed, inherited from his father. The three dogs darted in all directions around them, excited over the flock of birds overhead, and the sound of the boy's giggles was music to my ears.

It'd taken some time for him to trust that no one was going to hurt him ever again. The night terrors he suffered had only just begun to wane a bit, and oftentimes, I would wake to find him crouched in the corner of mine and Jericho's room, claiming that monsters were out to get him. Those were the nights I let him sleep between us.

Although he was estimated to be about nine, or ten, years old, his exact age was unknown. I'd asked Jericho how it was that Lustina had birthed him centuries before, yet he appeared so young. According to Jericho, time moved differently in Eradyę. What had felt like an eternity being trapped there amounted to nothing more than minutes. The fact that Elyon had begun to show maturing features over the last year proved his theory correct.

For Jericho, fatherhood seemed to have evolved over the last few months. Not having had siblings, or much responsibility over another young life, it didn't exactly come easy for either of us. Fortunately, Elyon proved to be both forgiving and patient, as we continued to learn with each day.

I tied the stems of the daisies together and set the pathetic looking crown I'd made from them atop my head. I'd planted the field in honor of Vespyr and made a point to spend the brightest days there, when the air was warm and fragrant. Unfortunately, Nightshade never really saw much sun, and seemed more overcast than anything, but it still made for some enjoyable moments. As I lowered my hand, I caught sight of an ant haphazardly crawling across my fingers, its movements jerky and slow. In its mouth, it toted a small crumb from the sandwich I'd eaten earlier. I held it up, noticing two of its back legs were missing. As it scooted itself over my knuckles, I set my other hand over top, to keep it from falling off.

Tingles tickled my fingertips and heat warmed the top of my hand. Little jagged threads of electricity danced over my skin, and on a gasp, I recoiled the hand which covered the other.

The ant scampered over my knuckles, its missing legs fully restored.

What the ...

I'd thought it might've been a different ant, if not for the crumb still in its mouth.

Staring down at my hands took me back to that day in the bathroom, after Jericho and I had first arrived in Nightshade, when he'd healed his wound just by touching it. I twisted my other wrist, marveling the few currents still crackling over my skin. Was it possible that I'd somehow acquired that ability with his vitaeilem?

Wearing an incredulous smile, I studied the tiny bug, who'd paused his scampering and was looking back at me. As if it was studying me, too.

"Myrmecophilous," I murmured, and set the ant onto the grass, watching it dart off with its food.

"I don't know how you can stand it out here." At the sound of Vaszhago's voice, I turned and smiled. He stood behind me, dressed in all black, of course, his hair pulled back from his face as he toyed with one of his bracers.

After Infernium, the demon had been set free, no longer bound to me, but for reasons I couldn't wrap my head around, he'd chosen to stay, serving as something of a guardian to Elyon and me.

"What? You don't like daisies?" I asked.

"I don't like the sounds of children."

Chuckling at that, I twisted back around, stealing a sip of chthoniac I'd poured earlier and set out on top of a picnic basket. "You know, it takes more muscles to frown than smile."

"Good. I'd hate for any of them to go lax."

I snorted and took another sip of the potent drink. I'd grown to enjoy the fiery liquor, a burnt cinnamon flavor that was deadly to most humans. An acquired taste, no doubt. I once made a slushy out of it, much to Jericho's horror. Food, in general, tasted so much better nowadays. Much more flavorful than before, which Jericho attributed to the changes I'd undergone since the claiming. "How did you become so moody?"

"What demon do you know who is spirited and optimistic?"

"Touché. Maybe you should break the mold. Be a trailblazer for a change."

His lip twisted with repulsion. "I prefer my cynicism. Keeps you optimistic types away."

"Well, good luck with that. Turns out, I don't mind you so much. Asshole." I turned in time to catch a *very* slight smile curve his lips upward.

"I still find you as pleasant as a thorn in my ass."

"Awww. That's so sweet of you."

Grumbling, Vaszhago stepped in the opposite direction.

"Hey, where you going?"

"I've had enough of the giggling for one day."

Eyes narrowed, I smiled back at him. "Is it the giggling which troubles you? Or the need to spy on the new *stable hand?*"

About a month earlier, Jericho had hired a new caretaker for the horses, a young girl of perhaps twenty. Completely human and entirely unaware of what Nightshade was. What any of it was, really, including Vaszhago. I'd caught her staring at him a couple of times, smiling, but as far as I knew, that had been the extent of their flirtations.

"I do not consort with human females."

"Ah. Then, it doesn't trouble you that she's grown quite fond of someone else?"

He ran his tongue over his teeth, his eyes assessing me. "Who?"

"What does it matter?" I asked, turning my attention back to Jericho and Elyon. "You don't *consort with human females*, anyway." I tried my best to copy his prim and proper enunciation, but sounded like an idiot.

"*Who?*" he asked again, and the impatience in his voice brought a smile to my lips.

"Cerberus, of course. Have you not seen the way she

frolics with him all day long? If you're crushing on her, I'd nip that in the bud quickly."

Exhaling a groan, he ran a hand down his face.

"You were jealous a second ago. Admit it."

"I will admit no such thing. Jealousy is a petty human emotion."

"Mmm." I took another sip of the drink and frowned. "Pretty sure Jericho said those exact words to me once."

"I've no time for these ridiculous conversations." Vaszhago turned back on his path toward the cathedral.

Before he got too far, I yelled over my shoulder, "Tell Nyria I said hello!" When I twisted a bit more, I caught sight of him shaking his head, and I let out a quiet chuckle.

"Mama! Look!" Elyon called out, swinging my attention back toward him and Jericho. "I did it!" Even after months of him calling me his mother, I still hadn't quite gotten used to hearing the name.

Smiling, I watched as he directed the birds to swoop and take flight, and clapped, while he hopped with excitement. Jericho strode toward me, pausing midway to glance back at Elyon, before he took a seat beside me on the blanket I'd laid out. The mere proximity of him stirred a rush of tingles beneath my skin. The result of the bond we shared, a sensation I felt every time he was near.

"He's a natural," he said, lifting my glass for a sip of my chthoniac.

"Like his father." I leaned into him, planting a kiss to his lips before licking the liquor from them. "He inherited all the best parts of you."

"Hopefully, he learns to use his wings easier than I did."

"When do you think they'll come in?"

"I was about his age, so I suspect not long from now."

"Great." I sighed, watching the boy guide the birds a bit too close to the treetops. "So I'm going to have to shadow him, to make sure he's not jumping off the top of the cathedral."

Jericho smiled and filled my glass with more liquor. "I'll refrain from telling you all the things I did when I was his age."

Watching him pour half a glass of the chthoniac, I raised a brow. "Are you trying to get me drunk?"

"Perhaps I am, yes." He pushed up to his knees, and his body forced me back onto my elbows. "I would very much like to meet you in the belltower this evening, Miss Ravenshaw."

I sucked my bottom lip between my teeth to hide my smile. "I don't know, Mister Van Croix. I've a number of appointments—"

"Cancel them. It's imperative that I show you a new trick."

My pulse purred, and I couldn't help the undoubtedly deviant smile on my face. Since the claiming, a number of things had changed. One of them being sex, in general. It'd become far more thrilling. Literally. Two nights before, he'd flown me up above the clouds, and fucked me in the sky with the moon as a backdrop.

Of course, those damn vibrating feathers had returned, too, which had inspired him to practice his edging technique on me. A torment that'd sometimes lasted hours, but made for downright obscene and filthy sex afterward. I hated how much I enjoyed the return of those vicious pleasure weapons.

"Well, in that case, I'll be there with bells on."

His brow kicked up, and he leaned into me, his lips only inches from mine, his breath a delicious cinnamon scent. "Very well. But *only* bells."

As he leaned in to kiss me, a bumbling force knocked me backward, as Cerberus plopped down between us without warning.

Jericho groaned as the hound intercepted his kiss, licking

my face, and I chuckled, petting the invasive beast. He'd lost the aggressive streak toward me, which I'd had no doubt was the result of Syrisa having taken over my body. After Infernium, Cerberus had become twice as protective over me. I'd sometimes wake from nightmares to hear him whining in the yard below my window. In spite of the lookalike I'd slain in Infernium, and the horrific visuals of it still clawing at my head, Cerberus put me at ease.

"Mama, look." Elyon strode up with Fenrir and Nero in tow, holding something in the palm of his hand. A bright purple butterfly, bearing a strange, pink-swirled design with a fine trim of thin, metallic-looking gold, took up the width of his palm, its wings gently fluttering.

The sight of it brought a smile to my face, as it somehow reminded me of Vespyr.

"She's beautiful," I said, and dared to run my finger over its soft, fuzzy wings.

"The symbols are cool. What do you think they mean?" Elyon asked, pointing to them.

"I'm not sure they necessarily mean anything."

"But they do. Everything has meaning."

The warm tingle of familiarity hit the back of my neck. The words he'd spoken were the same words my father had always said to me as a child. "Who told you that?"

"Augustus."

My heart gave a hard thud, and when I glanced back at Jericho, I caught his frown. I'd never spoken of my father in front of Elyon before. Not so much as a word about him. Whenever I'd grieved his absence, it'd always been in private. "Um. Who is Augustus?"

Elyon chuckled, running his finger over the butterfly's wings. "You don't know your father's name?"

Another glance back at Jericho, and I swallowed a gulp. "When did ... when did he tell you this?"

"A while ago."

Every hair on my skin stood on end, and I shifted on the blanket in my intrigue. "Where?"

The butterfly flew off into the sky, and Elyon lifted his head, watching it flutter higher, its colors bright enough to see against the blinding overcast.

"Elyon? Where did you talk to him?"

He pointed to his head.

"In your mind?"

He nodded.

"Do you speak with him often?" It was Jericho who asked the question that time, and Elyon nodded in response.

"He tells me stories sometimes. Of the witch's daughter and the baron. And Pentacrux, too. Can I go play with Cicatrix again?"

I reached out to squeeze his hand and smiled. "Of course."

When he ran off, Cerberus darting after him, the smile on my face faded. "How?"

"Perhaps a vinculum bond. Sometimes, demons are able to form a similar bond with humans."

"He's only a small fraction of demon, isn't he?"

"Yes. And angel. And human, too. Who knows what powers have evolved in him."

"Is it real? I mean, is it possible we'll be able to communicate with him? And my father still being alive?" As in, not having been cast into *absolute* death.

"Yes. It's real. And if Elyon can tell us which demon has claimed his soul, perhaps we can strike a deal with the Noxerians."

"You think they'd entertain such a thing? They didn't when you asked about my soul, right?"

"I've since essentially saved the fate of all five realms. I should be able to ask for anything my fucking heart desires, don't you think?" His comment made me smile only cautiously, but damn that glimmer of hope that glowed inside of me again.

"Personally, I think they should make you king, or something."

"I'd be a horrible, selfish king." He ran his hand across my thigh, and my muscles clenched, primed and titillated by his touch. "Ignoring all my responsibilities to keep my queen happy."

"Your queen is happier than she's ever been."

"And so shall it be for eternity." Cupping my cheek, he leaned forward and kissed me.

"Eternity."

It was a span I couldn't fathom. An endless horizon of perpetual sunrises and sunsets. Could one grow weary of such beauty? Tire of the moon and stars? Perhaps, but for then, I felt an almost gluttonous sense of contentment. A feeling beyond what I'd always known as love, as Jericho had once said. One that encompassed the all-consuming passion, devotion, the utter chaos of emotions that exploded inside of me whenever he was near.

All my life, I'd studied symbols and their meanings. I'd spent countless hours dissecting the way we associated emotions with particular words and objects. Turned out, the most complex and fulfilling, the intensity of what love *could* be, was more than just a scrawled heart on a page. More than the simplicity of affection and longing, caring and nurturing. I'd come to know there was a shadowed side of it, too. A much darker version, comprised of obsession, pain, and the unflinching readiness to sacrifice.

The single-minded selfishness to save one person over the good of the whole.

My definition of love had evolved into a multifaceted enigma, with endless planes sharp enough to cut me open, but strong enough to heal. From the heights of ecstasy to the abysmal depths of crushing pain, it was the most exquisite dichotomy. The only thing in the world which had the power to transcend time and death. And how fortunate I was to have found it twice:

In life and the after.

ACKNOWLEDGMENTS

It seems for the last couple of books, my acknowledgments have started out with an explanation of the stuff going on in my life that made writing a challenge, and this book is certainly no exception. It took me over seven months to write this one, which is not the norm for me, particularly when I had so many ideas constantly swirling around in my head. There were times I didn't touch the manuscript for a week, and those were the most maddening for me. However, what I have loved about this world is, no matter what, I can always fall right back into it.

I want to take the opportunity to thank those who were instrumental in helping me get this story out of my head and onto the page:

First, as always, my husband and daughters who've been patient and supportive as I continue to navigate this dream around their dreams. I love you.

My parents and siblings who continue to encourage and support me without judgement. Love you all.

My long-time editor and friend, Julie Belfield. So many things pushed this book back further and further and you rolled with it every time. You have the patience of a saint. Thank you for not giving up on me and telling me to go to hell, when you had every reason to do so 🤍 As much as I've tried to stick to deadlines, I have a sickening habit of working best under tremendous pressure, which is horrible for editing. I will get this figured out. In the meantime, thank you for being the supportive person you are.

My alpha reader extraordinaire and friend, Diane Dykes. You have also remained a tremendous support on this journey. Your kind and encouraging words mean more than you realize. They have effectively pulled me out of moments when I struggled with my doubt. You bounce these plots with me in a way that allows me to creatively implement new ideas. I'm so glad to have you in my life 🩶 Thank you for all you do.

Many thanks to the incredible talent of Hang Le. Once again, she produced a stunning cover that I'm excited to pair with Nightshade.

To Debbie and Kelly, my fearless beta readers, thank you so much for taking a chance on this manuscript and jumping into an unpolished version of the book without hesitation. Your feedback and encouragement is invaluable and I'm so fortunate to have you (both) on my team.

A big hug and thank you to all my ARC Team members who read the early copies of my books and leave reviews that make release day a little less terrifying for me.

To my Vigilante Vixens, thank you for creating a virtual home for me and always offering support. I feel so blessed to have every one of you!

To the bookstagrammers, booktokers, bloggers and readers who have shared their love of these books with gorgeous reels, edits and artwork, thank you so much. I can't properly express how much I've appreciated your enthusiasm for these stories and characters - it's what fuels my excitement for writing every day. I know this book took forever and I hope you felt it was worth the wait. 🩶

OTHER BOOKS BY KERI LAKE

STANDALONES
MASTER OF SALT & BONES
RIPPLE EFFECT
THE ISLE OF SIN & SHADOWS

THE NIGHTSHADE DUOLOGY
NIGHTSHADE
INFERNIUM

JUNIPER UNRAVELING SERIES
JUNIPER UNRAVELING
CALICO DESCENDING
KINGS OF CARRION
GOD OF MONSTERS

VIGILANTES SERIES
RICOCHET
BACKFIRE
INTREPID
BALLISTIC

SONS OF WRATH SERIES
SOUL AVENGED
SOUL RESURRECTED
SOUL ENSLAVED
SOUL REDEEMED

THE FALLEN (A SONS OF WRATH SPINOFF)

<u>THE SANDMAN DUET</u>
NOCTURNES & NIGHTMARES
REQUIEM & REVERIE

ABOUT THE AUTHOR

Keri Lake is a dark romance writer who specializes in demon wrangling, vengeance dealing and wicked twists. Her stories are gritty, with antiheroes that walk the line of good and bad, and feisty heroines who bring them to their knees. When not penning books, she enjoys spending time with her husband, daughters, and their rebellious Labrador (who doesn't retrieve a damn thing). She runs on strong coffee and alternative music, loves a good red wine, and has a slight addiction to dark chocolate.

Keep up with Keri Lake's new releases, exclusive extras and more by signing up to her VIP Email List:
VIP EMAIL SIGN UP

Join her reading group for giveaways and fun chats:
VIGILANTE VIXENS

She loves hearing from readers ...
www.KeriLake.com

Printed in Great Britain
by Amazon